[HEART BEATS]

*Jeannette
with love
Ava Marell x*

Heart Beats

Anthology created by : Louise Rogers-Thomas

Copyright © 2020

All rights reserved.

Cover design by: © Francessa Wingfield

Formatted by Bookaholic Formatting

This novel is licensed for your personal enjoyment only. This print may not be re-sold or given away to other people. If you would like to share this book with another person, please purchase an additional copy for each recipient. If you're reading this book and did not purchase it, or it was not purchased for your use only, then please purchase your own copy.

Thank you for respecting the hard work of these authors.

This book is a work of fiction and any resemblance to persons, living or dead, or places, events or locales is purely coincidental. The characters are productions of the author's imagination and used fictitiously. This work is copyright. Apart from any use as permitted under the Copyright Act 1968, no part may be reproduced, copied, scanned, stored in a retrieval system, recorded or transmitted, in any form or by any means, without the prior written permission of the publisher.

Contents

The Trifecta by M. B. Feeney..5
The End of Promise and Paine by Sam Destiny....................67
The Life and Death of a Rock Star by M.A Foster...............137
Creed by Amy Davies..157
Club Rife by C.H. Thomas..197
Wrath by Lacey Heart...261
Crashing Star by Xana Jordan..271
The Alpha's Star by Aimie Jennison......................................331
Opera of the Beast by Lilly Rayman......................................353
The Night I Fell For A Pop Star by Mandy Bee....................369
Wager by T.a. McKay...421
A Little Unsteady by Saffron Blu...453
Somebody Else's Song by Avery Hart...................................489
Kill-A-Queen by Bea Stevens..541
Marching Offsides by AM Williams.......................................637
Strip Down by Ava Manello...769
Park Life by Lucy Felthouse..805
Acknowledgements..821

Heart Beats

The Trifecta

by

M. B. Feeney

The Trifecta Series #1

Three best friends.

One last summer together.

Memories to be treasured forever, and not all of them are the good kind.

Having spent years in one another's pockets Ella Kerr, Justin Taylor, and Mikey Faulkner are on the cusp of adulthood as they are separated by their choice of university. New friends, new routines, and the lack of parental supervision are just some of the hurdles they need to overcome in order to make sense of their choices in life.

This coming of age story is the first in a series that reaches into the future they couldn't always plan for.

This is the first in a series.

Book two will be available Summer 2020.

Prologue
Summer 2006

It was five-year old Ella's first day in the new flat. Her daddy had been there for a couple of days, decorating; Mummy had told her he wanted her new bedroom to look nice for when she got there. Ella hadn't wanted to move to a new flat, but mummy had told her that her daddy had a new job and they'd needed to move to a different part of London, away from all of her friends at nursery.

She didn't understand about the grown-up stuff, but the flat was nice; they had a little garden because they lived at the bottom of the block, which they didn't have before. The garden of the flat had swings on one side and the other side had a trampoline. Ella hoped the children who lived in the other flats were nice and would let her play with them. It would be even better if they were girls, because she liked playing with girls more than boys.

"Mummy, I'm bored," Ella whined as she sat on top of a box of books in the living room, kicking her feet against the side of it. She'd already arranged her cuddly toys into the places she wanted them, with her very favourites – Mr. Sneezy, the elephant and Joey, the koala – on her bed. The rest of her room was full of toys and books, but she didn't want to play with any of them; it didn't feel the same as her old bedroom.

"I know, honey, but me and daddy need to get everything sorted out. Why don't you go and play in your bedroom?" Her mummy and daddy had made sure her bedroom was the first room to be finished, but the other rooms were still full of boxes that hadn't been opened yet, and they had a lot of stuff that needed to be put away.

"My new bedroom's boring." It wasn't, and Ella knew it, but she'd been feeling a little ignored by her parents.

Her mummy stopped emptying the box propped on the table and turned to face the young girl. "Gabriella Kerr, I know it's all new here but please, stop whining. I'm sorry I can't play with you or take you out, but I'm too busy to deal with you sulking all day." Mummy didn't sound cross, but Ella knew it wouldn't be too long before she was if she continued complaining.

Ella began to pout, but then thought better of it. She stood up and wrapped her arms around her mother's legs.

"I'm sorry, mummy." Ella spoke into her mother's jeans as she squeezed her legs tight in a hug. Before either of them could speak again, there was a knock on the front door. Ella's mum opened the door to reveal two small boys, both covered in a rainbow of paint. The taller, thinner of the two began to speak, waving his hands around. His friend, a small mixed-race boy, watched with a smile on his face.

"I'm Justin Taylor, and this is Mikey Faulkner, and we live next door. Not together, we're not brothers. He's brown, and I'm pink. He lives that side, and I live that side. Can she come to my house and play?" He didn't take a breath until after he spoke, his hands outstretched paused in their waving around, eventually pointing at Ella.

Ella's mum turned to look at her daughter, a question in her eyes.

"Come on, we're painting and gonna have ham sandwiches," Justin pleaded with the tiny girl, who looked up at her mum, unsure, while Mikey smiled widely at everyone around him.

Her mum nodded, giving her the go-ahead. Ella thought once again about the swing and trampoline, maybe one of them had a sister she could play with.

"Okay." Ella walked through the front door and followed the boys to the flat next door.

From that day on, *The Trifecta*, as Ella's dad referred to them as, was created and they were inseparable.

Chapter One
June 2018

"Hurry your lazy arse up!" Justin yelled out as he and Ella waited in his new, to him at least, car; a beaten-up old Citroen hatchback. Mikey had predicted it wouldn't last the year, and Justin ignored him; *Molly* was his pride and joy, even if she was a million years old. He'd saved up for her from his meagre part-time wages, and although she was cheap and most likely wouldn't last him a year, she was *all* his. He gripped the steering wheel, stroking it lovingly and making the ripped covering come away, itching to get on the road. "Mikey; if you're not out here in five minutes, we're leaving without you." He called out towards the block of flats they were parked outside of, his deep voice deafening Ella as she sat next to him.

"Alright, alright. Don't get your knickers in a knot." Mikey ran out of the flat he'd grown up in, and shoved his bag, sleeping bag, and rolled up sleep-mat into the boot before climbing into the back seat. "Are we ready to get this show on the road kids?" he asked his two best friends, leaning back against the pleather seats, his glasses resting on the bridge of his nose.

"Hell yes!" Ella and Justin called out in unison, as Justin put the car in gear with a crunch and began driving, the early morning sunshine shining down on the road ahead which was damp from the overnight rain. Their exams were over, summer was starting, and they were due to embark on the next journey of their lives. This road trip was their last chance for pure freedom and enjoyment, and the three of them were determined to make the most of it.

Two Months Earlier:

Gabriella Kerr sat fidgeting as she waited on the front entrance stone steps of the large school building, which was often imposing because of its sheer size. She checked her watch; only three minutes had passed since she last looked at it. Tapping her foot, she sighed, trying to control her impatience – not very successfully. Another five minutes passed before she looked at the time again; there wasn't long to go, and the three of them would be free for the entire summer.

"Hey, Ella." The tiny girl spun round to face the voice that had called her name. "You all done now?" The other girl, a tall brunette, had that tell-tale relaxation to her which indicated her exams were also over.

Ella stood and shook out her legs, which had started to go to sleep, causing her oversized jeans to flap around her slender legs, which was a relief in the growing heat of the summer air.

"Oh, hey Michelle. Yeah, I had my last one this morning." She may have been petite in stature, but her voice had a big quality to it when she spoke. Justin called her 'naturally loud', Ella liked to think of it as 'presence'.

"How come you're still hanging around? I'd have thought you'd have gone straight home to chill out or celebrate."

"I'm waiting for Justin and Mikey to finish up."

"Of course," the girl muttered before smiling brightly. "Well, I'm off to pack for my holiday. Have a great summer, and good luck with uni."

Ella smiled back at her, reclaiming her seat. The foot tapping resumed as she checked her watch again. Another five minutes had crawled by.

"Of course," the two words played on a loop through her head while she waited, and her thoughts wandered back to when she'd first met her best mates.

For the last six years, Ella and the boys had been students at Steppen Secondary, and one was rarely seen without the other two, just as they had since they met at age five. A lot of the other kids - especially some of the boys - had talked about them, thinking they were in a freaky threesome relationship or something else perceived as weird. The three friends didn't let it bother them; they were secure in their friendship, which is all it had ever been as far as they were concerned.

Ella was the perfect balance between the two boys. While Justin and his quick mouth often got them into trouble, Mikey's soothing manner and ability to talk his way out of most situations. Loud and often sarcastic, Ella was able to diffuse arguments between the boys and other people. Oil and water often came to mind when the three of them were observed for any length of time, but they made it work for them.

"Yo yo, Ella Bella." Justin's deep voice washed over her as he jogged down the stairs behind her. The moment she stood up, he wrapped his arms around her and planted a sloppy and noisy kiss on her cheek then let her drop back to the ground with an ungraceful thump.

"Urgh, you grotty bastard." Ella wiped her skin as she glared at Justin's cheeky smile, but her green eyes lit up with the smile she was suppressing. Before the tall boy could speak, he was shoved out of the way as Mikey's strong arms lifted her off her feet and swung her in a circle like a child.

"Put me down." She wriggled free. "God, I swear you two are overgrown children. Wait. I *know* you both are; I'm positive neither of you developed mentally beyond eight." Linking arms with the pair of them, Ella led them out of the school gates for the last time until results day. "So, what are we going to do with all this free time?" At just over four feet tall, she had to look up when speaking to them, a fact she was teased about on a regular basis, and not just by the boys.

"Well, right now I'm thinking having a few drinks is a great idea." Justin veered them towards the nearest pub.

"Sounds good to me, my man." Between the two of them, they hoisted Ella a foot off the ground by her elbows and began to walk faster than her short legs would allow her to keep up with.

"Wait! Put me down! Jesus, what is it with you two and picking me up? I may only be the height of a small child, but I am mentally mature you know, unlike some people." Both Mikey and Justin grinned down at her. "Anyway, we can't go to the pub." She crossed her arms as she glared at them.

"Why not?" Justin asked, not understanding her.

"Not all of us are eighteen, remember?" Her birthday was still a couple of months away; Justin's had been three weeks previously, while Mikey had turned eighteen more than two months before their exams had started. Another thing for them to wind her up about – not only was she tiny, she was younger than them both. As far as Ella was concerned, the two of them were lucky she loved them dearly at times.

"Shit. Right change of plan thanks to the baby of the group here. Off license and back to mine; my mum won't be home 'til late, and Craig's staying at his latest girlfriend's for the weekend." Justin's brother, who was almost five years older than them, was rarely ever at their flat anymore, which gave the three of them much more freedom while his mum worked long hours as a waitress. Justin and his brother weren't particularly close, but Craig had always looked out for him, and by extension, Ella and Mikey, while he was growing up. Now he had a part time job and was a serial dater, they barely saw him and that suited all three of them just fine.

Grins erupted all round as Ella and Mikey started walking again, leaving Justin to catch up.

At the end of the second week after their exams, Mikey and Ella loitered outside their shared block of flats, nervously waiting for Justin to return from his driving test. He was the first out of the three of them to even consider taking the test; both Ella and Mikey were still having lessons, but neither felt brave or ready enough. Justin naturally, had been confident in his 'mad skills' to book his test for a Saturday morning and he was due back any time.

"He's going to be a nightmare if he fails," Ella commented as she scuffed her already well-worn trainers against the wall she sat on.

"And we'll comfort him the way we always do, until next time; with beer and pizza." Mikey stood up a little straighter, bringing himself level with Ella and draped his arm over her shoulder. "It's what we do."

It was; Justin was an 'ideas man', and more often than not his ideas, especially those to make money, fell through. Every time it happened his best friends were there to make him smile and get over the disappointment. "But you know, he'll be even worse if he passes." Mikey continued, dryly, making them both laugh. Silence fell over them as they waited, Mikey's arm still draped over Ella's shoulder. She dropped her head onto his shoulder as they scanned the road leading into their estate.

"Oh, I think I see him." Ella squeaked her voice full of nerves. The pair of them straightened up and stood watching him park up.

A driving school car turned into the street ahead of them, both watched as it approached. Ella snuck a look at Mikey's serious face, his hazel eyes framed by his black-rimmed glasses, the uncertainty clear on his face that matched her own.

"Why the long faces?" Justin climbed out of the passenger seat, sunglasses covering his eyes. Ella jumped down off the wall and ran over to him, Mikey stayed where he was, watching them. Justin shoved the aviators on top of his short, light brown hair, exposing his ice-blue eyes that flashed in the sunlight.

"Just tell us." She could hear the nerves in Mikey's voice for their lifelong friend.

"You sound like you doubt my mad skills." Justin shoved a piece of paper into her hands and ambled over to lean against the wall next to Mikey. The pair of them watched Ella read, a smile splitting her face as the words sank in.

"Oh my God Justin, you passed!" She squealed, running over to them and jumping into his arms and hugging him. "I'm so proud of you, we both are." Four arms wrapped around her as the three of them huddled into the group hug that was as familiar to each of them as hugs from their families.

"Congrats man."

Ella rolled her eyes as the boys fist bumped; they never showed any emotions during occasions such as this. She loved both of them like the brothers they'd become to her, but she often got frustrated by them.

"Me and Dad are gonna go look at cars at the weekend. Can't you just picture it, me and my wheels, cruising?"

"Remind me not to go out when that happens, I don't want to have to fear for my life every time I'm out and about." Ella teased him.

"Funny. For that comment, don't expect me to take you anywhere. I'll make you walk, everywhere. Or even worse, get the bus."

"You evil bastard." Ella huffed, trying to hide the smile on her face. She never could stay mad at either of them, not even pretend mad.

"Awww, Ella. You're our little munchkin; like I'd make you do that." Justin pulled her into his arms and placed a kiss on the top of her head. He was a clear two feet taller than her, something he reminded her of often. "But we need to do something this summer, and once we have transport, we won't be limited to the estate." He waved his arms around for emphasis, making them look at the uniform brick buildings surrounding them.

"We need a road trip or something." Mikey joined in the conversation, leaning back against the wall and watching his two best friends.

"Yeah, but where?" Justin asked, excitement lacing his voice. The three of them walked over to the shop, more for something to do rather than the need to buy something. Before they made it in through the door, Justin stopped dead in his tracks and stood staring at the wall next to the shop that was constantly plastered with bright posters. Some of the older ones had peeling corners and fading letters.

"What's up bro?" Mikey asked him, sharing a confused look with Ella as they moved out of the way of the door.

"It's perfect." The tall boy's voice rose an octave in excitement. "It's so bloody perfect."

"What the hell are you talking about?" Ella stood next to Justin and looked at the wall, trying to work out what had caught his attention.

"That one." He flicked a folded corner of a black poster with fluorescent orange print. Mikey and Ella read the words out loud in unison.

Lakeside Music Festival

15 - 18 August 2018

"Look at the bands listed." Ella could feel her excitement rising as she pointed at one name in particular. *Chains and Locks*, her favourite band was headlining on the Saturday evening. Justin and Mikey groaned; both hated the all-girl guitar band that Ella loved, but there were enough other bands listed to pique their interest.

"A full, proper blowout weekend before we scatter to the ends of the Earth." Justin waved his arms dramatically.

"You idiot. We're only going to different universities, not moving to a new country." Although Ella teased him, she knew moving to a different city to both of her best friends was going to be hard for all of them. She pushed the thoughts out of her mind, determined not to worry about that just yet. Looking up at the two of them, she could see they were trying not to think about the separation either.

"Let's do this." All three spoke together.

Chapter Two

The journey took them a couple of hours, and they only got lost once due to Justin insisting he knew where he was going but ending up in the completely wrong town. Eventually, after Ella forced him to stop and ask for directions in a small pub – where they decided they may as well order some food and Justin tried to chat up the girl behind the bar - they pulled up at their camping pitch and set the large tent up.

"This is going to be a sweet weekend." Justin claimed as he lifted the cool box he had filled with beer and food and placed it inside the tent.

"I just can't believe that one of your ideas turned out to be a damn good one for once." Mikey quipped as he laid out their sleeping mats and bags in the middle of the main 'room'. There was more than enough space in the tent they'd borrowed off one of his cousins, but the three of them had decided they would all sleep in the same room, as they always had whenever they'd had sleepovers growing up.

"Oi. My ideas are always golden." Justin defended himself. Both Ella and Mikey knew he was full of crap as much as he did.

"Yeah, whatever. This one, however, is the best you've ever had." Ella managed to placate Justin as she grabbed a can of coke before heading outside the tent to see if anything was happening yet. "That girl behind the bar didn't seem to think your suggestion for a night out in a tent in a field was a good idea though." She sniggered as she joined him looking out over the growing sea of tents, many of them bright coloured to stand out, allowing the owners to locate them in the early hours whilst drunk. More than a couple even had huge flags attached to the top that fluttered limply in the light breeze that wafted over the fields. Ella wished she'd thought to bring a flag now.

They'd arrived, as had many others, the day before the festival was due to start. Their pitch was close enough to the main music area that they wouldn't have far to go when they wanted to watch an act, but not too close that they would be overrun by other revellers.

"Her loss. She obviously doesn't know a good thing when she sees one."

"Maybe she knows *exactly* what she saw when you were on the other side of the bar, mate." Mikey teased.

"Boys, I do believe this is going to be the best weekend ever." Ella wrapped her arms around each of their waists, not caring that her can fell to the floor with a splash as they joined her and stood either side of her, speaking quickly to prevent an argument starting between them.

"Ella, when you're right, you're right." Mikey pulled her in for a hug as they all looked out across the campsite towards the large stage in the near distance. All around them, tents were being erected, and they could hear music being played from car stereos as the hum of people's voices filled the air.

"Shall we go for a walk, see if anything's happening yet?" Ella asked the guys. They grabbed their phones and some money and began to weave their way through the campsite.

None of them had ever been to a music festival before, so as they walked around the rows of tents towards the main stage and refreshment areas with stalls not only selling food and drinks, but people selling handmade items, all three of them tried to take in as much as possible. The stage backed onto the water, while the refreshment area, roped off, was to the left, leaving a huge grassed area ready for the rest of the attendees to arrive.

A few were milling around, grabbing food and drinks, making them themselves comfortable at one of the many picnic tables before the crowds descended. The low hum of voices filled the air as the late afternoon sun glared down on them. In the distance, Ella could hear the tinny sound of Bluetooth speakers playing the music of the appearing acts.

"Some pretty fit girls around my man." Justin muttered to Mikey as the three of them bought some beers and hot dogs before sitting at an empty table. "Might get lucky this weekend."

Ella rolled her eyes before turning to face the two of them.

"You two are *not* bringing girls back to the tent for one-night stands. I don't need to hear or possibly see that."

"Hey, they have tents too you know." Justin informed her, his tone indicating that he thought she was a bit on the stupid side. In response, she simply flipped him her middle finger and went back to watching the others around them.

"You're a fucking animal Justin Taylor," Mikey commented as Justin ogled a group of girls as they walked past, their shorts short and crop tops flashing their midriffs.

"And damn proud." Justin excused himself to go and talk to the girls, leaving Mikey and Ella watching him and shaking their heads.

"He's never going to change, is he?" Ella asked Mikey as they finished their drinks and decided to walk around the site some more, leaving Justin attempting to work his 'magic'.

Mikey woke up to Ella's snoring desperate to relieve himself. Quietly, he extracted himself from his sleeping bag and left the tent, noticing that Justin hadn't returned for the night. He and Ella hadn't noticed earlier that Justin had stayed out all night as they'd made friends with their tent neighbours and spent the evening drinking having a pre-festival party.

Staggering more than a little, he made his way out into the night. Thanks to the day's high temperatures, it was still warm despite it being almost four a.m. He managed not to fall over onto any of the other tents as he stumbled his way around in the dark to the toilet block.

It was clear he was still drunk from their session with the group in the next tent as he made his way back to his own tent. The night was silent around him, everyone else having given up their partying for the night, but that didn't prevent him from getting momentarily lost.

"And where have you been young man?" Justin's voice sounded loud in the dark as he entered the tent after he eventually found the right one.

"Jesus Christ mate, you frightened the life out of me." Mikey whispered so he wouldn't wake Ella up. "When did you get back?" He crawled back into his sleeping bag, but remained sitting, just able to make out the details of Justin's face.

"About five minutes ago. Could do with some kip though, I'm fucking knackered mate." The grin on his face was wide and lewd, something Mikey ignored knowing that if he even mentioned where his friend had been, he would be inundated with gory details. All of them, multiple times.

"Well, get some shut eye, because you know Ella's going to be dragging us 'round all day later." Mikey looked over at where Ella was still fast asleep, although was no longer snoring.

"Yeah, I'm gonna need all my energy for tomorrow. I'm meeting up with... uhm..." Justin clicked his fingers until he remembered the girl's name. "Melissa."

"Maybe you should write that down, so you don't look like a twat tomorrow. Well, no more than usual." Mikey ducked to avoid the plastic cup that Justin threw at him, and then lay back down to try and get back to sleep.

The sounds of the campsite around them woke the three of them up a few hours later. Mikey was the first to actually clamber out of his bag and head outside. The heat was already starting to get oppressive and he could tell that it was going to get worse; he couldn't wait.

"Rise and shine dickheads." He called out to Ella and Justin who weren't morning people the way he was. While he waited for them to ignore him, he made a start on breakfast and coffee. Within minutes of the bacon starting to sizzle, Ella emerged from the tent, her short blonde hair all over the place, and her pyjamas rumpled from being rolled up in her sleeping bag.

"When did Justin crawl back?" She asked as Mikey handed her a cup of coffee, strong and dark.

"Not that long ago. I woke up to go to the toilet, he wasn't here when I went out, then almost gave me a heart attack when I got back. He had a smug look on his face, despite struggling to remember the girl's name."

"Of course. That's Justin all over."

"Taking my name in vain out here?" Justin emerged from the tent looking fresh and well rested, despite having had less sleep than Mikey.

"I fucking hate you." Mikey grumbled handing over another cup.

"Love you too Mikey boy. Don't hate because I not only scored a night with one of the hottest girls I've seen in a long while, but the fact that I look good the morning after the night before."

"No hate, but you *are* a dick."

"Enough bitching you two. Eat and drink up, then we can get this day started." Ella interrupted them before they got started. She held her hand out for her breakfast and dug in vigorously the moment Mikey handed it to her. It was the first official day of the festival, and the three of them wanted to make the most of it.

Chapter Three

Justin kept his eye on Ella as she danced under the floodlights beaming down onto the immense crowd. Although he knew she was capable of sticking up for herself, she was so tiny it would have been easy for her to become overwhelmed by the number of people around them. He didn't need to look at Mikey to know that he was doing the same; looking out for Ella was second nature to them, as familiar and automatic as breathing. It wasn't a thing they did because of a specific event, but more borne from the fact that Ella was so petite and easily overlooked by other people, drunk other people in particular.

While Ella appreciated them looking out for her, she often told them to stop in fear it was ruining their enjoyment. Thanks to joining in when Mikey had decided to go and train in kick boxing, while Justin had had karate lessons since he was a kid, Ella was no slouch at self-defence – her dad insisting she be able to look after herself because of her petite stature, wanting no one to feel they could take advantage of her - but they still continued to keep an eye on her.

As the music blasted out across the mass of writhing bodies, Justin couldn't help but smile when arms slipped around his waist from behind. The girl from the previous night had found him and things were already looking up for him.

"Shall we get out of here?" She yelled into his ear over the music.

"Nah, after the show ends." As much as he wanted to slip off and spend a few hours in her... in her tent, he was here with his best friends and knew they would crucify him if he fucked off without them again.

"Find me later then." With a kiss full of promise, she melted into the crowd in the general direction of the beer tent.

"I'm impressed." Ella sidled up next to him. He had to bend almost in half so he could hear her. "The same girl twice in a row. Could it be that Justin Taylor is growing up?" With a cheeky grin, she ducked out of the way of his playful slap to her arm.

"Shut up and dance."

Sticking her tongue out at him, Ella did as she was told. Smiling to himself, Justin watched her lose herself in the music, jealous that he couldn't completely let go. He wasn't a huge fan of crowds at the best of times, and this one was overwhelming him a little. Shuffling through the crowd, he managed to find a bit more space and was able to regulate his breathing better. He could still see Mikey and Ella, but he wasn't being jostled from all sides. The plastic cup of beer was almost empty, and warm, but he could feel the hip flask in the pocket of his jeans. It was a relief knowing he didn't have to move through the people around him to get another drink.

"You okay?" Mikey's voice was low, but loud in his ear.

"Yeah, fine." Justin turned to meet the concerned look in his best friend's hazel eyes.

"The crowd getting too much for you?" Naturally, Mikey ignored Justin's words and assessed the situation by the tension to his friend's shoulders and his tone of voice. Justin hated how well Mikey knew him and was able to do this every time.

Justin had never been good with large crowds, but never really understood why. He just hated feeling boxed in by so many bodies, particularly when the heat became oppressive. He hid it well from most people, had done since he was a kid, but Mikey had known him for almost his entire life and had seen him have a meltdown on a couple of occasions when they'd been out with their families when they were kids.

"Nah, I'm all good. It's hotter than Hades in this crowd though."

"You're not wrong. How about we grab Ella and head over to grab a drink and some grub? We'll still be able to hear and enjoy the music, but we'll have more breathing room."

Justin realised what Mikey was doing and was silently grateful.

"Come on then. This beer's a bit warm anyway."

After getting Ella, the three of them worked their way through the crowds, hand in hand, emerging into an open space at the edge of the immense body of people.

"I swear I'm going to wake up tomorrow with bruises in my intimate places." Ella groaned as they walked towards the cordoned off area that housed a large beer tent and a selection of food vans.

"Ella, I *really* don't need to hear about your 'intimate areas' thank you very much." Justin closed his eyes, instantly regretting it as he was assaulted by his imagination picturing her naked.

As they'd grown up, and became more aware of the opposite sex, Justin knew he was attracted to her. Knowing nothing would ever happen between them, he managed to quash those feelings, but every now and then they would resurface; usually when Ella said something innocent, but full of unintended double meanings that Justin was sure only he heard.

"Oh please. You two have both seen me half naked on multiple occasions. Don't act as if you haven't."

As Ella turned her back on them to get into the queue for the beer tent, Mikey and Justin glanced at one another, wide grins splitting their faces. It was then that Justin realised he wasn't the only one harbouring an attraction to the tiny girl they'd grown up with.

𝄞

Ella watched the crowd go mental for a band she wasn't a huge fan of as the three of them sat at a picnic table. The stage was surrounded by writhing bodies and she could almost feel the sexual tension wafting in the air. In fact, she was positive that she could see a couple getting down and dirty at the back of the crowd, but couldn't be sure; it wouldn't have surprised her though based on the amount of alcohol the revellers were drinking, the heat of the crowd, and generally being in close proximity to so many people. There was something about live music that was a turn on for so many people, her included. The anticipation of seeing her favourite band, *Chains and Locks,* the next evening had her on edge. It felt like the moments just before she'd had her first kiss, and she couldn't help but want more. It was a bit like being in a new relationship, especially the physical side of one; the feeling of not being able to get enough of the other person – not that she would know much about that side of things. Ella was still a virgin.

Justin and Mikey were also scanning the crowd, but she was sure that they were looking at something completely different to her. Justin was always on the lookout for pretty girls – he had a type. Tall, slender, and *very* blonde. She had a suspicion he liked them dumb, so he could sleep with them once then not have to worry about seeing them again. She didn't like how he treated girls and had often made her opinion very clear to him but it was his life. He never made promises to any of the girls, and made it clear it was a one-time thing for him; at least he was honest with girls he slept with, he had that going for him. She may not have liked how he did things in that sense, but she loved him for his big heart and crazy personality.

Mikey was less forthright in his approach to sex and relationships. He'd come out as bi to them when they started secondary school. It hadn't been a big deal for them, he was just Mikey. So what if he was attracted to guys as well as girls? Both Justin and Ella enjoyed pointing out good looking guys and girls to him, but none of them ever seemed to be right. Where Justin had a clear type, Mikey was a bit more 'choosy'. Again, it was simply how he was, and his friends accepted that about him.

Ella hadn't had a serious boyfriend. She'd dated casually, but nothing had ever progressed beyond a few dates and sloppy kisses accompanied by foreplay fumbling's in the dark. At one point, she thought there was something wrong with her, but both of the guys had assured her that wasn't the case at all. She sometimes wondered if other guys were put off by the fact that her two best friends were male, by how close they all were, but never had the courage to ask anyone about it.

Out of the corner of her eye, she could see the girl Justin had spent the night with approaching their table and rolled her eyes. Despite his attitude to girls, they couldn't help but be drawn to him. Tall with eyes so light blue that they stood out in the largest of crowds, he was good looking. He was also almost always smiling, finding something to enjoy, regardless of what he was doing. He'd been pretty popular in school – the other lads wanting to be his friend, and the girls wanting to be 'chosen' by him. It never really went to his head, he had Mikey and Ella to rein that in for him, but sometimes, when it was just the three of them, he would get a little over excited about the attention he received.

"Hi guys. Are you having fun?" There was a slight slur to the girl's words as she sat down next to Justin, almost slipping off the end of the bench.

"Yeah, it's great. You?" Mikey, ever the polite one, turned to face her as Ella remembered her name was Melissa.

"Oh yeah, we always have an amazing time here. No parents, the chance to do what the hell we want when we want, and live music. What more do we need?" She indicated the group of girls she'd come with.

Ella smiled at her. She *was* enjoying herself and wouldn't want to experience it for the first time with anyone other than Mikey and Justin, but she wondered what it would be like if she'd come with a group of girls instead. She didn't miss the idea of hanging out with girls per se; most of the time she couldn't cope with the constant bitching, judging, and general squealing that girls her age did when she saw them out and about, but every now and then she wondered if she was missing out on anything by spending all her time with the boys.

The group who had tagged along with Melissa wasn't large, only about four of them, but they'd clearly had a decent amount to drink. They were walking on unsteady legs and the more excited they got about what they were talking about, the louder and higher pitched their voices got. Melissa had clearly staked a claim on Justin as none of her friends did more than exchange a few words with him. Their attention was on Mikey most of the time. Ella couldn't blame them; he was a good-looking guy who was well built and stocky. There was an aura of safety to Mikey that was hard to miss. However, she noticed that beyond a few bright smiles and pleasantries, his attention wasn't on any of the girls, which didn't go unnoticed.

"Does he have a girlfriend who couldn't join you?" A curvy brunette in denim shorts and bikini top asked Ella when Mikey hadn't fallen for her fluttering eyelashes and tentative touches to his solid arm.

"No, he's single." Ella replied, taking a perverse pleasure in seeing a momentary flash of confusion then disappointment in the girl's eyes.

"Is there something between you and him then?"

Ella snorted, almost choking on the beer she'd just taken a mouthful of.

"No, it's not like that. We're all just best friends."

"Well, he watches you a lot when you're not looking, so while you might not think there's more to your friendship, he probably does." Before Ella could respond, the brunette stood up to wander over to another table that was surrounded by guys and beer bottles. Without thinking, Ella looked over at Mikey and caught his eye. He grinned at her as he lifted his beer bottle to his lips causing a ripple of heat wash over her.

Chapter Four

As the day went on, Mikey drank less and less; not only was the heat getting more and more stifling, especially in the crowds, but he wanted to keep his head clearer than he would if they back home. He was very aware that he didn't know the area around them, but also the people. No one had given him cause not to trust them, especially those in tents near theirs, but he didn't want to get blinding drunk and wake up to regret his choice.

Justin didn't seem to have the same concerns. Since they'd left the crowd and moved away from the stage, he'd downed beer after beer, and flirted with every girl who'd crossed his path. The group of girls were still sat with them, but only Melissa seemed to be paying them any attention. She was trying to sink her claws further into Justin, but he was treating everyone the same, showing none of the favouritism he'd bestowed on her the previous evening; it was obviously driving her nuts from what Mikey could see. Ella had clearly noticed it too; on more than one occasion he'd caught her eye and grinned at the growing frustration on Melissa's face and in her actions.

He was a little worried about Ella. Ever since they'd taken up residence at their picnic table, she'd withdrawn into herself a little – something she only seemed to do when she was uncomfortable. Outwardly, she was smiling and chatting to anyone who approached their group, but Mikey could tell her heart wasn't in it by the slight pinch to her eyes that didn't smile when she did.

"Hey, do you want to head back to the tent for a break?" He leaned over to ask her quietly. "You don't look like you're enjoying yourself the way you were earlier."

"I'm knackered if I'm honest. I might head back to grab a quick nap before this evening." She stood up and Mikey couldn't help but notice her vest top riding up and exposing a sliver of tanned skin above the waistband of her jeans.

"I'll come with you; I could do with a break from being surrounded by Justin's fan club for a bit."

The two of them let Justin know where they were going, ignoring the sly looks and grins from the girls surrounding him and Melissa, knowing that suspicions were raised as they always had been whenever Ella went somewhere alone with one of them.

Mikey hadn't planned to fall asleep next to Ella, but he woke with a start when Justin crashed into the tent.

"You two are a pair of antisocial bastards." His voice was loud and the two of them sat bolt upright, bleary eyed.

"What the hell Justin?" Ella moaned, wiping her face as her tall friend collapsed onto the floor next to them.

"You've been gone for nearly three hours. Everyone thought you were getting your freak on in here. I knew otherwise of course, but they wouldn't shut up about it." He grinned at the pair of them, clearly leaning towards being drunk. "Anyway, it's time to get some food before the main show kicks off on the big stage."

Although Ella was excited about seeing *Chains and Locks* the next day, Justin had been sold on the festival when his favourite British rapper had been announced as headlining the first night. He wanted to be as close to the main stage as he could be when *Devon MC* started his set.

"Okay, okay." Mikey could feel Justin practically vibrating with excitement as he started out across their legs. "Food's a great idea, soak up some of the beer you've been downing like water."

"You're really starting to sound like an old man Mikey Faulkner. You need to let loose and live; this is going to be a weekend to remember before we all go our separate ways to uni. You're holding back on us."

Rather than reply, Mikey gave Justin the finger as he crawled out of the tent to stretch the sleep from his muscles.

"Well...?" Justin looked at Ella with a grin on his face.

"Well what?"

"Have you finally succumbed to the power of Mikey boy's muscles?"

"You really are a massive twat." Once again, at the mention of something happening between her and Mikey, Ella felt heat course through her body up to her face. Silently hoping she wasn't blushing, she pushed Justin off her legs and followed their friend out of the tent.

"You really don't see it, do you?" He asked her, softly, before she could exit through the material doorway.

"See what?"

"How much Mikey's into you. Yeah, he's bi and all that, which is cool, but you're the one he wants."

"You're being ridiculous. That would be like me and you getting it on." Ella laughed at the face Justin pulled at her words. She couldn't imagine herself being anything other than friends with either of them, which made her reaction to people suggesting something between her Mikey all the more confusing.

"I can only tell you what I see in front of me. I mean, when was the last time you saw Mikey get freaky with anyone?"

Ella thought for a moment, ignoring Justin's choice of words.

"Well, we can't all be players like you, Justin." She teased.

"Jealousy does not become you Gabriella." He ducked out of the way of her tiny fist aiming for his bicep, laughing. He loved how easy their friendship was, the three of them rarely argued and could tease one another without upsetting anyone.

"You keep telling yourself that mate. Now, feed me." She jumped onto his back and they went to join Mikey who had wandered off to look across the crowd of tents leading to the festival area and head back down to the food vans.

𝄞

As they ate, Mikey thought about the conversation he'd overhead between his two best friends. Was it really that obvious he was attracted to Ella? He'd loved her as a sister for so long, he couldn't pinpoint when that love had shifted into something more. He knew Justin would go for a night with her if given the chance, but with him that's all it ever was. Justin Taylor didn't 'do relationships' as, according to him, there was no fun in them. He was more than happy playing the field until he was ready to settle down, if it ever happened.

Embarrassment coursed through Mikey as they'd playfully shoved one another around on the walk from the campsite to the cordoned off area for food and drink. He'd never expected anything other than friendship from either Justin or Ella and would continue thinking that. Maybe Justin was right, and he needed to let loose a little more. He was determined not to be the one to cause a rift in their friendship because he couldn't get over himself, even if that meant he *needed* to get over Ella as soon as possible. Maybe the only way that would happen would be by attempting to meet someone else.

Justin mulled over his short conversation with Ella about Mikey. When she'd said anything happening between her and either of them would be weird, it had stung a little, despite his being able to play it off. He knew that nothing would ever happen between himself and Ella, and was fine with that fact, but it didn't stop him secretly wanting it to. He was fine with them being just friends, and he would never stop caring about her, but sometimes there was a little feeling of wanting more which was squashed as far down in his body as he could manage.

Realising Mikey felt the same about her as he did wasn't much of a shock to Justin. There was something about Ella that drew guys to her; possibly her petite stature brought out the protective caveman in them or something, but it was her vibrant personality which made everyone fall in love with her in one way or another. He was glad he masked his attraction better than his best friend and hid behind the one night stands he was known for. Even though he enjoyed them immensely, and they satisfied him, he often found himself feeling empty a few days after the fact. He secretly wanted more from someone and hoped university would be the place he found them and it. Their wider circle of friends and acquaintances from school had put Justin on some kind of pedestal that he didn't always appreciate but often played up to as was expected of him. Deep down, he wanted a 'real' relationship with someone who legitimately cared for him, but for now, he was living his best life even if it didn't fulfil him completely.

Shaking himself from his dour thoughts, he wrapped his arms around the shoulders of the two best friends he would ever have and decided it was time to get their party started for the day.

"Right, who wants shots?"

Dancing as part of the huge crowd, Ella was jostled from all sides, but she didn't care. While she wasn't the biggest fan of *Devon MC,* she was getting caught up in the atmosphere of live music and the people around her. Justin had wormed his way through to the middle of the crowd while she and Mikey had stayed nearer the back where there was a bit more space, even though the crowd was heaving and moving insanely.

"I thought you hated him." Mikey yelled into her ear.

"I do." She grinned at him, alcohol making her happy and loose.

"Why do you look like you're enjoying every minute of his set then?"

"Because I am. It's not him, but all of this." She waved her arms around, indicating the crowd around them, almost hitting a few people who didn't seem to care. "Them enjoying themselves is making me enjoy myself; their fun is infectious."

"Makes sense. Shall we go and get another drink?" Without waiting for an answer, Mikey grabbed Ella's hand and pulled her towards the very back of the crowd and the beer tent. The further they got away from the crowd, the cooler the air became, even though the evening was still warm. They could breathe that little bit easier and the infectious fun from the other revellers began to ease off a little.

"I never thought I'd see the day I would dance to that arrogant dick." Ella commented, wiping her short blonde fringe from her sweaty forehead. The gentle breeze cooled her clammy skin as she walked side-by-side with Mikey. She couldn't help but notice the looks of appreciation he was getting from men and women around them.

"Neither did I. At least Justin didn't see you, he'd *never* let you live it down."

"You tell him, and I'll deny everything. He's more likely to believe me than you." Ella cocked her head to the side and fluttered her eyelashes, making her wide, green eyes appear bigger.

"Damn you and your wily feminine ways."

The pair of them laughed as they got into the queue in the beer tent.

"I know how to use them too, especially against you two."

"My lips are sealed; Justin won't find out the truth from me."

Ella hugged him tightly around the waist which shocked him slightly, not that she had never done it before, but his entire body was on high alert and full of adrenaline. After a moment, he wrapped his arms around her and placed a kiss on her forehead.

"Aww, you two make quite the domestic picture." Justin's voice made them both jump and spin round. They found their tall, somewhat skinny best friend behind them, a wide smirk on his face.

"Drink?" Ella asked him, thankful for the dark as her cheeks heated up, yet again.

"Does the pope wear red socks?"

"How the hell would I know?" Ella was confused by the question.

"General knowledge Gabriella dear, general knowledge; and by the way, the answer's yes; when drink is the question, the answer is *always* yes."

Rolling her eyes at him, she turned back to re-join the queue, leaving Mikey and Justin to wait for her at a table. She hoped Justin would move away from the subject of her and Mikey – something that seemed to be entertaining him greatly since they'd arrived. She was used to other people passing comments and making judgements about her and one (or both) of her best friends, but coming from their inner circle, the Trifecta, it was more than a little unnerving.

Once she'd been served, Ella turned to look for Mikey and Justin. When she managed to find them, her two best friends were once again surrounded by girls. Ella didn't recognise any of them as she put the drinks on the table and managed to squeeze onto the seat between Justin and Mikey.

"Excuse me, we were talking. You can't just push your way between us." A tall redhead looked down her nose at Ella from the other side of Mikey.

"Oh, I'm sorry. I didn't realise you saw them first and marked them. Please excuse my rudeness, I'll head back to my tent now and wallow in shame, reassessing my actions." Ella looked at the girl, a looked of apology on her face. Out of the corner of her eye she could see both boys grinning at her. "Uhm… Justin, Mikey. Which way's *our* tent again?" She asked them innocently.

Without another word, the redhead stood up and left the group, followed closely by her friends.

"Drink up boys, it's going to be a long night."

Chapter Five

The sun was bright as it shone through a gap in the tent's opening straight onto Justin's face the following morning. Groaning, he rolled over to try and get back to sleep, but it was too late. His bladder was screaming at him, and his head was pounding. The main downside to drinking – the hangover.

As he sat up, his stomach rolled dangerously, and the thumping in his head intensified to hammering. At least he hadn't woken up in some random girl's bed… tent, unable to find his way back to his friends. He looked around him to see both Ella and Mikey were both still fast asleep.

Grabbing his phone, he crawled out of the tent and stumbled in the direction of the toilet and shower blocks. The sun was dazzling, and the temperature was already ridiculously hot, which didn't help the nausea and other symptoms he was suffering from. It took him ten minutes to stumble the less than five-minute walk. Feeling as if he was going to throw up at any minute, he lurched into one of the toilets and relieved himself. Once he was back outside, he sat on the grass a few yards away from the block hoping the deep lungfuls of fresh air would help quell the storm raging in his stomach.

"You okay there?" A female voice spoke softly in his ear, causing Justin to open his eyes and blink against the brightness.

"I think so. Ask me again in an hour or so." He grumbled, not failing to notice she was extremely pretty. "But then again, I may be dead by then."

"What a tragedy that would be." She sat on the grass next to him and offered what looked like a protein bar. "This'll help you feel better, and then you can treat me to breakfast."

Justin took the bar and devoured it.

"So, I'm buying you breakfast? As a thank you for saving me?"

"That and the fact I think you're pretty and want to spend more time with you." She smiled at him, her eyes twinkling in the bright light. Yes, he wanted to spend more time with her, and if it cost him a breakfast so be it.

"At least you're honest." He glanced down at his phone as it buzzed with a text from Ella. He also noted it wasn't even 9 a.m. He ignored the text and turned back to the girl sitting next to him. She wasn't his usual type of blonde and leggy, but there was something about her. "Can you give me half an hour to get washed up and changed? I'll meet you by the food vans."

"Sounds perfect. See you then."

It wasn't until Justin had watched her walk away towards the shower blocks that he realised she hadn't told him her name. He climbed to his feet, surprised to discover his stomach was no longer threatening to violently excavate itself. Whistling softly to himself, he returned to the tent to gather clean clothes and his wash bag.

"So, you didn't swallow your tongue in your sleep then?" Ella remarked as she sat on top of her sleeping back, scrolling through her phone.

"Needed to pee. I didn't think you and Mikey would appreciate me pulling out my wang and pissing out of the door." He moved around the small space, gathering his things to go and have a shower.

"No, we most certainly would not," Mikey mumbled, sleepily, from where he lay.

"I honestly thought you'd crawled out of the tent to go and die somewhere. You were a mess last night." Ella commented, watching Justin move around. "You're in a hurry. The day hasn't even started yet."

"Well, I have a breakfast date in less than half an hour, so I'm not going to waste my time talking to you two, when I can be in the company of a pretty girl – no offence, Ella."

Rolling her eyes, she assured that no offence was taken. With a wide grin, Justin left the tent once more, whistling as he prepared himself for the day.

Mikey felt almost human again once he and Ella sat in the camping chairs outside their tent drinking a cup of tea and eating freshly made bacon sandwiches. When they'd finished, Ella took herself off for a shower and he sat looking out across the sea of brightly coloured tents. Their section of the campsite was starting to fill with the buzz of people waking up, but it was relaxing more than annoying. Mikey poured another cup of tea and sat back in his chair, making the most of the peace around him to think about how their time at the festival had gone so far.

Before they'd left London, they'd made a pact to stay together as much as possible. None of them had wanted to have this first-time experience without the others, but Mikey wasn't surprised that Justin had managed to meet a couple of girls. There were no expectations on him to not be himself, and both Mikey and Ella loved him for him.

None of them had expected to be spending some of their last summer together at this event, but Mikey was beyond glad they did. With the three of them going their separate ways for the next three years minimum, something he was dreading despite being excited about the next part of his life, he wondered if things would ever be the same between the three of them after this summer.

The main thing he hadn't expected was for this weekend away to make him realise how strong his feelings for Ella were. He'd tried to ignore them and push them away, but it hadn't worked. Both she and Justin had pointed out guys and girls they thought he'd be interested in, but all he could think was that they weren't her. As he sat listening to people around him recover from their hangovers, he wondered if he looked like the loser he considered himself to be. He'd known Ella since he was seven, surely by now he'd be over getting a lump in his throat every time he saw her for the first time at the beginning of the day. Surely, it was about time he grew up and let go of his teenage crush…

"Right, I'm all freshened up. How are we spending the day before *Chains and Lock* are on stage?" Ella asked him, disrupting his thoughts. He was grateful for the distraction, all the moping he was doing lately was annoying him, and it wouldn't take long for Justin and Ella to notice and pull him up on it.

"I don't fancy getting caught up in the crowds today, do you?" Ella asked once she'd put her stuff away in the tent.

"Not really, not in this bloody heat; at least not before the show starts up. I'm happy hanging back away from the crowds until I *really* need to get in the thick of things."

It was almost ten in the morning, and the pair of them were glowing from the layer of sweat on their skin.

"The heat's crazy, but I'm having the best time here. Just sad that it's almost all over, and we have to go back home to reality." Ella's face dropped at the thought. Not so much of going home, but what lay beyond the summer and being separated from not only her two best friends, but her family.

"I know what you mean. It's not long until we'll all be packing stuff up and moving away."

He couldn't help but look over at Ella as she blinked rapidly, a clear sign she was fighting the urge to cry. He rushed over to her and wrapped his arms around her shoulders. "Hey, don't let yourself get upset."

"I'm trying not to, but ever since I moved in, you and Justin have been the main constants in my life apart from mum and dad. I can't even begin to imagine having to get through a day, never mind three years, without seeing your ugly mugs every day." She sniffled, unable to stop a few tears escaping.

Mikey couldn't imagine not having his two best friends around all the time either. He and Justin had been friends from the moment they met at the ridiculously young age of around two; then Ella came along, and their triangle was complete. The three of them had discussed applying to the same universities, but it wasn't easy to find one that offered all the courses they wanted to do, so they'd have to separate.

"You little softie you. I give it less than a month before you've replaced us and are having the time of your life."

"Well, yeah. I could do with a friend upgrade, let's be real here." Mikey gasped, making Ella giggle through her tears.

"Well, if that's the way it's going to be, I won't come and visit you to torment you and tell your upgraded friends embarrassing stories about when you were little."

"You wouldn't dare!"

"Don't threaten to trade me in then."

Ella flew at Mikey and wrapped her arms around him, hugging him tighter than she ever had before. Looking up at him, he was struck by how bright her green eyes were.

"I'll never want to trade you in, I promise."

The overwhelming urge to kiss her came over him, but before he could even move, Justin approached and the two of them jumped apart before he could make any unwanted observations.

"Well, that's my night sorted tonight. Hope you won't miss me too much."

"Him... I might trade in, just for shits and giggles." Ella muttered under breath, making Mikey snort.

"What did I miss?"

Ella couldn't believe how close she had come to kissing Mikey before Justin had interrupted. She was stunned the thought had even crossed her mind – well, it wasn't the first time, but it was the closest she'd come to acting on the idea. As frustrating as being interrupted by Justin was, it was a good thing. The last thing Ella needed was for her friendship with Mikey to go wonky because of a moment of stupidity and emotion.

She'd meant what she'd said to Mikey; she'd never be able to replace the two of them in her life – she didn't want to. Yes, she knew she would make friends at university, but no one would *ever* measure up to the two boys she had gone through everything with, never. They may end up being separated by the miles, but they would always be friends; Ella was sure of that fact and it gave her a sense of inner peace she would carry with her for the next three or four years.

𝄞

    The three of them spent the day hanging around outside their tent, trying to stay out of the glaring sunshine and overbearing heat. Once *Chains and Locks* were due on stage, the three of them made their way as far through the crowd as they could so Ella could get a close as possible to her idols.

    Justin had passed a comment about being surrounded by 'emo chicks' which had made Mikey laugh, but he soon stopped when Andi, the girl he'd had breakfast with turned up, a bundle of excitement. Ella laughed to herself at the change in his attitude when the brunette told him she was a huge fan of the band. Thanks to how much Ella loved them and her constant playing of their music loudly in her room, he knew almost all the lyrics and was able to sing along, impressing Andi even more which was, no doubt, the aim of his actions.

    Ella hadn't been to many concerts, but she already knew that any she attended after this festival would pale in comparison. Even an hour after the music had finished for the night, she was still vibrating from the adrenaline coursing through her as she and Mikey made their way back to the tent. Justin had disappeared with Andi again, more than likely for the night.

    "Hey, I'm going to stop off at the loo. I'll meet you back at the tent." She called out to Mikey, who was swaying slightly and singing off key. Once he'd raised his hand to indicate he'd heard her, she took a detour, desperate to relieve herself.

𝄞

    Although he'd heard what Ella had called out, it took about a minute for the words to register in his brain. Mikey stopped walking, turned around causing himself to go light-headed for a moment, and then began walking to the toilet and shower block; there was no way was he going to let Ella walk by herself in the dark.

    As he approached the block, he heard a scream and, suddenly sober, took off at a run towards the sound. Rounding the back of the block, he saw

Ella fighting off a guy, twice the size of his tiny friend, who was trying to pin her to the ground as he grabbed at her chest. Her vest top was ripped down the front, displaying her bra, and he could see the abject fear in her eyes. Rage tore through him as he reached out his hands, ready to kill Ella's attacker.

"Get the fuck off her." He roared as he grabbed the guy's arm and yanked him away from Ella. The man stumbled and fell to the floor in a heap with a loud grunt. As he scrambled to get to his feet to run away, Mikey caught him with a right hook to the jaw which knocked him out. Leaving him sprawled on the ground at their feet, Mikey turned to Ella as the adrenaline surged through his body, leaving him shaking, his fists still clenched tightly at his sides.

She had tears streaming down her pale face as she tried to pull the two halves of her top together in a feeble attempt to cover herself up. Carefully, Mikey pulled off his shirt, putting it over her head gently to provide her with some modesty as he walked around the body on the floor between them to her and drew her into a tight hug. He'd always hated seeing her cry, but lately it was worse because of the feelings he was trying to deny.

Well, it made sense in his mind; at least he thought so.

Chapter Six

"I don't need to go home. I'm fine!" Ella was clearly trying to stop herself yelling at Mikey. She didn't blame him; he was only looking out for her after what had happened. "Look, festival security handed the guy over to the police. It's over; I'm honestly fine, a bit shaken up, but I'm not letting one dickhead ruin this weekend for me."

Mikey didn't know what to say. They'd spent over an hour with festival security and the local police giving statements over what had happened and were finally back at their tent. More than anything, he wanted to pack everything up and head home right then and there, but Ella was adamant she was staying. He'd tried to get hold of Justin, but the idiot's phone was off and all he could feel was rage at the guy he'd pulled off Ella. He wanted to believe she was okay, but she was still pale as hell, and there had been a quiver in her voice as she'd spoken to security and the police. Mikey trusted Ella completely, but an attack like that was bound to have an effect on her, even if she didn't want it to.

"Can you promise to at least sleep on it and see how you feel in the morning?" He asked finally, his voice soft, as Ella pulled a large t-shirt over her small fame.

"I promise to think about it, but I know I'll feel the same in the morning." The shake to her voice had gone, but he still couldn't help but worry. More than anything, she sounded tired rather than upset. Her tears hadn't lasted long, but despite the warmth to the night she'd started shaking from shock which he was assured was normal after something like this. Since then, thanks to copious cups of tea given to her by a lovely female police officer, she'd managed to get back to her usual self somewhat. Mikey knew 'normality' was likely to be temporary, and she would revert to shock at some point and was still worried sick about her.

What if he had carried on walking back to the tent? What if he'd not realised what she'd said and left her to deal with it on her own? Guilt surged through him for leaving her alone for just those few minutes.

"Stop blaming yourself Mikey. It's not your fault." She said as he wouldn't make eye contact with her, one of the tells she'd learned over the years indicating he felt guilty.

He looked over at her, hating how small she looked as she sat on top of her sleeping bag, her legs crossed as if they were back in primary school. Then again, at four feet two inches, Ella always looked small. But this time it was different.

"I should have been with you. If I had, he wouldn't have tried to attack you."

"He would have tried it with another girl; at least you showing up when you did stopped him, and he's not out there looking for the next opportunity to grab someone." Mikey considered her softly spoken words as Ella got to her knees and crawled over to him and wrapped her arms around his neck. She wasn't wrong, but it still didn't stop him from feeling guilty as hell.

"Please stop thinking about 'what if'. It's over with now, thanks to you. I'm never going to be able to thank you for what you did." The contact when her lips met the skin on his jaw felt as if it were branding him. She was the one who'd been attacked and yet he was the one being reassured.

For the second time in one day, Ella wanted nothing more than to kiss Mikey. Not just to erase the ghostly feel of a stranger's hand groping her breast painfully, but to feel Mikey himself. Was this a normal reaction after a sexual assault? Considering it had never happened to her before, she had no idea.

By the sound of his breath catching in the back of his throat, she could tell he wanted to kiss her too, so she was obviously surprised and disappointed when he gently withdrew her arms from around his neck and pushed her away from him a little. He was more worried about her, which she appreciated, but it didn't stop her from being horny as hell.

"Ella…" His voice, normally quite deep anyway, sounded even deeper to her. "Look, more than anything right now, I want to kiss you, but I don't want to push you after what you've just been through. Let's get some sleep and we can talk about it in the morning."

All she wanted him to do was to take her in his arms and help her forget about her attack. Although it hadn't been as serious as it could have been, she could tell he was worried about her suddenly freaking out. She knew it wasn't going to happen, but the look in his hazel eyes behind his thick, black-framed glasses told her that no matter how much she reassured him, he wasn't going to believe it until he saw it. And that hurt more than a little.

"I'm sorry Mikey." Ella withdrew herself away from him and started to crawl into her sleeping bag.

"Don't be sorry. It's not your fault, none of this is your fault." Climbing into his own bag, he rolled over to face her, disappointed she had her back to him. As he stared at the back of her short blonde hair, he was mentally kicking himself for turning her down, even though he'd done it for the right reasons.

"Ella, look at me. Please," he spoke into the air after a couple of minutes of excruciating silence. Eventually, she rolled over to face him. The light in the tent was low and dim, but he could see the shine of tears in her eyes. "It's not that I don't want to; it scares me how much I do want to, it really does. I just think it's a little too soon. Your attack was, thankfully, not as serious as it could have been, but it's still something you need to recover from. You might still have some kind of reaction to it once you've mentally processed it all."

"You're right, I shouldn't be taking my frustration out on you; if it wasn't for you, it could have been so much worse. Thank you doesn't seem to be a sufficient thing for me to say." Ella heard the crack in her voice as she spoke.

At her words, Mikey took hold of her hand, Ella hoped he'd missed the flinch at the sudden contact in the dark. Hating that she was suddenly scared to be touched because of one person, she let herself be pulled into his arms; resting her head against his chest, she soon fell asleep to the steady sound of his heart beating.

𝄞

Finding his two best friends sleeping wrapped up in one another's arms, was a bit of a shock to Justin when he returned to the tent in the morning. They were in separate sleeping bags, but there was an air of intimacy to them that made him back out of the tent immediately and sit down in one of the fold-away chairs. He pulled his phone out and began playing some music in the hopes it would wake one of them up so he could feel comfortable re-entering the tent.

Within minutes, Mikey was awake and had joined him. "Morning."

"That looked… cosy." Justin indicated the inside of the tent with a jerk of his head. He'd seen Mikey and Ella curled up together, snuggling, before – hell, he'd sat that way with Ella too, but seeing them the way he did this morning felt different.

"It wasn't what it looked like."

Mikey filled him in as he prepared the kettle on the gas stove to make cups of tea for them all. When he finished, he looked up at Justin, not surprised to see a look of thunder on his face coupled with sadness.

"Fuck… shit. Mate, I'm so fucking sorry I wasn't there with you."

Mikey could see that Justin was working himself up into a guilt fuelled frenzy, could recognise it in his friend's eyes as he'd felt the same after the attack. Ella had been right, the 'what ifs' didn't help and all they could do was deal with the here and now.

"Mate, honestly. It's okay, well it wasn't last night, but it is now. The guy has been dealt with, Ella's safe, and that's all that matters."

Mikey noticed a muscle in Justin's jaw clench as if he were struggling to hold in his rage. It took him a while to speak and when he did, his voice was thick with emotion.

"I'm so glad you were there for her when I couldn't be Mikey, seriously. I can't even-"

"Don't you dare finish that sentence Justin Taylor." Ella's voice made them jump. Both of them turned to see her sitting cross-legged in the doorway of the tent, looking at them with a fire in her big, green eyes. "Please don't go down the 'what if' route Mikey almost went on last night. It happened, it was dealt with, and is over. Please can we just enjoy our last day and night here before I have to face mum and dad."

Mikey explained to Justin that Ella had called her parents from the police station, ensuring them she was safe, and would be home as planned. They had tried to talk her into going back home early but had to accept her decision. He told them both how hard it had been listening to her speaking to her mum, trying not to cry as she had insisted that she was fine thanks to Mikey.

"Okay. We'll stay, but you are *not* going anywhere without one of us," Justin put his hand up to stop her interrupting him, "that includes the shower block. I won't take no for an answer Ella. We're not risking anything else happening, I don't care what you think. If you don't agree, we pack up right now and go home." He may not have been able to help her at the time, but he was damned if he wasn't going to protect her now.

Mikey nodded in agreement, and Justin could see from the look on her face that Ella knew that there was no way on Earth she was going to be able to disagree with them. Sighing, she nodded her head meekly and relief flowed through Justin at her silent agreement.

"Okay but promise me one thing, please." They both looked at her, waiting. "Don't hover and stop yourselves from having a good time because you're too busy looking out for me."

Neither Justin nor Mikey said anything. When they were alone, they would decide on an arrangement to keep an eye on her and still be able to have fun.

"I'm serious guys. I'm not going to lie, I've never been so scared in my life, but the whole thing's been dealt with and it's our last night before I have to deal with Mum and Dad, so please allow yourselves to have fun tonight." She looked at Justin. "I know you have someone lined up for tonight, so go and meet up with her, and Mikey; just let loose a little, please."

Eventually, both of them mumbled their agreement; they'd never be able to sway Ella's decision to make the most of their last night at the festival. With a huge smile on her face, she launched herself at the pair of them, hugging them tightly. She loved the pair of them and showed them often. Mikey realised making sure they had fun tonight was her way of thanking him for 'saving' her and for putting Justin's mind at ease so he wouldn't feel guilty for not being there at the time.

Deep inside, he was glad someone, anyone, had been with her. He didn't want to think about what would have happened if they weren't. It didn't matter who, just that someone was.

Chapter Seven

The 'beach' down by the lake was heaving with people. Justin walked through the crowds with Ella and Mikey looking for somewhere they could sit and watch the crowd with their drinks, but it was proving difficult.

A huge bonfire had been set up near a makeshift DJ booth, which were safely away from the water's edge, with large logs that had been placed around it in a rough circle, and finally the three of them managed to find a free space. It was tight, but they didn't care; once the music started, no one would be sitting for long anyway – at least that's what Justin hoped would happen when things kicked off and everyone started to dance.

Despite Ella reassuring both him and Mikey, he couldn't help but feel guilty as hell that he wasn't with them when she was attacked. He knew the police and festival security had done what needed to be done, but he was still angry he hadn't been given the chance to knock the creep out. Ella deserved to be treated like a queen, and he hated the thought that kept tracking through his mind; if she'd been completely on her own, she wouldn't have been able to fight him off. Deep down, Justin couldn't help but lay some of the blame at Mikey's feet, even though he knew it was undeserved. Mikey adored Ella as much as Justin did, if not more, and would beat himself up about leaving her alone for the short amount of time he had. He didn't need Justin piling it on as well, even if Justin did have a tiny little niggle at the back of his mind he desperately tried to ignore.

"Hey gorgeous." A female voice interrupted his thoughts. Turning to look at the girl who had spoken to him, he felt a wide smile split his face, grateful for the chance to get out of his own head for a while.

"Hey, Andi."

With a smile, the dark-haired beauty squeezed herself on the seat next to him.

"Looking forward to the party?" She asked as they looked around the crowd, beers in their hands as the atmosphere around them starting to pick up.

"Really am. Gonna be a great last night."

Justin vaguely remembered Andi telling him that this was her second time at the festival, so took it on her authority that the party was going to be pretty good. Seeing the bands live was amazing, but this party was supposed to be insane, and all three of them had been looking forward to it since they'd bought their tickets.

"You're quiet. Everything okay?"

"Yeah, just got a couple of things on my mind."

Before he could explain further, tell her about everything that had happened since he'd left her tent that morning, they were joined by Ella and Mikey who had gone in search of more drinks.

"Hey Andi," Ella grinned at the pair of them. Justin could feel the entire right side of Andi's body pressed up against the left side of his and realised it must look like more than it was to his two best friends, that and the fact he'd spent two nights with her – something he didn't do very often.

"I've heard so much about the two of you," Andi smiled at his two best friends. He really had told her about them which was also something he didn't often do with a girl he met.

"Shame we can't say the same." Mikey's answer made Andi laugh and Justin blush as the DJ began playing music, most of it by the artists who had been on stage over the weekend. The loud bassline prevented them continuing their conversation as the crowds around them began to dance and cheer.

"Go and dance with her." Ella whisper-shouted in Justin's ear, pulling him to his feet and giving him a shove towards Andi. "Mikey's with me, it's fine," she reassured him when he hesitated. At her words, his face was split once again by a wide grin as he took Andi by the hand and the two of them melted into the thick crowds.

"I think he might actually like this one." Ella muttered happily as she and Mikey watched them disappear, knowing that Justin's dancing resembled those weird inflatable dancing men. "And I think she likes him back."

As the sunlight began to dim, the organisers of the festival lit the huge bonfire. Heat, crackling, and flickering orange light filled the area surrounding it, drawing people closer and laughter surrounded Mikey as he and Ella watched the crowd.

As it got later, and night fell, the volume of the music lowered a little, but was still loud enough for people to dance and enjoy themselves and those talking no longer had to scream at one another.

Mikey and Ella had remained seated rather than go crazy like many other revellers who were looking to end the weekend with a bang. The two of them were content to sit and watch while they drank their beers. Neither were particularly in the mood to party hard but they were still enjoying themselves being surrounded by people who did and were.

"What's the betting we don't see Justin until after we've packed the tent up in the morning?" Mikey laughed catching sight of their friend and Andi leaving the beach hand in hand, heading in the direction of the vast campsite.

"Let him enjoy himself; we only have about a month before we pack up our lives and go off to uni, separately. Why shouldn't we make the most of tonight?" Ella spoke thoughtfully, not looking forward to going back home *or* being separated from either of her best friends.

"At least Justin's living his life how he wants to. I'm too busy trying to appear 'normal', worrying about how others view me, and you worry too much about what your parents think," Mikey spoke almost slowly as he cradled a bottle of beer. Out of the corner of her eye, she could see him staring into the flames of the fire in front of them. She wanted to be offended by his words but was unable to be. He was right; she did worry too much about her parents being disappointed by the choices she made. She knew, deep down, they understood that it was her life, but their certain expectations for her to do well at school, go to university and get a well-paid job afterward often felt claustrophobic.

When was she supposed to be a kid? She was still only seventeen with her whole life ahead of her, why couldn't she have the courage to live it the way *she* wanted to?

"I'm so scared about going somewhere new, meeting new people, and not having you or Justin around to back me up." She admitted after a moment of silence.

"I think uni's going to be good for you Ella," he held up a hand to stop her interrupting him. "I'm serious. No parents, no me or Justin to hold you back, and three years to make life your bitch while you make a fuck ton of friends. You'll have guys fighting for your attention and be able to have your pick."

"Ha." Ella barked out a laugh at the idea of university guys fighting for her. "And you two don't hold me back. You both let me be who I want to be without question or judgement, and *never* discourage me from anything. I love you both so much and can't imagine not having you around."

Ella could feel tears pricking at the back of her eyes. The last thing she wanted was to get sucked into a dark place on the last night of what had mostly been an amazing weekend. She shook her head and drank the last of her beer.

"Let's go for a walk." Mikey said softly, pulling her to her feet.

The further away from the fire and party they got, the dimmer the music and light from the fire got. Soon, they were far enough away on the manmade beach that they only had the stars and each other for company.

"You do realise that you're not losing either of us, right?" Mikey asked as they sat on the still warm sand.

"I know, but it's never going to be the same again is it?"

"No, it's not. But that's not necessarily a bad thing Ella. We may not be able to knock on a wall and know the other needed us, but we'll always be there for each other."

"It's just so hard to wrap my head around. Being in charge of myself, and not having the backup I'm used to; it's going to be so weird."

"It really is, but Justin drives, and we can get student railcards; we'll see each other all the time. Plus, video calls are a thing." Mikey wrapped an arm around Ella's shoulders and pulled her in close to his side as he planted a soft kiss on the top of her head. "Yeah, things will be different, but we'll always be *The Trifecta*."

Mikey hadn't heard, never mind said it out loud, the nickname for the three of them in so long, he'd almost forgotten about it. Ella's dad had always said they were three sides of the same coin which had never made sense to any of them, but it had stuck, and all of their families had referred to them by it for years.

"You promise?" She looked up at him, and he couldn't help but notice how big her eyes were. The thick, long eyelashes gave her the appearance of a Disney character and more than ever, he wanted to kiss her.

"I promise." As Mikey looked down at her, he realised that he'd never get this chance again, but he still hesitated, unsure how she'd react after the previous night. Shifting in his light embrace, Ella turned to face him and slowly, excruciatingly slowly as far as Mikey was concerned, pressed her lips against his.

At first, he thought he was imagining the fireworks; he'd obviously been subjected to far too many chick flicks, but then he realised that the dark sky above them was filling with bright colours as loud bangs and whistles drew them apart.

"I shouldn't have-"

Ella pressed her index finger against his plump lips.

"Don't you dare apologise, because I want to do that some more." Mikey smiled against her mouth as it crashed against his once more, the force knocking him onto his back. Instinct made him tighten his hold around her waist, pulling Ella on top of him as they lost themselves in one another and the sensations being brought on by frantic kisses.

When Mikey woke up in the morning, he and Ella were alone in the tent, which wasn't much of a surprise to either of them. What was a surprise was the fact that their sleeping bags had been zipped together and they were both naked.

"Mikey, stop acting so surprised. It wasn't a dream." Ella's voice, full of sleep, was muffled as she snuggled against his bare chest, his arm snaked around her tiny waist. He placed a kiss on the top of her head as he chuckled.

"I know it wasn't, I just don't remember joining our bags or falling asleep."

Ella shifted her head to look up at him, her green eyes flashing in the early morning light.

"I remember every minute, and I don't ever want to forget."

He leaned down to kiss her, but before they could get any further, Justin entered the tent, the smile on his face widening as he caught sight of them.

Chapter Eight

Driving back home was, emotionally, a mixed affair for Justin. He was happy for Mikey and Ella, whether anything came of their night together or not – he highly expected it to work. While he was attracted to her too, he'd always known she would never go for someone like him. He was the loud one, the one that needed to be reined in on more than one occasion, and he was the one who didn't get emotionally attached. That wasn't what Ella was looking for; she liked guys who were a little quieter, the type of guy who thought before he spoke, the type Mikey was. And he wasn't actually bothered by the realisation.

As he drove, he thought about Andi, the girl he'd gone back to more than once and who invaded his mind when he least expected her to. It was a foreign concept to him, to be left wanting more from someone, and he really did want more. He knew the number she'd given him was real as she'd sent him a text to say goodbye as she and her friends left the campsite, and more than anything he wanted to text and arrange to meet up. For the first time in a long time, it wasn't just about sex. He genuinely liked being in Andi's company.

"So, when are you seeing her again?" Ella asked as he drove along the motorway.

"Who?" He replied, concentrating on the road ahead. It was hard work to sound unfazed by her question. She leaned forward, placing her elbows on the back of his seat.

"Andi."

"No idea, probably won't get in contact." He tried to maintain his blasé air, not sure if he was managing it or not.

"You're such a bullshitter. You really liked her." Mikey joined in the conversation from the back seat. "Why can't you admit that?"

Justin didn't say anything. He was still trying to make sense of how he was feeling, and it was a little unnerving that Mikey and Ella had noticed he was putting on an act. It shouldn't have surprised him; they knew him better than he knew himself most of the time.

"Just call her in a few days and meet up, it's that simple." Ella told him softly, smiling when he looked at her in the rear-view mirror.

"Might do."

Ella turned to face Mikey next to her.

"He totally will."

Justin rolled his eyes as the two of them laughed at him. It wasn't the first time they had, nor would it be the last. He would, as always, take it in his stride.

They had a month left before they made their way in different directions for university, and he was determined that the three of them would spend almost every minute together until it was time to say goodbye. With a smile, he leaned over and turned up the music that had been playing quietly in the background as he put his foot down a bit heavier causing the three of them to hoot and holler as they made their way along the motorway.

When they arrived home, three sets of parents were waiting outside for them as if they'd been gone for months. Within seconds of her getting out of the car, Ella's mum and dad, who were standing a little away from Mikey and Justin's parents, had whisked her away into their flat leaving Justin and Mikey to do some explaining.

"Oh, that poor girl." Mikey's mum was shocked as the boys unloaded their stuff from Justin's car and dumped it on the ground. "I'm just glad you were there for her." She wrapped her arms around her son and hugged him tightly. Mikey turned his head to look at Justin who was grinning.

"Yeah, he was there for her alright."

Mikey flipped him the finger before disentangling himself from his mum's arms and started taking his stuff into their flat. He couldn't help but wonder what was happening between Ella and her parents; more than anything, he wanted to go over and help explain everything but knew he'd more likely make matters worse. The best thing he could do was wait for her to call or come to him; all he could do right there and then was sort his stuff out and take a long, hot shower.

He knew Ella's parents wouldn't blame any of them for what had happened, but he was worried they would try and pressure her into following it up with the police, something she'd said she didn't want to do. She'd made it clear to him and Justin she just wanted to forget about it altogether and make the most of the last of summer. He didn't blame her if he was honest with himself, even if he did want the guy to get locked up. The local police had told him and Ella it was likely he would go to jail, but it wouldn't be for long because he was 'interrupted' which made Mikey's blood boil. Just because some scrotum didn't manage to actually rape a woman meant he didn't get a decent sentence; but he was relieved Ella didn't suffer any more than she had.

For now, they would spend all their time together while they waited for their exam results. After that, they would be busy making arrangements with universities and organising housing and other stuff. It wouldn't be long before they were separated trying to adjust to new places and people.

"Hey, Mikey!" Justin's voice was right outside the bathroom door as he knocked a tattoo on the barrier between them. Mikey shut off the water and wrapped a towel around his waist, showing off the scar he usually kept hidden. Three angry welts stretched across his abdomen from a horrible football tackle when he played for the local under sixteen team; he'd never gone back afterwards.

"Missing me already?" He teased as the pair of them went into Mikey's room. Justin flopped down onto the bed while Mikey quickly dried himself behind his wardrobe door and got dressed.

"Yes sweetheart, I can't live without you." Justin deadpanned. The pair of them grinned at one another, relaxed in a way that only lifelong friends could be. Mikey noticed Justin's hair was wet, indicating a hot shower had been the first thing he'd done once he'd got inside his own flat. "I'm worried about Ella." Justin spoke quietly so Mikey's parents wouldn't hear them talking, even though they knew what had happened at the festival. "She's dealing with everything a little too well, don't you think?"

"Who are we to tell her how she should react and cope with stuff?"

"I know everyone deals with shit differently, but… I guess I don't know what I'm trying to say."

"I think I know. In films and on TV whenever anything like this happens, the girls freak out and stuff, but Ella's not like that. I mean, she was shaking after it all happened, but once the scum had been banged up by the police and security, she calmed down; maybe him being found so quickly helped her deal. Like… if he was still wandering around, maybe she'd be more on edge, wondering if he'd find her again. That kind of thing."

"Yeah, I guess. I wonder how much her mum and dad are freaking out right now."

"They weren't too bad actually." Ella's voice made the pair of them jump. Even though Mikey's room was quiet, neither of them had heard her being let into the flat.

She hovered in the doorway, unsure for the first time since she'd met the two boys, of where to sit. Justin made the choice for her by standing up and giving her a nudge towards Mikey's bed. As she fell onto her side, laughing, he pulled Mikey out of the chair by his desk, gave another shove and sat down in the empty seat.

"So, what happened?" Mikey asked her as she snuggled up next to him, something she'd done hundreds of times before.

"They wanted me to follow up with the police and take the guy to court, but I refused. I can't remember what he looked like, wouldn't be able to pick him out even if he jumped up and down in front of me. No, I told them to let it go so I can move on and enjoy the rest of summer."

Mikey didn't say anything. All he could feel was Ella's tiny, warm body pressing up against his side, conjuring up memories of them in the tent the previous night. Despite his shower, he could still smell her on his skin, feel her in his hands, and taste her on his tongue; all of which he wanted to experience again.

"Fair play Ella. But just so you know. If you did need to talk about it, or want to take it further, me and lover boy there will back you up one hundred percent. Whatever you decide, we've got your back, no questions asked." He stood up, a shit eating grin on his face. "But for now, I'm going to go home so you two can you know, be alone." With a lewd and over dramatic wink, he left the room, closing the door behind him.

Mikey turned his head to look at Ella who was laughing silently to herself.

"I love Justin, but I thought he'd never leave." She murmured as he lowered his head so their lips could meet softly.

Justin sat in his bedroom, his phone in his hand, scrolling through the photos he'd taken over the weekend. The ones he'd taken of performers on stage were blurry as hell or the artists were indistinguishable from the lights behind them, but he didn't delete them. They were his memories from what was mostly an amazing weekend, and even though they were a mess, they would trigger images in his mind of the festival.

He was still angry about what had happened to Ella, and guilty he hadn't been there to help Mikey stop that scum laying his hands on their best friend, guilty he'd been with another girl while Ella had been at risk of something that could have turned out so much worse than it did. He knew she wanted to let it go, but he couldn't stop thinking about it, about what *could* have happened. A hint of jealousy also ran through him at the thought of how close it had brought Ella and Mikey despite him constantly thinking about Andi and the possibility of the two of them being more than casual hook ups in a tent.

He didn't begrudge Ella and Mikey acting upon their hormones and feelings. Over the past weekend, and the last couple of months if he was honest with himself, things between the two had shifted a little. He'd initially put it down to exam stress as the two of them were the academic ones of their trifecta, where he wasn't, far from it. He may have been going to university, but as far as he was concerned, Media Studies wasn't a typically academic subject. He wasn't stupid, but Justin Taylor knew his limits, despite having picked a joint honours course of Media Communication and Marketing. He was going to make the most of his time at university, hopefully get his degree, then work out what to do and where to go next.

Justin had no idea what he wanted in life, other than to have fun, and where better to do that than surrounded by other party animals who would be up for pub crawls and getting wasted every night? Yeah, he could do the same at home, but it was time he was out on his own which sadly included being away from Mikey and Ella. Although, if they were going to be loved up and coupley maybe that was a good thing.

Dropping his phone onto his bed, Justin felt restless. He had all the spare time he'd ever wanted while at school, and nothing to do or anyone to do it with. Boredom wasn't good for him, but he didn't want to interrupt his friends just in case they were… indisposed. After pacing around his room for five minutes, he snatched his phone up of his bed and went outside to see if any of their other friends were around.

Chapter Nine

Results day came far too quickly for any of their liking. Justin had wanted to drive into school to get it all over and done with, but Ella wanted to drag it out for as long as she could and managed to talk the boys into walking the ten-minute journey. It took them, to Justin's dislike, well over half an hour. He wondered why their school insisted on doing it this way rather than via email the way a lot of other schools did.

"Ella, you're looking a bit green, you okay?" Justin commented as they approached the gates. He wasn't feeling too clever himself and was dreading opening his results.

"I've never felt so nervous in my entire life."

Mikey squeezed her hand in silent reassurance. Justin noticed they'd been hand-in-hand for the entire walk over and kept quiet for fear of Ella attacking him. He'd noticed she got 'testy' when plagued with her nerves; the build up to exam season taught him that after she bruised his arm when he laughed at her walking into a lamp post whilst reading one of her textbooks.

"You'll be fine; you're crazy smart and are going to pass with flying colours which means you'll be able to do anything you want." Justin put an arm around her shoulder and pulled her in for a hug. She didn't reply as they entered the building and saw their friends milling around in the lobby. Everyone he looked at was pale and looked petrified. That one, small slip of paper held the power to change their lives, in the best or the worst ways they could imagine, and that was bigger than Justin had ever realised until that very moment

He saw a couple of the other girls from their year had noticed Ella and Mikey holding hands, but knew Ella wouldn't worry about what they were thinking; there had been rumours about the three of them for years anyway, what was one more before she didn't have to see them every day?

"Let's get this over and done with" Mikey muttered as they walked to stand with their friends who were already clutching unopened envelopes.

Justin's mum and brother threw a party in their flat to celebrate all three of The Trifecta getting the results needed for them all to head off to their chosen universities. It was a loud affair and lasted the rest of the evening and into the night. Proud parents shed tears at the thought of their babies leaving home as they stood to one side, drinks in their hands, watching the kids play around as they had for years.

"It's not going to be the same without The Trifecta causing trouble wherever they go." Ella's dad commented as he toasted the three of them. "But, we're all so proud of you three. You're all going to do wonderful things at university and beyond."

Mikey could see tears in Ella's eyes as she hugged her dad. They'd been an official couple for a month and now, because they'd done so well in their exams, they were being separated for at least three years. It was going to kill him watching her, and Justin, leave. He was like a man who had been starved, then given food, and now it was being taken away from him again. He wasn't sure how he was going to live without Ella in his life constantly. They would keep in touch, sure, but it wouldn't be the same as touching her, holding her, kissing her, and more.

"You okay mate?" Justin sat next to him. Mikey didn't respond for a few moments as the pair of them watched everyone else in the room laughing and drinking as if it was New Year's Eve.

"Yeah... I guess." Mikey's sigh filled him with dread, and he knew Justin could hear it in his voice when he started to speak again. "I mean, I've known things were going to change for ages, but now... it feels too real. The three of us are going to be miles away from each other and things are never going to be the same again." Mikey could feel the lump forming in his throat and coughed to hide the possible onset of tears.

"It's shit mate, I know, but we'll always be friends, we'll always be The Trifecta."

With a gentle punch to Mikey's shoulder, Justin left the best friend he'd ever had to get his emotions under control; escaping out into the garden, he pulled his phone out of his pocket. He and Andi hadn't had a chance to meet up, but they'd been trading messages back and forth for almost the entire time since they returned from the festival. Something that surprised him just as much as him wanting to see her again.

Busy tomorrow? He waited while the three dots indicating she was typing bounced up and down on the screen.

Not yet.

Wanna meet?

Yeah, okay. With a grin, Justin typed out some arrangements before pocketing his phone and returning to the party. He thought it was nothing more than a booty call, but he was looking forward to seeing Andi again before moving away and living his life away from his mum and the confines of rules. University was a huge step, and Justin couldn't wait to take it.

The three of them had spent their final three weeks together before having to pack up the things they needed. Their time had flown by and before they knew it, the point had come to leave. They huddled together on the bed in Justin's bedroom one final time. Their voices echoed around the bare walls, devoid of Justin's film posters and photos, and it finally hit home for him that he was leaving.

"Wow, it's happening." He kept his voice low, not trusting his own emotions now that he could see his room, empty and without his personality everywhere.

"Mate, it's been happening for weeks now. You've been sorting through mountains of crap because you're a hoarder." Mikey teased him, not letting go of Ella's tiny hands that were clasped between his own.

"I know, but… seeing my room like this, blank and empty, makes it so real. Even though I'm due to leave in half an hour, seeing plain walls and my bed stripped makes it so much more… shit. It's happening."

The thump of his head hitting the wall behind him echoed around the room, and for some reason it made Ella giggle. The more she tried to stop, the more she laughed. Justin stared at her, not sure what to say as tears streamed down her face. She couldn't stop laughing and it was bizarre to see her surrounded by nothing but bare walls losing it when throughout his life the posters on his walls had always been the backdrop to their time in his room.

"I think she's finally gone mad." He muttered as he and Mikey watched the tiny girl between them.

Eventually, her laughter turned to real crying, and the two of them wrapped their arms around her to comfort her.

"I'm sorry... I just... I can't imagine what it's going to be like tomorrow morning and not having both of you next door. Not being able to just pop over whenever I want, not having the two of you tease me for being short... It's going to suck balls, and I hate it." Justin felt her body shudder as she cried and hiccupped between him and Mikey's bodies as they enclosed her in their arms.

"Shhh. Ella. There's no need for this. Three years isn't a long time, not really. Look how long we've been friends, and we'll *still* be friends during and after uni." Justin honestly believed what Mikey was saying; his best friend loved the two people sat on the bed with him, maybe one more than the other in more than one way. All three of them knew they would be friends for the rest of their lives. It didn't matter where they were – whether they were in the same city or not – they would always be there for one another until they took their last breaths. That was the sentiment in Mikey's words, Justin heard it and knew Ella heard it, even if she couldn't quite process it then and there.

"Ella, sweetie. Your dad's here." Justin's mum popped her head around the door. Although she was smiling softly, there was a sadness in her voice. "I'm sorry, but it's time to go."

The three friends stood up off the bed and followed her out of the flat and to the waiting car that was full of Ella's stuff, boxed up and shoved in black bags.

"Ready honey?" Her dad asked, his voice had the same tone as Justin's mums had.

"No."

Justin watched as she nibbled at the inside of her cheek, something he hadn't seen her do for years, and her inner turmoil flashed across her face.

He knew she wanted to go to university more than anything, to learn stuff and become great at whatever she chose to do with her life, but he could see she was scared. Scared at the thought of new things happening around her, scared at not having him and Mikey to back her up, scared at losing the new relationship she'd been building with Mikey. All these things had been verbalised over the past couple of weeks, and now he could read them all over her face and it killed him to see her in pain.

Eventually, after tight hugs and more tears, Ella's dad managed to get her into the passenger seat of his car. Justin and Mikey stood side-by-side watching as the car pulled away and disappeared around the corner.

"And then there were two." Mikey muttered before turning away to go back inside and get ready to leave himself without looking back at Justin. Within a couple of seconds, he ran back outside and wrapped his big arms around his best friend's body. He didn't know what to say as the two of them stayed like that for a few minutes in silence, but Justin seemed to understand as he hugged him back without saying anything. For once the oldest and first ever friend kept the quips to himself. Eventually, he let go and whispered, "I'll miss you mate" before going back inside to prepare to leave.

Justin stayed where he was for at least ten minutes, contemplating his future. He was facing 'the great unknown' and he didn't know how he felt about it. Yes, he was going to miss Mikey and Ella, but there was an undercurrent of excitement fizzing through him, and he actually felt guilty about that.

After a while, he turned and went back inside to look at his empty bedroom one last time. It was his turn to leave.

Epilogue

Ella walked out of her lecture and breathed in a lungful of the cold air, loving how it refreshed her after two hours of muggy heat from the radiators. It was almost the end of her first term, and she was more than ready to go home for the Christmas break. Despite her worry about leaving home, she'd loved every minute of being at university. She'd made a few close friends with some of the others who lived in her halls and had a healthy social life, but something was missing; two somethings.

Justin and Mikey had been in constant contact with her via text and email, but none of them had managed to visit one another, so she couldn't wait to see them when she got home, especially Mikey who she couldn't wait to feel in her arms, in her...

"Hey, Ella. All done for the day?" A girl from her class, Mary, jogged to catch up with her.

"Yeah. I've handed in my last assignment, and I'm ready to start packing to head home at the weekend. You?"

"Good God, yes. I'm not looking forward to the million-hour train journey back up to Glasgow, but it'll be great to be back home in my own bed for a few weeks."

The two young women smiled at one another as they walked back towards their halls of residence. They weren't very close, but they were friends and had spent a fair bit of time together, in class and socially.

"I bet you can't wait to get your hands on that boyfriend of yours." Mary teased, smiling at the blush covering Ella's face. She was thankful of the cold air which cooled her skin as Mary chuckled at her.

Ella's wall was covered in photos of her, Justin and Mikey, with a picture of just her and Mikey in pride of place on her bedside table. Everyone seemed to know about The Trifecta and how close they were. It gave her a thrill to see their faces whenever she went into her room, and she couldn't wait to get up there now and pack so she was one step closer to seeing them in the flesh.

"It's going to be so good seeing him and Justin, but yes. I can't wait to see Mikey in particular."

"Well, I for one am glad to hear that."

Ella felt as if she jumped a foot in the air at the sound of Mikey's voice behind her. She spun around, vaguely hearing Mary call something out to her, and her eyes found Mikey's. The hazel twinkling in the winter sun behind his glasses.

"What the hell are you doing here?" She yelled as she flung her arms around his neck and peppered his face with kisses.

"Thought I'd give you a ride home." He indicated the cherry red mini he'd been leaning up against as he'd waited for her; he'd passed his driving test not long after they'd all left for university, and his parents had surprised him with the car. It had been all he could talk about during one of their video calls, so much so that Ella had teased him about wanting to be alone with it.

"But I'm not packed, or anything."

"We don't need to leave right away. Tomorrow's fine for me."

There was a glint in his eye, which made Ella grin as he pressed his lips against her own. The kiss was full of passion, longing, and a promise Ella couldn't wait to cash in on. "Got any plans for tonight?"

"I have now."

The End

Heart Beats

The End of Promise and Paine

by

Sam Destiny

Promise and Paine rule the music world. She's the babe of rock music while he is the bad boy of country.

Have they ever been together on stage? No.

Have they been together everywhere else? Hell yes.

However, if the odds are against you, are you ready to walk away for the greater good?

Would you leave what you know for the person you love?

When everything is on the line, will they be strong enough to see this through—or will this be the end of Promise and Paine?

Warning:

If you are into angst, this story is for you.

If you are into getting your heart broken, this story is for you.

If you are ready to curse the author, this story is for you.

This story doesn't have a typical happy end.

Sometimes though, the end comes before the beginning, and if you like that kind of thing… This story is for you.

Chapter One
Maya

I woke to an empty bed.

Again.

Dating a musician sounded fun in theory, but there were moments when I was sure it was the worst thing ever. Sitting up, I listened, and sure enough, the soft notes of a guitar hit my ear.

For a few moments I allowed the haunting melody to engulf me, but then I decided that being close to Aiden now was more important than having him write new music. Wrapping myself in a knitted jacket, I ventured out and found him in the music room.

As always there was only a small lamp on, sitting right across from him on the desk he worked on. I didn't know why Aiden always sat at a desk when writing, but I had to admit he was a sight for sore eyes. His sandy hair was disheveled, and it could be due to sleep as well as him running a hand through it constantly. His back was bare, beckoning me with the tattooed shoulders and shifting muscles.

I crossed over to him, slipping my hands over his shoulders and he instantly reached for my hand. "I didn't mean to wake you," he whispered, kissing my palm before disposing of the guitar and pulling me into his lap instead.

"You didn't. I woke up because you weren't there." His expression softened, those tender brown eyes filling with affection.

He kissed me, soft and sweet, taking his time, and I felt it in every fiber of my body. "Being around you just inspires me too much, and I always worry I'll forget the spark of inspiration. It's crazy. I've written more in the last six days than I did in the eight months before."

That was how long there'd been tours going on, concerts everywhere, leaving hardly any time for us. But then, each time we saw each other again, it was as if no time at all had passed. "It's okay, I get it," I whispered and cuddled into him. I didn't care where he was holding me as long as he was holding me. "Wanna tell me about the song you've been writing?"

His face fell and he bit his lip. I pulled it free from its prison and then leaned in, soothing the sting with my own lips. "It's about…" He smiled softly, but the sadness was still there. "…us."

I shrugged as if I wouldn't know why he was hurting about that. "As long as you don't name anyone, you'll be perfectly fine to release it."

He shook his head, the sandy waves wild and tempting. "Nope, not this one. But let's not focus on that and go back to bed instead." He stood with me in his arms, leaving the music room, not caring about the burning light or the half-filled music sheets.

And I appreciated it because I wanted the time with him. God, I wanted every minute with him. At twenty-two he was everything a woman could wish for: tender, sweet, funny, smart, serious.

Yet hardly anyone knew that. I was lucky because he was mine, had been for the last two years. It was he who I returned to when the world threatened to drown me.

It was he who I called when my heart ached so bad, I didn't think I'd make it through another day.

And he always answered. Aiden was my life, and I had a feeling I was his in return.

He placed me on the bed, wanting to pull back, but I didn't let him. Instead, I drew him in, kissed him until I had my fill, and then I kissed him some more.

He sighed into my mouth and then covered my body with his. Everything was slow, unhurried, every one of his touches measured, as if he was trying to commit them to memory for bad times.

"I don't know if anyone ever told you, but you are the most beautiful at two a.m. in the morning, when dusk is far away and dawn will never come, in those moments when time seems to be suspended. Moments when only I will get to see and enjoy your perfection."

I smiled although I felt tears welling up. "You already have me in bed. You don't need to win me over," I pointed out and he chuckled, his lips going from my jaw down to my neck, nibbling and teasing. I surrendered everything I was to Aiden and he took it willingly.

I felt the trace of his kisses going down my body as he softly peeled the knitted jacket off me, letting my camisole and panties follow.

I wanted him naked as much as he wanted me that way, yet his movements immobilized me. I stayed where I was, letting him drink me in, knowing I'd get my way with him later, too. After all, we still had hours before the morning came.

My hands drowned in his hair on their own account as he reached the juncture of my legs, making my back bow off the bed.

He hummed in appreciation and I wanted to weep with his unhurried tenderness. Those moments, in the middle of the night, when nothing but the stars were out, witnessing what was going on between us, were my favorite, too.

It was Aiden and I then, two people helplessly in love in a world that would probably tear them apart. It seemed true love never was left alone, and may it be friends or family, someone was always trying to spread doubt.

I didn't know how we'd made it through two years and still were going strong. Maybe stronger than before.

All I knew was that I didn't see myself ever stopping to love the person that currently was trying to drive me crazy. "Aid... How about you come up and kiss me and give me what we both long for most?" I begged, knowing he wouldn't be able to resist.

As predicted, he chuckled, sighing, then came up to cover me with his body again. "Lose the sweatpants," I ordered and he claimed my lips, torturing me just a little longer.

Aiden

Taking my time was a great plan in theory, but I should've known Maya wouldn't go along with that. She never did. Yes, foreplay mattered to her, but whenever I asked her about it, she said sometimes it was enough to have me looking at her as if she was my whole world.

However, there was no 'as if'. She *was* my whole world, and I didn't know what I'd done to deserve her, but I'd sworn to myself she'd never once let her doubt that, even if we were thousands of miles apart.

Her hands slipped into the waistband of my pants and she pushed them down below my hips, my erection pressed between us as she struggled to get me completely naked. Having her wriggle underneath me turned me on more than I could say and so I didn't even bother trying to help her.

She dug her nails into my ass and I hissed, not because I was in pain, because holy shit, I was gonna lose it soon if she wouldn't stop. "I love you," I whispered against her skin. "I love you so much," I repeated. I'd learned a long time ago that you could never say those words enough to the person you were with because one day it might be over, and the last thing they heard weren't those words although they should have been.

"If you'd love me you'd give me what I want," she whined and I smiled to myself, biting her pulse while lifting my hips to let her continue with her mission. She kissed my chest while pushing the pants down until I could kick them off, then it was just us, skin on skin, and I closed my eyes, soaking up the feeling.

I grabbed her hands, bringing them over her head while her legs came around my hips, nudging me.

Her lips came to meet mine as I pushed forward, bringing us together in that ultimate connection you could only gain with someone you loved more than your own life.

Sex was fine and fun, but this? This was so much more. I didn't need a rush or hurried movements to get to the top as soon as possible. In fact, with her I didn't need anything but her moving with me and my body was ready to make her happy at any given moment.

We moved together, skin sliding against skin, and whimpers fell from her lips, making me harder than I thought possible. Maya made the cutest noise when we were together, and I wished I could bottle them up and keep them for those long, lonely nights on the road.

I let go of her hands and brought mine down to take some weight off her, but she didn't let me get far. "I need to feel connected to you from head to toe," she whispered.

"We're connected from heart to soul, isn't that enough?" I asked and she sighed against my lips, then kissed me. I wrapped her in my arms, holding onto her while I rolled onto my back, having her hover over me.

She closed her eyes, her strawberry blonde waves falling forward in a curtain of silk. I cupped the back of her head and drew her back in, needing her lips on mine like I needed air to breathe.

The way she was rolling her hips was out to drive me crazy and we both knew it. I could tell she was getting close, her movements getting more erratic, irregular, and I grabbed her hips, setting a new rhythm.

She stretched and the pale moonlight washed over her body, giving me a chance to appreciate her as if I was seeing her for the first time.

Was it supposed to feel that way? Was I supposed to fall for her again and again, never stopping, never going back to not wanting her? Would it ever change?

I didn't know, but I hoped it wouldn't.

At twenty-two we'd both seen the world, the bad and the ugly, had lived through things no one should ever live through, and I knew it made us older than our years let on.

Maybe that was why she and I were connected on a level that had taken me by surprise. It was cheesy, but the first time I'd seen her I'd heard wedding bells—real ones and metaphorical ones. High society wedding, some couple that split a year later, but Maya had been there in a soft pink dress, all flurries and laughter, and I'd known.

"Aiden..." My name on her lips pulled me back from my thoughts and I slipped my hands up her body, cupping her breasts, teasing her, playing her body until I felt her quiver.

I didn't need more to follow her over the razor-sharp edge, and I sat up, wrapping myself around her because I needed to be closer. I knew what she'd meant earlier with needing to feel me from head to toe, and I was willingly giving that to her.

Hell, if it were my choice, I'd never again change being this close to her. I helped her ride out her orgasm, held onto her a little longer before I placed her on the bed. "I'll be right back with a wash cloth," I told her, kissing her nose.

I cleaned myself up and then her, smiling to myself because she was putty in my hands. Once I crawled back into bed with her, my heart didn't calm down. It was late, the night still dark, the sound of the Pacific Ocean in the distance, and I wanted to write a million songs about how much I loved her.

Her, and no one else.

I wanted to name her in every single one of them because while I loved fan admiration, I didn't want to give them hope. Was it my duty to do so? Maybe. Musicians dealt in dreams, but honestly...

Couldn't that dream just be me loving her endlessly?

Chapter Two
Maya

"Paine? Promise?"

Aiden groaned at the voices echoing through the house. Last night had been perfect, but then, there was this.

"Coming," he called back, and I knew he hated to scream, but it was better than his manager, Neron, walking in on us.

"Hurry, you two are already late," he replied, his words echoing up the stairs and taking away the peaceful feeling inside of me.

Aiden leaned over and kissed the back of my neck.

"Come on, babe, we need to get up," he whispered.

I shook my head and then pulled a pillow over it. "I haven't heard anything. It's just Neron there. You go, I'll stay here pretending we can go out to the beach today, take the guitars and play a few songs together while the waves are crashing against the shore."

My heart ached because I wanted that, wanted the normalcy. Before he could reply, someone else called from the ground floor.

"Promise, move your sweet ass out of bed! You have the recording with Hunting Shadows first thing in the studio before Paine and you go in for your session," my manager, Dana, screamed. She always sounded hysterical although she rarely ever was. It was just something about her voice and her frazzled appearance that always made her look like a mad woman.

Aiden pulled the blanket lower on my body and kissed his way down my spine. "If you get up now, we can go shower together and can lock the door so we get some kisses in." I knew nothing more would happen because no matter how little I wanted to be out today; we still were known to be professionals.

"But... The bathroom is cold." I pouted, although we both knew nothing in this house was ever cold. Somewhere we had a housekeeper who was worth her weight in gold, and she was as stealthy as a ninja, making sure things were exactly the way we wanted them to be.

"I'll go ahead and start the shower, and you can linger one more minute, okay?" Aiden whispered against my skin, but once he pushed off the bed, I turned just so I could watch his naked form retreat.

"You are perfect," I called after him and his happy laughter drifted back to me, and I got out of bed, following that call as if he were a siren and I lost at sea.

The bathroom was huge and luxurious, all golden appliances and marble counters, and yet, today I didn't see that. Instead, all I saw was the man who slipped into the shower, his smile teasing, his body tempting.

"You are the only good thing about this morning."

He arched a brow while turning on the water. "I'm sure there'll be more. You were looking forward to that charity project."

And I had, because it meant Aiden and I were in the same city *and* the same studio without anyone noticing what there was between us. It also meant we'd be doing some promo together.

I'd never before been on the road with him, but my record company Joyful Tunes Records and his had worked it out.

Luckily.

He drew me in, kissing my nose before drowning his hands in my hair, making sure it was properly soaked. Aiden had a weird love about doing mundane things with me or for me, and washing my hair was one of those things.

I let him because holy hell, he gave the best scalp massages ever. Turning away from him, I let him do what he did best, and I closed my eyes, humming softly.

I'd meant to practice the song we were singing today, but since I'd never before sung with the Hunting Shadows, one of the most famous bands of our time, I couldn't exactly prepare. I liked harmonizing and I could do it in my sleep. I knew the lyrics, knew the melody, but I'd sung it in a million different ways so far.

Aiden and I had heard the same demo and yet, between us singing that song it could have been two different ones altogether.

After all, that was what happened when you threw together the bad boy of Country and the sweetheart of angsty rock.

Way too soon I was clean, Aiden's hands having relaxed me to the point of sleepiness, and he playfully slapped my ass. "Get out and take care of your hair while I clean myself."

I turned to him with a grin. "I could help and—"

"We wouldn't get clean then," he pointed out and opened the glass door for me. Cold air wrapped around me and I huffed, but then left the shower dutifully. I knew if we'd not be down in twenty minutes the latest, either of our agents would break down the door, and we didn't need that.

I took out the blow dryer after wrapping a towel around my body, glad that it would be just a study session day because it meant a loose shoulder-free top, jeans, and a messy bun on top of my head with low-key make-up.

Always pretty, always prepared to be filmed.

As I stood there, humming while I dried my hair, I couldn't help but feel excited. There'd be so many big stars, singers and bands I'd always wanted to meet but never had before, and because it was a charity project and some people needed to stick around for the behind-the-scenes video, my record company had cleared my schedule. I'd get to see some of the most famous people ever work, and it was a dream come true.

"No hope for the lost / no help for the lonely," Aiden sang, coming out of the shower, jumping in right on the line I'd just been humming.

I lifted my brush and lowered the hairdryer, getting into the performance. "And yet here we are / help on our minds only / Give them a break / Give some a pause…"

"We ain't here for the applause / We want the peace," we finished together and I loved it. I wished we'd be able to sing a song together, but somehow I didn't think that was ever going to happen.

Aiden

I walked down the stairs, Dana and Neron exchanging appointments in their schedules. They were luckily on board with us dating and had managed to sync some of our appointments so we'd have more time together, but it still felt as if it wasn't enough.

"I'm good to go," I announced. I wanted to kiss Maya goodbye again, but then we'd probably never leave because no 'one more time' would be enough. Besides, I'd see her in the studio and while we wouldn't be able to kiss and cuddle, we at least would be around each other.

And I'd be able to watch her sing. I loved her music, loved her voice, and yet had never been lucky enough to see her work the mic in a recording studio.

"Beanie," Neron pointed out without even looking up, and I reached up, my palm meeting only hair.

"Damn." For some reason that particular article of clothing had become my sign, and now I couldn't go anywhere without it… And still constantly forgot it.

Something hit my back, and when I turned, I spotted the gray hat on the ground and Maya at the top of the stairs, half dressed and sexy as hell. "You forgot something," she stated and I cocked my head.

Bending to pick it up, I grinned. It smelled of her perfume, fruity, like vanilla and peaches, and it would probably be in my nose all day.

I shook my head at her and then pulled the beanie on.

"Paine, can we get going? Yes, the two of you will be together in the studio, but you'll still need to appear separately. Come on."

I rolled my eyes at Maya, and then turned to Neron with a wide smile. "Ready."

I passed him and he said something to Dana that I ignored, then he was next to me. "There's been a change of plans. You'll be at the studio for three hours, then you'll be doing a press conference and meeting with the PR-reps. Step on Records is not happy with your latest numbers and we need to figure out what to do to boost it."

I froze in the door and it took Neron a few steps before he realized that. "What now?" he asked as if that wasn't obvious.

"My numbers aren't great?" Because that was news to me. News he had been supposed to inform me about.

He waved his cell in a gesture that told me to not mind. "You know, what we consider great and what they consider great is not necessarily the same thing."

I followed him to the car but knew there was more to this than he was letting on.

I knew his tell, and that was lowered lashes and constantly licking of his lips, which he was doing now. Once the driver had closed the door behind us, I nudged him with my knee. "What's going on?"

For the longest time I was sure he was going to placate me again, but then he sighed. "There are too many rumors about you. You know, too many women, not enough, too much sex, not enough. No one really knows anything about you and the record company feels like you should have a public fling. Something hot and bright, something that will get you back into everyone's minds. They want a high society love, one that burns bright and fizzles out soon."

I opened my mouth to say something, but he didn't let me. "And before you say it, I don't think Promise should be the solution. Besides the fact that her management needs her single right now since she has other plans—plans she needs to tell you about because that's what happens in a relationship—they also wouldn't want her name in an article with yours. Your reputation and hers... Let's just say, in their eyes they don't go together well. Plus, Paine, think about it. Do you really want to risk what you have with that woman by being in the public eye all of the time? There'd be press camping out in front of your doors twenty-four-seven and it would take only a few hours before they realize that the doubles walking into your cover-up apartments are nothing but that: doubles."

It had worked so far because no one had honestly bothered to find out where me and Maya were most of the time. There was hardly a scandal to be found.

"But Maya and I are a couple," I reminded him as if he hadn't just walked into our home and had called out for us.

"Promise and Paine can never be a public thing. Neither in music, nor in love. Her label will not allow it, and you know that."

Frankly, I did. I also knew what public love stories looked like and how they ended. However, having someone else on my arm? Impossible.

The closer we got to the city and therefore the studio, the more I wanted to take out my cell and text Maya. Hell, I wanted to talk to her, have her tell me what I was supposed to do. The thing was, I couldn't help but think that starting that conversation ultimately would be the end of Promise and Paine.

While we weren't our public personas at home, it would still influence us big time.

"Dana and I were thinking, maybe we could do it in a few months. Promise will be busy and away, so you wouldn't see each other anyway. If we spin it right, we can fit your public relationship into that time and then, once she's back, it'll already be done."

Yeah, it was that easy.

Not.

Chapter Three
Aiden

I was bent over the mixing console when a guy came in. He'd been running coffee errands all morning, and I knew he had a hard time looking unaffected by the stars walking through here, but hell, not even we were unaffected.

"Oh my," he gasped quietly, as if not wanting to interrupt anything when really, he couldn't.

Kevin, the guy responsible for recording in here, looked up. "What?"

"They are here," the guy replied and Kevin's jar dropped.

"Did you see them?"

Coffee guy nodded. "All five. They are recording currently. It's… Holy shit. Make an album with them and I swear, they'll break all records ever. Like… Everyone else can stop singing, there'd be no use."

Kevin stood, not caring that we were in the middle of a session. "Who is?" I finally asked although there were ten other people standing around that seemed to know as much—or as little—as I did.

Kevin and coffee guy paused in the door, giving me a look that should have me withering on the spot. "If you have to ask, then… You're more in the clouds with your head than I thought."

The two left and frankly, that caused a flurry of activity. Everyone followed, and so did I because I needed to know whom the hell we were talking about.

The studio they wanted to enter seemed to be filled to the brim, and even in the hallway people stood, trying to catch a glimpse inside. Once they spotted me, they decided to make room, having more respect than Kevin had had. I spotted Dana inside the room and she waved me over, but I froze where I stood when voices reached me.

Somehow, at some point, someone clearly had decided that headphones were a waste because they'd pulled the plug and everyone could hear the voices coming from the studio itself.

Through the glass I spotted Maya in the middle of Hunting Shadows, all four guys singing with her.

I knew technically she had only four lines to sing, two of them with me, but they were currently way past that part.

Pushing through, I reached Dana's side. "Can I find out what's going on?"

"Hush!" someone called and I gritted my teeth. I had to admit that the five were a perfect fit. The harmonies were smooth as velvet, and the wide smiles on their faces proved that they knew it, too.

They finished the song as if they'd sang it a million times before, but I knew that wasn't true. Once they were done and the tape ended, silence spread. Well, at least where I stood, because inside the people high-fived and hugged.

"Holy shit, Promise, you are something else," JC, lead singer of the band, announced. Maya waved him off, beaming with happiness. I saw it in the glow of her cheeks and the way she couldn't contain the grin.

"Hush, dude. You guys sound incredible. I mean... Hello, you know what you're doing. No wonder you reached stardom in a matter of months," Maya replied.

A blond guy, Seb, if I remembered correctly, pushed to take her side. "That was all you. I didn't think a female voice could push us the way you just did. Shit."

He wrapped an arm around her shoulder and squeezed briefly.

A guy with a bald head and a full beard leaned forward, pressing the button to talk to the five inside. "Okay, Aaron, take Promise's side. Seb, you stay where you are. We're running it again, but slower this time.

Try…heartbreak. You feel it in your soul. You crave that peace because you know every single person who's been hurt over the last decade."

Maya leaned forward. "Starting where? My line?"

"Nope, the beginning. Record's running. And… Go!"

The melody, slower this time, different, heavier with piano notes, sounded from the speakers and a dark-haired guy took Maya's side. They all stood close together although she didn't have to share her mic with anyone.

I saw the way she pushed her headphones back in position and then inhaled slowly. Seb formed something with his hands, and as if she knew exactly what it meant, Maya started first. Although Sebastian wasn't the lead singer, I couldn't help but think that he took the lead in there, because at another gesture of him JC started to sing and man, I hardly dared to breathe.

Dana suddenly nudged me, pulling me from the room.

She stood in the hallway and even out here the voices still were clear. I didn't think I'd ever had a studio session where I ran through an entire song, let alone twice, without being interrupted or corrected.

"The way you look at her, or the way you wished Sebastian to drop dead, is kinda obvious. You need to tone it down. Besides, shouldn't be you recording?"

I arched a brow at her. "Why are you here? Neron left the minute I was behind the mic. And I recorded my lines. In contrary to Promise there I didn't get the chance to sing more yet. Also, can you believe all those people?"

"Joyful Tunes wanted them together in a studio since forever. Like… Ever-ever. Rhys, Hunting Shadows' manager, refused it so far because he didn't think a girl could do their image any good, but man, this is a PR-team's dream. If they'd be singing a ballad together, you could shoot a video and it would be the…" She interrupted herself. "Anyway, won't happen because this time we'd refuse it. I haven't had a chance to tell Maya yet, but she'll be in Europe soon, and for an extended period of time. We cannot have any rumors about affairs and heartbreaks, so no Hunting Shadows duet. Although even I would listen to that all the time. Those five are a perfect mix."

It was then that it struck me how contrary our situations were. Maya's numbers were climbing, and so was most likely her net-worth, while I seemed to be a falling star—without even having realized it until that very moment.

Maya

After the fourth time singing the song, having switched positions around and eventually having shared a mic with Aaron, we were told to take a brief break. I was feeling high from the session because this hadn't been like a recording moment, but instead you sat in a garage with your friends and just sang together for the sake of it.

The Hunting Shadows were big since three years now, and although I didn't know their ages, I had a feeling that except for Luke, the rest was younger than me. Not by much, but that didn't mean anything.

JC had pulled me along to a room they'd been assigned, and it was weird standing in the silence of it.

"For the record... Holy fucking shit, you are Hunting Shadows and I just sang a song with you! Also, sorry for the language, but... Fuck!" I couldn't believe it. I'd not met them before, but I'd known of them and about them, and had realized a few months earlier that my favorite songs were from them.

Sebastian laughed, his blond strands falling into his eyes while Aaron pulled me in a hug. "There, now you were very close to them," he commented and I laughed, then dropped onto the couch next to Luke. He was dark-skinned and incredibly handsome. In fact, looking around I could tell that they had one for every girl: brooding Seb, bubbly JC, flirty Aaron, and hopeful Luke.

"This was..." I interrupted myself when the guys exchanged sheepish glances. "What?" I asked, dimming down my excitement.

JC was the first to clear his throat, and he turned, grabbing a black bag. "Would you mind… I kinda… You know, we promised some people to get some stuff signed by you, and… You know, well…" He shrugged and then held out a shirt and a handful of my LPs.

Staring at him, I needed a second to react. "Yes. Of course." I reached for the things and then took the pen he also offered. "Whom do I make it out to?"

I poised the pen, waiting for a name, and he cleared his throat. Again. Seemed it was a nervous habit. "To Jay."

I bit back a smirk at his reddening cheeks. "Which one?"

"All of them."

I didn't say anything to that and instead signed it all, handing back the things…only to be presented with more items from the rest of the guys. I was flattered, more than I could tell, and wanted to call Aiden right that moment. "Big fans, huh?" I asked, trying to play it cool.

"The biggest. We were freaking excited to sing with you. Well, all of us, except for Luke. Luke just gets excited about the current woman at his side," Sebastian explained and Luke threw a pillow from the couch we were sitting on, missing his band mate by inches.

"I was excited about meeting you," he insisted and I squeezed his knee.

"Don't worry. I didn't expect to meet fans here. I just expected to be one. So, I wonder if we'll be able to get a copy of that song just for my personal collection."

Before I could say more, or anyone else could reply something, Dana came in with a guy I didn't know but assumed to be Hunting Shadows' manager, Rhys.

"Promise, you were outstanding. I was just talking to Dana here about—"

"No."

I stared at JC in surprise. We'd spoken at the same time, clearly thinking the same thing. I saw Dana cross her arms in front of her body, smiling smugly.

Rhys' features darkened for a moment. "You don't even know what I want to say," he protested.

"You want us to sing together, make a touchy video, and then want us to promo together so we have rumors. Not happening though," JC replied.

Rhys huffed. "She's attractive and no one said you'd have to have anything with her in public."

I stood. "She's also quite capable of talking for herself and I'm with JC. We're not doing that. Their fans don't need anyone stepping in on their territory, and just because you want them in the press doesn't mean I'm ready to get my name dragged through the dirt for them. Also... My brand is not known for scandals. If I appear in the press with a guy, it'll be because I date him, nothing else."

"Amen. Promise, you're up in the next studio."

I nodded and then went around to hug the guys. "Leave your number with Dana, okay? I want to catch up with you, and I don't think IG will be the place."

Sebastian kissed my cheek, then JC, and there was something in his eyes that made me think they'd all appreciate friends. "We sure will. And we'll see you later when everyone's singing. We'll keep you a spot at our mic," he promised, then let me go while I followed Dana.

"Why did they change the plans? Wasn't I supposed to sing with Aiden before I did Hunting Shadows?" I'd not asked earlier because being professional meant you went with whatever you were told, and I had no doubt I'd see Aiden soon enough.

"The studio the two of you were supposed to be in was taken because some others clearly didn't know their lyrics. I mean, not even the two lines they were supposed to know. Anyway, it's Aiden and you now, but before you go in there with him, you need to know something."

I glanced around, but to my utter surprise the hallway we currently stood in was empty. "Yes?"

"Remember the movie role we talked about?"

I snorted. "The one from like... Nine months ago? I remember."

She nodded. "Yes. One of the guys liked you so much, he wanted to do a movie with you, but figured not having you sing would be stupid, so now you have a role in a movie about a girl following a musician on a road trip through Europe, only to be found by a label. It's like... All romantic and soft, you know, just up your alley. A lot of sunshine shots probably, cuddling by the fire and all. You know... *like you*."

I knew exactly what she was trying to say, and it was only because I was a professional that I didn't start squealing in that hallway.

Jesus, my life couldn't work out better, and I needed to see Aiden so he could be part of it all, no matter what.

Chapter Four
Aiden

There was only a handful of people in the room when I left it to join Maya behind the mic. She was still glowing and I wasn't the least bit surprised. I'd gotten the tone technician to send me a copy of every raw version of the songs, and she and Hunting Shadows were duet goals. I couldn't deny that.

I'd also come to realize that among all the stars that were here, some of them on stage for decades, those five were the biggest and most anticipated.

I didn't know what I was feeling, but I knew part of it was jealousy. My life was crumbling, and I had a feeling if Maya and I stayed together, we'd be crumbling right alongside it.

"Make sure they leave the mic off until I give you a sign," I hissed toward Dana outside the room and she nodded her understanding. I'd not be able to see her, but I knew she'd be seeing us. I had never understood why you needed one-way-mirrors in a recording studio, but today it made sense.

Today I wanted to pretend that it was just her and me singing together.

I entered the room and I could see in her eyes how much she wanted to jump into my arm. I plastered on a happy smile because she deserved it, and then told her I loved her. "The mics are out for a few minutes, because I needed to tell you that I've never been so impressed with anyone in a recording studio. You did... I mean... Hell, that was incredible. I still get goosebumps thinking about it."

I showed her my arm, proving my words true. She laughed, brushing her fingertips over my skin. To anyone watching it would look innocent enough. Her expression softened for the briefest moment, then she winked at me.

It was funny, but I think it was the first time ever that I could tell where Maya stopped and Promise began.

This was Promise in front of me, conscious of all eyes us even though we couldn't see them.

It was probably what made her better at the moment than I was. She never forgot what mattered if you wanted to stay famous.

Or maybe it was that Promise was the most fitting name, because she promised her fans to always be herself, and to be honest in her music. And she was. It was in her voice, in her eyes. Hell, when she sang, she had her heart on her tongue.

She went to the mic stand and grabbed a pair of headphones, turning to me. Without anyone else being able to see it, she formed, 'I wish I could kiss you. I have so much to tell you.'

I didn't reply and instead forced my eyes away from her. I didn't think how much more time we had, but when I grabbed a pair of headphones, too, a voice came through the speakers.

"You know your lines?"

"I know all lines," I replied. Just like Maya I'd read the lyrics often enough, had tried different versions. Fine, maybe I'd dealt even more with the song than Maya had, but clearly, she didn't have the slightest problem to fit in.

For a moment silence met us, then the guy was back. "Some people dropped out, and while they are trying to find some more, it seems not many are brave enough to sing with Hunting Shadows or Promise in there. If you don't mind, we're singing all lines together. Promise, you start. Two lines each, chorus together. Bridge... Do what feels right. It'll sound more natural if you two turn to each other. On three."

We both nodded our understanding and when I turned to Maya, her smile soft, I knew I didn't have to worry. I didn't care if there'd be a slow version coming now, the basic beats only, or a soft carrying melody telling us the speed, it wouldn't matter because together we could do this.

"Three."

I'd missed the rest of the count, but it didn't matter. We knew there were opening notes, and I had a hard time not humming them along.

"A burned ground / Destroyed house / a broken soul / meal shared with a mouse," Maya sung and it was like we were back in our bathroom, just singing for ourselves.

The lyrics flew from my lips, easy as if I'd written them myself, and we started the chorus, but before we got into it the music cut off.

"Paine, you are too fast," the tone technician announced.

"I wasn't," I replied, but one look at Maya's face told me I had been. "We were in sync," I protested.

She nodded. "I matched you because I figured they could just make the music fit, but you were getting faster."

I cleared my throat, turning to the mirror. "Sorry. From the start?"

"Yes," came the crisp answer.

I nodded and we started again, but this time we were interrupted even earlier. "Try not to overtake her voice when you sing together. You need to harmonize, not fight. From the beginning," the technician said, sound patient still.

Maya took my hand, coming closer. "I'll squeeze if you start being too dominant or fast, okay? One squeeze, too loud, two squeezes, too fast."

Once her palm was pressed against mine, I closed my eyes. I wanted to kiss it, wanted to have a moment to just be with her and soak up her presence. Maybe that would help. Sadly, I knew that wouldn't happen.

We started again, and this time it seemed to be smoother. We got further, and I brushed my thumb across her knuckles just to remind me that this was us. We could do this.

Hell, we could do anything.

"Okay, stop."

Even before anyone said anything, I knew I'd messed up again. "Wrong line," Maya whispered and I tore off my headphones.

I needed a moment, and I think everyone knew that.

Leaving the room, I wondered what in the world was going on—and sure as hell hoped it wouldn't be a permanent state.

𝄞

I found stairs and climbed them, pausing for a moment when I reached the door to the roof and found it ajar with a jacket between it. Still pushing outside, I made sure it wouldn't fall closed and then found a blond head there.

I crossed over. "JC, right? I thought I'd be alone up here."

He grinned at me, and his mismatched eyes caught me off-guard for a moment. It was an unusual feature and I had no doubt it was a hit with the ladies.

"Paine... I didn't think I'd be getting a chance to hide with you." He winked. "My escape is your escape. What are you running from?"

I didn't know him any more than I knew my next-door neighbor, and that guy I'd never seen before, and yet I felt as if I could trust him. "Ever been in love, and knew it couldn't last? Not because she didn't love you, but because it wasn't enough? Like… Love won't ever be enough to withstand the trials rockstar life is going to throw at us?"

He blinked. "You date someone in the biz? Brave you."

"I've been dating her for two years, and yes, I mean it, but no, there's nothing brave about it. It's all about love, and she is the one for me."

He smirked, but then lowered his head as if remembering something. "I wish I knew what that felt like. Won't ever happen for me because I cannot... You know, it doesn't matter."

I nudged him. "It does to me. What can't you do?"

JC licked his lips. "Date who I want, but that's really a story for plenty of alcohol and a long night," he replied. I held out my phone to him.

"Gimme your number. I think I'll have a need for one of those nights soon, and maybe we could do it together. Would mean I don't cry to a barkeeper who'd tell my whole life story to someone else for money."

He cocked his head. "Why would you need it?"

"Remember the beginning of the talk? Love of my life? Bestest person out there, only one I'd ever love..."

He grinned. "It vaguely rings a bell."

"I'm going to break up with her."

And as I said it, I realized it was true. Whatever she had going on, whatever would take her away from me for months, I knew it was just the next big step in her career, and what Neron and my PR-team had planned for me would only drag her down. If anyone ever figured out who we were, what we meant to each other...

Her career would take a hit while mine would thrive. It didn't matter that it would be unfair, or that not the woman should suffer, but she would.

And even if I wouldn't do all the PR-people cooked up, her career seemed to be going well while mine...didn't, if I believed my manager. I had already planned to check when I was home, to make sure he'd not lied to me, but I could feel it in my bones.

There'd been less interview-requests, less gossip magazines calling... Just less of everything, and I knew Maya would try to help me, would try to get me back on track, but again... Her career would be taking a hit then, and I couldn't risk it.

"If you love her, why break up with her?"

JC's question pulled me back from my thoughts. "What's most appealing about any star? Like… What makes us so appealing to our fans?"

He sighed. "Lies."

I chuckled. "I was aiming for availability. And what makes us more attractive? Being definitely single. You know, being out there, talking about living your best life, and there's no infliction in your voice because it's true. You don't have anyone waiting at home. You don't have anyone expecting you to call after an award show."

"Maybe she's not the right one if she has so much expectations."

I laughed. "She has them because that's what I do. I call her. She calls me. We talk, almost all the time, and you know why? Because we're not in the same place a lot of times. I know it hurts her when we're apart, but… She never lets on. And she's professional. Hell, you saw it. She knew what… Ah, shit."

There weren't many female artists here, and none except for Maya had sung with them.

"No way. Promise and you?"

If I wouldn't know how big he was in the industry, I'd expect him to be nothing more than a fanboy talking about his idol. His eyes were shining and his jaw nearly had hit the floor.

"Promise and me, yes," I confirmed. "We've been going strong since the Cassandra-wedding."

"That was… two years ago? Three? We were supposed to sing, just fresh out of boyband boot camp, but we didn't have time. But if you made it so far, why break up now? Holy shit, the movie news are true, aren't they? She scored a major role. Makes sense why they'd want her single for that. Most franchise works on the main actors having rumors about them."

I blinked. It couldn't be. I remembered Maya mentioning having auditioned for a role, but that had been months ago. "I don't know." But it made sense. And if he'd heard rumors about it... "But maybe. It would make sense. And my numbers dropping. My PR-team wants a public farce."

JC rolled his eyes. "It would be a few weeks, fake whirlwind romance, well-placed pictures, and Promise would know. I mean, for real. You can handle that. Plus, it will distract people from you and her."

I nodded. "She'd play along, for me, and I know she would, but there's no way she can ignore the pictures or avoid them, and I love her too much to ask that of her."

Clearly JC had an opinion concerning that, too, but he didn't get to tell me about it because Neron appeared in the door. "The roof, I knew it. Let's go back down and be the musician we both know you are, okay? Get a grip, Paine, or you'll feel that tomorrow."

I sighed, knocking my cell against the railing we stood at. "I'll call you."

JC grinned. "Sounds like you need it for sure."

With that I left, wondering if this was a lost cause or if I would be able to pull myself together enough to make it through today at least.

Maya

Aiden came back in and I jumped up, ready to wrap him in my arms, but knew I couldn't.

"I have an idea," I stated before he could say anything. I didn't need him to apologize to me or anyone else.

"Okay?" he asked, his tone doubtful, but I knew I was going to get him with that one.

I walked to the back and picked up an acoustic guitar. "It's not yours, I know that, but Sebastian had one. Seems he never goes anywhere without it. Anyway, I figured we try to have you play the guitar. You do the melody. It'll be easier for you keep the speed then, and I know you played it before. And then we'll sing."

He looked at me for so long, I wasn't sure he was going to play along, but then he took the guitar and wordlessly pulled me into a hug. I didn't let go of him until he was ready, and I didn't care who saw what or was thinking which way about this.

I'd also arranged for two chairs and so we took our spots.

"You got it, Paine. Whenever you are ready we are ready," the tone technician called. He'd been ready to postpone Aiden's and my session until Aiden had himself better under control, but I assured him we'd get it right this time. He'd complained about the guitar, but Dana had just reminded him that a good tone technician knew how to split the guitar from the voices and that was that. "First stanza and then the chorus for now, okay?"

Aiden nodded. "Yes, I got it."

He put his headphones on and I did the same, although this time only one of them because I'd need to hear the guitar to follow his rhythm even while hearing myself.

Once he strung the first few notes I knew this was exactly what he'd needed. The song went smoothly from there, and we weren't stopped after the first chorus, or even the second. Aiden didn't look at me, and I didn't need him to, I knew he was more than aware of me. This time we carried each other, our voices working together better than before. Once finished, he went right over into a second version, this time faster, closer to what I'd been singing with JC and the rest, and I realized he'd been watching, too.

Maybe it was better I hadn't been aware of that because maybe then I'd have been too nervous.

After all, he was Aiden, and if I wanted to impress someone in this world it was him.

Always him.

The second version went smooth, too, and after we were done, he set down the guitar, looking at the one-way-mirror as if he could see the people behind. "I'm ready to do it the way we should have earlier. I got it now. I promise."

The tone technician cleared his throat. "I won't lie, we don't have much time, meaning one run-through max. If you fuck this up—"

Aiden shook his head. "I won't. I promise. I'm sorry about earlier." He took my hand as if silently apologizing to me, too, and then nodded. "Let's do this."

I was ready, born ready, and not the least bit surprised when this time Aiden was outstanding. His voice caused me to melt next to him, and I sure hoped people missed the soft hint in my lines when singing. He was everything a woman could wish for, and his determination was as sexy as his fingers dancing across the strings of any guitar.

We actually finished that song, too, and were met with silence. I took off my headphones, and so did he, turning to me. "You knew what I needed."

I nodded. "You're a musician, one who's hands on. I figured a guitar would make this easier."

The door opened and Hunting Shadows filled in. "Let's do one together," Luke demanded. "I'm thinking that country voice, the female rockstar and we? It'll sound epic."

Aiden grinned, finally looking a lot more relaxed. "I don't think we have time."

Luke nodded toward the mirror. "Donny, we got time?"

The technician's voice came over the intercom. "We... of course. We'll run the slower version. Easier to catch up with everyone. You need me to tell you who starts?"

Someone shuffled in with more headphones, and they were plugged in while mics were adjusted, all in a rush.

"Nope, Paine will start, Promise and I will jump in, and then the rest. We'll figure it out," Hunting Shadows' Sebastian stated.

"Your song, Seb, your rules."

Aiden turned. "You wrote that song?"

I arched a brow. "You didn't read that when we got the lyrics? Yes, he did."

The guy in question blushed. "I usually do love songs, but hey, we all know pain and the loss of hope, right? I knew what I was doing, people approved, and here we are. Can we?"

He put on headphones, incredibly humble, and Aiden gave me a long look. I couldn't decide what he was trying to tell me, but it almost looked like he was somewhat jealous. "Your lyrics are incredible, too," I whispered, leaning in. "Maybe better." I winked and felt Seb nudge me.

He smirked and I nudged him back while Aiden shook his head, shaking off whatever it had been in his eyes.

God, there was a lot to dissect once we were home, but in the end it didn't matter because we'd be together, and together we could figure everything out.

Chapter Five
Maya

Coming home took forever. We'd been separated after the session with Haunting Shadows, and while I hadn't minded dealing with fans and press, I'd seen Aiden rush straight home. When I asked Dana if she knew what was going on, she'd put on an innocent face, just informing me that tomorrow she'd cleared my schedule based on Aiden's demand.

As much as that should excite me, I couldn't help but think that it wouldn't end well for me. Going in search of him I tried our bedroom first, finding him standing by the window.

"Aww, I missed your shower," I exclaimed and he turned to me, wordlessly, then crossed the space between us and then I was in his arms. He kissed me like he needed me to breathe, and I kissed him back as eagerly.

Everything about him screamed desperate and hopeless, and I wondered what was going on.

I pushed back, making sure I could look at him and cupped his cheek. "Wanna tell me what's going on?"

He licked his lips and since I could, I leaned in and did the same.

"Do you know how many people I've seen record? And how many of those were like you? I mean, I didn't see the start of your session with the guys, but I walked in when the rest of the rooms were empty because everyone was trying to listen to you, and you just...did it. You slipped right in and worked with them. You've been singing solo for..."

"Always?" I helped out because I'd never started out in a band in contrary to many others.

He framed my face, resting his forehead against mine. "Exactly. You've been incredibly professional."

I shrugged. "It helps that I know all their voices. I've been obsessed with their music before I knew it was their music. It made it easy."

He sighed and then stepped away from me. "I know. And guess what? When you and I sang together, it should have been easier, and it wasn't."

"Because you were off," I stated.

He cocked his head. "I think we all heard that."

I followed him when he went back to the window, pushing it open as if he hoped the ocean breeze would give him clarity. "I mean something was wrong with you. I saw it in your eyes when you came in, and I wonder what it is."

Aiden turned to me. "I heard a rumor that you got a role in a movie," he said, a small smile playing over his lips. There was pride in his voice and my cheeks heated in excitement.

"I cannot believe you heard a rumor about it already when Dana just told me between the sessions. But yes. Not the one I wanted, but a better one, it seems. I got some pages from the script and…man, that woman could have been me. Like it was written for me, you know? And… Europe, of all places. I'll be in Europe!"

He took a deep breath and then leaned in to kiss me. "That is unbelievable. What does Joyful say to that?" Yeah, I'd asked Dana the same once we were on the way back from the studio.

"Joyful Tunes Records got the contract adjusted so I'd be singing some of the songs. I will have to anyway, but I'll also get a chance to actually write some with the musical team for the movie. I have to read the script and then think it through. It's all still kinda so unrealistic, so far away, you know?"

I shrugged, meaning it.

"I'll be watching the movie a thousand times," Aiden whispered. "Maybe even more often. I cannot believe how big this is going to be."

Laughing, I leaned into him. "Actually, what if it flops? People are going to laugh about me forever."

He arched a brow. "How high are the chances? I mean—"

He couldn't finish as downstairs a door fell closed with a bang. "Promise?"

"That would be Dana. Come and let's find out what she wants."

I took his hand, but he pulled me back. "She'll tell you that someone leaked the material from today, you and the guys, and it's given your music a push that you cannot imagine. Also, them, too, which is kinda funny."

Exactly what I didn't want. "We agreed that there was no 'us' going to be anywhere except for the few lines."

"They want the song, Maya, and not every damn star in there. Just the band and you. The fans are screaming for it."

I shook my head. "Not gonna happen. That's a charity song, and it'll stay that way. Come on, I'm sure she wants something different," I insisted and then dragged him along.

The moment Dana spotted us, she exhaled slowly. "It leaked."

I nodded. "So, I've heard."

"Joyful Tunes decided to go with it."

I stopped where I was, and Aiden bumped into me, nearly causing me to tumble down the stairs. He grabbed me last second, and only when I rested against his strong body, I exhaled. This was too much too fast.

For a moment I stayed where I was, listening to his heartbeat, and then turned away. "No, Dana. They cannot do that without my okay, or that of the band."

My agent looked apologetic. "They can. They own you, Promise, and you know it, and Sebastian wrote the song. They can run it as often as they want, in any capacity they want, and guess what, there's also already a video being cut from the studio. I know you didn't see it, but Promise…"

I licked my lips, not sure why I was so against that. Aiden touched my chin, causing me to look at him. Maybe we should have gone down the stairs completely, but somehow this was poetic.

We were somewhere in-between, and I feared that no matter which way I'd be going, it would be the wrong direction.

Aiden

This was bigger than us, bigger than she'd thought, and I knew that. I'd checked my numbers upon coming home, but had been distracted by news and Promise's name appearing everywhere.

Yes, someone had leaked not more than twenty seconds, but it was going viral.

I'd never gone viral.

And I didn't think I was going to anytime soon.

"I'm not doing appearances with them. I'm not—"

Dana shook her head. "No, you won't. You'll be leaving for Italy in two weeks because the musical director will be there, and you wanted to be part of the writing process. You'll be gone, and you'll be busy doing that and the movie thing while Joyful Tunes will release an album of B-Sides in the wake of the release of Prayer for Peace. Hunting Shadows will be promo-ing for that gig and that song. You might be flown back for some interviews, but you will be out of the country for more than nine months, Promise. This was fast, but… It's going to be the one thing that will bring you in the hall of fame forever."

And Maya's agent was right.

"Also, there is one little detail I did forget to tell you so far."

I snorted. 'Forget' surely wasn't the right word, but then, I'd also not be brave enough to tell Maya what Dana so far had omitted.

For a long moment Maya just stood, staring at Dana and then at me. "Tell me tomorrow. I cannot take anything anymore today." She started up the stairs, but I caught her hand in mine.

"Listen," I pleaded and she met my eyes, her hazel eyes filling with tears.

She shook her head and I couldn't help but think that this should be the happiest day of her life, but it wasn't.

Because of me.

"This is too much too soon. I cannot… I need time to…" She stomped down the stairs and poked Dana's chest. "We had plans. We were meant to follow them. I was meant to have a break. I was meant to get a chance to release that charity song and do good. Instead, now that will be released and people will call me selfish and greedy. I… You need to go, and I need to spend the evening with the love of my life, and maybe tomorrow…"

Dana cleared her throat. "We'll release a statement. I already figured that out. We'll make sure people know you wanted it to be a charity song, and I talked to JC. You and the band will make a public statement that all profit from that song will go to exactly that organization it had been meant to before. It'll be the best way, the easiest way, and with you not promoting it, it'll be believable."

Maya met my eyes, a question in them. "It's the best solution, I think." And it was. Because Maya was right. She'd look horrible, but if she countered that…

"Joyful will not be happy."

Dana snorted. "What are they going to do? Fire you and the guys? The people making them the most of their money now? I doubt that. You'll have to sit through a meeting where they tell you they own you, you'll grovel, and then we'll leave and you'll be richer than you ever thought. Easy as that."

Maya nodded, then she walked the stairs back up, not telling Dana goodbye or anything. She was upset and I knew that, but it wasn't Dana's fault because she, too, was only a pawn in the record company's game.

"I'll tell her what you wanted to tell her, okay? And remember, no appointments tomorrow. I don't want to see you or Neron here."

Dana gritted her teeth. "Clearly clearing your schedule wasn't a problem, but hers... I'll have to lie about her having caught a one-day-bug, and I sure as hell hope you'll make sure no one sees her tomorrow."

I nodded. That was exactly my plan. "Count on it. And now, leave and don't come back before the day after tomorrow." With that I followed Maya up the stairs, finding her in the music room.

She was sitting at the piano, her fingers playing the same exact song she was probably currently cursing.

"Maya," I started, kneeling next to the chair and taking her hands from the keys. I kissed them, every fingertip, then her palms, and then leaned into them. "The movie contract states that you need to be single. And I don't think they'll tolerate what we have," I said slowly, wanting her to understand that I got it.

What JC had said made sense, and although there'd never be anything between Maya and any of the guys on set—she loved me that much—it wouldn't matter.

She didn't say anything, just inhaled slowly. I didn't think she was surprised. We were in the business long enough to expect things like that.

"Have you ever thought about the fact that love can *not* be enough? I mean, look at us..."

I kissed her, pushing up until we were almost the same height, and took my time. I knew we were counting down the hours, and I'd already packed a bag before she came. I didn't think she'd find it or notice the few things missing from my drawers now, but it didn't matter, either. "I love you, and I will love you in six months from now, and in four years. You are my endgame. You are my life. But—"

"I'm not doing the movie. I honestly rather appear greedy and have you than—"

My heart cracked as I realized that it was me who'd need to push her away. It was on me to make sure she didn't pass on this more than amazing chance.

It was on me to make sure that in a few years from now she wouldn't hate me for having given up her dream just because she couldn't see past us. "My numbers have been..." I shook my head, deciding I needed to start differently. "What happened at the studio today wasn't a one-time-thing." Total lie, but she didn't need to know that. "I've been off my game for a while now, and I need to find myself again. I need a break. I need to escape life. Give that to me tomorrow, okay? You and I, just Maya and Aiden, and then, tomorrow, we'll talk about how to proceed, okay?" I didn't know how often I could say okay, especially because nothing about this was okay, but in the end it didn't matter.

What mattered was that she'd be okay, and that, really, was what love was all about.

Chapter Six
Aiden

I'd not slept, and I didn't think Maya had fared much better, but we'd been closely cuddled up, almost breathing in sync, and it had been heaven.

Heartbreaking, torturous, painful heaven.

Once the sun came up, I'd slipped from the bed and prepared breakfast for her. I didn't think I'd be eating anything, but knowing I could feed her? It gave me a primal satisfaction.

She came into the kitchen, feet bare, shoulder free because my shirt was too big on her, and I loved her. I loved her more than I could say. "Morning," she greeted me, coming around the counter and leaning into me to kiss my shoulder. "I prefer you half naked. Actually, I prefer you completely naked, but I don't think that's on the menu today."

I turned to kiss her and then grinned. "Morning. We'll see what the day brings, and how much naked skin we'll discover. But for now... Bacon and eggs or would you rather want pancakes?"

She pouted. "I have to pick one? Aren't you mean?"

Predicting her answer had been easy, and so I surprised her by pulling a batch of pancakes out of the oven. She clapped, excitement shining in her hazel eyes, and I nodded toward the seat on the other side of the counter.

"Can't I stay here with you?" she asked, trying to steal some of the food, but I didn't let her.

"Go and sit your cute ass down on that chair, then you get pancakes, and if you're nice, you get a bite out of this..." I ran my hand down my chest, loving the appreciative way her eyes followed the movement.

She smirked as she met my gaze. "You know how to make a woman do what you want, huh?"

I didn't reply, just forced a smile, and couldn't help but think that if I'd know we probably wouldn't have to have this goodbye date.

Instead of saying that, I filled myself a plate with food and then leaned over the counter, closer to her, and she stole a strip of bacon from me. I didn't know why we'd never done this before.

Clearly clearing our schedules on short notice hadn't been as hard as I'd expected it to be, and this, us playing house, could have happened quite a few times before. The aftertaste wouldn't have been so bitter then.

I shook my head free from those thoughts and then watched her humming and enjoying the food. I tried to find something in her expression that told me she knew what this day was about, but she seemed oblivious.

Or maybe that was just what I wanted to see.

"So, after breakfast, what's next?"

I walked around the counter, now separated from her long enough, and wrapped her in my arms. "I was thinking you, me, a guitar, and the beach," I whispered and she sighed.

"Sounds like heaven."

And it was going to be. We had a private beach behind the house, and since no one suspected us here, I knew there wouldn't be anything to worry about. Once she declared breakfast done, we returned to the bedroom to get dressed.

Most of our time we didn't spend here together, and yet this was our room. Not once had I returned here and felt out of place, even after months of being away. Her tank tops lay next to my shirts, her yoga pants next to my sweatpants.

I'd miss it. I'd miss everything about this, and knew it would never pass.

I watched her as she changed, the task mundane and sexy. The way she wriggled into her jeans just because she felt like it, or the way she hopped from one foot to the other, pulling on socks while trying not to fall.

I'd missed out on so much with her, and I realized that only now.

"Stop staring, creep," she fussed and I lowered my lashes, turning away because I felt my eyes burning. I wouldn't allow those tears to fall, but damn, I suddenly wasn't sure I'd be going through with everything I should be doing.

Maybe I could stay a few more days… Weeks even. Maybe we could postpone this to another day. Maybe…

I didn't finish that train of thoughts and instead got dressed, too. This time I reached for the beanie as if it mattered, and when I faced Maya again, I saw she, too, wore one.

It was funny how such a little detail could make such a difference. She also pulled out round sunglasses, old-fashioned and probably cheap as dirt, but when she just beamed at me, I knew she'd make them look like a million dollars.

"Ready?"

She nodded and I walked ahead, more aware of her than I ever was. I grabbed my guitar, waiting for a moment. "You wanna take yours?"

It was a smaller model, not by much, but especially built for her, and I knew she loved it.

Had since she'd received it years back. "If I wanna play, I'll use yours. After all, it's kinda ours." She winked and my heart cracked. She was right, and when we were together, when either of us was writing, we used the same guitar, just because it made us feel closer. "It's like our favorite child. You know, we love the kids when we're apart, and each deals accordingly with the one they have, but when we're together…" She pointed at the guitar, "this one gets the chocolate."

I chuckled. "Did you just compare our guitars to children?"

She leaned in until she could kiss me. "Well, we don't have any of those yet, so yes."

I swallowed around everything I wanted to reply. We'd never before spoken about kids, and I hadn't even considered it with her, not with everything we were trying to reach, but the casual way she'd added the 'yet' got my heart racing.

Maya had clearly thought about it, and the way she'd put it she didn't think we'd have them now, but one day seemed to be a possibility.

And damn if that didn't take my breath away.

𝄞

Maya

Everything, every little gesture of Aiden's, screamed goodbye, but if he thought I was going to make it easy for him, he had another thing coming. Taking his hand as we went out the backdoor and followed the way down to the beach, I walked as close to him as I could without making both of us stumble.

"You know, if we'd ever have kids, they could probably sing before they could do anything else. And can you imagine me sitting at the piano with our daughter, teaching her songs? She'd be so little I'd have to have her in my lap and—"

"Maya, stop," Aiden pleaded, but I decided to ignore the obvious discomfort and pain in his voice. Yeah, I needed it to hurt so he'd know what he was trying to say goodbye to.

Blinking up at him innocently, I asked, "Why? I can see it. She'd be blonde, like you. Of course she would be. I mean, I'm technically blonde. Like… Real blonde, not this perfectly fabricated color. And the piano will always be with us. Her little fingers wouldn't be able to tease tones from the guitar, but a piano? And I think we'll also have a son one day…"

He stopped, turning to me, his eyes dark with pain and swimming with unshed tears. "Where does the kids talk suddenly come from? I mean, how... I..." He just shook his head, shouldering the guitar in its bag and cupping my cheek. "We've never talked about kids before."

I leaned into his palm, mainly because it was warm against my skin. Maybe I just felt cold because this felt all so final, so stupidly perfect that it could only be the end.

Or maybe it was that my body was already preparing for the heartache it knew was coming and therefore I didn't feel the cold surrounding us.

Either way, his skin seemed like balm against mine. "I've been thinking about it for a while. You know, after that movie deal, I'll be off. I'll be off for a while, and then I'll be in the studio. We're talking nine months. Longer. No one will have to see me. No one would have to know." And I didn't lie about having thought about kids. Ever since he and I had found out how great we were together the thought had been there, in the back of my mind.

It had been there, patiently waiting for a better time. The last thing I wanted was to ruin his career with this because... I didn't know. There were probably a million horror scenarios that could cost him all he had, and I didn't want that for him.

For me? I wouldn't care walking about because I'd be having all I needed. Last night, when he'd been restless next to me, his breath never really evening out, the images had been right there. I'd seen them so vividly, had seen everything that would be one day, and I knew it would be with him.

He turned away, continuing the way, and I waited for him to say something. I wanted to describe more scenes, like how the kids would come in one morning, the room flooded with sun, and they'd be jumping on the sheets.

Or days when we'd see Aiden in concert, the kids with thick, noise-cancelling headphones while I'd be screaming, cheering for him.

One day we wouldn't be secret anymore, and I knew it.

He didn't speak until the soles of our sneakers hit sand, then he dropped everything he'd been carrying and spun back to me, framing my face and kissing me as if we were the last two people on this Earth and he knew death was coming for us.

We didn't come up for air for the longest time, and I held onto him, loving the sound of the waves, the way his body was shielding me from the wind, and everything about the way he held me. The sweetness, the intensity... I wanted more. So much more.

"What if our kids have no musical bones? What if they are sports stars?" he asked quietly, wrapping his arm around me and taking my side while we watched the ocean.

The sky was filled with a field of angry clouds, only occasionally torn up by blue. It was perfect in its imperfection. I didn't need a sunshine day as long as I had Aiden by my side. "Easy," I replied. "You'll be singing national anthems a lot at all of their games."

He chuckled, but the sound was strangled. I realized then he could see it, too. He could probably see it as vividly as I could, as if he could touch the images if only he'd reach out.

Neither of us did, though, for fear of destroying what wasn't there.

"Maybe I'm staying home with the kids while you make the big bucks in music."

I placed my hand over his heart, looking up at him, but he didn't meet my eyes. "Rough patches aren't the end of the road, Aiden. They are the challenges we have to face in order to get to the four-lane-road with the smooth pavement. You know how fast our business moves. One day you're on top, and the next day you aren't, but then you'll be back soon. Whatever you think is happening with you right now has nothing to do with me or my career."

He licked his lips. "Maybe it does."

I shook my head. "No, it doesn't. And if it would, then it would be you instead of my career, Aiden. Always you. I have money, more money than I ever thought I'd own. I don't mind moving on from that, finding a smaller house, stretching it out, making it last. I can still write songs and make money that way, but... We managed for two years. What makes you think whatever is going on will change that?"

He shrugged and then let go of me to pick up the guitar again. "How about we take off the shoes and walk a little further? We don't need to solve any issues right now," he suggested and I liked the idea.

I also agreed. We didn't have to solve those issues now because I would not allow him to walk away from me.

Aiden

She knew. It was the only explanation I had for the way she talked, and damn, she was good. The image of her sitting on that piano with our daughter in her lap... It was buried deep inside my mind, no matter how hard I'd fought it, or how many times I tried to ignore it.

Maya had reached exactly what she'd wanted, and I wanted to tell her so, but didn't.

Instead, I wondered if maybe we'd be able to manage.

She *would* be gone for a long time, and she could probably ignore the talk. I'd hold hands with whomever they'd throw at me, and then we'd be good. After that, we'd return home, both of us together, and could work on that picture of the future she was painting.

Maybe this could work out.

Once I found a spot between the dunes, hidden from direct winds and with a log for sitting, I stopped us and settled down. Maya knelt in front of me, looking up at me. I didn't need long to find notes to play, and did so, for her and only her.

Some songs I'd written I'd never recorded. I was just playing them in the middle of the night for me, for her, even if she didn't know it. Those songs were mine, and mine only, and they weren't written with money in mind.

Only love.

She watched me, listened and hummed along, surprising me by knowing the melody although most songs she'd never heard in full. Maybe she was just that good about guessing the way I was writing them.

At some point she pushed to her feet, starting to walk toward the water's edge, and because the breeze was coming from behind me, I knew my notes would still carry. I sang, for her, for the birds, and the small insects hurrying across the sand, and when I had enough of singing, I put down the guitar and instead watched my girlfriend bathing her feet in the water, the breeze tearing on her beanie, the strands that showed underneath it, and her clothes.

If I'd have a camera, I'd capture that moment forever, but I'd left my cellphone back at the house and I knew so had she.

There couldn't be any emergency, industry- or family-wise that would be important now. Her parents had sold her off to the record company when she'd been fifteen and they'd never cared after that, only asking for money, and mine…

I'd lost mine. All I had was my brother, and he was currently on deployment. He was all the family I had, and if a call came in about him, there wouldn't be anything left to do for me anyway.

Army life was "fun", even if you weren't married to one of them.

We didn't have anyone else, and as I sat there and watched her, I realized we didn't even have close friends.

Hell, I couldn't name one person I'd consider a friend and would call if I needed to vent or cry to.

Well, besides Maya, that was. She was the person I'd always want to call.

"What are you thinking about?" she asked, joining me again, and I slipped off the log to sit in the sand with her. Maybe we should have taken a blanket, but I hadn't thought that far ahead. Instead, with my guitar and her I had everything I'd ever need in life.

"Tell me about that movie. Tell me about the deal. Tell me all you know," I pleaded just because I wanted to hear her talk. And when she was finished with what little she knew about it, I asked her about the songs she'd been writing, about the hopes she had for them.

I asked about everything I could think of because I wanted to know as much as I could, and I didn't get tired of her answers, of her dreams and hopes for the future.

She spoke about tours through Europe, about seeing the Eiffel Tower and the London Bridge. Maya wanted to see the world, and she wanted to meet fans. She wanted to have emotional performances, wanted to make a change.

She wanted to be someone young girls looked up to and knew they could have it all.

And I loved her all the more for it. I didn't think she realized that none of those things she talked about included a family, or that my bad boy image could blemish her perfect world.

I couldn't even remember how I'd come to that image. I knew it started with a shot of me half naked and people had started talking about my tattoos. Next thing I knew, me being out with the guys who played with me on stage had turned into an all-night-bender with women and booze.

Not in reality, just in the press, but who cared, right? And there were always women, at any given point in my life, no matter where I was, and it was enough of me to kiss one of them on the cheek and I had the next affair on my hands.

I was the guy who brought a beer out on stage and drank although you shouldn't do that, especially not when knowing there could be minors in your audience. I was supposed to be the role model Maya wanted to be, but I'd never cared.

And now it would come to bite me in the ass.

Country was a genre that had become increasingly popular, and it was harder and harder to withstand the current of new trends and still make it.

God, I was twenty-two and felt ancient among those guys coming up, doing a mix of rock and country and whatnot, and yet…

I didn't want to change who I was, and the fling Neron and my PR-team wanted would fit right into that image. Maybe it would help me to come out with Maya, but it would never do her any good.

"Aiden?" She nudged my shoulder and I realized she'd long stopped talking while I'd been drowning in my thoughts.

"If I'd have to fake a relationship, would you know it's fake? Would you believe me no matter which pictures you saw?" Because maybe then, if she promised me that now, I'd be ready to risk it.

Or rather, maybe then I'd be ready to try… Whatever she wanted; I'd try.

For her.

Maya

I turned to him. "Are you being serious?"

He closed his eyes, rubbing his hand across his beanie before pulling it off to play with the material in his hands. "I wouldn't… It would be just PR-stunt, and—"

I took his hands, making sure he met my eyes. "That's not what I mean. I was making sure you trust me that little." And it hurt. "We've been in this business long enough to know how it works. And I like how it would distract from us. But... Why? I mean, why would you even need that?"

Aiden licked his lips, a sign he didn't know what to say, and then cocked his head. "Because the record company wants it. They own me, I'll have to do it. The meeting would have been today, but I asked to postpone it because of us, of this. I didn't want to go anywhere and it was a good decision."

He kissed my knuckles while I leaned in, resting my forehead against his. "It's business, and you have been officially single for a while. I'm not surprised they want something more. Also, because of me you've stayed out of the press a lot. I was expecting something like this. But then... It's holding hands and showing off together. Nothing for me to worry about."

For a moment he thought, then he sighed. "There'll have to be private Instagram picture."

I rolled my eyes. "You and her and some couch, probably in some office, you kissing the side of her head, and everyone thinks it's some cuddly place. You holding her hand over a secret dinner, staged as we all know. I know the deal."

And I did. There was nothing that could shock me, and Aiden should know that. I knew he loved me. I had utter faith in him and he should have the same the other way around. I shifted. "Look, you and she can hang out in that fake apartment of yours. There's enough room and the couch is extremely comfortable. She can slip out in the morning, acting as if she didn't want anyone to catch her, and you, too, will be fine. Before you know it, the two of you are breaking up, she bawls her eyes out, you wear sunglasses and the entire female population is sure they can date you again."

He chuckled. "You make it sound so easy."

I smirked. "It is that easy. Business is business, and just think about it... There'll be paparazzi pictures from set. You won't be able to tell if they are behind the scenes or happened away from set because that's what those vultures are being paid for. Will *you* be able to handle seeing those without mistrusting me?"

"Of course," he instantly replied, then swallowed. "I didn't mean to imply you wouldn't trust me. I meant to imply that I don't want you hurting because you see some other woman constantly with me when it cannot be you."

I prayed for him to not mention Dana now, but sadly, no one seemed to listen to me.

"You know Dana and your Joyful Tunes would never go along with us coming out together."

No, they wouldn't, at least not now. For some reason they didn't think any press would be good press. Joyful Tunes was focused on positive press and avoiding scandals, hence having only the elite of poster-something musicians.

Hunting Shadows and I were the best examples.

And I didn't mind. I liked that people knew they could rely on me, and that they could count on me any time they needed.

Did that mean I didn't push boundaries? I did, with my music, with my involvement in charities, with my political voice, but there were no scandals in my file, no mental breakdowns, no shock to my record company or PR-team.

And I liked it that way because it was the type of musician I wanted to be.

I also knew Aiden didn't care how he was portrayed in the press, but usually it worked better for guys to be the dark, mysterious, brooding types anyway.

"They won't go along with us coming out together *now*," I replied, but one day they would have to be okay with it.

I didn't care what happened then, what people would think. Aiden was my forever, the end of every song, the last note I'd ever sing, and I knew that.

Hell, the way he looked at me sometimes he knew that, too.

For a few minutes he searched my face, then I saw a single tear roll down his cheek and his shoulders sagged with relief. "God, I love you. I don't know how or why I deserve you, but I love you. I love you more than anyone ever loved another person."

"Promise me you won't leave me," I requested, needing the verbal confirmation that he would not walk out on me or give up on us.

"How can I when you make it so hard? No, I'll stay, I'll hang around for the piano-lessons of our daughter, and the football games of our son. Or whatever else is coming. I'll be forever hanging around for *you*."

I shifted until I had one knee on each side of him, then I wrapped my arms around his shoulder. "Good, now that we solved that, can we *please* stop this depressing goodbye gesture thing you have going on and be happy instead? We have a rare day off together, and I cannot take that puppy-dog-look on your face any longer."

He laughed, the sound carefree and warm. "I did not have a look like that. I don't know what you're talking about," he protested, but I silenced him with a kiss. It seemed the crisis was averted, and damn if that didn't make me happy.

However, if there'd ever be a scandal I'd be willing to risk my career over, it definitely would be Aiden Paine.

Chapter Seven
Maya

Leaving behind the guitar and Aiden's shoes, we walked to the water's edge. For a few precious hours we could be just us, Maya and Aiden, a couple in love.

We talked about Europe and what I wanted to see, about the plans I had for my music once I was there, and how it would affect my writing. It was weird to think I could become a whole different person in another country.

Aiden's more relaxed demeanor made me breathe easier, too, and when he walked further into the water, rolling up his jeans, I jumped on his back, hoping—and knowing—he'd never let me fall, no matter how unexpected my attack.

And I was right. While he seemed to lose his balance for a second, his hands automatically reached for me behind his back and he steadied us both, making sure I stayed dry. I kissed the back of his neck. "Thank you for catching me," I whispered, rubbing my nose along his skin.

God, I didn't think I could ever feel for someone what I felt for Aiden Paine.

"Always," he replied and then spun with me on his back.

Any other person and I would have been worried about being dropped or him losing his balance and making us both tumble. He was too worried about me to be risky.

Still, the water splashed up his legs with every wave that was coming, and while merely my feet were wet, I knew he was half soaked.

Holding on tighter, I nuzzled his neck again. "Wanna go back inside? You know, I could help you out of these wet clothes, and make sure you warm up in a shower."

It was the beginning of October in California and he wouldn't freeze that easily, but... A wet Aiden could never hurt anyone.

Softly placing me on my own two feet, he turned to me and framed my face, there in the water, both of us knee deep as if the waves weren't going to try and pull us in. "I love you," he whispered against my lips and then kissed me, heating me from within.

We lived close to the water, always had, and somehow the times I'd been down here were still easily countable on one hand. Why, I couldn't say. But I knew this with him now was close to perfect, no matter how cold the water felt around my legs.

"This is…" I shook my head, unsure of what I wanted to say.

Aiden chuckled. "Yes?"

"Perfect," I finally decided for and he sighed.

"Comes pretty close, yes. But you know what would be even more perfect?"

I pulled back to meet his eyes. "If we could do it again tomorrow? And the day after? And the day after that? And then, could bring the kids one day?" Because that probably would be the only way I could see this being even more amazing.

He smiled softly. "You have a career, one that's just now taking off more incredible than you and I ever imagined. You were one of the biggest rockstars in the last years, but it seems you can go even further. And then… A movie. You. It'll be amazing. And after that? After that we'll have all the kids you want."

I nudged his chin with my nose. "You do have a great career, too. Just because currently it might be a little rocky doesn't mean anything. Just wait, you get to release all the romantic songs you wrote for me and people will think they'll be for your fake girlfriend, and it'll make you the heartthrob of the world. You'll be requested everywhere."

I believed that with every fiber of my being. Aiden had the chance to become one of those people everyone would still talk about in twenty years from now. Country maybe wasn't big in every part of the world, but the US and Asia definitely was enough to make a star fucking famous forever.

He licked his lips. "You really believe that?"

I nodded. "Of course. I know your talent. I've heard your songs. I hear them when they are raw. I know what you can do, and as soon as Neron and Dana get our record companies to agree, we'll make a song together. You and I, just imagine..." We'd be together a lot. So much, and it would do his reputation a world of good, that much I was sure about.

For a long moment he just brushed back my strands, combing his fingers through my hair, then he sighed. "How in the world did I deserve you?"

"You know," I stated instead of reacting to his words, "even if not, and your career crashes and burns, I'll still love you. And I might just hang mine up then, too. You know we have money. I know we have money. And I know we can be smart about it."

He laughed. "We just got to that age where we can enjoy every damn thing about life. We shouldn't be smart about anything. We have people to be smart for us, so... Let's not crash and burn just yet."

I didn't care. "Okay," I promised him anyway because clearly, he needed to hear it. He kissed me again, taking his sweet time, then finally agreed to let us walk back to the house.

By now I wasn't feeling my feet anymore because the water was cold, and I was glad once we walked up the beach again, the blood returning much warmer.

Aiden hummed, shouldering his guitar and then reached back for me, taking my hand as he led me back up to the house. I tried to figure out what song it was, but couldn't. Instead I simply enjoyed the tune, ready to cuddle up in front of the TV with Aiden later and do things normal couples did.

Hell, we'd probably suck at that because we didn't know what normal was any longer, but hey, I couldn't wait to try and see what it felt like.

Normalcy was something we hadn't known in a long time and yet, that day? I missed it something fierce, even if stardom had brought Aiden to me.

Aiden

Hope flooded every fiber of my body being out there with Maya. There was nothing I'd not do for her, and the way she made sure I understood we'd work together… It made my heart race in my throat. I wanted this, wanted this so bad, and maybe we could get exactly what we wanted.

As we made our way back up to the house, I held onto her hand tighter than before, wondering if she realized it. She'd been my life since I first saw her, and today she proved again that we were on the same side. The idea of leaving her had never been tempting, but it would have been a necessity I'd have dealt with.

Not leaving allowed me to breathe easier though.

"I'm gonna go and hit the shower," she announced the moment we were through the door and I laughed.

"You go ahead, and if you are too slow, I might just join you in a bit," I teased, kicking off my shoes. She climbed the stairs, humming, and I watched her, my heart cracking with how much I wanted to be close to her that moment.

Instead, I ventured into the kitchen and looked through the freezer. There'd have to be a meal we could only—

Oh, there was lasagna. I took that out, preheated the oven and then put it in. Somewhere in the distance bells sounded. Not loud, but loud enough to draw my attention. It took a few seconds until it settled in that it had to be Maya's cell.

I found it in the living room, Dana's name on the display, and I answered. "She's in the shower," I stated without a greeting, annoyed that Dana was calling even though we'd asked for that one day off.

While waiting for Maya's agent to speak, I picked up my cell, finding fifty missed calls, half from her, half from Gideon. My heart sank.

"What's going on?" I asked before she'd said anything. I usually appreciated the way she collected herself before speaking in anger, but today I didn't have that patience.

She swallowed. "If you ruin Maya's career, I'll personally come and send you to hell," she threatened.

"What? Why?"

She laughed, the sound almost insane. "I knew you were looking at her too long, and the wrong way. I knew people would be able to put two and two together. There are headlines online, making people question Promise's integrity. She promises to never lie to her fans, and now someone from the studio leaked the way she knew how to make you feel better and how you couldn't stop watching her. They talk about your relationship and the fact that she lied to the fans about it. The label called me right this morning, asking me if I hadn't taken care of that problem years ago."

I felt the blood draining from my face. "Wait..." We'd thought the Joyful Tunes had knowledge of our relationship and simply tolerated it as long as we didn't go public, but... "Are you saying you were meant to break us up when we started seeing each other?"

"Promise sells the truth. She's the poster girl for honesty. She's Joyful Tunes' female star. One of the biggest to come. She's going places and they know it, but imagine how many people would still buy her music if they found out all the longing she's singing about is fake because she's not alone. Or all the interviews she'd given before. To be honest, her contract states she needs to stay single. I realized quite soon she didn't remember that, or didn't know about the clause in her contract, but it's true. It's why Neron and I made sure you two would stay secret no matter what."

I had to sit. "Being with me could not only ruin what's coming now, but..."

Dana sighed, calmer now. "Yes, she could lose everything over this."

Breach of contract could cost her all the money she'd made so far. It didn't matter that she'd probably find sympathy for loving me, everything that was Promise would come crashing down around her.

"I'm going to talk to her. Don't call anymore today, okay? Just be here tomorrow at ten."

"As was agreed. She needs to be back at the studio for some fixing and rerecording of certain parts, so... I'll see you then."

"You will," I forced out and then hung up.

Before I'd walk up there, I needed to know what my manager wanted, too. After all, I didn't think he'd call to fuss at me for Maya.

"The fucking audacity you have. You could have at least answered knowing I'd be sitting in the deciding meeting for your career," he fussed without a greeting.

I blinked. "I thought that was cancelled. I asked for the day off, remember?"

He snorted. "Just because you wanted to have off doesn't mean they cancel meetings. They want that farce, and they picked someone. And I tell you, Paine, you'll have to make it real. Kisses in front of the press, and those better look as believable as you can. You'll be going on tour with Candace Lane. You'll be sharing a tour bus, and you better make sure the crew on tour believes the two of you are so in love or you'll be in a world of trouble."

"They know about the press and what they are saying about Maya and me," I concluded.

Neron sighed. "They do, and under no circumstances do they want you and the Joyful Tunes star associated. You know what that means, right? You cannot see Promise for the time you and Candace will be a couple."

"Did you know she could lose her contract over being with me?" I wondered why no one ever bothered to tell us.

Why did Dana it even allow in the first place?

"I did," Neron admitted. "In the beginning we thought it would be a fling. You know, one of those things where after two months everything fizzles out and the hassle wasn't worth it. But then... You didn't fizzle out, and it wasn't my job to take care of Promise's career. Your management never had problems with you seeing her in secret, and I followed that premise. Breaking you up would've not gotten any of us anything good."

I couldn't decide if I was still pissed at him or not, because early on it might not have hurt as much as it did now. "Neron..."

"Go, Aiden, and be with her. I'm sure things will sort themselves out."

I thanked him and hung up, wondering if they really would—or if maybe leaving the biz behind would be the best for us after all.

I'd missed Maya's shower, but I still snuck up behind her in underwear only, wrapping my arms around her.

"You took forever. I couldn't have been any slower," she pouted and I laughed. My heart was heavy, but she deserved the very best day, and in contrary to this morning, I didn't let on.

I couldn't.

"I put on lasagna and got lost in trying to figure out what the right heat and setting would be. Do you have any idea how hard those ovens are to use? I mean... What's the ideal setting for heating up but not burning? Ugh."

She turned, grinning. "And I missed it. I wish I could have seen you, all domesticated."

I pinched her ass. "You'll be seeing that when I pull out a perfect lasagna from the oven, put it on a plate all pretty and hand it to you. Ha."

Her eyes sparkled with amusement and I soaked it up. "Deal," she replied. "Now, are you gonna shower, too, or…?"

I shook my head. "Nah, I decided I can still do that before bed. I'm just gonna change into dry clothes." I pointed at my pants and she eyed them for a moment.

"I feel like we should put them into water to wash the salt out or something…"

I nodded. "Sounds good. Very… House-wifey of you."

She pushed my shoulder, but then drew me back in to steal a kiss. "Okay, get changed, I cannot wait to do nothing with you." She winked and then turned, slipping into yoga pants and a tank top, then she grabbed one of my hoodies to throw over.

I followed her with my eyes as she left the room, then hurried to change, too.

I found her in the living room, staring down on the remote for the flat screen we had in the living room. "Did we ever use that before?" I asked, realizing only now that I couldn't remember ever having watched TV with her.

She glanced at me, then back at the remote. "I did figure out how to turn it on, but couldn't find the Netflix button. I also somehow managed to turn it from TV to radio before I even had a picture, and now…" She huffed.

I chuckled and then grabbed the remote from her. "Let's see if I can fix it while…"

"I'm gonna go and look if we have some popcorn."

I doubted that. While neither of us was on a strict diet, there wouldn't be sugary treats unless we bought them ourselves, and I didn't think Maya would go for salty popcorn.

I turned on the TV, pressed a few buttons that made me think they could lead us where we needed to be and exclaimed in excitement when the red logo appeared, announcing me to having been successful.

"Sounds like you managed," Maya called from the other room and I followed her voice, finding her in front of the oven. She was crouched down, looking at the food, and damn, I wished we could have normalcy. I wished we could come home, cook dinner together, and then watch a movie every night.

"Looks good," she eventually decided and I leaned into the doorframe, watching her as she took out our food and then gave us each a piece. She wiggled her ass while doing so, looking happier than she ever had—and it broke me.

I didn't think I wanted to be a star any longer. Hell, I didn't think I wanted to have someone else dictate my life any longer, but I couldn't tell her that.

I also couldn't tell anyone else that because they'd think I had a mental breakdown, but as I watched her, knowing she and I couldn't pretend much longer that the world wasn't against us.

"You're watching me as if you ain't hungry so… I might just eat all of this alone," she stated and I grinned, walking closer to her.

We should have probably sat down to eat, but instead I stayed behind her on the counter, my body covering hers completely while we ate standing up. It was…intimate, cuddly, and exactly what I needed.

"You are a great cook," she decided and thanked her with a bow, watching as she rinsed the plates and then left them in the sink.

Maya joined my side, and I kissed her softly, letting her pull me back to the living room. We settled down on the couch as close as we could to each other without climbing on top of one another, then debated the movie choices for a moment. I honestly didn't care what we'd be watching, but I knew she liked having my input.

Half way through a romantic comedy I realized her fingertips were dancing over my thigh, and it wasn't in a playful way.

No, it was the way only a musician would recognize. I grabbed her hand and kissed the back of it. "You can go and sit on the piano if you want to," I told her. Yes, we'd wanted to take off, but if creativity struck, you sometimes had to listen.

She hesitated for a moment, thinking about it, but then settled back into my side. "No, no work today. I'm still gonna remember it tomorrow." She kissed my shoulder, then focused back on the movie while I kept watching her.

Maya wouldn't be able to live without her career, that much was obvious as her fingertips kept playing that song on my thigh even though she assured me over and over she wouldn't want to write now anyway.

I believed her, and yet I didn't. I kissed the side of her head. "I love you," I whispered. She briefly winked at me, then focused back on the movie, and it was the best damn evening I'd ever had—no matter what was waiting for us on the other side of the night.

Chapter Eight
Maya

Dating a musician sounded fun in theory, but there were moments when I was sure it was the worst thing ever. Sitting up, I listened, but this time only silence greeted me.

My heart sped up, my ears buzzing with panic. Things had been good. I knew I'd convinced him that we could do it. I'd seen it in his eyes.

Leaving the bed and not bothering with pulling anything over, I ventured out of the bedroom.

"Aiden?" I called, my voice already sounding hysterical as if my body felt him not being there any longer. "Aiden!"

There was nothing but silence greeting me and I felt the first sob leave my lips. My steps led me to the music room, but his guitar was gone, as were his latest lyrics. I searched for his favorite pen—a small thing, but something that would calm me down if I could find it. Musicians were superstitious creatures, and we always held onto things that we felt helped us get successful.

I didn't find it. I hurried down the stairs, but every room was dark. "Aiden!" I called again, but there was no different outcome than the first time.

The whole house was empty, and although it was highly unlikely, I searched the porch, too. I couldn't remember one single instance he'd sat there, but that didn't change my hopes. He had to be somewhere.

After an hour of searching and rechecking every room countless times, I finally gave up. Standing in the foyer I spotted my phone.

Grabbing it, I ignored all messages on my screen and dialed Aiden. It went straight to voicemail. I tried it again anyway, and a third time, too.

I tried Neron, with the same result and it broke my heart. This screamed black-listing. Pulling up the message app to type out a—most likely useless—message, I found a voice record from Aiden.

It had been one of those things I'd ignored in my haste to call him, and I was tempted to keep ignoring it.

Maybe if I didn't listen to the message he wouldn't be gone.

It was cold in the house and I sank down on the tiles, tears streaming down my face. I longed to have someone to call, like a sister or a best friend. I wanted someone who'd drop everything to come and sit by me now, someone who would hold me while I'd be listening to the message, but as it was, I didn't have anyone.

The person I'd call whenever I needed someone's shoulder to cry on was the one I would be calling about.

Dana crossed my mind, but she worked for me. She wasn't a friend in that sense, not someone who would be sympathetic because it was what she'd feel.

Instead, she'd be nice and soothing, but just because she got her money through me.

For a while I watched the moonlight wandering over the tiles of the foyer, the pale light shifting as birds flew by or clouds made their way past the moon.

When I finally lifted the phone to listen to the message, my hands were ice cold and I was cried out. I had no tears left to drop from my cheeks.

I swallowed and then hit the play-button.

"I don't know what to tell you. There are no words to explain to you how sorry I am about how things went down. Here's the thing… You might not care about your career, not care about what the media will turn my supposed relationship into, but I do. I cannot lose my career. It makes me. It makes the person I am. We are young, Maya. Very young. We have the best of our lives still ahead of us, and I know your career is currently running on its own.

"Had I told you I still planned on leaving, you'd have tried to talk me out of it. I know you would have, and for a few days I would've believed we can make it, but then... Maya, this thing between me and Candace, that's who'll be my girlfriend, needs to look serious. As serious as it can, and that will not work if I date you.

"I know this makes me selfish, but it's my career we're talking about. My music. My *life*." He paused to take a deep breath and so did I, feeling numb. I knew why he'd left, but the moment I'd get him on the phone or in person, I'd tell him we could work anyway. When he cleared his throat, I focused back on the recording.

"I know you probably would have picked me. You meant every word you said yesterday, about not caring what happens to you and your career, about finding a normal life, but... I'm, not like that. I want to go places, see the world more than I already have. I know you will get that because of Hunting Shadows, and we know that, but... I don't. And I want it. I'm jealous of what you have, and I want it, too."

I gasped. Never once before had we been that couple, the one where one had to be as successful as the other one. I couldn't believe what I heard.

"So, Maya, to cut to the chase. I need this, and I need it for myself, and where I'm going, I cannot take you with me. I need to be the change I want to get my career the way I want it. I'm sorry. I did not lie about loving you. I promise you that. But I did lie about not leaving you.

"In contrary to you I've never prided myself in being honest, and I'm the bad boy of country for a reason. You cannot count on me, and I'm sorry I faked it so well the last years, you thought you could. Don't call me up, because it won't change a thing. Be the woman I know you can be, the singer you are meant to become, and maybe one day you'll see that this was better for you, for me, for us. We were good together, but... You know."

No, I didn't know. I waited for the crack in his voice, for the rushing because he feared if he'd not get faster he'd break down, but it didn't come.

Instead, he sounded calm, controlled, as if he meant every word.

"In case you're wondering... What we had wasn't a lie. Not in itself. But it wasn't what you wanted it to be, either. I'm not old enough for forever, Maya. Not at twenty-two. I'm sorry. I love you, and in a way probably always will, but our song is over here. This is the End of Promise and Paine, and I know it. Time for you to realize it, too."

And that was the end of it. I replayed the message a hundred times, looking for inflictions, for hidden meanings, but nothing. I tried to message him, but I didn't get the feedback that the message was being delivered.

Aiden had walked out on me and in the process had cut all ties.

I didn't know what to think about that, but I knew that for me none of this had been fake. For me it had been everything I'd wished for and more. I had no idea what shock felt like, but I assumed it was the numbness I felt, the unwillingness to not move in case he'd be coming back.

Maybe shock also was the hope that in a few minutes I'd be waking up in bed and Aiden would be next to me, this being nothing more than a nightmare.

However, when the sun crept over the horizon, the morning light replacing the moonlight on the tiles, I knew I wasn't in bed.

I knew this was a nightmare, but I definitely wouldn't be waking up from it.

Aiden

I barely saw the headlights coming up the hill, I was crying so hard.

I was choking on air, too, pain cutting my throat like shards of glass. I'd somehow managed to deliver my message—my pile of lies—calmly and without a hitch in my voice, but then I'd broken down. I was sitting outside of the gate, my bag at my feet, my guitar next to me and morning was breaking over the horizon.

There'd been only one person for me to call, and he'd promised to come and get me.

The car stopped next to me and the first thing I saw were a soldier's boots.

I wanted to push to my feet, but I didn't have the strength.

"Aiden." I hadn't heard that voice in a while, and I hated myself for having gone this long without talking to my brother, especially considering he currently was stationed in the US, just four hours from here.

He held out his hand and I clasped it, allowing Austin to pull me to my feet. He wrapped me in his arms as if no time had passed and I couldn't tell him how much I appreciated it. "I missed you," I sobbed against his shoulder. "Thank you for coming."

"Always," he replied and his calm demeanor sorted my thoughts, sorted my pain until I could breathe again without getting light-headed.

He grabbed my bag, I shouldered my guitar, and then put it in the trunk of his jeep.

Once we were in the car and he turned it away from the house that held the woman I loved more than my own life, he cleared his throat. "How in the world did you manage to fall in love this hard?"

I laughed. It was breathless and broken, but still, genuine laughter. "You would have liked her. The private persona, Maya, not the public person."

Austin winked. "I like the public persona, too. She's pretty and a decent artist. Or at least that's what I think after googling her like crazy after you first told me you were in love with her."

He was older than me by two years, and yet he seemed so much more grown up. Must have been the army training.

"I cannot believe you dropped everything to come and pick me up."

He smirked. "I will have to be back at base in five hours the latest, so you'll be coming with me for now."

I chuckled. "Okay." I didn't have any other plans. In fact, I needed to call a lawyer and then have Neron sent over my contract. "You know, you are a surprisingly decent person for always having been an asshole when we were younger," I teased.

Austin grinned. "Just because I had you as a little brother." His smile vanished. "Besides, the army does that to you. It kinda puts things in perspective, and not everyone has your talent, you know?"

I nodded. "And still, I'll walk away as soon as possible."

For a moment Austin was quiet, then he glanced over at me. "Rushed decisions aren't good, you know that, right?"

Sighing, I wanted to pull out my phone and look at the pictures of me and Maya. "I don't want to be a bad boy any longer. And I know I owe the label another song, and probably this tour they just arranged, but... I don't want it anymore."

Austin cocked his head. "What's 'it' in this case?"

"People telling me who I can love. And me being at risk of ruining someone else's career."

My brother took a deep breath. "I don't think Maya would blame you. I read the rumors, read some of the articles. I'm not surprised you were calling me. I was expecting it."

I blinked. "What?"

"I'm your brother, and you might not call me often, but you usually do when shit hits the fan. You always have. It's what family is for, so... I knew it was coming. I was dressed and ready to go when you called. Call Neron though, so he won't worry. And make sure you sort yourself out before you walk away from what you always considered to be your dream. Just think of all the money you can lend me because you're fucking rich."

"Why did you choose the army after high school?"

Austin exhaled slowly. "It gave me a purpose. It gave me the chance to travel and still do good. Also, I look fucking incredible in uniform." He winked. "However, it also gave me a place I belonged. There wasn't much left of the family anyway, and I knew you were going to go places. I enlisted, knowing should you not become as famous as it looked, I'd be coming back for you."

"I wanna do good," I admitted.

Austin rolled his eyes. "In case no one told you lately... You are not a bad boy, Aiden. You're a good guy."

Maybe I was, but that didn't change that I'd craved fame, but now craved not being famous anymore. I wouldn't miss hiding who I loved.

I wouldn't miss people telling me what I had to sing or wear.

I wouldn't miss not being good enough for Maya.

I would miss her, but sitting there, I couldn't help but think that it would be the *only* thing I'd miss about the showbiz.

For a while we drove in silence because there was nothing much to say, but eventually I turned to my brother. "Austin..."

He arched his brows. "Yes?"

"Is twenty-two too old to join the army?"

The End (For now)

Heart Beats

The Life and Death of a Rock Star

by

M.A Foster

Rhythm & Riffs **Interview with Marcus King: Royal Mayhem front man, Marcus King, sits down with Miles Townsend for an exclusive, in-depth interview about life, family, the Mayhem Foundation, and** *Jaybird.*

By Miles Townsend

Marcus King doesn't shy away from the cameras. In fact, he's been deemed "The Gentleman of Rock 'n' Roll" by the media for a reason. King always makes time for his eager fans, whether it's an autograph or a quick selfie. He even takes time to answer questions from the paparazzi about his latest projects. But his personal life is off-limits.

"The media and I have a mutual understanding," King says. "Being in the public eye comes with the job. I'm happy to talk about my music with anyone, but my personal life—my family—is private."

Until today.

In this exclusive two-part, in-depth interview, Marcus King opens up about his life, family, and what's next for Royal Mayhem.

Marcus King and I are far from strangers. In fact, our friendship goes back nearly three decades to a place called Davie's Dive Bar. I'd been ten years old at the time, but I remember as if it was yesterday, when Marcus King and Andrew Wild walked into Davie's. I was sitting at the bar, doing my homework. My father and owner of Davie's Dive Bar, Dave Townsend, stood behind the bar taking inventory when the door opened and two teenaged boys came strutting in. One had dark hair and the other blond. The dark-haired one stood a few inches taller than the blond. Both wore determined expressions on their faces.

"We're closed," my father said as they approached the bar.

"I'm looking for Davie," the one with the dark hair said, as if he hadn't heard my father's warning.

My dad tucked his pen behind his ear and leaned with his forearms resting on top of the bar. "That's me."

"I'm Marcus." The dark-haired one held out his hand, and my dad shook it. He nodded to his blond friend. "This is my best friend, Andrew, but we call him Drew." The blond kid extended his hand and shook my dad's.

"What can I do for you?" Dad asked.

Marcus straightened his shoulders and said, "We were wondering if you had any openings for a house band."

Dad paused, taking in their appearance. "You look a bit young. How old are you?"

"Eighteen, sir. But we're not looking for a place to drink. We just want a place to play our music. You don't have to pay us or anything. We just want a chance to be heard."

Chance.

My dad was all about giving chances. "Life is all about chances. Taking chances. Giving chances. Second chances. Chance encounters. Chances lead to possibilities," he'd said often during my childhood.

So, he gave them a chance.

The next day, Marcus and Drew were back with their two other bandmates, Tommy and Chaz.

They called themselves Royal Mayhem. Marcus King was the front man. It was obvious from the way he presented himself the previous day that he was their leader. Andrew "Drew" Wild was the drummer, Tommy Stone played the bass guitar, and Chaz Vargas was lead guitar.

I wasn't allowed in the bar during business hours, so I never got to see them perform live for the patrons, but I did often get a front row seat to their practice sessions.

Even at ten years old, I knew Royal Mayhem was destined for success. Dad knew it, too. In just a few months, they had become a fan favorite and a regular paid gig at Davie's. Patrons were lining up at the door, and it wasn't long before the music executives began to surface.

Royal Mayhem's success story inspired me to become a writer. Four kids, barely out of high school, who went from playing for free in a dive bar to becoming one of the biggest rock bands in the world.

On day one of our two-part interview, Marcus enters the lobby of King Records surrounded by security with two young men in tow. He's dressed casually in a pair of worn jeans, black Chucks, and a faded black T-shirt with LAW printed in white across the front. He holds out his hand to shake mine, then introduces the younger men as Dylan, Marcus's nephew, and his friend Alex, who are interning at King Records for the summer. After the brief introductions, Dylan and Alex walk off, and Marcus leads me to one of the recording studios, which is currently occupied by Andrew Wild. On the opposite side of the glass are three twentysomethings in the middle of a jam session.

"Andrew." I extend my hand. "Good to see you again."

"You too, Miles."

I turn my attention to the three boys inside the studio. "Is that Lucas?"

"It is," Andrew answers. "He and his friends started their own band, LAW." He gestures to Marcus's T-shirt. "We're working on their first album."

I nod. "I'd love to hear it." I turn to Marcus. "We should probably set up an interview... soon?"

Marcus grins. "Absolutely."

Marcus and I have an unspoken agreement that *Rhythm & Riffs* gets the first interview with all of King Records' new artists.

Andrew leans into the mic. "Okay, boys, let's take a break. I want you to meet someone."

The large studio space looks like it's had a makeover since the last time I was here.

"What's up, Uncle Marcus?" Lucas says, clasping hands with Marcus and bringing him in for a hug.

"Lucas, this is Miles. He's an old friend and runs a magazine called *Rhythm & Riffs*."

Lucas nods. "I'm familiar with it." He grins and gestures to the kid behind the drums. "That's Ace." Then he points to the kid holding a guitar. "And that's Wes."

"Good to meet you," I say.

"Boys, let's go grab something to eat," Andrew insists before turning to us. "I'll be back in a few."

Once the boys and Andrew have left the studio, I quietly take in the spacious room.

"You've redecorated," I observe.

Two large sofas are situated in the middle of the room, a coffee table between them. A drum set is against the back wall with various amps and other instruments strewn around. A shiny black grand piano sits on the far side of the room with electric and acoustic guitars lining the walls.

"My wife did," Marcus admits with a chuckle. He gestures to one of the sofas before taking a seat on the one across from me. "My daughter and I were spending long hours in here working on a secret project. My wife wanted her to be comfortable."

And so we began our interview.

Does this mean your daughter is following in your footsteps?

Marcus: I wish I could say definitely, but I'm not sure she's ready to commit to it. She's young and ambitious, but she's also curious. I expect she'll try on several hats before choosing her career. As much as I'd like for her to thrive in the music industry, I also want to protect her from it. It's a tough business, and as with any job, there's always an ugly side to it.

When did you decide you wanted your own record company?

Marcus: About fifteen years ago. I'd witnessed too many talented artists passed over because they didn't fit a certain mold. We didn't bust our asses just to become another fad or flavor of the month. We were here to stay.

What or who inspired your love for music and made you want to become a musician?

Marcus: Music itself inspired me. It had been a part of my life for as far back as I can remember. It was my first love, my true love, and, at certain times of my life, my only friend. I loved all kinds of music, from classical to country to heavy metal. There isn't a band or musician out there who hasn't inspired me one way or another.

If you hadn't become a musician, what would you be?

Marcus: I believe I was born to be a musician, but if it didn't work out, I'd be a teacher. I love the idea of teaching, and in a way, I guess I am one anyway. I mentor a lot of inspiring musicians.

Where do you commonly find new artists?

Marcus: Clubs, college bars, word of mouth, social media, but mostly YouTube. Many aspiring musicians have a channel on YouTube. If I like what I hear, I'll get in touch.

Let's talk about *America's Voice*, the most watched show on television today. What's it like being a guest judge?

Marcus: I'm honored to be a part of *America's Voice*. It's been a wonderful experience so far.

Do you have any favorites?

I've got my eye on a few contestants, but we'll have to see what America thinks. The competition is tough.

    Thirty minutes into our interview, Andrew returns with the other two members of Royal Mayhem, Tommy Stone and Chaz Vargas.

"It's good to see you guys again," I say. "Would you mind hanging out for a bit?"

"Not at all," Chaz replies, propping his feet on the coffee table.

"Anything for you, Miles," Tommy adds.

What's new with you guys?

Chaz: Nothing special. Hanging with the family and enjoying some time off. Tommy's wife just had their twelfth kid.

Tommy: Fifth, asshole.

Congratulations. Boy or girl?

Tommy: Girl. Her name is Ruby. She is perfect and, thankfully, our last.

Let's talk about Royal Mayhem. How did you guys meet?

Marcus: Andrew and I met in foster care.

Andrew: We all grew up in the same neighborhood, but Marcus and I didn't really hang out with Tommy and Chaz until high school. We were all in the same band class together, so we knew they were capable of playing the guitar. And when Marcus and I decided we wanted to start a band, we asked if they wanted to join.

How did you come up with your band name?

Marcus: Drew had originally come up with the name Kings of Chaos, but with my last name being King, I felt like the name was centered around me. It wasn't just my band, it was our band.

Andrew: I played around with a few names, and Royal Mayhem is the one that stuck.

How does it feel being one of the most famous rock bands in the world?

Marcus: Our goal wasn't to be famous, it was to be successful. We're grateful to everyone who has played a part in our success, including our fans.

Chaz: Without our fans, we wouldn't have been able to do what we love.

Have any of you ever suffered from alcohol or drug abuse?

Tommy: Chaz and I enjoy the occasional joint and maybe a beer or two, but….

Marcus: We all indulge in a drink or two, but music is our drug of choice. We've seen what drugs can do to people we care about. We've lost several friends to drugs. My parents were addicts. We made a pact back when we first formed our band that we'd never allow alcohol, drugs, or women to come between us and our dreams.

What's the craziest thing that's ever happened on tour?

All fingers point to Andrew.

Drew: Fuck you, guys.

Care to elaborate, Andrew?

Drew: During our second tour, ironically called Consequences, I'd been hooking up with a groupie—for legal reasons, I can't give you her name. We'd become a sort of steady thing until one day she just stopped coming around. It wasn't uncommon because that's what groupies do—did. They got bored and moved on to other musicians. Many months later, said groupie showed up with a three-month-old infant and left him outside our tour bus for Marcus's wife and one of our bodyguards to find.

You confirmed the child was yours?

Drew: I did. After I freaked out, of course.

Marcus: I believe that sometimes even our biggest mistakes turn out to be blessings in disguise.

Drew: Lucas is the best mistake and biggest blessing of my life. If I could go back and do it all again, I wouldn't change a thing. He's a good kid and my favorite human. He's going to do great things with his band, LAW.

Chaz: (coughing) Shameless plug.

Marcus, you mentioned you'd been working on a secret project with your daughter. Can you tell me more about it?

Marcus: About a year ago, my daughter came to me with a notebook full of songs she'd written and asked if we could collaborate and put them on an album. It was definitely one of my proudest dad moments. Jayla had been writing songs since she was a little girl, but it was the first time she wanted to share them. I brought her into the studio, and we worked day and night for months. I gave her the full experience of what it's like to produce an album. I wasn't easy on her. I pushed her the same way I would push any new artist. The same way I pushed the contestants on *America's Voice*. Some days I pushed her to the point of frustration and tears. But she's strong and stubborn just like her mother and determined like me. When the album was complete, I decided there was no way I couldn't share it with the world.

You've kept Jayla away from the media thus far. How do you feel about sharing her with the world now?

Marcus: I'm torn. Jaybird is talented, and as her producer, it wouldn't be fair to her or potential fans to hold her back. As her father, I'm excited to experience this with her, but I'll always worry. I want her to be happy. Her happiness always comes first.

Will this be a solo album?

Marcus: No, this will be a Royal Mayhem album featuring Jayla. We all had a hand in putting this album together, and they're just as thrilled about it as I am.

What's the name of the album? And when will it release?

Marcus: *Jaybird* is scheduled to release next summer.

What's the significance of Jaybird?

Marcus: Jaybird is what I've been calling her since she was born. Jayla is derived from Jay Bird. It means "one who is special." My daughter isn't just special, she's a miracle. She's my Jaybird.

Will the album be different from Royal Mayhem music?

Marcus: No. It's still us and our sound. The album is a mixture of new, old, and even a few covers of our favorite songs.

Will there be a tour?

Marcus: Most likely, but no dates have been scheduled.

Drew: Since this was Jayla's project, we're leaving the decision to her.

Tell me about the Mayhem Foundation.

Marcus: The Mayhem Foundation focuses on putting music and performing arts back into schools. The foundation provides scholarships, instruments, and the necessities to teach students about music and performance. We're currently working with a private school in Florida that will host the first Project Mayhem class next fall. If all goes well, we hope to expand Project Mayhem to other schools.

What does Royal Mayhem want to say to their fans?

Marcus: Thank you for always supporting us.

Day two. It's late afternoon when I arrive at the King residence, a modern, two-story home made of stone and glass.

Marcus's housekeeper, a woman named Grace, greets me at the door, invites me in, and gives me a quick tour. The King residence isn't the ostentatious display of wealth and fame you'd expect to see from a rock star. It's an Italian-inspired five-bedroom, four-bath home. The entire bottom floor is an open floor plan with marble floors and a glass wall overlooking the Pacific Ocean.

Grace leads me out to the pool deck, where Marcus is lounging on an outdoor sofa looking completely relaxed. His bare feet are propped on the coffee table and crossed at the ankles while he strums a royal blue acoustic guitar.

"You have a beautiful home," I tell him as I sit on the adjacent love seat.

"Thank you," he says while continuing to strum lightly on his guitar. "It was my first major purchase after Royal Mayhem signed their first record deal."

I stare out at the ocean, the sound of the waves crashing against the shore bringing a sense of calm over me. I imagine Marcus spends a lot of his free time out here.

Is this how you would describe your perfect day?

Marcus: (chuckles) Pretty much. This is my favorite spot. I've written dozens of songs right here.

Emerson, Marcus's wife, steps out onto the deck with three bottled waters in hand and Grace carrying a tray behind her.

"It's good to see you again, Miles," Emerson says as she sets the bottled waters on the table. I stand from my seat, and she greets me with a hug before taking a seat beside her husband.

Marcus lowers his feet to the ground as Grace sets a tray on the table between us. Meats, cheeses, pretzels, crackers, and olives are artfully arranged on the tray.

"Thank you, Grace." Marcus smiles fondly at his housekeeper before she disappears inside.

Leaning over, I pluck an olive from the tray and pop it into my mouth.

How long has Grace been working for you?

Marcus: Since the beginning. After our foster mom passed away, Andrew and I moved into an apartment with Tommy and Chaz. Grace lived across the hall with her husband. They hadn't been in the States very long before he was mugged and killed on his way home from work. Grace had no family here. So, we became her family.

Emerson: I remember the first time Marcus brought me here. Grace hated me at first sight.

Marcus: She didn't hate you. She was being protective. She thought you were a groupie.

Emerson: (rolls her eyes) It was pretty evident from the start that I wasn't a groupie. She warmed up to me and eventually grew to love me.

How did you two meet?

Marcus: (smiles at his wife) We met on an airplane. I was catching a last-minute flight back to LA after the tour bus took off without me.

Emerson: I had just graduated high school and was on my way to spend the summer with my cousin before starting UCLA in the fall.

Marcus: When I sat down beside her, I noticed she was crying.

Emerson: Because I was nervous and scared.

Marcus: And heartbroken.

Emerson: (shrugs)

Marcus: I'd only gotten a brief glance at her profile before she looked away, but I knew she'd be the most beautiful woman I'd ever see in my lifetime. And when I finally got her to look at me, I was right. Even through her tears, her eyes were the brightest shade of green. She took my breath away. I was obsessed with her before I even knew her name. I was in love with her before the plane even touched down at LAX. I was afraid if I didn't make my move, I'd never see her again. I all but begged her to spend more time with me.

Emerson: A week later, we eloped in Vegas.

Marcus: We just celebrated our twenty-first wedding anniversary last month.

Do you believe it was fate?

Marcus: Absolutely. I believe that things happen when they're supposed to. We were two strangers on different paths who happened to be in the right place at the right time.

Emerson, what's it like being married to one of the most famous rock stars in the world?

Emerson: (smirks as she side-eyes her husband) That's a loaded question. Our first week together—before we were married—it was just the two of us existing in our own little bubble. After we were married, Marcus went back to work in the studio to finish up Royal Mayhem's second album, *Lovesick*, while I prepared for my freshman year at UCLA. About a year into our marriage, Royal Mayhem had become pretty famous. Suddenly, there were paparazzi lingering on the sidewalks outside the restaurants where we dined, and before long, they were hanging around outside the gate of our home.

Marcus: I chose to keep our marriage private mostly for safety reasons. A few photos of Emerson and I had also surfaced in some of the magazines, and there were speculations about our relationship. She was still a student at

UCLA and exposed to the general public, so our publicist gave some bullshit story that Emerson was just an intern working for the record label.

Emerson: Of course, with fame come the stories and the lies. I wasn't prepared for the photos of my husband splashed all over the tabloids with other women and their tell-all stories. I was still a teenager. I remember reading that garbage when I was in high school and believing every single word of it. I loved the drama. Never in a million years did I think one day it would be me at the center of that same drama. It put a lot of strain on our marriage.

Marcus: It was my fault. I hadn't taken into account that Emerson came from a different world. She was young and had been sheltered her entire life. We both had a lot to learn about each other, but it was my job as her husband to protect her.

Emerson: (grins) It's a good thing we're both stubborn and determined.

Marcus: Failure wasn't an option.

Emerson: One of the most important things I learned about Marcus King, my husband, and Marcus King, the rock star, is they're the same person. The man you get on stage and in the media is the same man we get at home. He's kind, charismatic, and genuine.

Marcus: There are too many fake personas in this business, and I can only imagine how exhausting it must be to keep it up. I've always prided myself on just being the real me.

What was your relationship like with the rest of the band?

Emerson: Andrew and I hit it off immediately. Tommy eventually warmed up to me a few months after Marcus and I were married. Chaz and I have a love-hate relationship. Most days, we tolerate each other. Other times I want to strangle him.

Marcus: Chaz adores Emerson, but he loves to push her buttons.

Emerson: I think he gets off on it.

Marcus: (chuckles) Probably.

How long have you been managing Royal Mayhem, Emerson?

Emerson: Sixteen years.

Marcus: She also manages me, our daughter, our home, and our everyday lives.

What was life like for young Marcus?

Marcus: The first eight years of my life were pretty shitty. My parents were drug addicts, and most of the time, they forgot I existed. The only good thing I remember about them was the one time they took me to a thrift store and bought me this little Walkman and a few cassette tapes. We moved around a lot and never stayed in one place long enough for me to make any friends. But I had my Walkman. One day my dad got pulled over. He and my mother were both high, and the cops found drugs in the car. My parents went to jail, and I went into the system. I never saw them again. I'd moved to nine different homes in four years, until I settled in with the Franklins when I was twelve. They were an older couple who were only able to care for kids who could fend for themselves. They were the first couple who treated me like a human being and not a paycheck. They made me feel safe. They were the closest thing I had to real parents. Six months later, Andrew moved in, and I had a brother. It didn't matter that we weren't blood. We were a family. The following Christmas, the Franklins bought me my first guitar and Andrew a drum set. Andrew and I would put on concerts for them. Mr. Franklin died during our senior year of high school. It was the first time in my life that I can remember ever feeling grief. Even after my parents had been taken away, I hadn't felt the loss. I don't remember feeling anything. Mr. Franklin loved Drew and me as if we were his own. He recognized our potential and encouraged us to chase our dreams. Losing him was the driving force to put ourselves out there. Sadly, Mrs. Franklin died less than a year later. I believe she was just too heartbroken over losing her husband. She passed away in her sleep, and Drew and I had to grieve the loss of the last person who ever gave a shit about us.

Do you know where your biological parents are?

Marcus: Yes.

Have you tried reaching out to them?

Marcus: No, and I don't ever plan to. Just because someone shares the same blood as me doesn't make them my family. I have a family, and I'm very protective of them.

Is there anything in your life and/or career that you wish you'd done differently?

Marcus: No. Every crucial choice, every decision I've ever made in my life, career or otherwise, has always been well thought out. I can be impulsive at times when I'm feeling passionate about something, but all of my choices and decisions are made with a clear head. I never want to look back and think "what if" because it all circles back to fate. Every choice, decision, good or bad, is what led me to this point in my life.

You've been working in this industry for nearly thirty years. What would you say is your biggest accomplishment?

Marcus: Success. I've accomplished everything I set out to do. I'm living my dream.

As the sun begins to set, the three of us make our way down to the beach. Marcus and Emerson walk alongside me, hand in hand.

What is life like for Marcus King these days?

Marcus: Surreal. I have good days and bad days. But most days I'm exhausted.

A year ago, Marcus was diagnosed with Glioblastoma multiforme (GBM), an inoperable brain tumor. After months of aggressive chemotherapy treatments, there was nothing more that could be done. Marcus was given a year, give or take.

Stopping nearly five feet from the shoreline, the couple squats down on the sand. "Sunset is my favorite time of day," Emerson tells me, leaning her head on Marcus's shoulder. "On the evenings when we're home, Marcus and I come down here to watch the sunset and reflect on our day."

I stare out at the orange and pink sky. "It's a beautiful sunset," I say, dropping down in the sand beside Marcus.

The three of us sit in comfortable silence for a few minutes, enjoying the tranquility of the waves rolling toward the shore and the backdrop of the California sunset.

"This is where I asked Emerson to marry me," Marcus tells me.

Emerson hums in agreement. "I thought he was joking. We'd only known each other a week."

"But I convinced her otherwise," he adds with a chuckle. "Since that day, this has become our spot. We've done a lot of thinking here. Had a lot of in-depth discussions and made a lot of important decisions in this very spot. It's also where I accepted my own fate."

What was your first thought after you'd been given the devastating news?

Marcus: I went into planning mode. Thanks to Emerson always being on top of things, my life and business investments were already in order. I started making a mental list of all the things I needed to do. Time wasn't on my side, and I had a lot of loose ends to tie up with lawyers, accountants, business partners. I already had a will in place; it just needed some updating. The *Jaybird* album was complete. I wrapped up my last season on *America's Voice* in May. Emerson will be taking over the Mayhem Foundation. And Jaybird will eventually take over Project Mayhem.

And now?

Marcus: Now I'm just taking life day by day, spending time with my family.

Are you afraid to die?

Marcus: No. I'm afraid of not being around to protect my family, particularly my daughter. I'm mostly sad that I won't be here to see her experience some of the most pivotal moments of her life.

How is Jayla handling it?

Emerson: She's not.

Marcus: We've been seeing a therapist. She comes twice a week to the house. One day she comes to talk with us as a family. The other is reserved for one-on-one sessions with each of us.

As a father, what do you want the world to know about Jaybird?

Marcus: She's just as beautiful on the inside as she is on the outside. She's talented, smart, kind, funny, and she has the biggest heart of anyone I know. She trusts freely and loves wholeheartedly.

If you could have your fans remember one thing about you, what would it be?

Marcus: That I loved them back.

Sadly, six months after this interview took place, Marcus King passed away at his Malibu home. He was surrounded by everyone he loved until he took his last breath. During his celebration of life, his daughter, Jayla, his Jaybird, stood before the congregation and paid a beautiful tribute to her father. With Jayla's permission, I've included part of that tribute here.

"Marcus King was just a man who loved his family. Music was his life, but family was his everything. He was an amazing father and husband. I can only hope that one day I'll be lucky enough to have a man love me as much as my dad loved my mom. What I've learned from this experience, this loss, is that at the end of the day, we're all human. Our titles, our social status, our money—none of that stuff matters when it's our time to go. I know he's in a better place, and he's at peace. I'm relieved that he no longer feels pain. Call me selfish, but that doesn't make me miss him any less, nor does it dull the pain of having to let him go. A pain so fierce it hurts to breathe because my heart is broken. I speak for my mom as well when I tell you that my dad was the moon in the night sky. The sun on a cloudy day. He was our life. Our world. He was our everything. I'll miss you, Daddy."

Marcus's presence in this world will be missed by all. Rest in peace, my friend.

The End

Heart Beats

Creed

by

Amy Davies

Rebel Hype Part 1

Being a rockstar is all I've ever wanted. So when the opportunity arose I snatched the f**ker right up.

Along with my twin brother Crossley and our best friends Bryce and Luther we formed Rebel Hype.

Just as we set out on our big, country summer tour, I see her. She makes my body buzz with need. I crave her touch; her flavour.

The life of a rockstar is fast and furious but our time is limited; so let's make the most of it.

Chapter One

My name is Creed Lawless, I am a twenty-two-year-old up and coming rock star with my band 'Sexual Neon'. I am here in California for a rock festival. Kevin picked us up in a dingy pub one night and here I am. Well currently I am dancing with a chick that is grinding her perfect fucking ass all over my hard dick in my jeans.

"Fucking perfect," I whisper into her ear. Girls love it when us men do that shit; they think it's sexy and intimate. I am only here to get my dick wet with all the free and willing pussy that is thrown at me. This chick though, she seems different, she has the girl next door vibe about her.

Wavy auburn hair, that reaches the small of her back, trim waist, perfect ass; plenty for gabbing and tits that I bet would fill my hands to the max. Her scent is driving me and my dick fucking wild, I need to be buried balls deep inside of her.

"I need to feel you wrapped around me, babe." I tell her, watching her skin break out in goosebumps. I smirk into her neck, laying a kiss in the one spot that drives the chicks crazy.

"So why are we still here?" she asks, looking at me over her shoulder. Fucking minx.

Smirking, I bite her bare shoulder, before stepping around her, taking her hand in mine and leading her away from prying eyes and the very fucking public dancefloor. Her giggles flow behind be, making me smile like a cat that just ate, or in this case is about to eat, the very sexy, tasty looking canary.

"Creed, slow down." Fuck, even her saying my name makes my dick twitch.

Slamming my left palm on the door leading to the tour bus we have for the summer. I keep dragging the girl to the back room. The bus already smells like sex, no doubt one of my three band mates already got their piece for the night.

We all grew up together, well I kind of shared a womb with one of them as he is my fucking twin brother, Crossley. The other two pricks that are in Sexual Neon are Bryce and Luther.

With a gentle but firm tug on her arm, I send her falling to the bed, her laughs fill the small room at the back of the bus. The scent of fresh sex in the air enhances my arousal; I know she feels it too.

"Before we go any further, I need your name and age, babe. Not being caught out again." I smile at her. With a nod, and a smirk covering her gorgeous face she gives up the deets.

"Fair enough. I'm twenty-one, my name is Taylen Blackwell. I am here for summer vacation with my family. Anything else?" she asks, moving to her knees while licking her lips.

"Nope. Strip for me." I growl. Her eyes widen but not in fear. I grip the back of my white t-shirt and pull it from my body, dropping it to the floor, just as she pulls off the strapless top she was wearing. Next go her short denim shorts, she is left in a black strapless lace bra with matching thong.

"Sexy." I growl, pushing down on my dick in my jeans. Her eyes eat up my upper body, taking in the pierced nipples, tattoos and defined abs. Being the drummer of the band I keep myself in good shape.

"I don't normally do this, Creed." She looks nervous suddenly, her innocence shining through. Fuck.

"Are you a virgin?" I ask, praying like fuck that she tells me no. I am a dick most days, but I not that much of a dick, a girls first time should be special. That's what me and Crossley tell our baby sister, Chole.

Shaking her head, "No. I mean this," flicking her wrist between us. "I'm not normally this wild; crazy. I am the calm and collected one of my friends."

She shrugs looking shy again.

"Well this is happening." I tell her, winking.

Biting her lip, I groan as the action goes straight to my dick. Moving forward I crawl over her, laying kisses over her thighs, hips and up her flat smooth stomach. I spy the tattoo on her rib cage, the urge to lick it is overpowering so I do just that I lick her skin, letting her flavor hit my senses and send my cock fucking delusional.

"Oh," she moans, arching her back into my touch.

Removing her panties, tugging them down her legs, I pull her to sit up, sliding her bra off her body. Kissing where the material just was, I look up at her, our eyes connecting making sparks fucking fly between us.

Shit I wish things could be different.

"Why the dreamcatcher?" I ask, laying more kisses over her naked body. Her body shivers at my touch and I smirk against her skin. The way women react to a man's touch is fucking crazy, talk about ego boost; but Taylen is different.

Normally I am an 'In, out and go' kinda of man but fuck she makes me want to devour her body; inch by inch.

"I used to have night terrors when I was a kid, they only stopped about two years ago, I thought that dreamcatcher on my body would help. It's a mind over matter thing, I guess. But it helps."

"Fair," moving my body up hers, I suck one nipple into my mouth while pinching and twisting the other one. Her body shakes and she moans into the space around us. The back room we are in will smell of her for fucking days after; this room is mine until I can't smell her anymore.

"More, harder." She pants, gripping my hair; holding me to her tit.

"Fucking hell, babe you taste good, I am going to feast on you all fucking night." I tell her meaning every fucking word. I need to have my fill of her before she leaves because she will have to leave.

Taking her lips in a deep kiss, our tongues battle it out. Pulling away from the kiss I move back down her body, needing to see what her pussy looks like; tastes like.

My rules just went out the fucking window. How the hell has she done this to me? I don't kiss girls and I never fucking eat pussy, but she makes me want to taste every inch of her.

Before I dive between her creamy thighs I stand and remove my jeans, not wearing boxers. I have always gone commando for a quick fuck, it's easier when fucking in a backroom or a restroom.

Her eyes widen when they settle on my cock, making me smirk at her. Taking my dick in my hand I pump a few times, seeing her eyes get darker and darker.

Yeah, she wants this; me. Don't they all.

"Spread them, baby." I tell her, my voice harsher than it has been, seeing her naked before me has my desire going haywire. She is making me crazy.

Chapter Two

Her pussy is pink, plush, swollen and ready for me. The glistening wetness that covers her pussy lips are calling to me, telling me to taste her, to suck on the plumb flesh.

Fuck me sideways, I'm going in.

Gripping her thighs, I dive in. Her scent invades my senses, kick starting my climax, my balls tightening just by the smell of her; sweet cherry blossom.

"Oh shit," Taylen cries out, as I suck on one of her pussy lips. She is completely clean shaven, I fucking love that shit, un-like Crossley who lives some bush to tug on, he says it makes the girls go crazy with sensation.

Laving at her pussy, her juices coat my tongue, sliding down my throat. My brain is cataloguing the taste and smell of her, no other women will ever come close to her.

She has fucking ruined me.

Moving one hand, I slide one finger into her hot channel, then add a second when she jerks from my touch. Pumping slow and deep into her hot wet pussy as my tongue flicks, nips and sucks on her clit; I hear her breathing pick up and her cries of passion fill the room, bouncing off the walls.

If the boys came back, they would know not to come charging in here. Fuck, I bet some of the roadies know what we are doing by the sheer volume of her climax.

"Shit, Creed." her voice bounces off the walls surrounding us. My pride rockets knowing that it is me that is making this sexy as fuck girl orgasm, screaming out my name.

Pulling my fingers out of her, I crawl up her body, making sure she sees me sucking her juices off my fingers. Her eyes widen but fill with lust. Yeah, she is a dirty girl at heart. What man doesn't love a dirty girl?

"You like that don't you, baby?"

With a nod from her, I lean in taking her mouth in a sensual, dirty kiss as her juices that coat my lips, rub off on hers. She moans into my mouth, making my cock leak all over her naked thigh.

"I want to taste you, too." She pants out breaking the kiss. Who am I to ignore a request like that?

Smirking down at her, then I kiss her once before rolling over onto my back, giving her full range of my body.

She has my stomach in knots and I am going against so many of my fucking rules for her. I never ever go down on a girl, I love pussy, but I love to fuck it and leave, and I never ever fucking kiss them.

Our gazes stay locked as Tay moves closer to me, the nerves showing in her eyes, she was a wildcat a second ago but now her shyness is coming through. Not wanting her to bolt or feel uncomfortable, I smile at her, offering her my hand to help her get into place.

"Do what you feel is right, this is all you, babe."

I may be a cunt to most women but Taylen has me wanting to be a nice guy for once. Totally fucking bewitched.

Her palms rest on my thighs, making me shiver and my cock jerks against my stomach. Her knees brush against my inner thigh as she shuffles forward to get closer to my cock. Moving in closer, she leans on one hand on my leg and the other grips my shaft.

"Fuck," I mutter when her soft hand tightens around my dick.

"I hope I do this okay, I haven't done it a lot," her voice confirms her nerves.

"Baby, you do you. Whatever feels right, like I said. No matter what you do I will enjoy, I'm a man after all, we all love a good blowjob." I wink at her, making light of the moment. With a slight nod, she moves her mouth closer to my cock, making the pre-cum to leak more in anticipation of her hot mouth wrapped round me.

My eyes are glued to her lips as they part, ready to take my cock into her mouth. My mouth waters watching her. She is fucking beautiful, sexy and she doesn't even know it.

Her hair falls like a curtain around her face, partially blocking my view. Reaching up I move her hair away from her face, gripping it in my fist behind her head, but I also use that to move her down my shaft, controlling her movement softly.

"Oh fuck," I moan, when she moves down more, taking me all the way back into her throat. My abs tighten, sweat covering my heated skin. She picks up her movements, sliding up and down my cock, taking me deep every time she slides down.

Still gripping her hair but tightening it now she moans around me, the vibrations hitting my balls. They pull up and I fear that I will blow my load inside her hot mouth, but I want to come in her sweet pussy that I bet my fortune on is tight as fuck.

"Stop," I all but scream at her. Her head shoots up, concern written all over her face. Smiling at her, I reach for her under her arms, yanking her up my body. She yelps causing me to laugh. Resting her body against mine, I take her lips again; our tongues duel, our flavors mix in our mouths, sending desire raging through my body.

"Ride me," I tell her, removing one hand from her body and reaching for the top drawer of the bedside table. Her eyes track my movements, showing her uncertainty. Once I have a foil packet in my and I hand it to her.

"Your choice here babe. We fuck or we don't fuck; up to you." I tell her keeping my gaze firmly locked on her. Taylen sits upright, tucking her hair behind her ears.

I take in her features, while she thinks things over. With my hands resting on her hips, her skin hot under my palms. Her cheeks are flushed, making her bright blue eyes pop. She has a few freckles scattered over her pert nose and cheeks.

Taylen brings her eyes back to me and she speaks, her voice sounding husky but firm.

"We fuck. Make it count, Creed, because I know that we only get right now. Leave your mark on me." Fuck me her words hit me right in the chest.

I wish like fuck that I can offer her more, even though we only met like an hour or two ago, I feel like I have known her for years. She makes me feel things that no woman has since Regina. That cunt tore me to pieces, and I said that no woman would ever hurt me like that again.

But Taylen, damn, this woman could make me break all the fucking rules.

"Then what are you waiting for," I nudge her, tapping her thighs. Biting her bottom lip, she bites the foil packet, ripping it with her teeth before pulling out the rubber and rolling it down my steel cock.

"I need you inside of me, Creed."

Her husky voice sends my need for her into hyperdrive. Growling, I lift her up and slam her down onto my cock, the need to have her ride me hard and fast is overpowering.

"Oh," she cries out into the room and I slam up into her over and over again. I rest my hands on her hips, forcing her to move fast and grind down hard. Her clit is rubbing against my pelvic bone and I can feel her pussy tighten with each thrust.

I am sweating like a whore in church and my heart is razing like a NASCAR driver. We moan, pant and cry out as we both orgasm together in the small back room.

Breathing heavy, Taylen falls flat onto my chest. Her tits are pressed against my chest, our sweat making us stick but to be fair I couldn't give a flying fuck right now, I am so fucking blissed out to have her there.

The sinking feeling hits me, that I have to let her go. I can't fucking keep her.

Chapter Three

Waking up disoriented, not even knowing we fell asleep, Taylen is still on my chest, both of us naked as the day we were born. By now the need to kick her out should be in full effect but I wrap my arms around Tay and hold on for dear life, because I know that when she wakes up, she will leave me. My chest tightens at the thought, but it also knows it's the right thing to do. She may make me feel but I know I am in the beginning of my career and I can't commit her, not yet. Way too much fucking temptation out there and I don't want to hurt her.

Burying my head in her neck, I breath in her scent, committing it to memory because fuck knows when I will see this woman again; I don't want to let her go.

Fuck me, I don't want to let her go.

Taylen said she was here on a family vacation, I am only here until Monday, why the fuck can't I have her all weekend. It is Friday morning now; I can get my fill of her and then set her free of any heartbreak that I might cause her.

A knock on the bedroom doors jars me from my thoughts of having Taylen anytime and anywhere over the next few days, if she agrees with my terms.

"What?" I call out, my voice sound like a fucking prickly frog is stuck down my throat. Taylen jerks awake, pushing up onto her hands, looking down at me with a sleepy smile on her flushed face; again, her hair forming a curtain around us.

"Hey, brother. You got rid of that piece of ass yet?" Cross says as he pushes the door open, not waiting to see if my company is still in here with me. He pauses and a smirk covers his face when he sees Tay still straddling my body.

Her body goes rigid at his words and her eyes widen. In a panic, I push her off my body, pulling the sheet up and over her to shield her from my asshole of a brother.

"Fuck off, man. I'll be out in a second." I tell him over my shoulder, making sure that he can no longer see Taylen. Breaking eye contact with Cross, I look back down at Taylen, who is bright red and her eyes look fearful but also hurt.

"Yeah, okay man, chill out yeah. Fuck, since when do you get wrapped up in one pussy. Damn she must suck you off like a fucking pro hoover, for you to keep her around."

If it was possible Tay's eyes went even wider and I shake my head at her to not to listen to him. My anger builds at my brother, my fucking twin who should be sensing some twin-to-twin shit right about now. Swinging my head back around to glare at him.

"GET. THE. FUCK. OUT," I growl at him. His hands go up in a surrender action as he backs out of the room.

"Hurry the fuck up, man, I'm starving to death." Cross bitches as he closes the door behind him. Shaking my head, I look back at Taylen and see her face is as bright as a lobster, her eyes are squeezed tight, like she is trying to forget what the fuck just happened.

Shifting my body slightly closer to hers, I lay my leg over her naked thighs and her eyes pop open, focusing on me. Bright eyes stare back at me and I can't keep the smile off my face at how fucking beautiful she looks right now.

"Hey, it's okay." I tell her cupping her jaw, then leaning in for a kiss but her head jerks back from me. Her eyes wide with shock now not embarrassment.

"It's not okay, Creed it is far from fucking okay. Oh my God," she jumps out of the bed, searching the room for her clothes. I lay there with a pounding heart watching her get dressed, muttering to herself. I can't make out what she is saying but damn she is cute doing it.

"Baby, he didn't see shit. He is used to walking in and finding random girls in here."

As soon as the words leave my mouth, I know that I fucked up and just blew the weekend with her. Swinging my legs over the side of the bed, I take in the anger on her face, she is fucking livid with me right now and I have to make this right.

"I am not some naive little girl who thinks she can tame you, Creed, but rubbing it in my face that you've sleep with a shit ton of girls in here, is not fucking cool. I'm out, thanks for last night." She scurries to the door, but I leap from the bed, pressing my naked body against her clothed one, trapping her between me and the flimsy door.

"I know that, I know that you know how all this shit works and I'm sorry for saying that shit, okay? Don't go. Let me take you to breakfast, I'm not ready to see you go yet,"

Her body sags a little in defeat and I know I've won; well this round anyway. Turning her in my arms I take her mouth in a kiss that leaves no room for debating whether I want her here or not.

Her arms wrap around me, holding me to her. The kiss is both sensual and forceful, our tongues battle it out.

Taylen has a shyness to her but I can see the wildcat in her too; she isn't a walkover. She is nothing like the other groupies that we hook up with and to be honest it is fucking refreshing.

"Come on let's go eat and I want to talk to you about something," I tell her, leaving the ominous statement hanging. Her eyes assess me and with a slight nod, I get my answer. I rush around the room throwing on clothes that I find, no fucking clue whose they are, all of the band share clothes; fuck we share more that clothes just ask Bryce and Luther.

Taylen stands and watches me get dressed, biting her lip as the hunger in her eyes grow but I know we need to get some food and have a talk before we go any further.

"Baby, I really fucking suggest that you stop looking at me like, I need to feed you."

Taking her hand in mine we leave the room. I can hear the boys before I see them, loud bastards. The smell of pot hits me the closer we get and Taylen's hand tightens in mine; yeah, she smelt it too.

"Hey, there you are man, fuck I'm wasting away here. I need me some fucking food. We fucked this chick last night that was freaky as hell, liked to be bitten and sucked on till no end." Luther pipes in as we enter the common space. Tay gasps and the boys try to look around me to see her.

"Fuckers, I don't need the dirty details of the girls you fuck." I bitch, tugging Tay over to the Captain's chair and pulling her into my lap. I kiss her bare shoulder, hoping it will calm her down, but her body is as stiff as a board.

My eyes flit between the boys, watching them as they watch Tay and me. I wink at them and their smirks take over.

"So, who do we have here?" Bryce asks.

"Boys meet Taylen. Tay, meet my brother Crossley, Bryce and Luther." I introduce the misfits sitting in front of us.

"I know who you all are, I'm a fan," she says, relaxing some. The boys smile at her, and her cheeks flush red again. My gaze finds my brothers and he winks at me with a knowing smile. We may fuck like the energizer bunny, but we also know that when we find the one, she is fucking it.

Even though I feel the pull with Taylen, I can't stop thinking about the tour I am about to embark on with my band. I'm not ready to settle for one pussy, even though I may live to regret letting her go, but first I need my fill of her.

Timing sucks ass right now.

Chapter Four

After we all went to breakfast, the band had to go and do a soundcheck. Taylen joined us after she went home to shower and change, then she sat on the end of the stage enjoying us fuck up and mess around, pissing Kevin off big time.

Her smile fills her face, her skin is flushed red with the sun and from the lust coursing through her body. In between songs I stalk over to her and have a taste, just like I am about to do now.

"You enjoying yourself, baby?" I ask, kissing her neck and sucking gently on her flesh. Her body shivers making me smile. I love the effect I have on her, but she has the same effect on me too. Her tiny hands grip at my jeans at my sides, holding me between her bare legs. She turned up wearing short denim shorts and a rock band tee that has been cut so it sits just below her perky tits, she has a bikini top underneath.

Sucking in a breath, she nods her head not giving me the words I want to hear. Moving my lips down to her collar bone, where her shirt has been cut into a wicked V, I suck harder making sure my mark is left where any fucker can see it.

"It's crazy being here with you, seeing how all of this works. It's amazing, Creed, thank you." Her words are breathy with need. My dick twitches in my jeans as she pulls me even closer to her body where I can feel the heat from her pussy.

"Baby, I love having you here, but you know we need to talk yeah?"

Giving me a nod, with a sad smile on her face breaks my heart but the pain will fade, we will move on and she will meet a guy that is perfect for her and me; well I will dominate the music world with the regret of letting her go.

"Brother, let's finish this so I can go and get my own pussy before the gig starts," Crossley yells across the stage. I groan against Taylen's neck, breathing in her scent; committing it to memory.

"You and me for the hour I've got spare before the show starts, yeah?" with a nod from her I rejoin the boys on stage and rock it the fuck out.

With one last kiss to her perfectly pink lip gloss covered lips I leave her sitting on a large storage box looking sexy and sweet all at the same time.

Reaching the microphone in the middle of the stage I turn to look at Tay and throw her a wink as I count us in on the drums. We belt out the song that we are singing to open our set tonight. Being here is a huge fucking step up for us and we are going to take the big ass leap and take every step up that we need to take over the rock world.

Song after song we sing, we beat the shit out of each track, nailing it every time. Sweat is pouring down my chest and back, so much so I grip the back of my t-shirt and pull it over my head, wiping my face before tucking it into the back of my black jeans. Taylen licks her lips, winking at me from the side of the stage.

My cock jerks at the little closet dirty girl that I am going to get my fill of for the next two days.

My dirty thoughts are halted when I see an old face, step up beside Taylen. Fucking Kitty. Zoning in on the two women, I storm over to them, when I hear 'fuck' coming from Crossley behind me and the pounding of boots catching up to me.

"Oh, yeah, he likes variety, that why I'm here, honey. You can leave now. I know what he likes." Kitty's whiney voice pipes up, saying shit about me again. This woman is fucking toxic.

"Shut the fuck up, Kitty. You were told not to come here. Stop fucking following me." I bite out, pulling Taylen to my side, wrapping my arm around her waist, keeping her tight.

"Oh, baby, now come on you weren't serious when you told me that," she steps up to me, running her false nails down my bare chest. Fuck, I forgot to put my shirt back on, when I charged in and get to my girl.

"He meant every fucking word, bitch, now fuck off." Bryce spits out from behind me. The boys hate Kitty as much as I do. We were dating last summer when I came back to the bus and found her fucking a roadie, while snorting coke off another one. We may be a group of misfits, who drink, and smoke weed but that is as much as we do, we do not do hard drugs. That shit fucked up Luther's childhood, so we don't allow it near us.

"Fuck off, ass-boy." Kitty spits out at Bryce, who lunges for her, but Luther stops him.

"Easy, baby," Luther says gently calming our boy down. Did I forget to mention that Bryce and Luther are bisexual? They fuck each other or add another woman into their bed, but never another man.

Bryce is as white as they come, and Luther is a mocha skinned sexy bastard. People often say shit to them about being together, but they just tell people to 'fuck off'

Love is love, brothers and sisters; deal with it.

"Leave, Kitty. You aren't fucking welcome here." I tell her again. She eyes scan over each of us, then stop on Taylen. Her eyes assess Tay from head to toe then she bursts out laughing, the noise grating on my nerves. Fucking hell how the hell did I ever think this woman was God's gift to men?

"This. This is what you are into now?" she jerks her hand in Tay's direction, almost catching her face with her nasty ass nails. Tay shrinks back, and Kitty gives us a sinister smile. Fucking hell, she is one ugly bitch.

"*This*," I say, looking down at Taylen and smile. "is more of a woman than you will ever be, and do you know why?" leaning down I drop a kiss on Tay's pink lips.

I don't wait for an answer as Kitty crosses her skinny arms, tapping her elbow her with nails, giving me a bored expression.

"Taylen is all fucking real, every inch of her beautiful body, inside and out. She doesn't act like she thinks I want her to act. She is real." I state loving the rage that is taking over Kitty's face.

"They only want the fame, Creed, your cock isn't that special," Kitty snipes back thinking she has hit her mark, but she is far from it.

"Maybe before. They were all like you, bitches who want the cock and the fame, but not my Tay. Now you know where the door is." I nod in the direction of the exit behind her.

"Can I just say something?" Tay speaks, her voice making me shiver. She notices and gives me a sweet ass smile.

"Yeah, baby. Say what you need before the trash is taken out." She leans in and kisses my jaw before bringing her gaze to Kitty.

"You don't know me and personally I am fucking thankful for that. You may have had Creed before me, but you most certainly will not have him after me. So, carry on walking and latch onto some other sorry guy who thinks the world shines out of that fake ass of yours,"

Everyone around us bursts out laughing, as a seething Kitty storms from backstage, going fuck knows where. To be honest I couldn't give a fuck where she ends up, as long as it's far away from me, my girl and my band.

"Fuck me, that girl is like sand, she gets in everywhere." Cross adds, making everyone laugh again.

Hearing Taylen laugh has my dick craving her. In a flash I stoop low and throw her over my shoulder, making her yelp, gripping the waist of my jeans. I slap her ass carrying her to our tour bus.

"Get it, baby," Cross yells after us.

"Fuck look at that ass, babe." Luther adds, making me stop in my tracks and turning to face them, the action also removes my girl's ass from their view.

"This ass is mine, brother. All fucking mine and I intend to have it," Tay tenses over my shoulder, until I run my hand over her plump ass, soothing her. Luther and Bryce smirk at me, and Cross nods, giving me his approval; not that I needed it.

Chapter Five

Throwing Taylen on the bed, her giggles fill the room and have a direct hit on my cock that is raging in my jeans. I rip open my belt and buttons and drop them, so I am as naked as a jaybird. Her flushed cheeks and beautiful smile send my desire to taste every inch of her into overdrive.

"We have a short time before I need to be on stage and, baby, I need you in every way possible. We need to savor this," at my last words her smile drops a little, but she recovers quickly. She knows we are coming to an end. The thought makes my stomach knot and my heart ache, but my head is telling me it is the right thing to do.

"Ruin me, Creed. Give me something to remember you by." Her sweet voice has my body racked with shivers. Smirking down at her, I move in and remove her shorts and panties in one swift action, then I pull her to sit up, quickly removing her tee and bra.

I love her tits; they are a perfect fit for my large callused hands.

The smile stays on her face as desire and lust fill her eyes. Heavy pants make her tits move up and down, enticing me to play with them, to taste them and savor them.

"I need to commit your body to memory, Taylen, because woman you will plague my mind for years to fucking come." Leaving it at that, I help her lay down and move down the bed.

Her tiny bare feet call to me to kiss and worship, so I do. Kissing her feet, moving up to her ankles, then her calves. Her skin is soft to the touch and she smells of strawberries. Her giggles fill the room when I kiss the side of her knee, my stubble adding to the sensation.

I plan on marking her, making sure that any dude within spitting distance can see that she is mine. Moving my lips up to her thigh, I give gentle sucks, leaving little red marks, then I bit as I get to the one place, I plan on spending the next few days, until we part ways.

"Your mouth feels so freaking good, Creed. I need you." She states panting. Her breathy words are a direct hit.

Without responding I run my tongue through her slit, making her jerk and cry out. Her flavor invades my taste buds and my cock cries out for attention, but the fucker will have to patient. After one hard suck on her clit, I remove my mouth, causing her to bitch at me.

"Hey why did you stop, that felt good?" her eyes are wide and dark, filled with lust for me. All fucking me.

"Patience, baby." Is all I say, before I start moving my mouth over her body again. I kiss her pelvic bone, then her hips, moving up over her ribs. Laying a sensual kiss just beneath her perfect globed tits, then I lick under each one, tasting her skin is getting to be one of my favorite things to do.

"Oh shit," she pants out. I smile against her nipple before sucking it into my mouth; hard. Taylen cries out, gripping the back of my head, holding me to her tit.

The pain shoots straight down my spine and to my balls, that are screaming for release.

My cock and balls clearly have different plans to my head and heart. I want to savor this woman; they want to get wet and explode.

Moving so we are face to face, our gazes connect. My heart stutters in my chest, no other woman has ever made me feel like this. So why do I feel the need to let her go?

With each of us searching for something, I slowly reach down and take my dick in hand and line him up, before slowly sinking into her succulent heat. Her eyes widen but they stay locked on mine.

Sinking right to the hilt, I bottom out, making her gasp and as a deep groan to leave my throat. The need to move but stay still is battling in my head; wishing I could stay here forever, but we both know it can't happen. I am sure she can read my thoughts, because she gives me a gentle nod and I start to move.

"Oh Creed, that…oh shit."

My hips move in a slow, sensual motion. Rocking in and out of her. I want this time to be slow and full of need and want, then I will fuck the shit out of her for the next two days.

"Oh, God." She breathes out again, as I just growl, lowering my head to her neck, breathing her in.

With a few deep thrusts, Taylen is coming all over my cock, soaking both of us, as my climax ruses through me taking me by surprise. Panting and trying to catch our breaths we lay in the bed, clinging to each other for dear life.

The inevitable is coming and yet we are both desperately trying to hold onto this moment.

"Creed." Tay says my name breaking the silence.

"Yeah, babe."

"Thank you. Just in case you fuck my brains out and I forget to say it."

I chuckle at her, twisting us so we are facing each other on our sides. The talk is needed now, even though I feel physically sick just thinking about the conversation.

"You are way out of my league, Taylen Blackwell. Way too fucking good for the likes a scruffy Rockstar." I tell her. She frowns at me and flicks my nose.

"What the fuck. Did you just flick my nose like a naughty dog?" I gripe rubbing my nose, scowling at her.

"Yes. Yes, I did, and you deserved it. You are not scruffy; you are a typical bad boy rock star but with a difference."

"Oh, yeah and what's that? A huge cock that no one else has?" I wiggle my eyebrows at her, making her laugh. Slapping my chest, she smiles at me, then leans in for a kiss. Before I can speak, Taylen talks, her face showing her sorrow.

"I know what this is, Creed. I never expected anything more; no promises, or marriage proposals. We are both young and free, with wild added to you." She says, winking at me.

"I hate this," I admit. It doesn't matter that we both know how this will end it doesn't make it any better.

"Creed, I am grateful for the experience, the time spent with you has been beyond the best and there are still memories to be made, right?"

"Fuck yeah. We don't leave until Monday morning, and I want to spend the rest of my time here with you. It's Friday now, so we have plenty of time to create sexy fucking memories with each other and ruin each other for any further partners." I wink at her, climbing onto her body, my cock hard as fuck between us.

I take her three more times before we get ready for the nights show. Having her in the wings of stage will give me the kind of high I have never experienced before.

Chapter Six

Sweat is pouring down my body, my shirt is long gone; Cross, Bryce and Luther are in the same state of undress as me. The ladies are eating it up but there is only one girl I want to get hot and sweaty with. Just thinking about her sexy mouth has my cock twitching behind my tight black jeans.

Spending time with her yesterday and last night at our first gig was fucking epic, I never thought a girl could make me feel like this again, but Taylen Blackwell has.

Last night after the show I took her to beach where I fucked her under the pier, then again on the bus. The boys had their groupies for the night but they stayed clear of the back bedroom so we could have it.

It was like watching us from the side of the stage was an aphrodisiac for Tay, she jumped me as soon as I reached her backstage. We were all hands, tongue and teeth well into the early hours of the morning.

I woke up this morning with her perfect mouth wrapped around my cock. Now that ladies and gents is the best fucking wake-up call known to man.

We spent the day together; thank fuck she told her family that she was spending a few days with me and the band. I could enjoy my time with her without looking over my shoulder waiting for the cops to pick me up for kidnapping.

The boys tagged along for a few hours but then Luther got fucking horny when he saw Bryce talking to some chick, so they left to go and play. Cross left shortly after to do whatever the fuck my twin does with his time when I am with a girl.

After the day together we came back to the festival set up and the band did a sound check again, as well as fitting in a few interviews with some local stations and music magazines. Getting our name out there is the main priority and seeing Taylen leaning against the wall watching us woo the female interviewers set my decision in stone, especially when the redhead asked us if we were single, because she heard that we like to 'play' with the ladies.

"So, boys, are there any special ladies in your lives right now? The stories I have heard are quite telling about how you like to 'play' with girls along the way." The redhaired music magazine interviewer asked.

"No special lady for me, I am enjoying the life right now, but I am not saying that shit won't happen." Cross says. My twin has always had that philosophy that when the right woman comes into your life, you will know it with one look, one kiss. I wasn't a true believer until Tay, who is looking sexy as sin standing against the wall behind the redhead. Her dress snug against her trim body, her bikini straps showing. The thought of me tying that strap this morning while I sucked on her tits has my cock twitching in my jeans.

"Creed what about you?"

I blink and tear my eyes away from Tay, smiling at the redhead. Shaking my head of the dirty thoughts, I answer her, but the words burn in my throat.

"Nope. I am just living the dream right now for however long this shit lasts. Can't tie my dick to one girl, he likes variety." I play up to the Rockstar persona, but I can feel the temperature in the room drop, as Tay's body goes rigid again the wall. Cross looks between Tay and me, then shakes his head.

I know there is a big chance that I just fucked things up for the rest of the weekend with Taylen. With our gazes locked, I hear Bryce and Luther take over, deflecting the conversation from me.

The crowd screams, bringing me out of my thoughts of how the day went with Taylen. I look over to see her leaning against a speaker box at the side of the stage, her smile in place but it seems forced since the interview. Even though she agreed to stay with me, I can feel the huge void growing between us.

I did that, but again my head, heart and cock are at war over her.

A part of me thinks this is the best way to end things, her knowing what a life with me will be like, but the other part wants to take her in my arms and never let her sexy ass go.

Throwing her a wink, I look back out at the constant movement of the crowd. The ocean and sunset behind the thousands of people, gives the most amazing backdrop. I hits the canvas of my drums, Bryce and Luther are gyrating with each other on the side of the stage, making the girls go fucking crazy.

Smiling at the people enjoying the music; my heart knows this is exactly where I want to be; need to be.

Music soothes the soul. It expresses what you are feeling. It is the beat of the heart for everyone that needs it.

"Are you sexy people having a good time?" Cross bellows into the microphone, spurring them on. Not loud enough for him, he ask again.

"I said, are you having a fucking good time?"

Screams fill the night air. The bass from Luther's guitar hits be square in the chest and it makes my heart fucking come alive.

Music is life.

Looking over at Taylen again, I see her smiling at the crowd and then bring her eyes back to me, this time her smile in genuine. And it causing me to smile and my heart to lighten. This is what she does to me.

"This one is our last song tonight for you fucking beautiful people. But we will be back tomorrow to please you again, are you up for that?" Cross asks the crowd.

The noise would raise the roof if we were under one.

"Fuck, yeah they do. They want us to fuck them through our music, don't you?" I say, smirking at the ladies.

Girly screams fill the air again, making me laugh and looking at my brother, I see him winking at a few of the girls in front of the stage. Fucking whore, but then again who the hell am I to say shit, I am just like him.

We finish up the gig and we leave the stage to chants for more from us, but the event manager told us that we cannot ever go over our set because we have some pretty big fucking names on this tour with us. I don't want to start off our career by pissing off some of the biggest bands in the industry.

The boys rush off the stage ahead of me, but I take my time making my way to Taylen who hugs Cross, Bryce and Luther before they walk down the steps to head to the green room that we have been given.

Closing the gap between us, I see her smile is still in place, her hands are tucked into the back pocket of her jeans shorts, pushing her tits forward, enticing me to play.

"Hey," I say to her, giving her a smile.

"Hey, you did amazing. You belong on the stage Creed." Her words make my head, heart and cock swell.

Fuck yeah, I do, I just wish that she could be by my side while I do it.

Chapter Seven

We are all sitting in the living space on the tour bus, Cross has a chick on his lap, while she kisses and sucks his neck, his hands firmly on her ass. Bryce and Luther are kissing while one girl on her knees alternates between their dicks. Taylen, well Taylen is sitting on my lap, kissing me, completely oblivious to what is going on around her. I am the center of her attention and I wouldn't want it any other way.

We know this is our last night together, and I have been playing on her good side since the interview. I hurt her I know that, even though we both knew it would end tomorrow morning.

The last few days have been a fucking whirlwind and Taylen Blackwell

"Cross, I need you," comes a whiney voice. I break the kiss and look over to Crossley and give him a slight nod and a smirk. Taylen is kissing my neck and can't see the interaction I am having with my twin brother.

What is about to happen will hopefully set the tone for tomorrow night when we say our goodbyes. Taylen needs to see what it will be like to be with a guy like me and be around the band on tour. I am not doing this to hurt her, I am simply showing her what my life is like now. I am way too fucking young to settle down, even if my body is at war over her.

"Get naked for me then, babe." Cross tells her. Keeping my eyes on what is happening across the small room, I feel Taylen adjust her body to see what is happening.

"Watch them, baby. This is the life of a Rockstar." I whisper into her ear, making her body shiver.

"I'm-I'm not sure. This isn't me, Creed." Her voice is quiet, but the tremor is clear.

"This is us, baby. Watch as Cross fucks this chick and makes her come all over his cock right in front of us." Smoothing my hands down her bare thighs, I see the goosebumps creep across her skin. "Look at Bryce and Luther. Have you ever watched two men go at it; kissing, fucking?"

Her head shakes no, but her rapid breathing and the heat from her skin tells me that she likes it. Bryce moves to the floor next to the girl and starts to remove her bra while kissing Luther's abs, over the girls bent body.

"Fucking taste me too, baby," Luther moans enticing Bruce to suck him off. Taylen shivers on my lap, from what she is seeing. Taking it one step at a time, I move her, so she is sitting on my lap facing the guys, with her thighs on the outside of mine, legs spread for me.

The denim skirt she is wearing rises with the parting of her legs, giving me better access to her pussy that I bet is soaking wet for me.

"How wet are you, baby" I ask her in a husky tone. Her body trembles with need.

"Have a look," she gasps when she speaks. Like she didn't mean for those words to come out of her mouth.

Moving my hand from her hip to her inner thigh, her body trembles beneath my touch. Sliding my hand against her silk panties, I move the material aside and find her clit, throbbing and hard. Pushing further down I find her pussy, wet, pulsing and hot.

"Damn, baby, I can smell how much you like watching the boys."

Hot and heavy breathing fills the small space, the smell of sex in the air. Rubbing her clit, moving back down to her pussy, making sure her juice coat my fingers, using it has lube to rub her to orgasm.

"Shit, bro," Cross pants out from across the room, eyes trained on my hands in Taylen's skirt. The girl he brought with him is riding him reverse cowgirl style. Her tits are bounce up and down, her moans are like a porn stars; this chick knows how to play it.

"My sexy bitch," I say close to Taylen's ear. Her pants become faster and faster. Speeding up my fingers on her pussy, my aim is to make her come on my fingers first, then I will strip her naked and fuck her in front of my boys and make her come over my cock.

Pinching her clit, she goes off like a fucking rocket, crying out her orgasm just as Cross's little chickie does. Kissing her neck, her hair covers most of my face and breathe her in. I close my eyes for a moment as I commit her scent to memory. Come daylight I know this woman will be gone from my life. My gut tightens but my heart agrees with my head, I have to let her go.

"Stand up," I instruct Taylen. She listens and I turn her to face me. Smirking up at this beautiful woman standing before me, I tug her skirt and panties down her legs, pooling them on the floor. She steps out and kicks off her flip flops, standing before me in just a cami and bra.

"Take them off." I instruct her and she obeys my command.

"Fuck, man you should see that ass on your girl." Bryce says from his place on the floor. I wink at him, turning her around to face them, her naked form on full show for them all to see. While they admire her, I remove my jeans and t-shirt.

"Fuck me, boy, I need to taste her." Luther adds. He is one kinky bastard, he loves kissing, licking and tasting the people he fucks. He goes to move off the sofa, but I shake my head. I can see Cross out of the corner of my eye smirking at me.

"All mine, brother. You can look but no fucking touching." I state, turning Tay back around to face me, her smile gives away her relief that I won't let these horny bastards lay a hand on her. But then in a flash she smirks down at me, then mounts my thighs, my cock nestling right between her wet, swollen pussy lips.

I groan at the sensation of how hot she feels against me, her juices coating my cock. My heart is racing, my body is buzzing, and my cock is throbbing. Sweat gathers on my brow from the heat of the room and this sexy as sin woman that is about to ride my cock.

"I want to try something, Creed." Her voice is sweet, serenading me into a sexual frenzy. Her request has me thinking that maybe she has been hiding her dirty girl routine all along with me.

Chapter Eight

"What's that, baby?" I ask her, moving my hands up over hips, curving to her ribs and reaching her tits, her nipples are plush pink and hard peaks wanting to be sucked and bitten.

Leaning forward, she forces my tit-full hands to rest against my chest. Her hair cloaks us in a curtain blocking out everyone else. Kissing me, her tongue plays with mine, before she gently bites down on my bottom lip, making my hips buck up into her.

"I want to suck someone off, while riding you, Creed Lawless. I want the ultimate experience with the drummer of Sexual Neon."

Smirking up at her, I see the unsure look on her face when she asks me this. Cupping her face, holding her close so our gazes stay locked, I explain a few things to her, making her feel more comfortable.

"I usually share with the boys, but with you I feel like I want you all to myself, but since we are giving you the ultimate experience; choose." I tell her before kissing her swollen red lips.

Her eyes widen when I pull back, I offer her a smile which she returns and looks over towards the boys. Cross now has his girl bent over the chair and is slamming into her. Bryce is fucking the girl that he and Luther are sharing while Luther is having his dick sucked.

Everyone is lost in the lust and potent sexual feel in the room. With the sound of skin slapping, heavy breathing. Grunting and moans, it like a fucking porno on the bus.

Taylen looks around the room again, her eyes focusing on Luther and Bryce. Thank fuck she didn't want Cross, not that my brother and me haven't shared groupies before but things with Tay are different.

Bringing her eyes back to mine, she whispers. "Luther," I lick my lips and nod my head. Without taking my eyes off her I call out to him.

"Luther, come join us," I call over to him. He doesn't keep up waiting long, I feel his naked thigh against mine. Taylen looks away from me and focuses on Luther sitting next to us. Her smile is small but inviting.

"I want to suck your cock, Luther." Her voice is firm now, but not full of confidence. He gives her a warm smile sensing the apprehension coming off her.

"Baby girl, you can suck me off any day of the week, as long as your man is okay with it." He tells her. Her eyes bounce between Taylen and me and I give hm a nod, to go ahead with it.

"Okay, then, but I need something first, baby girl." He says to her. She bites her lips and gives him a small nod.

"I want a taste. I know Creed said no earlier, but I need to taste those succulent lips and that fine pussy you are carrying around with you,"

"You okay with that, Taylen?" I ask her because I don't want her to do anything that she's uncomfortable with.

"I'm okay with that if you are." She says to me, smiling her beautiful smile at me. I nod, letting her know it is okay. With that she doesn't hesitate to lean over and kiss Luther.

He grips the back of her head, keeping their faces smashed together in a heated kiss. My cock jerks between Tay and me, leaking all over my stomach, ready and waiting to be buried deep inside of her.

"Damn, baby girl you taste good. Now how about you turn around and lay your back against my boys chest, so I can slip between your luscious legs and get a real taste of you. Bro, mind your giant cock, yeah." Luther winks at me and slides to his knees on the floor. Taylen kisses me one more time before she stands and turns around, doing exactly what Luther told her to do.

When her skin touches mine again it is my turn to shiver. She looks over her shoulder at me, leaning in for an awkward kiss. My hands grip her waist, before sliding up to cup her tits. Pinching her nipples, she moans and arches into my touch.

"Damn it, man look at that pussy." Luther groans from the floor, before diving in. I watch down her body, as he eats her pussy, giving her long hard licks with his tongue. Her bare pussy is swollen and shining with her arousal.

Pulling at her nipples and the attack on her pussy she cries out into the room, I look up and see that the other four people in the room have stopped fucking and are watching the three of us. I wink at the girl with the blond hair, making her blush further if that is possible after what my brother just did to her.

"Oh fuck, Luther. Yeah, suck right there. Harder, Creed." Taylen cries out into the room. Heavy breathing, her tits heave into my hand with every breath. I know how good Luther is with his tongue I have been told way too many times to count by Bryce and the girls they share a bed with.

In seconds, no doubt from Luther and the over charged atmosphere in the room, Taylen comes all over Luther's mouth. Sweat covers her delicious body, her skin is plush pink. As she sucks air into her lungs, Luther moves up her body and kisses her, taking her breath away.

I watch as their lips move together; like they have done it a thousand times before. Taylen fits right in with us. A shadow casts over us and I see Cross and Bryce standing in front of us. Bryce winks at me and moves Luther to the side, before leaning in and kissing Tay, taking the kiss deep.

Most men would get jealous of this but fuck, we are all brothers and do like to share, but even as Bryce kisses Taylen, I feel a connection forming among her and the band.

It will suck big fat hairy sweaty balls tomorrow.

Bryce and Luther step back and Cross takes their place, standing in front of Tay, he winks at me and leans in for a kiss. He kisses her sensually; like I do.

Fucking twin connection. He grips her tit in his hand and slides his other hand between her legs. She gasps but doesn't say anything.

"I can't get a full taste like Luther did, but I need to see what is driving my brother crazy." While explaining this, Tay's body arches off me, I look down and see that my brother has his fingers deep in my girl.

"I need to be in her now, man. Move over so Luther can join back in." I tell Cross. He smirks up at me, removing his fingers and bringing them to his lips. Even though I have done this with Taylen, she still gasps seeing my brother taste her too.

"I can see why. Lucky fucker," he mutters, walking back across the room.

Sliding the condom over my cock, that was left on the sofa I lift Taylen up and slide her down my shaft. She gasps at the intrusion, her pussy clamping down on me making me groan.

"Oh, shit, Tay. Fuck that feels good, do it again, baby." My eyes close, letting the feel of her surrounding me wash over my body. With my hands on her hips, I help her ride me, grinding down and rocking back and forth, taking my cock as deep as she can.

"God, Creed. Yes." Taylen pants. Her breathy moan making me want to take her harder. What is it about a woman moans that gets me fucking hotter? Or is it just Taylen?

I feel the cushion next to me dip and I force my eyes open, to see Luther back with us, with his big black cock in hand. Smiling warmly at Taylen, he brings his cock to her lips. Slowly he drags the head over her plump lips.

With the invitation there, Taylen takes it. She opens her mouth, sticking her tongue out, licking the head of his dick. He groans and grips the back of her head gently, pushing her down onto his cock, until she gags a little.

He fucks her mouth gently while she rides me. Back and forth she rocks, her clit hitting my pubic bone each time and her pussy spasms around me, causing my balls to tingle and tighten.

This is some sexy fucking shit.

Luther brings his gaze to me and I see the lust he has there, his usual brown eyes are now dark. He is puffing out big breaths of air, as Tay takes him into her mouth over and over again, alternating between sucks and licks.

"Oh fuck, her mouth is heaven. Fuck, baby, she could give you a few tips," Luther throws the joke at Bryce, who is watching intently, stroking his cock again.

"Fuck off, no one sucks your cock like I do." Bryce bitches back.

I would normally be up for this shit, but fuck this, I need to come, and I need to come now; so, does Tay if her pussy is telling my dick anything.

"She needs to come, man. Hurry the fuck up." I tell Luther through gritted teeth. Smiling down at me, he picks up the pace and so do I. I fuck her pussy, holding her so I can slam up into her. Luther holds her head so he can fuck her mouth, more forcefully now, but her moans tell us she is enjoying it as much as we are.

"Oh fuck, baby girl, I'm going to come." Luther pants out, seconds before he lets out a loud groan and comes deep in her mouth; Taylen swallowing every fucking drop.

When she has finished cleaning his cock off, he leans in and kisses her lips, more gently this time, a thank you of sorts, before he steps away and gets back into things with Bryce as the girl, they brought with them is passed out on the floor.

"Tay," I hold her chin softly, forcing her to look at me again. "You ready, baby. I need to fuck you hard, but I want to go into the back room. You okay with that?"

"Yes, Creed. I would love that." Smiling her beautiful smile at me, she goes to climb off me, but I grip her hips stopping her. Smirking I hold her tight and stand, still keeping us connected. My cock nestled in her warm, soaking wet pussy. I can feel her juices drip down onto my thigh, making my cock twitch.

Chapter Nine

Walking to the room, I leave behind the slapping of skin and loud moaning. This is our last night together and I want it to last. I want to take her as many times as her body will let me and then take her some more. Her skin needs to be smelling of me, feeling me for fucking years to come.

I want her body committing Creed Lawless to memory, so it knows if I am ever near her again.

Sitting on the edge of the bed with Tay in my lap, I kiss her. Taking her mouth in a kiss so deep, I have no fucking doubt she will feel it everywhere. Dropping my hands to her hips I help her rock my cock.

"Ride me hard, Taylen. Ruin me, babe." I grind out. My voice has taken a deeper tone, it always does with her. She makes my body go into sexual overdrive.

"Oh shit," she pants. Her eyes are closed, and her head is thrown back as the desire races through her body. Her body is flushed pink and is covered in a sheer layer of sweat.

Her hips rock back and forth, her hands resting on my knees and her body takes me for all I am worth. She is leaving her mark on my body.

"Baby, I am going to come, come with me. Get there," I cry out to the room, her pussy spasms around my dick, I know she is close but fucking hell so am I.

Sliding my hand across her flat stomach I angle my thumb down to her clit and press; hard. Her head snaps up and her eyes flash open, connecting with mine.

Taylen lets out a deep moan as her climax takes over, as that little touch sends her flying. Our gazes are locked in some deep soul-searching connection as we both fall over the edge.

I swear I go fucking blind there for a second, I have never come so fucking hard in my life. Taylen is beyond anyone in this world. My heart cracks even more, knowing the hours are counting down until she walks away.

Moving us up the bed, our sweaty, sated bodies stick together. Neither of us say anything as we lay there basking in the moment we just shared. My hands trace up and down her back, her hands firmly pressed against my chest, tracing the music tattoo I have there.

"Thank you," her voice is barely there but I somehow hear it. Adjusting my head, I kiss her lips, smiling at her.

Her glassy eyes say it all. Fuck. I swallow hard, the emotion of leaving this girl is fucking killing me. Her face starts to blur but I don't hide that shit, she knows how I feel, how I want things to be different. We talked for hours last night against my better judgement but fuck, I can't say no to this girl.

Taylen's breathing evens out and I can tell she has fallen asleep on me. Smiling I adjust her, so she is on her side curling into me. I pull her leg up, resting it on my thigh. The need to have her touching me is crazy; she just makes me want to be near her.

I wake a few hours later, with a mouth wrapped around my dick, lifting the sheet I covered us with earlier in the night, I see Tay between my legs with my dick hanging out of her mouth.

"Hey," she says, moving her mouth off me.

"Hey," I reply smiling at her then groaning when she takes me into her mouth again all the way to her throat. "Fuck, baby."

Flinging the sheet off us, so I can get a clear view of her. I watch as her head bobs up and down on my dick, her saliva making it glisten in the dimly light room.

"Harder," I growl and fuck me if she doesn't double her efforts. Resting up on my elbows I watch as her cheeks hollow out as she sucks harder making my balls tingle and I know now is the time to stop her.

"Baby, get up here." With a wicked smile on her face she crawls up my body, letting her tits drag across my skin making me buzz more for her. My body knows that we are coming to an end and it is wanting savor every second we have with her.

I hear you buddy; I fucking hear you.

Laying her lips on mine we kiss; it is deep, sexy and hits the spot. Not wanting to wait anymore, I flip us over, so I am hovering over her.

Her beauty hits me right in the heart. Smiling up at me with her large beautiful eyes and perfect fucking smile I lean in and kiss her again, it seems I can't stop fucking kissing this woman.

Reaching down I take my dick in hand and slide into her. Damn, she is fucking soaked and warm and soft.

"Oh, God, Creed. Make love to me. Just this once, please." Her voice breaks, her emotion clear as fucking day. With a nod I start to move.

My hips rock in and out of her in slow deep thrusts. Every now and then I grind in a circular motion making her cry out louder. With every thrust and motion our gazes stay locked, the fear of saying goodbye is right there between us but we both know it is for the best.

It is the most emotionally charged thing I have ever done in my life and an experience I am sure that I will never forget for as long as I live. With our eyes open I kiss her, soft pecks. Before I close my eyes and kiss her cheeks, her nose, eyes and forehead before resting back on her lips.

"I will never forget you, Creed. Never." Her voice breaks completely, and the tears fall. Nodding my head as the fucking emotion takes over me too, I kiss her tears away letting mine fall also. This is breaking my fucking heart; my soul.

"Come for me, baby. I'm close. Oh yeah, let me come inside of you, leave me mark on you inside and out." With that she comes all over my cock and her tight pussy gets even tighter and almost strangles my dick, making me come with her.

We both go flying and not wanting to come back down.

Resting my mouth on her neck I suck hard; leaving my mark on her.

"So good, Creed. Thank you," chuckling I slide out of her, pulling her close to me and we lay there just like we did earlier.

"Baby, you need to stop thanking for giving you the best sex of your life," Slapping my chest she goes up on her elbow, looking down on me. With a soft smile on her face she kisses me, then kisses over my heart. The frown appears but it is gone in a flash.

"One day you will find that one girl who will light up your heart like a neon light, Creed Lawless."

"Maybe." I reply. Tucking her tighter to me, we lay there until we fall asleep.

Dreams plague me of two little blond-haired kids running along the beach while me and Taylen follow behind them laughing and holding hands. They do always say that dreams have a way of speaking to you in the subconscious.

Chapter Ten

My head, heart and dick are not happy and all of a sudden do not agree with any past decisions they have made. Standing next to the tour bus, I watch Taylen say goodbye to Cross, Bryce and Luther.

Her smile brightens up even a sunlit parking lot behind the festival set up. I fucking hate this day. This day will go down in history of Sexual Neon as one of the worst days for the band, and my heart.

"The taxi is a few minutes out; bro. we'll leave you to it." I hadn't even noticed that the boys had finished their 'byes', I was completely locked on her. With a nod I walk over to her and wrap her in my arms.

She sobs against my chest; her cries break me. Letting her tears soak into my white t-shirt, I hold her until she is ready to talk. After fuck knows how long, not that I care, she pulls her head back and looks up at me.

She gives me a watery smile and licks her lips, giving me the cue to move in. taking her lips in a deep, sensual kiss; one that she will ever forget. No other man will ever kiss her like this, make her feel the way I make her feel.

A beep of a car horn has us breaking apart.

"I will never forget you, Creed. This weekend with you has been the best days of my life and that is saying something. Maybe one day we will meet again." I kiss her again just for the sake of it.

The car beeps again and I groan in frustration. Fucking taxi drivers.

"You Taylen Blackwell have ruined me for all other women. No one will ever compete with you. I want you to promise me that you will live your life. Finish school, get that nursing job you have always dreamed of. If you find a man that you fall in love with make sure he isn't a pussy and that he can take care of you in all ways. You get me?"

With a nod, she goes up on tip toes and kisses me again, branding me.

"Go," I tell her. Tears pour down her face again, but I hold mine back; for now.

"You've ruined me, Creed Lawless. One day soon," She says one more time before turning and climbing into the taxi. Before she closes the door, I reply.

"Until that day, Taylen Blackwell." A sad smile is thrown my way and she closes the door of the cab drives away, taking my heart with it.

"You've ruined me too, baby. I love you my Tay." I say to the air around me. Watching until I can't see the car anymore. My heart slows down, knowing that it won't fully function until the day I see her again.

"Dude, come on, the bus needs to leave." Cross calls to me. I nod and turn, closing the gap between us. He throws his arm around my shoulder, then speaks.

"One day, brother. One day." Crossley tells me, knowing full the meaning behind the words.

Climbing on the bus, I follow my brother but stop and look back at the road, not seeing the car anymore. I smile knowing that Taylen Blackwell has left her mark on me for the rest of my life.

"Until one day, Taylen baby. Until that day."

The End
Cross: Part 2 coming soon

Club Rife

by

C.H. Thomas

I am Logan Jagger.

I live my life by a set of rules that are NEVER to be broken.

But what happens when the unexpected occurs?

Will I throw caution to the wind and break all my rules?

<u>Unbroken Rules</u>

1 – Never sleep with locals.

2 – Never use my real name.

3 – Never have sex with holiday newcomers.

4 – Never take someone back to my apartment or villa.

5 – Never ride bareback.

6 – Never EVER do repeats; repeats lead to attachments.

Prologue

Fuck, I love my life!

Not many people my age can say they are living their dream, but I am.

Owning a nightclub has always been a dream of mine since I was a teenager. Music is my drug. It is deep-rooted in my soul. And now, at the age of twenty-five, I own a thriving nightclub, large apartment, and villa in Tenerife.

I'm living my life and loving every minute of it.

Don't judge me though. I'm not some silver spoon-fed wanker who wouldn't know a hard day's work if it slapped me in the face. I've worked damn hard to get where I am over the last few years, and I'm going to enjoy every fucking minute of it.

I lost everything dear to me seven years ago; my life stopped completely. Going off the rails was an understatement; I caused hell. Drinking, drugs, stealing. You name it, I did it. I'm surprised my friend's parents put up with me for as long as they did. Two months of complete hell I gave them. I was on the verge of having no family or friends, topped with the prospect of being homeless on my next birthday. If it hadn't been for the letter I received on my eighteenth birthday, I would have probably ended up in prison or worse, dead. At the time death didn't scare me; I welcomed the fear and went out of my way to find it. I had a death wish at seventeen, but that one letter changed everything in my life instantly. I stopped all the bad shit and put every ounce of energy I had into making something of myself and following my dreams. I started out small but fucking worked my arse off to get where I am and wouldn't change a thing. All those experiences have made me a better man, the man my family wanted me to be. I won't ever go down that road again.

Yes, I'm an arrogant twat with a big head most of the time, but the people close to me know why I'm like this. And for those that don't, it's none of their damn business. I stand my guard and don't let many people in unless I choose to.

Chapter 1

God, this chick is damn good at sucking dick! My eyes roll into the back of my head as I reach for the next track I'm about to play. I switch records as the girl on her knees squeezes my balls and takes my cock deeper into her mouth and swallows around me. I can feel my orgasm building as the song changes. The chick grabs my arse, making me slide even further down her throat, and sucks as if her life depends on it. For the second time in as many minutes, my eyes roll into the back of my head as my balls tighten as I shoot my load down her throat. God, she was good, but little did she know it was a one-time thing. She frees my cock from her mouth with a soft pop as I glance out over the top of the DJ booth across my crowded club, completely ignoring the girl. It is packed tonight. The last Saturday of the month is always a good night, Trance night and one I love DJing at. Being the Boss, I pick when I play and when I don't, but I never miss this one.

I fasten up my jeans and finally look down at the chick on her knees. I'll admit it now. I have no idea what her name is and to be brutally honest I couldn't give a shit. She has a look of euphoria on her face as she wipes her mouth on the back of her hand and smiles up at me with hope in her eyes. I know that look. It wouldn't last long; it never does. I don't do repeats, ever. It is a big rule of mine, no repeats and no attachments. That's why I choose holidaymakers to have fun with and normally ones that are due to go home within a day or two. I'd made the mistake of shagging some random pussy on the first night for her two-week holiday. She turned out to be a grade-A stalker, and I had to ban the crazy bitch from my club. Unfair, I know, but now I always check before getting my cock wet.

My life.

My club.

My rules.

Yes, that makes me a mean bastard.

I need to get this chick out of the DJ booth and fast.

"Thanks," I mouth to her as I reach over her to fade out the track mixing on the deck.

She tries to look shy and timid but fails miserably; no way was this her first rodeo. She was a pro at deepthroating. Before she could speak, I grab a few drinks tokens from my pocket and hand her a couple.

"Have a few drinks on me. Might see you around." It was a complete lie. I have no intention of ever seeing her pretty face again, and by the saddened expression on her face, she knows she's getting the brush-off.

Ignoring my outstretched hand for help to stand up, she climbs to her feet, snatches the drinks vouchers from me, gives me a fake smile, and walks out of the booth with her head held high. Like I said, not her first rodeo.

Living this life, I have a steady stream of girls wanting a piece of me. Every chick wants a piece of the DJ, and not just me. There are no exceptions, not even if the DJ is an ugly motherfucker. The girls flock to us. But no more close calls for me. I've had my share of clingy bitches. Some say rules are meant to be broken, but I never break my rules. Ever.

Chapter 2

The chick from last night left the club not long after I sent her packing. One of my bouncers had given me the all-clear after she had left with her friends.

My staff know how I roll and always keep a close eye on everyone within the club, including myself. I employ the best of the best: some locals, some friends from back home in England, and some that have been with me from the start, even if it has been on and off. I also like to help the students and travellers that are following their dreams of seeing the world. I'm not always a selfish git; I understand what it's like to have nothing, and seeing people following their dreams always makes me appreciate what I have, and what I've lost to get where I am.

The large apartment above the club covers the full top floor of the club below. Renting the four spare bedrooms to staff with the shared living area and bathroom has meant I've kept the master bedroom and en-suite bathroom for myself for late nights or, should I say, the early hours of the morning. We are like one big happy family, the only family I've had for the last seven years.

Grabbing a bottle of water from the fridge, I make my way to the rooftop terrace to find I'm not the only one who's up before noon.

"Morning, Boss," grumbles Todd from behind his shades.

"Morning. You look rough," I say, nodding at him as I take a seat on a sun lounger.

We sit in comfortable silence before all hell breaks loose when Danny joins us.

"Now then, fuckers!!" Danny shouts loud enough to wake the dead in typical Danny style. I wouldn't have him any other way.

Danny is my best friend from back home. He's been through everything with me. He even had my back when I put his parents through hell way back when. He helped me build Club Rife to what it is today and arrived here two days ago for a four-week vacation. Truth be told, I've missed the fucker, but I won't admit that to him.

"Well, aren't you two little rays of sunshine?" Danny says as he plonks his butt in the chair next to me.

Laughing at Danny, I glance over to Todd who's moaning from his chair, just before he rushes to his feet, covering his mouth with a hand. The poor kid only manages to topple over and puke all over himself. Being the caring, sensitive types that we are, we both burst into fits of laughter.

"I hope you're gonna clean up after yourself?" I laugh at Todd.

The kid has only been here for two months. He fancied a break from everyday life and as he's a cousin of a friend, I took him on for the summer. He can drink like the rest of us but suffers like hell the next day.

Looking up, Todd gives me the finger before heading inside.

"Well, that was fun," Danny sniggers.

"Never a dull moment here, man." I nod in agreement. "It's good to have you back."

"Ya damn right it is," he replies, grinning back at me like an idiot.

After checking the club's bars are stocked up and staffing is sorted, ready to roll for the next two days without me, I hand over to my manager Ethan. Ethan is another friend from school. He's been out here with me for three years now and has no desire to go home; he loves the lifestyle and we work like a well-oiled machine.

"See you Tuesday afternoon, Ethan," I holler as I exit the side door into the quiet afternoon streets.

"So, what's the plan?" Danny asks.

"Laze by the pool with a few beers?" I suggested.

After two days lazed by my pool drinking and catching up with Danny, I was ready to return to my baby.

My pride and joy.

Club Rife.

I loved my 'me time' but sitting doing nothing wasn't me. Being busy was good; it kept my mind from wandering to thoughts I've tried so hard over the years to keep at bay.

Strolling into my office, I find Ethan sat in my chair with his feet up on my desk, fiddling with his phone.

"Hey, Boss," he replies as he swings his feet off the desk.

"Hey, any issues over the last few days?"

"Nope, smooth sailing as usual."

"Great. Danny's gonna work behind the bar with me tonight to earn his keep," I said, keeping a straight face while I waited for some smart-arse comment from him.

"Yeah, whatever," he muttered. "Don't expect me to call you Boss though," he added under his breath.

The three of us quietly set up for the long night ahead and go out to grab some food before the rest of the staff starts to roll in for the evening. That's when the real fun always starts. A little after seven pm and we are all ready to work hard for the next eight hours.

The night started slow, which is typical, but soon picked up and the club is packed again. Full to bursting with holidaymakers.

"Logan, check her out," Danny shouts across the bar to me.

He'd been doing that for the last three hours. It was fun at first, but now that we are being run off our feet, it is getting old. I glance in the direction Danny is looking in, not sure what to expect as we both have very different tastes when it comes to the opposite sex. Which is a good thing; chicks never get in the way of our friendship. This new piece he is checking out is stunning but definitely not my type, and if I am guessing right, she is a holiday newcomer - a definite big no for me. When you've lived this life long enough, you can spot the newbies easily, even in club lights. Smiling back at him, I focus on serving drinks and keeping a close eye on the things happening around me.

"Danny, I'm having a quick break," I say as I walk past him. "Back in ten."

I am beat. The last five hours have flown by, and I'm not used to being behind the bar all night. It makes a pleasant change and I love it, always have. But as the owner, you get caught up in the other stuff. Making a mental note to cover the bar more often, I head to the staff room.

I settle on the break room sofa with a bottle of water from the fridge. I also stock the staff fridge with plenty of soft drinks or energy drinks. Drinking alcohol on the job is a no-no for all my staff, until the last hour when I let them have a few drinks on the house, and sometimes we stay after hours.

I flick through my Facebook feed. Nothing special going on as usual, just the boring everyday shit of what people are having for tea! I mean, come on; do they not have anything better to do? After wasting ten minutes, I make my way back to the bar, making a detour to the loo.

"Hi," a sweet voice says from behind me as I push the toilet door open. Pausing, I turn around to find a petite redheaded girl looking up at me with cute, blue puppy-dog eyes. I can't decide if it is her come-on look or if she's drunk.

"Hey," I reply. "Are you ok?"

"Err, yeah, I'm good..." She trails off and glances around, checking her surroundings. "I was just thinking..." She trails off again, squinting around. As quick as a flash, she leans up on her toes and starts attacking my lips with hers. Taking me completely by surprise, she manages to push me backwards into the toilet, all the while taking control of the kiss. By the time, she's backed me into the toilet cubicle, I've come to my senses and pull back, looking down at this little spitfire.

"Don't say a word," she says. "It's my birthday. I'm taking life by the balls."

I'm about to speak when she raises onto her tiptoes and kisses me again. This time I let myself enjoy it. Damn, she is good, but no way am I going to let her have control this time. Taking the reins, I grab her hips and turn us around so she is pressed up against the cubicle door. Pausing, I look down at her to find lust and pure need in her eyes.

She places her forefinger against my lips and whispers, "I've always fantasised about fucking a stranger in the men's room." She moves her body and starts rubbing against my already hard cock, making me moan in the back of my throat.

Grabbing her hips, I lift her and try to keep her still as she wraps her legs around my waist. Slowly kissing her neck and nibbling her ear, I whisper back. "Are you sure about this?"

Nodding is her only response as she pulls her legs tighter around my waist, causing me to moan again as my hard cock pushes against her warmth.

"Don't tease me," the little spitfire bites back with a smirk. "Just fuck me hard."

Fuck, how could I say no to that?

Pulling back a little, I pop open the buttons on my jeans, letting my hard cock free from its denim prison. While keeping her pinned to door, I seize a condom from my pocket.

"Always prepared?"

"Hmm, I never know when I'll need one." I always carry a supply of condoms in my pocket.

"Cocky much?" she smirks.

"Maybe…" I nod at her as I cover my cock with the condom.

Cock now safe and covered, I run my hands up her bare thighs to find her wearing no knickers.

Fuck me.

Her bare, wet pussy is so ready for me. Holding her ass up high, I position myself and tease her clit with my cock before slamming into her with one hard push. She lets out a loud scream of pleasure as I squeeze my eyes shut. She is wet and tight, and if I'm not careful, this will be over far too quickly. Taking a deep breath, I start to move in long hard strokes, pulling out all the way before slamming back into her warmth. Her moans grow louder with each movement as I pick up the pace. Slamming into her repeatedly, I can feel the tingling in my balls as they tighten. Knowing it won't last much longer, I push harder and faster, making the cubicle door rattle. She grabs my shoulders, pushing down on me as my cock pounds her tight pussy. Her head falls back and hits the door as her walls clamp down on my cock as we both come.

"Fuckkkkkk."

Resting my head against the door to catch my breath, I slowly lower the little redhead to her feet.

"Wow," she mutters to herself. "Even better than I dreamed it would be."

I don't know if she's talking to me or herself, so I don't respond. I just watch as she straightens up her clothes and looks into my eyes. I am half expecting the usual look of hope written across her face, but she surprises me once again.

She leans up and kisses me on the cheek. "Thanks," she says as she reaches to open the cubicle door.

I move to the side to let her out as she brushes past me. I stand here in a daze. It's not often I meet a chick that is just like me.

"Where the fuck have you been?" Danny questions as I re-join him behind the bar. "Ten minutes, you said!"

"Sorry," I say, looking up at him with a satisfied smile.

"Fuck!" he shouts. "You lucky bastard, getting laid while on the job."

"Perks of being the Boss, I guess." I smirk as I get back to work with a spring in my step.

Chapter 3

"Come on, man," Danny moans. "You've had me working for the last eight days straight. I need some fun. I'm supposed to be on vacation."

He is right. We haven't stopped over the last week. The summer holidays have started, and Tenerife is packed with holidaymakers. But there is no way I am going to let him laze about while he is here.

"Stop complaining. You've loved it. Wall-to-wall booty everywhere. You're only working nights, You have all day to yourself. Get up and do something instead of lazing about." I smile at him. "Anyway, you're worse than me. Different chick every night." I laugh. To be honest, I am proud of my boy, enjoying life to the max before going back home to his nine-to-five job. A job he loves doing, but soon he'll find the one and settle down. It's all he wanted when we were growing up. That life is definitely not for me though. "So, what do you wanna do then?" I ask.

"Waterpark!" he shouts with a child-like grin on his face.

"Let's do it," I agree.

Sitting on the waterpark sunbed with an ice-cold beer, I stare out at the pool before me. Watching families and friends enjoying themselves, it's at times like this when I miss them most. My parents and younger sister, but there is fuck all I can do now. I'm starting to get lost in my thoughts of all the things they are missing out on when Danny comes back holding a tray full of food.

"Here ya go," he says, passing me two cheeseburgers and fries.

"Cheers." I've forgotten how hungry running around like a big kid makes me.

Settling back, we eat in silence and enjoy the view. Half-naked women running around everywhere. What more can a man ask for?

"Fancy another drink?" I ask Danny. Probably a daft question, but hey, I have to ask.

"Yeah, why not?"

Returning with the drinks, I find two girls have taken up residence on my sun lounger, and they are in deep conversation with Danny. He must have seen me coming as he moves over to make room on his sunbed for me. He takes his drink without even looking at me.

"Hello," I say as Danny doesn't bother to introduce us. But as I look at his face, I understand why. He is mesmerised by the lass sitting opposite him. Paying no attention to them, I look at the girl's friend and the wind is knocked right out of my sails. Long dark brown hair that runs midway down her back, the most beautiful bright green emerald eyes I've ever seen, and don't let me get started on her body, wow. She is a perfect ten to look at.

"Hi," she says softly. "I'm Jenna."

"Logan." Shit! What am I doing? I never give my real name. Danny must have heard me as he looks up with shock on his face. "Sorry, would you like a drink?" I blurt out, needing a minute to gather myself. I never slip up.

What the fuck is wrong with me?

"It's ok. I'll go get them," Jenna says in a sweet, shy voice.

"What sort of gentleman would that make me?" I smile at her. My heart is racing, trying to beat out of my chest, but I can't let the panic I feeling on the inside show.

Giggling, she replies, "Ok, sir, I'll have a vodka and coke, please."

"My pleasure. And your friend?" I nod to her mate that I still haven't been introduced to.

"Same for her too."

"Coming right up," I say as I get up and walk away. I can feel my whole body shaking with what I can only assume is nerves or fear, but I don't know why. I have no reason to be scared or nervous. I am in control. I always am, but fucking hell, what was I thinking, giving her my real name?

Taking my sweet time to get the drinks, I wonder why I gave her my real name. Two seconds with her and I'd broken one of my rules. I need to get my act together. Maybe it's because I'm out of my usual hunting zone, my club. It comes naturally there to hide the real me. Here, having some downtime, I don't feel the need to hide.

As I walk back to our spot, I take my time to watch Jenna. She has a natural beauty about her; 'stunning' doesn't even come close to describing her. Jenna must have sensed me watching her, as she glances in my direction and gives me a little finger wave and a shy smile.

We spend the next few hours riding the water slides, laughing and joking, having a carefree time. Gone are all my thoughts about breaking my rules. Jenna and her friend Lou are really good fun and so down-to-earth. I can be myself around them and that terrifies me a little if I think about it too much.

"So, what do you two have planned for tonight?" Danny asks them.

"Few drinks, might hit a club. But we don't tend to plan, just go with the flow," Lou replies while never taking her eyes off Danny. "What about you?"

"We'll more than likely be in Club Rife," Danny says while giving me sideways glance to make sure I wasn't freaking out. Good job he can't see the thoughts running through my mind. "Come join us. It's down on the main strip. You can't miss it."

The girls agree they would see us there, and after saying our goodbyes, they head back to their apartment.

"What ya playing at, Dan?" I ask. Pissed off isn't even close to how I am feeling. Why the fuck would he do that? He knows the rules. After my big fuck-up earlier, I didn't think it could get any worse. He should have known better. Fuck, I should have known better than to blurt out my real name.

"Nothing man, it's just..." He trails off.

"Spit it out," I snap. I'm going to lose my cool and it isn't Danny's fault. Well, maybe it is. He invited them to the club, not me. He is pushing me way out of my comfort zone, but that's what Danny has always done.

"Well...they're cool. Why not spend some more time with them?" he questions.

"Yeah, but why my club? Why not somewhere else?"

"Cos it rocks, man!" he says with laughter in his eyes. "And we have the night off for a change. The Boss is a right wanker, makes me work all sorts of fucking hours." He finishes his rant but can't keep a straight face, making me forget what position he'd put me in.

Chapter 4

  I try thinking of any excuse not to go to Club Rife. Ethan is running the show, and I don't need to be there, not on my night off. But every excuse I think of makes me look like a pussy, and I am the furthest thing from a pussy. I love eating and fucking pussy, but I certainly am not one.

  "Come on, fucker. It's time to party!"

  Groaning on the inside, I shout back. "Dan, you're a fucking idiot. Grow up!" Good job I love him like a brother. God, tonight can't be over fast enough. In fact, I hope they don't show up.

  Dan is hammering back the drinks while I'm taking my time. I don't want the hangover tomorrow, but not only that. I want to keep my guard up, no more fuckups like earlier today. It is still at the back of mind. Niggling away as to why I'd dropped my real name. Trying to keep my mind off it, I look around the club from my seat in the VIP area. It's a great spot to sit and people-watch, I don't always have it as a VIP area, but during the summer when it's busy, I sometimes keep the area separate, letting it out for party bookings. That extra something while on holiday to make it memorable.

  I sense Dan before I see him, coming back to the table with more drinks.

  "Here," he mouths as he hands me another bottle of San Miguel.

  Nodding thanks back at him, I take a swig from the bottle. I look up at him just as a smile slowly creeps over his face. I know that look. It's the same look he always gets when he gets his own way.

  They are here.

  Turning around, I look in the same direction and fuck me! Twice in the same day, Jenna knocks the wind right out of me. As they walk towards us, I take my time to check her out. She has her hair down and curled over one shoulder, some strappy top and shortish skirt. Not so short that I'd be able to see her arse but midway between her knees and butt. She finished the look off with some sparkling high-heeled shoes I couldn't give a fuck about, but damn those legs and shoes would look really good wrapped around my waist.

Shit! Where did that come from? *Get your mind out of the gutter, Logan.*

Jenna isn't that type of girl. Everything about her screams the settling down type, the type of girl I avoid at all costs. Jenna is definitely not your one-night type of chick. She looks stunning though and not in a 'look at me, I'm gorgeous and know it' sort of way. She is beautiful but doesn't flaunt it like some girls.

Lou practically jumps into Dan's arms when she gets close enough. Shaking my head, I glance at Jenna who is also shaking her head and laughing at her friend.

"Hi," she says over the loud music. "VIP, very posh."

"We thought we'd treat you ladies tonight." Little bit of a white lie, but they will never know. I bend forward so she can hear me. "You look stunning, Jenna," I whisper just loud enough for her to hear. Not giving her time to reply, I ask, "Vodka and coke?" remembering her drink of choice this afternoon.

"Yes, please."

I move out of the booth and gesture with my hand for her to take my place. "Be right back."

After what seems like hours of drinking and dancing, I feel nicely buzzed, not wasted and certainly more relaxed. Jenna and I sit, taking a breather and chatting when Dan and Lou re-appear for the third time tonight looking very satisfied and slightly dishevelled. Knowing exactly what the dirty bastard had been up to, I choose to ignore the smug twat.

Jenna excuses herself to the ladies' room and I watch her walk away. She is perfect, but I really can't go there with her. I may be a dickhead when it comes to pussy, but I do have some remorse. I never slept with girls that were after more, and I can tell, just from spending a few hours with Jenna, she is the forever type. I'd even say a romantic at heart and that sure as fuck isn't me.

Fuck them good and leave them satisfied, is my motto.

As Jenna comes out of the toilet door, Todd comes racing up to me with a look of horror on his face.

"Boss, we have a fucking problem," he shouts.

This better be good and not another overreaction from Todd.

As I get up from my seat, I don't miss the look of shock Jenna shares with Lou.

Well, fuck me. Now we have two fucking problems. I didn't want to let that little cat out of the bag. But no hiding from it now. "Be right back," I say as I walk away and head to my office.

"Sorry," Todd says. "I know it's your night off, but…"

"But what, Todd? Stop fucking about and get to the point."

"I can't find Ethan anywhere and the bouncers are having issues outside." He takes a deep breath and continues. "Some jackass and his friends kicked off when they were searched, and we had to ring the cops."

Fucking great. Where is Ethan when he's needed? I bet you anything he's getting his dick wet!

After sorting the shit storm out front, I close the doors to more punters for the night. It is getting near closing time anyway. Ethan has finally been found and I let him deal with the rest. Four drugged up lads on holiday is now a problem for the police to deal with, not me. Drugs are something I will not tolerate, not in my club.

I grab some drinks from the bar and head back to the booth.

"Sorry about that." I smile as I sit down next to Jenna.

"All sorted?" Dan asks.

"Yeah, nothing I can't handle."

"So," Jenna says, leaning in towards me. "Bossman?" It's more of a question than a statement.

Well, there is no hiding it now. Dan will have said something while I was gone. "Yeah, Club Rife is my baby." I smile at her, trying my best not to look like a bighead showing off.

My look must have worked, as Jenna smiles and grabs my hand, pulling me off to dance again.

"Logan, I've got a massive favour to ask?" Dan asks once the club has shut and we are about to leave.

"Yea, what is it?" This isn't going to be good. He has a strange look on his face.

"Can the girls come back to yours?"

"Fuck, no!" Trying my best not to shout, I look around to make sure no one has heard me. "You know the rules, man. You can't ask me that."

"But…"

"No buts, Dan. If you're that desperate to shag her again, you go stay at hers."

"I can't. They're sharing a bed, for fuck sake. If I go there, where's Jenna gonna sleep?"

"Don't look at me like that. That soft arse look doesn't work with me." How the hell am I going to get out of this, without being a dickhead to my mate? It isn't my problem they are sharing a bed. And fuck me if I'm not starting to feel guilty for saying no already. OK, so maybe I lied that soft mushy look. My best friend's face was starting to influence me. Fuck!

"Come on, man, please," he begs. "It's not like you haven't broken your rules already."

Well, shit. I can't argue myself out of this one. My real name and my club. Fuck, I must be losing my mind.

"I like Lou," he says dreamily. "And I mean really like her."

Oh, shit. Dan has it bad. What the hell am I gonna do with him? Risk breaking his heart and pissing him off, or break another one of my rules?

Is it truly breaking a rule though?

I'm not taking a chick back to my place. He is.

I'm not getting laid tonight. He is.

So technically I'm not breaking my rules.

I must be drunker than I thought if that is my reasoning, but fuck it.

"Alright," I say, defeated. I better not regret this in the morning.

Chapter 5

My mouth tastes like shit.

My head is throbbing.

What the fuck happened to me keeping my defences up last night?

And why the fuck do I feel like I'm pinned down and sweating my cock off?

Slowly peeling my eyes open, I realise my biggest fuck-up yet.

My arms and legs are wrapped tightly around Jenna. Her body is pressed so hard against mine I don't dare move in case I wake her up.

Jesus, now I'm going soft. What the fuck?!

Slowly sliding each limb from under and around Jenna, I gingerly get up from the couch. Looking down at her, I thank the gods she's still sleeping soundly, and I don't have to make random small talk.

I need coffee, very strong coffee.

Sitting on the patio as I nurse my coffee, I can't help but think about the beauty still sleeping on my couch. What is it about her that is pulling me close? Three of my unbreakable rules, broken in twenty-four hours. Well, technically only two as the third doesn't really count. But there is some magnetic pull between us. If only I knew what it was, so I can avoid it. The only way I can think to stop it is to stay away from her. Very far away. But I know deep down that isn't going to happen. Not only am I Dan's wingman, but I also have this strange feeling that I wouldn't be able to keep away from her. It isn't just a sexual pull between us. Now don't me wrong; Jenna is drop-dead gorgeous. Any man with a pulse can see it, even if she doesn't. There is something else there that makes things so comfortable between us. No awkward silences; we are like old friends catching up after years.

A groaning noise behind me breaks me from my thoughts, which is a good thing. I was turning into a pussy.

"Morning, sunshine," I say to Dan. Fuck, he looks like death. I don't feel much better, but I'm gonna enjoy seeing him suffer today.

"Fuck off," he moans.

If he is wanting sympathy, he's come to the wrong place.

It's official. I'm going to kill Danny! I'd broken a rule for him last night, and now he's extended their invitation. I tried saying no politely but failed miserably, and he won again. So here we all are, sitting around my pool, enjoying the sun. Dan and Lou are acting like a pair of lovesick fools. You wouldn't think they'd been up all night shagging, and believe me, they had. Half of the island will have heard their screams.

"How long have you been out here?" Jenna asks. We've been chatting for hours, but I've managed to avoid any serious topics.

"Nearly seven years. I love it here, don't ever see myself going back to England."

"Don't you miss home? Family, friends?"

"Not at all, no. My friends are here. This is home for me." Please don't ask about family again. I don't talk about them. I never talk about them, not even with Danny. "It's far too cold and wet for me back in England. I don't think I'd survive." I laugh. Hoping to steer the conversation away from the F word, I get up from my lounger to turn the music up a little on the outside speakers.

"I don't think I'd have the guts to up and leave everything behind," Jenna says as she looks dreamily across the infinity pool.

I must admit the view is amazing, one of the main reasons I bought this villa. I have beautiful green hills and mountains to the left and the ocean out front. It is my peaceful place. I love sitting out here to relax and just think. It is the one place I let my mind wander to my family. This was their dream for me too.

"I think you'd surprise yourself, Jenna. Always follow your dreams. Life is too short." Right, things are getting too deep and serious; I need to do something to change that and fast. Jumping up from my chair again, I shout so the two lovebirds can hear me. "Time for cocktails. Let's get this party started." Fuck, I am going to regret this. What am I doing?

"About fucking time," is my only response from Danny before he starts sucking face again.

"Dan, leave her alone for five fucking minutes, will you, and help." I laugh at the sulky look on his face, but he reluctantly gets up and leaves Lou's side.

"What's that fruity girl shit?" Dan asks as I place the cocktail jug on the kitchen counter.

"Sex on the beach," I smile. "Live a little. It won't kill you."

Shaking his head at me, he grins and shouts. "Bring it on…Party for four."

This is going to get messy, but it's time to listen to what I preach and live a little.

"I need some munchies," Jenna murmurs and makes her way inside to grab some food.

I tell them both after the first jug had been polished off to make themselves at home. And they have, and to my surprise, I don't feel awkward. I'm enjoying having company, friends even, round to my private place, my sanctuary. Damn, these cocktails are strong.

"These the best cocktails ever!" Lou giggles, taking the thoughts straight from my mind.

I watch Jenna as she returns with a massive bowl of crisps. She's got a lovely pink glow to her cheeks, and it isn't from the sun. I need to be careful. She's getting under my skin. I think I'm having the same effect on her too. Jenna's eyes light up when we get close, and her breathing hitches every time our skin touches. I need a distraction, something to keep my mind clear and stop thinking about all the dirty things I want to do to her.

"Come on, Dan. Let's see if you've still got the magic touch on the decks." This would be entertaining. I knew Dan hadn't DJ'd in years, but it's like riding a bike. You never forget.

Looking a bit panicked, Dan gets up and pulls Lou along with him. As we move inside to my studio, I can't remember the last time I've mixed at home.

After a few failed mixes, Dan gets back into his stride, and we mix some classic tunes back to back. It feels good to have my friend back and to be doing something we both love. Jenna and Lou are dancing around the room without a care in the world.

"We're getting more food and drinks," Dan says as he and Lou leave the room.

Nodding at him, I look up at Jenna and wink at her, making her blush. God, I'd love to see that blush creep up her chest while screaming my name.

Fuck! *Stop it, Logan. You can't go there.*

But damn. With the alcohol flowing through me and the way she is swaying her body to the music, I can't help the thought running wild in my mind.

"Jenna?" I say while holding a record in my hand. "Come here."

As she comes close, I take off my headphones and hand them to her. "It's your turn." I smile.

"But..." She looks terrified. "I don't...I can't. What if I break something?"

"Don't worry. I won't let anything bad happen to you. Or my records, don't you worry."

Taking the headphones from me, Jenna puts them on. Placing the record on the deck, I stand behind her and explain what to do. Silently nodding, she follows my directions and slowly relaxes. I can feel her body moving to the beat. Giving her a helping hand, I lean around her and fade the song playing in her ear into the speakers and the track that is already playing. She'd nailed it the first time. Granted I'd given her an easy track, but damn. She'd done it.

Spinning her around to face me, I smile down at her and say, "See? Nothing to worry about. You smashed it."

The smile on Jenna's face is contagious. "I did it." She laughs as she reaches up and puts her hands around my neck, pulling me down for a kiss that takes me completely by surprise. Jenna pulls away, breaking the kiss, and looks towards the door. I'm not sure if it is nerves or if she is checking to see if we'd been seen. Deciding to break the awkward moment, I select another record for her to mix, something a little trickier this time. I stand behind her, holding her hips and moving along to the beat. I am ready to help, but she masters it, starting the track again and when the song changes, she pushes up the fader switch and boom. Perfect mix, again. The two beats match perfectly in time with each other.

This has to be a fluke. No way could she do that. Even some DJs with years of practice can't always do that. I'm in awe of her.

With my hands still on her hips, she spins around and gives me a shy smile. Looking down, I can't help but put my lips against hers. What is meant to be a quick peck turns into something more as she grabs my face with both hands and takes over the kiss. Her lips are so soft, and I can taste the cocktails we've been drinking. She owns me. I am gone. No way can I stop this now.

Where is Dan with the damn drinks and food?

I need saving. But as she presses her body harder against me, there is no hope in stopping this. Grabbing her hips, I take over the kiss as she melts against me.

Jenna moans against my mouth, sending the vibrations all the way to my already rock-hard cock that is begging to be set free from my shorts.

Running my hands teasingly under her top, my thumbs find her pert nipples and gently squeeze. A low moan leaves Jenna's lips as her head falls back, giving me room to nibble her neck.

"Please, Logan," she whispers.

"Please what, Jenna? I need to hear you say it." I shouldn't be doing this, but the desire coursing through my veins has other ideas. I need to make sure this is what she wants.

"I need you…"

"What do you need?" I moan in her ear as she grabs my arse, pulling me closer to her.

"I need to feel you…I want you."

"Last chance, Jenna." God, this is hard. My cock will never forgive me if she says no now. "Are you sure?" I question. "Last chance to say no."

"Take me now, Logan," she begs, and that is all the confirmation I need.

Turning us around, I walk towards the sofa and sit down. Jenna stands frozen in front of me for a brief second before shimmying out of her shorts. Gone is her shyness as she moves to straddle my hips. Biting her lip, she removes her bikini top; God, she is perfect and I can't keep my eyes off her. She leans in and bites my bottom lip, sending jolts of pleasure through my body. Holding her still so I can gain some control back, I take her lips in a demanding kiss.

She starts to move her hips, giving herself the friction she needs, and I can feel the heat and wetness of her pussy against my shorts.

"Jenna," I moan as I pull my lips from hers and push my hips upwards.

She takes the hint and lifts herself up, giving me just enough room to free my throbbing cock from my shorts. Jenna takes charge again as she rubs my cock against her wet pussy and slowly sinks down on my dick, making me growl. God, she feels good, so tight and warm, a perfect fit.

Jenna's movements quicken and her moans grow louder as I watch her bounce up and down on me, taking all the pleasure she needs. It was a beautiful sight. Moving one hand from her hip, I rub my thumb on her clit, making her eyes open to look at me.

"That's right, baby. Look at me when I make you come."

Pushing my hips up as her walls clamp tight around my cock, she squeezes the life out of it as she screams out my name. The look of pure ecstasy on her face has me tipping over the edge as my own orgasm takes over.

Resting her forehead against mine, I kiss her gently as we let our breathing calm. But the calm feeling I had is starting to evaporate fast as my cock softens and slips out of her warmth.

Fuck, no condom!

Fuck!

Jenna must have felt me tense below her as I realised, I'd fucked up again.

"Logan, don't worry. I'm on the pill."

Pill? That's doesn't stop my dick from falling off.

Why does she make my common sense fly out the window?

Chapter 6

After my major fuck-up a few days ago, I try to keep myself busy and away from Jenna. But it's hard; with Dan and Lou being inseparable, she's around the club and house a lot. In fact, Dan has moved Lou into my villa for the remainder of her holiday, which in turn means Jenna has moved her things in too. I was livid with Dan, but after he talked me into visiting their apartment, I soon changed my mind and backtracked on the stern no I'd given him. No way was I going to leave either of them there. Never in a million years would I leave Jenna alone in the dump they called an apartment. The place was a cesspit. Raising mould coming from all corners of each room, and don't get me started on the black mould in the bathroom. It was everywhere. The place smelt musty and damp. I have a feeling it hadn't been cleaned in months. The so-called kitchen had two small cupboards, an over-the-counter mini fridge, and a two-ring electric hob which had definitely seen better days. I wouldn't spend ten minutes in the hell hole, never mind sleep there. It was my place or Jenna and Lou were going to another hotel, and something tells me they probably wouldn't be able to afford another hotel.

So here I am. Between work and home, I can't get away from Jenna. If I am truly honest with myself, I am happy to see her around. When I'm not with her, I am wishing she was nearby. I can't win. I'd manned up too, and we had cleared the air between us after I'd fucked up.

The magnetic pull I feel whenever she is around is impossible to fight. I can't pinpoint what is drawing me to her, but I am like a moth to a flame. Her laughter carries across the room and I can't stop myself from looking up. She is beautiful, but when she laughs or smiles a genuine smile that reaches her eyes, she looks carefree and so full of life. That is a feeling I have never had, not for many years. But as I watch from my office, I realise I'm missing out big time. I'm twenty-five, have everything I wanted, but I never really let my hair down and live. And I mean really live.

Shutting down my laptop, I decide now is the time to live a little. I need to make a phone call.

"Ethan."

"Hey, Boss," he says sleepily.

"Sorry if I woke you, but I need a favour."

"Yeah, sure, what is it?" he asks, sounding a little more awake.

"You know you're always saying I should take time off?" I question.

"Yep," he says and goes very quiet.

Here goes. I can't believe I'm handing my club over again for a chick, but it's about time I had some fun. "Can you cover for the next week?" I feel nervous asking and I have no idea why. It's my fucking club. I make the rules. I run the show. Deep down I know Ethan won't say no. He's been pestering me for years to take some time off. Personally, I think he's been dying to get his hands on my baby.

"Damn fucking right I can," he shouts down the phone. "It's about time, Logan. Take all the time you need."

"Just a week, mate. Gonna spend the week chillin' with Dan before he goes back home."

"You betcha," I can hear the smile in his voice.

"Ok, then. Club Rife is all yours for the next seven days. Don't fuck it up." I laugh. It's a nervous laugh and I hope he can't tell. I know my baby is in safe hands with Ethan. "And Ethan?"

"Yeahhh,"

"Ring me if anything urgent comes up."

"Sure thing. Boss."

And with that, I put the phone down. Now, what do I do? I am already starting to feel angsty. I suppose it is time to give the others the good news.

"Done already?" asks Dan as I walk out of my office.

The girls look across to me and look hopeful. They have been talking about a dolphin and whale watching boat trip that they want to go on and who am I to shatter their dreams?

"Yep. All done for the next seven days," I say, keeping my face straight, waiting to see if he really heard me.

"Ya shitting me?" Dan bellows. "You never take time off and you've done it twice this week. What's got into you?"

"Fucked if I know," I smile. "Come on, let's go get that boat trip booked."

The look of delight and the girly squeal that leaves Jenna's lips makes it all worth it. Both Jenna and Lou jump around in circles across the empty dance floor as Dan comes over with a massive grin on his face.

"Thanks, man," he whispers.

"Come on then. Times a wastin', ladies."

Chapter 7

After booking some trips yesterday, we spend the remainder of the afternoon lazing on the beach and playing on the inflatables out in the ocean. The girls pass on the jet skiing, but of course Danny and myself have to have a go. And we clown around, having a blast. Probably a good thing the girls weren't on the jet skis with us. We'd have scarred them for life. It is something I've always been promising myself to do while out here but never really made the effort to find the time to do it. It's nice to break the everyday routine and let loose with my best friend. Having Jenna and Lou with us make it feel extra special and to be honest, deep down I am dreading the day they board the plane to leave. But I also can't keep handing things over to Ethan. Club Rife is mine and I love everything about it.

Today, though, we are halfway up Mount Teide, the island's active volcano. We sit in near silence as we ride the cabin car up the side of the volcano. Jenna occasionally grabs my hand to get my attention and show me something. The views are amazing and we can see for miles. We've been lucky to get a clear day with no wind so the ride to the top is smooth.

Reaching the top, I exit the moving car first and hold out my hand for Jenna which she takes without hesitation. Not wanting to let go, I keep a tight hold of her as we leave the cabin car building.

"Fuck me, it's cold," says Danny as he and Lou come to join us outside.

He isn't wrong. It's bloody freezing, but I guess being 12, 198 feet above sea level, it would be cold.

"Come on," I say while pulling Jenna along with me. "Let's keep moving to keep warm."

"I can think of something better to do to keep warm," whispers Jenna so only I can hear.

"Oh, you do, do you?" Something had sparked in Jenna yesterday, and I'm seeing a whole new side to her. Some cheekiness is starting to appear and I love it.

"Hmm," she replies while sucking on her bottom lip.

God, when she does that all the blood leaves my brain and heads south.

Leaning in close, I whisper. "Let's ditch these two and find a secluded spot just for us," I wink. "And I'll warm you up all right."

Unfortunately, there aren't any private places to have some alone time with Jenna. That would be something I will make up for when I get her home. But the views and spending time with Jenna are enough for now.

"It's like being on the top of the world," says Jenna with awe in her voice, and I can't disagree with her.

We sit snuggled up on the return cable car journey. I let mind wander for a few minutes to the what ifs. But that is only going to lead me to a dark place, one place I'm not going to go to. I am going to enjoy the time we have left together, and we have some more amazing things planned.

Chapter 8

The last couple of days have been amazing. We have packed so much sightseeing in. I've laughed until I've nearly pissed myself and worn a smile that hurt my face. Especially during the boat trip when we were lucky to find a pod of bottlenose dolphins that swam alongside our boat for what seemed like hours. Jenna was in awe of them and squeezed my hand the whole time, nearly breaking my fingers, but I didn't care. She had tried to secretly wipe the tears from her eyes but failed. I didn't let on that I'd seen, just held her hand a little tighter.

But now the melancholy is starting to settle in my gut. Tonight is the last night all four of us will be together. We'd partied hard during the week, so tonight we are having a meal out and few drinks. I know Dan wants to spend his last night with Lou alone, and to be honest I need to make the most of my last night with Jenna. Shaking my head to clear all gloomy thoughts from my mind, I knock on the en-suite door.

"Jenna, you ready?" I ask.

"Two more minutes and I will be."

"Ok, I'll wait out front. The taxi won't be long."

Heading outside, I find Dan waiting on the bench just outside my front door.

"Hey, man," I say, making him jump. "Sorry, dude," I snigger.

"Hey," he says glumly.

"What's up with you, sad sack?"

"Just thinking…Last night and all that."

"Arh, the thought of going home depressing you already?" I joke. "Well, you know where I am, and you're welcome back whenever you want, you know that," I say, patting him on the shoulder as I sit down.

"Yeah, I know. It's not that..." he drifts off. I know what is coming but am hoping to avoid it.

"Lou?" I question as he seems to have gone quiet.

"Yeah" is his only reply.

"She's only a few hours away from you back home. Maybe you can meet up at weekends or summat?"

"Lou said that too. I just hope the hundred and ninety miles isn't gonna get in the way."

"You'll figure it out. You always do. Now let's make the last night extra special, yeah?"

"Too fucking right!" he says as he jumps to his feet.

Talk about taking an emotional full three-sixty turn in moods.

All the doom and gloom leaves my body as Jenna walks out to meet us.

Fuck me! She looks drop-dead gorgeous.

She's wearing a little black dress and silver heels which make her legs go on for miles. I have no idea what she's done with her makeup, but the smoky 'come to bed' eyes and red lipstick just top off the look. Thoughts of cancelling the meal and me having my wicked way with her flashes through my mind and make my dick swell. And then it hits me...I am going to spend the night fighting off the urge to kill anyone that looks at her.

"Jenna, fuck...Are you trying to kill me?"

Shaking her head with a cheeky smirk, she doesn't reply, but the slight blush that creeps on her cheeks says it all. Her mission is accomplished. She has me by the balls for the evening. The little minx.

"Jenna?" I question as she runs her foot up my leg.

"Yeah?" she replies innocently.

She knows exactly what she's doing to me. She can feel my erection with her toes as she continues to tease me. Not only is she teasing me under the table, but the way she's slowly licking her cheesecake off the spoon is driving me crazy. Oh, I am going to get my own back on her.

"Jenna," I say breathlessly. "Come here."

Jenna moves slowly around the table, and I pull her onto my lap. Whispering quietly, I say, "You're going to regret teasing me tonight."

"I doubt it very much," she says as I hold on to her hip and lean in for a kiss. A kiss that soon gets heated and she melts against me.

"Hmm we shall see, later." I wink.

"For fucks sake, you two," Danny laugh. "Get a room."

"You've no room to talk, dickhead. You've been molesting Lou all night." What a twat! Leave it to Danny to break the moment. I suppose it's for the best. There's every chance I'd end up taking Jenna right here in the restaurant over the table for all to see, if we carry on.

Fuck, I'm dying to devour Jenna now that we are back home. I want to take my time with her, but with the way she's looking at me from the foot of my bed, there's no way I can hold back. All the teasing the little vixen had done during the night had made me a desperate man. Desperate to have her naked and under me screaming in pleasure, I am trying hard not to show it, but she's driven me crazy. I was hoping all the teasing would have been the other way around, but she had other plans. All I want now is my dessert.

"Logan," she moans as I kiss my way up her neck. How we made it to my bedroom I'll never know. I could have ripped her clothes off in the taxi.

"Hmmm" is the only sound I can make as my hand slowly slides up her bare legs, teasing her skin. I'll have her begging for more before the night is out. Serves her right for all the torment tonight. As my hands roam higher, I lift her dress up to reveal the sexiest black thong I've ever seen. Damn, this woman is something else.

Jenna's moans fill the air as I place feather light kisses across her lower stomach, the smell of her arousal making my cock ache even more. I don't know if I can drag this out like I wanted to. Her smell, her moans, are driving me wild.

"Logan...don't tease," she moans breathlessly.

I wanted her to beg tonight, but the sight of her flushed skin has me rethinking my ideas. Hooking my fingers round her lace underwear, I slowly drag them down her legs, letting them drop to the floor.

"The shoes stay," I growl as she is about to toe them off. Listening to my warning, she stands up tall and gives me a smouldering look that shouts, 'take me.'

Running my hands back up her legs, I pull her close. Her bare pussy is mere inches from my face. Teasing her more, I blow gently on her heated skin, making goose bumps appear all over her warm body. Leaning in close, I run my tongue over her sensitive clit, making her back arch as she holds onto my head, making sure I don't leave her wanting more. Swirling my tongue on her bundle of nerves, I add more pressure by nibbling on her clit. By the noises she's making, I know she's close. So, I nibble a little harder and her fingers pull at my hair as she screams my name.

After what seems like hours of sex, some slow and passionate, some hard and fast. Jenna has gotten under my skin, I can feel it deep in my soul. She finally passes out with a satisfied smile on her pretty face. Lying here watching her, taking her in, I imprint her to memory as this will be the last time for us. Tonight has been perfect. A one-off whirlwind holiday romance. Dare I say, romantic? Something I have never done before. I have broken far too many rules for her. It won't ever happen again. I can't let it. It shouldn't have happened with Jenna to start with, but now, breaking the rules again would just remind me of her. I honestly don't know how I'm going to forget about her and carry on with my life, I think as I drift off to sleep.

There was a sombre feeling all around the house this morning before they left, but now that I'm alone, it's even worse. I'm damn right irritable, and I can smell her all over the house. She's gone, but she's still everywhere. I love it, the faint lingering scent of her, and I can hear her moans of pleasure in my mind. But I also hate it. The memories are great, but they are a distraction I don't need, and a reminder of what I can never have. So I send a quick text to the cleaning company to book the villa in for an all-over deep clean next week.

I'd swapped numbers with Jenna at the airport when we said our goodbyes; I knew I would never use it. I couldn't, but I was being polite. She was a fantastic girl and would make someone very happy one day, but that wouldn't be me. I have to get back to my normal jackass self. I have a club to manage. A life to lead. And random chicks to fuck. But as I say, 'random chicks' out loud to myself, a sense of loss and dread hit me dead in the gut.

What the fuck?

It isn't because of her; it can't be, I'd lost my wingman; that was it. I'll be fine once I get back to my real life and back in the game. I know just where I must start. Club Rife. Back to work; booze and pussy on tap.

Chapter 9

Six weeks. Six long fucking weeks since they left. Since she left.

For the last six weeks, I've thrown myself into work, anything to keep myself busy. I've been walking around with a permanent scowl on my face. Making everyone around me miserable, I'll end up with no staff or customers if I keep this up.

I could kick myself for breaking my own rules. I did this to myself. By breaking my rules I've made my life fucking unbearable.

NO REPEATS EVER! Why didn't I fucking listen to myself?

Oh yeah, I know why. She got under my skin, and I couldn't keep myself under control. I blame my dick for taking all the blood and common sense from my brain. Damn perfect pussy too. And to top it off my dick is broken. Limp as fuck! She's broken me, and I have no idea how to fix it. I've tried everything I can think of. The only time it works is when I'm lying in bed or in the shower thinking about her. I need to stop this shit and fast.

Last night, I had a chick in my favourite place in the club. In the DJ booth on her knees sucking my cock, while I played to the crowd. But no. The damn thing didn't want to come out and play. Shrivelled up like a fucking prune. Never in my life have I had this problem. I even felt guilty for snapping at the chick when I threw her out of the booth, blaming her lack of oral skills for my soft cock. Poor lass ran away with tears in her eyes. I knew deep down it wasn't her fault, but fuck if I'm gonna admit it to anyone. It's taken me six damn weeks to admit it to myself.

I miss her. I miss her smile, her laughter, and most of all, just being near her.

As I lay back and relax in the bath, my mind wanders back to Jenna. I can't help but remember our last night together, how perfectly in sync we were with each other and the look of pure ecstasy on her face as she came. Groaning as my now rock-hard cock begs for some action, action I'm not going to say no to, even if it is by my own hand. Beggars can't be choosers at the moment. I need to release some tension before it drives me insane.

"Now then, fucker," screams Danny down the phone. I knew I shouldn't have answered the call without looking at the caller display first.

"Hey," I mumble back, trying to keep the glum out of my voice. "How's things?"

"Better than you by the sounds of things," he sniggers. "What's up, man?"

"Nowt, just not feeling myself." No way am I going to admit to him that my junk won't work. The prick would never let me forget it.

"Bullshit. What's the matter? Missing me or is it Jenna you're pining for?" I can hear the smile in his voice. Damn bastard knows me too well.

"Fuck off, Dan," I sigh. "It's that time of year again, you know." It wasn't a question. He knows damn well what this time of year does to me.

"I know, that's why I rung ya. Thought I'd try to take your mind off it for a few. Plus I knew you're missing the fuck out of me." He laughs.

"Yeah, yeah, whatever." I smile to myself. He always has a way of making me forget for a while. "So what's new? Have you seen Lou recently?"

"Two weeks ago, man. And it's a killer, but we talk and FaceTime nearly every day."

"Pussy-whipped asshole," I laugh.

"Fuck you, you're just jealous."

He isn't wrong, but I'm not gonna tell him that.

"Anyway, I got something to ask you," he says quietly.

"Shoot," I reply. God knows what it is this time.

"Err, I was thinking you should come home for a visit." He pauses briefly before continuing. "I can take a few days off, and the girls were saying it would be nice to see you again."

"Hell, I don't know, Dan. I haven't been back once since leaving, and to be honest, I don't know if I can face it."

"Of course you can. It's been years and even my parents are missing you. I have no idea why though," he giggles like a girl. "Just think about it for a bit. yeah?"

"I'll think about it but no promises,"

"Good, now tell me all the juicy pussy details I've been missing."

After giving Dan some bullshit about needing to leave the house, I finally got him off the phone.

Can I go back to the UK? I haven't been back since I left nearly seven years ago, and I'm not sure I want to.

"I need a drink," I say to nobody but myself and wonder what the fuck is wrong with me? I must be losing my mind or maybe it's because of the time of year. I always struggle a little around October. Normally throwing myself into work helps, but that doesn't seem to help with anything at the minute. So I'm taking the night to myself to try and pull myself out of this funk.

Sitting out on my patio, watching the sunset over the horizon, I wonder what they would have been doing now? Are my parents proud of me? I lean into the cooler box and grab another bottle of lager. These thoughts of my family never get any easier. I miss them now today as I did when I lost them. Closing my eyes to keep the tears at bay, I try to think of anything to make me smile. But with my lack of dick action and the anniversary, there is no stopping the red-hot tears from falling down my cheeks.

Chapter 10

After crying like a soft bitch last night, I felt much better when I woke this morning. I threw myself into the mountain of paperwork I had let pile up in the office.

Filing the last of the invoices and other crap, I stop dead in my tracks. Standing frozen to the spot staring at a box I'd not forgotten about but put to the back of my mind. Along with all the other shit going on in my head. I turn to leave the room, but something makes me turn back around and pick up the box. Walking with slow steady steps, I make my way to the kitchen table and sit down. The box is staring at me, begging to be opened before it burns a hole in the solid pine table. I've not opened this box since closing it just after my eighteenth birthday.

Walking away is my only option. I can't bring myself to open it again, not today. I stand near the patio doors, looking out over the mountains, and I swear I can hear voices telling me to man up and open the damn thing. If I open this box, I open an old can of worms I'm not sure I can deal with. But as I stand here contemplating my options, I know it's going to get the better of me and I won't be able to stop myself.

Heading back inside, I grab a drink and sit down to look at the offending box.

"Right, Logan, you can do it."

Do it for Megan, if not for yourself.

Removing the lid slowly, I peer inside, taking a look at the contents for the first time in years. And looking back at me is the last picture ever taken of all four of us. We were celebrating Megan's thirteenth birthday, sitting around the table laughing and smiling at each other. I wipe away the lone tear that is sliding down my cheek before it drops onto the picture. Flicking through the pictures I had kept, which isn't many, just the ones that really mean something to me, I come to the bottom of the box where I had stored the letter. The letter that changed everything on my eighteenth birthday.

Logan, my boy,

If you're reading this, then your dad and I are longer with you. I'm sorry, son, this isn't what we want, but our time has come to an end. You have come to the age where you need to make your own choices in life and we believe you can. Please look after Megan for us. Be the best big brother and role model you can. She has always idolised you, even though she drives you crazy at times. Especially when she follows you and your friends around, but she loves you and I know you love her. Oh and your dad says to keep an eye on that Danny. He has a thing for your sister. I don't see it myself. He treats her like the little sister he never had.

We will always be here watching over both of you, so don't do anything too crazy. Your dreams will come true if you work hard enough.

Now that you are eighteen, we can give you the insurance policies your dad and I had in place for times like this. We prayed it would never be needed, but life has a way of changing the path we are on. You know we have never been religious, but we do believe things happen for a reason. I know you won't see this now, but please, believe me, we didn't suffer, and we are happy watching over you. Please share this money with Megan and use it wisely. Make both your dreams come true.

We love you both very much. Don't let our death bring you down. We are both so very proud of you. You have become a strong, sensible young man. Find your dreams and go with the flow. Never look back and wish you'd done something differently. Always follow your head and your heart. They won't fail you.

There is also a letter for Megan. Please give it to her when you think she is ready. You will know when.

Love you more than life itself.

Take care, my Logan.

Love you forever,

Mum and Dad xxx

My mum was right, she always was. Apart from one thing. Megan wasn't lucky enough that night, she wasn't here to follow her dreams. She was with them, wherever they were. I hoped and prayed I was making her proud too.

I was going to make damn sure they were all proud of me.

I'd made my decision.

Grabbing my laptop, I search for a flight available in the next few days and book it.

No backing out now.

I was going back home to England.

God, I hope I don't live to regret this.

Chapter 11

Emerging from the arrivals exit at Manchester airport, I curse myself for throwing away most of my warm clothes. Fucking me! England is cold, and I'd forgotten about the biting wind. I snuggle further into my thin coat and head off to find my hired car. I told Danny I was coming home, but he couldn't get time off work until the weekend, which honestly suited me. I wanted a day or two to myself first. So, I hired a car and booked a hotel near to where I used to live before leaving for Tenerife. Finding the small car, I climb in, start the engine, and set the heater to high.

After driving the fifty-minute journey to my hotel in Leeds, I check-in and unpack, thankful it was early afternoon and the traffic had been light. I decide the first thing I need to do is buy some warm clothes. No way can I manage the next few days in t-shirts and the one thin coat I own.

Lying on the hotel bed after shopping and eating out, I send a text Danny to say I'd arrived in one piece and would see him at the weekend.

I am shocked. I still remember my way around Leeds after all this time away. But honestly, the place hasn't changed all that much. But the people certainly had though. Everyone seemed to be in a massive rush, pushing and shoving. I swear they had all forgotten their manners too. I don't know what made living abroad so much more relaxing. Was it the weather or the people, or just the pace of life? I wasn't sure but could guess it was probably a little bit of both.

I never thought I'd ever pluck up the courage to come back here. I didn't think I'd be able to face it. You see people in movies talking to gravestones and sitting in the cemetery for hours with their loved ones. I never thought I'd be able to do that. Always thought I would feel like a dickhead. But here I am, sitting by their graves. It feels good to talk to them again. I feel like a weight has been lifted off my shoulders for coming today. The dark cloud that has followed me around for the last seven years has gone. I feel lighter and ready to fight for the things I want. The things my family feel I deserve.

Looking at the headstones one last time, I stand and say my goodbyes. "I promise I won't leave it so long next time. Love you," I say quietly as I walk away.

Right, Logan, time to move on with your life.

Walking slowly back to the car, I smile to myself. I've never felt so relieved, so free. So happy. I wasn't this happy when I walked into Club Rife for the first time when I bought it.

I don't remember the drive back to the hotel. But I am showered, dressed, and more than ready for something to eat. My stomach had been talking to me all day. With the fear of visiting the cemetery, I skipped breakfast and lunch. I have one food on my mind, Indian. I've not had a traditional curry since leaving England. I know just where to head. I only hope it's still there.

To my delight, the Indian restaurant is still there and still just as delicious as I remember. After eating as much as I can manage, I head out into the cold fresh air and wonder what to do. If I head back to the hotel, I'll just lie there, unable to sleep. Not because I'm worried about anything, but for the first time in years I don't have any worries. So, I make my way over to the bar across the road. The bar is packed with office workers trying to wind down after a busy day. Luckily, I find a table near the window, so I can sit and people-watch inside and out. As I sit flicking through bullshit pages on social media, my phone vibrates with an incoming message.

Danny - Yo dickhead, I managed to get tomorrow off, so I'll be in Leeds just after lunch. Don't start the party without me.

How he has the nerve to call me a dickhead I'll never know!

Me - I don't plan to!

Playing it safe, I call it a night after a couple of pints. Knowing Danny is going to be around for the weekend, I know there's every chance it will get messy. And that is something I need to blow off some steam.

Chapter 12

I've lazed about in my hotel room all morning and am starting to get restless when I hear him coming. I can just imagine the chaos he is causing down the hallway. I swing my feet off the bed, unfortunately not quick enough as he starts banging on the door.

"Let me in, cockface," he yells so everyone can hear. I bet people in neighbouring rooms are dreading the night ahead with this buffoon about. Luckily for them and me, he is planning on staying with Lou tonight.

Danny bulldozes his way in the room as I open the door.

"Shower time and then we can get this show on the road," he says with an obnoxious grin.

"Afternoon. Nice to you see you too," I reply sarcastically.

He takes no time making himself at home and heads straight to the bathroom

Whistling as he exits the bathroom with the same stupid grin plastered across his face, he gives me a funny look and says, "Right, the girls will be out to party for seven tonight." He wiggles his eyebrows at me and continues. "What shall we do to kill the time? I don't wanna be shitfaced before they get here."

"Well, that's a first! Danny doesn't wanna get shitfaced." I laugh. "You're so pussy-whipped it's untrue."

"Fuck you!"

"We've got hours. Let's go see your mum and dad?" I look at him questioningly as he groans out loud. "They'll kill us both if we don't go visit while I'm here."

"Yeah, I know," he whines. "Come on then. Let's get the grilling over with so we can have some fun later."

The wait for the girls is torture. My nerves are shot, my hands are sweating, and I keep having to wipe them down my jean-covered legs. I have no reason for the tension that is flowing through me. I'm looking forward to seeing Jenna and Lou, well especially Jenna, but I've not made the effort to contact her since she left Tenerife. She's not texted me either, but she knew what happened back home was a one-time thing. A holiday romance of sorts. I hope the radio silence for the last few weeks isn't going to make things awkward and uncomfortable between us. I secretly hope we will be able to slide back into the friendship we had started. And yes, I was more than prepared for some hot sex again with her. Maybe I'm jumping the gun though. Maybe she doesn't want a replay our fun from the summer.

Danny nudges me in the ribs with his elbow, and I look up to find him staring up the street at the two gorgeous beauties walking toward us. But there was another person with them. One that makes me suck in a deep breath as turmoil starts to take me over for a second before I stop it.

What the fuck have I gotten myself into here? I am going to kill Danny for not telling me.

As Jenna and Lou get closer, I can feel the anger rising quicker than a speeding train. She looks beautiful and so happy walking down the street with a huge smile on her face. A face I remember so well, especially her expression when lying in my arms, in my bed. It's the twat walking next to her, holding her hand that has my blood boiling.

Why hasn't Danny warned me? Did he know she had a boyfriend? He better not have, or I'm going to kill him.

Lou runs the rest of the way down the street into Danny's arms, squealing so high-pitched only dogs can hear her. It's nice to see them both so happy, and I try to smile as she looks in my direction waving hello. But her smile morphs into something else when she registers the look on my face. Obviously, I'm failing at schooling my features and trying to hide my disappointment that Jenna is with someone.

I glance back up the street as Jenna stops walking to talk to the guy she's with. They look close. He's touching her face as they talk, and the wanker moves in for what looks like a kiss. A kiss I can't bring myself to watch so turn to avoid the nightmare coming to life in front of me, but I turn so fast I nearly fall over my own feet. I steady myself and look up to find Danny and Lou standing right in front of me, Danny still with his lovesick smile. He's completely oblivious to my discomfort.

Fuck, I feel like a giant nobhead. I bet I look like one too.

"Calm down, tiger," Lou says with a smile and touches my arm to grab my attention.

Calm down! Really?

Fucking hell what's wrong with me? I'm turning into a girl at the speed of light.

Where have my balls gone?

"Logan?" Lou says very quietly. "Put the beast away."

I can't manage to form any words, so I just look at her with what I hope is a blank expression.

"That's Luke from Jenna's office," she continues softly. "She's not his type."

She's not his type?...Wait, what?...Oh for fuck's sake!!

We stand in silence as I gather myself into some sort of order and take in what Lou just said. Not her type. I take a minute to think. Does Lou mean he's is gay? I bloody hope that's what she means. Only thing is now I feel like a right stupid cunt!! And I mean that literally.

How the hell do I get myself out of this hole without looking like an even bigger twat?

Besides me, I can hear whispering between Danny and Lou, but I take no notice of them as I look back up the street towards Jenna. She's walking towards me, alone. Fuck, I'd forgotten just how stunning she is, shy but beautiful. And boy do I feel like a complete idiot for jumping to the wrong conclusion about the twat that was with her. Surely every other hot-blooded male in my shoes would have come to the same conclusion, right? Glancing around the street I see no sign of the twat, Luke or whatever his name is. Thank fuck, I don't have to face him after I was just thinking breaking his nose for touching Jenna.

Just as Jenna gets within touching distance, I hear Danny burst out laughing and not just a little laugh. He's damn right laughing out loud for the whole world to hear, and I don't really need to guess what he's laughing at. I know well enough what they were whispering about now. Me, that's who. Me and yet another major fuck up when it comes to Jenna. He's never gonna let me live this down.

"Hey," Jenna says from behind me. "What's up with him?"

"Hey, you." I smile as I take her in. "Don't mind him. He's been a dickhead as usual." I reach for Jenna and gage her reaction as I pull her in for a hug. I thank the gods above that she doesn't flinch in my arms, but instead her arms circle my waist and she hugs me back. "How are you?" Lame, I know, but after so many weeks, where else do I start?

"I'm good thanks. Bloody cold. I hate this time of year," she smirks. "How have you been?"

"I've been good. Can I let you into a secret?" I question.

"You know you can." Jenna smiles at me.

"I'm an idiot for not messaging you after you left," I say as I watch her closely. "Honestly, Jenna, I've missed you."

Right, well it's out there now. Ball's in her court as they say.

"Have you now?" She grins. "Then why didn't you get in touch?"

"I needed to sort some personal things out before I could move on. Ya know?" I hope she understands without asking too many questions tonight. Going into the past isn't something I want to do right now.

"Yeah, I can get that," she replies, sounding a little deflated.

"Just family stuff, but it's all good now," I say quickly with a smile to ease the tension I can see growing in her eyes.

Jenna looks at me and nibbles on her bottom lip. "Jenna, don't." I groan deeply as I adjust my swelling cock. The little devil just looks to me as if she doesn't know what's wrong. "You know what that does to me," I say as she glances down to where my hand is trying to hide my growing erection. "Keep it up and you'll be naked, in bed before you've had a single drink." I can hear the breath she intakes, and I can bet anything there's a sexy blush creeping up her cheeks.

"Hey, Jenna, baby," Danny bellows as he breaks our little moment.

"Hi," Jenna says breathlessly.

Yes! She still wants me.

"Guess what Logan thought when you walked down the street with what's his face?"

Jenna looks at me puzzled before Danny dramatically fills her in on my mix-up from earlier.

Heart Beats

Chapter 13

I was the butt of all Danny's jokes all last night, but do you know what? I don't care. Every time Danny started going on about Luke and how green around the gills I was, Jenna moved closer to me or grabbed some part of me, which kept me level-headed and I just laughed along with him or more likely at him.

In the end though, I won the girl, so he can fuck off.

I've been lying in bed watching her sleep for what seems like hours. Creepy as fuck I know, but I don't want miss a single thing this weekend. She's got me by the balls; there's no denying it. There's no fighting it now. I might as well go with it and see what happens. One good thing though...my dick isn't broken anymore!

Jenna moans ever so quietly as she stirs and reaches across the bed to pull me closer.

"Morning," I mumble low, not really wanting to wake her completely.

"Hmm" is all she says as she lays featherlight kisses on my chest.

I hope she knows what trouble she's about to start.

Jenna continues to kiss her way across my chest as her hands slowly drift up my legs, making me sink deeper into the mattress. I close my eyes and enjoy the feeling of her touch. The bed moves and dips as Jenna settles herself between my legs. I love how her shyness disappears when we are alone. And this time I'm going to let her have control. I'm all hers do with as she pleases.

My back arcs off the bed as her tongue sweeps up my shaft, and I can't stop the low moan that leaves my chest. If she keeps up this slow agonising torture, I won't last long. I grab the bedsheets to stop myself from taking control as she takes me deep in her mouth. Jenna teases me with her tongue as it swirls around my cock before she takes more of me into her mouth again.

"Jenna...more," I beg.

She doesn't keep me waiting long before her head starts to bob up and down, switching between a soft and firm grip on my swollen cock. I can feel my orgasm building as my balls tighten, and the tingling starts to move up my spine. My orgasm takes over me, and I swear my whole body lifts off the bed and floats for a second or two as Jenna moans in delight around my cock.

"Fuck...Jenna," I say with a very satisfied sigh as she snuggles into my side and we drift off to sleep.

𝄞

Banging at the hotel room door could only mean one thing. Danny is back. I roll out of bed, pick my jeans up from the floor, and pull them up my legs whilst making my way slowly to the door.

"Yes?" I mumble as I open the door to find Danny and Lou standing in the hallway hand in hand, looking fresh and ready for the day ahead.

"Come on, you two. It's time for food," says Lou as she pushes her way in the room while bouncing up and down on her feet.

Just as bad as Danny, that one!

"I don't want to move," complains Jenna from under the duvet.

"But you promised," Lou whines like a four-year-old, making Jenna giggle.

"Lou, you're such a brat! Meet you in the bar in twenty minutes?" Jenna questions with a sigh.

"Ok," Lou replies as she skips out of the room with Danny hot on her heels.

"I don't want to go," moans Jenna again, looking at me with puppy dog eyes that make me want to cancel our plans for the afternoon.

"I know. Me either. If I could get us out of it, I would." Sighing, I take a breath and continue. "But just think, the sooner we get this over with, the sooner we can climb back into that bed and really enjoy ourselves." I smile and wink at her, making the sexy as hell blush creeps over her cheeks.

"Hmm... now that sounds delicious."

Fuck yes, it does.

We said our goodbyes to Dan and Lou earlier on in the evening and decided on a Mexican restaurant for dinner before heading back to the hotel for some quality time together. This is our last night together for a while, and I want to make it special. I'd made some arrangements with the hotel staff while Jenna was in the shower earlier. I'd never done anything remotely like this before, so I am really nervous. I just hope Jenna likes it and it isn't over the top.

As we return to the hotel, the receptionist gives me a little nod, indicating everything is set and ready.

Here goes.

Unlocking the door, I move to the side to let Jenna enter first, following close behind as I want to see what they have done to the room too. Jenna comes to a sudden stop and gasps, clasping her hand over her mouth.

It's perfect for her. For us. Or I at least I think it is.

Standing in the centre of the table is an ice bucket full of bottles of her favourite lager, a box of chocolates, and half a dozen pink roses in a vase. Scattered on the table and bed are a few pink rose petals but not too many though.

"Wow," she gasps. "Did you…" she trails off, not able to finish what she was going to say.

"Yeah, I did," I reply, not quite sure what to say next. But the need to know if she liked it is eating at me, so I have to ask. "Do you like it?"

Jenna is very quiet, and I wonder if I've gone over the top or if she hates it.

"I…" Turning to look at me with unshed tears in her eyes, she continues. "I love it, Logan. Wow. No one has ever done anything like this before for me."

"Well, they should have. You deserve it, but in a way, I'm glad they haven't. Because it means it's a first for both of us," I say fast but mean every word. Jenna leaps forward into my arms.

Thank fuck she likes it.

Pulling back just enough to look down at Jenna, I smile and say, "I'm so relieved that you like it."

"It's amazing. Thank you so much," she says and leans in for a kiss. A kiss I want to drown in, but I reluctantly slow it to a stop so we don't get carried away. I have one more thing planned.

"Drink?" I ask Jenna. A drink is the last thing on my mind now, but I need a minute to sort out the next surprise.

"Yeah, sure," she says as she sits in the chair and takes a rose from the vase. I grab two bottles from the ice bucket while Jenna inhales the scent of the rose and sighs deeply. "These smell beautiful."

I don't reply I as fumble around with my phone and Bluetooth speaker before pressing play. Before leaving Tenerife, I made a playlist for Jenna. Songs to hopefully remind her of summer and the fun we had together. As the music starts playing, she looks up and smiles at me. An all-knowing smile. This is the song she first mixed with at my villa. Handing her a drink, I pull her to her feet and wrap my free arm around her and start swaying to the beat.

"Logan," she whispers.

Looking down at her stunning blue eyes, I reply with a moan, "Yeah."

"Thank you for this."

"You're welcome," I say as I take the bottle from her hand and place it on the table beside us.

"Logan, I'm really going to..."

I don't let her finish the sentence. Instead, I pull her closer and take her lips in a slow sensual kiss. She moans into my mouth and her fingers start running through my hair. Within seconds, she's pulling and tugging on me, making me moan. She knows I love it when she gets all assertive and demanding.

As the kiss gets more desperate, it becomes a clash of teeth and tongues fighting for dominance. I soon put a stop to that as I bite her top lip hard but then slowly lick it better. She had her moment this morning. Now it's my turn.

I turn us so Jenna's legs are touching the edge of the bed as I bend down and rest on my knees. Jenna looks absolutely beautiful tonight in her little black dress with knee-high boots. I slowly unzip her boots and throw them to the corner of the room.

"Logan," she says on a low moan.

I reply by running my hands slowly up her smooth legs, lifting her dress as I go, revealing her sexy black lace thong. As my hands go higher, I stand to follow their lead, and Jenna raises her arms as I pull her dress over her head and drop it to the floor. My hands go around her back as my lips start kissing her neck and nibbling her on her soft spot under her ear.

"Oh no, you don't," I say as she tries to grab me and remove my shirt.

Jenna drops her arms with a sigh, and I struggle to hide my laughter. I won't keep her waiting long. Her torture is my torture too. I can't wait to be deep inside her.

I continue my journey with my lips, kissing my way around her neck as my hands unclasp her bra and she lets it fall off her arms. My lips slowly make their way to one of her nipples as my hands continue their way down her body to slide her knickers down her sexy as fuck legs. I can smell her arousal as she kicks her thong to the side.

I can't wait any longer. I need to taste her.

I gently lower Jenna to the bed, and she shuffles into the middle, giving me a "hurry the fuck up" look. So, I take my time removing all my clothes while she watches the show. I crawl up the bed toward her, spreading her legs as I go. Stopping at her sweet spot, I take in a deep breath. God, I love her scent. I take my time in teasing her with kisses before I nibble on Jenna's clit, which makes her moan as her hips lift off the bed.

"Please…." Jenna growls, making me smile against her heated skin.

"Please what?" I ask teasing her some more with my tongue.

"I need you now."

I can't deny her anymore.

I lean back on my haunches and grab the condom I placed on the bed earlier. Looking down at Jenna's hooded eyes, I can't fight the feelings I have for her anymore. I'm all in.

I hold myself up on my elbows so I can look in Jenna's eyes as I slowly enter her in one smooth motion. Fuck, she feels good. Jenna's eyes roll into the back of her head as I hold myself still, trying to control my cock before this ends too soon. Jenna wraps her legs around my legs and grabs my ass cheeks, moving her hips ever so slightly, taking me in deeper. Fuck! We start to move faster and harder as we both chase our orgasms.

"Fuck," I moan out loud as the tingle shoots up my spine, and I lose all my senses as we explode in ecstasy together.

I can't believe it's Sunday lunchtime already, and I have to say goodbye to Jenna.

"Logan," she said in a whisper. "I…"

"I know," I sigh. "I know." Fuck, this is harder than I thought it was going to be. "I promise to message and call all the time, Jenna. But please, promise you'll think about spending Christmas in Tenerife with me?" God, I hope she says yes.

"I don't need to think about it," she smiles and pulls me close. "I hate the cold over here," she giggles. "I'll be counting down the days until I can board the plane."

Thank fuck for that. We'd talked for hours last night about how our relationship would work with the distance. I have no idea how things will pan out, but fuck, I'll try anything if it means I can call Jenna mine.

Chapter 14
Christmas

I'm pacing the arrivals lounge, waiting for Jenna. Good job it's a concrete floor, or I'd wear a hole from one side to the other at this rate. Glancing up to check the information board, I see that Jenna's plane has landed safely.

We've talked every day since we parted in Leeds months ago. Fuck, I've missed her. I can't wait for us to spend the next two weeks together. Just Jenna and me. No interruptions. No distractions.

I continue to pace up and down, waiting for Jenna to breeze in through the door at my left. I feel like I've been waiting hours when in reality it's been ten minutes at the most. I've been waiting for this moment for weeks after she booked her plane ticket. But she once told me the ticket was booked, it became real, and I put my plans in motion to make this the best Christmas ever. For the last seven years, I've not celebrated the holidays. Club Rife has always been decorated and looks like Santa's elves have farted Christmas everywhere. But at home, I've never had a tree or even put up Christmas cards. This year was different though. I may have gone a little overboard with the decorations.

Stopping my pacing, I grab my phone to give me something to concentrate on and lean against the wall. As I'm scrolling through my emails, my phone beeps with an incoming text from Jenna, making me smile so much my cheeks hurt. I must look like a pussy-whipped douchebag.

Jenna - I'm off the plane waiting for my bags xx

My smile only grows wider. Not long now and she'll be in my arms. Right here she belongs.

Every time the doors slide open, I stop in my tracks and watch the sea of people walking toward the exit in the hopes of seeing her. But as time drags on, I get more agitated that she's not here yet. Just as I'm about to turn and start pacing again, there is she. Looking as beautiful as ever, even after being cooped up in a tin can, flying for four hours.

"Logan..." Jenna screams as she drops her suitcase and runs into my open arms.

So fucking good to hold her again and god she smells good.

Gently grabbing her cheeks, I lift her face so I can see into her sparkling eyes and say, "Fuck, I've missed you." I slam my lips to hers in a kiss that should be shared in private and definitely not an airport full of families. I reluctantly stop before I get too carried away and take her on the spot.

"Come on, let's take you home." I smile and grab her discarded suitcase, and we walk out into the bright sunshine and head to my car.

𝄞

It's Christmas Day, and I've been awake watching Jenna sleep again. It's become my favourite thing to do. She looks so peaceful and carefree. She's been happy since getting back here, but something is bothering her and I can't figure it out. Maybe I'm reading too much into it. I'm nervous as fuck about a couple of the presents I've gotten for her. So, maybe it's been me that's off it a little bit.

The suspense and wait are getting too much, so I gently stroke her cheek, trying to wake her up.

"Good morning," she says sleepily.

"Happy first Christmas," I reply, placing a soft kiss to her lips.

"Merry Christmas to you too," she says smiling. "Come on! Get up!" she shouts while jumping out of bed like a four-year-old, and all the sleepiness is gone.

I can't help but smile more as her giddiness is infectious.

We both sit cross-legged in front of our six-foot Christmas tree. We'd placed all the gifts under the tree before going to bed last night. I was very tempted to get a sneak peek during the night, but Jenna had other ways of keeping me occupied.

"You first," she says, handing me an envelope.

Turning the envelope over in my hands, I look up at her and she looks shy and nervous. Putting her out of her misery, I slowly open the envelope and pull out a single piece of paper. And start reading it.

Mr Bradley,

I have enjoyed my time working for your company, but it has come time for me to hand in my notice. I hereby give you four weeks' notice and will be terminating my employment on December 18th.

Thank you for all you have done.

Yours sincerely,

Jenna Richards

I read the letter twice before it sinks in, and I crawl across the floor to pull Jenna onto my knee, hugging her tightly. She did it. We'd spoken about this for weeks, or I should say, I've been begged her to move out of here.

"Seriously?" I question, still not quite believing it.

Jenna nods as a tear escapes down her cheek and I catch it with my thumb.

"I..." I'm lost for words so I show her how much I love her the only way I know how.

Epilogue
Jenna
Six months later.

Moving to Tenerife to be with Logan was the best decision I've ever made. My parents weren't happy with me. We'd only been dating a few months and out of those few months we'd spent a grand total of ten days together, but when it feels right, it feels right. I took a leaf out of Logan's book and said 'fuck em' and followed my dreams and my heart. It's paid off too. My mum and dad have been to visit twice since I've been here, and they love Logan just as much as I do.

The summer craziness is about to start with holidaymakers, but Logan has pulled back from Club Rife and handed over the reins to Ethan full-time. That doesn't mean he's not involved though. He does spot checks regularly and DJs at least twice a month. We often have a night out there to let our hair down and party like teenagers. But partying isn't everything anymore. We spend most of our evenings cuddled on the patio talking and watching the sunset.

As for me, I've started my own little business doing the accounts for English businesses owners in the local area. It's what I'm trained to do, so why not use it? No way was I moving out here and living off Logan. That's not my style. I need to keep busy and still be independent. I have a handful of clients, and that's enough for me. I certainly don't want to go back to working five days a week. I want to spend my time with Logan, enjoying our life and maybe one day starting a family of our own. Logan told me about his family's accident just after Christmas, and I was heartbroken for him. A family of his own is something he never thought he'd have again. He's scared rigid that something will happen to me or any family we may have. But he's changing his mind all the time and talking about our future and children. I won't push him. I never will.

Our future is bright as long as we have each other.

THE END.

Heart Beats

Wrath

by

Lacey Heart

Sinful Beginnings #1

A Dark High School Bully Romance

"Dreams are exactly that, girl. Dreams. A total waste of energy, and you sure as hell won't get far in life with that kind of attitude."

My momma had my life planned out for me, but it wasn't the life I wanted. I was nothing but a measly pawn in her evil and twisted games. And I wanted out... no matter the cost.

Preston Rydel was supposed to be my saviour. Only it turned out he had some evil plans for me too.

As the KING of Rivington Prep, there's no way he'd ever keep his promise to me. Instead, he has his heart set on destroying me. For good.

Prologue
Sophia

"Dreams are exactly that, girl. Totally make believe. And you won't get far in life with that kind of attitude—believe me." Her words ring in my ears and spin inside my head, making me feel nauseous and uneasy while my eyes sting from trying to hold back my heated tears as they threaten to fall. "You know your looks will only get you so far in life, and then all those men will only end up shitting on you anyway."

"But momma…" I choke out on a hiccup, just wishing for once in my life that she'd actually stop and listen to me. But unsurprisingly my momma doesn't pay any attention to me and my inward struggles. She never does. She's far too busy tending to her own wants and needs to give me so much as a second thought. Right now, she's far too occupied applying another thick coat of vibrant red lipstick, before finally lighting up her cigarette.

I continue to watch her, totally transfixed by her sheer beauty and I decide to settle myself down on her bed and I wrap myself up in my favorite tatty blanket as I silently try to hold myself together.

I sit quietly on my momma's bed for some time and I watch her every move as she tries to make herself look as presentable as possible. She doesn't need all that make-up though. She might not believe it, but my momma could walk about wearing a trash can and she'd still look good.

I don't know how much time has passed but my momma's eyes finally lock onto mine through the reflection of the dirty mirror on her dresser and when she sees me looking back at her, her face hardens.

"But momma, nothing." She snaps. "You think you've got it all figured out in that pretty little head of yours, don't you? Well, allow me to enlighten you. I don't know what kind of games you've been playing or what you're hoping to achieve, but life isn't some kind of fairytale, Sophia. It's a dark place. You'll meet a hell of a lot of nasty monsters outside these walls, that's for sure. Monsters just like your father. And they won't think twice as they prey on your innocence. Oh, no," she shakes her head and I hold my blanket tighter around my body. "They'll drag you in, make you feel special—like you're the only goddamn girl in the world, and once they have you, they'll tear you down and they won't stop. They'll continue until there is absolutely nothing left. The girl you were before will be nothing but a distant memory."

I squeeze my eyes shut and try to block her out, but I can still hear her. But I try my best to stay strong and fight my case, hoping that she might just listen to me. "But I want to go to college, momma." I stammer out the words before I have a chance to stop myself, and I await my punishment. I keep my eyes closed and brace myself for the inevitable—the sharp sting as my mother's palm connects with my flesh. A few seconds pass and still nothing has happened. Not so much as a single movement.

I slowly allow myself to open one eye to see if this is some kind of wicked test, but surprisingly I find my momma still sat down at her dresser. She doesn't say anything to me, but her small eyes narrow before a large cloud of smoke bellows from her mouth. My momma stays quiet—eerily quiet. My momma has never been a quiet person in all her days. She's always been the first to voice her opinion, and I know her current reaction should scare me—knowing it should prepare me for further punishment. I don't say anything to her, instead I remain tight-lipped, huddled up on the bed.

It's true.

I want to go to college. I want to go more than anything. I want to better myself. I want to explore the big wide world and I want to prove to everyone around me that I can actually make something of my life. I want to prove that I am more than capable of being better and worth so much more than the horrible woman sat before me—and I'm stubborn enough to do it too.

My momma doesn't say anything for a long time, and my heart beats louder and faster with each second that passes. I make sure not to make any sudden movements. I'm wise enough to know that would be a huge error of judgement on my part.

I know my role in this house, and I know it well. I'm to be rarely seen and never heard.

I'm taken by complete surprise when my momma suddenly throws her head back and lets out a loud laugh. It's not a nice laugh either. It's more like an evil cackle and it sends icy chills right down my spine, and my blood runs cold.

I guess a small part of me knows my momma isn't all bad. She's not a bad person, but that doesn't make her a kind person either. I know my momma does what she needs to and nothing more.

She feeds me, clothes me and bathes me every once in a while. Probably when she remembers or when my stench gets too fragrant to bear. That's about as far as her maternal instincts go.

My momma doesn't shower me with love or praise. But that's okay because I know I should be thankful that she's still prepared to keep me under her roof, and she does it without asking for much in return. Just that I keep quiet and stay the hell out of her way. Especially if she's entertaining her *friends.*

It's no secret that my momma hates the world and everything in it, and most of the time that includes me too.

"Oh, Sophia. College isn't a place for girls like you." She snarls some more. Her voice is laced with venom, and the harshness of her tone makes me flinch. "When I was nothing but a silly, naïve little girl like you, I wanted to go to college too. My momma wouldn't let me go, but I managed to escape anyway…"

"What happened?" I ask, not really sure if I want to know the answer, but then I've always been far too inquisitive for my own good.

Her eyes leave mine and trail off somewhere into the distance as though her memories are swirling fresh in her mind like they only happened yesterday. Maybe reminding her of all the opportunities she lost along the way.

My momma doesn't answer me straight away. But her cold eyes continue to search mine through the mirror, for what I don't know but I don't worry about it too much as the moment quickly passes as she concentrates on lighting up her cigarette once more.

"*You* happened." She finally says and it's barely a whisper on her vibrant lips, yet it stabs me hard in the chest, as though she's just shouted it from the rooftops for all to hear. I force back my tears and my fragile heart begins to race as I wait for my momma to speak again. Eventually, I manage to control my ragged breathing just before she clears her throat. "But none of that mattered. My momma was quick to make me realize my place in this world. She made me see that it was right here, doing what I'm doing. She told me girls like us didn't need to waste our time or our feelings on any of those monsters who prowl beyond these walls. You see, we have a gift, Sophia." I want to run away and shut out everything she's saying but the inquisitiveness inside me is holding me captive and I'm forced to hang on to her every word because my momma has never spoken to me like this before—like I mattered. She's never been one to give me advice or try to guide me. "My momma used to say, 'why risk your heart and give your body to them for free?' After all, we're only a useless, pretty vessel to them and the second they don't need us anymore, they drop us and discard of us like the dirty pieces of meat they think we are."

"Momma…" I try to speak but she quickly waves her hand to silence me and she continues.

"She also told me that you can keep your heart close to your chest and make money fulfilling their selfish needs." I watch as my momma's eyes harden some more and they pierce into mine, warning me not to argue with her. "College isn't for you either, girl. You were born with a vagina so you can bet your sweet innocent ass you'll be contributing to the family business when the time is right. And you'll do it whether you like it or not. It's non-negotiable."

"But…" My bottom lip quivers when the realization of what she's saying hits me hard in the chest while horrible images start to swim in my mind.

"Quit with the buts, girl." My momma sighs dramatically and her face scrunches with pure irritation. "That's enough chatter for one day. Why don't you make yourself useful and disappear for a while? Go and find that silly little boy and do silly, childish things while you still can." I shuffle off the bed with caution, still not knowing if this is some kind of trap my momma is setting me up for. I take another step and when she makes no effort to move, I decide she's actually just trying to get rid of me.

"I won't be long, momma."

"I don't care where you go or what you do. I need you out of the house for a few hours. Just make sure you're back for when it gets dark." Momma bats me off with a quick flick of her wrist and I know this discussion is well and truly over—before it even began.

My stomach is in knots, like it's infested with a thousand pit snakes desperately trying to eat their way out of my body. Then the fear slowly starts to creep in.

I need a plan, and fast. And I need to make sure it's a tight one. One that will allow me to escape from this hellhole, because no matter what my momma says. No matter how she tries to glamorize it, there's no way I can stay here now. Not when I know what my momma plans to do with me.

Momma might think it's totally acceptable, but there is no way I'm going to sit back and be used as a meaningless pawn in her sick and twisted games.

The difference between me and momma is that unlike her, I know my worth, and that certainly isn't being forced into becoming an emotionless whore.

Preston

My papa was an angry man.

Fierce, evil and feared by most. Feared by most, except me.

There was a time when I would have done anything for my papa. When I would always try to please him. I wanted him to see me—really see me—and be proud. But the more years that have passed and the more that I've grown I quickly realized that day would never come.

You can't force someone to love you.

But then I guess my good old papa didn't expect to knock-up one of his whores, only to find out she was with child when she was six months gone. And he sure as hell didn't expect her to die while birthing his bastard.

That bastard would be me. Preston Rydel.

Some would say I should be grateful that he took me on and didn't throw me straight into the care system. Maybe my life would have been better if he did. But it's a pointless effort thinking about what could have been.

Instead, he acts like I should grovel every time I see him. Sure, he kept me and raised me as best as he thought he should. But I know he didn't do that out of love.

Oh, no. No sooner was my mom lowered into the ground, the son of a bitch demanded a DNA because in his words, "ain't no one ever trust the words of a whore."

I know he thought he had it all figured out. The results would come back and I'd just be another innocent kid who was knocked up for money, not love. If the results came back negative his life would have been sweet. He wouldn't have to do shit. But unfortunately for me, those tests came back in a matter of days and they showed positive. That motherfucker created me and there wasn't a single thing either of us could do about it.

I guess dollar signs must have been flashing in his eyes as soon as the results came in and he finally got his head around it. After all, Gusto Rydel finally had a son. An heir—someone to finally pass down and help run his pussy empire. But I've never wanted to be apart of it, and that will never change.

It doesn't matter how many times I try to tell him this, he just won't listen. He thinks I'm still too young to be making any big decisions, but he's the one who doesn't know shit.

My mother was a whore for fuck's sake. She was a whore, and whether it was by choice or not, she was used, abused and degraded every single day of her short miserable life.

Whore or not, nobody thinks they'll end up dead at eighteen years old, but shit happens.

No one can change the past, but I can sure as hell make sure history doesn't repeat itself.

I might have Gusto's tainted blood coursing through my veins but that's where our likeness ends. I'm nothing like him, and I never will be.

"Preston."

I hear my papa slurring out my name and I grab my beats from the nightstand. I'm not in any kind of mood to listen to his bullshit today.

What the fuck do I care if his broads haven't been putting out or paying Gusto his cut? That's his problem, not mine. And it's like he says, I'm nothing but a stupid little kid anyways. This is his fucked-up circus and his cock-hungry monkey's, so he can damn well deal with it.

"Preston, you little motherfucker. Where you at?" he slurs again, his voice growing closer down the hall, and I place my beats over my head, hit play on my iPod and lose myself in my latest track.

Music is food to my soul, and it's the only thing which keeps me sane. If I didn't have my music, I don't think Gusto would have any blood pumping through his veins.

One thing I do know is the sooner I'm out of here, the better it will be for everyone involved.

PRE-ORDER WRATH: Sinful Beginnings #1 ready for release on June 15th.

Heart Beats

Crashing Star

by

Xana Jordan

Back Door Records

My band, *Crash*, was picked up by *Back Door Records* a year ago, and we have been working non-stop recording and promoting our first album, *Psychotic Beauty*. Finally, we're about to start our first tour, opening for *Zombie Butterflies*.

Well, at least we were before I mucked it all up.

Now, I'm stuck in this hell hole called rehab, dying a little each day. It isn't until I meet her that I realize what I have to do in order to set it all straight.

Prologue

"Kolton Dickson, you are charged with Driving Under the Influence, Transportation of Open Container and Possession of Dangerous Controlled Substance - cocaine."

Those are words I never thought I'd hear associated with me. Sure, I'm in a band with my best friends, and those things are easily associated with musicians, but that's never really been my scene. Although my bandmates and I do enjoy having a few drinks, we've pretty much kept away from all the hard stuff, even if it was easy to come by. Our band, *Crash*, was picked up by Back Door Records a year ago, and we have been working our asses off recording and promoting our first album, *Psychotic Beauty*. We're even about to start our first tour, opening for *Zombie Butterflies*. Well, at least we were before I fucked it all up.

Being my first offense for anything, the label's generosity in keeping the band's contract is my only saving grace at this point. Their ultimatum of either going to rehab or be released from the band was a no-brainer decision. As I'm being released from jail, I try my best to listen to the police officer and my label-appointed lawyer talk to one another, but all I can think about is our band being replaced on the upcoming tour because of my actions. How am I ever going to face them?

"We'll report all the details as soon as everything is confirmed." The label's counsel, Williams, shakes hands with the officer and I follow him and my agent, Aiden Marshall, to the car waiting for us.

"We have arranged for you to be admitted into *Brooks Treatment Center* at the end of the week," Williams informs me once we're inside the vehicle and pulling away from the building. "We'll help you get everything you need in order before then," he sets his briefcase near his feet.

"Thanks," I say in a daze. I'm grateful for their support, but facing my own demons isn't something I'm used to. "What will happen to *Crash* now?" I look between him and Aiden, hoping for good news.

"Right now," Aiden says, as he leans back in the seat across from me, "the band will be working on some press releases and minor appearances to keep the band's name out there. The album is doing well so we want to keep up with that momentum."

"What about the tour?"

"As long as you give rehab all your effort and stay clean, we're looking at a possible tour as early as next year." That's a relief. I really don't think I would be able to face my friends again if we lost everything we've worked for.

"Thanks."

"Don't thank me yet," he warns. "Don't screw it up." He's in the worst mood I've ever seen him in, and if he weren't the key to my future with the label, I'd probably tell him to kiss my ass.

Glaring at him, then Williams, I let my ego get the better of me and smart off, "Fuck this."

So, I messed up. It's not like I'm the first musician or person in the world to make a mistake. Doesn't mean they have to treat me like a naughty child without a brain.

This is going to be the longest six months of my life.

Chapter One
Day one

"Everything's clear," the orderly at *Brooks* says as he zips up my last suitcase. He's thoroughly searched every item I have brought with me, even the pockets of the pants I'm wearing. Damn, I feel so violated. "There ya go," he places my bags at my feet and then turns to the woman going over my paperwork.

"Thank you," she states as she smiles and nods in dismissal. Pointing a finger to the silent man who's been standing beside her, she says, "Mr. Dickson, this is West, your counselor, and he'll show you to your room so that you can get settled in. Your companion," she waves a hand to Aiden, "is more than welcome to help carry your luggage."

"Thank you," I reply and pick up a suitcase and my duffle bag. Aiden does the same with the remaining bags and we follow the counselor to the right and down a long hallway. My friends would have been more than happy to come with me this morning, but I didn't want them to. They've put up with a lot because of my stupidity as of late, and I don't think they need to deal with anything else. Aiden offered to come along, and I took him up on it because after all he's done for me and the band, I owe it to him to try and make amends. Besides, it's nice to know he still believes in me.

"I understand that this is all overwhelming right now, but it's actually a lot less complicated around here than it seems." West pats my free shoulder and gives it a strong squeeze. "We only use first names around here for privacy. If you want to share further information with any of the residents, that's up to your discretion."

"Good to know," I nod, relieved to have some sort of anonymity. It's bad enough the music world knows about my fall from grace. I don't need everyday people joining in on the judgment wagon.

"This is your room," he opens the door to my left near the end of the elegantly decorated hallway. "Nothing fancy, but you should have everything you need." He remains by the door as Aiden and I enter and set my luggage near the closet.

"Looks nice." I scan the room quickly and notice how sterile it feels. The light tan walls don't give the room a warm feeling like it normally would.

It only reminds me of where I am and what I nearly lost. What I still could lose.

"Well, I'll give you two a few minutes to say your goodbyes and I'll escort Mr. Marshall back to the lobby." West leaves the door ajar and steps across the hall and begins talking to the person living there.

"I'm not happy about what you've done to get here," Aiden states as he turns to face me. "But, I'm glad you're facing it head on and not running away."

"Yeah, well," I shrug, unable to say anything else. Why bother? Not like I had a choice in the matter so, it is what it is.

"I know you don't get any calls right away, but you have my number and don't be afraid to use it. I expect to hear from you," he cocks his head to the side expectantly. "The guys, too."

"Got it," I reply and mean it. Even though I already hate being here, I know they only want what's best for me.

"Good," he claps me on the shoulder then squeezes it firmly. "Well, I'd better head out so that you can get some stuff put away." I look down at my suitcases on the floor.

"Yeah, not a lot to organize," I scoff.

"You'll be out of here before you know it, man."

"I don't know about that," I mutter. Six months is a long fucking time. I sound ungrateful, resentful even, but I can't help it. This isn't exactly the place anyone *wants* to be.

"I do," he tells me before walking to the door. He stops just inside the door frame and looks over his shoulder. "Have faith." Having realized we're finished, West peeks his head inside.

"Lunch is at noon, and I'll be back by at eleven-fifteen to show you around before it's time to eat." When I nod in acknowledgment, he escorts Aiden to the main entrance.

Sighing, I sit on the twin bed, elbows on my knees, and run my hands through my hair, memories of being arrested forming in my mind.

Driving too fast without a clue where I was going, I was enjoying the joint I lit up after scoring some coke from some guy I'd never met before. The band had been practicing, practically non-stop for days and all I could think of was zoning out for a while. Why I thought drinking and smoking pot while driving was a good idea, I'll never know.

Aiden and the guys continue to believe in me, regardless of my idiocy, and the label's decision to uphold our contract is more than I could ask for. I'm surrounded by a support system bigger than I deserve. Everyone is doing whatever they can to help me succeed and I'm grateful.

However, even though there are people all around me, I've never felt so alone.

Chapter Two
Day Two

"Rise and shine," an unfamiliar voice yells out over the incessant knocking on my door. Whoever the fuck it is, they're pissing me off.

Slamming the pillow over my head, I roll over in the opposite direction and face the wall. Someone needs to chill their cheery ass the fuck out before I lose my shit.

"Breakfast ends in thirty minutes." There is a pause and I think they've left me alone until they knock again. Dammit.

"I'm not hungry!" I stick a finger in my ear and continue to smash the useless pillow into my head. The banging stops temporarily but the annoying voice is still there.

"Everyone has to go. It's mandatory or you lose points. Besides, the food's not that bad." That stupid point system I ignored when the counselor was explaining it is going to be a major pain in my ass. No question about it.

It's obvious this asshole is not giving up, so I grudgingly get out of bed and stomp to the door, more pissed off than before. Jerking the door open, I see the happiest grin on a guy I've ever come across. At least unmedicated ones. Fuck my life.

"Oh, hi," he says when I simply stare at him. I feel like shit and just want to sleep through breakfast. Is that too much to ask? Apparently so.

"I'm Greg and my room is across the hall." He gestures toward the door directly in front of mine. Oh, lucky me.

"Kolton," I offer with a nod, one hand on the doorknob and the other on the door frame. I'm not fully awake and use them for support as I try and focus on Cheery Chuckie.

"I can go grab us a table while you get dressed." This guy's never going to leave me alone.

"I guess," I sigh and close the door in his face. He's lucky I didn't slam it like I nearly did. Mornings and I aren't best friends even when I'm not tossing and turning all night.

Ten minutes later I find him waving at me from a table near the middle of the dining hall. At least it doesn't have cafeteria seating. Seeing as how everyone in sight is watching for my reaction I have no choice but to join him.

"Everything is the same set up as yesterday," he informs me when I'm in hearing range. "I grabbed us a pot of coffee unless you want to grab something else while you fix your plate." Why in the ever-loving hell is he in such a damn good mood?

I turn toward the buffet table without a word and get my food. It doesn't look half bad, but nothing really appeals to my stomach. Grabbing a banana and some toast I return to my self-appointed new best friend.

The meal isn't a total disaster since Greg did all the talking and all I had to do was utter a response now and then to keep up pretenses. He took it upon himself to fill me in on all the ins and outs he felt I should know about beforehand. You know, the 'who to stay away from' and 'what not to do' in therapy. Lord knows if I'll remember them all but I'm sure he'll be there to refresh my memory if I don't.

"I'm going to the gym before lunch," Greg tells me as we're leaving the dining hall. "You wanna come with?"

"Thanks, but I have to meet with the counselor." My meeting is at nine o'clock, so I doubt I'd have time to work out even if I wanted to. Going to the gym hasn't been top on my priorities list like it has been for my friends. Sure, I'll go for a run every now and then, or lift a few weights with them, but a daily exercise routine isn't for me.

"Oh, well I'll see you at lunch then." He turns in the opposite direction from me as I walk back to my room. I've more than likely been told where he's off too, but I wasn't paying attention, being more focused on going back to bed.

Once back in my room, I fall onto the bed and stare at the ceiling. Minutes tick by as I wait for sleep to claim me, but unfortunately, I'm more than awake. Apparently, Greg's constant chatter woke me up enough to push sleep away. How fortunate.

"Dammit!" I throw the pillow across the room and pull myself from bed. Might as well take a shower while I'm up. Not like I have anything better to do.

"Kolton," West greets me when I arrive at his office on the complete opposite side of the facility. Of course, Cheery Chuckie was more than happy to give me directions when he found me wandering down the hallway. I have a feeling that will be a common occurrence.

"Hello," I reply while reaching out to shake his outstretched hand. He ushers me inside and locks the door behind us, hopefully for privacy and nothing else.

"Take a seat," he motions to the two chairs positioned in front of his desk. They're more like armchairs instead of the straight-backed ones I expect to counselors and therapists to use; more like the ones in a doctor's office. They're pretty comfy.

Looking around his office, I notice there isn't much in the way of decoration, yet for some strange reason, it feels pretty warm and inviting. There are books on a shelf to my right and a window to my left looks out onto the back garden area. "Nice view," I comment, my attention focused on the people outside reading on the patio area. I wonder if they'd notice were they to look this direction.

"Yes, I was fortunate to score an office with such a good view and lighting. The sunshine that comes through is a wonderful mood lifter." He pauses for a moment to look outside with me. "They can't see inside. The window is tinted so that we have complete privacy." Is he a mind reader as well?

"How did…"

"I get asked that by everyone that's here for the first time," he explains, shrugging as if it's no big deal. "How has your morning gone so far?" Well, that was a quick subject change.

"It's gone," I shrug. I'm not in the mood to open up and talk about my feelings, or whatever it is he's trying to accomplish. It just isn't necessary.

"Are you finding where everything is?"

"Yep, Cheery Chuckie has made sure of that." I huff a short laugh then roll my eyes at the memory of his pounding on my door this morning. I swear, if that becomes an everyday event…

"Chuckie?" he raises a brow as his head cocks to the side. He's holding back a grin that leads me to believe he knows exactly who I'm referring to. Was I given that room on purpose?

"Grant," I clarify, my monotone voice clearly alerting him to how much Cheery Chuckie irritates me. His wide smile only pisses me off more.

"Oh, yes, *Greg,* " he nods as his grin grows. Asshole. "When did you two meet?"

With I sigh, I briefly give him a summary of my morning wake up and breakfast guest.

"He's good at making residents feel at home. I'm sure he'll be glad to help you if you ever have any questions about anything." Oh, he'll most certainly do that, unfortunately.

"Yeah."

"What I have you here for this morning is just a basic meeting where I explain what we'll be doing in our individual sessions, as well as those groups you'll be attending."

The next thirty minutes are spent with him going over rules and expectations for all sessions, what led me to be here and what I hope to gain from this whole experience. I'm sure all of his questions were necessary and innocent, but they felt more like an inquisition than a relaxed conversation.

I'm tired of this day already and could really use a guitar to escape from all these sharing sessions.

Chapter Three

"Finally," I say to myself when I enter the dining hall and find Cheery Chuckie nowhere in sight. I hope it stays this way.

Scoping out my options for lunch, I give in to my stomach and fill my tray with food that looks pretty decent and smells good, too. Finding a small table to myself isn't hard to do seeing as there aren't many people eating this late, so I sit at a smaller one off to the side and away from the other diners. Peaceful silence.

"Is this seat taken?" No sooner had I taken the first bite of my food, than these four words break my self-imposed seclusion. Who could possibly be bothering me now?

Looking from my plate, I'm stunned by the beauty standing in front of me. She's tall and gorgeous with red hair that falls to her ample cleavage and blue eyes that seem to twinkle from the overhead light. She's hot as hell in nothing but faded out jeans and a hockey t-shirt. I'm less irritated by her interruption, but why in the hell does she want to sit with me when there are so many other available tables?

"It's no big deal. I can sit somewhere else," she smiles then starts to turn away.

"No," I hastily object to her leaving, my hand shooting out on its own to catch her by the elbow. "You can sit here." How lame and desperate can I sound? She's probably just some groupie, anyway.

"You sure?" she asks, continuing to smile at me.

"Yeah," I gesture for her to take a seat. "You just surprised me."

"Sorry," she apologizes and sits right next to me. Not at any of the other vacant tables, but right beside me. We're close enough that I can feel her body heat, and her perfume surrounds me completely. It isn't overpowering or bold, more light and airy, but affects me just the same.

"No worries." Yeah, I'm back to one-word sentences due to lack of brain function. What the fuck?

"I saw you yesterday," she says quietly while cutting her spaghetti into near-perfect little squares with a knife and fork. If I didn't find it so damn cute, it'd be weird as hell. For all the time it's going to take to cut it up, I'm not sure she'll have time to eat that huge serving of chocolate mousse she's got on her tray. Why get spaghetti if you're only going to cut it up into mush like you would for a baby?

"Huh?" I reply more focused on what she's doing than our conversation.

"I saw you with Greg," she elaborates, turning her attention from her plate.

"Oh. You going to mash it up next?" I nod to her food with curiosity.

She looks at her spaghetti then back to me and grins. "Kinda crazy, huh?"

"Not if you're a toddler," I tease and she laughs loudly. Apparently, my brain isn't the only thing that loves her laugh, because my pants are all of a sudden not so comfortable. What the hell is wrong with me? "Why do you feel the need to mutilate it like that?"

"I guess it does look that way." She shrugs and her shirt slips to expose her bare, dainty shoulders. The smooth skin that appears has my mouth watering for a taste. "My dad always did it and he would cut it up for me when I was little. I suppose I just keep doing it out of habit."

"You are a weird one, aren't you?"

"Wouldn't be in here if I were normal," she winks and takes a bite of her geometric pasta. Even as unappetizing as she's made it, seeing her mouth wrap around that fork has my pants losing the fight against my growing erection. Since when did spaghetti become sexual food?

"Touché. Why *are* you here?" I've abandoned my own meal, completely infatuated with this gorgeous woman.

Tilting her head to the side and raising a brow, she says, "I'm not sure if I should divulge that information. I mean, I don't really know you or your name." Maybe she doesn't know who I am, after all.

"Kolton," I supply without thought. Can I look any more eager?

"Nice to meet you," she says, looking me over before taking another bite of her food.

"It's good to meet you, too…" I reply, lingering on the last word so that she will give me that information, but she does the opposite and keeps eating. Well played.

"You should eat before your food gets cold," she nods toward the plate in question and smiles as if she didn't just brush me off. Damn if the way she's looking at me doesn't do things to my head. Her angelic smile, while sweet and innocent, hints at something more wild and reckless. My Achilles heel.

"Are you always bossy?" I retort, chuckling at how easily she has me eating out of the palm of her hand, doing what she says willingly. Cutting off a piece of chicken with my fork, I take a bite and eagerly wait for her to answer.

"Depends on what you classify as bossy." She continues eating, unbothered by anything.

"Yeah, I just bet you are." I cut off another piece of chicken to eat and catch her staring at me, brow raised.

"You do, do you?" Her smile is now more of a cat-that-ate-the-canary grin than an angelic one.

"I do," I say confidently. There's definitely more underneath her surface than what she is showing me. I'd bet my life on it.

"Well," she drawls out as her eyes travel up and down me before landing on mine with a wink. "We'll just have to see about that."

"I'm sure we will. Are you going to eat all that?" I point to her dessert with my fork and she grins.

"Chocolate mousse is my favorite," she grins and smacks me on the stomach. "Don't judge me."

Laughing, I rub the offended area and chuckle. "No judgment here," I raise my hand in surrender, grinning like an idiot.

For some stranger that I've just met, this woman has me all in knots and I have no clue as to how or why.

Chapter Four
Day Three

"Fuck my life," I mutter as I enter the designated room for my mandatory group therapy sessions. It's been a long time since my days were this regimented. Even my high school's requirements can't compare to the level of planning this place uses.

Taking a seat just like yesterday, as close to the back of the room as possible, which isn't very far at all, I do my best to ignore the numerous sets of eyes trained on me, the 'new guy'. Can my life get any more embarrassing?

"Hi, I'm Cathy," the older woman a few seats away from me says as she offers her hand for shaking. She's in her mid-forties, if I were to guess, and has a warm smile that offers no pretense or implications of having some ulterior motive in speaking to me.

"Kolton," I offer, accepting her hand and shaking it briefly. I vaguely remember her from therapy yesterday, but I'm sure she wasn't sitting in the back like me. I made sure no one was.

"Nice to meet you," she moves one seat closer to me, yet keeps enough distance between us. It's as if she knows to stay away. "Just ignore them," she discreetly tilts her head to the side, eyes glancing toward the rest of the people in the room. "Their curiosity will be gone by the next group time."

"Thanks," I return her gentle smile. She reminds me of my mom's younger sister; gentle-natured and nurturing to the bone.

"No problem, sweetie. I'm always here if you need anything."

Before I can respond to her kind words, West enters the room wearing the most ridiculous looking outfit I've ever seen. Skinny jeans, a silky white shirt that looks more like a blouse than it should, and pointed dress shoes that resemble women's high heels and not men's loafers. It's beyond bizarre and on his tall, toned frame? I'm wondering why I'm the one in rehab and not him because he has to be higher than a kite to wear that on purpose.

"Good afternoon," West begins before taking his seat in front of everyone. Crossing his legs like a woman, he rests his hands on his lap and sweeps a gaze across the room, eyeing each one of us individually.

"Hello" and "hi" are muttered in response from everyone in the group except me. I'm still wondering what in the hell is going on.

"How is everyone?" he asks and gets the same sort of shortened responses as before. "That's good," he smiles, completely relaxed. This is all too weird.

"Well, now that we have added a few new members, I thought it'd be a good time to introduce ourselves and share a little before we get started. Why don't we start with you, Candace?" He motions to the woman sitting on the front row with giant blonde hair and bright pink lipstick.

"It's Candy," she corrects him sharply with a huff and crosses her arms. Several groans are heard from the group as she and West hold one another's gaze in what must be some sort of challenge. Why she wants to argue about being called Candy is beyond me and I don't care if I ever find out.

West remains mute and she finally gives in with a loud huff. "I'm Candy," she emphasizes, giving him a stubborn glare, chin jutting out in defiance. "And I've been at *Brooks* for a month. Unfortunately," she adds before jerking her head away and toward the side of the room, ignoring West further.

"My name is Carlton," a man on the other side of the room chimes in when it's clear *Candy* is done. "I'm twenty-seven and this is my second time in rehab. I was eighteen the first time and obviously, I didn't really take sobriety seriously." He shrugs with a chuckle from some of the other patients. At least he's honest he's screwed up.

I have no clue how much time passes as others share because I'm constantly wishing I were anywhere but in this god-forsaken place when I notice the talking has stopped and all eyes are expectantly on me. My left leg is shaking rapidly and my brain, which hasn't felt the best since I woke up, is pounding against my skull. These assholes need to mind their own business and look somewhere else. I don't need their stares or judgments.

"Kolton," I finally relent, giving them what they want so they'll leave me the hell alone.

"Hi."

"Hi, Kolton."

"Hey."

Cathy smiles sweetly and gives me a slight nod that I almost miss. Her reassurance isn't needed but appreciated all the same.

"As you can see," my therapist breaks the silence, "we're all here for different reasons. You'll begin to understand that while we all have some sort of addiction, we're no different on the inside. Everyone has their own story of how they got to be here, but each one of you is battling the same thing; addiction."

"Looks like you're dressed for a show," someone calls out, causing everyone to laugh, even me. Glad to know he's not normally dressed like that.

"I suppose it does," he laughs good-humoredly. "But we all have to realize that what we see on the outside when we meet people is just a mask. It's easy to make judgments of others based on what the eye can see. We do it every day when we hear about celebrities doing crazy things or making questionable fashion choices. It's easy to forget that they are people just like us and may possibly be hiding from pain like we are."

"Yeah, I'm sure huge celebrities and actors really have a lot to worry about," one guy scoffs, receiving glares from several other group members. Yeah, this whole thing was a set up from the get-go.

"Oh, shut up," another member snaps. "You're exceptionally cranky today."

"Whatever," he mutters.

West interrupts them before more snide remarks can be made, and I tune it all out. I don't care about their arguing bullshit. I need smoke more than air at the moment, and the sooner I can get this shit over with, the better.

Who am I kidding? I need more than a cigarette at this point to forget all the crazy shit running around in my throbbing head.

Chapter Five
Day Four

"Go away!" I shout at whoever is banging on my door. My head hasn't stopped thumping from yesterday and I feel like vomiting at any moment. Just being awake is nearly more than I can stand.

"Time for breakfast!" Cheery Chuckie's voice filters through my brain, making me groan in irritation. Food is the furthest thing from my mind at the moment.

"Not going!" I yell, more than thankful I had the presence of mind to lock my door last night so he couldn't just barge on in and make himself at home.

"They're having waffles and omelets." He knocks on the door once more and I cover my head with both pillows. Just the thought of sweet, sticky syrup and any form of an egg has my stomach rolling more than it currently is. Maybe if I don't say anything else he'll just leave me alone.

The banging continues a few more times before my jolly new pain in the ass finally decides to leave me be. Relaxing into the sheets, I maneuver myself into the least nauseating position I can find and remain as still as possible to calm my stomach. Falling asleep is going to be the only way I can get rid of this awful feeling.

"Time to wake up, Dickson," an unfamiliar voice penetrates my dreams. Where is it coming from? My covers are lifted from my body and the pillows moved from my head. A strong pat on my back has my eyes opening to see what the hell is going on. "Breakfast time."

"Ugh," I groan when the light in the room is too bright for my eyes to stand. Slamming them shut, I realize my headache hasn't gone away as I'd thought it would. Fuck. "Not hungry," I manage to grumble while burying my head into the mattress.

"Maybe not, but everyone has to attend all meals." The deep voice, although clearer than before, still doesn't give me any indication who this annoying person is and right now I just don't care.

Another pat on the back, much harder than the first, has me turning to glare at the asshole it came from. "Who the fuck are you?" I demand to know. Of course, they have a center uniform on, but my head hurts too much to read what the name badge says. All I know is that a giant of a man is standing before me with his hands folded across his chest and a glare on his face.

"I'll be your worst nightmare if you don't get your ass out of bed and come with me to the dining hall."

"Fine," I grumble and slowly make my way into a sitting position. "It's pretty stupid for me to go when I'm not going to eat anything."

"Doesn't matter to me if you eat or starve. My only concern is that you show your happy face like you're supposed to. Now, get a move on."

"Can I take a piss first?" I snap defiantly coming to stand face to face with him. He's not much taller than me at six-two, so I have no problem looking him right in the eye.

"Be my guest, princess. You've got three minutes." His smug smirk pisses me off.

"Maybe for you," I retort. "Takes me longer than that to get my huge dick out of my pants," I smart off, grabbing my junk and bumping into his shoulder as I head for the small bathroom. Asshole Giant.

As soon as Giant escorts me to the dining hall, I'm greeted by a waving, grinning fool otherwise known as Cheery Chuckie. My luck just gets worse. This day sucks ass already. "I hope we won't meet again under the same circumstances," Giant says, clapping me on the shoulder one last time before leaving me to sit with my welcomer.

"I was hoping you'd get here before I left," he grins as I take a seat across the table from him. It's not far enough away but will have to do.

"Yeah, I had a wake-up call," I mumble trying my best not to inhale too deeply so that the smells of the morning won't make my nausea worse. I'd hate to throw up in front of everyone here, but if it gets that bad, I'm not going to apologize for it. They should have left my ass in bed.

"I figured you would. They don't let anyone miss meals around here, much less any scheduled activities."

"So I'm beginning to learn."

"They do love their routines," he smiles annoyingly and I just want to throat punch him. No real reason other than it'd make me feel better.

"Coffee?" he asks, holding up a coffee carafe and motioning to an empty coffee mug in front of me. Although my usual response would be to consume a whole pot by myself, the mere smell of it makes my stomach cramp even more.

"Not even if my life depended on it," I frown and turn my head to the side and away from the direct coffee smell.

"Ahhh," he nods his head in understanding sympathy. "You've hit the detox stage. Here's some water." He pushes a tall glass of ice water in front of me and I gladly take it, drinking half of it at once. "Hydration is important."

"Whatever," I mutter, taking one last swallow before setting it down on the table.

"You should try to at least eat some crackers. You'll wish you had later."

When I don't reply or make any indication I'm going to eat, he excuses himself to attend a therapy session and promises to catch up with me later in the day. With my elbows on the table, I rest my face in my hands and close my eyes. At least now, I can enjoy the relative quiet the dining hall provides at this late hour.

Chapter Six

"Mind if I join you?" The heavenly voice from the other day interrupts my solitude. My head jerks up and I take in the sight before me. It's *her*.

"Sure," I reply clumsily. This stunning redhead is always knocking me off-kilter.

"You weren't about to leave, were you?" She takes the seat right next to me like she did the first time we sat together. I can feel the warmth from her body against mine and it's oddly soothing.

"Oh, no," I shake my head to reinforce my words. "I was just enjoying the quiet."

"I didn't mean to bother you," she hesitates and I hate that I've made her feel uncomfortable.

"You didn't," I take hold of her wrist to keep her from leaving me. "I had an uninvited wake-up call and escort down here." I roll my eyes at the memory. "Cheery Chuckie was waiting for me and tried to get me to eat."

"Oh, I see." She smiles sympathetically at me and covers my hand on her wrist with a gentle squeeze. "Nothing sounds appealing to your stomach?"

"Exactly."

"I completely understand. But, who is Cheery Chuckie?" She begins spreading cream cheese on a blueberry bagel and I have to look away from her plate before I vomit right on her.

"The guy across the hall from me. He's apparently my self-appointed best friend and newest appendage."

Her laughter, light and melodic, coupled with the angelic grin on her face, has all the blood in my body rushing to my second brain. That's not creepy at all. Shifting in my seat, I turn to get a better look at her beauty.

"You mean Greg, right?" she giggles, taking a sinful bite from her bagel slice. The vision of her wrapping those plump lips around something else had my cock harder than ever, begging to explore her further. I'm such a perv.

"I guess. Pretty sure it starts with a 'g' at least."

"That's him. He's very outspoken, that's for sure."

"That's an understatement," I agree whole-heartedly. "I have no idea why he's attached himself to me."

"Hmmm," she shrugs and takes another bite of her food. "Guess there's just something about you he likes. I seem to find myself looking for you, too." Excuse me?

"You do, huh?" Headache and nausea forgotten, I focus my attention on her as I try and decode what she means.

"Seems that way." Her casualness toward her statement intrigues me.

"So you look for me?" Lame, I know, but I can't help myself.

"Maybe a little," she answers between bites of food. "You really should try to eat something. Even water is crucial right now. Probably help with the headache."

"Okay," I instantly reply. Why does it sound like such a great idea when she says it, but my own mind tells me to stay away from everything?

"You can drink mine," she offers, sliding the glass next to my hand. "I need to grab some milk anyway." She smiles sweetly, then rises from her chair and walks over to the beverage station to get her milk.

Taking the ice water, I take a small sip to test out my stomach's response. The icy cold liquid tastes surprisingly good and I down half the contents by the time she returns to the table. "Taste good?" she grins setting her milk above her plate and another glass of water in front of me.

"Yeah." I take another swallow before setting the glass down. "Thanks for sharing. I didn't mean to drink so much." It's a lame apology, but it looks as if she expected it since she brought me a refill.

"No need to thank me," she giggles. "I know exactly how you feel."

"Yeah, it's no walk in the park, that's for sure."

"No, it isn't, but you seem to be handling it pretty well so far."

"I don't know about that. I was ready to throat punch Chuckie for pounding on my door earlier, and I'm pretty sure he'll do something even more irritating later."

"Maybe," she nods and takes a drink of her milk. "Try some crackers the next time nausea gets the best of you." She takes a package of saltines out of her pocket and lays them beside my hand. "It should help take the edge off."

"Why do you care?" I blurt out, immediately ashamed of how my irritated tone upsets her. I didn't intend to yell, but I did. I don't even know this chick and she's all up in my business like my mom. What's her angle?

Her face changes expressions in a flash, going from to surprise and irritation to anger and indifference. "I don't. Just thought I'd be nice and help out." She wipes her mouth and hands on the napkin and tosses it onto her half-full plate. Standing up, she takes her food tray and looks at me passively, not an ounce of emotion on her gorgeous face. Why in the hell did I have to act like an ass? "Excuse me." She leaves me sitting alone at the table once again as she scurries away to dump her tray and leave the dining hall.

Staring at the exit for far too long, I eventually shake myself out of the stupor I'm in and leave for the safety of my room, the offered crackers in my sweats pocket.

Heart Beats

What the hell is wrong with me?

Chapter Seven
Day Six

"How much more of this group bullshit do I have to sit through?" I snap when West asks me how things are going. I continue pacing in front of his desk, my hands wandering from rubbing my face to tugging at my hair.

"It's required of everyone," he deflects easily. It just pisses me off.

"Why would anyone want to air out their dirty laundry for the world to hear?"

"That's not what they're doing."

"I don't care. All of their incessant rambling drives me out of my mind. If I didn't already drink, they'd make me start."

"Drinking doesn't solve everything. Neither does cocaine."

"Sure doesn't hurt it."

"That's not what your record company thinks."

"Fuck you!" I wander over to the window and stare past the wandering patients into the tree line behind them. If I hadn't been in the front seat when Aiden drove me here, I'd never know I was in California. There's nothing but trees as far as the eye can see.

West remains quiet as I watch him write in his notebook from the corner of my eye. I bet that just gave him a shitload to report. My hands are shaking so badly, I shove them in my pockets to keep from pulling my hair out. I've tugged at it enough that my scalp is nearly raw. I can't help it. My muscles ache so deeply, I feel as if I'm about to be ripped apart from the inside out. I'd probably give my left nut for a hit of something right now. At least, I wouldn't hurt like a motherfucker.

"Why don't we talk about how you got to be here? You were pulled over for running a stop sign near the police department of all places and nearly hit another vehicle." Yeah, let's talk about that because it's the *happiest* topic of conversations you can have that concern me.

I refuse to discuss this.

"Not only were you drunk, but you also had small amounts of marijuana and cocaine in your pockets."

Still not talking about this shit.

"How long have you been using, Kolton?"

Using what?

"Marijuana may be legal in this state, but you can't smoke it in your car. You were holding a lit blunt when the officers pulled you over."

Stating the facts to get me to talk, are we? Not happening. I can stand here for the whole hour and not say a damn word. It's not exactly like I can focus well, anyway.

"Damn, I need a smoke," I mutter to myself and resume my pacing.

West continues to recite all the details of my arrest and incarceration. Incarceration. I never thought I'd use that word to describe myself. Then again, my step-father never failed to remind me how much I was like my good-for-nothing, always-in-trouble sperm-donor. I'm sure he's really proud to boast he was right about me all along.

A loud noise brings me back to the present and I stop walking. Turning around I see West stand from his leather desk chair. "That's it for today." He moves around the desk to stand beside me. "I know you're having a hard time with the withdrawal right now, but things will get easier. You just have to want it badly enough." He slaps me on the shoulder and gives me a sympathetic smile.

"You have no fuckin' idea," I snap, brushing out of his hold and leaving his office as fast as possible. All I need right now is a long nap before I hit someone.

Two hours of tossing and turning is all I'm allowed before a staff member is knocking on my door to remind me of activity time. Activity time is just a polite way to say forced socialization. Cheery Chuckie has, of course, appointed himself my activity partner. I've endured a lousy game of ping pong, a doubles game of pool and a two-hour workout in the gym that nearly killed me. Between the treadmill and rower, I nearly threw up all over the equipment. My so-called partner either didn't have a clue, or he just didn't care I was about to die.

"There's a basketball court outside. I thought we could shoot some hoops." Chuckie's eagerness to run around bouncing a ball for hours has me groaning on the inside. I swear he's only here to torment me.

Before I can give my opinion, I'm distracted by the beautiful sound of a piano coming from the sitting room. Without thought, I turn away from him and follow the soothing melody that's caught my full attention. Rounding the corner to where the music is coming from, I'm halted in my tracks to see who's playing such a mesmerizingly haunting song.

Her. Lunch girl.

"She's pretty good," my shadow says from behind me as I stare at her, completely entranced.

Good doesn't even describe her performance. The way her whole body moves with every note played is beautiful in itself, much like a private ballet. She's pouring all her emotion into every key she touches. Not only is it visible, but I can feel it in my bones. It's soul-tugging. Ethereal, even. I've never heard this song before.

"Everyone loves it when she plays, that's why there are so many people in the sitting room. Sarah doesn't do it as often as she used to, though. I suppose she doesn't really like having an audience."

I'm surprised she's even aware of the people around her. She seems to be totally engrossed in her music. It reminds me of my own time spent playing guitar and my hands flex of their own accord. My gut twists in response to missing the feel of it in my hands.

Her heartfelt melody stirs something deep inside I haven't felt before.

Chapter Eight

"Sarah." I let the name fall off my lips in an almost silent prayer, hoping for some insight into the beauty that's invaded my mind.

When she's finished with her song, the patients who've gathered to listen begin applauding. This sudden jolt of noise causes Lunch Girl's head to turn my direction. Her eyes widen to expose those icy blue irises of hers to my gaze. I'm mesmerized.

Instead of the smile I expect to receive, she frowns and looks around the room nervously. Sensing that she's about to make an escape, I quickly head to cut her off.

"Sarah."

My call stops her in her tracks, and she looks over her shoulder as I come to stand beside her. "Wait." I reach out to hold her hand but stop myself.

"What do you want?" She's aggravated with me and I can't say that I blame her. I wasn't the nicest person the last time we talked.

How do I say *I'm sorry, your playing was mesmerizing*, and *I want to taste all of you* without sounding like some freak who just got out of an all-boys Catholic school?

"Can we go somewhere," I shrug a shoulder nervously, "and talk?" She looks me over and glances once around the room before nodding slightly.

"Yeah," she mumbles and motions her head for me to follow her outside. I happily walk behind her through the French doors and over to an isolated bench near the back of the center's garden area. Even though it's a nice, sunny day, not as many residents are taking advantage of the grounds as I expected.

Taking our seats on each end of the small, concrete bench, we sit in silence for a few moments before I take the initiative and speak first.

"Look, I just wanted to apologize for being such a jerk a few days ago. I don't know what came over me, but you didn't deserve any of what I said or did." Far from it. She deserves so much more than I can ever give her, I just know it.

Questioning vibrant-blue eyes study my face and I feel more uncomfortable than ever. It feels like she's seeing past my flesh and bone and down into my soul, however twisted and damaged it may be. Her brilliant gaze holds me captive as I wait for her to dismiss my apology and decide I'm not worth her time. She'd be right.

"You were such an ass," she chastises me, a hint of a smile tugging at the corner of her delicate, pink gloss covered mouth. So kissable.

"Completely," I readily admit. My eager confession has her fighting to stifle a small giggle and she's so damn cute I can't resist reaching to brush my fingers over her shiny red hair with the pretense of wiping away a stray lock. Her hair isn't mussed by the slight breeze, but she doesn't have to know that.

"I suppose I can accept your apology." She releases her smile on me and it takes my breath away. "I should have remembered you're still new here and haven't detoxed completely. I know I wasn't exactly Miss Congeniality when I first got here, either."

"Yeah, I'm still not so pleasant most of the time right now, but I find it hard to believe you were ever anything like me. I know I'm an ass on a good day." My comment makes her laugh and it's nearly as entrancing as her music. I have an overwhelming urge to keep her this way, smiling and happy.

"I don't know about that, but I was a real bitch," she tells me, her face turning pink in embarrassment. "I hated everyone and everything and wasn't afraid to let it be known." She shakes her head and grimaces. "That feels like so long ago." Her voice is softer now and I wonder just how long she's been here and what her story is.

"I can relate," I sympathize to keep her talking. "My being here is all bullshit."

Her brows raise as she cocks her head to the side. "Oh, really?"

"Yeah. I don't have the problem everyone seems to think I do. I've just got shitty luck." Sarah bursts into full-on belly laughing, doubling over with her arms hugging her waist. She's all but snorting. It's quite a sight and has several residents looking in our direction.

"Wasn't that funny," I chuckle along.

"No, but that's the classic response," she giggles. "Didn't peg you as normal." Her amused grin is cute as fuck.

"I'm far from normal, sweetheart." She giggles again.

"Again, classic answer."

She's a tough one, but I like a challenge.

"So I suppose you're here for a different, less expected reason?"

"Oh, no," she beams. "I'm totally a classic rehab candidate."

"I didn't peg you as normal," I throw her words right back, smirking as I raise my own eyebrows and tilt my head to match hers. Fuck, I'm so lame.

"I guess I should have seen that coming," she replies with a smile.

The sun high in the sky behind her puts this glowing halo of sorts around her head as if she were an angel. I suppose in a way she is, having pulled my complete attention from running rampant to focusing solely on her.

Maybe I'm just losing my damned mind.

Chapter Nine

"So, Sarah, tell me how you get to vacation here at *Brooks*."

"Figured out my name, did you?" She flashes me another beautiful smile, one I'm becoming more addicted to each time she shares it with me.

"Chuckie," I refer to my instant friend. "He said you don't play as often now as you did in the beginning." Please tell me everything about you.

Sarah's smile falters then she looks away at something across the garden. Silence falls between us and it's unnerving how much I care about upsetting her. It's just like me to screw things up right after apologizing for being an idiot the first time.

"I didn't mean," I begin, scooting closer to her, but she interrupts me mid-sentence.

"Greg's right." She glances at me then back to whatever it is she's found to concentrate on. "I started playing the piano when I was a kid, about three years old. My grandmother had an organ and whenever I was there for a visit, she'd play it for me." She looks briefly at me and back to the garden.

"Seems like you two were close," I say only to get a small headshake in response.

"Not really. Both my dad's parents were a lot older than my mom's parents were. I guess they had my dad a lot later than usual for that time. Going to their house for a simple visit was way more formal than it should have been for family."

"Like, you had to call them certain names?" I can't imagine addressing my grandparents anything other than grams and pops, or at the very least mamaw and papaw.

"Oh, no. That wasn't an issue, although I'm not too certain she really liked being called mamaw."

"Isn't that what grandmothers want?" I know mine sure did.

"You'd think so, but I always got the feeling that it wasn't her first choice," she shrugs and frowns indifferently.

"That sucks," I say more out of disbelief than sympathy.

"Whatever. Anyway, she'd get out the songbooks from the piano bench and play away while I listened to her sing each song."

"What songs?"

"Oh, these were church hymns," she turns her attention to me then continues. "She even had one book with Christmas songs. You know, the really popular ones like, *Oh, Christmas Tree, Jolly Old Saint Nicholas,* and *Silent Night.* That was my favorite."

"The book?"

"Yep. It had *The First Noel.* It always called to me for some reason."

"That's not a typical song you hear at Christmas. I only heard it when we were at church," I add, the memory of my grandma straightening my tie before we entered the church coming to mind. She always tried to lick my stray hair into place and I hated it. What ten-year-old in their right mind wants granny spit in their hair? My ass sure as hell didn't.

"No, you don't hear it too often, but it was the first song I taught myself to play. Granted, it was only the melody, but I did it. The book was more of a beginner's one, and she taught me where middle C was on the music and keys. Eventually, I figured the rest out on my own. It was all top hand, but I would play it over and over again until she decided I'd played enough for the day."

"So, then you started lessons?" I'm so invested in her story, in *her*, that I have no concept of time. I only want to hear everything she wants to confide in me.

"Yeah," she sighs heavily. "My parents were thrilled to have what they considered to be a prodigy on their hands. Sent me to all kinds of lessons every day, sometimes twice, and I had to practice even more."

"Damn, that must have sucked all the fun out of it." Why are some parents so inconsiderate of how their children feel and put their own desires first?

"Oh, I absolutely loved it in the beginning. Just being able to play actual music instead of simply listening to it made me so happy," she smiles thoughtfully. It's as if she's a young child all over again while she relives that feeling just by talking about it. I know how that feels.

"Being able to make your own music come alive has a freeing quality that nothing else can provide."

"Yes, it does. You know something about that?"

"A little," I nod. I'm not too sure to what extent I want to share about myself even with how much her mere presence calls me to do just that.

"You should play sometime. It might help," she suggests. "It helps me sort through my thoughts."

"Maybe I'll try it sometime," I nudge her shoulder with mine. "What were you thinking through?"

Sarah lies her head gently on my shoulder and I'm thrilled by the action. The touch of her body on mine, even through our clothes, feels amazing. She smells so delicious, a combination of cinnamon and flowers, that I lean my cheek on her head to better indulge in her arousing scent.

"How I'm going to handle seeing my parents when I get out of here."

"You think it will be hard?"

"Wouldn't you?"

"Guess it depended on how much their opinions mattered to me. Right now, I wouldn't give a shit."

"Oh, I'm finally at peace with how they see me, but it's still not something I'm looking forward to. It'll be the 'same' them with the 'new' me."

"There's that," I agree. We fall silent in our own thoughts, and I'm brought back to Aiden's parting words on my first day here.

Have faith.

I don't know about faith, but I'm pretty sure things can't get any worse.

Chapter Ten
Two Days Later

"You've been spending a lot of time with Sarah," West notes at the beginning of my hour-long session.

It's been three days since my apology, and we've found ourselves doing more and more activities together. She's encouraged me to spend time in the gym when my body's craving for cocaine and any other drug I could get my hands on becomes too much. Sure, Chuckie and West suggested I try working it out of my system, but they don't make me *want* to do anything but throat punch them for being so damn...cheerful.

I glance his way, roll my eyes like a child, and look back out the window. The birds playing in the bird bath are more entertaining than this little interrogation. I think he's still talking to me, but all I can think about is that cardinal flying about over the other smaller birds playing in the water. He's taunting them, flying down to scare them out of his way only to pull away at the last minute and regain altitude above them. The more they scatter, the more he seems to enjoy it.

Suddenly, it's me looking down over all those who insist I have a problem that needs intervention. I'm daring them to push me out of their group and chirping loudly in delight when they flee in response. Fuck! If only I could simply fly my ass outta here, right over the perimeter fences and back to my life.

"Kolton." West nearly yells my name in order to snap my attention away from that wonderful daydream of flight. I turn my head in his direction and stare. "Wasting my time in these sessions isn't helping you get closer to leaving. In fact," he clears his throat and narrows his gaze, "it's only prolonging your stay."

"Why does everyone insist I have this huge drug problem that needs months of torturous intervention?" I bark back, my body twisting so that I face him completely. "I got caught smoking pot while driving," I shrug my shoulders. "Big fucking deal," I shake my hands in the air like I'm some cheerleader showing off her jazz hands. "I'm sure not the only one," I argue.

"That may be so, but you're the one who got pulled over for reckless driving while doing it. Not to even mention you had cocaine, which is not legal *anywhere*, in your possession."

"Whoopty-fuckin'-do, I smoke pot!" My hands flop around in the air in exasperation at this stupid cycle of round-and-round we always seem to do when I'm in here. "Doesn't make me an addict, or mean that I have a problem." How in the hell is it so damn cold in here? It's June for crying out loud. I shove my hands in my pockets in order to warm them up as much as possible until I can leave this office.

"No, but it's apparently not doing much for you if you're turning to cocaine to feel any effects. You can't see the way it's effecting you. That is a problem."

I remain silent as we stare at one another, neither willing to budge from our arguments. It's so freaking cold in here, my hands are stiff, and my arms are beginning to tense and jerk from the coolness in the air.

"Feeling chilly?" he asks, a small smirk tugging at the corner of his mouth.

"No," I deny quickly, but my voice wavers in betrayal.

"Let's see," he begins, tossing his notepad on top of the desk. "You've been nauseous, had muscle pain and fatigue. There have also been night terrors and now, you're getting chills." He's smug in his assessment or evaluation of my behavior for the past two weeks. I'd like to knock that cocky look right off his face. How in the hell does he know about my dreams? I haven't even mentioned them to Sarah, and I've shared the most with her.

I'm fine. He's delusional.

"Classic withdrawal symptoms of cocaine and other drugs." His flat, matter-of-fact voice grates on my nerves and I hate him for it.

"What do you want?"

"I want to help, but I can only do that if you want me to."

A knock on the door interrupts the tenseness that's suddenly developed. West gives me one last glance before walking away from his desk and answering the door. Hushed tones precede his stepping outside to deal with whatever is going on. Finally alone, I'm stuck with his words banging around in my head.

"What do I want?" I say the words aloud and walk over to the window that always has my attention. The birds are no longer fighting for time in the birdbath, the cardinal nowhere to be seen, and I'm envious of its freedom.

They're all wrong. I do not have a problem.

Chapter Eleven
Two weeks later

"I love it when you moan my name," I grumble against Sarah's neck as I slide my cock between her warm, wet core. My teeth nip and bite their way to her ear as I move in response to her inner muscles squeezing my shaft with enough force to hurt, but it only urges me on. There has never been a better feeling than when we're together like this, naked and vulnerable.

"Right... there," she instructs between breaths. The feel of her hot breath on my shoulder turns me on even more if that's actually possible, and I repeat the action she demands, pulling in and out of her at just the right angle to hit the spot she needs for release. Hearing her get off on what I'm doing is the best sound in the world. It's better than a riffed-out guitar solo or any high you can get from cocaine. I crave it.

"I'll never get tired of this," I moan when she shifts to wrap her long, silky legs from around my waist to straddle my shoulders. I'm so deep inside her I may pass out from the euphoria it creates. Thank fuck she's so limber.

It doesn't take many more thrusts before we both find what we need. Collapsing on top of her, I bury my face against the column of her delicate neck. She smells like flowers and sweat and sex and I could never smell another thing for the rest of my life and die happy. I'm in complete and utter heaven.

A bump to my shoulder jolts my attention back to the present and away from the dream I had last night. Damn, if it wasn't the best dream ever.

"So, did you sleep better last night?" Sarah repeats the question that triggered my little daydream episode. She's not quite sure whether to smile or frown and her expression is cute as fuck.

Rubbing my hands over my face, I release a deep breath before answering. "Still no bad dreams," I reply. She doesn't need to know that I woke up sexually frustrated from the naked time dream I had of us together. That's only for me and the shower to know about.

"That's great," she cheers, her smile as radiant as ever as we sit at a patio table by the indoor pool. The more time we've spent with each other over the past few weeks, the more my attraction to her has grown. I'm pretty sure she feels it, too, since she's always finding ways for us to spend time alone. Well, as alone as we can be under strict supervision from the staff. This place might be one of the nicer, laid-back rehab centers around, but they're not lax on the no-fraternization policy, gay or straight.

"Yeah, a good night's sleep is always better." I take her hand in mine when I'm sure no one is looking in our direction.

"I wish we were any place but here," she sighs and leans closer to me.

Taking the opportunity and living dangerously, I steal a quick kiss from her pouty mouth. It's nothing compared to what I'd like to do, but I'll take what I can get for now.

"Uhm," she pouts, her bottom lip sticking out. We both lean forward and touch our foreheads together. She's just as frustrated as I am about our situation.

"When we're both out of here, I'm going to take you away for a long, overdue vacation, just the two of us," I promise, meaning every word.

"Kol," she sighs her nickname for me as she leans back in her chair. Everyone else I know shortens it to Kolt. She's the only one to ever use that one and it pleases me to no end. "We come from two very different places."

"Of course, we do. So what?"

"You'll go back to your music and I'll go back to mine. Besides," she looks down to her hands that are picking at the hem of her light pink tee.

"Besides, what?" I lean back in my chair and fold my arms in front of me. She continues to look between me and her hands. "Tell me," I demand, careful not to raise my voice and have our conversation overheard.

"You're the lead singer of a hot new band. I'm just a pianist. Our worlds just won't mix well."

"You don't know that," I bark back with more heat than I intend.

"You'll be traveling on tours and all that goes with it. I live in a different city. We'd never make it work. Don't you see that?"

She has a mostly valid argument, but I'll be damned if I let something like distance come between us. Things like locations and schedules can be worked out. She has to understand that.

"You don't even think it's worth the try?"

"We barely know each other, Kolton."

"You know everything about me." In the past weeks, I've shared everything with her; my childhood, my parents, my screw-ups. There's just something about her, hell, between us, that wouldn't let me hide anything from her. "I have nothing to hide from you."

"A relationship will only complicate the already complicated. Can't you see that?"

"No, I don't." She shakes her head and glances toward the far side of the pool where several residents are heading inside for whatever idiotic activity the center has planned for today. "All I know is that this thing between us is important. It's real, and fuck no am I going to let it be dismissed as if it were an unwanted phone call."

"That's not what I'm saying," she begins to argue, but I interrupt her from spewing some lame-ass excuse.

"Bullshit," I lean my arms on the patio between us and lower my voice. "Don't rush to conclusions about us before we even get in that situation. Just take it day by day with me. That's all I ask."

I hold her gaze for an endless minute before quickly scanning the area for prying eyes.

"Day by day, huh?" she asks with a grin fighting to spill across her beautiful face.

"Yeah," I lean in closer. She giggles briefly, then covers her smile. "I guess I actually did listen to something West said, after all." Giggles turn into full-body laughter and I can't help but join in. "Don't let him hear that, though," I warn with failed authority.

"Never," she promises, saluting like a private on his first day in boot camp.

She doesn't know it, and I'm just coming to terms with it, myself, but she has the power to break me.

Chapter Twelve
One week later

"Knock, knock!"

That cheery voice can only belong to one person. Chuckie. I wonder what brings him to my room this time. He's over here at least five times a day, sometimes more, and there's never any guessing what his reason will from one visit to the next. He needs a hobby.

"Yeah," I call out, but he doesn't wait for me to answer and walks right on in like he lives here. Assuming bastard.

"Hey, man." He walks up to where I'm exercising and leans down to clap me on my upper back with a smile. "You have a package up front," he tosses his thumb over his shoulder toward the front desk area. What?

"Package?"

"Yep," he nods. "Pretty big one, too. Looks like a guitar or something." He shakes his head. "I didn't know you played."

"Guitar?" I forget the sit-ups I'm doing and rise up to stand before him. "It's a guitar?"

"Looks like one to me," he shrugs. How can it be?

My curiosity gets the better of me, and before I realize what I'm doing, I'm rushing out of the room and down the hall, Chuckie completely left behind. Passing several residents who are milling around, I barely avoid knocking over a cleaning cart. I shouldn't get my hopes up too high, but the thought of getting my baby back is too much to handle. I haven't felt whole without it.

Arriving at the desk I don't see anything remotely close to what Chuckie described. If this was some lame joke, I'll kill him. "I have a package," I tell the woman at the desk when she smiles up at me.

"Yes, Mr. Dickson. Your counselor actually just left with it. He was going to give it to you himself."

"I didn't pass him on my way here."

"Oh, you probably didn't. He was taking it to his office to get it out of the way up here because of its size."

"Thanks. I'll go find him."

"You're welcome, dear." She returns my smile and resumes whatever work she has on her computer. Wasting no time, I hurry to West's office while silently praying what Chuckie said is true. Being without my baby for so long is unexplainable torture.

Rounding the corner to West's office, I take a minute to calm the hell down and get control of my eagerness before it gets me into trouble. Even if there is a guitar, there's no guarantee it's for me.

"Kolton," he greets as he opens his door. "I was just coming to get you." His smile is wide as he opens his door further and steps to the side to let me enter.

"Hey," I nod and take my usual seat by the desk. Off to the side, I can see an instrument case leaning against the wall. It looks just like the one holding my baby. My hands are itching to open the case and take her out, but I refrain...just barely.

He walks around me and to the object of my attention, picking it up carefully and handing it over to me. "I talked with your agent, Mr. Marshall, a few days ago. He asked if he could be allowed to drop this off for you. He and your friends were adamant that this would help your recovery."

The guys are worried about me after I screwed things up? My gaze jerks from the case to him and he continues to speak.

"After some consideration, I came to the same conclusion that this could be useful. You haven't truly opened up and addressed the important issues, so I thought maybe you could use a little reminding of what's at stake.

That you could decide what you really want to happen while you're here and when you get out."

"Thank you." It's simple and to the point, and exactly what I feel. I'm thankful he took my music into consideration. Most people think musicians are separate from the music they create, but that is far from the truth. People like us live and breathe melodies and compositions and lyrics. It's just who we are as a whole. You can't have one without the other.

"You're welcome. You may not think it's true, but I'm also a musician and understand how it feels to be alone and without the one thing that's part of you." Wait, he's a musician, too? I've never gotten that vibe from him. Ever.

"You play?" I ask with undisguised surprise.

"Saxophone. All through junior high and high school." His amused grin is light and easy, quite the contradiction to how I've always seen him.

"Huh. Never would have guessed that," I comment, looking at my counselor in a new light. Maybe he does understand me more than I give him credit for.

"Most people don't. Wrong assumptions and stereotypes. Therapists can't possibly do anything creative because they're so analytical. I've heard it all," he shrugs with an indifferent smirk.

"Yeah," I agree lamely. I'm kinda dumbfounded by this whole discovery. "You still play?"

"The town where I live has a small community orchestra. I play with them whenever I can, doing all kinds of performances for different things throughout the year. We even play at some of the schools."

"That sounds pretty interesting." I've never given any thought to doing anything like that.

"I enjoy it," he agrees. "Kolton, use this opportunity to really think about why you're here and where you eventually want to be. Music is as big a part of you as it is me, so let it help heal you, too." He's right. Music has always helped center me and find a way to sort through my thoughts.

I haven't been doing a lot of that in the past year, though. Recording and moving to California has taken up most of my time. Looking back at it all, I can see now that I've gotten too far outta my own head and forgotten to take time to breathe. If I'm this fucked up after only a year and before our first tour, what in the hell would I be like after several years pass?

Opening the case, I gaze upon my favorite guitar and run my fingers along the fretboard, the feel of the strings against my skin filling me with a sense of contentment I've been lacking.

It's just you and me, baby.

Chapter Thirteen
A few days later

"Wow, I didn't realize you could play that well," Chuckie says from my left as I quietly strum away on a song that's been running through my mind a lot the last few days.

Between therapy and required meals and activities, I've spent most of my time outside in the warm, pleasant sunshine. There's a little bench in the shade in the back garden that gives me the freedom to play without too many witnesses while soaking up some much-needed vitamin D. I don't mind playing for crowds; love it, actually, but that's not what I want right now.

"Thanks," I reply not looking up from my instrument. Hopefully, if I ignore him, he'll soon leave me be.

"Don't worry about your band," he says lowly, the usual happy-go-lucky tone gone from his voice. This gets my attention and I look up at him. "You'll get everything sorted out and be on the road touring before you know it." He looks at me earnestly, hands in his pockets and shoulders slumped.

What. The. Hell?

"I've known who you were, although I've only really heard you sing," he declares bluntly. "I'm a huge fan from before you were even signed with Back Door Records."

"How?"

"Youtube is an amazing thing. You get to hear all sorts of bands without having to travel to see them. I stumbled on one of *Crash's* videos one night and have been a fan ever since."

"Thanks, man."

He shrugs his shoulders and gives me a small smile. "Look, I'm no music authority, but I know what I like, and your band is great. You guys have a real shot at making it big. This little addiction," he pauses to look around at our surroundings. "It's not gonna be easy, but you can shake it. I did, and I was way worse off than you were or are."

"I'm gonna try," I confess, getting a small nod in return. He then does an about-face and walks off across the grassy lawn and leaves me alone once again.

"What the fuck was that?" I mutter quietly as I watch him walk away. He confuses the hell out of me.

Shaking my head and forgetting about that weird exchange, I start playing my own version of *Somewhere Over the Rainbow*. I'm halfway through the first verse when a beautiful, angelic voice begins to sing along.

"Where trouble melts like lemon drops..."

My fingers continue to play as I look up to find Sarah standing there, a sweet smile gracing her already gorgeous face as she sings. I was so absorbed in the song I didn't notice anyone approaching. Smiling as she sings, she quietly takes a seat beside me and continues to sing as I play. She catches every little change in key and tempo I make, never missing a single note. She's amazing.

"That was a great twist," she grins excitedly when we finish our duet. I've never played for anyone like that, especially a girl, and it was beyond anything I expected. It's like she read my mind whenever I changed something or took the song a different direction.

"You were fucking amazing, babe." Her cheeks blush a bright pink as she lowers her head to look at her hands in her lap. She can't take a compliment for anything.

"I was okay," she concedes her fingers twisting together. Why is she nervous? "I've never sung with anyone like that," she confesses softly.

"A duet?"

She nods and says, "Never, really. I don't usually sing unless I'm alone."

"Why is that? Your voice is amazing."

"I was always the one playing the music. No one ever thought about me singing, I guess."

"Well," I lean closer to get a better smell of her perfume. It drives my libido insane, but I do it anyway. "That's their loss and my gain."

"Like that isn't the biggest line ever," she giggles, and I love to hear her so happy. That I made her laugh. "You're the singer, not me."

"It's true, though." If she were singing to me in a crowd, I'd thrown some clothing at her.

"You might be a little biased."

"Nope. Here, sing this with me." I start strumming the intro to *True Colors*. It's become more popular recently from some kids movie who used it, but I know it as an old Cyndi Lauper song from the '80s. As soon as she catches on to what song it is, she hums along.

"You with the sad eyes, don't be discouraged," we sing in unison, a perfect harmony that sounds as if we've performed together for years and not for the first time.

Our duet continues through each line verse and chorus, perfectly in harmony and the chemistry between us grows more intense with each note we sing. This song, while already heartfelt and soulful, seems to say more for the two of us. We're letting the other know that even through the times when it seems like we're insignificant, we'll always have the other to count on. It's a declaration that regardless of what persona we have to wear for the rest of the world, we will always see the real person inside the façade.

"I'll always be there when you need me," I promise when the song is over.

"Going to save the damsel in distress, eh?" Her amused grin doesn't fool me. My statement unsettles her even though I know her feelings are the same. She's proven it over the mere weeks I've known her.

"You're no damsel," I shake my head and she raises her brows in disbelief. "You're stronger than that."

The defensive pose she has softens and she gives me that magnificent smile I've come to crave. "Only you would say that. My parents don't think I'm so strong."

"They don't know you as well as I do," I lean in closer and run my nose along her cheek while no one is looking.

"They have known me all my life," she argues, but it's half-hearted at best.

"They know what they want to see. You're more amazing than they could ever hope for. That's what I see." Fuck her parents. They have no clue how special their daughter is, but I see it.

"Well," she starts to reply but the alarm on my watch goes off, signaling me it's almost time for group.

"Sorry," I apologize, hastily turning it off.

"No problem," she giggles. "You'd better go before you're late again. West will put you in detention," she teases. I have been late more than a few times and he's not going to accept it for much longer. It's the reason I've resorted to setting an alarm. I don't know what I'd do if my watch didn't have one.

With a quick glance around the mostly empty garden, I hastily place a kiss on Sarah's lips and stand up. Shifting my instrument in my hands, I turn to face her. "Meet me for dinner?" She rolls her eyes and grins.

"Do you have to ask? We've only eaten dinner together every night for the past three weeks."

"Just checking," I wink and head to the main building.

Just another day of faking my way through therapy, doing as little as possible, in order to keep up my good patient image. What's one more persona, right?

Chapter Fourteen
Group

"Kolton," West greets me when I enter the room. His smile is wide and full of shock when he notices I'm not late.

"West," I nod and take my usual seat the farthest away from everyone. They've learned by now that I prefer it that way. Well, except for Cathy. She's the only one not afraid to speak to or sit by me. Frankly, she's the only one I can tolerate in this whole group. Everyone else just grates on my nerves to the point I want to throat punch them. I don't know why, but that's how it is.

When everyone is here, West begins the usual 'how is everyone' and 'does anyone have anything they'd like to share' routine. We sit through a few people sharing about some of the experiences that got them here and how they now look at the situations, but I'm mostly thinking about how things are going with the band while I'm stuck in here.

Fifteen minutes into the hour, there's a knock on the door. We're all curious as to why someone is there since interruptions are usually prohibited unless there is an emergency of some sort.

"For the rest of our time today," West begins, "we'll be joined by a resident who's here to share their experiences with addiction and how treatment has affected how they deal with tough situations now." He walks to the door and ushers the knocker inside.

My heart stops when I see Sarah enter and take a seat near where West sits at the front of the room. What is she doing here and why didn't she mention it before?

"Hi," she addresses the room. "I'm Sarah, and I am dealing with addiction." She doesn't appear to be nervous and I have to wonder if she's done this before.

"Hi, Sarah," the group welcomes her almost in unison.

"I'm from a very affluent family that gave me everything I could have ever wanted, but not everything I needed. I started playing piano at a very early age and when my parents saw how good I was, they spared no expense to make sure I had the best teachers and lessons money could buy. I was so excited that I could learn to play the songs instead of just listening to them so playing every day didn't seem so bad in the beginning. I mean, what kid wouldn't love to do something they really like all the time, right?"

Her smile is infectious, and most everyone in the room is returning it, completely entranced with every word she speaks. I know I am, but for different reasons.

"As I got older, I began to notice how much they weren't really around. I went to a private school and saw the other kids talking about trips they took with their parents and the things they liked to do outside. I never really got to play outside like them and my parents certainly didn't take me anywhere fun. I was always the show pony. The prize possession they brought out for company or when they wanted to impress my dad's politician friends. He loved to brag about the titles and scholarships I'd won whenever they were near. It made his own political career even shinier and furthered his own ambitions. It was never about how proud he was of me."

"That's awful," Cathy chimes in, her head shaking in disapproval just like the other residents. Me? I'm livid. My own childhood wasn't exactly one to gloat about, but at least I got to do normal things. For the most part, anyway. When I finally meet her parents, because I will at some point, I'm not sure I'll be able to hold my tongue and be polite.

My angel's cheerful expression falters for a moment before resuming its optimism. I hate the fact that I can't hold her hand while she's spilling out her life story, but that wouldn't bode well for either of us. Damn fraternization policy.

"When I got to high school, drugs were easy to find. I'd heard enough talk about how they let you forget..." her voice trails and I dying to know what has her so quiet. I want to kill those demons for her.

"It's okay," West softly encourages her.

"Sorry," she apologizes needlessly. It's not like we don't all have baggage to deal with. "Needless to say, I took full advantage of what was available. Prescription or otherwise, it didn't matter. It gave me a break from all the pressure they placed on my success. By this time, they had me entering all kinds of competitions and when I didn't do so well, they'd lecture me and shove more practice my way. It didn't matter if I wanted a break or not. I did what they expected me to. As I'm sure most of you know, that only made my addictions worse."

Everyone nods in agreement, some mumbling their thoughts of sympathy.

"How did you finally end up here?" a guy near the front speaks up.

"Very much the same way most of you did, I assume. I hit rock bottom. I was in my third year of college and showed up higher than a kite for a piano lesson. Long story short, my high-priced instructor was blessed with quite the show. Got an earful, too. I'd just been informed that instead of attending a class trip to Europe for an English credit, I would have to stay in the States and perform for some event my parents were throwing."

"That blows," the same guy calls out among disgruntled comments and remarks from the group. I'm pissed. I had no idea it was that bad. I mean, she's told me most of this already, but the description of what her parents did to her wasn't this detailed. How can anyone treat her like that?

"It is what it is," she shrugs, smile still in place.

"I bet they were more worried about their reputation than your health," a woman grumbles.

"Unfortunately," she replies. "But I've learned how to deal with that. It took a while, but I've finally realized I'm old enough to decide what I want to do with my life. If that means leaving them behind, so be it. I'm responsible for my own happiness. Just like you are. You just have to make the choice to do whatever it takes to find it." Her eyes catch mine and linger there for a few stolen moments before she returns her attention to the rest of the room.

It's at this point that she begins answering questions from everyone and they continue for the rest of the hour. Her last words hit home and I'm left with them rattling around in my head.

If I'm responsible for making my own happiness, then what the hell am I going to do about it?

Chapter Fifteen
Three days later

"Where the hell are you?" I mutter while searching the common room for something, anything to keep myself occupied until it's time for my session with West.

It's been three days since the last time I saw Sarah. After she appeared in my group therapy session, we had lunch and spent some time outside singing together as I played the guitar. We talked more about her parents and she urged me to give rehab a fair shot.

"You have to deal with things and let them go," she'd said. She had some good arguments, but I'm not concerned about that at the moment.

I want to know why she didn't tell me she was leaving. Why she didn't inform me it was her time to be released. I didn't get to say goodbye or have the chance to make plans with her for when it's my time to blow this joint.

I give up and am on my way back to my room when I run into Cathy as she's entering the dining hall.

"You look stressed," she says, her motherly nature kicking in. I haven't slept well since I first realized Sarah was gone. She's looking me over, her eyebrows furrowed as she frowns at what she sees. I'm sure I look like shit, but I haven't felt this defeated since I first got here.

"I'm fine," I dismiss her worrying, smiling as best I can. She doesn't buy it, though, and shakes her finger in my face.

"Don't try that with me, Kolton. I know you better than that." With a hand on my arm, she moves us to the side of the entrance and continues. "It's a girl, isn't it?"

"What?"

"Who is she?"

"No, it's not a girl. Why are you saying that?" How in the hell did she know? I haven't ever talked to her about anything that personal, especially something that could get me into trouble.

"Oh, you can't fool me. I've had plenty of nephews around to know all about how they act when there's girl trouble. Now, tell Auntie Cathy what's wrong," she demands, and I have the strongest urge to just tell her.

"Nothing. Something. I don't know," I hedge, gripping the back of my neck in frustration while trying to decide just how much I want to give away.

"And?" she prods, waiting patiently for my explanation.

"We got to know each other pretty well, had some great chemistry. I really thought there was a strong connection between us, but she just up and left me without a word." There. I summed it up quite well if I do say so, myself.

"Do you love her?"

"I don't know if I'd say that just yet, but," I squeeze my neck harder and close my eyes, "I know I don't want to just let her walk away. I want to see where things could go. She's different from everyone else."

"So, you do the work, get out of here, and go after her." Yeah, like that hasn't crossed my mind already.

"It's not that simple," I argue, shoving my hands in my pockets.

"Of course, it is. No more avoiding the problem. It's time you started moving forward, honey." She's a foot shorter than me, but that doesn't intimidate her. She places her palm on my left pec and smiles sweetly. She really does remind me of my aunt. "You'll be just fine." Sliding her hand upward she pats my cheek then walks into the dining area without another word.

Stunned and completely confused, I make my way back to my room. There's another hour left before mealtime is over and I'm hoping a hot shower can help clear my head. So many thoughts are running through my mind I don't notice my cheery friend waiting for me by the door.

"Hey," he says when I reach him. "I was looking for you." When is he *not* looking for me?

"Yeah?"

"I have something for you. Hold on," he instructs, turning to retrieve something from his own room.

What in the world could he possibly have to give me? We're not close like that.

"Here," he says with a somber tone voice. "She wanted me to give this to you today." He holds a small, plainly wrapped package tied with a simple, skinny ribbon in his hands and offers it to me. Taking it from him, he claps me on the shoulder and walks down the hall.

Stunned yet again, I enter my room and sit on the bed. Examining the package, I see nothing to indicate who it's to or from. I hope with every fiber of my being that it's from Sarah.

"Just open the damned thing," I tell myself after who knows long. Pulling at the long end of the ribbon, I untie the bow and drop it to the floor. Running my finger under the flap on the bottom, I break the tape seal and tear away the paper to expose a white gift box of some sort. It looks to be about the size of some sort of jewelry item, but I'm not sure.

With a deep breath, I lift off the lid and exhale loudly when I find a small envelope bearing my name printed on its front. The box has some weight to it and my curiosity is getting the better of me. I take the note out and peel away the tissue paper underneath to find something cold and made of metal. Picking it up, I find an antique brass belt buckle in the shape of a moose head.

"It *is* from her," I say to myself. "Her and that chocolate mousse," I chuckle.

Hesitantly, I begin reading the personally written note. I read it several times, out loud and in silence before closing my eyes and bowing my head.

"Fuck me."

Find me when you're ready.

X Sarah

The rest of this story will be added to this and released as one full-length novel,

CRASHING STAR - Back Door Records Book 2.

Heart Beats

The Alpha's Star

by

Aimie Jennison

Oak Creek Bears: A Short Story

Silas West, bear shifter and Alpha of the Oak Creek Clan, has secretly had his eye on his best friend's sister for most of his life.

Knowing Ava Franco has dreams and a talent that will allow her to reach them, it isn't hard for him to take the steps to get her what she deserves.

Will he be able to let the woman he's always wanted walk out of his town to fulfil her dreams—or will his mating instinct be too strong after all?

Chapter One
Silas

The beat of the drums pulsates through my body and I close my eyes as I listen to the angelic voice singing words of unrequited love through the microphone, basking in the pleasurable shivers it sends rippling within me.

Ava Franco.

I've loved Ava Franco since I was a pimple-faced teen, but I could never make a move on her because not only is she part of our clan she's my best friend's little sister.

I guess I should back up a little. I'm a grizzly bear shifter and a clan is to us what a pack is to wolves. Sometimes we find mates within our clan but more often than not we try to bring fresh blood into the fold by mating with bears from elsewhere.

You'd think being the alpha of our clan would allow me to bend the rules a little but sadly it's quite the opposite, all eyes are on me and if I can't abide by my own rules why should anyone else?

I sense someone step up beside me but know it's Dante, my best mate and second in command, as his energy brushes against mine and his scent washes over me. He doesn't speak but I can feel his eyes boring into me.

I sigh. "What do you want?"

"I'm just wondering why you have your eyes shut? Have you got a headache or something?"

Opening my eyes I pin him with a hard stare. "I was enjoying the music and hoping if I kept my eyes closed everyone would get the message, and leave me in peace."

"Hmm...well, I think that got lost in translation. Want a beer?" Dante asks, his voice full of humour.

"Sure, thanks." I say focusing my attention back on the beautiful redhead on stage. Her hips sway as she finishes the song and I'm suddenly grateful that the scent of my arousal will be easily hidden with all turned on, gyrating people that fill the dance floor.

He may be my best friend and brother in all ways but the biological sense, but there is no way he would want me as his sister's mate. He's said time and time again he hopes she mates with someone low down in the clan, even someone submissive. Ava is powerful and dominant in her own right. She doesn't need a male to stifle her, and that is exactly what a dominant mate will do. He'll cherish her and protect her but he won't be able to control his natural need to do that enough to step back when she needs it and it will inevitably wear her down.

A beer bottle appears before me and I take it gratefully from Dante's hand. "Cheers, Mate," I state, before taking a healthy swig.

"I wasn't expecting to see you here tonight, Silas. You usually only make it to the monthly gatherings and that's only because you have to be there."

I chuckle at his words.

He's not wrong. I've made it perfectly clear I hate coming to the local bar. As an alpha you're at the centre of the clan-bonds. You connect everyone together and it can be overwhelming if you don't guard yourself from other's feelings. Unfortunately that can be a hard task in places that are bursting with scents and emotions like this bar is.

Once a month we have a gathering of sorts with other clans who live nearby. It's a way to have the opportunity for connections to be made and mates to be found. As the hosting alpha I have to attend those nights for a handful of reasons but mostly to keep everyone in check and to be sure no dominance fights break out. A number of other dominant bears coming into our territory looking to mate with our brothers and sisters is bound to be a time when everyone's tempers are a little on edge. Bears may not be native animals to Australia but just as this country is made up of many cultures have emigrated from across the world, there are plenty of non-native shifters among those cultures too.

We share our town with a wolf pack, the Oak Creek Pack, who do the same sort of thing on another night of the month. We're polite enough to make sure to stay clear of the bar on each other's nights. But any other night both species share the bar as we do most of the town, surrounding forest, and creek. It's only our home bases that are strictly our own territory. Thankfully we've managed to live in harmony for many years and as long as we stick to our firm set of rules we should be able to live many more like that.

"I'd heard Ava was singing and couldn't miss it," I admit, certain he wouldn't read anything into my words. I'd also needed to be close by to ensure nobody would make a move on her. Even though I couldn't claim her myself, it didn't mean I was going to let some other loser claim her. And in my eyes nobody is worthy of Ava Franco.

Her song ends and she thanks everyone, before introducing the regular act on stage. It takes all my will power to stay where I am leaning against the wall. A possessive part of me wants to go to the stage and escort her through the throng of people but she wouldn't thank me for doing it. I'm not her mate and therefore she's not mine to protect like that.

"You should have seen her getting ready, she must have tried on everything in her walk in robe and then I'm pretty sure she ended up wearing the first outfit she showed me." Dante shakes his head. "Women."

The woman in question bounds up to us a smile on her face that would give the Cheshire Cat a run for his money. She throws her arms around Dante's neck and he gives her a loving hug, lifting her off her feet.

"You sounded amazing, Ava. Mum and Dad would be so proud," he says as he places her back on the floor. His mention of their long departed parents doesn't do anything to take away her euphoria from performing. Her feet barely hit the floor before she leaps into my arms and I'm enveloped in her sweet scent.

"Hey Angel, you looked stunning up there like you'd just fallen from the heavens." I place her down and take a step back even though I want nothing more than to keep her in my arms and breathe in her scent.

She rolls her eyes as she bats at my chest. "Silas, you are so cheesy. No wonder you're still single."

I give her a hearty chuckle as I play along. I've always paid her compliments for as long as I can remember and she's always thought they were a joke. Like I'm saying them just to keep my best friend's little sister happy. I wonder what she'd think of them if she knew I meant every word.

Dante eyes me with a look I can't quite decipher, but he doesn't say anything so I focus back on Ava who is chatting to the pair of us, excitement clear in the high tone of her voice and the way she's bouncing on the balls of her feet.

"Did you hear them cheering when I'd finished? I never thought I'd have that kind of applause. They're used to hearing Melody," she gestures over her shoulder to the girl who is now singing without pausing in her speech, "so I don't know why they were so appreciative of me. She's like a superstar and I'm just…me."

If she could see and hear herself how I do, she'd have no doubts about why people reacted like that. She was born to be a star and I'm certain one day she'll get there… Providing her future mate doesn't protect her too much that he dulls her shine.

Chapter Two
Ava

The look in Silas's eyes is indecipherable. It's a look he gives me often and even though I've known him all my life I can never read what he's thinking.

He's a mystery to me. Maybe that's why I'm drawn to him like a bee to pollen. Maybe that's why I've had a crush on him for as long as I can remember. No, I'm pretty sure his long hair and muscled physique have more to do with that than his deep brooding looks. He practically drips sex appeal.

As I flick my gaze around the bar I spot more than half the female bears salivating over him and a number of wolves too, even though our two species never intermingle like that. It's kind of an unspoken rule our clan and their pack will not have sexual relations. I think it's what helps us to live in the same territory without killing each other.

"Here, I almost forgot." Silas's voice draws my attention from the females in the club and I find him holding out a bag of my favourite red frog lollies, a huge grin encircled with his neat beard. My heart practically explodes in my chest.

"Oh, mate. I'm never gonna wean her off them if you keep buying her them." Dante rolled his eyes at Silas.

I go up on my tip ties and give him a quick peck on the cheek as I take them out of his hand. "Thank you. At least Silas loves me enough to allow me my pleasures." My face heats as the words leave my mouth and I register how those words could have been construed.

"Ava Franco. Your sultry voice is just what Felicity Stone's been looking for in a supporting act for her next tour." I look at the guy who just approached us with wide eyes and can't help but feel grateful for his timing. "I'm sorry I should introduce myself. Ian Harris, I'm a PR at Golden Shade Records," he says whilst offering me his hand.

I place my hand in his and manage a quick greeting while my thoughts run wild inside me. Felicity Stone is the biggest female artist of the year. She has broken record after record and the hype around her doesn't look to be dying down anytime soon.

Mr Harris gives Dante and Silas the same polite handshake and I'm mortified when Dante opens his mouth.

"Wolf." The word sounds like a curse, and I suddenly connect what my nose had missed with all the excitement.

"I belong to the the Black Range Pack. I have permission to be here." The amused smirk on his face tells me he isn't insulted by Dante's actions but anger soars through me. How could he be such a dick to someone so important just because he's a wolf.

Ignoring Mr Harris he turns to Silas. "Where you aware of this?"

"Dante!"

Dante ignores my reprimand, his focus fully on his best mate and our alpha.

"Yes. I knew Mr Harris would be watching Ava tonight. I actually asked him here." Silas's words have my heart hammering in my chest as my mind tries to make sense of all this. Is this all some kind of joke? Or worse, is Silas paying him to be here?

A strong finger lifts my chin and chocolate brown eyes bore into mine. "Whatever you are thinking the answer is no. I told Ian we had a singer here who he might be interested in signing. That's all. He was under no obligation to even speak to you if he didn't like what he heard." The words are no sooner out of his mouth before I feel them as the truth. Being able to sense a lie has its pros. As far as I'm aware all shifters have such ability.

I nod in acceptance and Silas drops his hand. I immediately miss the feel of his energy against my skin. His scent lingers and I breathe it in.

"I'm grateful that Silas called me because you are exactly what I've been looking for in an artist. I need to iron out some kinks with the powers that be, but I'd definitely like to offer you a deal. You'd have to come to Melbourne with me and record a few songs and then you'll be the opening act for Felicity Stone's next tour. You'll be on a really tight deadline and it will be hard work. Do you think you're up for that?"

I glance between Silas and Dante, hoping to see something that will help me answer him. Since our parents died, it's just been Dante and me. I don't know how I feel about possibly leaving him alone. Although, he wouldn't really be alone because he'd have the clan. Both men give me wide reassuring smiles, Dante's concerns over the wolf clearly withdrawn since hearing about Silas's invitation, and I'm suddenly flooded with excitement. "Yes." I nod. "I think I am. Thank you."

"Fantastic." He glances at his watch. "I'm going to head back to my hotel and make some calls. I'll be in touch sometime tomorrow and we'll arrange a meeting to go over your contract." He pulls out a card from his breast pocket and hands it to me. "Here's my card. If you have any questions, don't hesitate to call. It was nice to meet you all," he says as his gaze travels over the three of us before he walks away with a final bid goodbye.

"Holy shit, my baby sister is gonna be the next big thing," Dante utters, pride clear in his voice as he pulls me into his arms and swings me around.

I laugh, filled with exhilaration as Dante finally places me back on my feet. I turn to Silas and throw myself at him planting a kiss on his lips. He stiffens beneath me before I can register what the hell I'm doing and I jump back. "Thank you," I say, faking confidence I don't have and hoping he doesn't catch the shake in my voice. "I don't think I'll ever be able to thank you enough for what you've done for me."

He shrugs nonchalantly. "You can always share your millions with me when you're rich and famous." It's only the gruff tone behind his words that tells me he's not as calm as he's acting. I can't take my eyes off his lips, the feel of them still fresh on mine.

"Come on, Sis, we've got some celebrating to do," Dante says as he throws his arm over my shoulder and drags me towards the bar.

I expect Silas to follow us but by the time we make it to the bar his energy is no longer brushing against mine and a quick glance to where he'd been propping up the wall confirms he's no longer in the building.

I tuck the card in my pocket and pull a red frog out the bag, popping it in my mouth before placing the bag in the back pocket of my denim shorts. The flavour flowing over my taste-buds, causing so many childhood memories to flow through my mind; many of them having Silas at the core of them.

Chapter Three
Silas

I can't stop thinking about her soft lips pressing against mine. It took more willpower in that moment than I knew I had to stop myself from licking at the seam of her lips, and begging for her to open up to me.

As much as I want to join in and celebrate with Dante and Ava, I know that I can't hang around without the risk of doing something stupid…

Like pulling Ava into my arms and kissing her senseless.

I leave the bar and make a beeline for my home, the urge to let my bear run almost overwhelming me. I quickly push him down, remembering the most important law we'd put together in aid to make the bar a safe neutral territory: No shifting in or around the property.

If the law was broken by either of the alphas it would instantly mean war between us and we hadn't lived in harmony for the last ten years just for me to ruin that all because of a surprise peck on the lips.

I break into a jog, and as my heart rate picks up, I concentrate on matching my footfall with the persistent rhythm. It does the job of calming me and as I pass the large cabin I call home, I pull off my tee without breaking my stride, dropping it on the ground. I slow to a stop at the tree line where my yard ends and strip out of the rest of my clothes, not bothering to fold or hide them. Anyone that may come across them won't even look twice since everyone that lives in bear territory is a shifter or a shifter's family member.

The general public knows nothing of shifters or other creatures that go bump in the night but we know our secrets won't be able to last forever. Technology and science are progressing more and more each day and it will only be a matter of time before one of us leaves some DNA in the wrong place. If a scientist looks close enough they'll see the vast differences between our DNA and a regular humans. Or some non-native animal ends up featured on someone's Instagram account. Our forest is private property and far enough away from tourist areas that we don't get any random strangers wandering about, but not all shifters have the security of that. Some groups have to hunt in national parks and highly populated areas.

Johnny, the Alpha of the Oak Creek Pack, has told me the wolves have a website of sorts where the different packs throughout the country can contact each other. He described it as Facebook for werewolves. Apparently they are trying to come up with a way to bring the werewolves out into the public eye without looking like the scary predators they are. Part of me thinks they need to broaden their reach and allow other shifters to join their site. Perhaps a cuter, less dangerous creature would be willing to step forward as the first to come out.

It only takes a minute or two for me to shift into my bear form, my bones breaking and reforming as my skin slides over them covered in fur. It's not the most comfortable of sensations but when it's something you've grown up with it's a pain you can bear. Unlike the wolves we aren't forced to shift with the full moon but we do feel the call and are usually a lot closer to our animals around that time. Our females tend to be able to carry children to term, for that reason only a small number of them miscarrying during an unexpected shift brought on by a sudden emotional outburst or because it wasn't meant to be just as happens with the humans.

Leaning forward on my front paws I stretch out the last aches of the change and shake my body, almost like a dog does as it comes out of water. I lift my snout and scent the air. The only fresh scent I can pick up on is Grayson's which isn't anything to be surprised about since he's on patrol tonight and my property isn't just my home; it's the clan's headquarters.

A safe haven for any one of my bears or their family, and needs to be protected as such.

As much as I felt the need to run earlier, my bear seems to have calmed with the distance between Ava and us, and is quite happy to just roam through our forest. After an hour or two I lose interest in chasing wallabies and other nocturnal animals through the trees and find myself back with the clothing I left strewn on the ground.

I shift back to my human form and pull on my jeans, walking barefoot to the house, the damp grass cold under my feet. I pick up my tee off the lawn as I pass it, throwing it over my shoulder.

The house is as empty as I expected. It's something I've gotten used to over the last couple years since my brother, Roark, moved into his own cabin as soon as he turned eighteen.

My mum chose to live with my sister and her husband after my father died and I took over as Alpha, complaining I was too much of a grumpy bastard to live with. I have a feeling my mood is why I don't often have many clan members as guests seeking out the comfort of their alpha or the safety of his home. Not that that is anything I'd complain about, I'd much rather have my own company than anyone else's.

Heading straight to the bathroom, I turn on the water as I strip out of my jeans, dumping them in the hamper with my sweat soaked tee, before stepping under the steaming rain head. The heat and the pressure do wonders for the tension across my shoulders. Once the water starts to cool I step out and dry off.

Pulling on a pair of sweats I head to the kitchen in the hopes of finding some food I could cook up quickly.

The smell of pan-fried steak hits my nose and my mouth starts to water at the thought of eating it.

"If I'd have known you were gonna take that long in the shower I wouldn't have started cooking until you were out. I hope you like it cold," Dante announces, nodding towards a plate containing a juicy looking steak and a serving of veggies, as he goes about washing the dishes.

I sit down and start to eat whilst wondering why he'd felt the need to follow me. I'd have expected him to go straight to the home he shares with Ava once the bar kicked out. I eat in silence waiting for him to get whatever might be on his chest off. "Thanks," I say after I finish the last mouthful. "Even cold it was delicious."

He throws me a grin over his shoulder. "I'm not a Michelin chef for nothing."

I grunt and he laughs.

"You love her, yet you're gonna let her walk away and become a star."

Ah…that's what he's here for. I weigh him up trying to see how he feels about the fact that I love his sister but his face is guarded so I can't read him.

"Don't deny it. I've watched you love her from a distance for as long as I can remember."

I give him a raised brow and another grunt.

"So why did you call the wolf in?"

"She's destined to be a star." I shrug. "I wanted to be able to give that to her."

He frowns. "But she'll have to leave and you're Alpha, you can't go with her. I'm your second and I can't go with her."

"No. I'm sending Roark. He's a good fighter and can blend in with the wolf's security detail. She won't like it but she'll understand that I wouldn't let any of our females out unprotected." I've thought things through and even spoken to Roark about it. He's more than excited to be able to travel the world and rub noses with the rich and famous.

Dante nods. "Okay, that sounds as good a plan as any but what if she meets someone? What if something happens between her and Roark? Could you really live with it if they came back mated?"

I want to say yes but I can't. I know I'll never be able to handle that and he'd hear it as the lie it would be if I voiced that. "I'm willing to face the consequences of this decision when the time comes." He gives me a worried look and I forge on, "If I didn't call the wolf, didn't give her this opportunity… I'd be snuffing out her flame. And she'd slowly lose everything she is just to be the alpha's mate. I can't do that to her. She needs to live the life she wants."

"Huh…" Dante places the last plate in the cupboard and dries his hands on the tea towel. He gives me an approving look and shakes his head. "You're a stronger man than I am," he states before walking out the door without another word.

"We'll see about that," I whisper to the empty room.

Chapter Four
Ava

I've only been up for about an hour when my phone starts to ring.

"Are you gonna get that or do I have to come and smash it to smithereens?" Dante shouts through the house showing his grumpy side. He loves his sleep and hates mornings so if he gets woken up, he really is the epitome of a bear with a sore head.

Ignoring Dante I pick up the phone, hitting the accept button before I really paid attention to the number or name on the screen. "Hello."

"Morning Ava. Ian's emailed your contract over. Megan's reading over it now, so if you want to pop round she'll got through it with you and you can sign it and send it back over." Silas's deep voice chimes through the phone and I find myself momentarily distracted by the sound. "Or not. If you don't want to take the offer you don't have to it's entirely up to you."

The uncertainty in his tone pulls me out of my stupor. "No. I mean yes. I don't want to leave home and everyone I love, but if I want a career in music it's something I'll have to do." I nod agreeing with myself even though nobody is here to see it. "I'll be right round."

I hear him grunt into the phone, a sound that makes me weak at the knees whenever I hear it. I'm pretty sure it's not a normal reaction to such a sound but I can't help it. Silas does things to me without even trying; he'd probably be mortified if he knew about it. "Okay. See you in a few."

The line went dead and I slip my phone in my lightweight viscose shorts pocket before heading out the door. Excitement bubbles inside at the possibility of my dreams coming true but what I said to Silas is the truth: The thought of leaving Dante behind tugs at my heart. I don't like the thought of leaving Silas either. I won't know if anyone's making moves on my man. Not that he'll ever know he's my man, but in my heart he always will be.

I let myself into Silas's cabin via the kitchen door and make my way towards the voices I can hear rumbling through the walls.

"It's a really good deal. I can't see anything untoward about it at all," Megan states, surprise clear in her voice. "They must really want her."

I walk into the boardroom that Silas regularly uses for meetings and find Megan hunched over a pile of papers, and Silas standing over her clearly reading over her shoulder. My bear doesn't like to see him so close to another woman but I remind her for the hundredth time he isn't ours.

"Yeah, I thought the same when I read over it earlier," Silas says as his eyes lift to meet mine. I expect him to look away but he holds my gaze, his bear there to see in the flickering golden orbs.

"Silas," I say my voice sounding strained to even my own ears. It isn't often I see him like that, his bear so close to the surface; it unnerves me. I break the eye contact and focus on Megan. "Megan, I haven't seen you in a while. How have you been?"

"Keeping busy. Not as busy as you'll be if you sign this contract. You are gonna be working your butt off for the next eight or nine months."

Silas lets out one of his sexy grunts and I have to make an effort not to react in any way. Megan closes her eyes and I have a feeling she has the same problem as I, which, although it makes me realise I might not be so strange after all, it also means I'm not the only one who has an attraction to Silas.

I don't like that one bit.

"Come, sit," Silas demands pulling out the chair beside Megan.

I stare at him without moving. Having grown up with him I've made sure to never allow him to order me around without a reasonable excuse. Alpha or not.

He rubs a hand over his face and lets out a breath. "Sorry, Ava. I'm a little on edge today. Do what you like, but you'll probably be more comfortable sitting."

I nod and stride over to them running my hand down his arm as I pass him, aiming to give him at least a little comfort from the touch.

"Do you ladies want a drink? Perhaps tea?" he asks already making his way out the room no doubt needing a minute or two to talk his bear down.

"Tea sounds fab. Thanks Silas." I wish I could ask him why his bear is causing him so much trouble but I know it's no use. He'd never be so open in front of Megan.

I turn my attention back to Megan to find her staring at me, mouth wide in surprise. "How the hell did you do that?"

I frown.

"Ignore his order and then get him to apologise for it. I've never heard him apologise like that before," she clarifies.

"Practice. He's my brother's best friend. We pretty much grew up together and I learnt from a young age if I didn't want to be some little slave to them I had to have a spine of steel."

"It's a shame you're gonna be leaving town. I could really do with picking your brains about…someone." She glances at the door and I know she means Silas but doesn't want him to hear her. A shifter's hearing is heightened and although he may be in another room he'd still easily hear any conversation we have in here.

My heart sinks with the knowledge that the beautiful blonde next to me has a thing for Silas. She could have any guy out there with her big boobs and smart brain and yet she wants the one guy I can't have. Not wanting to encourage her one bit I turn my attention to the papers on the table. "So, what's the deal? How much of my soul are they asking for?"

Megan grins. "You're soul's safe were it is."

"The closest they'll get to your soul is in the songs you write and it's up to you how much you put into them," Silas states as he places a tray containing a teapot, three cups and a jar of honey on the table. He goes about pouring the tea while Megan gets down to business.

"Okay, so they're initially offering you an album deal. You'll have three months to write and record it. Then one month to nail down the performances and any choreography that might go with it. The royalties they are offering you are pretty good, I did some research and spoke to some colleagues last night and it's a better percentage than most unknown artists get offered. Then they want you to be the supporting act for Felicity Stone's tour, which is a five month around the world tour. There is also a clause stating that providing your album gets enough sales, they'll want you to headline your own tour not long after that to ride the hype out. That's when they'll look at renewing your contract for another album too."

I clasp my hands together on the table to stop them shaking. "Holy shit. That's…"

"Fucking epic!" Megan finishes for me.

I laugh nervously. "Yeah. That."

"If you want my professional opinion, sign it. It's nine months. If you hate every minute," she shrugs, "you come home at the end of it and don't look back. If you love it…all the better. We'll milk them for all we can with the next contract." The laugh on her lips makes me think she really loves that side of her job. She slides the paper over towards me. "I've got to head off to the office, I wasn't kidding earlier when I said I was pretty busy. I've marked where you need to sign and Silas can sign as witness and then you can email it straight back to the PR guy." She reaches for a briefcase I hadn't even noticed on the chair beside her and after giving Silas a brief peck on the cheek as she passes, she leaves the room. My eyes don't leave her retreating back as I suppress a growl of dislike.

"I haven't seen you stare daggers at anyone like that for a long time. Maybe it's not safe to let you out in the general public after all." The grin he flashes me is one he doesn't share often, making his dimples pop on the edges of his neat beard.

"I'm pretty sure it's safer for everyone if I do go." My smile drops from my face as my earlier worries about Dante hit me hard. "You'll look after Dante for me?"

He reaches out and places his hand over mine, giving it a gentle squeeze. "You'll only be gone for nine months, he can't get in that much trouble, surely."

I raise a brow at him. "We're talking about Dante."

"Hmmm. True. Okay," he places a hand on his heart. "I solemnly swear to try my damnedest to keep one Dante Phillip Franco out of trouble whilst you are sharing your beauty and talent with the world."

My heart skips a beat at his words and the conviction behind them. Not wanting him to see what I'm feeling I drop my gaze to the papers before me and reach for the pen Megan had left on the table.

"I guess with the I's dotted and the T's crossed all that is left for me to do is sign on the dotted line."

Silas does the one thing that guarantees I can't focus…grunts. Thankfully Megan was true to her word and marked all the places I needed to sign clearly enough that I didn't need to concentrate too hard on the task.

Chapter Five
Ava

Two days after signing that piece of paper I find myself standing outside a black limousine. A chauffeur is playing Tetris with the suitcases I'd packed. Roark's one and only duffle bag takes up barely any space at all, which does a wonderful job of making me feel guilty about my amount of luggage.

Silas had told me Roark was to come as part protection, part comfort, which if I'm being honest I am really grateful for. Roark and I have always gotten along and became pretty good friends over the years. I did once have the smart idea of trying to make Silas jealous by dating him but that backfired majorly when Roark told me he was actually gay. I promised to keep his secret and he promised to keep mine. So, having him with me will be like taking a piece of this place along, which I think will help me avoid getting home sick.

I glance around at the small group of people waiting to wave us off: Roark's mum, sister, and Dante.

"It's time to hit the road," Ian states as he slides into the car, via the door the chauffeur holds open.

I give Dante one last hug as I peer up the street over his shoulder hoping to see Silas. That stupid dreamer inside me is hoping he'll come running down the street to claim me as his mate and beg me to stay.

A hand touches my back and I can't hide the disappointment when I find Roark, a sad smile on his face. "We better go."

I nod and give the rest of Roark's family a hug before slipping into the car behind him.

"He couldn't face waving us off," Roark states as soon as I'd closed the car door.

I can't hide my sullen look. "You. He couldn't face waving you off."

Roark shakes his head. "You are as blind as he is. No. Silas already said goodbye to me. He couldn't trust himself to let you go."

Out the window I spot a familiar figure, with messy hair brushing his shoulder standing on the porch of Silas's cabin as we head out of town. A guttural bellow pierces the air and my bear is desperate to call out in return.

He couldn't trust himself to let you go.

My mind takes Roark's words and runs with them, writing the best fairytale it can come up with.

A fairytale where the prince chases after the princess and they live happily ever after.

Sadly that isn't how real life works…

My story is far from a fairytale.

Read the rest of Silas and Ava's story in Silas, Oak Creek Bears: Book One, coming soon

Need more in the meantime? Join my reader group to keep up to date with the news of all my upcoming releases.

Heart Beats

Opera of the Beast

by

Lilly Rayman

Paranormal RH Romance

This is an introduction to a Paranormal RH novel coming in 2020.

A chance meeting with a wise woman sets off a chain of events the repercussions of which would resonate for decades.

More than thirty years later, a young girl's audition might just be the catalyst which connects the past to the present.

Prologue

36 years ago

Exhaustion filled her bones, weighing her down as she stood, trembling with fatigue at the bus stop. Rain fell in sheets of icy curtains beyond the narrow shelter. It reflected her mood of late, she thought, the unrelenting sensation of impending doom. A bitter scoff left her dry cracked lips in a twisted sigh of self-deprecating laughter. Pregnancy hormones had really done a number on her usually bright and bubbly personality. Or maybe it was the borderline abusive attentions of the domineering bastard who had put her in this situation. He had swept her off her feet, literally, seven months ago. Scooping her up in his big burly arms, he raced her away from the runaway car, which had been careening the wrong way down the one-way street. There had been a gleam in his dark eyes as he fixed them on her own blue ones. Something that caught her attention and stopped her from saying no when he offered to take her for coffee, which turned into drinks before morphing into a wickedly sensual affair.

It was only after she had fallen pregnant despite being on the pill that he asserted his control, demanding of her how she should manage her pregnancy. She had wanted to terminate, a child was the last thing she wanted, not when she had worked so hard to get a foothold in the music industry. It had been the first time he laid hands on her in anger, wrapping his fingers around her arms so tightly, her hands tingled. Hauling her up so her toes dangled inches above the carpeted floor, he growled into her face that she if she killed his baby, he would kill her.

She recognised the menace in his tone and relented, promising she would keep his baby.

"You only need to carry him for nine months, you selfish bitch, and then I will take him away. Go live your life child-free and think no more of me or our son!"

His words still rang in her ears four months on. She didn't want to leave her child with him, had grown attached to the baby growing inside her. The bonding had begun when she felt the first movements and, although she felt battered and bruised from the frenetic energy of the child within her, she loved him.

The wet swish of braking tyres in puddles of water masked the hiss of automatic doors opening but served to bring Chrissy back to the here and now. Sucking in a deep breath, she lurched out of the dry shelter, biting back a squeal as icy water sluiced down the back of her jacket before she boarded the bus. The artificial heaters worked overtime to keep passengers warm, yet only managed to congeal the multitude of scents from so many different bodies into a nauseatingly cloying perfume, which kicked Chrissy in the guts in a vomit inducing way.

Paying her fare, she moved, sluggishly, towards the seats, smiling tiredly at the elderly woman, who moved her bags allowing her to sit near the front and not push further into the overpowering smell of humanity in close confines.

"Thank you," she murmured as she breathed in the tranquil aroma of sage smoke.

"You're welcome, child," answered the old woman. Her native accent was as thick as the two braids that lay across each shoulder, and the deep grooves of age creasing the beautiful nut-brown tone of her skin. "May I?" she asked, her gnarled hand hovering above the gentle swelling of Chrissy's abdomen.

For a moment the word "no" hovered on Chrissy's tongue, her usual response to strangers wishing to paw over her baby bump like it would bring them all the luck in the world. Only today, with this old native lady she paused. A tender warmth seemed to seep from the hand that didn't touch, melting through the ice of the miserable day. With an awkward nod, Chrissy consented to the contact of a stranger.

With a soft smile the old lady nodded before closing her eyes and emitting a harmonious hum that seemed to vibrate through Chrissy. The baby reacted, rolling around violently for a moment before stilling when the gnarled hand contracted from a caress to a grip. The old woman's eyes flew open, locking Chrissy in their clouded gaze as the woman began to chant.

"Two wolves, one black, one white, fight for dominance within you. Neither one is stronger, yet a dark alpha will pit one against the other. Balance cannot come until Harmony can be found between them.

"Take the white wolf and run from the dark alpha, keep him safe until Harmony is found."

The clouds in the old woman's eyes vanished when she blinked. Her hand relaxed its grasp and with a soft pat she pulled it back to her lap.

"What did you just say?" asked Chrissy on a shaking whisper.

The old lady frowned, deepening the lines that framed her face, "I said it's twins, child." The bus lurched to a stop and the old woman hauled her wizened frame to her feet. "This is my stop. Good luck, dear."

Chrissy watched in disbelief as the cryptic lady shuffled off the bus and disappeared into the downpour outside the false light of the bus.

Only that morning her doctor had told her she carried two babies. The information had not yet sunk in, and she had been aimlessly wandering around town ever since. She hesitated to return to Victor fearing to tell him. She wanted her baby, babies. Needed them. She knew though that Victor would be true to his word. As soon as she gave birth, she would never see him or her babies again. While he would be no great loss, her children would be.

She needed to keep the second baby a secret, and she could not do that if she remained under his thumb. She needed a plan.

Chapter One
Present Day
Raul

The music danced around his head, the notes floating with a teasing inaccuracy on the curving staves that twisted through his subconscious mind. The melody was the same. Every night it spun and pulsed through his dreams. It coiled around his very soul and awakened his senses with embarrassing intensity. Every waking moment it continued, taunting him with the repetitive nature of the refrain. The haunting strain that followed the signature beat and rhythm of his usual compositions tormented him because he was unable to pin down the notes or even recreate the music on his piano.

With a snarl, he slammed his fists down against the aged ebony and ivory keys he usually caressed with loving skill. The harsh jangle of off-key notes jarred through his ears in stark protest to the abuse of his aggression. Lip curling back in frustration, he swept the horrendous mess of useless crotchets, quavers and minims blotted on the crumpled sheet music away from the top of his piano. He stood up so swiftly, his velvet cushioned stool crashed to the rugged floor with a muted thud of protest.

The growl that rumbled from his inner beast burst from his chest with more hostility than the few who knew him had ever experienced. Stalking across the soundproofed room of his mother's gated Upper West Side mansion, he breathed deeply to try and find control of his emotions once more. His behaviour was out of character. He was known for being cool, analytical. A mastermind of his time when it came to compositions of any style or genre of music. He could play the piano with his eyes closed, was adept with the guitar and passable with the violin. The only instruments he had been unable to master, although understood their ranges and strengths, were the wind instruments. The damage to the right side of his face put too much pressure on his mouth to allow him to get the right breath for those instruments.

His mother was the powerful mogul known only as the Phantom Queen, behind the successful music company, Phantom Records. For years she had marketed the company she had started, from the ground up, on the mystery of not knowing the identity of the person behind the mask, or even the name of the powerhouse behind the label. Raul was barely toddling around the shabby apartment hidden in the warren of back alleys of Hell's Kitchen when he had first started to play music. He tinkered on the keys of the piano in the recording studios his mother hired by the day. A way to get her artists recorded, so they could be launched through the radio stations of Soho and

Broadway until she had the artists selling their hits by the million. As fast as the company grew with each successive talent Phantom Queen promoted, Raul became even more proficient with every instrument to which he turned his hand. From the piano to the strings he was composing and playing music. In all his thirty-five years of playing music, he had never struggled to write anything that had come through his mind.

His pacing stopped when he spotted the light gleaming across the polished wood of the lower body curve of his guitar hanging on its rack on the wall. His head leaned to one side, while he considered the music plucking from the strings. The unscarred side of his face twitched with the faintest of smiles as he moved towards the instrument. His fingers caressed lovingly around the neck before he closed his hand around the neck.

The door opened before he could lift it from its pegs. His face dropped to a scowl as he turned to face his mother. Her lush, raven hair was fixed into her fanciest up-do, the once-upon-a-time costume tiara had long since been replaced with one of delicate silver work encrusted with twinkling Swarovski crystals. Her piercing blue eyes gleamed with excitement from behind the signature mask of Phantom Records, her crushed velvet black cape brushed with a whisper of sound across the floor behind her as she swept through his personal space towards him.

"You are really going through with this thing then?" he asked her as he observed her public appearance, his scowl deepened when he noted the second mask she held in her tiny hands. Hands that had held him through many a nightmare from as far back as his memory could stretch. Hands that would join his on the piano when he was young, to teach him the beautiful complexities of playing a duet.

"Raul, my beautiful son. We've talked about this. Television is the way of the future. With so many networks running talent and singing shows, the competition is getting fiercer. If I want to keep Phantom Records at the forefront of the pack of launching new careers for new talent, I need to grow and allow the company to move with the times. I thought you were with me on this. Too many months have gone into setting up this process. Scouts have held preliminary auditions across the country for the past four months, leading up to tonight. The first ever live auditions, televised from Broadway Theatre of all places. It would mean the world to me, if you came with me, Raul, supported me in this." As she spoke, his mother, known to the wider world as Phantom Queen, to her small, intimate circle as Chrissy, and to him, simply Maman, approached him. Her head, even with her artificial curls piled on top of it, barely reached his broad shoulders. She reached for him with one hand, allowing her cool fingers to slip against his hotter digits. "I love you, Raul, but you know this company, it means everything to me, and I want, no, need it to succeed."

Raul looked down on his mother, her head craned back to regard him with a pleading intensity that she knew always buckled him. "You already have made it a success, Maman—" he saw her open her mouth to argue, so he shushed her with a fingertip to her lips. "Let me finish, I understand you, I am just worried, for so many years you have worked hard to stay hidden, won't this make it a little harder? So far, you have only submitted to written interviews and the odd photograph, hiding behind the mask, the brand. A ploy that has not only been a brilliant marketing strategy but kept you safe. Now, you want to risk that by being in front of a camera. Putting your voice out there, for all, for him, to hear? Can't you just let someone else from the company front for you?"

Her smile was gentle, the softness of it tinged with a deeper sadness steeped in the truth of his words. "I haven't been hiding myself, my beautiful boy—" Raul's mouth twisted with distaste and he looked away with a barely audible scoff at her words, "—Don't dismiss yourself, or me like that, son. Beauty is found far deeper than the surface of the façade presented to the world. Your father is the prime example of that. It is him I ran from, a picture of beauty that masked the cruellest and ugliest of natures. You are nothing like that beast of a man, and you, my beautiful, yes, beautiful boy, have the tenderest of souls within that gruff exterior you show the world." His mother dropped her head and looked away, a pinched look to her mouth, told Raul she was frowning behind her mask. "You made me forget my train of thought. Oh, yes." She looked back up at him, the intensity of her stare was almost unnerving. "It is you I have been hiding, not me. Victor made himself perfectly clear he was happy to have nothing to do with me when I ran away from him—"

"Then why?" interrupted Raul.

"Because it was you, he wanted, not me. I just couldn't let you be raised by that bastard, and I certainly couldn't live with him, he would have killed me as soon as you were old enough, I am certain. It's been long enough now, that I think I can take the risk. I haven't heard anything of him in the last couple of months. Besides, you are a grown man, he would never be able to hurt you now."

Surprise reeled through him, "Maman? You never said anything before."

"No. I haven't needed to. Tonight, however, I did. I need you with me, Raul. I need to do this."

Raul closed his eyes. He hated the sliver of light which always shone through the bottom of his right eye lid. The scarring he had carried from birth meant his right eye never closed properly. Just another reminder of the monster he believed himself to be. He could make himself forget he couldn't play wind instruments, or smile properly, when he did neither of those things, but unless he lived in continual darkness, he could not escape the constant light. It was something he had tried to do when a child once he realised, he was disfigured. His mother never allowed him to stay hidden for long. She would pull him out of his darkened room and make him feel the sunshine on his face. He would never admit it to her, barely even to himself, but he loved the sensation of it stroking across his skin. He still lurked in shadows, a deep hood over his face when anyone but his mother was around.

Her love wrapped around him with her silent presence. Gritting his teeth, he opened his eyes and took the hated mask from her hand. It may hide his hideous face from the world, but it rubbed against his face and left his scarring feeling over-sensitised. "Let's get this show on the road then." He sighed out as he lifted the mask up to his face.

Chapter Two
Harmony

Wrapping her two-foot ponytail around her hand, Harmony tugged on her hair in frustration. It was a habit she had picked up, a throwback to her childhood when she lived in Monterey, California. What she remembered most was running around the big house her father had worked in. She had grown up with Dante, the only son of the terrifying man her father worked for. Dante used to tug on her black hair when they were children, and she hated it. Yet when she left the West Coast for her scholarship to Juilliard, she had started pulling on her hair when she was nervous or stressed. It always brought to her the ruggedly handsome face of Dante, grounding her with the mesmerising dark eyes that drilled through her very soul, even from her memories.

With another tug of her hair, she could smell the salt and hear the crashing waves against the rocks of Pebble Beach. Dante lowered his head and glared at her, the water breaking on rocks behind him, framing his displeasure with the moonlit crystal drops of water which hung suspended in the air for a moment before falling back to join the rest of the turbulent tide.

"Are you kidding me?" The incredulous voice pulled her back to the bustling activity of the backstage of Broadway Theatre. "No wonder you barely finished Juilliard's. If this is all you can hand me in written music and expect me to accompany you. You are crazy."

Indignant of the condescension being spat at her by the arrogant musician in front of her, Harmony arched her perfectly groomed brow and snatched the sheet music back. "If you need a full score in front of you, when all I need is you to play what I give you, then you, sir, are an incompetent wannabe pianist."

Aggression reeled off the man in front of her as he stepped into her personal space and grabbed the sheets from her, lifting it above his head out of her reach as he spat, "Not even the Ghost of Phantom Records could play anything with this chicken scratch you call music!"

"How dare you! Give that back now!" yelled Harmony, trying to jump to reach her precious music notes, only to have the jackass withholding it from her put a hand on her shoulder to restrict her movement. Tears burnt at the back of her eyes, yet she refused to let them fall. She would not ruin the makeup her roommate had painstakingly applied for this first televised audition on the inaugural Phantom Records Talent Quest.

Anger and hurt swirled within Harmony at the audacity of the man she had hired to accompany her, to belittle the music she had provided. At the back of her mind, she knew he was probably right. She had struggled to pin down which notes she needed to be played on the piano while she performed the music on her guitar. The song had been teasing her mind for months. At first in just her dreams, accompanied by the writhing images of her body entangled with a man she had never laid eyes on before. Or at least, she didn't think she had, after all, besides a gleaming eye piercing her in the sultry darkness of the bedroom, she never saw his face. The music began to torment her through the days as well, yet no matter how hard she tried, she was never able to capture the notes. Picking up her guitar, had allowed her to recreate the music, or at least some part of it, but she knew it was missing the harmonising notes of the piano.

A dark and brooding presence loomed over the odious toad of a man in front of her and took the music from his clenched hand. With a tender movement, he smoothed out the crumpled sheets and dropped his hooded head to look at the handwritten music in his hand. "What is it I am not supposed to be able to play?"

Harmony gasped with shock as she took in the sight of the shadowed phantom mask over the face hidden in the shadows of the black hoodie. Toad-face made a strangled noise before he found his voice. "This silly little upstart thought she could scratch out some random notes on the stave and expect an accomplished pianist to be able to accompany her while she plays her silly ditty on stage for the Queen of Music herself!"

"Silly ditty?" reeled Harmony, "Why you—"

"An accomplished pianist could follow these notes," commented the Ghost as he lifted his glittering black eyes to stare down the mouth-flapping man in front of him. "If you can't see the beauty of the music within these few poignant notes, then you may as well call yourself a wannabe and quit music now." The last word came out as a dangerously rumbled growl. Simultaneously, it sent a thrill of pleasure through Harmony's core and frightened the fool into a stumbling run as he backed away to turn tail.

Harmony sucked in a sharp breath when the Ghost turned his face towards her. She was instantly captivated by the familiarity of the dark shining eye which penetrated her from behind the mask. His right eye, however, was not as dark as the left. Instead it was clouded, a white scar-like stripe breaking through the glassy orb.

"I'm curious to know, where you found this music." His voice was a soft rumble, like distant thunder that vibrated through her very being.

"I didn't find it, I wrote it. Or at least I tried to. Despite the music being clear in my mind, the notes themselves seem to be extremely reluctant to be committed to the stave." Harmony flushed red, and her head drooped. "Sorry, that probably sounds crazy to you."

"Not at all," he murmured, and reaching out a curled hand, lifted her jaw with his index finger, his thumb resting on the tiny dimple in her chin. "I seem to have the same affliction at the moment." He lifted the music into her line of sight, "These notes seem to be similar to the ones which torture me, cavorting through my mind yet elusive when I try to commit them to paper. Tell me, have you managed to write the piece you intend to play with your guitar?"

His hand held her head while as his eyes continued to hold her mesmerised. Wordlessly, she managed to shake her head in reply.

The left side of his mouth twitched. "Will you do me the honour of allowing me to share this music with you? Let me play beside you, let me follow you?"

His words evoked flashes of entwined bodies dancing in her mind to the tormenting strains of the music she intended to play. Her lips parted; the tip of her tongue darted out to moisten them. She felt her chest begin to rise as her breathing increased. Lyrics began to curl around her, complementing the instrumental piece she had been obsessing over. It was almost as if he was the key to unlocking the music within her mind.

"Can you do that?" she asked on a breathless voice a couple of octaves lower than her usual tone of voice.

"I can do anything I want." His answer was laden with a heat that threatened to sear her with a burning lust she hadn't felt since she was last in Dante's company.

A nervous laugh left her lips as she stepped away. "I meant won't it be against the rules if the Ghost of Phantom Records accompanies one of the contestants as they audition?"

"You let me worry about the details, you just capture the music and be ready to woo the crowds, your soon-to-be-adoring fans." He remarked, his one good eye glittering in the filtered light of the backstage. He tapped her nose with the softest of touches before he turned on his heel and disappeared into the shadows, her sheet music still in hand.

Chapter Three
Dante

A sense of restlessness filled Dante as he moved from one extra-large picture window overlooking the woods, to the next. He needed to do something, yet he wasn't sure what exactly he was supposed to do. He looked behind him at the desk overflowing with paperwork. He hated it but it was a necessary evil if he was to be alpha. His father was the true alpha of the Briar pack, but although still alive, he had been reduced to an almost animal-like state, needing to be locked up within the cellars of the expansive Spanish styled home of the pack's gated estate.

It had nearly killed Dante to challenge his father, and then have him locked up. Had Adam, his best friend and Walter, his father's beta not been there to inject their alpha with wolfsbane while he was locked in vicious combat with his son, Dante would be dead. The ramifications of a rabid alpha, from a powerful pack, on the loose would have been devastating for the human inhabitants of Monterey. It would have also resulted in the council, which operated in the deepest shadows of the supernatural underworld, destroying the whole pack for bringing them unwanted human attention.

The beast below awoke from his slumber and began snarling, hurling himself against the reinforced concrete walls of the silver lined cell. It broke Dante's heart. A fact he hated, knowing his father when in his right mind would have sneered at him for holding such sentimental connections.

He'd been taught from a very young age that emotional attachments to anyone was undesirable. His father was a cold, cruel man and he had worked as hard as he could to harden his son to be the image of him and had succeeded in influencing some elements of Dante's life. The worst of them was allowing Harmony to believe he had no feelings for her, in essence pushing her away until she fled to the opposite side of the country. His father hadn't completely destroyed the heart within him, though. Dante had been unable to kill his father, the only parent he knew, since his mother had died in childbirth.

The snarling grew louder, the very sound of it a knife jabbing through Dante's back. In a moment of swift decisiveness, he grabbed his bike keys from the desk and stalked towards the door, snagging his leather jacket off the hook before he swung it open.

He would head over to see whether Adam wanted to join him for a ride through the mountain trails, then maybe they could go for a run in their wolf forms when they reached the remotest section of the ranges.

The ride through the quiet roads of the pack's estate was quick, and Dante wondered where everyone could be on a Saturday night. He hadn't seen a single teen, or couple wandering the pack grounds. It was unusual not to spot another vehicle, or pedestrian, despite the fact the Briar pack all lived in a gated community of forty homes exclusive to pack members. It was never completely quiet.

Adam opened the door within moments of Dante ringing the bell. As always, he greeted him with a strong arm shake and back slapping hug. "Hey, man, how's it going?"

"Quiet, where is everyone?" questioned Dante as he stepped over the threshold into the comfortably furnished home Adam shared with his mate, Sadie.

Sticking his head out the door and having a quick glance around the neighbourhood, Adam shrugged before he shut the door behind them. "Probably glued to their TV's. There is a new show just airing tonight. Live auditions for the Phantom Records Talent Quest. Sadie kicked me off the sports channel to watch it."

Rolling his eyes Dante followed Adam into the den where Sadie was curled on the sofa, leaning forward towards the large flat screen. "Not another reality t—" words failed him when he saw a face from his past flick across the screen. She was as beautiful as the day she had left Monterey for a scholarship to Juilliard. It had been the hardest day of his life watching her stumble through her goodbye. Despite her desire to pursue her dreams, she had awkwardly tried to let him know that she would stay if he felt anything other than friendship for her. He did, of course, but he could never admit it to her. Not with his father's voice in his head telling him love was for fools. He wouldn't have put it past his father to hurt or even kill Harmony as a lesson to his son. Instead, he had wished her luck and felt his heart break before it hardened when she walked out of his life.

Now he was watching her walk onto a stage, her curves and flowing raven locks highlighted by the artificial lighting. She was everything he remembered, and more. He felt his groin stir with lust as she spoke, announcing her name and that she would be performing a song she had written herself.

With the encouragement of the judges, she positioned herself on a bar stool, set her guitar and started to strum. The chords were eerily haunting, flowing from the speakers of the television. It curled around him and teased every one of his senses. Even his wolf sat up and took notice from deep within his psyche.

The rhythm of the guitar was matched by the minor, somewhat discordant notes from an unseen piano. It was harshness and gentility blending together in a magical combination that stirred the soul and made a person want to float away on the strains of the music.

As the music came to an end, Dante was jarred back to his current surroundings. He hardly heard a word said by the judges in response to the performance.

"Ohhh…she was amazing. I never saw the piano, though. I wonder if she used a recording to accompany her?" gushed Sadie.

Adam chuckled before wrapping his arm around her shoulders. "Does it matter, babe?"

"I guess not. I wonder who she is?"

Dante sighed. "Harmony Maurice. Her father was the antique book specialist who worked for my father when I was younger." The desire for a bike ride left him, and he found himself walking out of his best friend's home without saying another word. He missed the look shared between Adam and Sadie while he mulled over his body's reaction not only to seeing Harmony again, but also the music she played.

It was a connection he couldn't ignore, and he needed to see her again.

His father's words be damned.

To Be Continued

The Night I Fell For A Pop Star

by

Mandy Bee

Heart Beats

A flat tire.

A chance meeting.

Two complete opposites, one a pop star and one a homebody.

Can one night together change their fate?

Chapter One

"Um hello....?" I hear someone holler from the back door of the church.

Crap, we're almost finished cleaning up. I slowly walk to the back, hoping whoever it is has already left since they didn't get a reply. It's been a long day for me. The annual hotdog and BBQ sale makes good money every year but it's murder to work. Some people are so rude you just want to hit them, but it's probably not a good idea to hit them while they are buying food from a church.

When I make it to the backdoor, I see a broad figure filling the doorway. If this man was any taller he'd be hitting his head on the door frame. When his eyes meet mine, they stop me dead in my tracks. What in the world is he doing here? How is this possible?

His deep sapphire blue eyes rake over my body before he flashes me a cute little smile and I can't stop myself from smiling back at him. Smacking myself mentally, I straighten my shoulders, and erase all emotions from my face. There has to be a reason the biggest pop star in the world, Xander Kelly, is standing at the backdoor of my parent's church, in the small town of Hinton West Virginia.

"Yes, can I help you?" I ask him tentatively. My voice soft, but I managed to not sound as confused as I felt.

While most girls from ages of five to eighty are in love with Xander, I'm not. He just turned twenty-two, which makes him only three years older than me. However, this just makes everything you see about him that much worse. He should know better by now that you can't act like a spoiled brat all the time. Just last week it was all over the internet that he was caught storming out of a five-star restaurant in Miami because the chef wouldn't make him tomato soup and grilled cheese sandwiches. Who does that? I'm praying my face isn't reflecting my thoughts.

"Hi, I just got a blow out, and saw the sign for food. Are you guys still open?" He asks, bringing me out of my thoughts.

While I'm tempted to turn him away, I don't. "Yeah, we are cleaning up but come on in." I answer him passively, turning to walk back towards the fellowship hall of the church.

"I'm Xander by the way." He introduces himself like I wouldn't know who the hell he is. Yes, Mr. Megastar even us little people know who you are.

"I know who you are." I can't contain my eye roll but I'm walking in front of him so I know he can't see me, not that I'd care if he did. "All we have left are hotdogs." I tell him as we enter the fellowship hall.

"Sounds good, I'll take three with mustard, please." He says coming around me, but I turn before he can step in front of me and make my way toward the huge kitchen that is connected to the fellowship hall. There's a small window connecting the two rooms, just like at a restaurant.

"Kate, can I get three hotdogs with mustard please?" I dip my head to ask her through the small window.

At this point of the day it's just me and Kate working, she's the pastor's wife. I don't think she would know who Xander is, however her grandkids would be having a fit if they were here.

"You hate mustard Nia." She answers me as she grabs three buns from the steamer.

"It's not for me, we have one last walk in." I smile as I turn around. Kate is one of the sweetest women I know. She'd give you the shirt off her back but never mistake her kindness for weakness. She can be hell on wheels when she needs to be.

"Ok, be ready in a minute."

"Thanks."

"Do you want a drink?" I turn, calling over to Xander.

"Sure, what do you have?" He walks over to me, invading my space giving me the urge to step back, but oddly, I don't.

"Coke, Sprite, and Water." I answer him.

"Water's fine. So, your name is Nia?"

"Yes." I answer him, but I can't force my eyes to meet his. I wonder if he is waiting for me to freak out or fan girl over him. Maybe he thinks no one is a small town like this would even know who he was.

I hand him a bottle of water from the only ice cooler we had left. We usually start with seven, but we always end up with only one left at the end of the day. Kate helped me dump the ice just a few minutes ago so everything is still cold.

"Here you go, everything is cleaned up and I'm heading out. Can you lock up after or do you need me to stay?" Kate asks from the kitchen while holding the hotdogs out for me to get. I want to beg her to stay because I'm not at all comfortable being alone with Xander, but she's been here longer than I have.

"Thanks. You can go. I'll be fine." I wave to her as she walks out of the side door that leads to the parking lot. I wait until I hear the bolt click, telling me she used her key to lock the door before I turn around. Xander's on the other side of the room looking at a cross stitch that my mom made.

"Here's your food."

"This is really pretty." He points to the cross stitch. "Who did this?" He asks as he walks over to me.

"My mom I did." I answer proudly.

"It's beautiful."

"Thank you, it took her six months to make."

"It's really beautiful. I could never do anything like that. How much do I owe you?" Mom hears that every time she does a new cross stitch.

"Again thank you, and don't worry about the money." I answer him as I grab my bag and head for the door.

"Wait, I need to pay you for the food." He says from behind me.

I'm already out the door and waiting on him; one turn of the key and I'm free.

"No, don't worry about it." I'm trying to be nice dude just take the food and go. "I already locked the cash box before you got here." I want to go home.

"I don't think I have ever seen anyone turn down money." He chuckled under his breath.

Is he laughing at me? Oh for the love of God I'm not sure how much more of this I can put up with.

"Can you exit the church so I can lock the door, please." I gesture with my hand for him to walk outside.

"Sorry." He whispers as he walks by me.

Finally! I shut and lock the door before turning to face him. "It's ok." Is all I can get out before my jaw drops. I must be dreaming, the Jeep of my dreams is parked right in front of me. With a once over of the beauty I look down and see the flat tire. Well shit, this is his Jeep.

Chapter Two

I can feel him watching me, but right now I'm eyeing this Jeep. Oh man I love this car; no love doesn't even begin to describe it. It's an old CJ-7 but it's been completely redone. He's put a lift kit on it, new paint job, and looks like the inside has be updated too. It's black with white stripes around the bottom. I have dreamed of having one just like this. I'd go riding around with the top off. Maybe even make someone else drive so we can go off roading and listen to music as loud as possible while I stand up in the back and let the wind wrap around me. I glance over my shoulder at Xander who is just standing there with a big ass smile on his face.

Those charming eyes of his are assessing me again, but differently this time. I know I'm not like the models he's used too but I'm not ugly. So what if he's probably ten inches taller than me? So what if I'm not a size freaking two? And so what if I don't wear makeup, or use all that hair gunk shit? I square my shoulders and give him my best smirk.

"You like my Jeep?" That wasn't really what I thought he was going to ask but ok.

"Yeah, I like your Jeep. I've always wanted one like this. What year is it?"

"1986, it's a CJ-7 but I had her rebuilt."

Her? I roll my eyes. "I know it's a CJ-7, and you also put a lift kit on her and new paint. Looks like you redid the inside with leather, but I hope you didn't do too much to the engine they always built these Jeeps to last." His eyes widen with wonder. Did I shock the poor boy?

"Yeah, I did black leather inside, but I had the engine rebuilt to brand new, with just a few updates nothing too over the top. You know about cars?"

"Cars? No, not really. But I've always wanted a CJ-7 just like this one." I answer as I'm walking closer to his Jeep. I don't care what he says I want to get a better look.

He jogs past me. I think he's going to tell me to get lost but instead he opens the door allowing me a better look. Xander Kelly the nice guy, this side of him would shock the world; it was starting to shock me.

I walk up to the waiting door and bend in part way to get a good look. I take a deep breath of the overwhelming polished leather smell. It sends goose bumps up my arms. The black leather matches the black paint of Jeep perfectly. Not all black interiors are the same breed when it comes to cars. He has a hot stereo system and mind-blowing speakers in the back. I bet this cost a pretty penny, but hey it's not like he's hurting for cash.

Stepping back, I say. "Wow, I love this Jeep!" I know I'm grinning like an idiot, but I don't care. I really love this Jeep and it may be the only time I get to see one like this. I look at him and his eyes are all bright, with a prideful shine to them.

"Glad you like it, wish I could take you for a drive right now but," He points at the flat tire. "that will have to wait." A drive in my dream car? This is just my luck that it would have a flat tire.

"I can't imagine you having Triple A but have you called for a tow or something yet?"

"Yeah, but the tow company said it would be two to three hours to get here. That's when I saw the sign for your sale and hoped I wasn't too late to get some food." He smiles. He really does have a nice smile. Wait what am I doing? I can't get caught up in his deep blue eyes, nice smile, and perfect car.

"You got there right before the buzzer, ten seconds later I wouldn't have let you in." I tease him.

"Buzzer? Don't tell me you know basketball too?"

Is he teasing me now or is he for real? I can't tell.

"What? A girl can't know basketball? I'm not a huge fan of professional basketball. I like college basketball more than anything." I know he loves pro basketball because he's always being photographed at different NBA game.

"I didn't mean it was because you're a girl. I mean it's cool that you know about both. What college is your favorite? I'm a Duke boy, and why no NBA?" He leans against the front of the Jeep and crosses his arms.

"You're a Duke fan? No way! That's my team, I love Coach K!" I'm a little impressed that he likes Duke. I would have guessed he was a UCLA fan since he lives on the west coast.

"You seem surprised by that, and you still didn't answer my question about the NBA"

"Well, don't take this wrong ok? I feel that if a man gets paid millions to play then is it really worth watching? In college they are fighting to win and fighting to get to March Madness. They have to keep their grades up to play and I respect the guys that have good GPAs and play good ball too. I get that in the NBA they are playing to win the title at the end of the season but still if you're earning millions of dollars a year, what do you have to lose if you don't win?" He looks a little overwhelmed by what I just said so I mutter "Sorry." I think I just need to get in my car and go home.

"Wow." He says making me look back up at him. "I've never met someone who had a real reason for not liking the NBA. Most say, 'because I don't' but you have really thought it out."

"Yeah." Is all I can come up with, but I try to smile. "Um, when did you call the tow truck?" I ask hoping it was long before he came into the church.

"Like five minutes before I walked over to ask for food." He laughs.

Damn, that was only like fifteen minutes ago. Should I let him stay here and just go? I don't know what to do. He must have seen I was fighting with what to do because he said. "You can go, I'll be fine, I'm a big boy." Laughing again but kinda shy at the time.

"Yeah, you're a big boy Xander." I playfully roll my eyes. "But it will be dark in less than an hour and if one of your crazy fans comes and kidnaps you, I think I may feel bad about it."

I consider just hanging out at the church, but I could take him to my house. I only live three blocks from here and my family is away this weekend.

I promised to help with the hotdog sale, and it got me out of a family reunion, and in return I get some peace and quite time at the house. But now maybe a few hours with the real Xander Kelly would be kind of fun…maybe.

"No one knows I'm here, only you. I needed to get away from everything, so I took a drive. I packed a bag and drove off. That was four days ago. My mom and the important people in my life know I'm safe, I check in daily. But I don't tell them where I am. So, unless you go on twitter and say something, I think I'm safe."

He takes two steps closer to me, shutting the door on the Jeep as he reaches me. "What…" I stuttered.

"Nia, I can trust you right?" He asked, his eyes locked on mine searching for something, the truth maybe?

My heart started racing and a small gasp left my mouth before I could stop it. It took me a second, but I quickly stepped back and shook my head, breaking the weird trance he had me in.

"You're not on my twitter so you're safe from your obsessed teeny poppers but nighttime around here, not so much. Look we can either go back into the church or you can ride out the wait at my house. It's just a few blocks away, but you need to call the tow company to get an update and an ETA. If we go to my house, you need tell them that too."

Oh my God! Did I just invite this guy to my house? Yup, sure did. I don't know what I'm doing. I could blame it on the awful day I had but I know that's not the real reason I just asked Xander if he wanted to come home with me. Maybe I'm still under that trance from a minute ago. Maybe I've lost my mind. Or maybe this could be a good thing. It's not like I have anything urgent to do tonight. Maybe a couple hours with a pop star won't be so bad.

Chapter Three

"You're inviting me over to your place?" He asks with a smile that looks like he is laughing at me.

"Look, I'm not being rude or anything but like I said before, yeah I know who you are. I didn't say I liked your music or was a fan or anything like that now did I? I'm trying to be nice. You shouldn't be alone in the dark with a flat tire. We don't have a high crime rate around here, but you'd be a sitting duck for any punk who came around. So, no I'm not going to let you just stay here alone. You pick, the church or my house." I cross my arms to let him know to pick fast and that I'm a little annoyed with him.

"Trust me Nia, I could easily tell you weren't a fan and that was a good thing for me by the way. I don't care if you like my music, not everyone does and that's ok. I know you're being nice; you've been nothing but nice. If you think I shouldn't stay with my car then I pick your house."

I want to pick apart everything he just said but I stop myself.

"Fine my house it is, but first call the tow company tell them you are going to a…" What should he tell them? A friend's house? But we aren't friends. "Just tell them you are going to leave your Jeep because it's getting dark and to call you the minute they get here. I'll run you back over." I'm nervous, and even I can hear it in my voice.

"Ok, give me a minute to grab my bag I don't want to leave it here." I wait by my car while he makes the call and grabs his stuff. "Ready?" He asks as he walks up to me.

"Yup." I jump in and start the car. My little ten-year-old mustang is nothing to his Jeep, but it's clean and runs great. My sister passed it down to me when she got a new SUV last year. First thing I did was deck everything out in sugar skulls. My dad says it looks like the day of the dead threw up in my car.

Xander has to bend low to squeeze his broad body in to the small seat and I bite my lip to keep from laughing. I put the car in drive and pull out of the parking lot. One turn onto the main road, one turn onto my street and then we are pulling into my driveway. Took us less than two minutes to get to my house. I could have walked to the church, but I sometimes help with deliveries for the sale and I hate driving other people's car's.

Getting out of the car, I don't even bother telling him to follow me because I know he's already right behind me.

My house is nothing grand but it's home. My family has lived here for over ten years now. My sister is in her last semester of college. After this summer she has plans to move out. Mom and Dad were thrilled that she stayed home during college, they want me to do the same thing. I'm still undecided. I want to go out into the world and be on my own but at the same I'm scared I'll fail and end up back at home anyways. I still have the rest of the summer to decide so I've been trying not to think about it too much.

We have a standard three-story house. A finished basement, main floor, and top floor. We are by no means rich, but we are blessed. We have nice things and never go hungry. I look around and think he can't say anything bad, and if he does, he'll get an ear full that's for sure. I'm sure our home is nothing to what he's used too, but it's our home and I'm proud of it.

I take off my shoes on the back porch before unlocking the door because I like being barefoot. He starts to take his off, but I stop him. "You don't have to do that I always do because I like being barefoot."

I head for the front door to get the mail. Turning around I see him looking at my chess set that on the coffee table. I have a small collection of chess sets. Most are put away and only come out when I want to show them off. He is looking at a marble one that we keep out in the living room so dad and I can play.

I lay the mail on the table and ask. "You like chess?"

"Yeah, a friend taught me how to play a few years ago. But your set is really nice."

"Thank you, this is one of my marble ones. I have several that are put up in storage. This one and the onyx one, that is in the china cabinet in the dining room, are the only two out right now."

His eyes go all wide again. "You have an onyx chess set? Wow, can I see it?"

"Sure," I shrug and walk towards the dining room. "This is it." I point at it. I love this set. The grey and white mix in a perfect swirl pattern. Beautiful is an understatement for this set. "My mom brought it back from Mexico."

"It's amazing! I love the colors. Can I look at some of the pieces?"

He wants to touch it? No, I don't think so.

"Um no, I don't let anyone touch it. Sorry, not even my family. My dad and I play on the marble one." I start to walk into the kitchen because I need coffee, but he stops me by grabbing my arm.

"You play as well?" I give him a look that tells him I'm not ok with him touching me. As he lets go, my look softens. "Would a person really collect chess sets if they couldn't play the game?" I tease him. "Yes, I play as well. My dad taught me when I was ten. Mom and Mindy don't play so it's just me and him."

"Who's Mindy?"

"My sister, she lives here too. We both live with our parents. Well, not for much longer. Mindy is almost done with college; she wants to move out once she finishes."

"That's cool, I live with my mom too. Or she lives with me. We fight over that, but I always say I live with my mom." He smiles one of those all-American boy smiles and I can't help but smile too. It was in that moment that I took a really good look at him. He's wearing a black t-shirt and nice fitting jeans. Every time you see him online, he has these big baggy jeans that fall down showing his boxers and not in a good way. But right now, he looks like any other guy, no drama, just a guy named Xander.

I turn to go make my coffee. I ask if he wants some and he says sure, so I make a full pot. As I wait for it, I get the sugar out and my creamer. I gather the cups and stare at the coffee pot. I didn't even hear him come up beside me.

"You really want coffee, don't you?" He asks.

I squeal then hold my hand over my chest trying to slow down my heart. "The kind at the church tasted like crap and I have the house all to myself this weekend, I don't plan on sleeping much." Wow, that came out wrong.

"What do you plan on doing?" He raises an eyebrow.

"That came out wrong. I was hoping to write this weekend." I blush.

"You write too?"

"Yeah, I write short sorties and poems. I've been wanting some time alone for a while now and sitting at Starbucks doesn't count as alone time. Not when most of the people in there don't know the meaning of indoor voices."

The coffee pot dings, giving me a reason to turn away from his personal question. I go about fixing my cup just the way I like it then let him fix his. He drinks it black. I would choke on black coffee. I need sugar and creamer.

"Nia, you know about basketball and love jeeps, you play chess and write. I would bet you read a lot too. But I would also bet you love music and movies too. Is there anything you don't do or don't know about?" Is he teasing me again? I wish I could tell with him.

"I do love music and movies. And I do read a lot. You win both bets. And yes, there's a lot I don't do and a lot I don't know about." Walking into the living room I curl up on the couch and sigh into my coffee.

"I thought you were going to write?" He asks sitting at the other end of the couch, making me want to move to the a chair. But I don't, not wanting to hurt his feelings.

"My laptop is upstairs, and I very rarely let anyone read my writing let alone let someone watch me write." I know what is coming next, I hear it from my family all the time.

"You write but you don't let people read it?" See, I knew he was going to say that. My family, mainly my sister, has been on me for years to publish some of my work, or at the very least let them read it.

"It's no big deal, just short stories about things that could happen but never would in real life. Now the poems there are about five that I have let my family read and only two have my name on them."

"You're a private person then?"

"Yeah in a lot of ways I am. Did you ever eat your hotdogs?" I'm just realizing that I don't think he did.

"Um no they are in the Jeep. I got caught up in talking to you and kinda forgot." He looks away from me. Is he blushing?

"Guess I should fix you something to eat then." I jump up and head back to the kitchen, happy to busy myself. This is something else I can do; I can cook better than most of my family. Here he comes right after me. It's like having a puppy following me. Can't say I hate it, but I won't say I love it either.

"You don't have too. I'll get something later." He tries to say but I know the guy is hungry. I go to the fridge to take inventory of what we have. I could make a chef salad, pasta with chicken…Oh yeah baby Nia's famous pork chops coming right up.

"You want some pork chops, with green beans?" I ask him with my head still in the fridge.

"So, I guess I'll be adding cooking to the list of things you do. Yeah that sounds great can I help?" Cooking with Xander Kelly? Wait, I need to think of him as just another guy named Xander, forget who he is and what he does. This way is easier. I'm not hosting a pop star at my house. I'm just being a nice person, who is helping out someone who needed it.

"Um you can set the table." I show him wear everything is and start cooking.

I love cooking and this is a recipe that no one has. I created it one night just messing around and my family raves over it. I've made it for a few friends, and they loved it too. Hope Xander loves it too.

Chapter Four

It doesn't take long to get the green beans ready. I put them in the steamer and hit them with some garlic power. My famous pork chops are all rubbed down with my mix of spices. The pan is ready, so I gently place them in and smile when I hear that searing sound. I love that sound. I'm cooking for two instead of 4 or more so in no time everything is ready. The table looks nice. He even rolled the silver wear.

"Nice" I say then ask. "What would you like to drink?"

"What do you have?"

"Well let's go look." I walk back into the kitchen and as I'm opening the fridge door, I almost hit him in the face.

"Hey, don't break the face" He laughs.

I roll my eyes again and smile "Yeah, I think five million girls would kill me if I broke anything on you." I laugh. "We have lemonade, diet coke, water, beer and wine."

"Lemonade sounds good."

I grab the pitcher and two glasses and follow him to the dining room. I pour our lemonade and sit the pitcher on the table then start plating our food. I watch him sit and take a deep breath.

"This smells wonderful." I blush at his compliment.

"Thanks, do you say a blessing before you eat?" I don't know much about him just want the internet says and it's not very nice to him.

"Not all the time but we can if you want too" I can see he's not use to this, so I say a quiet prayer and then look up at him. We start to eat, and I laugh just about every time he moans. It's like he has never had a home cooked meal.

"Your mom does cook right?" I ask.

"Sometimes but not like this." He answers while trying to chew.

As we start to eat he asks me about my college plans. I tell him about getting accepted to Marshall University but how I would like to take online classes instead of going to campus. He found this a little odd because most teenagers are dying to leave home, go to college, and live it up. That's just not me.

I guess I'm what most people would call an invert or a homebody. I'm not a complete hermit, I do leave the house, but I just don't like to be around a lot of people. I still want to get my own place, eventually.

My parents want me to take at least one on campus class. They think it will help with my social skills. It could, but maybe I'm ok with not having social skills. I plan on majoring in English with a minor in business. I want to open an online tutoring program. None of that means working outside of my house.

When we finish eating, he takes both our plates and starts to clear the table.

"At my house the cook does not clean." Don't rich people have others who do things like this for them?

"Ok, just wipe everything off into the trash can and leave the plates in the sink."

"No, I'll wash them if you show me where your soap is." He's really going to do dishes? Where is my phone I wanna YouTube this?

"You don't have too, just clean everything off and I'll wash them in the morning."

"Just show me where the soap is and go sit down." Bossy Xander, fine if he wants to do the dishes then I won't stand in his way.

"It's under the sink Mr. Bossy." I laugh and walk into the living room. "I'm putting some music on but don't worry it won't be yours."

I can hear him laughing over the water running. "I'm not worried about that. What are you going to put on?"

I turn on the TV and go to my country radio channel. I'm a country girl but I like a little bit of everything. Florida Georgia Line 'Get Your Shine On' comes on. I turn it up so I can't hear him telling me to change it, not going to happen. I curl up on the couch and close my eyes because I love this song. After that a good mix of some of my favorite songs play. I'm in music heaven right now. I didn't even hear the water stop or him walk in.

"Hey." He says causing my eyes to pop open and me to jump up turning the TV off.

"Hey, done already?" I try to hide that me caught me in a music trance.

"Yeah, dishes are all done, but the tow company just called." Oh, he's leaving. Wait isn't this what I wanted? Why am I sad?

"Ok, I'll grab my keys."

"No, that's not it. The tire I need isn't in stock and will have to be ordered. The guy said it probably won't get here until late tomorrow night." Oh, so what do we do now?

"Um…ok…so where are they towing your Jeep?"

"To the local dealership. I guess I need to call a few hotels and see what's available."

Before I can stop myself, I say. "You could stay here."

What the hell just came out of my mouth? I don't know who is shocked more, me or him. We stare at each other, both with that deer in the head lights look.

"You're asking me to stay?"

"Yeah, I guess I am." I say trying to hide the nervousness in my voice.

"Are you sure because I could just get a room and wait on my Jeep to get fixed. I wouldn't want to mess up your 'alone time' weekend."

I don't know what to do. Do I want him to stay? Yeah, I kind of do. Do I want him to go? Not really. When I think of him as just Xander, a very sexy male who is also sweet and kind, I'm happy to let him say. When I think of him as Xander Kelly, mega pop star who is plastered all over the internet as the biggest playboy ever, I want to kick him out and lock the doors behind him. Problem is, he's both. I don't know what to do, yet I've already asked him to stay.

"How are you going to go to a hotel and not let everyone know you're in town?" I ask, wanting to convince him that staying is a better option.

"I see your point, but I'm worried you're just doing this to be nice not because you want too."

"Trust me, if I didn't want you here you wouldn't be. I don't do anything I don't want too. I don't mind if you stay." I say with a shrug that I hope looks casual.

"Well your house is better than a hotel, and your cooking is better than take-out. I'd love to stay."

Xander Kelly just agreed to stay at my house. The blush I just had from his compliments is now gone, as all the blood rushes from my face leaving me pale and somewhat queasy. I gotta pull myself together and quick. He is just a guy, nothing more. I'm doing a good deed, for a man who needs some help.

"So…yeah…um you can stay in the guest room. Come on I'll show you." Bad idea Nia! That room is across from yours!

I start to walk up the stairs and I know he's following me, my body can feel him behind me. I turn on the hall light, open the guest room door and flip the bedroom light on.

"Nice room."

"The bathroom is downstairs. I have a book collection in the hallway if you want to read or something. Sorry there's no TV. This use to be my brother's room and he took it with him when he moved." Great now I'm rambling.

"You have a brother? What's his name?"

"Joe, he got married and moved to Washington."

"Cool, I don't care much about TV."

"I'll let you do whatever." I leave, heading for the sanctuary of my bedroom. Once inside I take the first full breath since Xander entered my house. Being around him has really messed with my emotions. Why am I so drawn to him?

"Guess this is your room." He says, startling me.

"Don't do that! My heart about stopped!" I manage, trying to catch my breath. "Yes, this is my room. Remember that thing about me being a private person?"

"Sorry, didn't mean to frighten you. I remember, but when you walked out of that room." He points across the hall. "You looked like you might be uncomfortable with this situation."

"Xander, I said it was ok for you to stay here, just take me at my word. I wasn't uncomfortable, I just feel…uncertain around you and I don't know why." I move us both out of my room, making sure to shut the door, and head downstairs. I need more coffee. Just like a little puppy Xander once again is following me.

"Hey, don't feel that way around me please. I thought we were getting along. Is it because of who I am or is it because you're uncomfortable with someone else here with you?"

"It doesn't have anything to do with who you are or what you do, it's more about…I don't do things like this ok."

"Like what? I'm at loss here Nia, just tell me what's wrong and I swear I'll try to fix it." God, he sounds like he really cares about all this.

I go get a fresh cup of coffee, knowing I'll need it to help me through this.

"Ok here's the thing. I don't just talk to random guys, then let them stay at my house, alone with me. The private part of me is screaming 'what the hell are you doing' but for some reason I don't want you to go. You're not as bad as the internet makes you out to be and you don't act like what I thought people like you would act. You're nice, but it freaks me out some that this has all happened in a matter of just about," I look at my watch. "two hours. I'm sorry but it's a little unnerving. There you have it. If you don't want to stay I'll understand." I turn so he can't see the fear in my eyes. I don't want him to go but him staying is against everything I'm used to.

"I like talking to you too." I hear him say. "The internet loves saying I'm some type of bad boy, but they never put the good stuff about me. My mom told me a long time ago to get used to it and I have. As to acting like people like me, I don't know what you mean there, but I'm guess it means famous people. Well if we were at my house and you were staying with me then I would be a big show off and show you everything that I thought you would like. The time thing freaks me out a little too. I know this girl for two hours and she has given me food, twice now and taken me home so I wouldn't be sitting in the dark in my broken-down Jeep, ready to be kidnapped by a fan." That got a little laugh out of me. "I don't want to scare you." I feel him next to me and this time I look at him. "But you have to know it freaks me out too. I don't know what the do's and don'ts are in your house, you must have some rules. But I'd still like to stay and if you don't want me upstairs, I'll sleep on the couch. Ok?"

I just smile and shake my head before saying. "No, you don't have to sleep on the couch, and as to the rules I may have to make some up." Now we both are laughing. "Ok, so from now on we can be fully honest with each other. Blunt but nice."

"Deal, but you know I will be asking a lot of questions right?" He teases. I figured this much.

"Yeah I know, I'll try not to ask you too many." I promise him.

"Ask whatever you want, I don't mind." He says. Yeah but I do, well kind of.

"But if you're going to stay till tomorrow night, I need to call Kate and tell her that I can't work the sale tomorrow, which I had planned to do anyways."

"I could work it with you, if you want?"

"Um no, if you don't want people to know where you are, you are going to have to stay indoors. Like in the house"

"True." He says, a sad twinge in his voice and looks away from me. He looks lost in his thought, maybe he's sad he can't go out like a normal person without being mobbed by fans. I let him be and go grab my phone, I head to the front porch to call Kate.

Chapter Five

"Kate it's Nia, I have bad news I can't work tomorrow." I say as soon as she answers the phone.

"Don't worry, I think we can handle it, plus with the rain coming we may even close early." She doesn't even ask why I can't come in, which I would've had to lie to her, but I would've had no choice in it without outing Xander.

"Thanks for understanding Kate, see you later, love ya." I hang up fast and dial my sister.

"Hey girl! Taking a writing break?" Wow my sister is way too perky for this time of night.

"Not really but I need to tell you something and you can't tell mom and dad ok?"

"What is it, are you alright?" Perky is gone and now she's got her worried voice on.

"I'm fine but I had a friend come in from out of town and he's staying for one night. His car got a flat and the tire he needs had to be ordered. Please don't tell mom and dad they would flip out!"

"Nia, you hate it when family comes to stay with us, and you're letting a guy stay? Who is it? Is it someone I don't know? I don't see how that could be because we know all the same people."

"He is just a friend from out of town I can't really tell you right now, he doesn't want anyone to know where he is. But he is not running from the law or anything like that he just wanted time away from his life and ended up here."

"I promise to keep this from mom and dad but when he leaves I want to know everything." She says.

"I promise to tell you everything. I'll call you after he leaves."

"Nia," she pauses, her voice goes to a whisper. "you're not going to have sex or anything right?"

"WHAT?! GOD NO! Why would you ask such a thing?!" I know I'm screaming too loud but oh my God Mindy!

"Chill out I was just asking. Don't get your panties in a twist sis." She laughs as she hangs up on me.

I walk back into the house, stunned from the call not watching where I'm going and run smack dab in the strong figure known as Xander, "Were you listening in on my calls?"

"No, I heard you scream and went to the door then saw you on the phone and was walking away when I heard the door open."

"You didn't hear anything?"

"I swear, all I hear was you screaming." He sighs. "You didn't tell them about me, did you?"

"No, I didn't use your name. Kate didn't even ask why I wasn't coming in, which was fine by me. But I had to call my sister to let her know someone was staying with me for a night. I told her a friend from out of town was staying and to keep it from mom and dad. She didn't know what to think, knowing sis she probably thinks an old boyfriend is spending the night." I'm laughing while he stares at me.

"So, I'm a friend from out of town?" His smirk is back.

"Sure, unless you want me to call her back and tell her I have Xander Kelly at the house and to please call the papers." I hold my phone up teasing like I'm going to dial, reaching out he easily takes it from my hand.

"No, I think I like being the unknown friend from out of town."

"Can I have my phone back please?"

"I don't know, I don't think I trust you with it just yet."

Say what? "What does that mean?" He puts my phone in his jean pocket and heads for the couch.

"Hey give it back." I grab his arm and we are suddenly in a fun little twist and turn match. I laugh every time that I almost have it and then he wiggles away. He's laughing at everything too. This is fun, but I want my phone. An idea hits me. I stop and say. "Fine you want the phone for the night go ahead keep it." I wink at him.

"I win, right on!" He cheers. "Wait, are you up to something?" I just smile at him.

"I think I'll go change be back in a few." I say heading up the stairs. He better not follow me.

I go into my room and swiftly change into a tank top and pajama pants. Looking out my door, I notice that his is still open, slowly I head for it. I'm half a step in before I'm flipped around, and he has my wrists captured in his hands! Damn it!

"Whatcha doing?" He asks his face an inch from mine.

"Trying to be a good host. I was going to turn your bed down." I glance down at my hands. "You know you're still holding my wrists, right?" My voice is low, almost a whisper. My heart feels like its about to beat out of my chest.

"I know and I know you're lying." He doesn't let go of me.

"Fine, whatever. I wanted my phone back so I came in here hoping to find yours so we could just trade."

"Now that I believe." He smirks at me.

"You're still holding my wrists."

He's looking me dead in the eyes, I want to look away, but I can't. This is starting to freak me out. He leans in and kiss on my forehead then lets go of me. He takes a couple steps back but keeps his eyes focused on mine. What? Did he just kiss my forehead?

I go to walk out, well more like almost run out, but his words stop me as he offers. "Here, you want this?" I turn and he hands me my phone. "I put my number in there." He winks at me.

"Thanks." I smile, tucking my phone in my bra, I walk over to the large bookcase that takes up one whole wall in the hallway. Books are sometimes my safe haven. I start searching for one to get lost in tonight.

I feel him walk up behind me, his warm breath tickles my neck. "You have a nice collection. I don't get much time for reading but I have time now, got something I can read?"

"Sure." I playfully hand him a Dr. Seuss book that we have for when Mindy baby sits. Grabbing an old favorite of mine I saunter back into my room, not closing the door. He stands at the doorway and watches me.

"Well as much fun as Dr. Seuss is, I was thinking about something more along the lines of an unknown author."

"Um I don't think I have anything like that." Shit, he means my writing.

"Yeah you do, come on let me read something by you, please?"

"I don't let anyone read my work, I told you this."

"But here's the thing, you don't have to tell anyone that I read it. I trust you. I know you're not going to go to the papers about me being here, even after I have to leave. So, let me read something. This weekend is basically our little secret. Why not share with me what you won't with others?"

He has a point I'm not going to run and tell the papers I spent the night with Xander, because they will paint me to look like a slut. So yeah, he can trust me, but can I trust him?

"I don't know, you have a point, but no one has ever read my writing. So, if you did and didn't like it…"

"You are too hard on yourself you know that? When I started out I was the same way but the stress from all of the worry about killed me. I had to learn to let go of the fear. You need to do the same thing. Why don't you trust anyone to be in your world?"

He really doesn't want to know the answer to that question and I really don't want to answer it. I cross my arms and bite my lip to look like I'm thinking. I could just let him read a poem and be done with it.

Chapter Six

"Fine, one poem."

"Oh no, no poems I want a story."

"Xander no, I can't, I just can't." I turn around. I'm blinking back tears, not wanting to cry.

"Hey, no don't do that, I'm sorry I pushed. I'd love to read one of your poems please." He pulls my arm until I turn around, I try to hide my gaze from him, surely he'd see the fear in them. He wraps me in a hug, my arms go around him like it was a natural thing to do. We stand there captured in a perfect moment that seemed to go on forever. Having him hold me like this just felt so right. The peace it brought me should have me running scared but I actually made me want to hug him closer.

Then I felt him stroking my back, just up and down with one hand, just the fingertips of one hand while the other one is on the small of my back. Gently I pulled away from him, he let me go with a sigh.

Sitting on my bed I loaded my laptop, browsing my files, contemplating poem or story? Stand strong or give in? I pick a poem, it's titled Gone. I let him sit by me, secretly pleased by the closeness, and move the laptop stand to wear we both can see the screen. I watch as he reads. It's a poem about a friend I lost. I watch closely as he reads it twice. My mind is racing as he read it. What if he hates it? What if he thinks it dumb? What if he laughs at it…at me?

"That is touching." He finally says. Wow is all I can think. I pull the laptop back, making the screen no longer visible to him.

"Thank you." I whisper softly.

"Is that one your family has seen?"

"No."

"Why did you choose that one for me?"

"I don't know, I saw it and thought it had feeling to it."

"Yeah, it had feeling. It was so sad, dark like, then right at the end, I don't know it was like there was....hope."

Well yeah that's kind of how I wanted it to be. I thought. But having him say it was nice.

"Thanks."

"Who was it about?" I should have expected him to ask that.

"I lost a friend a while back, it was about her." I can't look at him.

"You're really good at putting feelings into words."

"Thank you, no one's ever said that."

"No one gets to read these so yeah no one's ever said it. You're good Nia and I bet your stories are too. I'm not asking to read one, but I bet they are great. You need to put yourself out there a bit and let everyone see you."

"Have you been talking to my mother?" I roll my eyes at him.

"No, but I'm guessing I would like her." He laughs while laying back on my bed.

"You would get along with most of my family, as long as you're like this, down to earth Xander, not pop star Xander. But I know you're both." I don't know why but I sighed.

"I try to be down to earth Xander all the time but that doesn't sell albums, from what my people tell me. I love my music. Being on stage is like nothing I can even explain. It's home to me. The studio is the same way. Writing music, taking it from paper to tape, it's hard to explain but it's part of my soul. But with every good thing there's something bad that comes with it.

The bad to my music is the media craziness. My agents want me in the news at all time, so they get to me to wear a crazy outfit or get caught doing something dumb, and they make sure the press knows all about it. It's nuts but even when they talk trash about me my sales go up. That's why I needed to take a drive. They wanted me to get caught kissing some fan and let the story blow up. The girl was fourteen, I'm not into jailbait. So, I packed up and drove away for a few days." He reaches over and takes my hand. "And met you."

"Wow so that's how it works." His life sounds kind of sad. He sounded passionate about his music, but the media stuff sounds awful. Does he ever just get to be Xander? "I will have to remember that next time I see you wearing your jeans so low I see the bottom rim of your underwear." I laugh trying to lighten things up. I take my hand from his and playfully smack his leg.

He groans. "I hate wearing my pants like that, but everyone around me says that's the in thing right now."

"Yeah trust me not all of us like to see it. There is a right way and a wrong way for guys to show their boxers.

He looks at me while still laying on my bed. "Really? Do tell."

Now this time I can tell he's teasing me. The look he is giving me is playful but there's heat behind those beautiful eyes. "Ok, the way you do it in the photos is the bad way, the really bad way. The right way which can be very sexy, is to wear jeans that fit your body type but if you reach for something over your head or bend down and your shirt rides up, then just about an inch or so of nice looking boxers show. That can be really sexy because it looks like you're trying not to show your underwear which makes seeing them almost forbidden."

He's just starring me; I don't like this, his sapphire eyes seeing me. I turn to look at my computer and he sits up with his hand laying behind my back. Not touching but I can feel it there because he's putting his weight on it and pushing into my bed.

"Do you have a well thought out answer for everything? Don't get me wrong I like it, but I have never met anyone like you."

"Anyone like me? Yeah right back at ya!" I laugh and shut down my laptop and roll the table away. I should stand up; I need something to do but he's still sitting there. What should I do? "Well you must be tired, if you want to shower like I said before the bathroom is downstairs feel free to use whatever is in there."

"No, I'm not tired, and I must smell bad if you're telling me to go shower."

"You don't smell bad; I was just being a good host. Oh yeah, would you like me to go turn down your bed for real this time?" I can't help but laugh.

"Sure, why not." That's not what I thought he would say.

Fine I'll turn down his bed and go get more coffee. I walk into his room pull the comforter halfway down at an angle then push the pillows up some. Then I turn and walk out. He's in the hallway watching me, I pass right by him smiling.

After making my way to the kitchen, I rinse out my coffee mug and make myself a new cup. All the while thinking about Xander. He has me feeling crazy yet calm at the same time.

"You must be thinking of something really important or that bottom lip just taste good." I jump back, almost spilling coffee on myself.

"Stop doing that! I need to put a bell around your neck!" I put my hand over my chest and take a deep breath. Good God what is he doing to me.

He reaches to get a coffee cup and his arm rubs my arm. I take a step back. I don't want to feel anything. I don't want to feel anything. I don't want to feel anything. I repeat this mantra. Problem is I do feel something and it's not good.

"So, what do you want to do now, or did you have something planned? I could lock myself in the guest room if you want to be alone." I can tell by the look he's giving me he doesn't want to do that, but I also know if I asked him to he would.

"Um I don't have anything planned and I don't think I could write right now anyways so……yeah."

"So, it's just the two of us drinking coffee and not knowing what to do for the rest of the night. Is this what tomorrow is going to be like?" He's still smiling so I know he's joking.

"No tomorrow I plan on torturing you with a five-movie marathon. Can Xander say Twilight?" I giggle and walk into the living room.

"Twilight?" I hear him groan. He walks in and sits closer than before.

"Good boy." I tease him. "I'm team Edward and I have all five movies on DVD. And I have a Breaking Dawn blanket my sister got me for Christmas. I planned on watching all them while huddled under it."

"Aren't those movies for little teeny boppers?" He groans again.

"Probably, but I'm nineteen, so I'm technically a teeny bopper to some people, even though I'm also considered an adult. But in my opinion the books and movies are both timeless. I loved them when they came out, and I'll love them fifty years from now."

"Well, I've only seen two of them, they aren't that bad, but you have to share the blanket." My heart stopped. What did he just say? I try to blow it off.

"No beans, you can use another one, I will not share my twilight blanket." I turn on the TV and Sugarland starts singing 'Baby Girl.' I lean back. "I haven't heard this one in a while." I say. Then I hear him move closer, I keep my eyes shut and focus on the music.

"Yeah it's a good song." He says, God he must be right beside me.

I look over and yup he's dead beside me and reaching. What is he reaching for? Then I see what it is, he wants the remote! Oh, it's on. I grab it from the side table.

"Oh no you don't."

"Come on lets channel surf." He whines.

"You don't like TV remember, and I know you'll put on music I can't stand. My house, my rules."

"You never did tell me the rules of the house." Well, he's right about that.

"Fine, this is a rule then. If I don't like what's on the TV, I change it till I find something I like. Got it."

"Fine. What if I ask if we can turn it off all together and do something else?"

"Like what?" Music boy doesn't wanna listen to music?

"Well we could talk, we could sit quietly and feel awkward, we could play a game." I stop him there.

"What kind of game." I'm holding back a smile, but I know he can tell because his just got bigger. Oh Lord my heart is racing.

"What kind of games do you have? Or we could make up a game." His eyes are shining. Oh, hell no! Not that kinda of game.

"We have a few decks of cards, but I'm guessing you're not good at poker."

"Oh yes I am. I love poker."

"Fine let's go play poker." Oh, this will be fun! I go to the china cabinet and get a deck of cards from the drawer. He follows a little too close this time, but do I really care? Nope.

I turn around and hand the deck to him "You can deal." I walk past him and sit at the table.

"Do you wanna play for money or something else?" Oh, hell yes! Wait, what? NO! My mind has got to stop this!

"Well you have a little bit more money than me, but when I play with my sister and friends we play for points."

"Points?" He asks.

"Yeah every hand you win is worth 5 points. Whoever gets to 50 points first wins." Simple and easy.

"We could play strip poker." He says starring right into my eyes.

Chapter Seven

Strip poker?!?! What? No way! I must be twenty shades of red right now and totally in shock. Control yourself Nia, show pretty boy who is boss.

"I think not, but right now I'm thinking I just want to forgo it all." I stand and try not to run out of the room.

Strip poker? He is out of his mind? I mean I'm not a prude or anything, but I haven't even known him a full day!

Heading back to the living room I turn the TV back on and turn the music up loud. But he came in right after me.

"Hey, can you turn that down? I'm sorry I shouldn't have said that, it was just a joke." I try to play like I can't hear him, then the TV goes off. What the hell?

"Hey!" I jump up.

"I was trying to say I was sorry and that it was just a joke."

"Well your joke wasn't funny, and don't ever turn off my music!" I snatch the remote and throw it onto the couch.

"What is with you? We were all good, laughing and joking. What did I do?" He looks like a deer in headlights

"Xander it's nothing you did ok? First, I'm not used to hosting a 'pop star' and I don't know. I know we were getting along and stuff but..."

"Hey I'm not a 'pop star' tonight, I'm just Xander remember?"

"I don't get you at all, you're nice and kind of sweet when you wanna be. Then it's like for some unknown reason I'm scared of you." My voice isn't raised anymore but I'm not calm either.

"Scared of me? Why? I'm not going to hurt you or anything."

Yeah physically but you can hurt me other ways. How can I feel like this knowing this guy for like less than a day? I always thought I hated Xander Kelly. His music, the crazy stuff he's always getting caught doing. But he did tell me that they fake some of that stuff. However, now that he has been here at my house and we have been talking and joking, it's like I'm one of his fourteen-year-old fans. No, I'm not! I keep going back and forth with myself, in my head, until I'm dizzy.

"I know you're not going to hurt me. Xander, you're just..." I let out a deep frustrated growl. "You're starting to make me feel crazy!" I try to walk past him to get to the kitchen, but he won't move. "Please move."

"No, because I know what you mean."

"What?" I take a step back.

"You make me feel crazy too Nia. I mean I started out with a flat tire, and have ended up at a beautiful woman's house, where she cooked me dinner and is letting me spend the night." Beautiful? Did he just call me beautiful? "But here's the thing." He goes on. "I like talking to you, I like joking with you. I just like you. I don't know how or when or what, but for some reason it feels right. But if this is going to be a problem I will go to a hotel. I don't want to hurt you or drive you crazy." I stare at him; he feels it too.

"I don't want you to go. But it's not like me to feel like this. I don't...I just don't..." He would never understand so I'm not about to tell him.

"I don't want to go either. And it's ok, I won't try anything, and we can just be friends." I can see he means it; he gives me a half smile. I roll my eyes.

"Fine, but I'm still not sharing my Twilight blanket." I tease trying to break the tension.

"We'll see." He smiles his shy smile.

"Well it's getting late we should hit the hay." Yeah bedtime, well more like quite time for me.

"Need a hand locking up?"

"Nope I'll get it just wait by the stairs." I go around turning the lights off and locking all the doors. The last light is the one at the bottom of the stairs.

"Last one, you can go on up now." I reach and turn it out. The light from the stairway is the only light still on.

"Ladies first." He says. I start up the steps and pray that he's not watching my ass. I stop outside of his room, he comes up and stands in front of me.

"Do you need anything?" I tell myself I'm trying to be a good host.

"No, I'm alright, goodnight."

"Goodnight." I walk across to my room and open the door.

Wow what a day. I get into bed and roll my computer table over to me. I left my door open. I can see into his room from here and I can see the bottom of his bed. I see his feet under the blanket so he must have laid down, good now I can write a little. I open my laptop and check my e-mail and Facebook, nothing good there. I open my latest short story and read the last little bit and try to think about what should happen next. I hear something move; I look up to see Xander is in the hallway. He's looking at my books.

"Um I just wanted to borrow a book, is that ok?" He looks over at me.

"Yeah that fine, just don't go above your reading level."

"Very funny, you working on a story?"

"Kinda, why?" No, you're nothing reading it.

"When I walked out here you looked like you were deep in thought. Sorry I bothered you."

"You didn't bother me; I'm stuck on this one anyways." Why did I tell him that? I know what's coming next.

"Need some help?" See I knew that was coming.

"No, that's ok." You're not reading it and you're not helping to write it either.

"Come on, you can bounce ideas off of me, we could be a good team."

"Xander, my sister has tried all that in the past and it never worked. You will not get any farther than she did, sorry"

"So, I get to read some of them then?"

"What? No." I'm shocked, why would he ask that?

"You said your family has read some of your work, so if I only get as far as your sister that means I get to read some of your stories, right?"

"No, my family has read a few poems, you already got a poem. Feel lucky no one outside of my blood line has gotten to read anything by me."

"What do you mean I got a poem? You wrote one about me?" He winks, he knows what I meant.

"No, before tonight I hated your name." It came out before I could stop it.

"And now not so much?" He's still standing at my doorway, and now has a big ass smile on his face.

"Well I don't hate you or anything, but I really don't think I'll be writing a poem about you anytime soon. Now do you need help picking a book?"

"No, I think I'll just go plug in my headphones, see you in the morning."

"Goodnight." He goes back in his room.

About an hour later I have finally found a flow with my story and I'm happy with how it's going. Then I hear music. No wait its him, he is SINGING! Xander Kelly is not only staying at my house, he is singing in his sleep? Who sings in their sleep?

I get out of bed and walk as quietly as I can to his door. He has he's headphones on and his eyes shut. Now I can understand what he's singing, it's 'Iris' by the Goo Goo Dolls. I love this song. He doesn't have a bad voice for this type of music. I stand there for a minute. He opens his eyes, and I'm caught red handed.

"Hey." I whisper.

"Did I wake you?" He asks while pulling off his headphones.

"No, I was still up. I thought you were singing in your sleep. I came to check on you."

"You came to check on me? Do I sound that bad?"

"No nothing like that. I love that song by the way." I try to smile, don't know why the only light is coming from his iPod and I don't think he can really see my face that much.

"Yeah it was their best, you still working?"

"Yeah I was about to take a break"

"Break for sleep or....?"

"A break for a snack, aren't you tired?"

"Snack? I'm in. No, I don't sleep much."

"Yeah me either, I sleep maybe 3 or 4 hours a night." I flip on the hall light and turn to walk down the stairs. I know he's going to follow so I don't bother asking. I turn on the lamp by the steps and then go to the kitchen and flip the overhead light on. I hear him come down the steps and I smile. I shake my head. Don't go there, I tell myself. What do I want for a snack?

"What kinda snacks do you eat?" He asks.

I look over at him and my jaw drops. He's shirtless! He has changed into baggy basketball shorts and no shirt. Oh My God! He doesn't have any socks on either. What is it about naked feet on a guy? I try to shake my head and act like I have to sneeze, I think he bought it.

"I like popcorn, chips, pretzels, simple things for this time of night."

"Cool, got any popcorn?"

"Yeah." I walk over and open the back door and reach up into the built-in open cabinet and grab two things of microwave popcorn.

"It will be just a few minutes." I say locking the back door.

"Two bags? What you don't wanna share one?"

"Sure, I can split one bag into two bowls."

"No, microwave popcorn does not go into bowls. It's meant to be eaten right out of the bag." Where is he going with this?

"Umm...ok." I guess we are staying up together then.

I put one bag of popcorn in the microwave and hit the start button. I go to the fridge and get a bottle of water. Thinking he may want one too I hand the first to him and get me another.

"Thanks. Where do you want to eat?"

"You're welcome. The living room I guess."

"Ok but I'm moving the coffee table and we are eating in the floor." He says walking out of the room.

"What? Popcorn is not Japanese food." I yell from the kitchen.

"So what? And bring the cards, we'll play slap jack." Oh, I love slap jack! Ok this could be fun.

I get the popcorn and the salt, grab the cards and walk into the living room. He has moved the coffee table and is sitting on the floor looking up at me. Right now, there is a shirtless Xander Kelly sitting on my living room floor!

"Here," I hand him the popcorn and the cards. "Do you like salt?" I ask.

"Yeah, do you?"

"Yup just asking before I put some on the popcorn." I sit down and take the popcorn back, open it and shake the salt over it. Waiting for him to deal the cards I look up and see him staring at me. "What?" I ask taking some popcorn and handing him the bag.

"Nothing, so slap jack?" There is that shy smile again.

We sat there for the next two hours playing game after game of slap jack. The popcorn is gone, and we are still sitting in the floor. We have been laughing and having a great time, maybe he's not so bad after all. He does have great eyes and a nice smile.

"Hey." He says and catches me off guard.

"What?" I ask.

"You looked like you were in space there for a minute. What were you thinking about?"

"Oh nothing, sometimes I space out."

"Another game?"

"No, I'm good. Don't you need to try to sleep? You're going to have a long night tomorrow after they get your Jeep done." Then it hits me, he'll be gone tomorrow.

"I'm not tired. I haven't really thought about all that though."

"Where will you go after here?" Do I really want to know?

"I'm not sure, I know I have to be in New York by Friday so that gives me six days to make my way back."

"Cool…um…I'm going to get another water." I jump up and rush into the kitchen.

"You know I could hang around this area for a few days. I mean not stay here because your family will be back, but we could hang out or something."

My heart starts racing. He wants to stay here and hang out with me? Fine by me. Wait no, this is a onetime thing remember? He's a rich pop star who will never look at you again once back in his world. But what do I tell him?

"I don't think you would like Hinton that much. And you can't really go out, I mean without being spotted."

"Well I was online earlier, on my phone, and saw these cabins that aren't far from here. I could rent one for a few days and you could come hang out with me. Not like overnight unless you wanted too, but during the day and stuff." I look at him with my mouth open and my eyes wide, what did he just say?

"I really don't know what to say to that."

"Say you'll help me book a cabin."

"Help you?" Now I'm lost.

"Yes, help me, I can't call them and tell them who I am. So, I usually have someone call and book it under their name, but that person is usually with me. But I do have a fake ID with me so you could make it under that name, and I can check in myself."

"Ok, I'll help you, but I will not check you in, you're using that fake ID. However, it's almost 5am and I don't think the offices for those cabins are open." I hope not because I don't wanna call at 5am.

"I know it says to book one I have to call between like 10am and 2pm."

"So that gives us five hours." I say feeling awkward.

"Yeah, you feel like sleeping?" No, I feel like kissing. Wait, what!? Where did that come from? My mind needs some soap.

"No, I don't think I'll be sleeping tonight. The coffee you know." Still awkward.

"Yeah me either. So…" He feels it too, I can tell.

"We could get a head start on the Twilight movies." I smile, yes movies nothing else just movies.

"Sure, I guess I need to get a blanket because I hear I can't share yours."

"That's right, you can pick one from the closet in the dining room, I'll go get the DVDs and my blanket." I all but run up the stairs to grab the movies. Walking into my room I get the blanket then think, two could fit under here. We'll see. I go back downstairs and he has moved the coffee table back and gotten his own blanket. I put the first movie in, take the remote sitting it by my side of the couch and sit down tossing the blanket over me. He sits down right beside me.

"Too close?" He asks. No, not at all.

"No, you're fine." I say a little too low. I hit play and I'm ready for some Edward.

Chapter Eight

Something jolts me awake. I look at the TV the first movie is close to being done. I lift my head up now aware that I'm laying on top of Xander and my head was on his chest with us both asleep under my blanket! What the hell?

I go to slowly move so not to wake him, but his arm comes around me and pulls me back to him. My head is back on his chest and we are cuddling. What? He groans a little and I can't tell if he's really asleep. I lay there listening to his heartbeat. I take a few deep breaths and try to get up again. I free myself from his arm but when I stand up to move away from him, he grabs my hand.

"What's wrong? Where are you going?" He's still half asleep.

"We fell asleep and ended up a little too close. I was going to move to the chair." I whisper.

"No, you don't have to do that. What's wrong with how we were laying?" He has let go of my hand but has sat up still covered with my blanket.

"Just go back to sleep." I start to stretch; he stands up pulling me into a hug.

"Why can't you just let whatever is happening happen?" He whispers in my ear.

"Because I will not get my heart broken by someone who says he wants to stay, but in reality, I know he can't stay. It can't work like that. You're Xander freaking Kelly, you have girls throwing themselves at you. You don't need me; you don't need this." I'm still hugging him, but I know we should let go, but I don't want too.

He leans back a just hair but doesn't break the hug. "You listen to me, I don't make a habit of letting strange women take me to their place. I feel something for you. I can feel you don't want to rush anything because yes, I will have to leave for work. But I will come back to Hinton. Even if you say you can't do this and will not see me again, I will still come back and wait for you." He has been looking me dead in the eyes. I can feel a tear roll down my cheek, he wipes it away with his thumb.

"I won't lie, I do feel something for you, but it scares me. I couldn't stand you or your music or the crap they put on the internet about you. Then you walk into my life and it's like Dr. Jekyll and Mr. Hyde!"

"A few of my friends have said that too. I try to tell my PR people that I don't want to be known as the 'bad boy heartthrob' but the truth is it's all about the money. My world comes with a price. Maybe it's time I put my foot down with all their shit. I would hate that me trying to have a normal private life would get out to the press but so far it hasn't. This is not the first time I have taken one of my drives. It is the first time I really don't want to go back."

Not knowing what to say I just lay my head on his chest. We stand there for a few minutes before finally sitting down on the couch, together. He pulls my blanket over our laps and just holds my hand. My mind is in overdrive. Could this ever work, even just as a friendship? He would get bored after a while of coming back and not being able to go out.

"If you don't want this to go anywhere," He breaks into my thoughts. "I will pack up and leave for New York as soon as my Jeep is ready. But if you will at least explore what we are feeling I would love to rent that cabin and even meet your family, if you want."

I'm in utter shock. He will go if I don't want this but will stay and meet my family if I do. I can hear my dad saying very bluntly that he doesn't like his music, well I kind of did that too.

"Can we just be friends and work on that? If it does grow into something more, then we can talk about that. But right now, can we just see if we can be friends?" I know he can tell that I'm not sure about all this, but he has that shy smile on his face, and I start to melt a little. He lays back on the couch pulling my arm asking me to lay back down with him, just without saying it aloud. I lay down with him, my head on his chest. We are all curled up under my blanket, yes this is cuddling for sure. It's nice. I lay my arm over his waist; his arms are around me just holding me. I hear the movie ending, I reach for the remote and turn it off. Sleeping sounds better than twilight, sleeping while cuddling with Xander sounds better.

I close my eyes and start to drift off. This last thing I remember is him kissing the top of my head saying, "Sleep baby, it's all ok." After that I'm off to dream land.

I turn over and stretch. Wait I'm in my bed! Was it all a dream? My phone rings. Without looking at answer it.

"Hello?"

"Hey miss me?" It's Xander! "Come get some breakfast, your coffee is waiting on you."

"On my way." I don't know how I got into bed, but I'm fully dressed, so I know nothing happened, Xander isn't that type of guy.

In the last twenty-four hours I think my whole world has changed. Xander showed up and I don't think I'll ever be the same now that I've met him.

As I'm going down the steps, I think to myself, whatever this is, whatever we are feeling, I'm just going to go with it. Looks like I have a cabin to book.

Epilogue
Six Months Later

"Are you ready yet?" Xander asks from the doorway.

We are at his private cabin. He bought this place last month. He claims it's because he was tired of renting one almost every weekend. I think he truly just wanted us to have our own place together. We've officially been a couple since the day after our first night together. I think I fell in love with him that first night, but every weekend after that our love grew more and more. However, the press thinks we've only been together about three months.

That first month after the news got out was the scariest of my life. People actually camped outside of our house just to get pictures of us. I got death threats, hate mail, and someone sent me a lock of hair asking me to pass it on to Xander.

It took a couple of weeks but it finally died down. We still make the papers at least once a week but it's calmer now.

"I'm getting my shoes on. Did you load the bags in the Jeep?" I ask him as I slip on my sandals and grab my phone.

"Yup, let's go." He takes my hand and all but pulls me out the front door. I can't help but giggle.

Xander got us tickets to see Duke vs. North Carolina, but not just for us, he got tickets for my whole family.

I'll never forget the first time Xander met my parents. We were both extremely nervous. We had been seeing each other for only two months, I thought it was a little to early too introduce them, but daddy pretty much ordered me to bring Xander to the house. He wasn't happy with me disappearing to the cabins just about every weekend.

However, everything went great. My parents love Xander, so does my sister. He's become part of my family. I can't lie, I secretly hope one day he will truly be part of my family but I don't know if he is ready for all that yet.

He holds my door open for me, and helps me in. I'm still in love with this Jeep. I sigh happily as he closes the door.

We meet everyone at the airport. Xander tried to convince us to let him rent a private plane but it just wasn't necessary in my opinion. When he wears his shades and hat you can't tell who he is. He did hire security that will meet us at the airport in North Carolina, there was no way around that since we'll be in a big crowd and all.

The one-hour flight really did beat the five hour driving time. Xander's security was there when we got off the plane and rushed us to a waiting SUV. No one even had a chance to see who any of us were. It took another half hour to make it to the game but once we got there I was bouncing in my seat.

You'd think for someone who usually hates crowds I'd be scared to death, but I wasn't. Over the last six month Xander has truly helped me come out of my hiding place. I still get nervous but I no longer feel the need to always be at home. I was looking around at everything and enjoying the excitement all around me.

The teams were warming up on the court. This was going to be an amazing game.

Xander wrapped an arm around my shoulder and pulled me closer to him.

"I have a surprise for you." He whispered in my ear.

"What did you do?" I asked him. Anytime he said he had a surprise for me usually meant he bought me something.

"Come with me." He stands, holding his hand out to help me up. I take it but raise my eyebrow at him. When he starts to walk us onto the court I stop. "It's ok, it's part of your surprise." He assures me.

As we reach the middle of the court a referee hands Xander a mic. Then I hear the announcer says. "Ladies and gentlemen here to single the Star Spangle Banner, Xander Kelly."

Holy shit! He didn't tell me he was doing this! I try to jerk my hand away so I can run back to our seats but he won't let me go. Instead he pulls me close to his side as he sings our nations song. When it's over the crowd goes crazy. I look around at all his screaming fans and can't help but smile. Their cheers pause, but only for a second, then I hear an excited gasp right before they start applauding again. A small tug on my hand tells me why.

Turning I found Xander down on one knee with a light blue ring box in his other hand. My heart stopped, my eyes filled with tears, and all the breath left my body.

"Nia, you are my heart, my soul, my reason for living. We met by accident but if you'll have me, we'll never be apart again. Will you marry me?"

With tears streaming down my face I somehow got the word "Yes" out.

Xander's strong arms wrapped around me, spinning us both around, he kissed me deeply as everyone cheered. I felt him slip the ring on my finger. I glanced down at the rock this man just put on me. The size of the stone was way too big, but I loved it.

Mom and Dad hugged us when we made it back to our seats. Mindy took hundreds of photos of us. My family welcomed him into our family. My heart felt complete.

I couldn't tell you who won the game, I don't really care either. All I cared about right then was Xander. He said I was his heart and soul, I hope he knows he's my heart, my soul, my everything.

No matter what happens in the future I know I'll never regret asking Xander to come home with me. It was the craziest thing I've ever done, and the best part of it is I get to see a side of him that not many people see. I plan on loving him with all my heart. And who knows, I may even let him read one of my stories. Or I could just write a story about our first night together. The night I fell for a pop star.

Heart Beats

Wager

By

T.a. McKay

What do you get when you add together a guitarist from an up and coming band, a best friend who thinks he's funny, a lost bet, and a boxer with a chip on his shoulder?

You get Brayden's life, and he's regretting playing that game of poker with his fellow bandmate.

Actually, he doesn't regret playing, he just hates that he lost. Especially now he has to come face to face with a guy who looks like he's ready to rip him apart.

A losing streak and lies got him here, but he can't back down, not when he has to repay The Wager.

Chapter One
Brayden

"You're going down fucker."

I roll my eyes at Tony because he might like to think he's about to win the poker game, but the truth is, he's going to be eating his words. This hand is the decider, and I'm determined to win because it's time for Tony to suffer. I want to pretend that I'm good, but the ratio of wins to losses for me doesn't show that. This time I'm going to win. The fact that I'm running eight games down shouldn't matter, not when I'm holding a fucking fantastic hand. "You keep believing that."

He looks smug as hell, but as I look at the four of a kind I'm holding, I know that tonight is mine.

"Why do you two do this to each other every time?" Conner sits on the other side of the dressing room, playing his guitar softly. He never gets involved when the competitiveness comes out between Tony and me, but he always likes to make comments on it.

"At least it's not for money anymore." Tony speaks, but he doesn't look away from me, a twinkle bright in his eyes.

"No, because you'd both be broke. Now you play to be able to humiliate each other."

It's true. We used to play for cash, but once the competitive nature kicked in, the amounts we would bet would get stupid. When the pot hit nearly five thousand one night, we decided to make things a bit more interesting without making us broke. Now the winner gets bragging rights, but more than that, they also get to choose a forfeit for the losing person. Even with that, we started tame, like making the loser strip in a room full of people, or the time that I made Tony eat an entire tube of wasabi, but now the forfeits are getting riskier, so I need to win today so that Tony doesn't have me fucking swimming with sharks or something equally as stupid.

"Don't worry, Con, Bray can handle being beaten again." Tony sounds cocky, but little does he know that it's only going to last until my cards hit the table.

"Yeah, yeah. Just remember that you're friends." Conner turns his attention fully back to his guitar, blanking us as we pick up cards.

Poker started as a way to pass the time while we waited to go on stage, but now it's fuelled by revenge. Or at least it is for me. I can't have Tony besting me, not again. Today is going to be a win, and I have the perfect task for Tony when he loses.

"Ten minutes until stage." The runner shouts into our dressing room before vanishing quickly.

"Time's up. Ready to show?" It might not be in the actual rules to finish a game at this point, but when time is against us, we make shit up as we go along.

"Age before beauty." Tony is still smirking, and for the first time, I feel doubt building. He knows we're about to show our hands, so why would he seem so confident?

I push that thought out of my head as I place my cards on the table and fan them out, letting Tony see the hand that will have him singing I'm Too Sexy by Right Said Fred on stage. Oh god, I can't fucking wait to see that.

"Read 'em and weep, fucker." I have to admit I am feeling smug, but when Tony's smile never fades, my stomach clenches.

"My thoughts exactly."

No, this isn't good. His smile is still plastered to his face as he drops his cards, and I feel like screaming when I see his hand. I thought I had him this time, four of a kind is hard to beat, but I'm looking at the perfect run.

"Royal flush."

"No fucking way. You cheated." My voice is loud, but I can't help it. Conner bursts out laughing as he pats me on the shoulder.

"Take it like a man, Bray. But now let's move before the crowd gets hostile." Connor cracks his neck and heads to the door. Tony gets up from his seat to follow Con, but the smile never leaves his lips.

"It's okay, Bray, I'll go gentle on you." He messes up my hair, and I slap his hand away.

How the hell did I lose with almost the best hand in poker? He must have cheated, but there's no way to prove it. I need to accept whatever the hell Tony is going to think up, and I know for a fact I'm going to hate every minute of it.

Chapter Two
Brayden

"Thank you, Leeds. It's been a pleasure, but now it's time to get fucked up!" Tony holds the microphone above his head as the crowd goes crazy, and the feedback when he drops it onto the floor makes me cringe. He does that every bloody gig, and still, I'm not used to it. I don't know why he needs to drop the fucking thing. I made the mistake of bitching about it once, and now he likes to make sure he's standing next to me when he does it. I hate the arsehole sometimes, and I would totally kick his arse if he weren't one of the best frontmen I've ever seen. He's the one that holds the band together, not that I will ever admit that to him because he would be a nightmare to live with if I did.

I leave the chants behind me as I head down the back stairs away from the stage. As I pass, I high five Donny, the lead guitarist from Shatter, the band following our performance, and he yells about us warming up the crowd for them. I throw him the finger over my shoulder, and I don't need to see him to know he's laughing. Donny is one of the nicest guys I know, and since our bands have been playing the Summer Rock Tour around the UK for the last three years, we've gotten to know each other well. Twelve dates with twelve headline acts makes it one of the UK's largest rock events every year. Our band, The Crave, was picked up three years ago after one of the organisers heard us play in a local bar. It might have helped that I gave him an orgasm he will never forget, but the second year we were invited back told me the reason we were here was our talent.

"How long before we leave?" Connor cracks his neck as he stretches out. We are a middle rung band, meaning that we don't go on early when the crowd is only just arriving, but we also aren't one of the groups that everyone is here to see. We have a following now, but we aren't as massive as the main headliners, Satan's Crush. Those guys are the ones that I want to be like, because they exploded a few years back and they have been unstoppable ever since. I've followed their career carefully since they came from not too far away, and when I heard they were going to be joining us this year, I had to hold in my inner fangirl. Not that I've managed to meet them yet, but I'm working on it.

"We're heading out about eleven. Connie said if we aren't in the van by then, she's smothering us in our sleep."

Tony smiles when I mention Connie, and I can only imagine the depraved things he's thinking. He has it really bad when it comes to her, and the more she turns him down, the harder he tries to get her attention. The first time he caged her in backstage, I nearly jumped to her rescue, but less than five seconds later I realised that she didn't need anyone's help. One knee to Tony's balls and he was lying on the floor groaning in pain. I still remember her face as she walked past. The smile on her face was utterly innocent, and it made her look like she hadn't just left my friend rolling about the floor. That was the day that I knew that the band needed her in charge, and now, two years later, she's still dealing with our shit and making sure we are where we need to be. She isn't really a manager, but she is the one who deals with booking gigs and making sure we get there. Basically, if it weren't for Connie, we would be fucked.

"Did she say what she would smother us with? It could be worth it." Tony wiggles his eyebrows and I can almost picture what's in his mind.

"That's fucking gross. The picture in my head is something I don't need." I strip my t-shirt off over my head and throw it towards my bag on the couch.

"I know you don't like lady parts, but that's just rude."

I walk to the table at the side of the room and grab a bottle of beer, opening it and taking a long swallow. As soon as my thirst is quenched, I turn to face Tony, keeping a serious look on my face. "It's not the visions of Connie that makes me want to puke."

"Fuck you. You know you want me."

I burst out laughing at the look of horror on Tony's face but refuse to give him an answer as I make my way to the small sink at the side of the room. This is one of the nicer dressing areas we've had on the tour, and it's great having a sink to use. I run the water, making sure to keep the temperature cool, and when it's perfect, I grab handfuls of it and splash my face and neck. I might not move much on stage, but it doesn't stop me from sweating like I've just run a marathon. The lights and equipment create a furnace-like heat, but then you add in the high temperatures from the hotter than average summer weather, and it's like performing in the middle of the desert. As soon as my skin feels like it isn't about to combust, I turn off the tap and run my fingers through my hair, pushing it back from my forehead. What I actually want is a shower, but that won't be possible until we turn up wherever Connie is taking us. Maybe we shouldn't put so much trust in her, asking more questions about what's happening, but the truth is I don't care.

As long as she gets me to where I need to be on time, I'm perfectly happy to have her running my life.

"I'm heading out." Connor shouts across the small room from the hall, and I wave at him as he leaves. One of the good things about not being on later in the night is that we still have a chance to go out and party before the final act finishes.

"See you in a few." Tony strips off his t-shirt and grabs a clean one from his holdall.

"Where are you two heading?"

Tony runs his hands through his hair to try and tame his curls. "There's a get together on Shatter's bus. Billy is leaving for the rest of the tour, so we are giving him a proper send off."

How the hell did I not know about this? "He's leaving?"

"I swear you need to listen more. He told us a few days ago that his daughter is having surgery and he needs to be there."

"Shit." I don't remember any of that, and I wonder where I was when it was mentioned.

"They'll be finished their set soon so come over when you're ready." He pats me on the shoulder as he heads out, leaving me standing in the room on my own.

My friends are used to me zoning out when they speak. I seem to spend my life trying to catch up with the conversation, and that usually means missing important shit. I want to pretend that it's because I'm thinking about something important, but sometimes it's the oddest of things. Granted, the most bizarre thoughts can lead to the best songs, but it means I miss a lot of things. I shake my head, deciding that I can't change anything now, and grab my own clean t-shirt. When it's on, I grab all my toiletries and pack up my bag, not wanting to have to come back later to collect my things. I can drop them at the van before heading to the bus to have a drink, and it means I can just collapse into the van after having a drink. That was a lesson I learnt quickly, that if I rely on my drunk self to get my shit together, there's a good chance that I will leave something important behind. It's how I lost my favourite t-shirt, and I still curse myself for it. Since I don't want that to happen again, I grab my bag and head to the van.

"You hiding in here?"

I look up to find Donny standing at the bathroom door. He's leaning against the doorframe with his arms folded across his chest, looking like the damn meal that he is. I came in here about ten minutes ago to get some quiet, hoping that the peace would help settle my spinning head. I've been drinking some concoction that Connor made up in the sitting area, and now I'm so fucking wired I can almost see sounds. "Don't drink that pink stuff, it's not good for you."

Donny laughs and closes the door before taking a seat across from me in the cramped room. We are in Shatter's tour bus, and theirs might be small compared to a lot of the bands that are travelling with us, it's still bigger than our pitiful van. At least they get a bed to sleep in at night, instead of having to fight for a section of back seat like I have to. The Crave will hopefully be at this level one day, but Shatter have been around a lot longer than us, so we have a few more years of work to get there.

"I never drink anything that doesn't come straight from a bottle." He holds up a beer to prove his point, and I wish I'd done that tonight. I don't know what was in the shit that Connor made, but I feel torn between giving in to the dizziness and wanting to run around the bus a few times.

A water bottle appears in front of me, and Donny shakes it to get my attention as I stare at it. "Thanks." I open it immediately and down nearly half the bottle in one go, hoping that it might clear my head a little.

"I thought you might like it. You need to dilute all the sugar that's in your system."

"I think it's more the alcohol that's the problem."

Donny smirks, and I can't help but stare at his mouth. He's such a gorgeous guy, and anyone would be blind not to notice. He has long hair that lies around his shoulder in waves, and the sun always seems to glow off it, highlighting the almost blue-blackness of it. It's not the first time I've noticed how hot he is, but with the alcohol giving me a little more courage, I permit myself to check him out openly. I let my eyes drift from his face downwards, a pleasant tingle spreading through me as I get an eyeful of his toned body. He looks like he spends hours a day working out, not that I'm complaining since it gives me a fucking fantastic view. His arms look like tree trunks, and his chest is solid, and I have the sudden urge to touch it to see if it's as hard as it seems.

"If you keep looking at me like that, there's a good chance you won't get out of this bathroom without being fucked."

As his words register in my brain, my dick wakes up, showing instant interest in Donny's words. He might have said them as a warning, but I don't see any problems with what he's threatening me with. There's no mistaking how fucking hot Donny is, and I could think of worse things to happen in a bathroom than bending over for him. Leaning back on the sink, I smirk at Donny, trying to encourage him to make a move. Getting him to take the lead means that if I wake up in the morning and regret it, I can pretend that it was all Donny's idea.

"Wow, I would just hate for that to happen." I stand up and Donny matches my movements, standing opposite me as he stares at me, almost challenging me. When I don't back down, he takes a step towards me, crowding me, so I have to lean back to be able to see his face still.

"It's probably not a good idea. You've had a lot to drink."

I still have the pleasant buzz from Connor's strange concoction, but I can still make good choices, and what I'm thinking is I would love a little bit of what Donny is offering. It's been a while since I was with someone who could fuck me like I wanted, and I'm convinced that Donny could be the guy who could make my toes curl. "Not enough to know that it would be fun not to be able to sit down tomorrow."

Donny growls before he attacks my mouth. His kiss is forceful, and it makes my dick ache. It's everything that I'd hoped it would be, and as I melt into his body, I let him take full control of what's about to happen.

Chapter Three
Brayden

I drop the screwdriver into my toolbox and glare at the engine in front of me. I have no idea what the owner has been doing, but a car this new shouldn't look this bad, especially when it's not a cheap car.

"How's she looking?" I turn to look at my boss Colin, shaking my head before throwing my oil rag under the hood.

"It's not good. I'm pretty sure that the catalytic converter needs replacing, and that's fucking with the engine."

"How the hell is the cat damaged?"

"There's a dent on the side of the casing, but I honestly think that somethings been added that's caused it." I wanted to find the real cause, but that's the shitty thing with car engines, sometimes you can only see the problem. Most of the newer cars have an onboard computer that tells you what's wrong with the car, but not how it happened.

"Fucking boy racers." Colin grumbles some more as he walks away, probably mentally adding up the cost of fixing the car.

I lower the bonnet and grab the worksheet. I need to report my findings so Colin can give the owner all the info they need. I hate this part of the job because paperwork fucking sucks. I've worked here for about three years now, and Colin is a great boss. Not many company owners would let me take time off when I need it for gigs, then work extra time to make up my hours when I'm available. Maybe one day I will be able to make enough money from the band to live off, but for now, I need a regular job, and Colin helps with that.

The overhead bell goes signalling a call, and it follows my journey as I head to the coffee pot. I've just poured myself a cup when Colin pops his head out of the office and yells.

"Bray, there's a call for you!"

I nod my head before heading to where he's holding out the phone. "Hello?"

"Hey, dickwad. How's it hanging?" Tony sounds cheery on the other end of the phone.

"A little to the left. How goes the big bad world of banking?" Every time I talk about Tony's job as a financial advisor, it still shocks me. I've never understood how a guy like Tony, one who likes to drink his body weight in alcohol before usually doing something stupid, the guy who is the perfect frontman for a rock band, can be such a sought-after whiz with money. He has enough clients that he could give half of them away and still make enough money a year to support the whole band. And he does support the group. He takes a smaller cut from the money we make and then there have been times he's paid for the travel and accommodation for us all.

"Busy, busy. What are you up to later?"

"I'm finishing up at four, but after that, I've got no plans." Today is an early finish, but it might be my last one for a few weeks. Everyone must know something I don't, like maybe there was an announcement I missed because we are fully booked out with services.

"Fantastic. I need you to be ready for six, and I'll pick you up."

It's not unusual for the guys to call with plans for rehearsals or drinking, but I get a feeling that it isn't that. For one, he sounds too fucking excited for it to be anything good. And another reason, Connor is away for the week shadowing an up and coming tattoo artist. This young guy is apparently a fucking genius when it comes to watercolour, and Connor wants to learn his technique. "For what?"

"Oh, bitch, it's time to pay up."

𝄞

I get changed into workout clothes and slam the locker door. I glare at Tony where he sits on the bench with a fucking smug smile on his face.

When he'd called me earlier, I'd hoped that maybe he wanted to catch a pint or something, but no, he called to cash in on his poker win. So here I am, using my early finish to come to the gym so I can go head to head with some boxer. Yeah, that's right, my forfeit is to go a few rounds with some semi-professional boxer and try not to get killed. Thankfully I won't be fighting the guy tonight. Tonight is about getting some one-on-one training with him before that happens.

"You look upset."

"I'm sorry, I was trying to look fucking pissed off. I'll try harder." I grab my water from the bench and march past him, trying to ignore his laughter. I go straight to the running machine because I want to warm up before this guy turns up, and Tony follows close behind me. I start slowly, not wanting to tire myself out too much before the real exercise start, but fast enough that I warm my muscles up. Tonight is going to hurt no matter what, but maybe I can try to limit how much pain I'm going to be in tomorrow if I prepare.

"I wouldn't use up too much energy, Bray. This guy's a fucking beast."

I glare at Tony, wishing that I could hurt him with my mind. This is taking the forfeits too far, and if I get injured, it might affect my guitar playing. I would say he hasn't thought about that, but I reckon he has, it's just not enough of a risk to ruin his fun. "You can go now."

"There's not enough money in the world to make me miss what's about to happen."

"I'm glad you're getting so much pleasure from this." I might sound pissed, but the truth is, I wish I'd thought of this as punishment. I always draw a blank when it comes to thinking of something cruel and unusual, and next time I win, I need to top this. Maybe it's time for Tony to get a tattoo? Something penis-shaped on his bicep.

"Oh, you have no idea how hard this is making my dick, and it hasn't even started yet. Come on, and I'll introduce you to Eli."

As much as I want to leave, I'm not one to bail on a punishment, even if this one is going to cause me pain. I stop the machine and collect my water, glaring at the back of Tony's head as I follow him to the back of the gym. I take a few deep breaths as I resist the urge to run away screaming, and as soon as my feet hit the mat and I see the guy I'm going to have to fight, I wish I had.

"Eli, my friend. Come and let me introduce you to Brayden."

I stare at the man-mountain in front of me and wonder how the fuck I'm going to survive the training, never mind the actual fight. Okay, so it's not going to be a real fight, but at this moment, that fact doesn't make me feel any better. The boxer, Eli, must be about six foot three, which is a lot more than my five-eleven, and he outweighs me by probably a hundred pounds. Putting all the physical differences aside, he has a look on his face that says not to fuck with him. Maybe it's just the fact that I'm about to stand toe to toe with him, but I seriously wish he didn't look as though someone had pissed in his cornflakes.

Eli stands with his arms folded across his chest, and even though the next few hours are going to hurt, I give myself a few seconds of pleasure by running my eyes over him. Yes, it's terrible timing, but if he's about to kill me, at least my last memory will be of some really hot guy. I'm not a small guy by any stretch of the imagination, but Eli makes me feel small, which is something I look for in a fuck buddy. Not that he'll be fucking me, well at least not in the fun sort of way.

"Hi." It has to be the lamest greeting I've ever come up with, but now that it's out there, I just have to roll with it. It doesn't help when Eli just continues to glare, and I'm left standing there feeling awkward. It might be that he is trying to throw me off kilter before the training, but the whole angry meathead impression is fucking with my head.

"So," Tony claps his hands. "I'll step to the side and let you two get on with things." He pats me on the shoulder and I shrug him off. "Enjoy."

He walks to the side of the mat and takes a seat, leaving me in the silent stare-off with Eli. I try my best to keep the silence up, but I get to the point that if he doesn't speak to me, I might just leave. "Is this whole silence thing part of the training, or are you just the quiet, serious type?"

"Put your hands up and protect your face."

"What?" I'm not a novice when it comes to working out, and yes, I especially enjoy using the punch bag to get a good sweat on, but I've never actually boxed in my life. I thought that he might show me a few moves before I needed to protect anything.

"Put your hands up. Like this." He holds his own hands in front of him, but where my hands are bare, he is wearing black wraps. "Keep them up no matter what, the aim is to stop me from punching you."

All the words make sense, but none of them settles my sudden nerves. There's no way in hell that I'm going to be able to do this, and when the fucker connects with me, it's going to hurt. I look over to where Tony is sitting, and he looks far too happy about what's going to happen. He's definitely getting a tattoo next time, on his fucking dick. A smack to my head brings my attention back to Eli, and it's the only notice I get before his fist comes at my face.

Chapter Four
Eli

What I want to do is knock this fucker out, but my conscience tells me that he isn't a boxer, so I need to go easy on him to begin with. I promised Tony to give him a few hours of training before taking him in the ring, and I'm a man of my word. This whole thing had started as a simple favour for a friend, but now it's become really fucking personal.

"Don't I need wraps or something?" There's a waver to the arsehole's words, and it gives me a great sense of satisfaction. I want him to feel scared, let him know what it feels like not to be the powerful one.

"Don't worry, Brayden. You won't be hitting me." The colour drains from his face, and I want to cheer. I shouldn't let personal feelings come into this thing, but after what Tony told me, it's difficult not to. Teenage me wants to smash his face in, finally getting payback on the guys who made my life hell. Guy's like this one in front of me always think they are better than me, like I'm what's wrong in the world, and I want to show him that he is nothing.

I don't let him catch up with what I'm saying before I smack him on the head. It's not hard, but it's enough to get him lifting his hands finally. I hit out a few times to gauge his skill level, smirking when he struggles to keep up with me. It doesn't make me take it easy on him, and there's a sense of satisfaction when I connect with his jaw.

"Fuck." Brayden drops his hands, and I instantly use that advantage to get another hit in. His head flicks back, and he stumbles away from me. "Calm down, dude."

"What's wrong, can you not handle yourself against this meat-head who fucks men?" Anger rises inside me as I remember the shit that Tony had told me about Brayden. The guy is a typical homophobe, and according to Tony, thinks all bodybuilders are thick fuckers. I'm not sure why Tony hangs around with a guy like that, but I'm only too happy to make him suffer for his backwards views. Brayden gives me a strange look, like he has no idea what I'm talking about, but I'm not in the mood to have a discussion with him. No, he needs to just deal with the shit I'm about to give him because the real training is about to start.

I work him hard over the next hour, and by the time I'm finished, Tony's friend is lying on the ground panting like he's about to have a heart attack. I'd feel sorry for him, but the arsehole deserves everything he gets. There's a pat on my shoulder as Tony walks past me. He kneels in front of Brayden and hands him a towel, smiling the whole time. I still have no idea why the two of them are friends, and it makes me wonder if I know Tony like I think I do. He has no issue with me being gay, but if he's hanging around with folk that have a problem with the LGBT community, is he the sound guy I think he is? Maybe it's time to find someone else to look after my investments.

"Will see you next week." I don't wait for a response before I spin on my feet and head to the changing room. I think the sooner I get out of here, the better. I grab my towel and shower gel from my locker as I go past, and head straight to the showers. I strip off my vest and shorts, throwing them on the floor before getting under the water. I don't hesitate before pouring the shower gel onto my hand. I scrub my hands through my hair, using it to work out some of my anger towards Brayden. My entire life has been filled with people judging me for being gay, but for some reason, I've let this guy get under my skin. He hasn't even said anything to my face or treated me differently, but I can't get what Tony told me out of my head.

I probably shouldn't tell you this, but Bray isn't the biggest supporter of gay people. He's a great guy, but I don't think I'll say to him that you're gay.

That's when I should have walked away, but like an idiot, I thought that I would be able to control my anger. Maybe my brother Anthony was right, and I'm not the sharpest tool in the shed. I turn off the water and grab my towel, wrapping it around my waist before picking up my discarded clothes. I stuff them into my bag and roughly dry my skin. I'm just slipping my legs into my grey jogging bottoms when Brayden hobbles into the changing room. He glares at me before heading straight to the showers, not even stopping to get his towel. The sound of the water hits my ears as I tie my shoelaces, and as hard as I try, I can't stop my eyes from flickering towards the shower.

Brayden's standing under the water with his head dropped and one hand on the wall like he's trying to hold himself up. My eyes drop down his body, taking in how hot the guy is. He might be a screaming homophobe, but he's fucking sexy. Spending the last hour watching Brayden move showed me that I might hate the guy, but my dick doesn't seem to care. Yes, it's shitty to check out a guy that hates me for who I am, but I'm human, and he's nice to look at. His body is slim but not thin, telling me that he is probably in a manual job opposed to working out. His hair is dark and does that floppy thing that lies across his forehead and frames his piercing grey eyes. It's a real shame that the guy is a fucking tool.

I force my attention away from Brayden as I grab my t-shirt from the bench next to me. I pull it over my head, and when I can see again, Brayden has come back into the changing area. He sits on the bench next to my bag, and I zip it up before lifting it and throwing it over my shoulder. Brayden flinches when I get close to him, and I want to hit him a few more times. My anger takes over, and I run my mouth before I get a chance to filter my thoughts.

"You know what, fuckhead, it isn't contagious. You won't catch it if you spend too much time close to me." I refuse to give him a chance to reply before I slam out of the room, leaving the dickhead behind.

"Who kicked your puppy?"

My brother Anthony smacks me on the back of the head as he walks into the kitchen. I've been sitting at the dining table stewing over my run-in with Brayden, and I hate that I've given him time in my head. Letting people like him under my skin does nothing but cause me grief, and I'm usually really good at leaving all that shit behind as soon as I walk away. Maybe it's because I'm going to be meeting Brayden again that I keep thinking about him.

"No one. How was your day?" I take a bite of the eggs that I made when I first came home even though they're now cold. Sharing a house with Anthony is great, but at times like this, it can be annoying. He knows me better than anyone in the world, especially since he's my twin, not that people would be able to see that if they just looked at us. I am tall and built like my dad with his dark hair and even darker eyes. Anthony is about four inches shorter with my mum's delicate build and almost white-blonde hair. We couldn't be more opposite if we were born from different parents, but the way we think and act is practically identical.

"Busy but productive. I finally got the approval for the trip I want to take my class on, and they all seem excited to go."

That's another area that I differ significantly from Anthony. He's a teacher at the local primary school, and he spends the day moulding the minds of our next generation, where I spend my days making peoples gardens look as amazing as I can. I admire what Anthony does, but the thought of being stuck indoors all day makes me shudder. I wasn't sure what I wanted to do when I left school, but a weekend job with a local landscaper showed me that I had a passion for gardening, and it changed my life. "That's great."

He turns and looks at me, and as he stares, I go back to eating. "Out with it."

I lean back in my chair and run a hand through my hair. I always attempt to keep things from Anthony, and I don't know why I try. I'm not sure if it's a twin thing, or if it's simply that I'm not as mysterious as I think. "Just some guy pissed me off."

"Possible partner?" Anthony leans on the worktop and gives me his full attention.

I snort before I respond. "Not a chance. He's just the run of the mill homophobe."

This gets Anthony's attention, and I can see the anger in his eyes. It takes a lot to get my mild-mannered brother to lose his temper, but anyone being a dick about my sexuality will do it instantly. "Who do I need to hurt?"

I burst out laughing, loving him for his protective streak. He's always willing to jump into a fight to protect me even though I outweigh him and tower above him. "It's fine, Ant. I can handle this guy."

"Except it's obviously bugging you."

He's right, but I still don't know why. It's the reason I've been sitting here so long, trying to talk some sense into myself. "I'm not one of your students."

"Well, I know that, they all act more mature than you." He gives me a sweet smile, and I give him the finger. He laughs and starts making himself something to eat. "Stop avoiding the point. Why are you giving this guy headroom? It's not like you."

"The truth is, I don't know."

"Helpful. How did you run into him?" Anthony throws me a carrot, and I catch it, taking a bite before answering him.

"I'm training him before I beat the fuck out of him."

This stops Anthony in his tracks. "I'm not sure which one confuses me more. Okay, so why are you beating him up, and why are you training him first?"

I spend time explaining to Anthony about the favour I'm doing for Tony. He looks as confused as I'd been when Tony had approached me with his proposal because I'd never met anyone that had wanted me to hurt their friend. Apparently, Brayden had lost some sort of bet and Tony wanted a forfeit that he would hate. There were also stories about Tony being forced to streak at a show or something, but I stopped listening because they were disturbing. All I know is that the two of them, who are in a band together, sound like they would fit in well with my brother's young class.

"Great friend." Anthony shakes his head when I finish talking.

"Which one?" Tony might sound crazy for setting his friend up, but then I can't get past the lowlife that Brayden is.

"Yeah, good point. They both sound like it would be worth staying away from." He turns his back to me as he searches through the fridge, and I take another bite from the carrot.

As I crunch down on the vegetable, my head races. Not having anything to do with Tony isn't an easy solution since he's my financial advisor, but I only need to see Brayden another twice. He's going to be nothing more than a tiny blip in my life, but for some reason, he's making waves in my usually calm thoughts.

Chapter Five
Brayden

I can't believe I'm back here willingly. Last week was painful and humiliating, and I should just tell Tony to stick his forfeit up his arse. But here I am, standing at the side of the gym watching Eli as he warms up on the punch bag. I try to convince myself that I'm not checking him out, but there's no denying that shit. The guy is fucking gorgeous, even if he has this major chip on his shoulder and he confuses me every time he opens his mouth. It's like he thinks there's a problem with him being gay, which makes no fucking sense, but after hours of not being able to sleep thinking about it, I've decided that I'm not going to make a big thing of it. This whole thing is going to last a few hours at most, and I refuse to stress over such a meaningless encounter.

"Come on, loser. Last chance to practice your non-skills before the big day." Tony looks so happy with himself, and I swear that it takes so much self-control not to tackle him to the ground and show him how much I picked up last week. I might want to complain about everything I experienced, but the truth is, Eli was a great teacher, even if his people skills are shit.

Since that plan isn't going to happen, I follow Tony slowly and repeat the plan I devised in my head. After the second night of obsessing over Eli, I decided that today I would come in, listen to what Eli is trying to teach me, and then get the fuck out of here. If I don't give him a reason to be pissed off at me, then he might be half-human. It's a simple plan, but as Eli turns to glare at me, I'm not sure it will happen.

"Ready?"

I take a deep breath and nod my head, stepping onto the mat and straight into the lion's den. Pain met me at every move over the last week, and I discovered muscles I didn't know existed. It took so long for my body to recover from the beating it took, and now I'm back to suffer some more.

"Hands up and protect your face."

Seriously, this guy must have something against my face because he's forever trying to do damage to it. I'd had the idea that maybe I'd met him before and offended him, but there is no way I would forget a guy that looks like him. So no, I haven't said something that would make him hate me, but I pity anyone who has. To have this guy angry at you must be scary because having him mildly put out by me is bad enough.

    He starts circling, and I rush to raise my hands. The first thing I learned last week was that this guy isn't playing around. Pulling punches isn't something Eli will do, and I still have the bruise on my jaw to prove that point. We spar for a while, and I'm feeling proud of myself because I'm stopping a few hits this week. Okay, so the ratio is still on the side of his fist connecting, but at least it isn't a total whitewash like last time. When he slaps me on the side of the head, I'm starting to rethink how positive I feel, but then he follows that up with a few body hits, and I finally lose my temper. I'm sick of this arsehole giving me attitude, and I'm ready to fight back. I widen my stance and try to remember everything I've been taught, and when I lash out, hitting Eli on the shoulder, he smirks like he's just won the lottery.

    "Oh, let's do this."

    I instantly want to take back what I did, to tell Eli that I'm sorry and I want him to keep taking it easy on me, but I don't have a chance to speak before he comes at me. If I thought that holding my own had been hard before, I have no chance now. I can't even see the punches before they land, but I can feel them, holy fuck can I feel them. He's ruthless in his attack, and I'm trying to shake off an uppercut when a large body connects with mine. The next few moments happen in slow motion, and when my back connects with the matt, a huge thud sounding through the gym, the breath is knocked out of me. My lungs cry out for air as I try to get control over my body. My eyes are wide as I struggle, and I cry out when I finally get air to move into my body.

    "Holy fuck." The words come out a little strangled, and when I hear a huff of laughter from above me, I finally pay attention to the huge guy that's lying on top of me. He's got a smirk on his face that tells me he's really fucking happy with himself, and if I were a better man, I wouldn't find it hot. As things are, I'm not that guy, and I can't help when my dick hardens with the pressure of his body on me. My body might ache, but I'm only human. Eli is a walking wet dream, and I can't ignore the fact that he's pressed against me and if I'm not mistaken, he's hard.

    "What's wrong, you can't handle yourself against a shirt lifter? That must be a blow to your manhood?"

    Okay, he keeps saying shit like that and I have no idea why. He's talking as though I'm not gay, and I'm just about to ask him what the fuck he's talking about, but he chooses that moment to notice my hard on. Conversation completely stops as Eli grinds his erection against me, and I feel a little smug that I'm affecting him when he doesn't want me to. My eyes roll as he gives me one last grind, and I can feel his lips next to my ears.

"You better watch out, Brayden, you might have a secret in there somewhere."

My eyes flash open, but before I get a chance to say anything, he's off me and heading to the changing room. I drop my head back to the mat, knowing I should chase after him so I can set him right about a few things, but the safest thing is to give myself a minute to calm down. Apparently, me having a boner is a trigger, and I would like to avoid possibly getting my face punched in for real.

"You okay, bud?" Tony leans his hands on his knees as he watches me, a look of satisfaction on his face. He's getting far too much enjoyment out of this whole thing, and I swear, the next time he loses, I will be on the sidelines watching every second of pain he endures at the hand of the tattooist. No, he's going to get something pierced. I just need to decide between his dick or his nipples.

"What is up that guy's arse?"

Tony's eyes glisten, and there's far too much humour there for him not to know anything. Now Eli's attitude might make a little more sense.

"What the fuck did you do?"

Tony bursts out laughing, and that's all the confirmation I need that he's set me up in some way. "I might have mentioned that you were a raging homophobe, which Eli wasn't impressed with since he's gay."

Well, at least that explains why the guy wants to take my head off at every opportunity. "Which means you didn't tell him I was gay?"

"It slipped my mind." He holds out his hand, and I take it, pulling myself up off the matt.

"You are a dick. The guy hates me and is trying to kill me whenever he can." I start to unwrap my wrists and head to the changing room, hoping to catch up with Eli so I can finally explain the situation. I would want to kill me too if I'd been told the shit he had, and hopefully, once he knows the truth, he might take his frustrations out on Tony instead.

"Oh, come on, like you wouldn't have done the same. I just wanted to add another layer to your training." He flutters his eyelids at me and the move is a little disturbing. He might be trying to look innocent, but he's looking creepy as fuck.

"Another layer of pain maybe. All I will say is you better win cards next time." I push open the door to the changing room and take a deep breath, bracing myself to face Eli again. I might know why he wants to kill me, but that doesn't mean he'll give me the chance to speak since that seems to be a nasty habit he has. I look around the room, but it's empty, and I curse myself for taking so long. I need to get this shit sorted, but it seems like it will have to wait until next time.

"You're two beats behind, Bray."

I crack my neck and take a deep breath. I've been off all afternoon, and it's starting to drive the rest of the guys insane. I want to pretend I don't know what has my head fucked up, but there is no hiding from the reason. There's absolutely no reason for my head to be a mess over Eli still thinking that I'm homophobic, but it doesn't stop my mind from focusing on it completely. It's been the only thing I've managed to think about since the gym the other day, and my concentration has been shit since then. Colin has noticed it, and he told me to get my head out of my arse before he kicked some sense into me. "Sorry."

"You need to get your head sorted, man. We only have a week before the next concert, and this new song needs to be solid."

"I know. I'll get it." Right, time to get this. Counting the beat on my guitar, I attack the song head-on, but as soon as instinct takes over, my mind drifts right back to Eli. I'm not sure I've met anyone who's built like him. He reminds me of Van Damme in his heyday, just a hell of a lot better looking.

It's his eyes that I noticed first, and even though he only looks at me with disgust and loathing, there's a fire that burns in them. The masochist in me wants that fire aimed at me in a much different way, and I wish there was a way to get it.

"Fuck it, Bray." I look up to find both Tony and Connor glaring at me.

"What?"

It's Connor that takes the lead for a change, letting me know that I've fucked up big time. Connor is a quiet guy and tends to take a back seat when it comes to laying down the law, so to see him pissed off, I think that it's maybe time to step away. "You are completely off. Is there a problem with the song, or are you just being a dick?"

I put my guitar on the stand and head straight to the fridge where we keep our alcohol supplies. We hire out the back building of Colin's business, and it didn't take us long to set it up as our rehearsal space. We have couches and a kitchen area, and when we come here to practice, we can spend days here without having to leave. Tonight though, I want nothing more than to get the fuck out of here, but that's not going to happen. First, I have to face two very pissed off band members and try to convince them that I'm just having a bad day. I collapse onto the sofa and take a drink of beer.

"The song is great, it's just me. My head isn't in the game tonight. Maybe I just need to go and get laid."

Connor takes a seat next to me, finally looking a little less pissed off. "You need to do something. I've never seen you like this before."

I pick up a discarded t-shirt from the arm of the chair and throw it at Tony, who gives me a knowing look in return. He's fully aware of what's fucking with my head, but he stays quiet, letting me sink deeper. "Maybe Tony could help out, by maybe talking to someone for me."

Connor looks between us, but neither of us enlightens him. It only takes a few moments for him to roll his eyes. "I should have known that this would be something to do with both of you. Is this to do with the bet?"

Tony bursts out laughing, and Connor holds up his hands.

"I don't want to know, it's safer that way. Just get this shit sorted before I kick both your arses. We have two weeks to get this song nailed, and I refuse to fuck it up with some kid like bullshit that you two have pulled."

I take a long pull from my beer, glaring at Tony over the top. He smiles smugly at me, and I suddenly wonder if I could get Eli to kick his arse.

Chapter Six
Eli

I slam the shot glass onto the bar and take a deep breath. I shouldn't be drinking so much since I have a client before lunch tomorrow, but the whole situation with Brayden is fucking with my head. I don't even know why, because I've come face to face with guys like him my entire life. Being openly gay brings out the lower levels of scum, so Brayden's attitude shouldn't be a surprise. Go to the gym on any given day, and I can hear some fucker spouting off about queers invading their space, but it usually just goes over my head because I'm numb to it.

For some reason, this thing with Brayden is getting to me, and I fucking hate that fact. The next two shots go down easy as I stew in my anger, but when a slim body comes to stand next to me, far too close to be anything other than a come on, I look in that direction. Unfortunately, the body belongs to a beautiful woman, and not the guy I'd hoped it did. For the tenth time tonight, I curse Richard for bringing me here, to a straight club, so that he could hook up before he fucks off to Australia for a month. I tried to explain to him that Australia had women too, but he wanted one more English girl before he left. So here I am, trying to fend off drunk women who would like to become friends for the night.

"Hi." The woman flutters her eyelashes at me, and with the alcohol flowing nicely through my blood, I decide that I've had enough.

"Sorry." I spin away from the bar, leaving my wannabe friend standing staring at me. I storm out the front door and head towards Twilight, the nightclub I wanted to go to in the first place. I'll be on my own, but that shit never bothered me in the past, and if it means I get some action tonight, it's totally worth it. I think I need to fuck my frustrations out, and I'm never going to manage that playing Richard's wingman all night. I'm a good friend though, so I shoot him a text before I walk into heaven.

The bass from the music vibrates through my chest, and I feel my shoulders relax as I step into the place I belong. This is what a nightclub should look like, with wall to wall half-naked men. I don't bother with the bar, thankful that I drank before arriving so I don't have to struggle through the crowd that's three bodies deep. Even as I think that, I see a guy at the back of the crowd that I wouldn't mind tangling with. His arse is a perfect bubble, and the way his tight jeans mould against it, makes my mouth water. I should walk to the edge of the dancefloor and wait for him to get his drink, but I throw caution to the wind and walk up behind him. I make sure I don't touch him, knowing that there's no worse feeling than someone touching without permission, but I get into his personal space, so he's aware that I'm interested.

Being this forward isn't the way I normally act, but I need to fuck someone before I explode. I'm not usually the aggressive type, which surprises most people because I'm a big guy, but tonight I'm craving control. I think it's because I've felt so out of control with Brayden since the day he walked into the gym, so tonight I want someone to bend to my will, and I'm hoping that Mr Perfect Arse will be that guy. I crowd in behind him and when I inhale, his aftershave swirls around my senses and my dick instantly goes hard. Maybe tonight I won't be left turned on without release, which seems to be a constant problem the last few weeks. This afternoon was the worst, and that's why I'm out tonight. Feeling Brayden against me, his erection pressing against mine, had nearly made me do something stupid like lean down and kiss him. The only thing that stopped me doing something stupid was knowing that he's straight, but that gave me such a bad case of blue balls.

The guy slips through a gap in the crowd, and I follow him. I should probably feel like a creep, but I convince myself that since I'm not actually touching him, it's all good. I also choose to ignore the fact that I'm achingly hard after just smelling him because that would make me feel kind of desperate. Hot guy huffs when someone pushes in front of him, and when he takes a step back to avoid bumping into the queue jumper, he collides with me. The whole length of his body presses tightly against mine, and I give in to the urge to put my hand on his waist. I don't hold tight, letting him move if he doesn't feel comfortable, but he doesn't put distance between us, and my dick twitches in happiness. He must feel it because he leans into me more, his perfect arse rubbing me in all the right ways. I drop my nose to his neck and inhale as I slip my hand to his stomach, pulling him tightly against me.

The world slips away as I enjoy having a guy that wants me. Okay, so finding someone isn't a struggle for me, but I've been so stuck in my head over Brayden, that I haven't let anyone in the past few weeks. Again, I shouldn't have given him any headspace, but that didn't stop me from entertaining his hatred, so I force myself to push away all thoughts of Brayden, determined not to let him spoil the night for me. That's all good and well until a few minutes of grinding later, the guy with the perfect arse turns in my arms, and I'm left staring at the one person I can't get out of my head. My hand drops instantly and I take a step back, putting distance between us while I try to work out what the fuck Is happening. Why would a guy who hates gay people be here, in a well-known gay club? Is he here to cause shit? But if he is, then standing at the bar isn't exactly the protest that most people would go for.

When I realise that none of those answers matters to me, I turn on my heels and head towards the exit, planning on getting the fuck out of here. The last thing I want is to cause a scene by punching the guy in the face, so it's easier to walk away. I make it to the corridor where the bathrooms are when my arm is grabbed. I slow my steps and Brayden appears in front of me. The thought of speaking to him again makes my anger grow, and I pull my arm from his grip. I expect him to shy back, but my anger is met with his, and when he looks around, I wonder if this is the night I get to finally kick his arse. Before I get a chance to do anything, I'm manhandled into the single toilet that a guy walks out of. There are grumbles of protest as we push in before the guys who are waiting in line, but Brayden doesn't seem to care. I'm about to give him a mouthful of abuse when he holds his hand up, silencing me before I get a word out.

"I know, but let me speak before you punch me."

The fact that he realises that I'm angry makes me feel less mad. At least he knows that I hate him, and that gives me a strange sense of satisfaction. "Why are you here?"

"There's so much to explain, but let me start with Tony is a dick. He did all this, but he refuses to sort it out." He scrubs his hand through his hair, and if I didn't hate him so much, I would think that he looked fucking cute with his hair mussed up.

"Agreed." Tony's a great financial advisor and a good friend, but there is no getting past the fact that the guy is a bell end. A nice one, but there is no denying that he's a friendly smile away from a punch.

"So, here's the thing, I'm gay."

I stare at Brayden, trying to work out if he's telling me the truth, or is he just trying to avoid a fight. It would explain why he's here, but it doesn't explain why Tony said all that shit about him. And just like that the whole thing makes sense, and I curse myself for not seeing it before. Of course, Tony wouldn't be friends with such a homophobic person, and that only leaves one solution. "He lied."

Brayden nods his head like everything depends on it, and there's a look of relief on his face. "Yes, he did. He thought that maybe you would hurt me a little more if you thought I was homophobic."

"Fucker!" I'm going to kill him. I can't believe he used my sexuality against me, getting me to hate someone for no good reason.

"My thoughts exactly." Brayden smiles and now that the anger towards him is gone, I can fully appreciate how cute he is.

"I'm sorry."

He shakes his head again. "Don't be. I'm just glad I found out because I was starting to think that you had mental problems." He lets out a small huff of laughter. "All the times you spoke about me having problems with you being gay, I thought this man is insane."

I laugh along with him and pretend I don't notice the fact that I've taken a step towards him. It's not a big one, but it's enough that the distance between us lessens. Brayden must realise because when he looks into my eyes, the tip of his tongue flicks out against his lips. The memory of being on top of him this afternoon rushes back to me, the way that his erection was as hard as mine, and I want to be back in that position. I'd been sure he would rush home and scrub his body in the shower, determined to rid himself of the lust caused by a man, but now I wonder if he jerked off like I did. God, I bet he looks fucking glorious with his dick in his hand, and I suddenly want to see that now.

"Eli?"

My eyes flicker up and away from Brayden's lips, only to find him closer. It's my turn to wet my lips, and I need to find out what his mouth feels like against mine. I'd spotted him in the crowd when I arrived, and I still want to give in to the urges I had when I first saw him. "I hated you so much," Brayden lowers his eyes as I speak. "But I think it was because I wanted you so much."

Brayden inhales deeply and it breaks the spell that's been holding me back. There's no denying that Brayden caused so much anger in me, but I think it's because I couldn't lie to myself and pretend that I didn't want him. From the moment he walked into the gym, my body has been trying to get closer to him. I had to fight against all the instincts that were telling me to claim him, and that was what was messing with me. Now all those hurdles are gone, and I can take what I want. I grip him by the back of his neck and drag him towards me. When my mouth crashes down on his, he melts against me, opening instantly so I can finally kiss him like I want. Our tongues tangle together, and when he licks across the roof of my mouth, I think I've died and gone to heaven. He doesn't give in to me completely, and when I press him against the wall behind him, he doesn't become submissive. He fights with me, and that only turns me on more.

Brayden breaks the kiss, but when he speaks, I can't be upset about it. "Come home with me. I want you so fucking bad, but I don't want it here. I'm not OCD, but gross."

I laugh at his comments, but that changes to a groan when he sucks the finger I'm using to brush against his lip into his mouth. He's so tempting, and I'm so fucking happy he's gay. There is no worse feeling than lusting after a straight guy, especially if that guy is a big fat homophobe. "On one condition."

It takes Brayden a few moments to open his eyes, and when I see the heat in them, I nearly cut the night short by coming in my boxer's. "Name it."

I brush my lips against his. "After I fuck you into the mattress, we go and kick Tony's arse."

Brayden laughs and he might think I'm joking, but I'm not. The guy needs a good kicking, especially when I think that I might have missed this night with Brayden. Yes, it might be only one night, but I have a feeling that it's going to leave a lasting memory. Thinking about not getting this chance makes me angry, and I think that's it's only fair that Tony gets that anger.

"Oh, one hundred percent a deal. For both things."

The End

Heart Beats

A Little Unsteady

by

Saffron Blu

A Running Hearts Short Story

What leaves *you* unsteady?

For Darius, best rapper out there, it's seeing his sweet drummer Kamil in a situation you don't want anyone in.

Suddenly there are feelings he didn't anticipate.

Feelings he shouldn't have.

But... In the end, what can it hurt if those feelings leave him *a little unsteady*?

*Trigger warning for violent situations.

Chapter One
Darius

I smiled nicely at the camera once again all the while thinking my face was going to stick in this grimace for the rest of my days if this meet and greet didn't end soon. Sometimes these things could be fun but today I just wasn't in the mood, which made me hate every second.

Don't get me wrong I played a good part, I smiled and chatted to all the VIP fans, and gave them the attention they'd paid for, but boy, was I ready for some drinks and downtime with the crew. That in itself said a lot, since I was usually looking for any excuse I could find to avoid the after-parties.

"I can't believe I've actually met you." The girl in front of me was giddy with excitement her palm felt sweaty as it rested in mine.

"It was my pleasure, sweetheart." I lifted her hand and pressed a gentle kiss to the back of it.

She squealed as she looked over her shoulder at her friend. "I'm never washing my hand again. Like, ever."

I laughed. "I'm pretty sure you will," I said as I threw her a wink and dropped her hand.

I gave Trevor, my head security guy, a nod and he clapped his hands together catching everyone's attention. "That's it folks. Darius has to call it a night or else he'll have nothing to give at tomorrow night's show and you wouldn't want that for all the fans coming tomorrow."

There was a round of headshakes and shrugs from the people in the room and I quietly snuck out a door at the back, while Trevor ushered them out the other way.

Needing a few minutes to myself before heading down to the event room that the after-party was being held in, I decided to go to the green room where we usually chilled out before the show. I reached out to open the door but paused with my hand on the handle as a dancer called out from down the corridor.

"I wouldn't go in there if I was you. Kamil's having a gangbang."

I frowned at his words. Kamil wasn't one to do that kind of thing. He was out and proud, but I'd never seen him getting it on with anyone backstage. There was no way he'd be involved in a gangbang. Ignoring the dancer I opened the door and couldn't believe what I was seeing.

Two guys from the support act, Crimson Pandas, were standing over the sofa with their bare backs to me; it was easy to see the trousers bunched up around their ankles.

"Shift over it's my turn," the one on the right stated.

As they shuffled about I could see Kamil laid face down on the sofa, naked from the waist down. His ass was in the air making me think he must have a cushion under his pelvis. The fact that he wasn't moving or making any noise had all kinds of warning bells going off in my head.

"What the fuck is going on here?"

One of the guys jumped seemingly startled by my voice but the guy who was lining himself up with Kamil's raw and abused hole didn't seem to bat an eye. "Having some fun. You're welcome to join."

Ignoring his comments, I stepped closer and when I got a clear view of Kamil's face mushed into the cushions I could tell he was clearly out of it and not conscious enough to give his consent. Anger bubbled up inside me at the sight. "Get the fuck off him, right now."

"If you aren't gonna join in, piss off." James, the lead singer of the Crimson Pandas, stated as he pushed his hips forward.

I saw red.

Reaching out I pulled him off Kamil and without any thought threw out my fist clocking him in the face. When he went down, unable to stand up as his trousers tangled around his feet I reached for him again and pummeled him.

Punch after punch.

I felt hands grip at my shoulders but I was too angry to stop.

They'd *violated* Kamil.

Sweet Kamil.

Clearly taken advantage when he was unconscious and unable to defend himself. It was now up to me to set this straight.

To make sure they didn't touch him again.

"*Fuck!* D, he's down. You need to stop." Trevor's voice pulled me out of my rage-filled haze. As my eyes focused and landed on the beaten face of James, I couldn't believe I'd done so much damage in such a short time. I knew there'd probably be consequences for my actions but in that moment I didn't give a damn. All I cared about was Kamil and his welfare.

"Yeah, were gonna need a couple of ambulances and the police." My eyes darted to Trevor as he spoke into the earpiece he always wore.

I hoped the ambulances arrived before the police so that I would at least know Kamil was getting the help he clearly needed before the police took me away.

I crouched beside Kamil's unconscious form and stroked a hand over the back of his head. "Kamil, can you hear me?"

There was no movement in Kamil's body at all and panic overtook me as I worried that he may have suffocated while the fuckheads were abusing him. I shoved at his shoulder and rolled him over. He may only be a small guy but he was a dead weight and it took a lot more muscle power than I'd expected. When I finally got him over, my eyes trained on his chest and when I saw it rise and fall with his breathing a small amount of relief flowed through me.

He was alive.

As my eyes took in the rest of his naked form I quickly reached for a blanket that was hanging over the back of the couch. I needed to cover him because I didn't want anyone else seeing his body without his permission. My stomach churned afresh at the thoughts of the violation he'd already had at the hands of the two fuckers I could hear whimpering behind me.

"Kamil. Open your eyes for me babe." I gently tapped his cheeks to try and rouse him but he was completely out of it. My hands shook as anger started to rise within me again.

I knew he wasn't into drugs. He'd watched a close friend die from an accidental drug overdose and hated the stuff because of it. "What the fuck did you give him?" I shouted, my rage obvious in the growl behind my words.

"He... I—" One of them stuttered nervously.

I pinned him with a glare. "Don't try and blame this on him. He doesn't even touch over the counter painkillers. You gave him something." My words made it clear I wasn't taking any shit from them.

"We gave him a roofie." The guy had the gall to look ashamed as he spoke and I just wanted to beat the shit out of him too. "James said it would loosen him up a little and...I didn't realize it would knock him out completely."

"Yet when you realized it had, you still took it in turns to fuck him?" I shook my head trying to dispel some of the rage. "Trev, get them out of here. If I have to listen to one more word I'll..." I left the sentence hanging because I didn't want to voice how far I would go because I was ashamed to say it would be too far. I'd get locked up for a long fucking time.

As Trevor marched the upright and talking guy out I focused back on Kamil, ignoring the whimpering groans coming from James on the floor. I didn't know how much damage I'd done there but those noises meant the fucker was alive and I at least wasn't getting sent down for murder.

A couple of EMT's entered the room and seeing James on the floor went straight for him.

"Leave him. This guy is the one you need to look after first."

One guy came straight over while the other stayed with James. "I'm sorry sir but we have to treat them according to the order of urgency." He looked Kamil over and started asking questions. "Can you tell me what's happened here?"

"Those fuckers roofied and raped him." I didn't try to mince my words because I wanted James to hear those vile words because I had a feeling that isn't what he believed went on here. You heard it so often, the attacker believed the victim wanted it and they were just having sex, but that wasn't what happened when you needed to drug someone to take away the chance for them to say no. That doesn't make it any less rape then if they'd forced them kicking and screaming.

If anything it makes it worse because the drug he gave Kamil is known to make people forget what happened and if I'd not come in here he'd maybe have woken up tomorrow thinking he'd gotten blind drunk and have no memory of the night.

"And that's why he's in the condition he is over there?" he asked, gesturing towards James with a nod of the head.

"Yes." I didn't allow my voice to soften in shame, and I didn't hide my bloody and bruised hand out of sight because I wasn't ashamed. I wasn't proud of my actions either, but if we could relive the moment all over again, I wouldn't change it.

Chapter Two
Kamil

My head throbbed before I even opened my eyes and I couldn't help but wonder what the hell happened during last night's after-party. When I tried to think back, my mind just went fuzzy, so I pushed my concerns away thinking I must have had way too much to drink.

The bed felt rock hard and I was very aware of being hot and sweaty, which wasn't really a concern since we'd been living in hotels the last few weeks and not many of them were the high end kind with beds that felt light a fluffy cloud. God, what I'd give to be able to bring my own bed along with me on these tours.

As I cracked open an eye I was immediately aware that I wasn't in a hotel room and something had gone very wrong last night.

The machine at the side of my bed was all I needed to see to tell me I was in a hospital. I tried to sit up but the room spun and I lifted my hands to cradle my pounding head. "Fuuuuck."

"Kamil?" A sleepy voice said from somewhere beside me. "Oh, thank fuck. They expected you to wake up hours ago." I knew it was Darius— I'd recognize his sultry voice anywhere, no matter how foggy my head might have been.

Slowly I lifted myself into a seated position. I frowned as I tried to think back to last night. "How the fuck did I get here, D?" Without giving him time to answer my question I carried on. "I remember coming off stage. I remember chatting to some of the Crimson Panda guys." I squeezed my eyes shut trying to picture who it was. "I can't even remember which fucking guys it was...D, what happened?"

As Darius swallowed, his hardened eyes softened and he reached out to take my hand. I dropped my gaze to our joined hands before focusing back on his sympathetic stare. "Kamil..." He visibly struggled to find his words, it was like he was trying to choose them carefully and I knew he didn't want to be telling me whatever it was.

"Be straight with me."

He nodded and I watched his shoulders straighten as steeled himself to speak. "I don't know what happened before I walked into the green room, but I found James and Leon tag-teaming you. You were unconscious and when pressed they admitted they'd slipped you some Rohypnol."

My eyes practically popped out of my head with the shock of words. *I was drugged and raped?* I couldn't believe it. Surely that would be something I'd remember, to some degree at least? "By tag-teaming, do you mean…"

"Fucking you. They were taking turns to fuck you, Kamil."

My stomach rolled at his words. I wasn't a bottom, so if this was the truth that would mean the first time someone fucked me…

That thought didn't help my stomach at all. I flicked my eyes around the room looking for somewhere to vomit.

Darius must have seen something on my face because his hand left mine, and a cardboard bowl was suddenly there in my lap and I quickly emptied my stomach into it. His hand smoothed my hair over my head, the movement was soothing and I was suddenly overwhelmed with emotions.

I felt dirty. And stupid for letting them do such thing to me. Angry tears rolled down my cheeks and I roughly brushed them away with my knuckles.

"Hey…" Darius stilled my hands taking them in his. "Don't hurt yourself. Please…" he begged, his voice breaking.

Seeing his emotions so close to the surface seemed to wash my anger away. The tears didn't stop, instead they rolled down harder, and faster, and I suddenly found my self pressed to Darius's chest, sobbing as he whispered words of comfort.

I didn't know how much time had passed but my face was dry of tears and my soul felt a little lighter by the time there was a knock on the door.

"Hi, I'm Officer Schmit," the tiny brunette woman announced as she stepped into the room without invitation. "I was wondering if you'd feel up to going over what happened?"

My hands started to shake at the thought of replaying what happened which, to be honest felt crazy, because I knew I couldn't actually remember it. I clasped my hands in my lap to ease the shake. "I'm not sure how much I'll be able to help. I can't exactly remember anything. Darius will probably be able to tell you more, he walked in on it all." I gestured towards the man beside me.

Officer Schmit gave me a small smile. "Mr. Hayes has already given his statement and been charged."

I frowned at her words and wondered if the haze from the drugs was lingering making me misunderstand. "Charged? He wasn't involved with what happened to me."

"No but he—" She clapped her mouth shut and made it obvious she was choosing her words carefully. "If you could tell me what you remember and then we'll discuss Mr. Hayes and his charges." She quickly glanced at Darius. "If that's okay with Mr. Hayes?"

Darius nodded stoically and I wondered what the fuck was going on. I felt like I was missing something really important.

"Sure, but like I said I don't really remember much." I closed my eyes as I thought back to the concert. "We'd just played the encore and given the last bow. I usually spend some time in the green room while I wait..." I gave Darius a sheepish look. I was pretty embarrassed to be admitting this in front of him but I felt like it was important. "While I wait for Darius to finish his meet and greets." Darius's eyes widened in surprise and I forged on. "Darius hates the after-parties and would give them a miss if he thought he could get away with it, but just like anyone else he needs to unwind. So I've been waiting for him most nights knowing he likes to have a breather in the green room before leaving the venue."

Darius shook his head like he couldn't believe what he was hearing. I didn't know if it was a good thing or a bad thing. We'd become pretty tight friends since I joined the last tour as his drummer. I liked to think we both valued our friendship because although we are both openly LGBTQI—me representing the G and Darius the B—we'd never overstepped that boundary even as far as a drunken fumble.

Touring can become so lonely and it's no surprise that many marriages are broken up over the things that happen on tour. So two free and single guys not hooking up in the name of friendship, no matter how much sexual attraction might be sparking between them, is pretty big in my eyes.

"I'd only been in the green room for maybe five minutes—I'd not even had time to pull my phone out of my pocket, to read like I usually do—when two of the Crimson Panda guys came in."

"Could you state their names for me?" Officer Schmit questioned.

I shook my head. "I've never really socialized with them. They've always come across a little homophobic so I've always kept my distance. One of them was the lead singer, James. The other guy though I'd be able to point him out, but his name could be anything." I quickly flicked my eyes to Darius, knowing he'd mentioned a name earlier, unfortunately I'd been so focused on everything else he was telling me I'd not really retained the name. I didn't bother mentioning that though incase Darius wasn't meant to talk to me about it, having made a statement already. Maybe they'd think we'd been getting our stories straight or something. You see all kinds of things like that on TV.

"That's okay. We'll arrange a picture for you to look at, at a later date. What happened next?"

"The guy whose name I don't know made a beeline for the fridge and James came over to the couch and sat beside me. No-name guy asked if I wanted a beer and even though I was a little weary of them because like I said before, I knew they were a homophobic, I said sure. I figured keeping it relaxed and not giving them a reason to be pissed and start with the slurs was a good idea." I shrugged feeling like I was probably over explaining but I didn't know how much detail I needed to give.

"James started talking to me and by the time the other guy made it to the sofa the lids were off the bottles and he was handing them out."

"Did he offer them out in any specific way? Like did he make sure you grabbed a certain one, or anything?" Officer Schmit asked.

My brow creased as I thought about her question. "Thinking back on it, there's nothing that I can say stood out to me. No." I said with a shake of my head. "We talked shop. You know…concerts, music, song writing, that kind of thing. Everything else is a little fuzzy from then on."

"You did great. Thank you. We'll still need you to come to the station in the next couple of days to make it formal, so if anything else comes to you, you can add it then." Officer Schmit closed her notepad and stood. She nodded towards Darius. "Mr. Hayes, I'll leave it to you to explain the charges against you to Kamil."

I watched her leave and once the door closed I turned my attention to Darius. "What was that all about? Why have you been charged?"

Darius sighed. "I've been charged with assault and battery. I lost control and went too far when I pulled James off you."

I gave him a questioning look. "*You* lost control? You're the most calm and chill person I know."

Darius shrugged nonchalantly. "Not last night, I wasn't."

I couldn't imagine Darius losing his temper. He might be a rapper and have the bad boy vibe in spades but he was always against violence, the closest he got to confrontation was when he'd jump in to break up a fight.

I knew it wouldn't have been a nice thing to see, knowing someone was being taken advantage of but for him to go against all his morals and do enough damage to someone to be charged with battery, he must have had something more going on in his head.

I couldn't help but wonder if someone he was close to had been in a similar situation in the past or something because his actions just seemed so over the top. I mean, we were friends but I wouldn't think he'd get that ticked off about *me*.

Chapter Three
Darius

"I'm gonna go grab a nurse. They'll probably want to check you over now that you're awake." I rushed out of the room needing to be away from his questioning stare.

I'd sat beside him for the last few hours wondering why the hell I'd lost it like I had, and I was struggling to come up with a reasonable answer. Yes, he was a friend and James was doing unimaginable things to him but did that really warrant me to beat the man half to death?

If Trevor hadn't have pulled me out of my rage-filled haze, I could have killed him.

I could hear raised voices and as I made it closer to the nurse's station I recognized the head nurse giving Officer Schmit a piece of her mind. "He has not been cleared to speak with you yet. I'll be putting a complaint in with your senior officer, and if you do something like this again I'll be making sure security knows not to let you in the building at all."

Officer Schmit attempted to apologize but the nurse wasn't having any of it; she turned on her heels and headed my way. As her eyes landed on mine she gave me a warm smile. "I'm just about to check on your boy now. The Officer told me he's awake and talking."

I nodded. "I was just coming to get you."

"You do realize you could have just pushed the button beside his bed and someone would have been with you straight away?"

I'd not even considered that when I'd left. I probably should have called them in when he first woke up but I'd been too distracted with explaining things and the officer coming in. I'd only really come for the nurse now because I'd needed to get out of the room and away from Kamil's demanding stare. I was worried that he'd read more into my actions than I wanted him to see. I was too scared to even think about my reasons myself. I wasn't ready for him to start asking questions.

"I didn't want you guys to think it was some emergency and I needed to stretch my legs anyway," I said to appease the nurse.

We entered the room and found Kamil wobbling at the side of the bed his ass hanging out of his hospital-gown.

I immediately rushed over to him. "What the fuck are you doing?" I asked as I gripped on to his biceps to offer him the support he clearly needed to stand.

He struggled for a minute, his hands tugging at the open sides of the gown but after a beat it seemed as if he gave up on the impossible task. "I needed to pee but then when I stood up I realized my legs wouldn't be getting me across the room."

The nurse disappeared and the door closed, I couldn't help but wonder if she was trying to give Kamil a little privacy but then I almost laughed at that thought because nurses see all kinds of shit. A bare ass hanging out of a gown was nothing.

"Why didn't you say something before I left?"

Kamil sighed. "I didn't need to go until you were gone."

"You should have fucking waited."

The door burst open and the nurse came in pushing a wheelchair along. "I do wonder when people are going to listen and actually push the button when they need a nurse." She stopped beside us. "Right, Darius sit him in here. I'll get you to the bathroom and comfortable in no time, Kamil."

Kamil's face flushed as he swallowed. "I…i…if you can just get me to the bathroom, I'm sure I can manage from there."

"I'm sorry but you are too unsteady to be left without aide. If something happened because I wasn't there helping you, I'd lose my job." The nurse's words sounded honest and forthright.

Kamil's shoulders straightened as he allowed me to lower him into the waiting wheelchair. "Okay. Let's get this over with."

I was itching to offer my help but I knew he was a proud man and if he wasn't happy with allowing a nurse helping him when it was her job to do such a thing, something told me he wouldn't accept a hand from me.

As I watched the nurse wheel him into the bathroom and close the door behind them, I decided now was a good time to get some information about what was happening with James and Leon from Trevor. Being our security detail he should have access to the ins and outs of the investigation and if not, surely he'd know someone who did.

I pulled out my cell and hit his name on the screen.

"Barnes." His bassy tone rang in my ear.

"Trev, do you know what's happening with James and Leon? The police wouldn't tell me anything when I gave my statement."

I heard him sigh and the noise in the background faded off making me think he must have found a quiet spot wherever he was. "You're part of the investigation D. I'm not allowed to tell you anything."

"Come on, Trev. Kamil's awake and I'm sure as soon as he has a minute to take things in he'll be asking the same questions I am. He deserves some answers," I begged, not caring that he could probably hear the desperation in my voice.

"Okay." His voice was muffled and I pictured him running a hand over his face as he spoke which he did whenever he was tired. "The evidence is pretty clear cut from the rape kit and the test on the beer bottles. Both James and Leon have confessed so they'll be charged first thing in the morning."

"Pfft... They were quick enough charging me, yet *they* won't be charged until tomorrow? That sounds fair." I couldn't keep the venom out of my voice.

"I'm sure they would've charged James earlier if they weren't patching him up at the hospital." I opened my mouth to speak again but before I could get a word out Trevor forged on. "Fuck. Darius. I shouldn't be telling you this...James has dropped the charges against you. The state could still charge you but I have it on good authority that given the circumstances, that won't happen. I assume you'll get the official word tomorrow. You're a fucking lucky bastard." My shoulders sagged in relief at the news.

The bathroom door opened and the nurse backed out with Kamil in the wheelchair.

"Sorry that took so long, I had performance issues," Kamil stated sounding mildly amused. I was hoping he wasn't masking his real feelings behind humor but the realistic part of me felt that that's exactly what he was doing. Maybe it was something he needed right in that moment.

"I'm going to have to go, Trevor. Thank you." I said into my cell before ending the call and slipping it back into my pocket.

"Can't pee with an audience?" I asked Kamil.

"Evidently so."

The nurse clicked her tongue. "I told you I wasn't watching anything but your legs to make sure they were going to keep you upright." She helped him back in the bed with the strength and efficiency you wouldn't expect a woman of her age to have, before checking hooking him back up to the machines and checking his obs. "That all looks good. The doctor will be round in about an hour to do his own tests. So I'll leave you two to it."

Chapter Four
Kamil

I bit at the piercing in the corner of my mouth as I watched Darius stew on his thoughts. I only lasted a minute before I had to break the silence.

"What's up? Did Trevor have bad news?" I asked having heard him say bye to Trev when I came back from the bathroom.

Darius seemed to startle like he didn't even realize he was lost in his thoughts until I spoke. "No. Actually he had some good news. Both James and Leon confessed to everything."

Leon...so that was the other guy's name. It didn't ring a bell so there was no way I could have given that to the police.

"And James isn't pressing charges against me so I should get a call with the official word about that tomorrow, providing the state doesn't feel the need to follow through with the charges. Trevor seems to think under the circumstances they won't, but I guess only time will tell."

I placed my hand on his and he looked down at it in surprise. "That is amazing news. So why do you look so miserable?"

"I think it's all just catching up with me. I'm sure I'll be excited once I've had a nap." I could tell he wasn't being completely honest but I was doing the same thing. I'd been focusing on him to avoid thinking about what happened to me and I would probably be doing that for a while. I wasn't ready to face up to any of that yet. Maybe I never would be.

"You should probably get yourself back to the hotel and to bed. You need to be fresh for tomorrow's show."

We had another two nights of performances before we moved on to another town and another show. We were only one month into a five-month tour and it was already taking its toll; Darius didn't need any added exhaustion.

Darius shook his head. "No, I'm good. I'll at least wait to see what the doctor has to say."

To pass the time while we waited for the doctor we talked about anything but what happened that night. I told him about my twin sister, Abigail, and the baby she'd had a few days before we left for the tour. Abigail send's me daily photos of my nephew, Isaac, and every little face he pulls. It helped me get through the days without feeling like I was missing too much of his little life.

We had a weekend coming up that was free from shows because of the Grammys and Darius's nomination for one, so I'd be taking those few days to fly home and spend what time I could with my sister and nephew. I was all they had and although I knew she could manage alone she was forever telling me how much she missed me. This opportunity was too hard to pass up.

The door opened and a guy cleared his throat, effectively cutting our conversation off. "Kamil. It's good to see you awake. It took a lot longer than expected." The guy was wearing a long white coat with an ID-badge hooked on the front pocket. I couldn't quite read the name from here but there was no denying he was a doctor of some sort.

"Is that a bad thing?" Darius asked.

The doctor shook his head. "Not at all. Everyone reacts to drugs differently and the fact that your man here is awake and so alert, that is a very good sign." As the doctor came to stop beside the bed he offered me his hand.

I stared at it dumbly, the words *"your man"* running through my mind and giving me thoughts I'd never dreamed of thinking before.

"Hello Kamil." His voice quickly pulled me out of my stupor and I shook his hand. "I'm Doctor Thompson. I'm just going to go through a few little tests, is that okay with you?"

"Sure."

He did the usual doctor things like taking my pulse and checking my eyes with a flashlight. "I'm pleased to say the drug seems to have worked its way out of your system. You'll have to come back and have some STD tests over the next few weeks, the nurses will give you a pile of pamphlets explaining everything to do with that along with your discharge papers, which I'm happy to go tell them to write up now. It might take them about thirty minutes or so to organize. How about you get changed while you wait?"

The doctor left the room without waiting for my answer and I turned to Darius. I was pretty certain that if I'd been clothed when I arrived the police would have taken them for evidence. I asked as much. "Do I have any clothes?"

Darius stood and strode across the room. "Yes...Well no. After I left the police station I went to the hotel to grab you a bag of things. Unfortunately, I couldn't get into your room so I brought you some of mine." He lifted a duffel bag onto the bed and gave me a concerned look. "Will you need a hand or..." he gestured towards the door, "do you want me to wait outside?"

I took a quick moment to assess myself and although the grogginess had faded and I felt steadier on my feet this time around, I figured it was probably best to accept the help. "I'd be grateful if you could make sure I don't topple over." I gave him a grave look. "I don't exactly want to stay here any longer than I have to."

Chapter Five
Darius

A piercing scream filled the darkness and I jumped out of bed and ran for the dividing door between Kamil's room and mine.

Thankfully I'd had the forethought to leave it open in case he needed the bathroom and couldn't manage to get there on his own.

I could easily make out Kamil's stiff figure on the bed, in the moonlight shining through the window, the crisp white sheets tangled around his legs.

I had to climb on the large king bed to reach him in the middle. He didn't react to my weight in the bed, so I reached out and placed a hand on his clammy bicep. "Kamil?" I called out in a calm soothing voice even though I felt anything but calm.

His screams subsided to a whimper that tore at my heart. It was a sound I never wanted to hear coming from my friend again.

"Kami, wake up, it's D."

Like magic his eyes popped open and he scooted back on the bed clearly trying to get away from me. Understanding his intention, I quickly moved until I was just perched on the edge of the bed and there was over half an empty bed between us.

"Hey, it's only me. You were having a nightmare."

He reached out and the small reading lamp at his side of the bed came on. "Fuck. I'm sorry."

I shook my head. "You've got nothing to be sorry for. I'm just glad I left that door open."

Kamil shuffled into the middle of the bed and sat with his back against the headboard. He dropped his head into his hands and took some deep breaths. No doubt trying to calm down his racing heart.

I found myself breathing a little deeply too, because my heart was beating erratically and I hadn't been the one having nightmares. "Do you want me to go?" I asked after a minute.

Kamil lifted his head his gaze connecting with mine. "Could you stay for a little bit?" The wounded look he gave me had me agreeing instantly.

"Of course. Do you mind if I sit next to you?"

He shook his head and patted the space in invitation, so I placed a pillow against the headboard next to him making sure to leave a little room between us, not wanting to make him feel crowded.

Once settled, we sat in silence for a good minute or two. It was only when I couldn't handle the silence any longer that I had to break it. "Do you want to talk about it?"

After the words had left my mouth I realized he could have taken that two ways. Either he'd think I was talking about the nightmare or perhaps what happened to him in the green room. And in that moment I knew I wouldn't mind either way as long as it helped him. He didn't deserve what had happened to him. And he certainly didn't deserve it haunting him for the rest of his days. Or nights as it seems to be.

"I don't know if it was a memory or just what my mind has imagined after hearing what happened," he starts, his gaze staring straight-ahead. "I couldn't move. I was…helpless. Me? How could *I* ever be helpless?"

From an outside perspective you would completely see what he meant, he was not a small guy. The physical exertion of his drum playing keeps him fit and muscular. He was tattooed and had a number of piercings. No, Kamil didn't *look* like he could ever be helpless. But he was trusting and sweet, and sadly, he put that trust in the wrong person that day.

I slid my hand over to his and interlocked our fingers. "You were. But you won't be, never again."

When his eyes locked onto mine I hoped he could see the truth of my promise in them, because I meant it. I would do everything in my power to make sure he wouldn't feel like that again. And that started with getting our supporting act replaced before we hit the stage again.

Kamil slid down the bed so that he was lying on the pillow facing me, our hands still connected between us. "Thank you."

Spotting the time on the clock and knowing the sun would be rising sooner than I'd like, I moved myself down the bed too. "It's all good. Now lets get some sleep, before the sun comes up."

𝄞

"Darius! Darius!"

An incessant screeching woke me up.

"Darius. Where the bloody hell are you?" The British accent had me rubbing my bleary eyes.

"I'm here, Sadie." I grumbled loudly. "In Kamil's room." I clarified, even though she'd probably be able to follow my voice through the adjoining door.

As the little fiery woman stepped into the room dressed in a navy pantsuit, her blue eyes were on her phone as she tapped away at the screen. Sadie's blonde chin length bob was dead straight and flawless as usual. She had a baby face and looked about eighteen, even though she was actually twenty-two; she called it a curse but I was sure as she got older she'd be glad of her youthful looks.

"Good, you're awake. Why didn't you answer me when I first called your name?" She lifted her gaze off her phone then and her eyes widened as they fell on us. Kamil curled into my side still seemingly asleep regardless of our not so quiet voices. "What the..." She waved her hand dismissively. "Nope it doesn't matter. I've got more important things to worry about right now."

Kamil shifted beside me turning his body to look at her. He was still close enough that I could feel his leg brush against mine, making my morning wood throb and me wish I'd pulled on some sweats before running in here last night. "It's okay. There's no scandal I just had a nightmare and D graciously offered to sit with me."

"The public know Darius is bi so it wouldn't matter if something was going on with you two." Sadie's face softened as she really weighed up Kamil. "How are you feeling this morning?"

"I'm fine."

She gave him a raised brow.

He sighed. "Honestly…I'm not sure how I am. But I promise to speak up if I feel like I'm anything but okay."

She nodded seemingly satisfied. "Okay. I'm happy with that answer. I have a number of good therapists on speed dial when you are ready to talk," she said, making it clear he would talk to one at some point and there would be no arguments about that.

"Thank you."

"Now, I do have a serious question to ask you. Do you feel up to performing tonight? I have another drummer on standby if you don't, so it won't be any trouble."

Kamil frowned and I sat up beside him wanting to have a clearer view of him so I could read whatever he might not be saying. "I think I'll be okay playing. I just don't want to go in the green room again." His eyes widened as he looked at me. "And I don't want to see the Crimson Panda guys."

I smiled. "That won't be a problem, I kicked them off the tour. They were informed to clear their shit out before they left the arena last night."

His breath hitched. "No. No. No. No. You can't just kick them off the tour. They have a huge fan base. It'll—"

I placed my hand on his arm and his rambling stopped. "If I let them stay on the tour I'd be condoning what they did and I will *never* do that."

"Besides, he's got some friends in high places and managed to snag someone way better than Crimson Pandas," Sadie said, excitement lacing her voice.

I rolled my eyes at her enthusiasm but couldn't hide the smirk playing on my lips. "I gave Saxton a call."

"Saxton. Like *the* Saxton." Kamil sounded just as thrilled as Sadie at the mention of his name, if this went on much longer I'd have ended up with a complex. My people are supposed to like me the best.

I nodded. "The very one. Running Hearts are happy to open a few shows for me."

"That is fucking brilliant. I've always wanted to see them in concert." Kamil's words had me shaking my head.

"And here I was thinking I was your favorite." I held a hand to my chest in mock heartbreak. "I guess I should be thankful Saxton already had a drummer in the family, or I might have lost you to them."

"Maybe you should." Kamil laughed and playfully tapped at my cheek with his open palm. "Stop pouting, you've got the best drummer there is and I'm not going anywhere."

"While seeing you two like this gives me all kinds of ideas for your fans to ship, we've got a lot of shit to do before the show tonight. The police have been trying to get ahold of you both, so you guys need to get up and call them straight away. I'll order you some room service for breakfast and then we'll discuss the rest of what's on today's agenda." Sadie may only be young and when she first started I thought I must have drawn the short straw because I'd assumed I'd ended up with the crappy intern, but she really knew what she was doing and was super efficient.

Chapter Six
Kamil

I walked into the arena expecting to be overwhelmed by panic and fear but nothing happened. It was just like any other day. Darius kept watching me far too closely for my liking not doubt expecting some reaction, similar to what I had been waiting to hit. I knew he was only concerned but I feared seeing pity in his eyes. I didn't want people to pity me for what happened, least of all Darius.

Waking up curled into his side that morning had my heart hammering and gave me thoughts I'd never had about Darius before. I'd had to pretend I was still sleeping for much longer than I actually was, just so that I could mentally talk my hard on down. Hearing Sadie's voice did a good job of helping with that thankfully.

Instead of going to the 'original' green room, Darius led us around the other side of the arena and to a room I'd never seen before. It was still essentially a green room but it didn't have a sofa. Instead the room was lined with half a dozen hard plastic single chairs, like you'd find in a school. I did wonder if the style change was for my benefit, or just because they had no other sofas available.

It didn't go unnoticed that he seemed to take us the long way around from the back entrance we used, to avoid passing the original green room but I didn't bring it up. Maybe he had reasons that were nothing to do with me, and everything to do with him having lost his temper. Maybe he didn't want reminding the fact that he'd practically pulverized James in that green room. He could have easily lost his career over it.

Thankfully after we'd gotten out of bed and called the police, Darius had been told the charges against him had been dropped, just as Trevor had mentioned the previous night, and they informed me about the confessions of James and Leon. It was assumed that because they'd both confessed that they'd probably take a plea deal so I wouldn't be needed to stand up at a trail, which was a relief, to be honest. I just wanted to forget it ever happened and no long dragged out trial meant the sooner I could do that.

"There you guys are," Sadie stated as she walked into the room only minutes after we stepped in ourselves. "Running Hearts are just finishing up their sound check and then you'll need to head on stage to do yours."

"Are the other guys here?" Darius asks obviously talking about the rest of his band. D might be a rapper—*the* artist everyone is there for—but he still had a group of musicians on stage with him, guitarist, keyboard player, someone on the decks, and, of course, me and my drums all playing a part in bringing his sound together.

Sadie nodded. "They're all side stage watching Running Hearts rehearse."

"Oh, I wanna see. Come on." Without any conscious thought, I grabbed Darius's hand and dragged him along behind me. We ran through the corridors and it was only the fact that his hand tightened around mine, that I noticed I'd brought us right past the original green room. That knowledge didn't diminish my excitement about catching the end of Running Hearts sound check, so I kept running for my destination.

I skidded to a stop at the side of the stage causing Darius to barrel into my back.

"Jesus," he said as he steadied himself with his hands on my shoulders. "I wasn't expecting that."

I laughed. "What did you think I'd do run out onto the stage like a crazy fan?" I felt the loss of his hands as he stepped up beside me, and I turned to see a cheeky grin on his face.

"You did seem a little fanatical when I'd mentioned Saxton's name earlier."

I slapped at his upper arm. "I was not fanatical," I said as I turned my attention back to the act on the stage. I could see the rest of our band across the other side with Sadie, who must have chosen to go the other way when we ran off.

They sang another song before everyone was happy with the sound and finally put down their instruments. We walked out and met them in the center of the stage.

Darius pulled Saxton into a manly hug. "Thanks for coming."

"We're happy to help you out, " Saxton stated as he took a small step back. He glanced at me but before he could greet me Kat, his sister, and the band's drummer elbowed him in the ribs as she passed to get to Darius.

"Don't let him fool you that it's all for you, it gives us a chance to try out a couple of our new songs live and he'd be lying if he didn't say we're all excited about that." She threw her arms around Darius. "Hi Big D, it seems like ages since we last saw you."

"Probably because it has been," Darius said as he hugged her back. "It's good to see you too, Beautiful."

"Stop chatting up my sister," Saxton complained. "She knows all about your bad boy ways and isn't stupid enough to fall for it."

Darius grinned and I shook my head. Saxton had just set Darius a challenge and he'd enjoy doing it just to get a rise out of the other guy. "Maybe she likes a bad boy. You'll have to watch this space, Saxton."

"The pair of you. Stop it!" Kat reprimanded as she shoved Darius's arms of her shoulders and stepped around him heading for me. "Hey, Kamil. It's good to see you again."

I returned her gentle hug and although she hadn't mentioned or hinted at what happened the fact that I knew they all knew made me suddenly feel uncomfortable. "You too," I stated quickly before letting go and striding over to my drum kit, needing to some space between myself and the others.

Sitting down I picked up the sticks I always kept beside the kit and started tapping to a gentle beat.

"I guess that's Kamil's cue for us to get started." I heard D say to the others but I didn't react, I just allowed the beat to calm my mind.

Within minutes everyone had their hands on their relevant instruments and Darius stood in the center of the stage with his microphone. We all knew the song list so I changed the beat to the one we always used for sound check, the other guys jumping in with their own instruments right on time.

Chapter Seven
Darius

After two songs we managed to have the sound how it needed to be and the guys left for the green room, leaving just Kamil and me on stage. Kamil was still tapping out a rhythm that didn't belong to any of my songs and I headed over to him.

I'd noticed he'd acted strange when Kat hugged him, practically running away from the contact. I wanted to outright ask him what it was about but knowing what he'd been through I didn't know how much of a knife's edge he might be on. I didn't want to distress him anymore. Instead I decided to ask him about the beat his drumsticks were making.

"Have you been moonlighting for someone else?"

The beat stopped and he looked at me with a frown, clearly not having any idea what the hell I was talking about.

"I haven't heard that beat before," I clarified, nodding at the drumsticks lying loosely in his hands. "It was quite mesmerizing."

He shrugged. "It was just something I could feel. Something I needed to put out there."

It reminded me of how my raps came to me; random words that I had to release and which eventually pieced together made something more. True musicians were like that.

Just like other artists who had to draw what they saw, or authors who wrote the stories they felt needed telling. We were all creative beings. Sadly what I'd noticed is we tended to be more emotional, more sensitive.

Kamil and I may have been just friends for a long time but something had changed within me since seeing him being taken advantage of. I had a ridiculous need to protect him; to help him heal.

To give him experiences to wash away the touch of those other people who never deserved to look at him let alone touch him in the ways they did. Those thoughts scared me since it wasn't a feeling I was familiar with.

"I guess we should go out back and get psyched up for the show," he stated as he stood from his stool.

I followed him through the corridors to the new green room in silence, when he reached out for the door he paused with his hand on the handle. "I'm okay." He turned to lock eyes with me. "Honestly."

I could see the determination in his straight back and clenched jaw and knew he was telling the truth. Maybe I'd been over thinking things after all.

We stepped into the room and the news anchor was chatting excitedly on the big screen TV that was hanging on the wall. "The music industry has been rocked today with Crimson Pandas having been dropped from not only rapper Darius Hayes tour, but also their recording contract. A source close to the situation has told us two of the band members drugged and raped someone on Darius's team. Neither Darius nor the record company have been reachable for comment."

Beside me, Kamil grabbed at his throat as he stared at the woman on the screen with wide eyes and started gasping. All the color had drained from his face.

"Shit. Someone turn that off," I yelled not caring who was there and listening, just that someone did as I asked. I maneuvered Kamil into a chair before crouching in front of him, hating the sound of his panicked gasps.

"Breathe, Kamil."

His ice blue gaze locked onto mine, his terror easily visible.

"Breathe. In and out."

His eyes never left mine but he did as I said and we breathed together.

"It's just a panic attack. Keep breathing. In and out."

After a long few minutes of slow deep breaths his body relaxed beneath my hands on his biceps that I didn't even recall gripping.

"Can we have the room for a minute?" I called out to everyone behind me.

Kamil shook his head and glanced behind me. "That's not necessary. You all witnessed my freak out. You deserve an explanation."

"You don't need to explain anything to us." Kat stepped up beside me and placed her hand on his shoulder. "If you want to talk about it, then, by all means, I'm here for you, but you don't *need* to tell me anything you don't want. I'm pretty sure everyone else in here feels the same." She glanced around the room and both Kamil and I followed her gesture seeing a number of nods of agreement.

"Thanks." Kamil sounded shy, which wasn't something I was used to but having just had a panic attack in front of everyone I guessed he probably felt a little raw and unsure.

After a second's hesitation conversations picked up and everyone started chatting between themselves. With on gentle squeeze of Kamil's shoulder Kat strolled off and out of the room. I focused my attention back on Kamil and seeing that he actually had color back in his cheeks, I stood to my full height. My legs ached from squatting for such a long time, so I took a moment to rub my thighs before taking a seat next to Kamil.

"Thanks for helping me out of that. It hit me so quick; I didn't even know what it was at first. I just couldn't breathe and…"

He didn't need to finish; I was there. I witnessed his panic and fear overwhelming him.

"It's what friends are for." I gave him a warm smile and hoped he felt like I was more than just someone he worked for.

The smile he gave back didn't last long before it fell, and he was again sad and serious. "I think I need to call my sister and tell her what happened. It's only a matter of time before my name gets out there and I don't want her hearing it like that."

What he said made sense. As much as we'd want to keep his name out of it, leaks happen and in this business they usually happened pretty fucking quickly. "Yeah, that's probably a good idea. Why don't you go use my dressing room?" I glanced at my watch and made some quick calculations. "I won't need to be in there for at least another hour. So take as long as you want."

With a determined nod, Kamil stood and made his way out of the room without another word.

Saxton dropped into Kamil's vacant seat as the door shut. "How are you doing?"

I gave him a questioning look. "Me? I'm fine."

"I heard you beat the living the shit out of James. That is a sure fire sign to say you ain't fine."

I didn't bother arguing, because he was right; my actions definitely said I wasn't fine.

"You're into Kamil." It wasn't a question but I answered anyway.

"Yeah, not that I knew it then. But he makes me…a little unsteady." I couldn't think of another way describe how I felt when it came to Kamil.

Saxton laughed. "That's not exactly the words I'd use, but if you say so."

I chuckled at his phrasing and sighed, needing to change the subject. "How are you after the divorce from the Aussie beauty?"

His whole demeanor changed, his eyes filling with sadness, and I suddenly wanted to bite off my tongue for bringing up what was obviously a touchy subject for him.

"I wasn't actually married." His voice was flat and emotionless, like it was some well-rehearsed answer.

I'd known he wasn't married. I, along with everyone else in the world had seen the statement he'd made explaining that whole misunderstanding. But I'd also seen him with Aimee, and heard from reliable sources that they were head over heels in love with each other.

"I'm sorry mate, I didn't—"

"Oh you fucking didn't just mention she who should never be named?" Matt stated cutting me off. He sounded pissed and I had to look at him to see if there was any humor behind his words. The anger in his clenched jaw told me there wasn't. The Aussie beauty seemed to be a sore point for them all.

Saxton got up without a word and left the room leaving me staring after him regretting ever opening my mouth.

A heavy hand fell on my shoulder and I turned away from the door to find Will, another member of Running Hearts, standing beside me. "Don't worry too much. All those new angsty songs will be full of emotion tonight. The fans will get a great fucking show." He threw me a quick wink and followed after Saxton, and although my heart still felt heavy for him, Will's words had eased my guilt a little.

Chapter Eight
Kamil

I stared at my reflection in the mirror as I waited for my twin sister to answer the call. I looked tired as fuck and suddenly felt it too. It was like the visual made it be.

"Hey Kam," she called cheerily into my ear.

I suddenly had second thoughts about telling her. I didn't want to take away the happiness I could hear and replace it with worry.

"What's going on? Is it something to do with what I just saw on the news?" she guessed.

I'd obviously hesitated a moment too long and now I had no option but to tell her, because I knew my sister well enough to know she wouldn't let the subject drop if she felt she was on to something.

"Yes. Last night…" I didn't know how to word it. Thankfully I didn't have to.

"It was you," Abi stated blandly. "Do you want me to come visit? I could probably still get a flight tonight if you want me there."

I chuckled, knowing she was probably already checking flights on her iPad. "Abi, you can't just jump on a plane, you have a newborn baby."

"Isaac is just over a month old, Kam. I'll be perfectly fine on a short distance flight." She sounded so confident that a selfish part of me wanted to take her up on her offer but I couldn't put her through that. We were so busy on this tour we'd be moving to the next destination in a couple of days, it just wouldn't be worth the hassle for her.

I told her as much. "I'd love to see you both, but it's so busy with the tour I'd hardly see you and it'd be a waste of your money. I get the weekend off in a few weeks and my flight is booked. I'm looking forward to seeing you both then."

She sighed unhappily down the line but didn't argue. "Okay... If you need to chat you know I'm up feeding Isaac at all hours so just call, no matter what time it is."

"Scout's honor." I promised.

"You were a scout for one day. It doesn't count." I could imagine the eye roll she was giving me.

The one she gave me every time I called myself a scout.

I laughed. "You're only jealous because you weren't one at all."

Isaac cried in the background and I heard rustling through the line before she started quietly shushing him. "You go sort him out—"

"No." She cut me off. "I don't get to speak to you often and he's happy now he's getting a cuddle."

Hearing that he had actually stopped crying, I took her at her word and we spent the next thirty minutes talking about Isaac. She doted on him and it made me want the next couple of weeks to pass so I could go and see the bundle of cuteness with my own eyes.

I was just leaving the dressing room as Darius rounded the corner. It was time for us to get ready for the show. I felt relaxed after the mindless chatting and I was more than to go out on the stage and watch the crowd treat Darius like the Rap God he was.

𝄞

By the time we made it back to the hotel I was exhausted, the previous day's events having caught up with me. I barely managed to get a quick shower before falling face first on the bed and falling asleep to the sound of Darius's shower running through the open door between our rooms.

There was weight on me and I struggled to breathe through the musty smelling material that my face was pressed into. I knew I should do something but something wasn't right but my limbs were heavy and my mind fuzzy. My heart raced erratically.

"Kami. Wake up." Darius's worried tone pulled me out of my dream, like it was a command I couldn't help but follow.

I opened my eyes to find his chocolate brown orbs brimming with concern staring back at me. I took a deep breath. "Thanks." I said as I made an effort to take slow steady breaths in the hope that my heart would follow the pace.

He gave me a small reassuring smile before sitting back against the headboard on the other side of the bed.

"I'm sorry I woke you again." I admitted as I sat up and mirrored his position on my side of the bed. Darius was the person those thousands of people paid to see each night; he needed his sleep. It wasn't like he could perform with half the energy and he certainly couldn't be replaced if he wasn't feeling well enough.

Darius shook his head and placed his hand on my thigh, the feel of his warm, soft skin against mine making me hyper aware of how intimate the touch was. "You need me? I'm here. No questions asked. No complaints." His eyes slowly traveled from his hand on my thigh and up my body, setting every nerve in my body on fire before landing on my eyes. "I care about you Kamil. Probably more than I should." That last sentence was barely a whisper but I heard everyone of those words and everything it implied.

Something ignited inside me and I was no longer on my side of the bed. I'd crushed my lips against his to show him that I felt exactly the same way about him. Darius didn't reciprocate, but he didn't push me off either. It was almost like he was frozen with shock.

I sunk my hands into the dark brown strands at his nape, tugging his head back to get a better angle at his lips as I licked at the seam begging for him to open up for me.

He did.

In that moment the world melted away and all that was left were a drummer and a rapper, making a different kind of music in the darkness of night.

Look out for *A Little Unsteady: A Running Hearts Novella* to find out what happens next for Darius and Kamil, coming late 2020.

In the meantime join my <u>reader group</u> to keep up to date with news of my new releases.

Somebody Else's Song

by

Avery Hart

When life kicks you down, how much would you give to climb your way to the top?

Everly Rae is what some may consider a failure: a high school dropout turned traveling musician. Her "gigs" consist of her singing at hole-in-the-wall bars, and most don't even have stages. But when she meets Nolan at one of the dive bars she stops at, her luck finally changes. He is the manager for one of the world's most famous bands, and he wants Everly to be the opening act on their tour.

Life could be perfect ... except for the band's lead singer, Camden. He's a hotshot and superstar who's loved by millions. He also hates the idea of taking Everly with them.

Will Everly Rae finally catch her big break? Or is she destined to sing someone else's song for the rest of her life?

Chapter One

"Thank you for coming," I said as I handed Mrs. Haywood her change.

"My pleasure dear." She smiled sweetly. "You have yourself a good night."

The little bell hanging over the door tingled as the last customer of the day exited the store. I waved goodbye through the window as she made her way down the town's main street and towards her home on Bluebell lane. As soon as she was out of sight, I took a seat on the rickety wooden stool and placed my head in my hands. Although things had been slow, it still had been an extremely long twelve-hour day of work, and money troubles had been weighing heavily on my mind for months now.

Sighing, I popped open the register and began counting the cash, knowing it wasn't going to be much for the day. The customer flow had been minimal, which wasn't shocking since it had been slowly declining for the past six months. Still, I hoped each day would bring a change for the better.

It never did, though.

One-hundred and forty-three dollars. That's how much the shop pulled in for the day. I jotted it down in the ledger book and added up the totals for the week. Bills were due, and I had put them off for as long as I could in hopes for some sort of small miracle. As I stared at the pile that was delivered this afternoon, the bright red lettering stamped on the papers reading *"PAST DUE"* mocked me, and I knew they couldn't be put off any longer.

I separated the stacks, sorting them by which bills were already late, and which had only just come due. Adding up the earnings for the week and comparing them to the previous weeks had my stomach dropping. Once again, each week there was less and less. On top of that, my overhead kept increasing. At this rate I would be out of business before the year ended.

My chest constricted at that thought. My miracle wasn't coming. At least not in time to save me.

I switched on the radio, an old, beat up unit that belonged to my dad from the late eighties. I'd had it since my teenage years, so I was surprised it even worked anymore. It wasn't anything to look at. The once-shiny black surface was now marred with scratches and scrapes, but the speakers sounded fine and that was all that mattered to me. It was far from the modern-day CD players and iPods, but that made no difference. I had grown up listening to my parent's old cassette tapes, and when I wanted to hear newer music, I just switched to the radio—when I was actually able to tune in to a station that came in halfway decent. Kind of a hit and miss thing around there.

I turned the knob, and the speakers crackled as I passed over the stations before finally landing on one where the song came through clearly. Turning the volume up, I hummed along and let the music wash over me. It brightened my mood even as I put together the meager deposit I needed to take to the bank before they closed tonight. Then I could mail out some payments tomorrow.

Checking my numbers again, I sighed in relief. If nothing else, at least I'd be able to make the shop's rent for this month. Last week I hadn't been so sure. The other bills? Well, that was a different story. It seemed as if I'd have to dip into my savings account in order to tackle those. But at least the rent was covered because it meant the shop would live to see another month. If something didn't give, and soon, I really didn't know how many more I'd have.

Slipping the deposit into my purse, I gathered the bills that were spread across the countertop and slid them in, too. I'd write the payments and get them ready to mail once I got home and had something to eat. At the thought of food, my stomach growled loudly. Since I overslept this morning I hadn't had time to pack a lunch, and with money so tight, I couldn't spend any extra. Not even to eat.

My nightly ritual of cleaning up and preparing the shop for tomorrow came next, except there wasn't actually much to do. It was more of a habit than a necessity at this point, but I went through the motions nonetheless. After all, I had been doing it for so many years—since I was a girl just helping momma out actually—that it was second nature to me. That and it helped me keep the memory of her alive.

God, I missed her. She always brought such a light into the shop, one that couldn't be extinguished. No matter how tough or bad things got, she always managed to keep a smile on her face, and it had been contagious. I didn't know anyone that could be in her presence without beaming. Well, anyone except my father.

When Momma had first gotten sick, I'd been only ten years old. Dad decided it was high time for him to pack up and move out, leaving the two of us behind to fend for ourselves. Neither of us heard from him after that day. Not even once. To be honest, I'd never really missed him one bit. Leaving like that had ... well, it was wrong. So wrong I'd never be able to forgive him for it. Even then, though, Momma always wore that smile on her face. I envied that about her now when I couldn't muster one up to save my life. I had no idea how she had managed it.

It was then, at ten years old, I had begun helping Momma out at the shop. When school let out for the day, I'd walk the five blocks there, quickly do my homework, and then she would teach me how to run everything. How she stocked the shelves, how she rang up customers, and at closing time she would show me what to do in order to get things tidied up and ready for the following day.

I had always been a fast learner; picking up on everything in half the time it took for her to train a new hire. After the first two days, I'd been able to close the shop on my own, which gave Momma a chance to lay on the small couch in the back and rest.

A week later and I could ring up customers, stock the shelves without asking where things went, and I even managed to learn a good portion of how to do the bookkeeping. It was a lot of work, but I did what I had to in order to help her out.

By the time I turned fifteen, Momma had gotten a lot worse. Barely able to work a few hours a time, she spent more time at doctor appointments than anything else. She hired extra help but they could only do so much. The rest fell on my shoulders, and the hours I'd been putting in after school just weren't enough to get everything done at the shop. There was no way I could continue going to school and keep running the shop. The place meant everything to Momma. She'd opened it and built it from nothing. When she got sick and couldn't be there as much, it caused her pain. Plus, I didn't have to be a genius to realize how much she stressed about money. If we didn't keep the shop open, we wouldn't survive. Weighing the options, I did the only thing I could think of in that moment. I dropped out of high school and worked full time, filling Momma's shoes the best I could.

I remembered the day I told her my plan as if it were yesterday. She wasn't happy about the idea, but she also knew we didn't have a whole lot of options.

"Everly, sweetie, why don't you head out. Go out with your friends and do something fun. I'll take care of closing up tonight," Momma said as she came to the front, her usual smile donning her face, although it didn't quite reach her eyes.

I could tell she was tired, exhausted even though she just woke from a nap, but she was trying hard to hide it. She always did.

"That's okay, I got it." I made my way to the door, flipped the sign from open to closed, and locked the door. "Why don't you go home and get some rest?"

"I've been resting all evening." She yawned and wiped the sleep from her eyes. "Go on now, let your momma take care of things for a change. You've been spending so much time here lately, I can't remember the last time I've seen you with friends. Or doing anything for yourself for that matter. You need a break or you're going to wear yourself out."

"I'm fine, Momma. Promise."

And I was. To be honest, I had grown to enjoy being here and working. It was comforting in a way, and I was able to keep an eye on her should anything go wrong. Sure, it was tough for me in the beginning not being able to go out and hang with my friends, but as the years passed, I cared less and less about that. It seemed insignificant in the grand scheme of things. Besides, I had my guitar to keep me company during the slow times and when I was home. Playing and singing brought me more joy than being out and about ever would.

"I insist. Now, you scoot your little behind outta here and let me feel useful." She popped open the drawer to the register and lifted the cash tray from it, placing it on the countertop.

"You can feel useful tomorrow. Cadance took off for the day, remember?" I approached her and placed my hand on top of hers, halting her movements and bringing her attention to me. "You need to save that energy and rest up as much as you can before opening tomorrow. You haven't worked many hours in a row for a while, not like you'll have to tomorrow. Your body is not used to so much exertion anymore."

"You're all grown up now, aren't you?" Momma said, wiping a tear from her eye. "Where has the time gone? You've spent so much time here helping me that you've missed out on so much of your childhood."

"It's okay Momma, I don't mind. I love working here, and you've needed the help. That's what family is for. To be there for one another when they need it most." I scooped her into my arms and gave her a giant hug. "I'll always be here for you. Promise."

I released her from the hug and took her hand in mine, guiding her to the small sofa. "Can we sit for a minute? There's something I need to talk to you about."

"Of course. What's on your mind, baby?" she asked as we sat down.

"I don't think you're going to like this idea, but please hear me out."

She nodded, so I continued. "You've been getting weaker and needing to rest more. I've been doing all I can when I'm not in school, but it's not enough. You need more help during the day, and we need this shop so we can pay the bills."

"Everly, sweetie. I know where you're going with this. You think you need to drop out of school so you can be here all the time. I can't let you do that, though. You need to finish your schooling."

"And I will. I can do it at home, at night once the shop closes. I'll continue my studies. I don't need a piece of paper saying I graduated. That paper isn't what will make me smart. It's what's in here"—I tapped myself on the top of my head—"that does that. It'll be okay, Momma. Everything will be okay."

We'd argued about the idea of me dropping out of school the entire night that night, but eventually she realized we didn't have much of a choice if we wanted to keep the shop running. And that was something we *needed* to do. By the following week, she'd officially pulled me from school and I was working full time at the shop. It was a lot of work, and I'd been exhausted, but I'd felt so much better knowing things were being handled.

Life had a funny way of working itself out, and just like that night when I told my momma everything would be okay, I repeated those words to myself now.

"Everything is gonna be okay, Everly," I said to the empty room. Everything is gonna be just fine."

Chapter Two

I pulled up to the bar—which was situated behind a truck stop off the main highway—and parked in the spot closest to the front door, which was the only area in the lot that had any semblance of light. It was a raggedy hole in the wall from the outside, with the wooden siding looking quite a bit worse for wear. A few cars were parked sporadically in the lot, and the dimly lit sign had more than one busted letter, making it impossible to read the actual name of the place. If I hadn't called ahead to make sure they were open, I likely would have assumed the building had been abandoned.

It'd only been a month since I closed the shop, which was the hardest decision of my life. It just wasn't making money anymore, and there was nothing else I could do. I'd tried everything. I couldn't allow myself to fall further into debt just to hold onto something that was my mother's love. It had been time to let go of that last piece of her and move on with my life, so I decided to take to the road for a while and follow *my* love. Singing.

Although the place wasn't even close to what I had been expecting or hoping for, I didn't let it deter me from my plan. I was still getting used to playing in front of people again, so I was happy it'd be a small crowd and not a packed house. Even if there was only one person in there, I'd perform as if my life depended on it. And in a way, maybe it did.

I climbed out of my car and popped open the trunk, smiling as I pulled the old guitar case out. I'd had this case since I was fifteen—the last present my mother bought me—and although it was extremely beat up, I knew I'd never part with it. It meant too much to me. Besides, it was nothing a little duct tape couldn't fix, and the Lord knew I'd used my fair share of that on it.

Walking around the car, the gravel crunched under my boots, echoing loudly throughout the open area around me. I paused at the door, taking a few deep breaths to steel my nerves before I reached out and placed my hand on the cold metal.

The knob squeaked as it turned, and when I pushed against the door to open it, the thing didn't budge an inch.

"What the heck?" I muttered as I tried again, mustering a little more power than the first time.

Still nothing.

I jiggled the doorknob, turned it the opposite direction, and pressed my shoulder against it, shoving with everything I had, but no amount of force could move the darn thing.

Maybe it wasn't open after all. I let out a huff as I picked up my guitar case and turned to leave.

"Just my luck," I muttered as I kicked a piece of gravel, an utterly defeated feeling crashing through my heart.

"Having trouble?" a deep voice asked. I startled, jumping so much my guitar case slipped from my fingers. It hit the ground with a loud *thud*, but at least it landed upright.

I turned and my eyes shot up to see a man standing a couple feet away, a big smile on his face as he looked down at me. He was older than me, probably in his late thirties, and his perfectly-ironed clothes were clean. Not how I'd expected a patron of that bar to be dressed.

Normally, running into a strange man in a darkened lot would put me on high alert, or at least send me running in the opposite direction, but there was something about him that made me feel more at ease than I knew I should be. He wasn't menacing, either. In fact, when my eyes met his only kindness shone from them.

"Sorry, I didn't mean to scare you." He reached down, picked up my case, and opened it. "I hope I didn't break your guitar."

"It's okay." I returned his smile. "I just didn't expect anyone to be behind me. Honestly, I thought this place was closed." I signaled to the bar with my thumb and shrugged my shoulders.

"Why do you say that?" he asked, looking puzzled.

"Door won't open. Figured it must be locked."

"Mind if I give it a try?"

"Knock yourself out."

I stepped to the side, giving him room. He reached out, turned the knob, and with both hands he shoved. Of course the damn door swings wide open ...

"After you." He held the door open with one hand while signaling me through with the other.

"How did you ..."

"The knob is finicky," he said before I'd completed my sentence, already knowing what I was going to ask. "You have to lift it while you turn, and then give it a little shove. It's the only way it'll open."

"I'm taking it you've been here before." His knowledge of the door made it obvious so I had no idea why I'd even made that statement.

"Once or twice." He winked at me—but not in a creepy way thank goodness—as he followed me through the doorway and into the bar.

Once inside, I took in my surroundings, surprised to find the inside looked nothing like the outside. It was actually quite comforting and cozy. The walls, tables, counters, and everything had been made out of wood. Paired with the dim lighting, it reminded me of a cabin nestled deep in the woods.

Tall tables were scattered over the floor, complete with stools. On the far wall, wood booths and benches took up the space. Across from that was the bar, which was considerably bigger than I would have thought, its wall behind lined to the ceiling with bottles of alcohol.

"So," the man said, bringing my attention back to him, "you playing tonight?" He nodded towards the case I was gripping like a lifeline.

"Oh. I-I don't know." My cheeks heated.

His head titled to the side. Maybe I should have asked when I called earlier. Showing up guitar in hand while not knowing who ran the place—or anything about it really—probably wasn't one of my smartest moves.

Feeling the need to explain myself, I continued. "I mean ... I was hoping I could, but I haven't even spoken to anyone about it yet. I guess I figured I would swing in and see if they'd allow me to." The entire thing sounded ridiculous now that I'd said it out loud. I contemplated turning and walking right back out the door, getting in my car, and driving far away from the little bar.

"I see," he said as he rubbed his fingers along the short stubble of his chin, a contemplative look spreading across his face. "What kind of music do you play?"

"I can play anything really, but my favorite is Country."

At my words, his face lit up as a smile spread his lips, making crinkle lines form at the corners of his eyes. He looked as if he'd just hit the lotto, but I didn't understand his reaction. His eyes roamed from the top of my head to my feet. I squirmed, and a sinking feeling hit my gut because I was incredibly unsure of what I'd been planning on doing all of a sudden. Maybe my initial thoughts about the man had been wrong. Maybe he wasn't as innocent as I'd originally assumed ... The possibility sent a wave of nervousness through me.

"Country, huh?" There was something in his tone that piqued my interest. It also kept my feet glued to the floor, which was good because part of me wanted to hightail it out of there. "Well, lucky for you I happen to be a huge fan of Country music."

He paused and I cocked an eyebrow, wondering where he was going with this. Why was I lucky he liked it?

"Don't go anywhere." He straightened and took a few steps towards the bar before turning back to me. "I just so happen to know the owner of this establishment, so let me see what I can do about getting you to play tonight."

As he walked away, I thought my jaw would surely hit the floor from shock. Being honest with myself, I half expected to be turned away the moment I stepped inside. Never had I expected to run into someone who knew the owner.

While I waited for him to return with news of my future plans, my eyes scanned the room again. My insides did little somersaults when I realized the place held more people than I'd initially realized.

From the outside, the building had looked almost abandoned, and when I first entered, there'd only been a couple of people inside. Then again, I hadn't had much chance to look around before the man had spoken to me and pulled my attention back to him. But with him off speaking to his friend, it gave me the perfect opportunity to check the place out. Voices I hadn't noticed until then flooded my senses.

There were a few people standing at the bar to my right chatting with the bartender. The booths to the left were half filled with people laughing and joking while they sipped drinks and ate finger foods. The tables in the middle were empty, but even with that, I still counted a good fifteen, maybe twenty people inside. It might not be a large crowd, but it was still more than I expected when I first pulled up and definitely more than the last bar I had played in.

I couldn't spot a stage area, which made me wonder where I'd play. Luckily I had my guitar, though. It was the only thing I needed to perform.

My thoughts were interrupted as the man approached with a petite brunette walking next to him, her arm linked through his.

"Well hello there," she said as they came to a stop in front of me. "You must be the little lady Nolan here was telling me about."

Nolan, I repeated to myself, silently smacking myself for not thinking to ask his name before.

"Well aren't you a pretty little thang?" She reached her hand out and I took it, giving a little shake. "It's so very nice to meet you."

"It's a pleasure to meet you too, ma'am."

She beamed at me, her smile so kind it could brighten the darkest of rooms, and instantly I felt at ease with her. "Please, call me Celia. Ma'am makes me sound like an old fuddy-duddy and believe you me I am *far* from that."

"I'd say *far from that* is a bit of a stretch," Nolan chuckled.

"You bite your tongue, Mister. Just because you're all grown now doesn't mean I can't still give your ass a whippin'." Celia elbowed him in the side, eliciting a laugh from both of them.

"You know I'm just kidding with ya, Mom," said Nolan.

My eyes widened. "Mom?" I gasped. There was no way she was old enough to be his momma, although it did explain the loving banter between the two of them and the way she looked at him with nothing but admiration.

"Don't look so surprised, sweetie. I had my baby here when I was still a baby myself at sixteen years old," Celia said, answering my unspoken question. No wonder they look so close in age.

"Wow, that must have been very difficult for you, raising a child when you were so young yourself." Taking care of my momma and running the store had been a lot of work for me when I was not much younger than that, but I couldn't imagine how hard it must have been to raise a child.

"It had its moments, yes, but we managed just fine. I was lucky that his father, rest his sweet soul, stuck by my side and helped me raise him. This boy was quite the handful when he was younger, let me tell you."

"Mom," Nolan groaned. "Can we not?"

"Ah yes. Always the businessman." She rolled her eyes but I could see the amusement that danced behind them.

"As I was telling you before, this is—" His words halted as he quirked an eyebrow at me.

"Everly. Everly Rae," I finished for him as I realized I'd never told him my name either.

"This is Everly, and she plays guitar." He gestured to my case sitting on the floor at my feet. "She was hoping she'd be allowed to play for us tonight."

"Well, Everly, I'd certainly love to hear you play," Celia said. "Unfortunately, there isn't much of a crowd on Thursday nights, as you can see." She swept an arm toward the few patrons.

"That's alright, I don't mind." I smiled at her. "That is, if you'd be so kind as to let me play."

"There's just one little problem. I didn't know we'd have a musical guest tonight, so we don't have any equipment here. Nothing for you to plug your guitar into."

"What kind of guitar do you have?" Nolan asked.

"Just an old acoustic I've had for ages." I popped open the case to show him.

Nolan nodded in approval. "That'll work just fine. It's not like the place is packed, and we definitely don't have a concert hall here. As long as the music is turned off, we should all be able to hear the guitar just fine."

"You have a good point," Celia said to her son. "But what about for her to sing? The microphone from the karaoke machine broke a couple days ago, and I haven't had time to get a new one yet." She looked at me with apologetic eyes.

"Without the guitar being plugged in it's better for me to not sing into a mic," I explained. "That way my voice doesn't drown out the sound of the guitar. I prefer it that way, actually. It's more pure, intimate. At least in my opinion."

Nolan looked to his mom and she gave a slight nod.

"In that case," she said, "let's get you situated, shall we? Once you are settled, I'll let everyone know what's going on."

"Really?" I squealed, unable to contain my excitement. "Thank you *so* much! This means a whole lot to me."

"Follow me, sweetie. I'll show you where to set up."

Excitement coursed through me as I scooped up my case and turned to follow Celia.

"You two go on. I'm going to make myself a drink and grab a seat." Nolan signaled towards the bar. "Looking forward to hearing your performance, Everly."

I beamed at him and made my way across the room, following his mother's lead.

Chapter Three

I inhaled deeply, trying calm the nerves that snuck up on me once the initial excitement wore off. Before I'd hit the road, I hadn't played in front of anyone since my momma passed. I'd grown up in a small town in Alabama named Pinkerton. Everyone knew everyone there, so it was like playing for family. There had been nothing to worry about, nothing that made my anxiety rise to the surface. Once I left home, though, everything had changed.

I shouldn't have been so nervous. It wasn't like I'd never performed in front of people before. Heck, I'd been driving around and playing at random bars for the past few weeks, and some of them had larger crowds than what was here tonight. But something about tonight felt different. I just didn't know what.

You can do this. I repeated the words over and over in my head as my hand slid silently over the neck of the guitar that was propped on my knee. Readying myself, I positioned my fingers over the metal strings.

The music was off, and the voices and laughter from not long ago faded away. There wasn't a single noise in the bar except for the heavy pounding of my heart. I felt all eyes on me but hadn't been able to pull my gaze up and meet their stares. Who'd have known silence could be so incredibly deafening?

My eyes closed as I strummed the first chords of the song, the guitar gently vibrating against my body. The sound soothed my soul like nothing else could, making the nerves melt as my lips parted to sing.

The first notes were soft and faltered slightly, but the music wrapped around me like a cocoon and, within moments everything became effortless. The tempo sped up, my voice grew louder, and confidence surged through me as I belted out my own rendition of Dolly Parton's "Jolene."

Halfway through the song, claps sounded in time with the beat. "Whoop, whoop," was shouted from various patrons, too. Opening my eyes, I raised my head and took everything in. People smiled and sang along, clearly enjoying themselves. A few had even left their booths to stand closer to me, sitting on the stools at the tables in the middle of the room. It might not mean much to someone else, but to me it meant the world.

The song came to an end and everyone cheered, which filled my heart with happiness. Despite it being a small crowd, I felt as if I were on top of the world. I was meant to be there.

"Thank ya'll so much," I said as the patrons quieted down. "I just wanted to thank Celia for allowing me to play here tonight, and Nolan for telling her about me."

My eyes scanned the room, finding Nolan still standing by the bar with a drink in his hand. When our eyes met, he raised his glass and smiled.

"This next song is one I wrote myself, and it is dear to my heart."

I'd never played this song for anyone so I wasn't sure how it'd go, but something inside told me to do it. I wasn't sure what it was, but I'd always been taught never to ignore an intuition.

My fingers moved again, the notes slower than the previous song. *This one's for you, Momma,* I said silently in my head.

The atmosphere changed the moment I sang the ballad. Silence encompassed the room, the only other sound coming from the shuffling of feet as a few more people took a seat in front of me. Their eyes never left me as they inched forward, trying not to make a sound.

Emotions poured from me as I sang the song I wrote for my mother after she had passed away. The pain in my voice rang clear, the emotion raw. Even I could hear it, which made me wonder if the people could too. Glancing out at the crowd, I took in their stillness, but I couldn't read their expressions. No matter what they thought, it felt good to open myself up like that, to finally play that song for someone else. Still, apprehension crept in. Did they like it? Or did they hate it?

As I continued, my eyes found Nolan in hopes to find approval. It didn't make sense. He was a complete stranger and I'd only just met him that day, but for some reason he comforted me.

What I hadn't expected was to be met with the same unreadable look as everyone else in the room, nor the pang of sadness it caused inside me. I blinked away the tear that formed in my eye and allowed the single drop to roll down my cheek, leaving a warm trail of moisture in its wake. Something flashed across his face, but I couldn't tell what. Maybe that was a good thing.

I belted the lyrics to the last lines, my voice wavering as I sang my goodbye to Momma while strumming the final few chords. When I finished, silence greeted me. Not a single person even moved. They all just stared at me. I shifted, completely and utterly uncomfortable.

This was a bad idea.

I considered ending things there, packing up my guitar and hightailing it out of the place, but then something amazing happened.

A single clap sounded, then more followed. Within moments, cheers and applause filled the bar, even louder than I thought possible due to such a small crowd. One by one the patrons stood, smiles stretching their cheeks. That was the moment I realized their lack of expressions hadn't been what I'd originally thought. They never hated my song. They were struck with awe. Stunned into silence. One lady even dabbed at the corner of her eye with a napkin, her eyes glassy with tears. I did it. I had touched them with something I'd written, and the pride that I felt in that moment was indescribable.

The rest of the performance went along better than I could have ever hoped for. A couple more people came in and were immediately drawn to me. Everyone sang along to the cover songs I played, and they even enjoyed the other songs I had written. I played until my throat was dry and my fingers were sore. By the time I finished, though, I barely noticed. I hadn't felt this happy in ... well, a *really* long time.

"Wow! That was incredible." Celia came at me from the side and squeezed me into a hug, which I angled myself to return. "You have some set of pipes on you. Where'd you learn to sing like that?"

"Singing's always come natural to me, ever since I was a little girl." I shrugged. "Same with playing guitar. One day I picked one up at a booth at the town fair and the rest is history. I'd never held one before, and had no idea what I'd been doing, but somehow I managed to make something beautiful come from it. My momma always told me I was a natural, that it ran through my blood."

"Well, I'd have to agree with your momma," Nolan chimed in. I hadn't seen him walk up. "You have a talent unlike anything I've seen before."

"Thank you." My cheeks heated at the unexpected compliment. "That means so much to me."

He nodded and rubbed his chin, something I noticed he did when thinking. At least in the few hours I'd known him anyways. I wished I could read him, know what was going on inside his head. I could see the wheels turning, but I had no way of knowing why they were.

Leaning down, he whispered something into his mother's ear and she nodded enthusiastically.

"That's a great idea, Nolan," his mother said. "I'd be willing to bet those here tonight would gladly come back tomorrow, and would likely bring friends, too. Along with the usual Friday night crowd, I imagine we would have our hands full."

"Yes, I'd say we would," Nolan agreed. "And if you need help, I'd be more than happy to jump behind the bar and lend a hand."

What on earth were these two going on about?

"Won't you be busy with …"

"We have a few days to relax." He cut her off mid-sentence. "Besides, I'm sure they'd be happy to have a couple hour's break from me being up their asses."

"Okay," she replied. "Then that would be wonderful. You know I miss having you to help around here."

"Then it's set." Nolan seemed excited, but I couldn't help but think there was more to it than spending time helping his mother out. "We should let everyone here know about tomorrow before they leave and ask them to spread the word." He turned to leave but Celia put her hand on his arm, halting him in his tracks.

"You're jumping ahead of yourself, son. Don't you think you should ask Everly here before anything else? I mean, for all we know she may have another gig, or plans of her own."

"Oh." Nolan turned back and looked at me, a sheepish grin shining from his face. "I'm so sorry, Everly. I got lost in the excitement."

"It's quite alright," I said. "Ask me what?"

"Well, Mom and I were hoping, if you didn't have prior commitments, that you would come back tomorrow night and play another set? I know it's short notice. Actually, it's not much notice at all, but we would love to have you back. And this time we will have the proper setup for you."

What? They want me to come play again? Tomorrow? I could barely believe the words that came from his mouth. I looked to Celia for confirmation this wasn't a joke, and the smile on her face as she nodded confirmed what he'd just asked. *They want me to play again!*

"We'd be happy to compensate you for your time as well," he continued. "It wouldn't be much, but I'd like to offer you one-hundred dollars, and of course drinks on the house."

"I'd love to!" I blurted out before he finished, afraid if I waited I'd wake up from what had to be a dream.

I'd never been offered money to play. Truth be told, I'd been more than happy playing the small gigs I'd managed to get. Every bar that had allowed me to perform at no cost to them had been experience for me. But I'd have been lying if I said I wasn't relieved to be offered some money. The little bit I'd had in reserve was almost gone, and I'd been sleeping in my car the last couple nights as to not incur any unnecessary expenses. Luckily, the temperatures at night had been lovely, and the owner of the bar I'd played at last night lived in a small studio apartment above the place and allowed me to shower there. She'd been such a sweet lady.

"Everly?" Nolan's voice cut through my thoughts and pulled me back to the present. "Does that sound okay to you?"

"I'm sorry," I said, embarrassed to have wandered off in my own mind. "What did you say?"

"I asked if you could get here at seven tomorrow night. That would allow time to set up and make sure everything is working properly for you. I figure you could start your set at eight. If that works for you?"

"Seven. Right. Yes, I can be here by then." It's not like I had anything else going on, so I'd be there whatever time they told me to be. Heck, if they'd told me to jump through fire at that moment, I'd do it. I was so incredibly thankful for their offer.

"This is going to be the best Friday night we've had to date!" Celia stated, excitement obvious in her tone. "On that note"—She signaled to the bar where a few patrons stood waiting—"I'd better get back to it. The bar won't serve itself."

With a final hug, she left, nearly skipping her way over to the waiting customers. I liked the woman a lot. She reminded me of my momma before she got sick. They both had the same bubbly personality, and a smile that could light up any room.

Nolan and I talked for a little longer and exchanged numbers in case one of us needed to reach the other about tomorrow night. Before long, the adrenaline from my performance wore off, and my eyes got heavy. I said my goodbyes and headed to my car.

I slid my guitar into the trunk, laid across the backseat of my car, and smiled as I replayed the night in my head. Before long, I drifted off into a peaceful slumber.

Chapter Four

"Everyone, can I have your attention please?" Celia spoke into the microphone, drawing everyone's attention to her. "We have a *very* special treat for y'all tonight. As luck had it, last night an extremely talented young lady walked into this here bar and graced us with a performance that brought chills to everyone."

A couple whistles sounded. As I glanced at the crowd, I smiled when I recognized some of the same faces from last night. It was crazy that these people enjoyed my performance so much that they'd returned to watch it again, but it tickled me pink, too.

"Her voice is unlike anything I've heard before, and she was kind enough to return for an encore tonight." Celia beamed at me, her eyes twinkling in the bright light that shone onto her. "So please join me in giving a warm welcome to Ms. Everly Rae!"

The crowd erupted in applause as I made my way into the makeshift spotlight where Celia stood. She reached out and pulled me into a hug before she whispered, "Knock 'em dead." She spoke into my ear, then made her way to the bar.

I took my knee-length floral dress into my free hand and gave a little curtsy to the crowd, which was considerably larger than last night. Seating myself on the stool, I propped one foot on the rung and rested my guitar on my knee, adjusting the microphone stand so it would be in a good position for me.

"Hi ya'll, I'm Everly Rae. It's an honor to be here again tonight." With a gulp, I tried to calm the nervous energy shooting through me. I'd never performed in front of this many people before. All their eyes were on me, and it hit me hard. Anxiety made me a bit jittery, but excitement grounded me enough that I could push through.

"I'm just going to jump right in with a song I'm sure many of you've heard before. I'm gonna do it a little different, but if you know the words, feel free to sing along."

I strummed my guitar and the notes echoed through the small amplifier they'd set up for me tonight, making the sound feel like it was flowing right through me. I'd considered starting with Dolly Parton's Jolene again after the reaction it received last night, but in the end I decided to begin with something different: my own rendition of Johnny Cash's "Ring of Fire." I knew it was different from the way people knew it, but I hoped they would love it all the same.

As I played, I was not disappointed by the crowd. They sang along to the songs I covered and their enthusiasm filled the room. When I played one of my own songs I'd written, they listened intently and cheered just as much at the end. The whole thing felt surreal, like I was living in a dream and could wake up any minute.

"Alrighty, I've got one more for ya'll. It's a song I wrote for my momma after she passed away. I'd always kept it to myself, but those who were here last night heard me play it for the first time in front of anyone. Tonight, I'd like to play it for all of you. Hope ya'll like it."

I'd always planned to keep this song private, something I sang when I was alone and missing my momma. It felt too intimate to share. Too raw. But last night something called to me—something I couldn't ignore—and I knew I *needed* to put it out there. Maybe it had been a sign sent from Momma from above, or maybe it came from deep within me. Either way, I had put it out there and it felt so … right. Therapeutic maybe? I wasn't quite sure how to describe it.

As I played my gaze drifted over the crowd, allowing them to see my expression, to see the pain I felt when I wrote that song. I hadn't wanted them to just hear the words, I wanted them to *feel* them. To be touched by them. And from the looks on their faces, there wasn't a single person left unmoved.

My eyes landed on one particular booth closest to where I sat, filled by a group of guys around my age who were speaking in hushed whispers. All except one. With a baseball cap pulled low, his eyes were fixated on me. He was oblivious to the others' conversation, and as he stared—even though it was hard to tell with the dim lighting and the shadow from his cap—I felt like he was reaching deep inside my soul. A shiver swept through me while my heart picked up speed. Why was he staring at me like that? Sure, everyone in the room had their eyes on me, too, but his stare was different because I could feel it. I just didn't know if that was a good thing or a bad thing.

Not knowing what else to do, I closed my eyes and concentrated on the end of my song. I focused on the feelings inside and belted out the chorus one last time before slowing the tempo and delivering the final line so soft it was nearly a whisper.

The room erupted in applause and, just like the night before, I received a standing ovation. No words could describe the way I felt in that moment. It was nothing short of magical.

I looked to the booth again, curious to see what the mystery guy's reaction would be, but he was no longer there. Disappointment rattled me as I took in the empty seat, but I shook it off. I didn't have time to dwell on it. What did one stranger's opinion matter anyways, especially when there was a bar full of people cheering for me?

Within moments people flocked around me, offering compliments and gushing about how much they loved my songs. The booth guy faded to a distant memory.

Chapter Five

The area around the bar was packed with people waiting to order their drinks. Celia and Nolan bustled, their impressive speed serving the crowd as fast as they could manage. If I knew more about bartending I'd hop behind the counter and help them because they could use another set of hands. Still, they moved effortlessly together, like they were locked in a fast-paced dance they'd done their entire lives side by side. If they were overwhelmed, they sure didn't show it.

With my throat dry from singing, I desperately wanted a drink, though it looked like I'd have to wait a bit until the crowd simmered down. Right now, I couldn't even get close to the counter. Next time I'd have to bring a bottle of water, or even a glass of sweet tea when I had a gig.

"Everly!" Nolan spotted me and gave a wave, signaling me to move forward.

I shook my head, not wanting to intrude on those around me. He either didn't see it or chose to completely ignore me.

"C'mon guys, make some room. Let her through." He motioned for the people to move aside.

A few grumbles rang out, but once the people saw it was me cutting through them, they inched away and made a path for me to squeeze through.

"Great job tonight, Everly," Nolan said. "Can I get you something to drink?"

His hands kept filling drink orders and serving them, almost like they had a mind of their own.

"A sweet tea would be wonderful when you have a chance. No rush though, take care of the others first."

"Nonsense," he replied. "Mom," he called to Celia who was working the other side of the bar. "Can you grab a sweet tea for Everly, please?"

"Of course! Coming right up." Celia grabbed a glass, filled it with ice, and poured the brown liquid in. "Heads up."

She pushed the glass and it slid across the counter, somehow not spilling more than a couple drops over the rim. Nolan stopped it with his hand and grabbed a straw, sliding it into the glass.

"Here ya go." He handed me the drink.

"Thanks so much." I opened my wallet, took out a five-dollar bill, and extended it to him.

"It's on the house, remember?" He smiled sweetly and shooed my money away.

I knew it was what he said when they asked me to play tonight, but I didn't feel right not paying. Somehow, I knew arguing with him would be pointless so I settled on leaving it on the counter as a tip.

The cold liquid soothed my throat as I sipped it, and my taste buds exploded in my mouth. It was by far the most delicious sweet tea I'd ever sampled, and I greedily drank down the entire glass in a matter of seconds.

"Your voice is absolutely incredible." Warm breath fanned over my ear, the voice so low I knew only I had been able to hear it.

I startled at the closeness even though the area was packed and everyone was pressed against each other. Still, I hadn't expected to feel someone's breath in my ear, nor had I expected the way my body would react to it.

I turned to face the guy, needing to know who it was that made my heart flip flop with a single sentence. A gasp escaped my lips as I realized it was the guy from the booth, the same one that pierced through me with his stare even though I could hardly see his eyes.

His hat was still pulled low, and the shadows prevented me from seeing his whole face, but his gaze was just as intense inches from my face as it had been from across the room.

"I'm sorry?" I questioned, unable to formulate a coherent thought when he was this close to me.

"I said"—His breath was sweet and had a hint of bourbon on it—"you have an incredible voice."

His voice was smooth like velvet, and my insides involuntarily clenched at the sound. I knew I should have said something, but I was rendered speechless at that moment. The corner of his mouth arched upwards in a half smile, as if he knew the affect he was having on me.

"You're insanely beautiful as well."

My breath hitched as he lifted a hand and tucked a curl behind my ear that had fallen loose from my messy bun. His skin barely made contact with mine, yet it left a burning trail in its wake.

I needed to see his face, needed to see who it was that caused my body to react in such a way. Before my mind had a chance to catch up and stop me, I lifted my hand and slowly raised the brim of his baseball cap.

He flinched at first and his hand shot up, halting mine. But then with a deep breath, he allowed me to continue. The shadows lifted inch by inch and revealed each of his features one at a time: his perfectly pink lips, chiseled cheeks that were covered with stubble, and finally after what felt like forever, his eyes. One was a deep blue, and the other a dark green with brown speckles. As I stared into them, it was like I was being swallowed by an endless black hole. I could get lost in them so easy, but I didn't know if I could ever manage to swim back to the surface if I let that happen. Or if I even wanted to.

He was handsome, *so* very handsome, and unlike any man I'd seen before. So why was he standing in front of me like I was the only person in the entire room?

I rose on my tiptoes, continuing to raise the brim. He was much taller than my five-foot-five self. Our faces got closer and his tongue darted out and swiped across his lips, wetting them. Mine parted slightly as he brought his head down, our mouths so close we were breathing one another's breath. He was intoxicating. Had I moved my face forward just a tiny bit our lips would have met. He was a stranger. I shouldn't be thinking like that. The idea excited me nonetheless.

Before I could make a fool of myself, I lifted the cap the rest of the way until his messy brown hair was freed from under it. Bringing it down, I held it in my hands, afraid if I made any sudden movements he would grab it and put it back on to hide his face again.

His eyes regarded me as if he was waiting for me to react. Once he saw I wasn't going to, he released a breath I hadn't realized he'd been holding, a relieved look on his face. Why would he be relieved, though?

"So," he said, breaking the trance, "what's your name?"

"My name?" I was confused as I had announced it before I began my set.

"Yes." He chuckled. "You know, the word that people use to get your attention?"

My face reddened at how stupid I must have looked. "Everly ... Everly Rae," I squeaked, finally breaking eye contact for the first time. I wanted nothing more than to run off and hide under a rock.

"Relax." He laughed again. "I was just joking with ya." He took his hat from me and placed it on his head, only this time he wore it backwards so his face wasn't hidden. "Well, Everly, it's nice to have a name to go with that beautiful face of yours. I got here a bit late, so missed the beginning of your set." He looked to me apologetically.

"Oh," I replied, feeling much less embarrassed. "Now it makes sense." No wonder he hadn't known my name. "And you are?"

His body tensed and his eyebrows furrowed as he examined my face closely. "You don't know?"

"Of course not. We only just met, and you've yet to tell me."

He smiled then, and it was enough to light up the entire room. A dimple formed on his right cheek, giving him a boyish look that didn't quite match his masculine face.

"I'm Camden."

"Well, Camden, it's nice to meet you." I held my hand out and he took it in his.

I had meant to shake his hand, but instead he brought my hand to his lips and kissed it. His lips lingered for a moment and his breath ran over my skin causing goosebumps to raise down my back. What was it about this guy that caused my body to go haywire?

"You're not from around here." Camden stated matter-of-factly, and I wasn't sure how he could be so certain of it.

"How do you know?" I asked, hoping to find out.

"I've never seen you around Willow Peak before." He shrugged as if it had been the most obvious thing in the world. "And believe me, I'd have noticed you."

My cheeks flamed again. I wasn't used to all the compliments, either, so I had no idea how to respond.

"Oh, um. No. I'm from Pinkerton, Alabama. This is my first time here."

"You're quite a ways from home. What brings you out here to bumblefuck South Carolina?" He signaled to Nolan, likely wanting to order a drink.

"I don't know, really," I responded. "I've been travelling and when I passed through here, I figured I'd stop and see if I'd be able to play anywhere. I got real lucky when they allowed me to play here."

Camden opened his mouth as if to say something, but Nolan's voice rang out, cutting him off.

"Hey, Camden. Glad you decided to show." Nolan reached over the counter and bumped fists with him.

"Yea, well, there's not much to do around here so figured I might as well."

"Aw, way to make a friend feel loved," Nolan joked, pretending to punch him on the shoulder. "I see you've met Everly." His eyes shone with excitement.

Did I really make that much of an impression with my performance?

"I did." Camden nodded.

"Good. Saves me the introductions when things die down. So, you enjoy the show?"

"Absolutely. I was just telling Everly here how amazing her voice is."

"I told ya, man." Nolan beamed as if I was some long-lost treasure he'd found. Which really didn't make any sense to me. "She's really got something special. Anyways"—He paused as he signaled to a customer to give him a second—"we'll talk more later. What can I get ya?"

"I'll take a bourbon, on the rocks. And don't be giving me none of that cheap shit, either." Camden looked to me. "What about you?"

"Oh, I'm okay. I don't really drink but thank you." I gave him a wide grin to show I was flattered by the offer.

"C'mon, Everly. It's rude to turn down a gentleman when he offers to buy you a drink." His dimple made an appearance again, and I knew I wouldn't be able to say no to him.

"Okay … just one." There was nothing wrong with having a drink to celebrate the night.

"Now you're talking. We'll take two."

Nolan rolled his eyes, but I noticed him chuckle to himself as he turned to make the drinks.

"So, how do you know Nolan?" I turned to face Camden.

"We've been ... uh, friends ... for quite some time."

I remained quiet, waiting for him to continue. When he didn't, I knew there was more to it, but I didn't want to pry. Since I didn't really know either of them, it wasn't my business.

Nolan returned with our drinks, breaking the awkward silence that had fallen between us. I was thankful for that.

"Here ya go, guys." He slid the glasses on the counter to us. "I'll add it to your tab?"

"Thanks, man." Camden picked up his glass, saluted Nolan, and took a long swig of the brown liquid.

I followed suit, bringing the other glass to my lips. The fervent scent invaded my nostrils, and I nearly gagged at the smell. Not wanting to look like a wuss, I held my breath and took a sip.

The liquid burned as it made its way down my throat, but at the same time it tasted much better than it smelled. Hints of vanilla and caramel swirled around my mouth and I was surprised to find that I sort of enjoyed the taste despite how strong it was. I took another sip, then another. Before I knew it, I emptied half the glass.

"Easy there, killer," Camden said. "This here packs quite a punch. Especially if you aren't used to drinking."

"Don't be ridiculous." I smiled to him. "It's only one drink. It's not like I'll get drunk from it or anything."

"Don't say I didn't warn you." He shook his head and chuckled as I drank the rest of the glass.

Chapter Six

A couple hours and a few drinks later and I was feeling odd. My body tingled and felt hot, but I'd been having the time of my life talking and joking with Camden. He was good company, funny, and the fact that he was hotter than a summer day in Alabama certainly didn't hurt.

So, this was what being drunk felt like. At least I thought I might be drunk. A little. I had nothing to compare it to since I'd never had a single drink before. The thought made me giggle, but I didn't know what was so funny.

"I need to use the restroom," I said to Camden. "I'll be right back." I turned and stumbled a little as I tried to take a step forward.

"Woah, easy there. You okay?" he asked, catching my elbow and steadying me. "Want me to walk you?"

"I'm fine." I straightened my shoulders as if that would prove my point. "I'll only be a minute."

As I made my way to the ladies' room across the bar, I managed to stay upright despite the slight spinning of everything around me. A couple people stopped me on the way, complimenting me on my performance again and telling me they hoped I'd be playing here again soon. I thanked them and promised I'd be back again some time. And I meant it, provided Celia would have me.

After I did my business I washed my hands in the sink. My cheeks were flushed with heat when I looked in the mirror, and I hardly recognized the girl that stared back at me. There was something about her, something wild and careless—so unlike the girl that had left her hometown and life only a couple short months ago to follow her dreams. I didn't know what to make of her. It was frightening and exhilarating, but I decided not to give it much thought.

Splashing cold water on my face, it refreshed me and cooled my overheated cheeks. I dried off with a paper towel and nodded my approval in the mirror before I spun around, opening the door and running smack-dab into a hard chest. I stumbled back a step or two and a set of strong, muscular arms wrapped around me, pulling my body close. I should have been freaked out by the gesture, by a stranger's arms wrapped around me, but I knew before I even looked up that it was no stranger. Well, not exactly anyways. The immediate electricity that sparked between our bodies was a dead giveaway.

"What are you doing here?" I asked, looking into a set of mesmerizing eyes.

"I wanted to make sure you were alright," was all Camden said.

I didn't quite understand why he'd said that. I'd only went to the washroom, and I couldn't have been gone more than a couple minutes.

"You've been gone for nearly twenty minutes," he said, answering my unspoken question.

Twenty minutes? Had it been that long? I wondered to myself, but then I remembered being stopped by a few people on the way. I guessed more time had passed than I'd realized.

"Aww, did you miss me?" I smiled at him with hooded eyes, and I swear his darkened a few shades as he brought his face close to mine.

"Maybe," he replied, his voice soft and deep.

My insides did a little somersault at hearing that word come from his mouth. What the hell was going on with me? That wasn't like me, to have such an intense reaction to another person—especially a man. But I wasn't about to question it, nor was I about to stop what happened next.

My mind shut off, which was a good thing since I tended to overthink everything. The little hallway we stood in was dark, only a single lightbulb above us casting a dim light to the area. We were alone, I was a bit intoxicated, and my body moved on its own accord.

My arms wrapped around his body, snaking their way up his back and pulling him even closer. Heat radiated from him, and my body soaked it all up.

"What ..." His breath hitched and he cleared his throat as I rose on my tiptoes and placed a feather-light kiss behind his left ear. "What are you doing?"

He nuzzled his face into my neck, his breath quickening and caressing my skin.

"I don't know," I whispered. And I didn't.

One of my hands trailed the back of his neck to his head, pushing his hat up and off as my fingers tangled in his hair.

His tongue flicked out, licking a tender spot on my neck and I couldn't stop the little moan that escaped me. My body shuttered at the foreign contact. He trailed kisses down my neck, his lips barely brushing my skin as he guided me back until I bumped into the wall. He kept his touch light, his kisses gentle, but my body wanted more. Craved more.

My other hand, which was still wrapped around his body, inched its way up the back of his shirt. My fingers glided over his smooth skin just above the waist of his jeans, and within seconds, goosebumps rose under my fingertips. His body shuddered and he pulled his head back just enough so I could see his face. I whined at the loss of contact.

"What is it you want?" he whispered. "Tell me." His lips tickled as they barely grazed mine.

The smell of the bourbon we'd been drinking invaded my nostrils, and mixed with the sweet scent of him, it intoxicated me. Made me delirious. His eyes boring into mine, he panted and I lost the remaining bit of my senses.

The world around us ceased to exist as I closed the last bit of space between us and crashed my lips to his. His hand flew to my cheek, holding me to him as if he was afraid I'd pull away. That wouldn't happen, though. I was too lost in him. Too frenzied with need.

His lips parted and our tongues met, swirling together in perfect unison. It was the kind of kiss you only saw in the movies, yet here I was, living it. It may have been my first *real* kiss, but my body knew exactly what to do.

"Yo, Cam." A voice rang out, breaking the spell we were under. "I've been looking everywhere for you. The guys are about to head out and wanted to see if you need a ride back to the hotel?"

Camden pulled away, his hands dropping to his side as he turned to face Nolan. I instantly missed his closeness, and I whimpered at the sudden loss of heat.

"Shit man, I'm sorry. I didn't know you were ... Everly?" Nolan looked shocked as he took in the sight before him.

My hand going to my hair, I tried to tame the unruly mess I knew it must be. Embarrassment flooded me as I realized what I'd been doing: making out with someone who was practically a stranger. In the middle of some public place. Where anyone could have seen.

"Hey," I said and quickly averted my eyes to avoid Nolan's intense scrutiny.

I didn't know why Nolan seeing Camden and me kissing bothered me so much, but it did. He was just as much a stranger to me as Cam was, but the tone he'd said my name in made me feel like I'd let him down. I knew how silly that was, but I couldn't change it.

"Yea, a ride would be cool." Camden bent down and picked up his hat before tucking his hair back and placing it on his head. "Just gimme a minute, okay?"

"Um." Nolan looked to him, then to me, and back to him again. "Sure, I'll let them know. I have to finish up a few things here and I'll meet you guys there in a bit."

"Alright, thanks man."

Nolan turned and left the same way he'd come in and Camden turned his attention to me. He took a step closer and reached up, cupping my cheek in his hand. His head bowed and his lips ascended towards mine. As much as I wanted to kiss him again, the embarrassment over what just happened won over. I was surprised at myself, unsure what to make of it all, and I needed to clear my head—something I knew wouldn't happen with him near.

I breathed him in one last time before pulling away and putting space between us.

"I, um ..." I trailed off, struggling to find the right words. My body begged me to stay, while my mind knew what I needed to do. "I better get going."

I turned and left, not stopping to look back. If I had, I wouldn't have been able to walk away again, and I didn't stop until I made it out the exit.

The cool air outside hit me and I reveled in it, letting it wrap around me and cool my hot skin. The more distance I put between Camden and me, the less cloudy my head felt. Sure, I was still a bit drunk, but at least I was thinking more rationally. *What the hell was I doing before?* I wondered to myself. That hadn't been me back there. I'd never done something like that in my entire life. A little voice nagged at me from the back of my mind telling me it *had been* me, and I'd gladly do it again when it came to Camden.

I pushed the voice back, not ready to deal with that thought just yet. After I slept off my alcohol-induced stupor, I'd deal with what I'd done. My keys jingled as I pulled them from my pocket. They slipped from my hand and tumbled to the ground.

"Son of a biscuit!" I mumbled to myself as I crouched, my hands roaming the gravel.

The door to the bar opened and a bunch of voices talked and laughed, but one came louder than the others.

Camden.

Great, that was *not* what I needed after I just ran out of there without so much as a goodbye. My fingers fumbled for another moment before landing on my keys. *Yes!* I brought them up and made quick time of putting them in the keyhole and unlocking the door to my car. I cracked it open and slid inside, closing it as quietly as I could so I didn't bring any attention to myself. Good thing I'd brought my guitar out earlier in the night. I ducked down and reclined the seat back so that I'd be hidden from view.

Before long, car doors slammed, the voices stopped, and I heard tires on gravel as a vehicle made its way out of the parking lot and on to the road. I peeked out the window just in time to see red taillights disappear.

Plopping back down, I sighed in relief at not having to face him, but then my heart clenched at the realization that I may never see him again. And that thought hurt. I thought about climbing into the backseat to stretch out, but before I could muster the energy my eyes grew heavy and sleep dragged me down.

Chapter Seven

A sudden sound jolted me awake and my heart pounded in my chest. *What the heck was that?* I blinked my eyes a few times to clear the sleep from them.

Rap. Rap. It sounded again and my eyes darted to the window. I nearly jumped out of my skin when I saw a dark figure standing outside it.

"Easy, Everly. It's just me. Nolan." His muffled voice came through the car as I sighed in relief.

"Nolan? What the heck are you doing? You scared the daylights out of me." I popped my seat up and rolled down the window.

"I was about to ask you the same thing. What're you doing sleeping in your car? It's freezing out here."

I shivered as a gust of wind blew inside and pulled my jacket tighter around me. He was right; the temperature had dropped.

"I, um ..." Glancing around as I tried to come up with an explanation, everything spun a bit, reminding me I'd been drinking. "I had a bit too much to drink, so figured I should sleep it off."

"In your car? Why not call a taxi or ask me to drive you?"

I shrugged in response. "What time is it?"

"Half past eleven." He blew a puff of warm air onto his palms and rubbed them together.

It surprised me how little time had passed. I'd only been asleep about half an hour.

"C'mon," Nolan said, opening the door. "Let me drive you to wherever you're staying."

"It's okay, really. I'm fine." I didn't want to have to tell him I'd been sleeping in my car more than just that night.

"Well, you can't stay in your car all night. It's way too cold for that. Don't want you catching a cold or anything. It'd be a shame if you couldn't use that pretty voice of yours for awhile."

"Well." I took a breath, knowing I'd have to tell him I didn't have anywhere to go. "I don't exactly have a place I'm staying."

"In that case"—He held his hand out, not even questioning me—"c'mon. You can come back to the hotel we're all staying at."

Gaping at him, I knew that wouldn't be a good idea. No way could I go stay in a hotel room with a stranger.

"I'll get ya your own room, don't worry. It's the least I can do. And come morning, I'll bring you back to get your car."

I contemplated his offer for a moment, figuring if I had my own room then it was perfectly fine. Besides, the thought of a hot shower and a comfy bed to sleep in sounded delightful, and I'd have been lying to myself if I said the possibility of seeing Camden again didn't make excitement rush through me.

"Okay." My mind made up, I nodded and opened the door, placing my hand in his. "Thank you.

Nolan helped me from the car and I popped my trunk, grabbing my guitar. I knew I didn't need it, but since I'd left home I hadn't gone anywhere without it. It'd become my security blanket, so to speak.

Hopping in his car, I stayed quiet as he took off, not knowing what to say. The drive took about fifteen minutes since it was just past the border and into the next town. I was thankful Nolan had turned up the music when we'd gotten in his car and hadn't tried to make much conversation. He hadn't brought up my lack of sleeping arrangements, hadn't asked me to explain my situation. Instead, he allowed the comfortable silence to stretch around us as the music played.

    We pulled under the overhang outside the hotel's front door and made our way into the main lobby. Once inside, I stopped dead in my tracks. The place was beautiful, the lobby open with a winding staircase on each side leading up about two stories and meeting in the middle. The stairs were covered by a deep-blue runner with intricate gold designs around the edges. The walls were perfectly white, and the main floor a white marble with gold flakes scattered throughout. In the middle of the room between the two staircases sat a shiny black grand piano with couches and chairs surrounding it. Two enormous columns stretched from floor to ceiling and hanging between them was a gorgeous glass chandelier that must have been ten times the size of me.

    "This way," Nolan said as he placed the palm of his hand on my back. "Let's get you checked in, shall we?"

    "Nolan," I whispered. "I can't afford to stay at a place like this."

    He tried to nudge me along, but I kept my feet planted on the floor.

    "You don't have to worry about that. When I told you I'd get you a room, I wasn't expecting you to pay."

    "I can't let you do that." My eyes roamed the room, taking it all in. I'd never, not once in my life, seen anything like it. And it was likely I never would again. "It's too much. It's *way* too much."

    "You don't need to worry yourself about that. Now, are you gonna come with me or am I gonna have to pick you up and carry you over my shoulder to the desk so we can get you your room?"

    I squared my shoulders, ready to argue with him since I figured he wouldn't hold true to his threat. When I opened my mouth to protest, he proved me wrong by reaching forward and grabbing me by the waist. My feet lifted from the ground and I squealed as he stepped forward. His grip on me faltered, and I nearly dropped from his arms.

    "Okay, okay! You win. I'll walk, just put me down."

"Well, that was easier than I expected." He did as I asked and set me down, a smug smile spreading across his face as he picked up my guitar case and made his way to the counter.

I had no other choice but to follow, especially since he now held my guitar as ransom.

"Okay, here you are," Nolan said as he came to a stop in front of a door marked 306.

He handed me the key card and waited as I unlocked the door, swung it open, and flipped the switch to my left. A warm white light spread through the room and I couldn't believe my eyes. The room was *huge*. It mirrored the decor from the lobby: perfect white walls, the same marbled floors with gold flakes, and the king-sized bed had a navy-blue comforter with gold trim.

Opposite the bed was a large jacuzzi tub that could easily fit four people. I let my fingers glide over the edge as I walked past. I'd never been in a jacuzzi. Heck, I'd never even seen one in person before. But someone once said "there's always a first for everything," right?

"I hope this is okay. This was the only room they had left near ours. I'm sorry it's so small." He placed my guitar case on the floor and looked around, shaking his head in disapproval.

My eyes widened to bulging. "*Small?*" Was he looking at the same room I was?

"Yeah, it's much smaller compared to the others. They didn't have any suites left or else I'd have gotten you one." He frowned apologetically.

"You're crazy if you think this is small. I mean, you could probably fit my entire home in this space. It's amazing, really." I may have been exaggerating slightly, but it wasn't far off.

"Well, as long as you like it that's all that matters." Nolan shrugged and flashed me a smile. "Alright, well, I'm two doors down in 310. If you need anything, just knock." He turned and made his way to the door. His phone sounded with a text and he stopped to read it. "If you're hungry, the guys just ordered food. They always order more than they can eat, and we'll be up hanging for awhile if you want to join us."

"Thanks, but I'm pretty tired. I think I'll just take a bath and head to bed if that's alright." I yawned then as if to prove my point.

"Okay. If you change your mind, everyone's in room 307. It's right across the hall."

The door closed behind him and I immediately turned on the tub to let it fill with hot water. As I waited, I stripped out of my dress and draped it over the back of the chair. I grabbed a pair of black leggings and an oversized tee from the small bag of clothes I brought and set them on the bed. It was my go-to outfit for lounging or sleeping.

After a few minutes the tub filled and I slipped into the water. The heat cocooned me and I sighed. With a push of a button the jets turned on and I leaned back, allowing them to massage my tired back. It was heavenly, and just what I needed.

Twenty minutes passed and the water began to cool, signaling it was time for me to get out. I stood reluctantly, pulling the stopper to drain the water and stepping out. When I wrapped one of the navy and gold towels around my body, its softness enveloped my skin. Once dried, I dressed in the clothes I'd laid out and climbed into bed, pulling the comforter over me.

I'd opted to skip washing my hair because I hated trying to sleep if it was wet. Since I hadn't brought my blow dryer with me, I'd just wash it in the morning; it'd give me an excuse to soak in the jacuzzi again before I had to leave. That thought alone was enough to make me smile. *One could get used to this,* I thought.

Finally laying down, I closed my eyes but opened them again after a few minutes. If I'd thought sleep would come easy, I had never been more wrong in my life. I laid there staring at the ceiling, willing my eyes to close but they wouldn't. Muffled laughter flowed through the door and I couldn't help but wonder what everyone was up to, who everyone was for that matter. Was Camden with them, sipping a glass of bourbon? Was he thinking of me? Did he even know I was here?

My mind was going a mile a minute, asking too many questions now that the initial excitement of being here had worn off. How could Nolan afford to stay at a place like this? How could any of them?

"Ugh!" I groaned, throwing the comforter from me. I knew there was no way I'd be able to fall asleep no matter how tired I'd been.

Curiosity took over, along with the desire to hopefully see Camden again. I stood from the bed, slipped on my slippers, and made my way out of my room and across the hall. Raising my hand, I rapped on the door before I could change my mind, tuck tail, and run back to my room.

The door swung open and Nolan greeted me with a huge smile, beer in hand.

"Everly! I was hoping you'd change your mind," he said and gestured for me to enter.

I stepped in and Nolan closed the door behind me.

"Guys, I'd like you all to meet someone."

Everyone quieted as soon as Nolan spoke, and I couldn't help but squirm when all eyes focused in on me. What was I doing here, in a hotel room with a handful of men I didn't know? My momma would be rolling in her grave if she knew what I was doing.

"This here is Everly. Everly Rae. She's the one with the beautiful voice you all heard tonight at The Weeping Willow." He paused and looked to me. "Everly, these are the guys." He pointed to each with his beer bottle as he said their names. I gave a little wave to them. "Landon. Harry. Caleb. And I believe you already met Cam."

My heart fluttered in my chest as my eyes met his. He'd been so handsome when I first saw him at The Weeping Willow, and even more so now in the bright lights. He gave a wink and my cheeks heated at the memory of him and me from earlier that night.

"Come on in and make yourself at home." Nolan signaled to the living area the guys were sitting in. "Can I get ya a drink?"

"Sure, that would be great." I needed something to calm my nerves. Taking a seat, I made sure to pick one on the couch that had nobody else in it.

"Wicked performance tonight," Caleb said, drawing my attention to him. "You've got real talent." The others nodded in agreement.

"Thank you." I beamed at him, flattered by the compliment and happy the guys enjoyed the show. "It was so much fun. I was really lucky when I ran into Nolan and he introduced me to his mom. And she was amazing for letting me play at The Willow since I'd walked in off the street with no warning."

"Celia's an amazing woman, so it doesn't surprise me she let you play. She's the type of person that'd give you the coat off her back if she saw you needed it. She's like a mother to all of us."

It warmed my heart to hear Caleb talk so fondly of the woman. I'd only just met her the day before last, but I really liked her. You could tell she was a kind soul.

Nolan returned and handed me a beer. He grabbed one of the chairs, turned it backwards and sat on it, hanging his arms over the back. I sniffed the bottle and scrunched my nose. It smelt awful, but I didn't want to be rude so I brought it to my lips and took a sip anyways. It tasted just as bad as it smelled.

Sensing my disgust, Camden stood and walked to me, taking the beer from my hand.

"Here," he said, offering the glass of brown liquid he'd been drinking from. "I believe this is more your taste."

"Thanks." I took a sip and smiled when I realized it was the same bourbon we'd been drinking earlier. Much better.

Camden took a seat on the couch next to me and propped his foot on his knee, taking a swig from the bottle he'd just taken from me.

"How can you drink that?" I asked him, wondering why someone would willingly drink something that tasted so ... well, gross.

"It's not so bad." He shrugged.

"If you say so."

An hour or so later my sides were hurting from laughing so hard. The guys really were great to be around and I hadn't had so much fun in as long as I could remember. Not one of them made me feel uncomfortable in the slightest. On the contrary, they put me at complete ease.

"Hey, if you don't mind me asking," Harry said, "why are you playing in a small bar like The Weeping Willow? I mean, don't get me wrong, it's a great place to hang and grab drinks, and you know how much we love Celia. But man, you should be doing so much more with the talent you have."

Camden's body tensed beside me, but I opted to ignore it, shaking off the odd feeling it gave me.

"Long story short, I've never had the opportunity to pursue singing, or anything else, before now. Growing up, I had to put most things on hold so I could focus on taking care of my momma when she got sick."

"I'm so sorry," Harry said.

"Don't be." I gave him a reassuring smile. "I did what I had to do, and I wouldn't change it for anything. But now? Now I'm just trying to figure out where I belong in this world."

"Well, if you ask me, you belong on the big stage where the world can hear you. People *need* to hear you."

"I couldn't agree more," Nolan chimed in. "Which is why I wanted to talk to you guys about something."

"What's up?" Caleb asked, curiosity lacing his voice.

"As you guys know, we're set to hit the road in a couple days to finish the second half of the tour."

Tour? Huh? What was he talking about, and why did I suddenly feel like I was intruding on a private conversation?

"Unfortunately," Nolan continued, "I got word that Nalia is going to need vocal chord surgery and won't be able to join us as planned."

"Ah, hell," Landon exclaimed. "What are we supposed to do now? It's too late to find a replacement opening act."

The guys looked to one another for an answer and mumbled under their breath about how "screwed" they were. I just sat there in silence taking it all in. So, the guys were in a band? And a touring one at that. *Wow.*

"Under normal circumstances I'd agree with you," Nolan began. "It'd be near impossible to find someone last minute to finish the tour with you guys. However," he continued on. "I think we've already found the solution to our problem."

I wondered what band they were in and if I'd heard them before. They must be pretty big if they were staying in a hotel like the place we were in. I looked around, taking in the room before me and realizing just how enormous it was. I'd thought my room was giant but this one was easily twice the size, if not more.

"Not gonna fucking happen!" Camden shouted and jumped from the couch, jolting me from my thoughts and back to reality. "*She,*" he said as he pointed at me, anger lacing his voice, "is *not* coming on tour with us."

Woah now. What? I was so confused as to what was going on and inwardly scolded myself for not paying attention to the conversation that had been going on around me.

"Cam, calm down and hear me out." Nolan stood and put a hand on Camden's shoulder, but he angrily shrugged it away. "It's the perfect solution. You guys need an opening act, and Everly has just the talent to be that. Plus, it'll get her foot in the door in the industry and provide her an opportunity to be noticed the way she should be. It's a win-win situation."

"I said it's not gonna happen. No fucking way in hell."

"Don't I get a say in the matter?" I said as I finally found my voice.

"No!" Camden exclaimed, his tone short.

At the same time, Nolan spoke, too. "Absolutely." He signaled for me to speak.

I inhaled deeply. "You." I stood and poked Camden's chest with my finger. Hard. "You have no right to decide what I do or don't do. You don't know me, or anything about what I've been through."

His eyes darkened in anger and his fists clenched at his sides. He obviously didn't like being spoken to in such a manner.

"This has been a passion of mine for as long as I can remember. Due to certain circumstances, I'd never had an opportunity to follow my dreams. And that's okay. I wouldn't change anything about my past."

I paused and looked from one guy to the next, seeing the excitement in their eyes. I could tell they wanted me to do it, that they believed I was good enough. And that meant more to me than anything.

When my gaze landed back on Camden, however, my heart sank. He was angry. *So* angry. And it didn't make any sense to me. Earlier tonight, he had been telling me how amazing my performance was at The Weeping Willow. He was sweet, funny, and *kind.* But now? Now he was nothing like the man I'd met earlier. I didn't understand why his demeanor had changed, but I brushed it off the best I could and continued.

"I never expected this to be happening. Not in my wildest dreams. And to be honest, I have no idea who ya'll are or what you play, but if ya'll are willing to give me the chance, I would *love* the opportunity to come on tour and perform. Even if nothing comes from it, just the fact that someone believes in me is more than I could ever ask for, and something I will never forget."

"So, does this mean it's a yes?" Nolan eyes found mine, hope shining from his.

Before I could answer, a glass flew across the room and shattered against the wall.

"Fuck this!" Camden roared. "You guys do whatever the fuck you want. But if *she* comes," he spat, "then I'm out. You can find another singer and finish this tour without me."

He stomped across the room and grabbed the bottle of bourbon before storming off down the hall. Moments later, a door slammed shut.

The room was dead quiet as everyone looked at one another. Confusion marred their faces, and I bit the inside of my cheek to keep from crying. What the hell just happened?

"I-I'm sorry." I hung my head low as I placed my glass on the coffee table and made my way to the door. "I'm going to go. I'm so sorry for whatever problems I've caused."

My fingers grabbed the doorknob and turned, pulling the door open. I stepped into the hall and took out the keycard for my room. As my room's door swung open, a hand fell on my shoulder and stopped me in my tracks.

"Everly?"

Nate's voice was low, sad. I didn't turn, though. Tears welled in my eyes, and I didn't want him to see how Camden's words affected me.

"He'll come around," he said.

I nodded once before stepping into my room, letting the door click shut behind me.

Chapter Eight

The alarm clock buzzed, the sound loud and intrusive. I groaned and rolled over to hit the button, turning it off.

I hadn't slept that night, not even for a minute. My mind was a mess and I didn't understand what the heck had happened. Camden had gone from hot to cold, and none of it made any sense. Not only that, but the guys I met were in a band—an actual band—and they wanted me to join them on tour. I should have been happy, elated even, but instead I spent the rest of my time there crying until all my tears had run dry.

I rolled out of bed and changed into clean clothes. It was early still, only seven in the morning, but I'd wanted to make sure I was out of there before any of the guys woke. I had been too embarrassed and hurt to face any of them.

Half an hour later a taxi pulled up. I grabbed my guitar and bag and slid in, giving the driver the address to The Weeping Willow. I hadn't wanted to spend money on things I didn't actually need, but I figured I could spare it this one time.

As we pulled away, I didn't look back. I didn't need to be reminded further of what had happened the night before. The ache in my heart was reminder enough. My dream had been dangled in front of me, but before I could grab hold of it, someone had snatched it away.

I hated Camden for what he had done. Going on tour was something that should have been *my* decision, not his. Who did he think he was, anyways? My blood boiled in anger the more I thought about it, but at the same time my mind kept replaying the night at The Weeping Willow. The way his voice had nearly brought me to my knees and the way his touch set my body on fire.

"Thank you," I said to the driver as I handed him the money. "You have a nice day."

"You too, Miss," he replied.

The gravel crunched under my boots as I walked to my car. I popped the trunk and placed my belongings inside. As I turned the key in the ignition, I wondered if any of the guys were awake yet. If they even knew I'd left.

I felt guilty then. I should have said goodbye to Nolan; or at the very least I should have left a note. He'd helped me so much the past couple days, and I'd be forever grateful for what he'd done. He was willing to take a chance on me, someone he barely knew, because he believed I had what it took. I only wished things had turned out differently.

The drive home to Pinkerton was long. I hadn't realized just how far I'd travelled from there. Somewhere in the tenth hour of driving, I found myself pulling into the driveway of my momma's little house, the one that became mine when she passed.

It felt good to be home, even if I didn't plan to stay long. I just needed a few days to clear my head and forget all about Camden and what he did. I didn't need him or his stupid tour to make it in the music world. He'd see. When I made it big and had my own tour *I* was headlining, he'd look back and wish he'd taken me with them.

The next morning, I sat on the front porch watching as the sun rose. I sipped a glass of sweet tea and thought about where I was going to go from there. I wish I had asked the name of their band when I had the chance, that way I could've looked up where they were touring and made sure I went in the opposite direction. The last thing I needed was to run into Camden again.

My cell phone rang, and I looked to the small wicker table next to me where it sat. A random number lit up the screen. I reached over and pressed the button, sending it to voicemail. I'd had enough of the sales calls lately; they were getting ridiculous. You couldn't avoid them, though. Every time you blocked one of the numbers, three more called.

The phone rang three more times in rapid succession before I finally caved and picked up.

"Whatever ya'll are selling, I'm not interested. I'm sorry, but can ya please stop calling my phone?"

I was about to hang up when a voice sounded from the other end, causing me to freeze.

"Everly?"

"N-Nolan?" I stuttered his name, caught completely off guard. He was the last person I'd expected to call me. "How did you …" I trailed off as I remembered we had exchanged numbers before my second night playing at The Weeping Willow.

"Where are you right now?" he asked, his voice rushed.

"I'm back home. Why? Is everything okay?" I couldn't help but worry that maybe something had happened. He didn't sound like his normal self.

"Everything's fine, but I need you to do something for me."

"Um, okay …"

"I need you to pack your things."

What in the heck was he going on about? Pack my things for what?

Before I could ask, he spoke again. "We're on our way. Bring whatever you think you may need, and don't forget your guitar. You're coming on tour!"

The End… for now.

Kill-A-Queen

by

Bea Stevens

Someone out there has a homophobic grudge and the money to act on it. Kill-a-Queen, an underground operation, is attempting to eradicate homosexuals in key positions in order to frighten the gay community and send them back into the closet.

Their next target is handsome rock star Max Avery, the guy Tom Fraser is trying to protect. Trouble is, Tom is also the guy who's been hired to kill him…

Chapter One

'You'll be fine. It's only high treason if you kill *the* queen, not *a* queen.' Ryan reminded his mate with a wry grin.

Tom shrugged. 'Great, so I'll only get a life sentence."

"It could be worse." Ryan always looked on the bright side.

'How?'

'Hmm, I haven't actually worked that one out yet.'

Tom rolled his eyes.

'Who is the guy, anyway?' Ryan asked, chugging the last of his tea.

'Max Avery—whoever he is.' Tom shook his head and reached into his pocket. 'I've got a picture.'

Ryan was already staring at him, his jaw almost hitting the table of the back street cafe. His expression turned to one of recognition as he glanced at the photo in his friend's hand. '*The* Max Avery. Man, how did you get this job?'

'What? You're going to say he *is* actually royalty and I could get hung, drawn and quartered for this?' Tom couldn't help feeling surprised at his reaction.

'You don't know who he is, do you?' He sighed. 'Tom Fraser, I don't believe this. That guy's good. I mean, really good. Not to mention hot. But I'll bet you're about to tell me you hadn't even noticed that, aren't you?'

Tom narrowed his eyes, putting the photo back in his pocket. 'Well, *you* obviously had.'

'That's only 'cause I'm not blind.'

'Neither am I. I'm just professional. It's a job.'

'Killing a rock star. Yeah, just a day's work, isn't it?' Ryan sneered.

'A *day*? Hell, why would it last that long? One pull of the trigger and it's done. It's only the likes of you who'd take all day over a thing like that.' Tom chuckled.

'Yeah, well, maybe I'm not as cold blooded as you.'

'Or maybe you're just too damn *hot* blooded. There's no room for sentiment in our job, you should remember that.'

Ryan stood, beaming at his friend. 'I'll remind you of that once you've met him.'

Tom chortled as he followed him out of the cafe. If Ryan Forbes thought he'd get his head turned by a pretty face, he'd have to think again. Work was work, in Tom's eyes. He'd never mix business with pleasure—although he couldn't deny the singer was quite fit.

By the time the two guys reached the police station on the other side of town it was getting dark.

'I thought something had happened to you,' Inspector Grimley barked as soon as they arrived in his department.

'I did call to say... ' Tom knew he may as well talk to the wall, but he wanted to make his point, anyway.

'Well, you're here now,' Grimley interrupted. 'Get those wires off and meet me in here.' He headed towards his office, mumbling something unrepeatable and, luckily, inaudible.

'He's all heart. I'll fetch some coffees.' Ryan went over to the machine in the corner of the large office, while Tom had his wires removed by Bill, another of their colleagues.

'Think you'll get used to these things?' Bill asked with a grin.

'I hope so. They're not the most comfortable though, are they?'

'They're not supposed to be. As long as they do their job, it's all we can ask for.' Bill shook his head. He was a nice man, with grey hair and a kind smile.

'Thanks.' Tom grinned and followed Ryan into the boss' office.

'Hope you brought me one of those.' Grimley nodded at the cups in Ryan's hands.

'Of course.' Ryan placed one on the desk in front of him.

'Sugar?'

'I gave you four.'

Grimley grunted, before taking a sip of his drink as the other two sat opposite him.

'Is it political?'

Tom sighed. 'It's hard to say at this stage.'

Grimly leaned forwards, casting a shadow over the two men. 'Well, what the heck *did* you find out, then?'

'The man I spoke to said he was called John.'

Grimley rolled his eyes. 'Aren't they all?'

Tom squeezed his lips together in frustration. 'John Pettit. He said my job was to kill this guy.' He pulled out the photo and handed it over. 'His name's Max Avery and he's a singer, apparently.'

'*Rock star*,' Ryan added, quickly.

Tom gave him a sideways look, and shook his head. It seemed his friend was quite keen on the guy.

Grimley grunted again. 'Look him up. See how much of an impact his death would make.'

'I will.' Ryan jumped in.

Grimley raised an eyebrow, clearly surprised that the guy was actually volunteering for work—it was quite unusual, to say the least.

'As we thought, Kill-a-Queen is an underground operation that hopes to eventually clear all the homosexuals out of the country—or, at least, force them back into the closet. They've got pockets of sympathisers all over Britain, who are all working for the same outfit, according to Pettit. They're picking out key gays to get rid of, in the hope that their followers will get frightened back into the shadows, as it were. Oh, and the calling card the killer's been leaving with the 'Q' stands for 'queen', not 'queer', as we first thought. The killer's proud of what's being done in his name and wants the world to know who's behind it.'

'So, who's the bigot at the centre of all this? Our Mr Big?'

'Some guy called Harrington. I didn't get to meet him, of course, but I got the impression he was here, in London. Pettit hinted that the guy had some kind of personal vendetta against homosexuals—that's why he put his millions into the operation.'

'Sheesh! More money than sense,' the inspector groaned.

'Actually, this guy, Pettit, seemed to think he was doing quite a good job, so far.' Tom remembered the look of admiration on Pettit's face when he spoke about the guy.

'Two minor politicians and a soap-star?' Grimley sneered. 'Hardly world domination, is it?'

'It's three murders we've yet to solve, sir,' Tom reminded him. 'And God knows how many more if we don't shut down this operation soon. The guy's only just getting started.'

Grimley opened his mouth, studied the faces of the two men in front of him, then closed it again. It couldn't be easy for him, putting two gay officers on the job, but sometimes you just had to fight fire with fire.

'You just make sure you're not the next victim.' He nodded at Tom.

'Don't worry, I've got no intentions of becoming that,' Tom assured him.

'Only the good die young,' Ryan interjected with a snigger.

Tom rolled his eyes, assuming it was a line from one of Avery's songs. *How original!*

'You're going in there as one of his security team,' Grimley announced. 'That should give you every opportunity to keep an eye on him.'

'Isn't that a bit obvious, sir? I mean, cop to security guard?'

'Yeah, couldn't he be a backing singer or something?' Ryan piped up with a grin.

'D'you sing?' Grimley raised his eyebrows at Tom.

'A bit.'

'Good. You can do both. Give you an even better position to find out what's what.'

Tom narrowed his eyes at Ryan, who was grinning like a Cheshire cat. Singing in public wasn't exactly his forte—and Ryan knew it only too well.

'You make damn sure you keep me informed of everything that's going on, you hear?' Grimley was pointing at Ryan. 'And you,' he indicted to Tom, 'keep in contact at all times. No heroics. Understood?'

'Of course.' Tom nodded as he and Ryan stood.

'I want to know who this Harrington-guy is, what the hell he thinks he's doing, why—and how the heck we can stop him. Got it?'

'Yes, sir,' they chorused before leaving the room.

'You sure you're okay with this, mate?' Ryan asked quietly, as they walked out of the building. 'I mean... you know.'

Tom nodded. 'Yeah, I'm fine.'

'You should've told Grimley, I reckon.'

'Nah. It was a long time ago, and it's not going to affect my judgement, trust me. I want those guys brought down for *all* the gays, not just Charlie.'

'I still think the boss should be aware.'

Tom stopped walking in the middle of the car park. He stared at his friend, jutting out his jaw. 'If he finds out, I'll know exactly who told him.'

Ryan put his hands up in a placating manner. 'I'm not saying anything. It's your call. None of my business, really.'

'You got that right.'

'I just wouldn't like this to bring it all back for you, that's all.'

'It's never gone away.' Tom sighed, running his hand through his tousled, dark waves. 'Look, Charlie's death has nothing to do with this. It was three years ago, for God's sake. Just a drunken brawl, nothing like what we're dealing with here. This lot's premeditated and built on hate. The guy who killed Charlie had no idea he had a heart condition, and was just fooling around, really. Charlie was unlucky.' He shrugged, before continuing to walk to his car.

Ryan nodded. 'Okay, man.'

Tom pulled the keys from his pocket.

'You wanna go for a drink tonight?' Ryan looked doubtful, and Tom appreciated the gesture. 'After you've changed out of that get-up, of course.'

Tom grimaced at his smart, black suit. He hadn't been quite sure what a killer would wear, so he went with the Kray twins' look. 'No thanks. I've got a pop star to gen up on, remember?'

'Rock—he's a *rock* star.'

'Same thing.' Tom shrugged again.

'Man, you've got a lot to learn. Get on back and do your homework. Listen to some of his stuff—you'll be surprised.'

'You like him, don't you?' Tom gave a half-grin.

'His music's good.'

'And... ?'

'Okay, he's a looker, you know? But I'm spoken for. Jarred would go mad if he thought I was lusting over some singer—you know how he is.'

Tom chuckled. Jarred Jones was probably the most possessive guy he'd ever come across. Ryan seemed to like it, but there was no way he'd tolerate all that jealousy in a lover.

They reached his car and he unlocked it before turning back to his friend. 'I'll be making an early start tomorrow,' he said, frowning. 'The guy's doing some rehearsal in town, so I'll get the Tube over.'

'The Tube?' Ryan raised his eyebrows.

'I'm not getting snarled up in traffic on my way in,' Tom said, with a nod. 'Wouldn't make a very good impression on my new employer if I turned up late on my first day, now, would it? Besides, you'd be surprised what you overhear on public transport.'

Ryan shook his hand, before giving him a hug. 'Good luck, mate. I'll be listening out for your calls. You just let me know if you need anything.'

'Thanks, mate.'

Sneddon Studios was in a back street just outside Camden Town. Tom straightened his back as he walked up to the door and pressed the buzzer for entry.

'Jack Chester to see Tobias Cross.' He straightened his tie for the umpteenth time. It was clip-on and managed to keep digging into his neck. He hoped he wouldn't have to wear a suit every day in this job—this was killing him.

'Come on in, Mr Chester,' a young girl's voice replied, as a low droning sound indicated that the door was unlocked.

'Thank you.'

A man of about fifty, with an immaculate haircut and well-manicured nails met him in the foyer. His Armani suit and shoes wreaked of money, but Tom wasn't in the least impressed.

'You're our latest recruit, I presume?' The guy stretched out a hand with nicotine-stained fingers. His weak handshake spoke volumes, but Tom just smiled politely, nodding.

'Jack Chester.'

'Welcome aboard, Jack. Come on into the office.'

'Shouldn't I sign in first?' Tom eyed the visitors book on the reception desk.

'Don't worry about that.' Tobias led the way into a really pokey room with only a very small desk and one chair either side of it. 'Sit down.'

Tom did as he said. 'Thank you.'

'You came with impeccable references,' Cross told him, sifting through some papers on the desk. 'Are you any good?'

Tom nodded. 'The best.'

Cross was clearly taken aback and raised his eyebrows, as though impressed. 'Good. That's what we need. Max is a good guy, tends to do as he's told, but you'll need to keep an eye on him when he's had a drink or two.'

'I'll be watching him the whole time,' Tom assured him.

'Says here you sing, too. That might come in handy.'

Tom said nothing, wondering just how Grimley had managed to get that little gem into the CV at short notice.

'You've been on the team of a couple of rock stars, I see. You must enjoy the work,' Cross went on, skimming through the papers in front of him.

'Yes, sir.'

Tom wracked his brain to remember what had been put in that document. He'd looked it over last night, along with a whole load of research about Max Avery, the twenty-nine year old singer who'd topped the charts before revealing that he was gay. His admission had brought about a lot of adverse publicity, though it seemed he still had quite a following.

'And you've been charged with the protection of a minor royal?' Cross sat upright, clearly taking a deep interest in his past work.

'Yes, sir.' Tom refrained from rolling his eyes. Grimley sure had laid it on thick.

'I think you'll be more than suitable for the position.' Cross abruptly put the papers down in front of him. 'You've already had a list of your duties, I take it?'

'Of course.' Tom nodded.

Cross clasped his hands in front of him. 'You will know of the recent publicity concerning Max, I take it?'

'Yes.' Tom frowned.

'What is your take on it? Do you think Max was right to admit his sexuality, having already made a big name for himself, or should he have kept it private?'

Tom studied the older man. His jaw was clenched and his eyes narrow. He had very short, fair hair and pale grey eyes. His mouth was small, with thin lips. It was clear from the way he asked the question what answer he was hoping for.

'I think he should have done whatever felt right to him,' Tom replied, maintaining the man's stare.

The slight flare of Cross' nostrils told him all he needed to know. The guy wasn't happy. There was an awkward silence for a few moments.

'So, you're on the fence?' The smarmy look on the man's face made Tom's fist itch.

'Not at all.' He fought to keep his cool. 'I think that Max Avery is a grown man and can make his own decisions about how to run his life.'

'But what about his career? You don't think this revelation was commercial suicide?'

'Not necessarily.' Tom shook his head. 'I think the guy put a lot of thought into his decision and did what he felt was right for him.' He remembered reading several articles about how Max had debated making the revelation, but felt, ultimately, that he had to be true to his fans as well as himself. He knew some would desert him once they found out that all those love songs weren't written with some girl in mind, but his true followers would stick by him.

'So, you don't think he should have considered the rest of us? How it would impact *our* future?'

'He's the brand that makes you the money. If he makes less, you make less. I get that. But he's also a man, a human being. He's living his life under the spotlight—doesn't he deserve to portray his *real* life, not someone else's fantasy of who he should be?'

Cross clenched his lips, a flash of anger in his eyes. It was clear they weren't going to agree on this matter, and Tom could see he was in for a rough ride with him. Nevertheless, he had never compromised his principles, and wasn't about to start now.

'Max is in the live room. You can go and watch him, if you like?' Cross went to stand up.

'I'd rather take a look around the building first, if that's okay? I need to get a feel for the place, and check out the security measures here.'

Cross' eyes widened. 'Of course.' He glanced at his watch. 'I can spare a few minutes to give you the guided tour.'

'I don't want to take up your time. I can take a look by myself,' Tom offered.

'No, it's fine.' Cross flounced towards the door, and Tom followed.

'You'll have seen reception on your way in,' Cross waved a disinterested arm in the direction of the foyer, before leading him down a corridor. 'And this is where all the action happens. These are vocal booths. They're used for singing as well as voice-over work, that sort of thing.'

Tom nodded. The rooms were smaller than he'd imagined, with about enough space for one person to sit comfortably and look into the monitor in front of them. In fact, the whole building was much seedier than he'd expected.

'This is one of the machine rooms,' Cross went on, showing him a large room, which, like the vocal booths looked out onto the control room. 'This is used for noisier equipment that could interfere with the sound quality if it was too near to the singer.'

Tom noticed a couple of humungous power amplifiers against one wall. It was clear to see where the money was spent in this place.

'Over here we have the isolation booths.' Cross led him around a corner, with small rooms that also looked out over the control room.

'Of course, for loud instruments,' Tom cut in before the boss could make his explanation.

They turned another corner, where there was more hustle and bustle, and Tom looked through the glass into the studio.

'This is the live room, where the magic happens,' Cross told him, patronisingly.

Tom ignored his attitude, clearly brought on by the realisation that he already knew all about recording studios, how they were generally laid out and what each room was for. He recognised Max talking to another man, and nodding. He was even more handsome in real life, and Tom felt his stomach burn.

Max looked up and gave him a gleaming smile, which Tom reciprocated. He was dressed casually, in jeans and a white sweater. Tom envied him, hoping it wouldn't be too long before he could get back into his comfy clothes. He also looked edible, much to Tom's surprise—even more handsome than in his photos. Max indicated for him to go around to the door, but Cross stood in front of him, barring his way.

'You can't go in there,' he said. 'It's restricted access only. As is the control room. You can watch through the glass, of course, but you can't actually go in.'

'Why not?' Tom frowned, his jaw clenching hard.

'It's the rules. Only certain personnel are allowed in.'

Tom seethed. 'I'm security. That means I need access to *all* areas.'

Cross gave him a smarmy look. 'Well, I'm afraid those are the rules.'

'Whose rules?'

Cross suddenly looked flummoxed. 'It's just the way it is, I'm afraid.'

Tom was tempted to thump that supercilious look from the man's face, but they were interrupted when Max joined them.

'Is everything all right?' He looked from Cross to Tom, warily.

'Of course. I was just explaining the rules to Jack Chester, your new security guard.'

'And *I* was just explaining that, without access to all areas, I can't be your security guard. I wish you luck.' Tom nodded to each of them before heading towards the foyer.

Chapter Two

Tom's whole body shook with anger as he marched down the corridor. God only knew what he'd do if he didn't keep this job, as it was the only way he could convince Pettit that he was going to kill Max, and, at the same time, the only way he could save the poor guy's life. He wasn't about to be pushed about like that, though, even for an undercover job.

'Wait. Jack.'

His heart lurched as he recognised Max's voice calling him back. He'd been willing for someone to stop him, knowing how badly he needed to stay here—especially having seen Max Avery in the flesh. He turned around and stopped.

'Please, Jack, don't go.'

He sighed. 'I'm sorry, man. I can't keep you safe if I'm not allowed in certain areas. No one can. To give you the protection you deserve, you need someone with you all the time, and that's just not possible with all those rules. If I can't do the job properly, I won't do it at all.'

'Of course, you get access. I've no idea what Toby's on about. We've never had a problem before.' Max's big, blue eyes pleaded with him, and Tom felt his stomach burn again.

Just then, Cross caught up with them. Max swung around to face him.

'What the fuck, Toby? We need Jack. What d'you mean, he has restricted access?' Max put his hands on his hips as he confronted his manager, and Tom couldn't help feeling impressed at his confidence.

'Well, he's only just started today. We can't give him full access yet. He'd need a security pass and everything.'

'Then get it.' Max's voice was curt. Cross bit his lip, looking over at Tom. 'It might take time.'

'Then you'd better start now. I've got no security, thanks to you, and I need Jack here. Wherever I go, he goes. You said yourself, I need to watch my back.' Max glared at Cross, who, in turn, scowled at Tom.

'Right. If that's the way you want it.' He put his hands up and backed away.

'Jack, I can't apologise enough,' Max said, his entire body visibly sagging. 'I don't know what the heck he's playing at, but I need you to take this job. I'll double your salary if I need to. I saw your CV and you're the best. Please ignore what he said and reconsider. I need you.'

Tom felt a twitch in his nether regions as he looked into Max's gorgeous eyes. He longed for the guy to need him in other ways, too, but he had to dampen his thoughts and keep to the job in hand. He cleared his throat.

'I'll give you the best protection I can,' he promised. 'But, if that fuckwad of a manager interferes, I'm out of here, understood? I won't put up with his shit.'

Max heaved a huge sigh of relief, but it was nothing like the one Tom inwardly sighed. He wasn't used to bluffing, and it terrified him every time he tried it.

'Thanks, man. I owe you one.' Max gave him a beaming smile, which did nothing to cool the fire in Tom's stomach. 'Come on, let me introduce you to everyone. They're not all like Toby, honestly.'

Tom followed him back down the corridor and around to the live room.

'Everything okay?' a young guy with a weird haircut asked, as soon as they went in.

'Yeah. Just Toby being an arsehole, as usual.' Max shook his head. 'Honestly, I don't know what's wrong with him lately.' He turned to Tom. 'Jack, this is Stuart, one of the audio engineers. Stu, meet my new bodyguard, Jack Chester.'

The men shook hands. Tom was pleased that this guy's hand wasn't as limp as Cross' had been.

'Good to meet you, Jack. I hope he doesn't give you too much trouble.' Stuart grinned, tipping his head to indicate Max.

'Hey, watch it. I don't want you putting him off the idea—Toby's already tried it once.' Max smiled.

'You look like the kind of guy who can handle the likes of Toby Cross,' Stuart said, looking Tom up and down, admiringly.

Tom nodded. 'I've got his measure.'

'Good, we don't want a repeat of the last one.' Stuart grimaced.

Tom was about to ask what happened to his predecessor when they were interrupted by a slightly older guy wearing jeans.

'Well, if you've all finished your meeting, perhaps we could lay this track down some time today?'

Max grinned at the irritable guy, totally unperturbed by his manner. 'Just introducing my new bodyguard, Jack Chester. Jack, this is Rick Foster, the record producer.'

Rick threw Tom a cursory look, before heading back through to the control room.

'Is everyone always this friendly around here?' Tom mumbled.

'You'll get used to it,' Max said, chuckling as he pulled on his headphones.

'You can sit there, if you like.' Stuart pointed to a chair, and Tom immediately sat down.

'Say that again,' Max was clearly listening to Rick through his headphones, and cocked his head to one side. 'Right, no probs.' He took a sip of water from the table to his side, as Stuart left the room.

Moments later, Tom was treated to a beautiful rendition of Max's new song, *If you were Mine,* a cappella style, although he was quite sure the music was coming through Max's headphones.

He'd heard some of the guy's music before—most of it last night while he was learning all about him, as though cramming for an exam. He'd liked what he heard, but it was nothing compared to having him singing right in front of him—*to* him, it felt like.

Max's eyes were locked into his, and he sang as though he meant every word. When he finished with *'I'd love you til the end of time'* holding the last note, Tom felt his heart melt. The sultry wink Max gave him when the song ended made Tom's breath hitch., especially as he held his gaze a little longer.

A tap on the window from the control room made them both look up, and Rick gave the thumb's up.

'It's a wrap,' Max said, beaming as he removed his headphones.

'It sounded great,' Tom said, standing up with a smile.

'Thanks, that's really nice of you.'

'I mean it. I've heard some of your stuff—which is cool, by the way—but that was the best so far.'

'Oh, so you're an expert on rock music now, are you?'

The man's sneer made Tom turn on his heel and he glared into the face of Tobias Cross.

'I know what I like.' His teeth were clenched.

Cross gave a derogatory sniff. 'I'll bet you do.'

'D'you want to discuss this outside?' Tom offered, taking a step nearer the door.

'Not particularly. I've got work to do.' Cross' scornful expression was getting on Tom's last nerve.

'Good. Does that mean you've got my pass sorted out so I can do *my* job now?' Tom feigned a smile.

'Yeah, did you get it?' Max chipped in, coming to join them. He looked expectantly at Cross, who said nothing, just handed over a plastic lanyard with a card attached.

'Thanks,' Tom said, taking it with a supercilious smirk. He put it around his neck before turning back to Max. 'What's next?'

'I thought I might practice a few more tracks while we've got the studio booked,' Max replied. 'I've got an album coming up, as well as Saturday night's concert, and I just want to make sure I get these last ones perfect.'

'So, what are *your* plans?' Cross asked. 'Just sitting around here watching all day?'

Tom gave a half-smile, though the idea was tempting. 'Actually I wanted to run through Max's schedule for the next few days. I also need to know how many more are in the security team. I'll want to check out Saturday's venue beforehand and acquaint myself with it. Do you keep his diary?'

'Yes, but—'

'Great. I'll leave you to sort it while I nail these tracks,' Max said with a nod.

With a huff, Cross marched towards the door, closely followed by Tom. He didn't relish the idea of spending the next hour or two in the man's company, but he had work to do—and part of his job was to find out what was biting the older guy's hairy arse.

He followed Cross into the little office, where the older guy slammed the door shut after them.

'Now, let's get one thing straight here, shall we? You're a security guard, nothing else. You do as I tell you, not the other way around, d'you understand?' He was standing on the opposite side of the table, his knuckles bent on the mahogany veneer. His face wore the snarl that Tom was now used to.

'I understand that I'm employed by Max Avery, the same as you. I take my orders from *him*. You're *his* manager, not mine. Do *you* understand?'

Cross' face turned bright red and he puffed his chest out as though he was about to explode. 'Now you listen here—'

'No, *you* listen. I don't know what your problem is, and frankly, I don't *want* to know. You've been on my case ever since I got here. Now, I've been appointed in charge of Max's security, and I intend to do my job to the best of my ability—with or *without* your co-operation. But I'll tell you something, if you get in my way and try to hinder my job *you'll* be the one to regret it, understood?'

'Get in your way? You've only been here five minutes and you think you own the goddamn place.'

'And in that short time I've seen enough to know that things aren't right around here. Now, I don't know if you're interested in protecting that guy or not, but one thing's for sure, not everyone around here's singing from the same hymn sheet.'

Cross gulped, staring at him. 'What? Just what are you saying?' His voice was gruff, demanding.

'I think you know.' Tom narrowed his eyes at him. 'And you can email me that schedule. I haven't got time to wait around all day.' He turned and left the room, careful not to slam the door on his way out. Cross might like to draw attention to himself, but it wasn't *his* style.

He stopped at reception, where a pretty girl smiled at him.

'Can I help you, sir?'

'Yeah. I'm Jack Chester, Max Avery's bodyguard, and I just wanted to ask you a few questions, if that's okay?'

She raised her eyebrows. 'Of course.'

'Does he come here often?'

She giggled. 'Shouldn't that be, do *I* come here often?' she joked.

Tom chuckled. 'Yeah, I can see how that sounded.'

'He comes here quite a bit when he's working on a new album. He's a cool guy.' She leaned forwards, lowering her voice. 'Such a shame he's going through all that shit in the papers.'

'Do you get any hassle from the press while he's here?'

'No. We're not the most salubrious of places, so most people wouldn't expect someone like Max to be working here. I think that's why he likes it. Besides, we've got the intercom on the front door, so no one gets in unless they're expected.'

He nodded. 'Good thing, too.'

'Yeah, until someone goes off in a strop and decides to lean on the buzzer for hours at a time.' She rolled her eyes.

'I can imagine. Who was that?'

'The guy that was here the other day. Max's other bodyguard. Had a row with Mr Cross, who threw him out the building. Next thing, he was leaning on the buzzer insisting that he needed to come back in. Said it was urgent. I wasn't allowed to open the door, though. We called the police in the end, and had him removed.' She shook her head. 'Shame, though, he was a nice man.'

'Do you know his name?'

She frowned up at him. 'Sam something-or-other.' She thought for a moment. 'Haskell, that's it. Sam Haskell. He was really polite and everything—I was shocked that Mr Cross was so horrid to him.'

'You don't know what it was about, I don't suppose?'

'No. He went into the office and all I heard was Mr Cross yelling at him, then he threw him out.'

'Didn't the guy say anything?'

'He said something about Mr Cross needing to listen to him, but... well... you know Mr Cross.' She muttered.

'I do now,' Tom replied with a grimace, guessing she'd just heard him and Cross raising their voices in the office.

'I don't think anyone's ever stood up to him before,' she whispered, leaning a little closer to the hatch.

Tom smiled. 'Now, why doesn't that surprise me?'

She giggled.

'Well, thanks... um... ?'

'Pippa.'

He nodded. 'Thanks, Pippa'

'You're welcome, Mr Chester.'

There was a loud noise as a door opened nearby. 'Nothing better to do than chat up the receptionist, eh?' Cross sneered.

Tom turned to him, frowning. 'My job is security. You don't think the receptionist's job is, too?'

Cross looked incredulous and opened his mouth to speak, but Tom got there first.

'You think the intercom system's just there for convenience, do you? That the signing-in book's just there for the hell of it?' He pointed to the book by the hatch. 'Maybe we could just give the lady the day off. Leave the door open for anyone to just walk it, shall we?'

'Very funny!' Cross stormed off down the corridor, while Tom rolled his eyes. The receptionist giggled once Cross was out of sight.

'Thanks again,' Tom told her with a smile, before following the cantankerous git.

As he turned the corner, he saw Cross going farther down the corridor until he came to another door, which he opened and went inside. Tom frowned. How come he hadn't been shown that room? And what the hell was Cross doing in there?

Chapter Three

Max was singing a great rock song when Tom caught up with him in the live room.

'Almost finished,' he called over to him after the last note.

'Sounds good,' Tom told him, 'but there's no rush.

Taking a sip from his bottle of water, Max raised his eyebrows. 'Everything okay?'

'Yeah. I was just wondering what's in the room down at the end of the corridor past the instrument booths? The one in the corner there?'

'The other machine room, I think,' he replied with a shrug.

'Right. I haven't checked it out yet and just wanted to make sure I wouldn't be interrupting anyone if I took a look around?'

'Wow, you're thorough.' He looked impressed as he smiled at Tom. 'No, we've got the place booked out until twelve, so there won't be anyone else using the room. My musicians aren't in today.'

'Great, I'll just pop down, make sure it's all kosher, in that case.'

Max waved as Tom left the room, then Tom heard him talking to someone in the control room. He looked across and noticed that both Rick and Stuart were in there, working with the equipment.

Tom went down the corridor again and stood outside the machine room, pressing his ear against the door. He could hear voices inside, one which he recognised as Cross', but the other he didn't know.

'I don't think he'll be a problem,' Cross said, and Tom could just imagine the supercilious expression on his face. 'The guy's got a big mouth, but it's full of bullshit. He'll be no match for the hitman, once he finally gets here.'

'Do we know how much longer it'll be?'

'Nah, they're hardly gonna announce his arrival, now, are they? I'm expecting to hear from Pettit any day, though, with an update.'

Fuck! Tom didn't know whether to be more shocked that Cross was in on the intended murder, or that the fucker seemed to think *he* wouldn't be a match for the hitman! At least it proved he wasn't onto him, though that was only a small consolation.

Hearing a creak near the door, Tom quickly moved out of the way and hid around the corner by the instrument booths. He took out his mobile to pretend to be on a call, when he heard the footsteps get nearer and then veer towards reception.

'Well, I'll catch up with you soon, Jim,' Cross was saying as he and a middle-aged guy shook hands in front of the reception desk.

Tom used his phone to take a photo of the guy, and then slipped quietly back to the room the men had just left. He knew he wouldn't have much time, as there was a possibility Cross might return after seeing his friend off, so he took a quick look around, and snapped a couple of pictures with his phone. The room had some large pieces of equipment he didn't recognise, and a stack of tables and chairs at one end. It was probably used for storage when not in use, he surmised, noticing the dust on the furniture.

He heard footsteps outside, but it was too late to make his escape, so he hid behind the tables. The door opened, and he heard Cross speaking to someone.

'Yes, I know all that, but this is important,' he hollered. 'I don't care where he is. Either he gets back to me this afternoon or I'll be speaking to Harrington himself, got it?' He stood in the middle of the room, yelling, and Tom could only assume he was on his phone, as he was sure no one else would take that shit without answering him back if he were face to face with someone.

Luckily, Cross left shortly afterwards, and Tom climbed out from his hiding place and checked there was no one about before letting himself out of the room. It occurred to him that if Cross was in on the plan to kill Max, then the two shouldn't be left alone—not that he thought the older man would try anything here, but he couldn't be too sure what his intentions were.

On returning to the live room, Tom was surprised not to find Cross there, waiting for Max to finish. The other two guys were still accounted for, in the control room, so he turned and headed back towards reception.

Pippa was on the phone, so he peeped at the visitors book. There was no sign of a 'Jim' written in it, so he waited for her to finish, hoping to ask her about the guy.

'We're about to leave. Shouldn't you be doing something other than hanging around here?' Cross called as he came around the corner of the corridor.

Tom bit his lip, toying with whether to ask him who he'd been speaking to, but then thought better of it. Having Cross not view him as a threat would work in his favour, so he decided not to divulge what he knew.

'There you are.' Max came up behind Cross and gave Tom a huge smile.

Tom smiled back, determined not to let himself get rattled by the older man. 'Where to next?'

'We need to grab some lunch. I don't know about you, but I'm starving. There's a café down the road that we often use while we're over here.' Max went to follow Cross out of the building.

'Don't you need to sign out first?' Tom queried as they reached the door.

'The receptionist can do it,' Cross grumbled.

'No. It's the visitor's responsibility to sign in and out, not hers,' Tom pointed out. 'That's the whole object of the exercise.'

Cross frowned. 'It's what she gets paid for.'

Pippa blushed, looking over at them.

'No, it's not. It's every visitor's personal responsibility to sign in and out of the building. It's called a *security* measure, as well as being part of the health and safety rules of the building. Or didn't you read the notice?' Tom indicated a laminated sheet on the wall, right beside the fire instructions, by the front door.

Cross looked incredulous. 'Who's got time to read all that?'

'Anyone who's interested in keeping safe, I should imagine. Or is that not a priority in your job?' Tom raised his eyebrows.

'It should be everyone's priority,' Max interjected. 'Jack's right, Toby. We should all be more careful. Especially right now.'

Cross seethed, but took the pen that Tom offered him and scribbled into the book. Max grinned as he followed suit, and Tom winked at Pippa as he did the same. She beamed.

'So, this café you usually use, has it been checked out by one of your security team?' Tom asked, joining the others in a large, black car. Max sat in the middle with him and Cross at either side. The seats were made of soft, plush leather and there was plenty of room for all of them.

'You *are* the security team,' Cross told him, bluntly.

Tom stared at Max. 'I'm *it*?'

'I've got Ronald, the driver,' Max said, nodding to the back of the guy's head, 'but that's it. I did have a team of four, but they all left. I thought the last guy would have stayed loyal to me, but he went, too.'

'Why did they leave?' Tom looked pointedly at Cross, already guessing the answer.

'They had their reasons.' Cross gave him a dismissive look and then gazed out of the window beside him.

'What reasons? You don't just lose your whole security team overnight.' Tom seethed. Max Avery was too big a celebrity to not have a good number of staff looking out for him.

'I honestly don't know.' Max looked sad as he shrugged. 'I thought we all got along well, you know? We had lots of fun, drank together, all that. But they all seemed to just fall by the wayside.'

'So, it wasn't just because you came out?' Tom had to ask.

Max sniggered. 'They all knew I was gay. It's never been a big secret. I just hadn't actually announced it before. It was Toby's idea to make it official. I was just going to let the public find out for themselves, but he thought it would have a detrimental effect. Like, the press would suddenly blast it all over their pages as though I'd done something wrong. I suppose he had a point.'

Tom stared at Cross who still hadn't returned his attention from the window.

'So, it was *you* who wanted to make the announcement?' Tom asked him, pointedly.

'Not quite. I didn't expect it to be done in the way it was,' Cross said, rolling his eyes, as though speaking to a tiresome child.

Max frowned. 'You said I should tell the world. Be proud, and all that.'

'*You* wanted it to be made public.' Cross raised his voice indignantly as he turned to Max.

Max shook his head. 'No, what I said was that I didn't have a problem with fans knowing my sexuality. I'm proud of who I am and if they don't like it then I'm sorry, but that's me. I didn't say we should make a big announcement or anything, just that it shouldn't be kept a secret.' He turned back to Tom, rolling his eyes. 'I'm not ashamed of being gay, but I didn't really expect it to be made into a big deal.'

'You lost a lot of fans over it,' Cross pointed out.

'Then they weren't real fans, were they? It's more important to me that people follow me because of my music, than for me. They don't know me, and probably never will, but they can always listen to my songs.' Max shrugged.

'I couldn't help thinking it was an odd time to disclose your sexuality,' Tom remarked, his mind whirling. 'I mean, it was right after two politicians had been murdered for being gay. Not exactly the safest time to go public.'

'He said he wasn't afraid,' Cross butted in. 'Max is proud of his sexual preference and won't be intimidated by what other people think.'

'So, you take care of his publicity as well as managing him?' Tom asked thoughtfully.

'Of course. It's all part of the job.'

'Well, it is now,' Max agreed with a nod.

'But it wasn't always?'

Max shook his head. 'No, I had a publicity manager, Annabel Crawford. She was really instrumental in getting my name out there. I'm so grateful to her. But she left.'

Tom noticed his unhappy expression. 'Why did she leave?'

Max shrugged. 'I don't know. Toby just said she handed in her notice and went. She didn't even say goodbye to me, although I thought we were good friends.'

'Where is she now?'

Max turned back to Cross. 'I wish I knew.'

Cross sneered. 'Good riddance to bad rubbish. She obviously wasn't as loyal as you thought she was.'

'What did she write in her letter of resignation?' Tom asked.

'Just that she'd got a better offer.' Cross turned back to gaze out of the window again. They'd been stuck in traffic for the past ten minutes so the scenery hadn't changed since he last looked.

'So, she's with another celebrity? Can't be that hard to find out who.' Tom was thinking aloud.

'Puh! Good luck with that one, Sherlock.' Cross sneered.

'There are ways and means of finding people,' Tom assured him, sick of his attitude. 'If you want her back you'll just have to make her a better offer yourself,' he told Max.

'You think she'd come back and work for me?' His face lit up.

'If the only reason she left was that someone gave her a better offer, there's no reason why you couldn't just up your own offer. I'm surprised she didn't come and speak to you about it in the first place.' Tom shrugged.

'Me too. I was gobsmacked when Toby told me she'd just up and left. I had no idea she was even looking for another job. We got on so well, we had such a good laugh. And she was brilliant with the press and stuff.'

'That's what you need,' Tom replied, sighing.

'Meaning?' Cross glared over at him.

'Oh, Toby, he didn't mean it like that,' Max cut in. 'All Jack meant was that I need someone who's an expert at publicity. You're doing a great job, but you have to admit it'll be a lot easier if we can get someone in who knows their stuff.'

'*I* know my stuff.' Cross looked ready to kill.

Tom snorted, turning to stare out of the window on his side. Two could play at that game.

Chapter Four

Tom insisted on scoping out the café before Max left the car. It was a regular, purpose-built establishment with one front door, a back door out from the kitchen, and a fire door in the small passageway that led to the toilets. It wasn't too busy, considering it was lunchtime, and he chose a table that enabled him to keep an eye on all the exits.

'I've never felt so looked after,' Max said with a grin, sitting down.

Toby snorted, causing them both to stare at him. Tom was secretly glad of the diversion, as he felt his face heating up at the compliment. He liked the idea of taking care of the gorgeous guy—and he certainly seemed to need it.

The waitress who took their order recognised Max and asked for his autograph in a whisper before heading back to the kitchen.

'I'll bet you get that a lot,' Tom said with a grin.

'A bit.' It was Max's turn to blush, as he fiddled with his napkin.

'Not so much lately, though, eh?' Toby grumbled.

'It's fine. I'm sure all the hype'll die down soon,' Max assured him. 'Besides, it's nice to have a meal in peace.'

'Oh, the pressures of stardom.' Tom put the back of his hand to his forehead in mock despair, causing Max to burst out laughing. Tom liked the sound, and vowed to make him do it more often.

'Something like that,' Max replied with a grin. 'Anyway, tell me about yourself. Are you local? Need a place to stay? We're renting a house not far from here, if you need somewhere?'

Tom swallowed hard. It would make sense for him to stay with Max, if he was going to stand any chance of guarding him. Although the look on Toby's face spoke volumes.

'I'm sure there's no need for that,' the older guy butted in, just as their meals arrived.

'Actually, I'm staying at a hotel. Do you actually have a spare room at your place? It sure would cut costs and enable me to keep a closer eye on things.' Tom held his breath waiting for the reply, his heart beating like he'd just run a marathon.

Max's grin spread right across his face. 'Yeah, there's a couple of spare rooms,' he assured him. 'And you're right—I think I'd feel a lot safer with you around twenty-four seven.'

Toby couldn't hide his annoyance. 'Oh, that's hardly necessary,' he protested. 'And you know how much you value your space after a long day, Max.'

Tom put his hands up. 'Look, I don't want to be in the way or anything.'

He was thrilled to see a look of horror cross Max's handsome face. 'No, honestly, it would be great to have you there.'

'Well, only if you're sure?'

'Positive. Can you move your stuff in this afternoon? I've got another appointment later, but you can get yourself settled before then.' Max glared at Toby as he spoke, reserving his smile for Tom.

'No problem. Just give me the address and I'll be right over.' Tom prayed he didn't offer to come with him to fetch his things, but luckily Toby interjected just then.

'It's only for a couple of nights, while we're working on this album,' the older man pointed out, through a mouthful of chips.

'So, who else is staying there?' Tom asked, turning back to Max and ignoring the remark.

'Just Toby. I don't exactly have a large entourage, do I?'

'Actually, that's something that's surprised me,' Tom admitted. 'I thought all you superstars had a bunch of hangers-on flocking around you wherever you went.'

'Nah, it's hardly my scene,' Max assured him with a smile. 'I don't like to be high profile—honestly. When I had Annabel and the guys with me I felt like I was just showing off if we went anywhere together.'

'You must have felt safer, though, surely?' Tom nibbled at his chicken, not really feeling much like eating.

Max smiled. 'I did, to be fair.' He lowered his voice, leaning into Tom, who breathed in the rock star's expensive aftershave. 'I have to admit I feel quite vulnerable at the moment, especially with the backlash of that damn press statement.'

'Well, I've got to say, you picked the wrong time to announce your sexuality, what with the hate crimes and all.'

'That was actually the point.' Toby's voice was loud and curt.

'It was madness.' Tom rolled his eyes.

'You think it was a bad idea, too?' Max looked sad, and Tom kicked himself for being so blunt.

'Two people had just been killed. What made you think you wouldn't be next?'

'I'm hardly massive,' Max said with a self-deprecating smile that made Tom's stomach burn. 'I'm sure whoever's doing all this won't have heard of me.'

'Neither of those politicians was that well-known,' Tom pointed out. 'And the soap star last week only ever had bit-parts.'

'They still had a large following,' Max said, putting down his knife and fork. 'That's why the story was so big.'

'Maybe you're *too* big,' Tom pointed out. 'Anything happens to you and there'd be uproar.' He turned to face Toby, who seemed to have taken a great interest in the pattern on his plate.

'That's a very flattering thing to say,' Max said, with a smile.

Toby snorted but still didn't look up.

'Are you going straight back to the house now?' Tom asked, as the waitress retrieved their dirty dishes.

'Yep. I'll get my head down for an hour then we need to do some planning. I've got a one-off concert on Saturday and then a tour in the pipeline, so Toby's been busy securing venues.'

'Let me guess—you used to have a guy to do all that for you?'

'Yeah.' Max nodded, sadly. 'I really need to get more staff hired, but Toby says everyone who applied so far's been rubbish.'

'Just can't get the staff, eh?' Tom sniggered, looking over to Toby, who just scowled back.

'Are you guys going to be together the whole time? I don't want you going off on your own while I'm not there.' Tom spoke firmly.

'Don't you worry. Who do you think looked after him before you came along?' Toby rolled his eyes.

'We'll be stuck like glue,' Max promised, as they all stood up.

'I'm counting on it.' Tom picked up the bill, but Max held out his hand.

'It's on me. Business expenses,' he said.

Tom thought for a moment. He was used to paying his way, and it seemed odd not to, but his boss had a point.

'All right.' He relented as he handed it over. 'Thank you.'

The waitress came back to clear their glasses, so Max handed her some notes. She blushed when he told her to keep the change, and went off to get his receipt.

'You'll need the address,' Max pointed out while they waited. He smiled at Tom, making his heart melt.

'Yeah, of course.'

'Give me your number and I'll text it over.'

Tom wasted no time in divulging his mobile number, and it was less than a minute before his phone pinged to say he had the message—and the rock star's telephone number.

Tom took the Tube home and called in to update Ryan as he packed a small case.

'At last!' Ryan moaned. 'I hope you've got some news for us after all this. We've been worried sick something bad had happened. Grimley's talking about having you wired twenty-four seven.'

'Max Avery's asked me to move in with him.' Tom told him with a smirk, as he threw some clean underwear into his case.

'What?'

'You heard. I'm packing my stuff right now.' Tom grinned, trying to ignore the butterflies racing around his insides.

'Well, that was quick. I take it you like him then?'

'Yeah, he seems like a nice guy—and you're right about his music, it's great.'

Ryan chuckled. 'I knew you'd fancy him.'

'I didn't say that, exactly.'

'But it's true.'

'Okay, so I like the guy. But we've only just met and the only reason I'm moving in is to keep a closer eye on him. Trouble is, I think it's Toby Cross I need to watch, too. I heard him on the phone, and I'm sure he's in on it. Luckily, it turns out he's staying at the same house as Max, so I might get my chance.'

'Hmm, I've been looking into him and he's got a good record as far as celebrity management goes.'

'That's as maybe but he's not what he seems .He wants me to think he's against Max announcing he's gay. After all, he doesn't want to lose his cash cow, does he? But it turns out it was *his* idea to tell the world in the first place. Something's not right there, mate.'

'I went back through the media coverage, and Cross looks quite happy about the situation. Said some complementary stuff about Max being honest and respecting his fans' right to know about him.'

'That's what I thought. So why does he want me to think he was actually against it? Says he only went along with it because it was what Max wanted.'

'That doesn't add up,' Ryan agreed.

'And there's another thing,' Tom went on, I need to find out who this Jim-guy is who he had a secret meeting with at the studio. I'm sending you his picture now.'

'I'll see what I can find out,' Ryan promised. 'Think you'll be able to bug Cross' phone any time soon?'

'Leave it with me. I'm about to move in with the guy, remember?'

'Oh yeah. Your ménage a trios.' Ryan chortled down the phone.' Enjoy it—and keep in touch.'

'Yes, Mum.' Tom chuckled as he hung up. He suddenly had a vision of being in bed with Toby as well as Max, and he shuddered in disgust.

Spending the night in the same house as a gorgeous rock star might be anyone's dream come true, but for Tom it was a nightmare. Having endured the evening being sneered at by Toby, he was now in bed, where sleep was eluding him.

Max's appointment turned out to be a photo shoot, which was a delight to see. Tom watched with interest as he struck different poses, and he was sure when the gorgeous hunk smiled, it was at him, not the camera in front of him.

The house was quite salubrious, in Notting Hill, with four double bedrooms, all with en suite bathrooms. His was next to Max's, with Toby in a larger room across the corridor. A very nice housekeeper, Mrs Robertson, took care of the home and cooked delicious meals for them until nine at night, and after that they were left to their own devices. Luckily, the lovely lady was adept at keeping the fridge well-stocked, so the guys would never go hungry.

Tomorrow was going to be a busy day, as they were visiting the venue of Max's upcoming event. Tom dreaded the thought of organising a security team for the concert, but there was no way he could control everything on his own. Toby had raised massive objections when he'd tried discussing it earlier, but Max had overruled him, saying that if Tom felt it necessary, then he would go along with it. Toby was bound to be in a hell of a mood again tomorrow, but Tom could handle the grumpy bastard.

Tom must have fallen asleep, as he woke the next day to the sound of his alarm. A shower refreshed him, and he pulled on his smart trousers and shirt, dispensing with the tie today.

'Morning.' He was thrilled to see Max already in the dining room when he went down to breakfast

The guy beamed at him, making his insides melt just a little.

'Morning Jack. Did you sleep okay?'

'Eventually,' Tom admitted.

'Toby didn't keep you awake then?'

Tom shook his head.

'He snores like a goddam pig,' Max explained with a grin. 'That's why he sleeps across the corridor. You can still hear him from there most nights, but it's not as bad as when we have to share a room together.'

'When you're on tour?' Tom clarified.

'For concerts, anyway. Luckily I haven't had a tour since losing my security guard. Toby had to stay with me in Manchester last week, just to be on the safe side. Neither of us was happy with the arrangement, but he could hardly guard me from the other end of a hotel corridor, could he?'

Tom's heart lightened, hoping that it would now be his turn to share a room with the gorgeous singer.

'I can't believe you've had to manage with no security,' he said, as Mrs Robertson placed a plate of bacon, eggs and mushrooms in front of him. He thanked her and she nodded.

'It wasn't by choice,' Max replied with a grimace. 'I don't know what happened between Max and Sam, but it must have been bad to make him just walk out like that.'

'This is Sam Haskell?' Tom asked. 'Surely he must have given you some indication that he wasn't happy?'

Max shook his head while sipping his coffee. 'Not a word. Although, I knew he was getting pissed off with Toby's damned attitude.'

'If the guy's losing you all your staff, shouldn't you sort it out?' Tom asked, reaching for the toast.

'Oh yeah, you'd like that, wouldn't you?' Toby was standing in the doorway.

'Oh, morning, Toby. I didn't see you there,' Tom lied with a smirk. He'd purposely sat in a position where he could keep an eye on the kitchen and the door at the same time. It was second nature.

'Clearly,' Cross snarled. 'So, you think it's *my* fault the staff have all left, do you? And just what do you propose to do about it?' He huffed as he slumped into the chair opposite Tom.

'It sounds that way,' Tom said, crunching into his toast. 'But it's not my place to do anything about it. That's up to Max.'

They both looked over at the boss, who turned a cute shade of red. Tom couldn't help feeling bad for putting the poor guy on the spot like that. 'Of course, the most important job is to recruit more staff to replace them,' he said. 'You can always discuss the rest later.'

Max nodded, looking gratefully at Tom. 'Yeah. We desperately need to get the staff up to scratch before next week. How, though, if all the candidates were useless?' He turned to Cross.

'Well, if you can't get new ones, how about trying to re-hire the old ones?' Tom tried to sound flippant, but wasn't surprised at the evil look Cross offered him.

'That's actually a good idea,' Max replied with a smile. 'Like you said yesterday, if I offer them more money, they might just come back.'

'Of course, you'd have to find out why they actually left in the first place. If it was just getting a better offer, you've got no problem. If it's anything else, you'd have to address whatever was troubling them so they'll *want* to come back.' Tom tried to hide a grin as he felt Cross' beady eyes boring into him.

'That's true,' Max replied, thoughtfully.

'We'll need to look through their letters of resignation, see what their beef was,' Tom went on, matter-of-factly.

'Okay, can you dig them out for me, Toby?' Max asked, standing up. 'Once we know what we're dealing with we can see about putting it right.'

Toby said nothing, but just glared at both of them.

'Thanks for the breakfast, Mrs Robertson,' Tom said, grabbing the last slice of buttered toast from his place as he, too, stood.

'You're welcome.' She smiled and he got the impression she wasn't used to being appreciated.

Brushing against Cross on his way past the older man, Tom managed to knock his phone off the table.

'Careful!' Cross barked, as it clattered to the floor, causing the back to fall off.

'Oops, sorry,' Tom lied, deftly attaching a bug before putting it back together and replacing it. 'Nothing broken.'

Cross grunted but took up his cutlery as Mrs Robertson served up his breakfast.

'Jack, let me show you where the concert's going to be on Saturday,' Max said with a smile. 'It's not far. Toby, why don't you finish your breakfast? We won't be long.'

Tom happily followed Max out to the car, while Toby sat glowering. This was going to be a fun day, Tom could feel it in his bones.

Chapter Five

Max was playing at the Hammersmith Apollo, about quarter of an hour away from where they were staying.

'It's a sort of pre-tour event,' he told Tom as they were driven south. We need to put the feelers out to see what the mood of the fans is. If they don't come out to this, there's no way they'll be interested in a tour.'

'Hey, I'm sure it'll be okay, mate.' Tom put a hand on Max's arm to comfort him, and was amazed by the zing of electricity that coursed through him.

Max smiled. 'I wish I had your confidence.'

'I think once we've got a proper team in place to keep an eye on you, you'll feel much better,' Tom said. 'Do you know how to get hold of Sam Haskell?'

'Toby kept all the staff details,' Max said, glumly. 'Although...' He whipped out his mobile. 'I've got his number, but Toby said I should delete it as Sam was going to change his phone so as not to be bothered by me.'

'*Bothered* by you? I thought you got on?'

'So did I.' Max shook his head. 'I've no idea what happened, but Toby said the guy didn't want to speak to me anymore—said he'd sue for harassment if I tried to get in touch.'

'Does that sound right to you? I mean, you both got on okay, and then suddenly he has a row with Toby and doesn't want to speak to you anymore. Could it be *Toby* that doesn't want you to speak to Sam in case he tells you exactly what went on between them?'

Max pursed his lips. 'I did wonder about that at first,' he admitted, thoughtfully. 'But then I was worried that maybe I'd got the guy all wrong and he really might sue me for contacting him.'

'Why don't *I* try? I can sound him out,' Tom offered. 'As his successor, I'm sure he won't have any objection to me calling him—and if he has, he can just hang up.'

Max's eyes lit up. 'Good idea. I love the way you think, Jack.' He smiled as he sent over the phone number.

Tom hoped that wasn't the only thing the guy loved about him. He hadn't known Max more than a day, but was shocked at the feelings he already had towards him. He had to remember, though, that the guy was off-limits. And Tom had a job to do.

Kensington was really busy, so it took longer than expected, but they eventually pulled up outside the theatre.

'Eventim Apollo,' Ronald, the driver called out to them as they stopped.

'It'll always be the Hammersmith Apollo to me,' Max said, rolling his eyes at the name-change.

Luckily, Tom had attended events at the venue, so was quite familiar with the general layout, though he'd never been backstage before. They signed in after a warm welcome from the receptionist, and were told to go through while she contacted the duty manager.

'We're planning a mixture of seating and standing,' Max explained as they entered the auditorium. That gives us a maximum capacity of three-and–a-half thousand.'

'You'll want a good security team,' Tom reminded him. 'I can't do it all myself.'

'Toby's onto it,' Max assured him. 'He usually hires from an agency for events like this.'

'Good. I'd like to rehire some of the old staff too, if that's okay with you? Might be best to have some familiar faces around on the night.'

Max smiled. 'Good luck with that.'

'You think it'll be a problem?'

'I think Toby will try to make it a problem.'

'Let him. Just get me their numbers and I'll do what I can. I've got a feeling they'd rather not hear from him.' Tom shook his head, wondering just what kind of bullying tactics the manager had implemented to get rid of them all.

'Hey, Max, it's good to see you.' A guy in a snappy, black suit greeted them as they stood admiring the large stage.

'Paul, how are you?' Max beamed as he held out a hand to the guy, causing Tom's stomach to jolt. He'd never considered himself the jealous type before, but he really didn't like the way the good-looking manager was grinning at his ward.

'I'm great,' Paul replied.

'Good. This is my new bodyguard, Jack Chester.'

Tom nodded at the guy and held out his hand, glad to see that his expression hadn't changed. He hoped it was just his job to appear friendly with clients.

'Jack, it's good to meet you. I'm Paul Tuner, manager here at the Apollo.'

'Nice to meet you, Paul. Do you have time for a few questions?'

'Of course.' Paul frowned. 'What happened to Sam?' He turned back to Max.

'He left,' Max replied with an uncomfortable shrug.

'We're looking into getting him back on board,' Tom said, confidently. 'Hopefully, just a minor hiccup. I'll be in charge of Max's personal safety for this event, though.'

He was rewarded with a smile from Max.

'Okay, well, I'm happy to help with anything you need to know, Jack.' Paul offered him his business card. 'Feel free to call me anytime. In the meantime, why don't I show you around a little? Max has already performed here in the past, so you should have a copy of the building's layout, but I'll get Helen, our receptionist, to give you another copy of the plans on your way out.'

Tom nodded. 'Great. How many exits are there?' He followed Paul as he gave them a guided tour of the building, and was impressed at how thorough the guy was. Afterwards, they were invited to join him and one of his team, Aaron, for a coffee in the manager's office.

Having made a mental note of the number of CCTV cameras, Tom excused himself to visit the gents'. On his way he took a closer look at the Fire Exit, and was pleased that it was properly secured. The building was patrolled by security guards, and he was aware of one of the cameras turning its attention to him as he peered through the open door to what appeared to be another office. Good. These guys were on their toes.

Content that Max was in safe hands for a short while, he pulled out his phone and called his predecessor.

'Hello?'

'Hi, my name's Jack Chester, is that Sam Haskell?'

'Yeah.' The guy sounded suspicious, and with good reason.

'I've just taken over as bodyguard to Max Avery and wondered if I could speak with you for a minute?' Tom tried to sound relaxed and cheery.

'Good luck with that. What do you want to know?'

'I'm having a little trouble with the manager, Tobias Cross, and wondered how you'd found him?'

There was a snigger down the phone. 'The guy's a bastard. What more can I tell you?'

Tom chuckled. 'Great. It's good to know it's not just me, then.'

'No, he hates everyone. Except Max, of course.'

'Do *you* have a problem with Max?' Tom held his breath.

Sam huffed. 'Well, put it this way, I didn't *think* I had a problem with the guy. Turns out he couldn't stand me and wanted me off the job. Pity he didn't have the guts to tell me to my face, eh?'

'That's not true.' Tom spoke quickly, afraid the guy was about to hang up.

The phone went silent and he was afraid that maybe he had.

'Sam? Are you there?'

'Um… yeah. What do you mean?'

'Max was told you didn't want to speak to him. He was devastated that you left. Cross reckons you threatened to sue him if he tried to get in touch. I think you need to call him.'

There was another unnerving silence before Sam spoke again.

'Are you sure?'

'Absolutely. Look, we're doing a recce at the Apollo right now, but should be through in about half an hour. Would you be able to call Max? Sounds like Cross has been playing you two off against each other.' Tom bit his lip.

'Told you he was a damn bastard.' Sam sounded vicious. 'Of course, pal. I'll give him a ring later.'

'Thanks, Sam, I appreciate it, mate.'

Tom smiled as hung up and made his way back towards the manager's office. He had a long way to go, but he'd made a good start on figuring out what the hell was going on around here.

By the time the guys got back to the house, both were feeling a lot more relaxed.

'I could've come with you, you know,' Cross snarled, looking up from his lap top.

'There was no need,' Max told him, flippantly. 'I just wanted Jack to see the place and meet the guys.'

'Yeah, it was a very fruitful meeting.' Tom couldn't resist the jibe.

'Really?' Cross couldn't have sounded more disinterested if he'd tried.

'Thanks, Mrs Robertson.' Max accepted a cup of coffee from her just as his phone rang. He checked the screen and stared for a second. 'I just need to take this.' He glanced up at Tom, who gave him a knowing smile before he headed out of the room.

'Max said you were hiring a security team for the event,' Tom said, pulling up a chair opposite Cross at the kitchen table.

Mrs Robertson presented him with a mug of steaming hot coffee. 'Thanks very much, Mrs R.' He smiled at her and she blushed.

'What of it?' Cross snarled.

'It needs to be a large team. That place has got too many nooks and crannies to leave anything to chance. Great venue, though.' He took a sip of his drink.

'Max has performed there before, you know?' Cross was clearly irked.

'I know. But he had his whole team behind him them, as well as the extra security. It's a bit different now.'

'In what way?' Cross frowned.

'Well, I think he's lost his confidence a little, having had all his staff disappear like that. He seemed to regard them as friends as well as colleagues.'

'They were his employees,' Cross pointed out. 'Nothing more.'

'You can be friends with your staff, you know?' Tom told him. 'In fact, it makes for a much more harmonious atmosphere when everyone gets along, don't you think?'

Cross grunted. 'They need to know their place.'

'You think some of them were getting a bit over-familiar?' Tom frowned.

'It has been known. He's a big star now, *some* people find that attractive.'

The look Cross gave him made Tom wonder if he'd guessed how much he liked the rock star. He swallowed hard.

Just then Max re-appeared with a face like thunder. 'What the hell have you been saying?' he bellowed at Cross.

The older man balked in surprise. 'What?'

'Why did you tell Sam that I didn't want him as my bodyguard anymore? The guy's just told me everything you said, so don't try lying to me.' Max stood over Cross with his hands on his hips.

'It wasn't like that,' Cross replied, dismissively. 'The guy got too big for his boots. He was rude to me. What was I supposed to do?'

'Tell the truth, for one.'

'I didn't want to worry you with stupid staff issues,' Cross protested. 'It's my job to protect you from unnecessary stress. Besides, it was all dealt with at the time.'

'No. You told him I didn't want him around anymore. He got the impression he'd overstepped a mark or something. And why tell him I didn't want to speak to him, when you'd told me it was *him* who was avoiding *me*?'

'Oh, he obviously got the wrong end of the stick.' Cross waved a hand dismissively through the air. 'He never was the brightest star in the sky.'

'He was great at his job.' Max's voice rose as his face went redder.

'What exactly did he say?' Tom asked, trying to calm the situation.

Max huffed, momentarily facing Tom. 'He said that Toby sacked him. *My* staff. Who the hell gave you the right to do that?' He was already looking back at Cross now. 'Is that what happened to the rest of them? You decided you didn't like them so you told them I was firing them all?'

'Not exactly.' Cross sighed as thought Max was a tiresome child, which did nothing to alleviate the rock star's anger.

'So, you got rid of them all? Why?' Tom frowned at the older man, while Mrs Robertson made herself scarce.

'They were no good. You need a dependable team behind you, Max. None of them were as loyal as you thought they were. They were always bitching about you behind your back. I didn't want to tell you because you seemed to think they were friends, or something. But that wasn't the case. They were just after your money and your attention.' Cross quickly closed his mouth, a sure sign he'd said too much.

'Meaning?' Tom probed, just as the doorbell rang.

Max sniggered. 'Send them straight through, Mrs Robertson,' he called out.

Tom stood as they were joined by three other men and a woman. His heart raced. This wasn't what he'd expected when he'd spoken to Sam. He thought the guy would just explain what happened and leave Max to decide what to do. By the look of the crowd in the kitchen, it looked like he'd already made up his mind.

'Welcome, everyone,' Max said, smiling at them. 'I'd like you to meet my new bodyguard, Jack Chester.'

Tom stood to shake their hands, noticing how Cross was fuming.

'Jack, this is Sam, Annabel, Damon and Bernie.' He turned to Cross. 'And, of course, you all know Toby Cross.'

Judging by the looks of anger and disdain, they all knew Cross only too well.

'Thanks for coming over, guys. I realise you've all been fed a load of bullshit from Toby, so I wanted you all to get the chance to hear the truth from the horse's mouth, as it were. Grab a seat.'

They all sat down as Tom's phone rang. It was Ryan.

'Could you excuse me just for a minute?' he said, heading toward the door. He didn't wait for an answer. Something must be up.

Chapter Six

Tom hurried outside to take the call.

'You need to keep a close eye on Cross,' Ryan said, as soon as he answered. 'That guy he was talking to yesterday, Jim Cresswell, is one of Pettit's mob.'

'Shit. It looks like Max is about to fire the old man,' Tom replied.

'Don't let him. We need him where we can see him.'

'Got it.' Tom was already walking back into the house, where he could hear raised voices as he hurried into the kitchen.

The team were all pointing and shouting at Cross, who was denying everything, as expected.

He shoved his phone into his pocket. 'Guys, let's just take a deep breath,' Tom urged them, holding his palms up. 'This is getting us nowhere.'

Max huffed. 'You're right, Jack. It seems Toby fired all the staff, telling them it was *me* who didn't want to keep them on.'

'You must have had your reasons,' Tom turned to Cross. 'Why don't you explain yourself?'

Cross screwed his lips together angrily before speaking. 'I didn't think they had Max's best interests at heart following his announcement,' he said, sulkily. 'I heard them all talking about it behind his back.'

'Only because we were concerned about him,' Annabel pointed out. She turned to Max. 'We didn't agree with Toby's idea to tell the whole world, right after those poor people had been killed. We couldn't understand why you'd think it was a safe thing to do. But you know that, you and I had already discussed it.' She shrugged.

Max nodded thoughtfully. 'Yeah, we did.'

'And I told you how I felt before you announced it,' Sam added.

The other two chipped in with similar comments.

'Well, it looks to me that there's only one person who needs to lose their job around here.' Max glared at Cross, who looked bewildered.

'Now, hold on a minute…' Cross leapt to his feet, letting the chair fall over behind him. He put his hands out in a futile attempt to placate his boss.

'No, you hold on,' Max told him, rising elegantly from his seat. 'It's one thing to give me bad advice, but when you then sack my staff for not agreeing with you I think it's time to call it a day.'

'Hang on.' Tom went over to Max, placing a hand on his shoulder.

Max gaped at him.

'I think we all need to calm down,' Tom said, softly. 'Could I have a word?'

Max nodded and followed him through to the living room, where they sat on one of the large, squishy sofas.

'I'm sorry, mate. I just didn't want you making any rash decisions in there,' Tom explained, calmly.

'I want him out. Not only did he tell them all I wanted them gone, but he made up stuff about me not feeling comfortable around them. Then he said I'd sue if they contacted me after they'd left. It's all bullshit, Jack.' He shook his head. 'I don't' know what the hell's got into him, but he has to go. I can't have him lying like that.'

Tom nodded. Nothing would have given him more pleasure than to see Cross thrown out on his ear—but it just couldn't happen. Not right now.

'I get that he's a cantankerous git and he's given you bad advice, but you need to box clever here, mate. The last thing you need right now is a load of adverse publicity on top of everything else—and, we've seen what a great liar the guy is. He'll have connections everywhere and before you know it, he'll have made up another great story that'll have your credibility plummet quicker than a rat down a drainpipe.'

'But, I can't let him get away with it.' Max shrugged. 'Not only for everyone else's sake, but also for mine. What will the staff think if I keep him on? They probably won't come back if he stays, and it'll look like I'm not even supporting them.'

'I hear you, mate, but we have to be careful. Now's not the time. You've got the new album, the concert on Saturday, and then the tour to worry about. You can't do all that without your manager. I know he's a bastard, but we have to admit he's good at his job. Except the advice bit. He's shit at that.' Tom's lips twitched and he was pleased to see Max giggle.

'You got that right.'

'Trust me. That guy's so deep in the shit with you right now, I'd hazard a guess he'll be as good as gold from now on. He needs this job, don't forget. And I hate to admit it, but you need him, too.'

Max sighed. 'What about the others? They were all keen to come back.'

'If they're as loyal as you think they are, they'll understand. You'll need to read the riot act to Cross in front of them, but if you make it clear it's because of the timing and how much you need support from *everyone* right now, I'll bet they'll see it your way.'

'I hope you're right.' Max grimaced as they stood up.

'Don't worry, mate. I've got your back,' Tom assured him with a grin.

'And I'm truly grateful for it.' Max turned back and placed a hand on his arm, making Tom burn for him. 'I don't know what I'd do without you, Jack, I mean it.'

His big, blue eyes gazed into Tom's and for a second the world stopped turning. Their lips got dangerously close before Tom came to his senses and cleared his throat. Max smiled, an indication that he understood.

'Timing, huh?'

Tom nodded with a smile. 'Unfortunately.'

'You can say that again,' Max said, heading for the door.

Tom followed him, taking deep breaths to calm himself down.

Another row was ensuing in the kitchen when they returned.

'Okay, everyone, listen up.'

They stopped as soon as Max appeared.

He turned briefly back to Tom, as though for reassurance, and he nodded his support.

'Firstly, I want everyone back on the staff, if you'll come?' Max said, firmly.

'As long as he's not here,' Damon piped up, followed by nods and murmurs of agreement.

'Now, that's another matter,' Max went on, confidently. He turned to Cross.

'Why shouldn't I sack you on the spot?' he asked the older man.

Toby looked surprised at the question, and Tom guessed he'd expected to be fired straight away.

'I didn't mean any harm,' Toby protested. 'I heard them all bad-mouthing you and thought I was sticking up for you. I'm sorry if I did the wrong thing, I was just being loyal, that's all.' He actually looked quite apologetic.

'You *did* do the wrong thing. Firstly, you've got no right to fire anyone—that's not your job. And secondly, if you had any doubts about the integrity of the staff you should have reported it to me.' Max pointed at him as he spoke.

'Now, apart from giving me crap advice, and sacking my whole staff, I have to admit you're actually quite good at your job,' he went on calmly. 'Oh, but I think we'll leave the publicity to Annabel in future.'

There were titters of mirth from the team, though Cross still looked worried.

'Sounds good to me,' Annabel said with a smile.

'Great. Now, I know it's going to be a bit of a strain getting back to normal, but I'm doubling all your salaries for the next three months as a consolation for what's happened and for still having to work with Toby after all that he's done. I know he deserves to be sacked for what he did to you guys, and he'll be apologising to you all personally. The only reason he's still got a job is because of the timing. I'm sorry, but it's going to be a rough ride for me right now and I need him. I need all of you. I hope, as my friends as well as colleagues, that you understand that?'

Silence descended for a moment before they all started nodding and agreeing with him. There were even whoops from Damon and Sam.

'*You're* not on double pay,' Max clarified to Cross, after they'd all quietened down. 'You're just lucky to still have a job.'

Cross nodded, and whispered a thank you.

Tom grinned. It was good to see Max looking so confident, and he sure seemed happy to have his old team back.

There wasn't much work done for the rest of the day, as they were all getting re-acquainted.

'I think you should all move in while we get our act together,' Max announced as they all sat around in the living room, with tea and biscuits.

'Have you got room?' Annabel asked, her eyebrows raised in surprise.

'Of course. We'll manage.' Max looked quite relaxed as he smiled at them. 'Jack can bunk in with me, Damon and Bernie can have his room, and Sam can share with Toby. That leaves the other room for Anna.'

Tom felt a burning sensation in his stomach, especially when Max winked at him.

'Fine by me,' Bernie piped up, nodding at Damon, who also agreed.

'Not on your life!' Sam interjected. 'Even double pay's not enough for me to put up with his snoring.'

'I do *not* snore,' Cross objected, irritably.

'You can come in with us,' Damon called over to Sam. 'Though you're not getting *my* bed.'

'Oh, you're all heart,' Sam replied. He was good-looking guy, probably in his thirties, with short, dark hair and a wicked sense of humour.

The whole team clearly got on well, although Cross tended to keep himself to himself, having spent most of the afternoon in his room. Damon and Bernie were really close, and it turned out they'd been friends for several years before coming to work for Max. Damon was fair with a slender build and thin face, while Bernie was rounder, probably in his forties, with reddish hair. Annabel was a pretty blonde, with a slim figure and a fiery temper, by all accounts.

Before dinner, Max arranged for cars to take them all home to retrieve their belongings. They all lived in London, so it wasn't too far for any of them, but the traffic in the city is a force to contend with at the best of times.

Tom and Max were in the living room watching the early evening news when they both suddenly gaped at the screen.

A male teacher has been brutally murdered in Derbyshire today. The man, who has not yet been named, is known to be homosexual, and the killer left a calling card with the letter 'Q', nothing else. The murder is thought to be possibly linked with that of two politicians and a young actor who were found in similar circumstances over the past few months. All had the same calling card, which is thought to be short for the word 'Queer' or 'Queen'. Police are concerned that this hate-crime is escalating and are currently following leads on all of the murders.

Max's face turned ashen as he stared, open-mouthed.

Tom felt his phone vibrate and quickly checked the screen. Ryan had sent through a copy of the press release. Too late. He'd have liked to have been warned before the rest of the world heard about it.

'It's getting worse,' Max mumbled, eventually.

Tom switched off the TV. 'They'll get them soon.'

'You think?' Max looked incredulous. 'It's been three months since the first incident and there's been nothing about the police catching anyone yet. How many more people will have to get killed before they pull their fucking fingers out and do something?'

'They're doing their best. And they *are* following up leads,' Tom assured him, putting his hand on the guy's arm.

'How the hell do you know? There's been absolutely nothing about who they're questioning or how close they are to finding out who's behind all this. They're probably not bothering—after all, it's only gays who are being killed. It's not like it's *normal* people, is it?' Max spat the words out, taking Tom by surprise.

'Of course they're bothered.' Tom pulled back from him, irritably. 'Murder's murder. It doesn't matter who it is—it all warrants investigation. Besides, what about the number of gay officers? Civilians don't get the monopoly on being homosexuals, you know?' He hadn't meant to shout, but his raised voice shocked them both.

'I suppose I hadn't thought of that,' Max admitted, shamefully. 'I'd just assumed—'

'Yeah, maybe that's the trouble,' Tom snapped before leaving the room.

He went upstairs to get his own things together. The guys would be back soon, and they'd need his room for their stuff. He was already wondering if it had been such a good idea to agree to bunk up with Max. It was hard enough to keep his hands off the guy as it was.

'I think someone's coming,' he heard Cross say, as he passed his bedroom.

He shook his head. Ryan would give him the details of his conversation later, so he didn't need to worry about that. Not that he really wanted to hear from his colleague right now, anyway. By not giving him the heads up in time, Ryan could easily have just made him blow his cover.

He let himself into his room and threw his things into his bag. Then he sat on the bed and rubbed a hand over his face. It wasn't really Ryan he was pissed off with, it was himself. If he'd let slip who he really was it would have been his own stupid fault, no one else's.

He went through to the bathroom and had a quick wash, which actually made him feel much better. There was a knock at his door.

'Hi.' It was Max, looking rather sheepish.

'Hey, Max, I was just about to come down.'

Tom backed away from the door to let his boss in, and Max tentatively followed him into the room.

'Look, I'm sorry for what I said earlier,' Max began. 'I was just sounding off.'

'It's fine. We all need to vent sometimes.' Tom smiled. 'Sorry if I overreacted.'

'It was just the shock,' they both said at the same time, then sniggered.

'I'm scared,' Max admitted as they both sat on the bed. 'I know that probably sounds big-headed of me, but I can't help thinking that I could be in the firing line. I never should have made than damn announcement.'

'You don't think people would have known you were gay, if you hadn't?' Tom spoke softly.

Max giggled. 'You've got a point there.'

'That calling card's a bit odd, don't you think? It doesn't really make sense that it stands for 'queen', as, judging by the victims they're not exactly flamboyant, are they? I mean, I get that they're queer, but not necessarily queens.' He was really thinking aloud.

'I dunno, one of those politicians was a drag-queen in his spare time, according to the news,' Max suggested.

'Yeah, that's true.' Tom sighed with a smile.

'Look, if you'd rather stay in here, I can always get one of the others to share with me?' Max offered, eyeing the packed case on the floor.

Tom's heart hammered. Having him this close, in this bedroom, was hard enough, but he knew it would be harder to resist the guy in his own room. All night. Still, he heard himself chuckle and say 'No, it's fine. I'm happy to do whatever you want.'

'Really?' Max stared at him, licking his lips.

That was when Tom realised what he'd said. 'I mean... about the sleeping arrangements... as in... you know... where you want me. Oh God!' He shook his head. 'What I meant was...'

'I know,' Max said with a chuckle. 'I was just teasing. Sorry, my bad. I just couldn't resist.'

Tom rolled his eyes. 'Try harder next time,' he said, his voice much deeper than he'd intended.

Max raised one eyebrow seductively. 'And if I don't...?'

Tom chuckled. The ambiguity of this conversation was just getting worse, and was doing nothing to extinguish the fire in his belly.

Luckily, a kerfuffle downstairs distracted them, and they both headed for the door to see who was back first.

'Hey, hope you've got a big room up there,' Damon said, heading up the stairs with a huge suitcase.

'So do I. I hate to think what's in that thing, but I sure as hell don't want it cluttering up the living room,' Max told him, in mock horror.

'I'll just grab my bag.' Tom went back into the room and retrieved his belongings while Max helped Damon.

'You haven't got Bernie in that thing have you?' Max asked, puffing after helping lift the case up the stairs.

'Very funny. It's just a few things, that's all,' Damon replied, rolling the case towards the bedroom they'd just vacated.

'Including the kitchen sink, I'd guess.' Max shook his head before showing Tom into the room next door.

Max's room was spotless, with everything put neatly in its place.

'I've cleared this wardrobe for your stuff,' he said, walking over to the far wall. 'And you've got those drawers. We've got separate bathroom cabinets too, so just make yourself at home.'

'Thanks.' Tom smiled, trying to hide his nerves.

It was stupid to feel like this just being in the same room as the guy—even if it was his bedroom. For some reason this felt even more intimidating than being in the room next door. More… personal. How on earth would he cope with spending the night with the gorgeous hunk?

Chapter Seven

'I asked Roland to stop at the dry-cleaners for your stage outfits,' Annabel announced, as soon as Max and Tom joined them for dinner. 'They're in the living room.'

'What would I do without you?' Max squeezed her arm as he pulled out the seat next to her.

'I'm a bit concerned about your backing singers,' Sam said, as they helped themselves from large pots of beef casserole, potatoes and vegetables. 'This looks lovely, by the way, Mrs R. Thanks so much for catering for us all at short notice.' He gave her a cheeky smile, making the poor woman blush again.

'You're welcome. I come from a big family so I'm used to this sort of thing,' she assured him.

'I should have consulted you when I asked everyone to stay.' Max looked devastated. 'Mrs Robertson, I'm so sorry. I just didn't think.'

'It's fine, really. Will Mr Cross be joining you tonight?'

It hadn't gone unnoticed that the older man wasn't at the table, and the atmosphere was much lighter because of it.

'He can help himself whatever he decides to do,' Max told her. 'Why don't you get off home, and we'll load up the dishwasher once we're done?'

She beamed. 'Thank you very much.'

'That poor woman,' Max admonished himself as she left the house. 'Whatever must she have thought?'

'I meant to tell you, Roland's gone back home, too. I said you'd ring him if you needed him. Hope that was okay?' Annabel said, reaching over for more carrots.

'Yeah, of course. He only lives down the road from here. In fact, that's how he got us this place. A friend of his owns it, apparently.' Max took a sip of his wine, looking over at Tom, who smiled back.

'It's a lovely place,' Bernie piped up. 'Does Mrs R come with it?'

'I'm not sure. Roland just said he'd sort out a housekeeper.' Max shrugged.

'She's a diamond,' Damon added. 'We should have her whenever we've got a London gig.'

'You guys live here,' Annabel pointed out. She lived a little further afield, preferring the countryside to the city.

'Yeah, but it's better when we're all together like this,' Sam said. 'Cheers everyone.'

They all lifted their glasses in a toast.

'Are the musicians all sorted for the concert?' Damon asked after they'd all started eating.

'Yeah. Toby's got them booked,' Max replied. 'I'm sure he's sorted the singers, too. He said everything was under control.'

Tom suddenly felt unnerved about the whole event. 'Has he got a security team booked? Apart from us, of course.'

'Talking of which, I'm not actually sure what my role is here,' Sam piped up with a frown.

Tom's face went hot. He'd taken the guy's job, for goodness' sake.

'Well, if we haven't got all the singers we need, Jack will have to step up so you'll be back to your old position,' Max said, with a smile.

With a splutter, Tom almost choked on his wine.

'You okay there, mate?' Damon patted him on the back.

'Yep.' He quickly regained his composure and cleared his throat.

'Where is Toby, anyway?' Annabel asked, looking around. 'We need to discuss all this and he's the only one who knows exactly where we're at. We've only got two days, as it is.'

'I assume he's still in his room,' Max replied with a shrug. 'But you're right, we could do with him here.'

'Shall I fetch him?' Tom offered, getting up.

'If you don't mind?'

'Of course not.'

Tom left the room and quietly made his way upstairs. He could hear Cross mumbling in his bedroom, and put his ear to the door as soon as he reached it.

'Well, if he doesn't get here soon we'll have to go ahead with the damn concert,' Cross was moaning. 'I thought you said he'd be here by now? I need it to be done before Saturday or there's a whole show to organise. What the hell's Pettit playing at?'

The silence indicated he was on the phone.

'Oh, come on, Jim, you can do better than that. Pettit definitely said he was sending someone over this week. He knows there's a concert planned—or, at least, it's supposed to be planned. I've got no musicians, no singers, the only thing we've got is the ticket money in the account that can't be touched until after Saturday. I can't afford any delays.'

There was a short silence before Cross cut in. 'Hang on, I think I heard something. Gotta go.'

Tom quickly retraced his steps stealthily before going back to the door much more noisily. Cross already had it open when he arrived.

'Oh, hi. Max was asking where you were.'

'So he's sent his lackey to find out, eh? At least you're learning your place, at long last.'

Cross locked his door and followed Tom downstairs. Halfway down, Tom turned back to him, much to the older guy's surprise.

'I saved your damn arse for you today,' he hissed. 'Now I'm not expecting any thanks or anything, but you'd better prove to Max that he was right to listen to me. That concert needs to be spot-on, d'you hear me? He needs you to do your job and you damn well better do it properly.'

'Or what?' Cross sneered.

'Not only will you be out of a damn job, but you'll have ruined the whole event for Max. I thought you said you cared about the guy. Why not start showing it?'

Tom took another step before Cross' next remark stopped him in his tracks.

'Not in the same way you care about him, of course.'

He swung back around. 'I'm his bodyguard, nothing else.'

'Then you'd do well to remember that,' Cross sneered. ''Cause from where I'm stood it looks like you're hoping to be a darn site more to him.'

Tom grabbed him by the collar and pushed him up against the wall, his blood boiling. 'What the hell are you talking about, Cross? You think I'm a faggot or something?'

'There you are.'

Max's voice permeated the red haze in his head and Tom wanted to die on the spot. The supercilious smirk that Cross gave him was enough to make him clench his fist hard, but he knew he couldn't hit the guy. Not with a witness, anyhow.

He slowly turned to face Max, whose gorgeous face looked hurt and distant.

With a shake, he let go of Cross' collar and slowly made his way downstairs. Max was already on his way back to the dining room, and Tom knew it was a waste of time trying to talk to him right now. Besides, he was still enraged about Cross, and even more so now.

'We wondered what happened to you,' Damon said to Cross as he and Tom took their seats.

'I was working,' Cross replied, reaching over to the large casserole pot. 'I hope you've saved me some.'

'Yeah, there's loads,' Bernie assured him, passing up the potatoes, too.

Cross piled up his plate while Tom just stared at his own, having suddenly lost his appetite. He wanted to leave the room, but it would be too obvious, and, anyway, what would it achieve?

Knowing that Cross hadn't even organised the concert properly was gnawing away at him, but he couldn't say anything. It wasn't his place. All he could do was stand back and watch the car crash. Damage limitation was all he dared hope for now. Max's career was on the line, as was any hope for a future together.

'Annabel picked up my outfits for Saturday,' Max began, the excitement having left his voice. 'I've got the new one upstairs for the big number, and the new shirts. How are we doing with the singers and musicians?'

Tom wanted to cry as he looked at Max's expectant face, as he questioned Cross.

'All in hand,' Cross lied.

'Thank goodness for that. Max was going to have me up there doing backing vocals if you hadn't got everyone sorted,' Tom said, sounding as cheerful as he could.

He'd hoped Max might snigger at least, but the guy didn't even look his way. Damn. He could feel the cold emanating from his boss, even from this distance.

He knew it was a horrid thing to say, but he was trying to throw Cross off the scent by pretending to be straight. It was the perfect cover, especially if he acted as though he was repulsed at the very thought. He just wished there was a way of explaining that to Max. He felt physically sick. That word, that horrid word, should never have left his lips. It wouldn't have usually. He hated it. Faggot. Just the sound of it was derogatory and demeaning. It was supposed to convince Cross that he wasn't remotely interested in Max, but instead it had just proved what an absolute arsehole he was.

Chapter Eight

Tom awoke the next morning with a crick in his neck. He'd gone to bed before Max, thinking it was the easier option. He'd heard the guy come up a while later, and watched him undress in the dark. Max had a ripped body, and Tom was glad of his bedcovers that hid his 'appreciation' as he ogled his fit outline.

Max didn't speak to him, and he assumed the rock star was expecting him to be asleep. He wished he had been. With the gorgeous hunk in the bed across the room from him it was impossible to keep his mind off him.

Eventually, Tom had waited for the steady rhythm of Max's breathing to indicate he was asleep, and headed downstairs. The sofas were large enough, but the arm was at the wrong angle to be used as a pillow. He'd settled for a night on the floor after that, and was now paying for it.

His phone had woken him, which was just as well, as he'd hate to think of poor Mrs Robertson coming in to find him here in just his boxers. It was another text from Ryan, who had actually kept him company with messages way into the small hours.

It transpired that the reason his colleague had been a little tardy with the message regarding the news was because he was busy listening in on Cross' conversation.

Tom had already gleaned that Cross was concerned about the killer not having arrived to murder Max. Jim Cresswell had promised to speak to Pettit about it, which he'd done that evening. It turned out that Pettit had confirmed that the killer was here, and Cross had been speculating about which one of the team had been hired to kill the boss. According to Ryan, Cross' money was on Bernie, as the guy was known to have financial difficulties.

It had occurred to Cross that he, Tom, might have been the killer at first, but then realised that it was unlikely as he was obviously attracted to Max, and would clearly have a problem going through with the job.

Tom had berated himself all night for making that stupid comment. In an attempt to put Cross off the scent as far as his personal feelings were concerned, it seemed he might have just unwittingly have played straight into his hands on a professional level. How stupid could he be?

Ryan had worried him further, however, when he said that Pettit had apparently been furious that he hadn't heard from Tom. He was afraid he was getting cold feet, and had arranged to attend the concert, in the eventuality that the deed hadn't been done by then, to witness it for himself. Tom was now expecting a call from Pettit to hurry him along, in no uncertain terms. Shit!

Grimley was hoping it might flush Pettit from his hiding place, and had sent instruction to Tom to assure the guy it would take place the following day—now today. When it didn't happen, Pettit would hopefully follow through with his plan to come to the concert, where the cops would be waiting for him. The only fly in the ointment was Harrington—they still had no idea where he was.

Taking the bull by the horns, Tom quickly sent a message to Pettit confirming that he was on schedule to murder the rock star tonight. He knew he was playing with fire, but it was part of his job.

He grabbed his blanket and headed upstairs, wondering if Max would have missed him. It was nearly six and the cacophony of grunts and heavy snoring coming from Cross' room was the only sound.

Tom lay on his bed, glad to see that Max was still asleep. He didn't know how to explain everything to him, and just hoped that he got the chance before it was too late. The hurt in those beautiful blue eyes had haunted him all night and he had to do something.

A few minutes later, Max huffed, throwing his covers back. He looked over to see Tom watching him.

'You came back, then?' Max whispered.

Damn.

Tom nodded. 'Cross' snoring kept me awake so I went downstairs,' he whispered back. 'You were certainly right about him. He could wake the fucking dead.'

It was just light enough for Tom to see the glimmer of a smile cross Max's lips.

'There's something you should know,' Tom went on, clambering out of bed. He took his blanket for modesty's sake, and perched on the side of Max's bed. He held his breath, afraid that he would be told, unequivocally, to go away. He wasn't.

'Yesterday, Cross made a comment about us. Well, me, really. He thinks I fancy you.'

'It's okay, I heard you put him straight, remember?' Max's expression was unreadable and there was a coolness in his voice, albeit a whisper.

'I'm gay.' Tom blurted it out.

Max frowned.

'I'm sure you guessed,' Tom went on, 'but I hadn't reckoned on Cross picking up on it, too. I made that horrid comment to put him off the scent.'

'Why?'

'What?'

'Why bother? What difference does it make, what he thinks?'

Tom bit his lip. 'I think *he* fancies you,' he admitted.

Max snorted. 'What?'

'Shh.' Tom put his finger to his lips, reminding Max that he'd just made a noise.

'Sorry, but—seriously?' Max looked incredulous.

'I can't be certain, but I'm afraid it's what his problem is. The team said he got quite personal about how you didn't want them around, and that you were sick and tired of them. That's not how a boss talks about his staff, no matter how friendly they are. I think Cross is jealous of the time you spent with them, and that's why he got rid of them—or tried to.'

Max frowned. Tom was desperate to elaborate. He also thought that Cross wanted them out of the way so they couldn't interfere with Max getting killed. It was clear they all felt close to Max, and would do anything to help him. That's just what Cross was afraid of. But he couldn't reveal that. Not yet, at least.

'I think you've got it wrong, mate,' Max whispered. 'But I'm really flattered—I think. Actually, no I'm not. It's a horrid thought. Cross is practically old enough to be my dad.' He sniggered, and Tom rolled his eyes.

'I might be barking up the wrong tree, but it's one theory,' he said.

Max shuddered. 'I'm glad you didn't tell me that last night—I'd have had nightmares,' he giggled, giving Tom a playful punch on the arm. 'I hope to God you're wrong,' Max whispered, a little more seriously. 'But what about Toby? Was he right?'

Tom thought for a minute before realising what he was asking.

He nodded. 'Yes,' he admitted.

Max came closer but Tom forced himself to pull back. Max frowned.

'Listen,' Tom whispered, softly. 'I really like you, and I'd like to see where things go, if you're up for it?'

Max nodded. 'Of course.'

Tom smiled with relief. 'But... I know this is going to sound really old-fashioned, but I don't want us to start anything just yet.' He noticed Max's face fall and immediately put his hand on his arm, causing him to look up again. 'I'm your employee right now, but only until the concert. After that, Sam can take over his old job.'

'What about you?' Max frowned again.

'I'll be around, of course, just not as your employee. Then we'll be free to do as we like. Do you get me?'

Max nodded slowly, a grin spreading across his face. 'You're too proud to sleep with the boss.'

Tom shrugged. 'Yep.'

'And does that include kissing the boss?'

'Yeah, I'm way too proud for that,' Tom told him. 'I never kiss anyone before I've brushed my teeth.'

Max threw a pillow at him, but Tom had already jumped off the bed and was heading for the bathroom.

𝄞

'We need the backing singers and musicians to meet us at the theatre for a rehearsal,' Max told Cross when they were all sitting at the breakfast table.

'I'll give them a call.'

'Is it the same people we had for the Manchester set?' Max asked before biting into his bacon.

'Yeah. They were okay, weren't they?' Cross enquired.

'Yeah, great.' Max looked much more relaxed than Tom expected, but then, he reckoned, the poor guy trusted Cross.

'What time can they get there?' Tom asked.

Cross gave him a derisory look. 'What's it to you?'

Tom rolled his eyes. 'We all need to be there. It's not just Max who'll be working tonight, you know?'

'Yeah, tonight, but not today. *You* don't need to be there for the rehearsal—unless you're seriously considering joining the singers?' Cross chortled.

'Haven't you read his CV?' Max frowned at Cross. 'Jack can sing.' He turned to face him. 'Actually, I'd really like you up on stage with me. What better position for a bodyguard than up there?' He beamed with excitement. 'What d'you reckon?'

'Don't go getting any ideas there, boss,' Sam interjected, placing his palms up.

'You're safe. I've heard your singing,' Max assured him with a chuckle.

'I rest my case. Carry on, Jack.' Sam laughed.

'Thanks, mate. I thought we were in this together,' Tom objected, playfully.

'We are. Right up until the time you get on that damn stage.' Sam sniggered.

'If you're desperate I'll go up there, but if all those professionals can manage without me, then I'd sooner watch over you from the wings, if you don't mind,' Tom told Max with a smile.

Max rolled his eyes in jest. 'I dunno. You were right—you just can't get the staff.'

'Hey, watch it,' they all chorused. Except Cross, of course, who wouldn't know a joke if one bit him on the bum.

'Right, we're going down in two cars today. Bernie, are you okay to drive the Range Rover?' Sam asked.

'Of course.' Bernie grinned.

'Great. You take Damon and Anna. Toby, you're with me, Max, and Jack.' Everyone nodded.

They finished up breakfast and then headed to the Apollo.

'I'm looking forward to meeting your backing singers and musicians,' Tom said, as they were driven in the direction of the river. 'Do you always have the same ones?'

'Mostly,' Max said with a nod. 'Although they do work with other people, too, so it's usually a case of booking them well in advance.'

'How much notice did you need to give them?' Tom asked, looking over at Cross.

'Enough.' He had a face like a bulldog chewing a wasp.

Max threw him a look, which Cross chose to ignore.

'I just wondered,' Tom said with a shrug.

'Why? You after my job next, is that it?' Cross grumbled.

'God, no. I wouldn't be any good at all that admin,' Tom said, putting his palms up. 'I take my hat off to anyone who can juggle everything like that. The responsibility to remember it all must be enormous.'

Cross snorted.

'Toby, that was a compliment,' Max told him.

'Yeah, right.'

Tom shook his head guessing that he had the older guy on the back foot. Cross didn't seem to know how to take him, and that was just the way he liked it.

Chapter Nine

If there was one thing Tom Fraser prided himself on, it was being prepared. So, when—surprise, surprise—the backing singers and the instrumentalists 'failed to turn up' he was able to offer a solution.

Knowing that Cross had done very little to organise the concert, he'd asked Ryan to source the necessary replacements. Of course, he had to make it look like it was *he* who managed to come up with the goods at the eleventh hour, thus is one of the perks of being undercover.

Another perk was that Ryan had already had the guys checked out before booking them, so there were no last-minute hold-ups, and Tom could be confident about their backgrounds.

'Thank God you've got contacts in the business,' Max said, sighing with relief once everyone was in place and the first couple of songs had been successful. He beamed at Tom gratefully.

'I have my uses.' Tom winked at him, making him giggle.

His phone buzzed, so Tom indicated to Sam to keep an eye on proceedings while he went to answer it. It was a message to call Ryan as soon as he had a minute.

'We've got news on that murder ring.'

'Go on.' Tom was now outside the back of the building.

'We've got the killer of the teacher, though it hasn't been announced yet.'

'That was quick.'

'He was an amateur. Struck too soon. Apparently someone was getting twitchy about another murder not happening on schedule so this guy was drafted in at the last minute. He was supposed to wait for further orders but saw an opportunity and took it.'

'Pettit's been trying to get hold of me.'

'You're playing a dangerous game, mate. These people are pure evil.'

'Has the guy been talking?'

'Yeah. Harrington got dumped by his husband, who then went on to die of AIDS, courtesy of his lover. Harrington had the lover killed.'

'And now he's working on the rest of the world?' Tom shook his head.

'Yeah. The guy's body—or, what was left of it—was found in a shallow grave up north.'

'Shit.'

'These people are brutal. The guy we've arrested said he's actually relieved to have been picked up by us before Pettit got hold of him. He still fears for his life.'

'Any clues where they're operating from?'

'We're homing in, but can't pinpoint them yet. We're also still trying to find out more about Harrington. I'll be in touch, but, for God's sake, be careful, mate.'

'Of course.' Tom hung up, just as he heard a sound behind him.

Cross was coming out of the side door.

'Making secret phone calls, eh?' The older guy sneered. He sauntered up to Tom, his hands on his hips.

'A man can have a private life.' Tom narrowed his eyes, wondering just how much he might have heard.

'Hmm. Seems there's lots of privacy and secrets surrounding you. Where was your last job again?'

'Right now I'm more concerned about my current one. We've got a concert to organise, remember? Oh no, you seem to have forgotten, haven't you? No singers, no musicians—and where's that security team you're supposed to have booked? Or did you manage to forget them, too?' Tom strode towards the door, but Cross barred his way.

'Funny how you managed to get fill-ins so quickly,' Cross sneered. 'And I didn't see you do one single security check on either of them.'

'I've worked with them before. All my contacts have been checked. What about this security outfit you're supposed to have booked? Have they all been checked?'

'Of course.'

'And where are they?'

'They'll be here.'

'You're running out of time, Cross. In case you hadn't noticed, this event happens tomorrow. When are you planning on detailing these guys? Introducing them to everyone who needs to know them?'

'It's all in hand.'

Tom threw him an incredulous look. 'Is it? What, like all those others you'd got organised?'

'Not my fault if they got a better offer.'

'Yeah, from who? You know any other big names out there with concerts tomorrow night and managers who failed to book the necessary back up?'

'Just keep out of my way.' Cross snarled at him before turning and going back into the building.

'It's you that's in *my* way, actually,' Tom said to the back of the guy's head. 'I saved your job for you and it turns out you haven't even been doing it. Just what the hell *have* you been doing with your time, old man?'

It hadn't been his intention to confront Cross right then, but Tom saw red. This guy was not only lazy, he was dangerous.

Cross turned around and took a step towards him, getting right in his face. 'Talking to our mutual friend,' he muttered. 'Turns out I'm not the only one who hasn't been doing their job.'

Tom stared at him. *He knows!* His whole body turned hot and he could hear his heart thumping. 'Yeah, but at least I *intend* to do my job,' he muttered back through gritted teeth.

Cross sniggered. 'Yeah, but which one?' With that he stalked back down the corridor, leaving Tom doing his best to steady his nerves.

Just how much does he know?

The atmosphere was electric the following day when they all returned to the theatre. Fortunately—or not—Cross' team of security guys actually turned up. Tom knew there was no point in asking if they'd all been checked, as Cross would only lie. There was a good chance they were all Pettit's men—Harrington could even be among them, for all he knew.

He'd received an enraged call from Pettit last night, following the lack of murder.

'Cross got in the way. What the hell does he know?' Tom had demanded.

Of course, Pettit denied involving the older man and threatened to kill Tom himself if he didn't get the job done today. Tom sensed the nervousness of the guy on the phone, and reported it to Ryan.

Grimley immediately instructed Bill to meet Tom at the café near the theatre, where they went into the gents' so Bill could wire Tom up. Although Tom was quite happy to accompany the other guy into a cubicle and strip off his shirt, Bill wasn't so keen.

'I'm just not used to this,' Bill complained in a harsh whisper.

'You haven't lived, mate,' Tom teased.

Although he'd never admit it, Tom felt a lot more secure knowing that he was wearing the wire, and could call for back-up at any time. He was half-expecting Pettit to show up and confront him before the start of the concert, but luckily there was no sign of him.

He'd toyed with the idea of a bullet-proof vest, but decided against it. Not only would it draw attention to himself, but it would also indicate that he was expecting trouble, which would surely unnerve the whole team. No, tonight had to go as smoothly as possible for everyone's sake—and that included the thousands of ticket-holders.

Ryan was posing as one of the theatre's own security team, located in the surveillance office to monitor the cameras. Having spotted Pettit among a group of about six other men, he was relaying his every move to Tom, who'd picked him out of the crowd and was surreptitiously keeping a close eye on him.

'I didn't realise it was a sell-out.' Max peeped around the side of the stage, his face shining with excitement.

'You're obviously more popular than you thought.' Tom wasn't about to tell the guy that he recognised a good number of the audience as undercover police officers interspersed among the crowd, most of them near to Pettit and his gang.

Max beamed, his confidence level visibly rising. 'Let's get on with the show.'

The crowd went wild when the music started up. They were soon on their feet, dancing along to the songs, and Max looked like he could burst with happiness. Tom was glad for him, he was clearly doing what he loved.

He looked over for Cross, but he'd already deserted his position.

'I've lost Cross,' he murmured into his hidden mic.

'He went behind stage.' Ryan was already onto him. 'He's on his phone.'

Tom's eyes immediately went to Pettit, who was talking with the guy next to him.

'Who to?'

'A woman.' It was Bill's voice this time. 'She's local.'

Tom raised his eyebrows. 'Personal?'

'Nope. He's confirming everything's in place.'

'We don't know of any women being involved in this racket,' Ryan interjected.

'She sounds well-ensconced in the operation,' Bill replied. 'Told him to keep a close eye on you, Tom.'

Finding out new information at this stage in the game was unnerving, to say the least. It made Tom wonder what else they didn't know.

The music was great and the audience lapped it up. Max hadn't stopped smiling since the curtain had risen, and Tom could tell it was genuine. His heart went out to the guy. It must be scary being so much in the public eye and then wondering if said public had all turned against you. Fame was a fickle thing, and Tom was glad he wasn't into the scene. A terrifying thought niggled at the back of his mind, though: if they became a couple after all this, as they were hoping, how the hell would he keep out of the limelight? Max was such a massive star, it would be impossible for his partner to go unnoticed. And after the scandal about the singer's sexuality, how would the public take to seeing him with his new partner?

There was no break in the middle of the set, and Tom was surprised how quickly the time went. He'd seen the schedule and knew Tom had two more songs, then he'd say a few words, the curtain would fall and then he'd be back for a two-song encore.

'Pettit's on the move,' Tom muttered into his mic, noticing the guy along with his entourage, making his way to the end of their row.

'Cross is outside,' Ryan offered.

'He's on the phone,' Bill said. 'The woman from earlier. We've traced her to West Kensington, there's a team on their way there now.'

Tom's heart hammered, but he managed a smile when Max looked over his way. He was beginning to wish he'd opted for the bullet-proof vest, after all. He just prayed nothing kicked off in the auditorium.

To the audience, nothing untoward was happening. To the trained eye, however, it was clear that a group of officers were following Pettit and three of his gang down the corridor that led to the gents'. Two officers were already in place, one in the cubicle and one by the sink.

In the auditorium, a female officer engaged one of Pettit's guys in conversation.

'Cross is on his way to the toilets,' Ryan reported, 'stand by'.

Officers were strewn between the auditorium and the gents, and a couple of Cross' security team were also patrolling the area. From the little information the police had managed to glean about those guys, they seemed clean, and there were no grounds for suspicion that they were involved with Pettit and Harrington. As for their professional credentials, it seemed not one of them was properly trained for the job, unfortunately.

'This is the last in the set.' Sam came over to Tom, smiling.

'Yep. Gone well, hasn't it?' Tom forced a smile.

'Thank God. He deserves this.' Sam smiled fondly at Max.

'You guys really like him, don't you?'

'Yeah, he's a good guy. Pity he's had such a rough ride.'

'Cross isn't the best person to offer advice to anyone,' Tom said with a nod.

'It's not just him. His mum doesn't help matters, either. She's always been against his sexuality and since her best friend lost her husband to AIDS she's been trying to convince Max to keep quiet about being gay.'

Tom frowned. 'But Max wouldn't listen?'

Sam shook his head. 'Not exactly. He just wasn't prepared to try to hide it. It was Toby who convinced him to make that announcement, saying it would ingratiate him more with his fans. His mum was one of the reasons Max was against it. He was right, too, his mum disowned him after it went into the press.'

'And it was Cross who made the announcement?'

'Oh yeah. Made out he was speaking on behalf of Max, of course. Max was devastated, especially about his mum. Cross has continued to insist it was the poor guy's idea all along. As if.'

'Get his mum's name,' Ryan urged into Tom's ear.

'So, his mum won't be here tonight? Do you know her name? I might check the ticket list, just in case,' Tom replied.

'Na. She wouldn't come. Max's birth name is Atherton, but his mum goes by her name of Smithson. Mary Smithson. I've never met her but Max still dotes on the woman.'

'Running it now,' Bill said.

'Cross is talking with Pettit. Sounds like its going to kick off right after the final song,' Ryan informed him through his earpiece.

The crowd let rip as the song ended and Max waited for them to quieten while he stood by the microphone. He couldn't have looked happier.

'They love him,' Sam said, smiling.

'Where did Damon and Bernie go?' Tom suddenly realised the guys weren't waiting in the opposite wing anymore.

'Must be out back,' Sam said with a frown. 'Anna's still there, I'll check with her.'

'We need to be ready when the curtain falls, in case Max needs anything,' Tom said, trying not to sound as concerned as he felt.

'I'm on it.' Sam disappeared through the back.

'Mary Smithson is good friends with a Gwendoline Mitchell,' Bill's voice came over the earpiece, in an urgent manner. 'Mitchell's maiden name is Harrington—and her nickname's Queenie.'

'Pettit's gang in the toilets are armed with pistols,' Ryan added quickly, 'and they're heading back to the auditorium.'

Chapter Ten

Tom felt like everything was happening in slow motion, while he scrambled his thoughts.

The curtain fell to raucous applause, following Max thanking the audience and band. There was a clatter as a couple of the musicians threw down their instruments and ran for the backstage toilets. Annabel rushed across the stage and took a towel and a clean tee-shirt to Max, who was covered in sweat, but beaming. Tom noticed him look around for him, his eyes shining.

'Pettit and the gang are getting back to their seats,' Ryan said.

Tom ran over to Max, catching a glimpse of his ripped chest as Annabel rubbed a towel across his body before helping him on with the shirt.

'Need anything?' Tom asked.

Max offered him a wink, making them both chuckle. 'Later,' he murmured.

Annabel shook her head, rolling her eyes at them with a smile.

'Two songs is your limit,' Tom told Max, as the musicians quickly resumed their positions.

'Okay boss.' Max grinned.

'You're learning,' Tom replied before making a hasty retreat back to his position in the wings.

'Cross is coming to find you,' Ryan said into Tom's ear. 'He's been told to keep an eye on you until they make their move. He's coming up the corridor now.

Tom swiftly dodged behind the screen to the back of him and headed towards the largest dressing room. With any luck, he could keep any action away from the stage, especially while Max was still performing. He just prayed the guy had taken him seriously about not prolonging the encore.

The room was in darkness, but Tom could still smell the feint scent of Max's aftershave hanging in the air. He switched on the mirror lights and delved into the holdall on the chair. His heartbeat nearly deafened him as he reached in and took out Max's spare towel and stuffed the rest of his belongings into the bag.

'What the hell d'you think you're up to?'

As predicted, Cross found him.

'Getting Max's stuff ready for when he comes off stage.' He didn't even look at Cross, and tried to ignore the guy's sneer. 'Have you got the cars waiting?'

Cross frowned.

'Oh, come on. You know the drill. We get him out of here as soon as he leaves the stage. We'll never get him home otherwise. Have you seen how many people are out there?' Tom somehow managed to keep the tremble from his voice.

Damon came into the room. 'He's on the last number.'

'Great. Can you take this out to the car? We need him out of here as soon as he comes off.' Tom handed him the holdall, then followed him out the room.

'Just what's your game?' Cross snarled from behind him.

'I could ask you the same thing.' Tom went back to his position in the wing, aware of the older man following. He just prayed Cross wasn't armed under that jacket, for Max's sake.

'How long does it usually take to get him to the car?' Tom whispered, nudging Cross. He could feel there was no gun on the guy's left side and, as his jacket momentarily opened on the right, he was glad there was nothing there, either. He'd have seen it under his arm, and the jacket would be too heavy to swing open if it were in the pocket.

'Depends.' Cross was his usual, unhelpful self.

'Everyone in position,' Ryan instructed, as the curtain descended.

'Let's go.' Tom ran over to Max, closely followed by Cross.

'I need to pee,' Max insisted.

'There's no time, mate.' Tom ushered him across the stage and down the steps at the back.

'My stuff.'

'It's in the car.'

Damon was already in the back of the car when Tom pushed Max inside, and Annabel climbed in after, while Tom yelled to Roland to start driving.

'Aren't you coming?'

'I'll follow on,' Tom promised. 'Go.' He slammed the door, aware of another car waiting with its engine running just up the alley. The car pulled out in front of Roland, and another joined from behind before they reached the road.

'What the…?' Cross had clearly noticed the cars, too.

'Who the hell's that?' Tom was good at bluffing. He frowned.

'Someone's following them.' Cross was clearly a fan of Captain Obvious.

'Is it staff?'

'I fucking hope so.' Cross scowled as the car's lights disappeared, 'Or Max is in big trouble.'

'What do you care?' Tom mumbled, just loud enough to be heard.

'Has he gone?' Bernie came running out the back of the building. 'The fans're starting to swarm the front of the driveway.'

'Yeah,' Cross replied, authoritatively. His phone buzzed and he stepped away to check it.

'I think Pettit's looking for you,' Ryan said into Tom's ear. 'You'd better get back inside.'

Tom did as he was told, as casually as he could. He bumped into one of the roadies carrying a large, black case. 'Great gig.' He nodded at the guy, standing back to let him through.

'One of the best.' The guy said, smiling. He got as far as the door when Cross tried to get in.

'Out of my way, you imbecile.' Cross shouted.

'Fuck off.' The guy barged through, forcing Cross to back out of the door and give way to him.

Tom heard the two of them arguing, but ignored it and went back up to the wing of the stage to peer through the side screen.

Most of the audience had left, but Pettit and his gang were down in the standing area, probably waiting for him. Several other people were milling about, some dressed casually, chatting while clearly en route to the door, while others were smartly dressed, some with clip-boards. Tom smirked, guessing they were all his colleagues from the station.

'We've got the building surrounded. Cross has just come in the back,' Ryan was saying. 'Stay out of sight as much as you can, but don't go backstage. We can't get enough back-up down there without it looking obvious.

'He let him go,' one of the men shouted over to Pettit. Tom guessed he was the one who just rang Cross.

'Find him!' Pettit was furious, as he looked around the room.

Hearing Cross behind him, Tom grabbed a sheet of paper and stepped out onto the stage, as though reading it. His heart was in his mouth as he glanced over to see Pettit and the gang heading for him.

'They've just arrested Harrington,' Ryan said into his ear. 'Take it easy, mate.'

Cross rushed out from behind a side screen, coming up behind Tom.

As Tom turned to face him, Cross ran at him, a knife in his hand and hatred in his eyes.

Tom grabbed the guy's arm, but the blade was longer than he'd hoped and pointing towards his neck. Cross' arm shook, but he held onto the handle for grim death. Tom's death.

'Don't stop.' Pettit ran onto the stage, a gun in his hand, also pointing at Tom.

'We've got you covered,' Ryan's words were music to Tom's ears. For a fraction of a second, he really thought he'd been forgotten.

'We're waiting,' Pettit urged Cross, menacingly.

'Can't you just shoot him?' Cross' voice was strangled as he struggled against Tom's grip.

'Where would be the fun in that?' Pettit sneered.

'He's saving the bullet for you, you fool,' Tom spat out, having already guessed Pettit's game.

He felt Cross' body sag very slightly as his words sank in, and at the same time there was a kerfuffle in the standing area in front of the stage.

Tom hoped it was the police making their presence known to Pettit's gang, but there was no time to look as he seized the opportunity to twist Cross' arm as he squeezed it, causing the guy to drop the knife. Pettit stepped forward to retrieve the knife, but Tom was too quick for him. Grabbing the handle, he stabbed the blade into Pettit's leg, causing the guy to howl and fire his gun into the air as he stooped down to nurse his injury.

A couple of lights rained down in pieces, but two officers hit the stage before they did, both with guns pointing at Pettit. They must have been waiting in the wings.

Tom snatched the gun from Pettit's trembling hand before one of his colleagues pulled the guy's arms behind his back and cuffed him.

Adrenalin pumped through Tom as he looked around to see the cops leading away the whole gang. The other officer on the stage cuffed Cross, who was puffing like a steam engine, clearly in shock.

'I didn't do anything,' he wheezed.

'Not for the want of trying,' the officer barked at him, before pushing him towards the side of the stage and down the steps.

'You okay, mate?' Ryan's calm voice was in Tom's ear again.

'Yeah. Did Max get back all right?'

'Yep. The escort reported that they're all back inside having a stiff drink. A couple of officers stayed with them to explain what was going on. Looks like you might be offered a permanent job over there when they hear what a hero you are.' He chuckled.

'Nah. I already resigned,' he assured his friend.

'Now that's interesting, I want to hear more.' There was click as Ryan disconnected the equipment, and Tom chuckled, guessing he was on his way.

Inspector Grimley ambled towards him as Tom climbed down from the stage, pleased to see that nearly everyone else had gone by now.

'Fucking hell, Fraser!'

'Thank you, sir.' Tom shook hands with his boss.

'I want you in my office tomorrow,' Grimley told him.

'But it's Sunday tomorrow,' Tom moaned, knowing full well it would do no good.

'So? You're lucky I'm not taking you back with me tonight.'

'Oh, sorry to interrupt.' Ryan joined them with a big grin on his face.

'You know what I mean.' Grimley actually looked embarrassed.

'Oh sir, don't spoil it,' Tom teased. 'I thought it was my lucky night.'

Grimley took a step backwards. 'Eleven sharp tomorrow. Both of you,' he barked at them, shaking his head as he made for the door.

Ryan put an arm around Tom, as they giggled. 'I've got to admit I was worried for a second back there,' he told him. 'Pettit's a nasty piece of work. You were right about Cross being his next victim.'

Tom nodded. 'I guessed.'

'You need a lift back to the house?' Ryan offered, pulling out his car keys.

'Thanks, mate.'

Tom could hear loud voices as he walked up the path to the house. A mixture of excitement and horror. Who could blame them?

The curtain twitched and Annabel waved from the window. 'He's here,' she called to the others, who crowded around the door.

'Everyone okay?' he checked as he joined them.

'Christ, man, I've been worried sick,' Max said, going over to put an arm around his shoulder. 'What the hell happened to you?' He stared at Tom's shirt and it was only then that the cop realised he had blood splashed up his front.

'It's all right, that's Pettit's,' he assured Max.

He felt the guy relax in his arms.

'The cops told us what was going on when we got back here,' Damon explained, as they all sat in the living room. He offered Tom a beer.

'No thanks.'

'Not while you're on duty, eh?' Bernie piped up, with a knowing look.

Max stiffened beside him and Tom swallowed hard.

'My name's Tom Fraser,' he said, slowly.

'We know.' Max sounded a little pissed off.

'I was undercover to save you from getting killed. Pettit hired me to murder you, on Harrington's orders.'

'Queenie.' Max nodded. '*Auntie* Queenie, when I was a kid.'

'I heard she was a friend of you mum,' Tom went on, warily.

'Her husband, my so-called Uncle Harry, left her for a man who gave him AIDS that killed him. I think Queenie went a bit mad after that.' Max shook his head. 'She still loved him.'

'It must have been hard.' Tom accepted a glass of orange juice from Annabel, who was also handing out more drinks to the others.

'The hardest part was when she got to my mum.' Max shook his head, ruefully.

'Mum knew I was gay, but Queenie managed to convince her that we were all evil killers. In fact, that cop said it was Queenie who was the killer. Killer Queen. Who'd have thought it?' He gave a huff.

'Kill-a-queen. Killer Queen,' Tom muttered. 'We thought Harrington was a man, at first. No wonder it took so long to track her down.'

'Do you think your mum was involved, then?' Bernie asked with a frown.

'No.' Max was adamant. 'The cops have already interviewed her. She had nothing to do with it—she was horrified when she heard what her so-called friend had been up to, and that she'd planned my murder. I've already had a message from her. She wants me to meet her for lunch tomorrow. Said she's hoping to build some bridges.'

'That's great news,' Tom said, giving the guy a quick hug.

'Yeah, I'm looking forward to seeing her.' Max smiled.

'Queenie probably went after you because it was too close to home, you being the son of her best friend, and all.' Sam spoke softly.

'That cop said she was trying to target gays in prominent places, so that puts you right up there,' Annabel added. 'Judging by your support tonight, your death would have devastated a lot of people. It's a good job she failed.'

'Was Toby in on it?' Sam turned to Tom.

'He knew Pettit had hired someone to kill Max,' Tom admitted, 'and he eventually guessed it was me. I think Pettit pressured him to make sure I did it, that's why he pulled a knife on me.'

'A knife?' Max's eyes went wide.

'He didn't hurt me,' Tom assured him, rubbing a hand over Max's knee. 'But Pettit wanted him to. Trouble is, Cross didn't seem to realise he was being played. Pettit would've killed him next.'

'I knew Toby was stupid but I never took him for dangerous,' Sam said with a whistle.

'Yeah, and just how thick does that make me? I had no idea Toby was involved in anything like that.' Max shook his head.

'You weren't to know. You just trusted him, that's all.' Tom squeezed his arm. He was taken by how vulnerable the rock star appeared, and realised that, despite the fame and everything that went with it, the guy was as insecure as anyone else. He smiled to himself. Charlie had never seemed insecure or vulnerable. That might have been why his death was such a shock. His heart had been a ticking time-bomb, the elephant in the room. For the first time since losing him, Tom actually felt content, happy.

Max narrowed his eyes at Tom, clearly unconvinced. 'No wonder you don't want to work for me anymore.'

Tom smiled, shaking his head. 'It's got nothing to do with that, and you know it. Sam's your bodyguard, remember?'

'So, what does that make *you*?' Max's big eyes widened with hope as he spoke.

'Why don't we discuss that upstairs?' Tom winked, stood up and reached for his hand.

THE END

Marching Offsides

by

AM Williams

College football, hot jocks, and…a band nerd? Camden is in the marching band, but doesn't understand football. She plays her music and calls it a day. But when she's paired with King University's star quarterback for a class project, she discovers that football might not be all that confusing. Jackson is the big man on campus and star quarterback. People love him and flock to wherever he is. He doesn't realize how much he hates it until he meets Camden, a girl that acts like she doesn't know who he is. Can two people from different social groups overcome the expectations placed on them to find true love?

Chapter One
Camden

Camden couldn't believe her luck. She also couldn't decide if her luck was good or bad.

She was leaning toward bad.

She climbed the stairs in the library, dragging her feet as she walked toward the study room in which Jackson Dove, starting quarterback and big man on campus, would be waiting for her. She felt sick just thinking about it.

Of all the things she thought would happen while she was in college, working with the quarterback in a class was not one of them.

The study rooms came into view and she slowed to a stop.

She knew she was acting crazy. She felt crazy too.

She didn't know Jackson. She'd never had a class with him. She'd never talked to him before. The closest she'd ever gotten to him was when she was at the football games with the marching band.

She was one of the girls that hung out in the background and she was fine with that. Really. She didn't want to be in the spotlight with people looking at her.

She was fine with her band nerd existence.

Except… now she probably wouldn't be able to avoid some of it.

People flocked to Jackson. He simply existed and people wanted to be him and be around him.

She saw it the other day in class when they were exchanging information for their project and people came up. They ignored her, pushing her out of the way, even though she'd been there first.

It was a weird experience for her and one she couldn't say was remotely pleasant.

She shook her head and blew out a long breath. Standing creepily outside the study rooms wouldn't change anything that had happened.

So what? It was Jackson Dove, the most popular guy at King University. He was just a guy.

A guy that was rumored to be going pro after he graduated.

A guy that was rumored to be one of the nicest guys on campus.

A guy that was rumored to have done all sorts of things at the football parties.

She huffed out another breath. There was nothing special about him.

She forced herself to take a step, and then another one. She glanced in the rooms as she went by, taking in the groups that were working diligently.

When she reached their room, the last one on the row, she paused just out of view of the doorway.

Jackson was already there, his books on the table, a notebook open with a pen lying on a blank page.

That wasn't what got her attention though.

It was the other person in the room.

Camden thought it was one of the head dancers, but she couldn't be certain. She only knew what the dancers looked like because they would sometimes practice with the band when they were getting ready for an upcoming halftime show.

Her palms started sweating as she watched Jackson and the girl. They weren't doing anything x-rated or inappropriate, but Camden really didn't want to go in there. Jackson looked relaxed, but the girl was practically sitting in his lap and was leaning into him. She shuddered to think of what they might start doing in a few minutes. That doubly made her want to turn and flee.

She needed to go in, though. She and Jackson had a project to work on and she didn't want to have to spend more time than necessary working with him.

She threw her shoulders back and stepped into the room, flashing Jackson a brief smile before dropping her bag into a chair and unzipping it.

"Who are you?" the girl asked.

Camden glanced at her and saw that her eyes had narrowed as they scraped over Camden.

She tried not to glower as the girl looked her over, making her skin crawl. It was obvious this girl was staking her claim.

"Lisa, really?"

Lisa flicked her gaze to Jackson, and she visibly melted, which allowed Camden to breathe a sigh of relief.

"I just don't know this girl and I don't want some random person coming up to you and taking advantage."

Jackson chuckled and Camden tried hard to not pay attention to what he was saying to Lisa, but it was hard considering they were all in a room together.

"Random person? I told you I was working with someone on a project. You think some random girl would come in here?"

"Well, no…"

"Exactly. Besides, you have no say in who I spend my time with."

Camden's eyes widened at Jackson's words and she kept her gaze pinned to the things she was pulling out of her bag. She really didn't want to be here for this conversation, which had now taken a very awkward turn.

Lisa huffed. "Really, Jackson?"

"Really, Lisa. We're not dating."

Camden glanced out of the corner of her eye toward the duo and studied their body language.

Jackson still looked relaxed as he leaned back in his chair while Lisa looked like she was ready to claw his eyes out.

Her shoulders were high and tight around her ears and her face was growing red in what she could only imagine was embarrassment. Camden was sure Lisa was going to blow a gasket any moment now, and she was debating abandoning her stuff there and going down to the coffee shop on the first floor to give them a minute to finish their conversation.

"You need to go," Jackson said.

What he said wasn't really the problem, though it wasn't nice; it was how he said it that had the hair on the back of Camden's neck standing on end.

His voice was devoid of emotion and there was a flatness to it that seemed to warn Lisa of what might happen next if she didn't leave.

"I need to get to work with my partner."

Lisa huffed and started muttering under her breath as she finally stood and left the room.

The heaviness of the air dissipated as soon as Lisa walked out and Camden tried not to sag with relief.

She wasn't one for confrontation. She'd rather walk away and hope that the problem would go away than face it head on. But she didn't think Lisa felt the same.

"Sorry about her," Jackson said, pulling Camden's attention to him.

Camden shrugged. "Don't worry about it. You don't need to apologize for her. I didn't mind waiting."

"You shouldn't have to. We're here to work together and she was encroaching on our time."

Camden made a non-committal sound as she pulled out a chair and sat down. She looked at Jackson again and saw him smirking at her.

"What?"

"Why are you all the way over there?" he asked, gathering his things together and sliding a few chairs over so that there was only a chair between the two of them.

Her face heated. "No reason."

Jackson chuckled, but said nothing.

"Okay, so our topic is…"

Jackson pulled the assignment sheet toward him and quickly read it aloud. Camden wasn't paying attention to what he was saying. She was too busy looking at him and trying to calm herself down.

Jackson Dove was sitting close enough that she could touch him and she was trying not to freak out.

He had bright blue eyes that crinkled at the edges when he smiled. Sharp cheekbones accentuated a face that was handsome to look at. He had a nice and easy smile. In fact, she couldn't recall a time when he wasn't smiling.

He had dark hair that he kept a little long, the ends curling over his ears and the collar of his shirt.

He was hot in that all-American way. He looked like the boy next door.

And she was perilously close to acting like a stalker. She needed to snap out of it.

She forced herself to pay attention to what he was saying and gave her own ideas for their group project.

She was an education major and was just starting out with her low-level education classes. Jackson was one too, which wasn't something she knew about him.

They were paired up—randomly—to complete a lesson plan unit on a subject of their choosing.

She was really excited to be in the class and working on the project. It was the working with Jackson that she was unsure about and that was mainly because she didn't know him and he didn't know her. What if they didn't work well together, and they bombed this assignment?

It was the start of a new year, which meant football season was in full swing. Would that impact their working together? Would he flake off because of practice and games? She hoped not, but she'd have to wait and see what turned up with it.

They spent the next hour listing different topics and narrowing it down to five different ones.

"So we'll meet up next week with our research and figure out what one to do?"

Camden nodded. "Yeah, sounds good."

Jackson smiled and opened his mouth to say something, but was stopped when someone spoke from the door. "Jackson, my man. I found you!"

"You found me." Camden's eye twitched when she heard the tone of his voice. Much like earlier, his tone was flat, but she could hear some happiness in there.

Camden worked on getting her things back into her bag and checked the time, wincing when she saw how late it was. She only had thirty minutes before she needed to be at band practice, which meant she wouldn't have enough time to run to her on campus apartment and drop her stuff off.

She sighed as she heaved her book bag on, wishing she'd paid more attention.

"See you Thursday," Jackson said as she stepped out of the room.

She raised a hand in a wave and tried to ignore the knifelike prick in her chest when she heard the question out of the guy that joined them at the end. "Who's the chick?"

She hurried away, not wanting to hear Jackson's response.

Chapter Two
Camden

"You're cutting it close today," Corey, one of her roommates, said as Camden yanked her locker open.

"I know, I know. My study session ran a little over."

"Oh, really? Do tell. And I'm being serious. Tell me all about it. You've been mum about this study thing you have going on."

Camden shrugged. "Not much to tell. I have a group project in my lesson planning class and we're trying to get a head start on it."

"Hmmm…" Corey said and Camden didn't have to look at her to know that Corey was studying Camden and her body language. "I think you're hiding something. You've got that look you had about you freshman year right after the seniors hazed you."

Camden cut her eyes to Corey. "Really? You're going to bring that up right now?"

Corey shrugged and turned back to her locker, flicking her long brown hair over her shoulder. "I'm just saying. You look like there's something you don't want to talk about and it mimics the look you wore then. You'll talk to me when you're ready. Now, come on. The dance team is here today to do some run-throughs with us."

Camden groaned and banged her head against her locker. That so wasn't what she needed. With her luck, Lisa would see her and recognize her. She'd probably say something to Camden, which would draw the attention of the other band members and possibly even the instructor. She really didn't want to deal with that shit right then.

As she walked outside with Corey toward the practice field, she hoped that she would be lucky enough to avoid Lisa and whatever cattiness she might throw her way.

Upon arriving at the practice field, she breathed a sigh of relief when she saw that the dance team was already stretching on the other side of the field. Camden hurried to join the band and tried to get toward the middle.

They ran through their scales to warm up before getting into formation and running through their show for the upcoming football game. It was the first home game of the season and they had a lot of new people in the band this year, so it was simple.

It was a variation on one they'd done the previous two years, so she could let her mind wander while they went through the steps.

The dance team eventually joined them and they switched over to some of their pep band songs to make sure their timing was right.

Once that was done, they did one more run-through of the halftime show before they were released.

Camden sagged with relief. She was hot and sweaty and more than ready to head back to her place for something to eat and a nice shower. She needed to make sure she paid attention more so she didn't have another day like today.

"You, girl," she heard from behind her.

She ignored the voice, assuming it wasn't directed at her, her mind focused only on getting home.

"Hey, I'm talking to you!"

A hand gripped her right bicep and yanked her off balance.

"What the—" she yelped as she was jerked around to face a fuming Lisa.

"What's your problem?" Camden asked, pulling her arm from Lisa's vice-like grip. She rubbed her bicep and checked her skin. Lisa had a tight grip, and she worried she'd bruised her.

"My problem is you. You were ignoring me."

Lisa glared at her and Camden's eyes widened. "What?"

"You heard me calling to you and you kept right on walking."

Camden snorted in disbelief. "I heard you say something ambiguous and kept walking because I didn't think you meant me. I have a name. If you'd used it, I would have stopped."

Camden went to turn around, but was stopped again by Lisa grabbing her arm.

"Don't walk away from me."

Camden glanced around and saw that they were drawing a crowd. "Don't grab me. What's your problem? I don't even know you, so I'm not sure why you want to talk to me."

"I want to talk to you about Jackson."

Camden's face screwed up in confusion. "What? Why? I don't even know the guy."

Lisa laughed and shook her head, tossing her hair over her shoulder. "You think that innocent act will work on me? I see through that shit. You have that wide-eyed doe look about you. I bet you've been waiting for this opportunity for years and think this is your chance. I'm here to tell you it won't work."

Camden's eyes got wider the more Lisa talked. "What the fuck is your problem?" Camden burst out. "We were assigned as partners, that's it. I just want to get a good grade."

Lisa rolled her eyes and cocked a hip to the side as she crossed her arms over her chest. "Puh-lease. All girls are the same with him. You think that because you get some mandated alone time with him for a class that it'll make a difference in your relationship and status at the school. It won't. You're just a band nerd and he'll never look twice at you."

"What's the problem here?" Dr. Foster said as he pushed through the crowd of students surrounding her and Lisa. "I could hear you inside the building."

She glared at Lisa, who cowered slightly before suddenly standing tall again. She smirked at Camden and said, "This girl tried to start something with me."

Camden's mouth dropped open. "I did not! I was walking away when you grabbed me and started going on about something I don't care about!" She held her arm out, which was still red from where Lisa grabbed her.

Camden glared at Lisa, who glared back. Dr. Foster looked between the two of them. "Right. This is what we're going to do. You're both going to leave and avoid each other. I don't want to hear anything more about the two of you and we'll call it done. If I or someone else has to deal with the two of you again, you'll be dealing with me and the dance coach. Understood?"

Camden nodded, as did Lisa, and Dr. Foster walked away.

Lisa huffed before stomping away.

"Jeez," Corey said, coming to stand next to her. "What crawled up her ass and died?"

Camden shrugged. "No idea."

She had an idea, but she wasn't too sure she wanted to voice it right then. There was still a large group of people clustered around them and she didn't want to give any more fuel to what had just happened.

Camden pushed through the crowd and to her locker, quickly gathering her stuff and putting her flute away. She tapped her foot as she waited for Corey to get her things before almost jogging to get away from the band, most of whom were still staring at her.

"Wait, slow down!" Corey said, panting slightly as she jogged to catch up. "Did Lisa bother you that much?"

Camden glanced around and breathed a sigh of relief when she saw there were far enough away from the band building that they were almost to the main quad. She didn't have to worry as much about someone hearing what she was about to say.

"How much did you hear?"

"Just the part when Dr. Foster came out. What was that about anyway?"

Camden concentrated on the concrete sidewalk as she tried to figure out what to say. "Lisa came to talk to me about my study group."

"Okayyy..." Corey said, drawing the y-sound out. "Why?"

Camden sighed and stopped walking. She looked at her best friend and said, "Because my partner is Jackson Dove."

Corey blinked at her blandly for a few moments before her mouth dropped open and her eyes widened. "Jackson Dove? As in the star quarterback for the university and the hottest guy on campus?"

Camden gave a short nod. Corey's mouth opened and closed a few times with no sound coming out. "Why didn't you tell me?" she finally asked.

Camden shrugged. "I don't know. I didn't want it getting out. You know how people can be. Lisa is a perfect example of that."

Corey stared at her for a few moments before she said, "I think you need to start at the beginning and tell me what happened today."

They started walking again and Camden spent the rest of the ten-minute walk telling Corey what happened from when she got to the study room and until Dr. Foster came out.

Corey said nothing immediately. As they scanned their ID cards to get into their building, Corey finally said, "You're fucked."

Chapter Three
Jackson

Jackson stood on the sidelines and watched the second string quarterback run through some plays with his offensive line.

The guy was good, he'd give him that. But he wasn't as good as Jackson, which was why he wasn't worried as he watched them line up again. The only way Roscoe would get playing time was if Jackson got injured or they were creaming their opponent.

"Dove!"

He jerked his head to the right and saw his head coach standing there, glowering at him. Coach Smith jerked his head and Jackson knew he was being called over.

He ambled over, slapping hands with a few teammates as he went by until he was standing next to his coach, who was watching the action on the field.

"What's this I hear about a cat fight involving you?"

Jackson's brows rose, and he looked at the coach. "What? A cat fight?"

Smith jerked around to face Jackson and glowered. "I just got a phone call from the band director. Apparently two girls were having an argument about you at practice and he wanted to tell me to handle it. He didn't need one of his best musicians getting distracted by the likes of you."

Jackson's mouth fell open. He honestly didn't know what to say. He had no idea what two girls the coach was talking about and he made a point to not get involved with girls who were filled with drama.

"I don't know who you're talking about, Coach. I'm not seeing anyone."

Smith glared harder, if that was possible, and Jackson felt a small bead of sweat work its way down his back. Smith was a hard coach, but he was fair. Jackson had never had a run-in with him like some other guys on the team. He kept his nose clean and concentrated on getting good grades and staying out of trouble. He didn't want to ruin his chances of going pro because he stuck his dick somewhere he shouldn't have or because he got in trouble.

"You need to talk to whoever the fuck it is that's doing this, then. This is a big year. I need you focused on the game and staying on top of your grades and not chasing some loose pussy around campus."

Jackson nodded and just barely stopped his lip from curling in disgust. His coach was old school and had no issues speaking his mind. It was something Jackson appreciated. But he really didn't like how he talked about women.

"Go on and shower off. Figure out who you need to talk to. Foster said it was some dance chick and a flute player."

Jackson's brow furrowed as he turned toward the locker room. He pulled his practice jersey off and dropped it into the bin by the door and started unbuckling his pads as he considered what Smith had said.

It was obvious who the dance team member was. Lisa. There was no doubt in his mind that she'd started something with someone. He shook his head as he thought about the girl. They'd ended up working at the same marina this past summer and partied together a few times.

But she was interested in riding his dick and he wasn't so interested in her doing that. She was shallow and mean, two qualities that he didn't particularly care for in a girl. He had shown no interest in her besides being friendly. But she seemed to take that as meaning they would get together, especially now that they were back at school.

The other person who coach mentioned was the one he wasn't sure about. He didn't know anyone in the band that might talk to Lisa about him. He tried to think of the band and all he could call to mind were their uniforms and where they sat at the games he played.

It didn't make sense.

He pulled his pads off and dumped them in his locker before stripping the rest of the way down and grabbing his shower gear. He showered quickly before throwing his clothes on and walking out of the locker room, still pondering the second girl.

He pulled his phone out and did a quick search on the school's website, finding the webpage for the marching band. He navigated to the page that pictured the different sections and looked over the faces.

A few looked familiar, making him think they'd probably had classes together at some point. But it wasn't until he got to the picture with the flutists that he paused.

The smiling face of his partner greeted him. Camden North. She was in the band.

His mind flashed back to what happened at the library earlier, and he closed his eyes as he groaned. He should have known that Lisa would try something. He had no idea that Camden was in the pep band, otherwise he would have tried to warn her.

"Fuck," he said as he exited out of his browser and pulled up his text messages.

He went to the thread with Camden and quickly typed out a message.

Jackson: Where are you?

He stuffed his phone back in his pocket and started walking toward the edge of campus where the football house was. Technically, only seniors were supposed to live there, but because he was the starting quarterback, they let him move in his sophomore year.

His phone dinged, and he pulled it out to see that Camden had responded to him.

Camden: At home. Why?

Jackson: Where do you live?

Camden: Why?

Jackson: I need to talk to you in person.

He watched the three dots jump on the screen before disappearing. They started again before stopping. Finally, she responded with her building and he saw that she wasn't that far from him, so he turned toward where she was and continued walking.

He passed several people that recognized him and called a greeting. He nodded and smiled, but didn't stop to chat. Normally he wouldn't mind someone stopping him to talk about an upcoming game, but he needed to talk to Camden to figure out what the deal was with Lisa.

A part of him knew that he didn't have to talk to her right then. He'd see her in two day's time and that wouldn't make a difference in anything. But he couldn't help but worry about what had gone down. He wanted to make sure Lisa hadn't tried something, and that Camden was okay.

He had no idea why he felt that way about the situation. He didn't even know Camden. He was sure he'd never seen her before they had class the previous week and were paired up together.

The only time he'd had a conversation with her had been earlier at the library when they got together to work on their project. And all he got from that was that she was nice and easy to talk to. She hadn't brought up football or anything related to that. In fact, she seemed to not even know who he was.

He hadn't realized how refreshing it was until she had already left and Jones had found him in the room with her.

Yeah, he didn't know her, but she intrigued the fuck out of him.

He saw her building and sent a quick text to let her know he was outside.

As he drew up to the front door, he saw it open and Camden stepped out.

She was looking down at her phone, so he used the opportunity to quickly scan her.

She'd changed from earlier and was now wearing a pair of yoga pants and a loose t-shirt. She'd pulled her hair back into a messy bun. It didn't look like she was wearing makeup, but he didn't think she'd been wearing any earlier to begin with.

She was sexy in a subtle way and he wondered how he didn't realize that earlier in the day when they were studying together.

"Hey," he said as he drew closer.

Camden looked up and smiled at him. "Hey, yourself. What's up?"

He glanced around and saw that there weren't many people nearby. He was grateful because he wasn't sure how this conversation was going to go. He didn't know Camden well enough to know if she would freak out about what he was going to say or if she'd be stoic.

"Sooo..." he said, stuffing his hands in his front pockets and rocking on his feet. "Coach approached me today about something that happened between Lisa and someone in the band."

He was a believer in straight-shooting and putting things out there. He probably could have been better at easing her into the conversation, but it was out there and they could talk about it now.

Camden's eyes widened and her face grew red. "Wh—what?"

He licked his lips and glanced away briefly before looking back at Camden. "The band instructor called my coach and said that two chicks got into an argument about me at the end of band practice today."

Camden's mouth opened and closed a few times and he could practically hear the gears turning in her head. He remained silent and let her work through things and figure out what to say.

She finally cleared her throat and patted a hand along her hair before asking, "Why'd he call?"

Jackson shrugged and lowered his gaze. "I'm not entirely sure. But I guess he thought it was bad enough that I needed to handle it? He didn't give details; just said that it needed to be fixed."

Camden sighed and brought her hands up to her face. "Oh my, God. I can't believe this is happening."

He looked at her and smiled when he saw that she was freaking out. He couldn't help it. It was kind of cute.

"So what happened?"

Camden blew out a loud breath and waved toward a bench outside the door. "You might want to sit."

He shrugged and dropped his bag to the ground before sitting and turning toward her.

He listened as Camden told him what happened with Lisa. The more he heard, the angrier with Lisa he grew. He couldn't believe that she'd had to nerve to go up to someone and threaten her because she was a jealous bitch.

"Are you okay?" he asked when she finished.

"Yeah, I'm fine. More surprised and shocked than anything, you know?"

Jackson nodded and ran a hand through his hair. "I'm sorry she said something to you. We're not dating. Never have, never will."

"You don't have to apologize or explain anything to me," Camden said when he took a breath. "Really. I don't know why she came up to me about you considering we only have class together and today is the first time we've really talked to each other. I'm sure it'll blow over."

Jackson wasn't so sure, but he nodded his head. "Okay, if you think so. Let me know if there are issues."

Camden nodded. "Oh, for sure."

He was sure she was placating him at the moment. That was fine. He had ways of finding out what was going on if she wouldn't tell him. But she didn't need to know that.

"Well," he said as he stood and grabbed his bag. "I guess I'll see you Thursday."

"Yep, Thursday."

He nodded to her and turned to walk home.

As he walked, he turned over the brief conversation with Camden in his mind. She was like no other girl that he'd met. He knew that she knew who he was now, but she still hadn't acted like it mattered.

He couldn't decide if his ego was wounded because of it or he liked that she acted that way.

He knew working with her would be something else, that was for sure. He couldn't wait to see what the semester held.

Chapter Four
Camden

After how the week started, Camden fully expected the rest of the week to follow in a similar fashion. She was surprised when it didn't. Lisa glared at her whenever she saw her, while Camden just ignored her.

She talked to Jackson briefly in class, but they hadn't texted each other again.

By the time she was getting into the stands for the game Saturday, she'd put what happened from her mind. She wouldn't forget what happened with Lisa earlier in the week, but she wouldn't dwell on it either.

She rarely ran into Lisa in the normal course of her day, so she doubted that was going to change, which helped ease some of the nerves she had about the girl.

She stashed her things below her seat before grabbing her flute and making her way down to the field for their opening show.

It was the first home football game of the season, so the stands were packed and a dull roar sounded all around her.

The university was crazy about its football team. They were good and from what she understood—which wasn't much—they were predicted to go far this season. She wasn't too sure what far meant, but she knew it was important because it hyped people up to see how this game went and to see how Jackson played.

As they drew closer to the game, it was all the people on campus could talk about.

While waiting for coffee, the baristas discussed it.

While walking to class, everyone she passed speculated on how the game would go.

Even some of the other members of the band were making bets on who would win.

It was insane.

She'd been in marching and pep band since high school, so she'd seen her share of football games. But that didn't mean she understood it.

She knew there were two teams and eleven players each on the field. If they ran into what was called the end zone, it was six points. If they kicked it through the large yellow goals, it was three points or one point. She had no idea what made it one or the other.

Everything else made zero sense to her.

She was just there to play her instrument and enjoy herself.

And she did. Some of her best friends were in the band with her, so she got to hang out with them while attending football games for free. Yeah, she had to play an instrument and perform at halftime, but that was a small price to pay to get to spend the day with her besties.

"Look alive!" the drum major called out as he went down the line.

Camden double-checked that her music was clipped to the end of her flute and brushed a hand over the jeans she was wearing. She was thankful that they only wore their official uniforms later in the season and that she didn't have to sweat buckets during the game.

It was late August and their game was at mid-day. It would have been brutal. It was going to be tough no matter what because their section didn't fall into the shade until the sun moved behind them. But at least it would be more bearable in regular clothes.

At the signal from the major, the band surged forward and started the opening show.

She could hear the cheering of the crowd and the booming voice of the announcer, but she tuned them out and concentrated on making sure she stayed in formation.

They reached their final spots and fireworks went off along with a cannon as the football team ran out of the tunnel and streamed past them.

She felt a frisson of excitement course through her at the theatrics.

There was just something about attending a live football game—even when she didn't understand the sport—that was so much fun. The excitement was contagious and she couldn't help but get amped up along with everyone else about the game.

As the teams went to their respective sides, the band filtered into the stands and she soon found herself at her seat, playing the fight song for the university as they geared up for kick-off, one of the few things she understood about football.

The game passed in a blur, as did their halftime show, and before she knew it, they were being dismissed as the clock wound down the final seconds of the fourth quarter.

She was sweaty, and she was certain she smelled, but she wasn't the only one. Everyone around her looked just as bedraggled, but they were all smiling. They'd won and that meant the campus would be alive with revelers.

She hooked her arm through Corey's and they quickly got to the car and drove back to campus. After showering quickly and changing into shorts and another shirt, they left their building and headed toward the quad, which already had a large group of people gathered there.

Every home game that they won, people would congregate on the quad to celebrate. The football team would eventually join them before people would fracture off and go to whatever party they were going to that night.

When that happened was when she and Corey would usually return to their apartment for the night.

Tonight was different though.

As they were getting ready to head back, her gaze caught Jackson's, and he curled his finger in a come-hither motion.

She'd arched a brow and checked around herself before pointing to herself, certain he didn't mean her. She could see him laughing as he motioned her toward him again.

She grabbed Corey's hand and jerked her friend behind her as she started walking, dodging the already drunken partiers around her.

She ignored Corey's protests as she wound closer to Jackson.

"Hey," Jackson said when she stopped in front of him.

"Hey," she said back, hoping her face wasn't as red as it felt.

"I'm Corey," Corey said as she shoulder-checked Camden, "her best friend and roommate."

"Nice to meet you," Jackson said, shaking her hand. "Y'all enjoy the game?"

Camden nodded while Corey launched into a long recap of her favorite plays of the game.

Where Camden had no idea what was going on most of the time with football, Corey was a fount of knowledge. Her dad was the football coach at her high school and she spent a lot of time on the field from what she'd told Camden.

When Corey lost steam, Jackson looked back to Camden. "Y'all going to a party tonight?"

"Oh, no—"

Corey cut her off. "We haven't decided yet."

Jackson smirked and Camden was certain Jackson knew what Camden was going to say before Corey talked over her. "You should come to the football house. We're throwing a party tonight. Invitation only."

Camden didn't have to look at Corey's face to know that her friend's eyes were wide and she was likely throwing a pleading look at Camden.

Going to a party at the football house would be a dream come true for Corey. She idolized the football players at the school and always talked about trying to get in with them. If Camden said no, Corey would never let her forget it.

"Sure. When should we get there?"

Corey squealed and Camden shook her head while Jackson laughed.

"I see I've found a football groupie."

"That's putting it lightly," Camden said, smiling at her friend who was now calmer, but waiting anxiously for the word on when to go.

"Walk back with me. I'm heading there now."

He turned and Camden and Corey fell into step behind him. "I can't believe that we got invited by the quarterback to the football house for a *party*," Corey whispered in her ear. "This has to be a dream. Pinch me."

Camden reached over and pinched Corey hard on the arm, making her friend yelp. "You didn't have to do it for real."

Camden glanced at Corey, who was rubbing her arm. "Don't ask for what you don't want."

Corey tried to mean mug her, but a smile broke over her face and she threaded her left arm around Camden's right, squeezing it tightly.

"I was being stupid and didn't mean for you to."

Camden rolled her eyes and stayed silent. Corey chattered away in her ear while they followed Jackson through the crowd. She noticed how everyone wanted a piece of him, but she couldn't tell if it annoyed him or not. He always smiled, shook hands, bumped fists, or whatever it was while he moved through the crowd.

It was something to watch.

He glanced over his shoulder at her and met her gaze, smiling before slowing down so she was next to him.

"You don't have to come if you don't want to," he said as they finally left the last of the crowd behind.

There were still a lot of people around, standing in clumps, but it was much quieter than it had been on the main quad.

"If I don't go Corey might murder me in my sleep."

Jackson chuckled. "Wouldn't want that."

They lapsed into silence and Camden realized they were closer to the football house than she thought when she caught sight of it lit up and people spilling out of the front door onto the lawn. A heavy bass beat jarred her and she could feel it working through her body.

"Oh my, God!" Corey said as they followed Jackson into the house.

The crowd quickly swallowed him while she paused at the door, taking in the sea of heaving bodies around her.

Though he said it was invitation only, she wondered how many invitations they had handed out based on the crush of people inside and the ones she'd seen outside.

"Let's find a drink," Corey shouted in her ear as she grabbed her hand and led her through the crowd and hopefully toward a keg.

Chapter Five
Camden

It was slow going through the crowd, but they finally found the kitchen, which had a keg in the corner. They each handed over five bucks and grabbed a Solo cup that they filled with flat beer.

Camden wrinkled her nose at the taste of the beer, but beggars can't be choosers. She wouldn't put her nose up to some cheap beer since she hadn't even planned on going out after the game.

Corey cheered beside her and she looked over to see her friend joining the crowd that was surrounding a guy doing a keg stand.

Camden shook her head and tried to push her way through the thickening crowd to the back door. She was sure the backyard would be just as packed as the front, but she didn't care. It would be outside and away from the sweaty bodies covering every surface inside.

She finally got to the door and breathed a sigh of relief as she stepped onto the back deck. It surprised her to see that there was almost no one outside. A few people sat to the side smoking cigarettes, and she thought she caught the hint of weed as well.

She ignored them and went down the steps to the grassy backyard.

There were a few people clumped in the yard, but it was fairly empty.

The music was still loud and the bass still trilled through her body, but it was more bearable outside.

She sipped her beer and saw a lawn chair off to the side beside a small inflatable kiddie pool. That was a weird thing to see in the backyard of the football house, but who knew what these guys got up to in their downtime.

When she reached the chair, she dropped into it and sighed.

She had been invited to her first major party at the football house—only took two years and some change—and she was all too happy to escape the main action and sit outside in the backyard.

If Corey wasn't with her, she'd probably ditch the rest of the party and go home.

But she didn't want to leave her friend in the house by herself. It wasn't that she didn't trust the people inside, but she didn't know them. She'd stay outside until she finished her beer and then find her friend. Maybe she could convince her to leave the party and go home.

That was wishful thinking. Camden knew she'd probably have to pry Corey out of the house when she was falling down drunk. It wouldn't be the first or last time she had to do it either.

She leaned back in the chair and gazed at the stars. It was a clear night and the indigo of the night sky spread out above her. If she ignored the thumping bass, she could almost imagine that she was back home on the farm, lying in her backyard, staring at the stars with her siblings as they pointed out the constellations.

But she wasn't home. That was made very clear a few moments later when she heard shrieking.

She picked her head up and looked toward the deck where a large group of people were now congregated.

She recognized a few football players by their sheer size. Chances were the girls with them were dancers or cheerleaders. Those three groups spent a lot of time together.

"Jackson! Come on!" a deep male voice yelled into the house.

A few moments later, she watched as Jackson stepped outside and was absorbed into the crowd.

She couldn't figure out what they were doing, and she honestly wasn't sure she wanted to know.

She didn't think they were doing anything illegal. But she couldn't know for sure.

The group started hooting and hollering before dispersing. Most of the people went back into the house while a few spilled out onto the lawn.

Jackson, or who she thought was Jackson, stayed on the porch leaning against the rail.

A girl sidled up to him and she watched as the girl wrapped herself around him.

Though she couldn't make out his features, based on the way he was standing and not encouraging her, she didn't think he wanted whatever the girl was likely suggesting. But he didn't push her off until she tried to lean up and kiss him.

"Back off, Lisa," Jackson said, straightening and shaking her off.

"Come on, Jackson. Why are you fightin' this?" Lisa asked as he walked down the stairs.

Jackson didn't answer and walked away from the porch, becoming swallowed in shadows.

Camden felt like a creep sitting there in the chair, watching what was happening on the porch, but she was too scared to move now. She didn't want Jackson or Lisa to see her and think she'd been spying.

Technically she had been, but she'd been outside before them. It wasn't like she'd witnessed anything she shouldn't have, anyway.

She turned her attention away from the porch and tilted her head back to stare at the sky again, blocking out the surrounding noise.

"Why are you hiding out here?" Jackson asked a few moments later, making Camden jerk and slosh her beer out of the cup while a strangled scream escaped her lips.

"Jesus, fuck! Calm down! It's me, Jackson."

Camden pressed a hand to her chest to calm her rapidly beating heart and blew out a low breath. "I realize that. Don't sneak up on someone."

"I thought you heard me," he said as he dropped into the chair next to her.

Camden snorted. "Right. Wear a bell next time and maybe I will."

"What are you doing out here? I thought you were inside."

Camden shrugged and sipped her tepid beer. She grimaced at the flavor, but she was determined to finish it since she'd paid for the cup. "I wanted some air, so here I am."

Jackson said nothing, so she let her head fall back again to stare at the stars.

"What are you looking at?" he asked her a few moments later.

"The stars."

"I feel like that was an obvious answer."

"You asked an obvious question."

"I did."

They lapsed into silence and Camden let it wash over her.

"This really isn't your scene, is it?"

Camden laughed. "What gave it away?"

"Do you really want me to answer?"

Camden lifted her head and looked at Jackson. His head was still tilted back looking at the sky, but she was now more interested in him than she was in looking at the stars.

"Sure."

Jackson lifted his head and she could just make out his facial features, though they were cast into shadows. "Well, where do I start?"

He paused and sipped from the bottle that she realized he was holding. "Your friend seemed more excited about the invitation than you did. And you're outside when everyone inside is raging. Doesn't speak to being a party animal."

"What can I say?" Camden said dryly. "I like to keep things fresh."

Jackson laughed. "Then there's that, your sense of humor. You don't act like most girls that I'm around."

"How do you mean?" She wasn't sure she wanted the answer, but she asked anyway.

"You had no reaction to me in class that first day or when we met for our project. None. I thought you had no idea who I was."

"I knew who you were."

"I realize that now. You're in the band. You'd have to be stupid to not."

He sighed and took a long pull from his bottle. Camden sipped from her warm beer, looking down in surprise when she realized that she'd just drunk the last of it.

"You out?" Jackson asked.

"Yeah." She shrugged. "Whatever."

"I'll be right back."

Camden watched Jackson walk away, curious about where he was going and what he was doing.

He didn't go up the stairs to the house. Instead, he skirted around the side of the house and disappeared from sight.

She watched the last place she'd seen him for a few moments, but he didn't reappear, so she shrugged and turned her attention to the back porch.

More people were outside, and she recognized Lisa as one of them. It looked like Lisa was looking for something or someone because she was scanning the yard.

Camden shrank back into the chair and was thankful she'd worn a dark-colored shirt. She shuddered to think of what might happen if Lisa realized she was sitting in the yard and who she'd been sitting with.

Lisa turned back to the people behind her and Jackson slipped around the corner of the house and quickly walked toward her.

Camden looked at the deck and had to laugh as she realized that no one realized Jackson had just walked by them.

"Here ya go," he said, handing her a cold bottle.

"What's this?"

"A wine cooler. The girls sometimes stock up the fridge in the garage. I thought you might like it more than the keg beer."

"Thanks," she said as she sipped from the bottle.

Her tongue was pleased with the sweet, fruity flavor of the cooler. It was much better than the taste of the beer.

"Tell me about yourself," Jackson said.

Camden slid her gaze over to him. "What do you want to know?"

"How does a girl like you end up at a party like this?"

Camden laughed. "Well. Funny story. This guy I know from class is kinda a big deal on campus. You might know him. His name is Jackson?"

She cut her eyes to him and she couldn't be sure, but she was positive he was grinning at her. "Oh, really. What about him?"

"He invited me and my roommate to this party. She's obsessed with football, so I just had to agree to come. She never would have let me live it down."

"What about her roommate?"

Camden's brows furrowed, and she looked back at Jackson. "What?"

"You? Are you obsessed with football?"

Camden snorted. "God, no. I barely understand that there are two teams. I have no idea what's happening most of the time."

Jackson laughed. "Really?"

"Yep. I'm clueless. Corey is diehard though. Her dad is a coach and her brothers all played. I think she tried to play actually, but the school wouldn't let her or something. She refused to cheer, so she joined the band. And here we are."

Jackson snorted. "Wow. I need to chat with her, see how serious she is."

"If you do, you'll probably blow her mind. I'll hear about nothing else for weeks."

"She's obsessed?"

"I told you that," she said, sipping from her bottle.

"You did that. Should I be worried she'll go hide in my room or someone else's room to spy? Try to steal our skin for a jacket?"

Camden snorted and winced as the sugary drink went up her nose. "Oh God, that burns."

She blew her nose furiously, trying to clear it while coughing.

"You good?" Jackson asked when she stopped hacking.

"I'm great," she wheezed. "Don't say shit like that when I'm drinking."

"I'll try to remember."

She cleared her throat and said, "To answer your question, no you don't have to worry about it. I'll make sure she leaves with me."

Jackson just made a humming noise and didn't say anything else.

They lapsed into silence again and Camden realized that it was comfortable. She didn't feel the urge to fill the silence—not that she normally did—and it was nice sitting outside in the yard with the cicadas singing around her.

She pulled her phone out and checked the time, grimacing when she saw that it was almost one in the morning. "I need to find Corey," she muttered, quickly finishing her drink.

She made a face at the sickly sweet taste and stood.

"Let me help," Jackson said, standing next to her.

She shook her head and jerked her chin toward the porch, which was filled with even more people than earlier. "I think you better stay here. You leave your little sanctuary and you'll be overrun. I'll be fine. She can only be so many places."

"Let me know if you need help."

"I'll send out the bat signal, don't worry," she said before turning and walking toward the porch and pushing her way inside.

Chapter Six
Jackson

Jackson watched Camden go and pondered the conversation he'd just had with her. His earlier thoughts about her were spot on. She was very different from most of the girls he came into contact with.

He liked it. And he was starting to like her too.

He sighed and drained his beer before deciding he should head back to the party. If he didn't rejoin it soon, people would probably come looking for him. He slowly walked toward the porch and smirked at the people that called his name as he stepped into the light surrounding the porch.

"Jackson! There you are, man!" Ethan called out. "We wondered if you'd found some bunny to keep you warm tonight."

"Nah, man. Just chilling."

His eyes slid to the right and met Lisa's. If looks could kill, he was sure he'd be incinerated. Maybe he should have lied and said he had found someone to cuddle up with to get her to back off.

But as soon as he thought that, he knew he couldn't do it. While he might not like her much and wished she would move on, he wouldn't lie his way to getting her to back off. He just needed to be more direct.

"You see the highlights earlier?" Ethan asked, pulling him into the conversation with some other players.

"Nah, what were the scores?"

Over the next hour, people started leaving the party until it was the group of guys that lived at the house and their girlfriends plus a few people hanging around hoping to score. What they were hoping to score, he didn't think about because he wouldn't be a party to it.

He finally said goodnight a little while later and made his way up the stairs to his room on the second floor. He dug his keys out of his pocket and unlocked his door. Once he was inside, he locked it back up, not trusting that someone wouldn't try to come inside it if they knew he was in there.

He was one of the lucky few rooms in the house with an ensuite bathroom and he was thankful for it right then.

He shed his clothes and stepped into the shower, turning the water to the hottest setting he could handle and letting it cascade over him.

He closed his eyes and his mind turned back to Camden. He didn't know what it was about her that was making him obsess so much. That was a lie. He knew exactly what it was.

She was different.

She didn't care that he was the quarterback, and it was nice.

While he didn't mind people knowing who he was and talking to him all the time, it got tiring to constantly be on just in case someone recognized him. He was always smiling and always willing to chat with someone. He didn't want to risk one day of being off and it potentially being detrimental to his career.

But sometimes he wished he was anonymous and could get by with people ignoring him. It was easier in the spring when football season was over. He wasn't constantly in the spotlight with interviews and games.

He could fade into the background until late summer when football started up again.

Talking to Camden was like talking to someone that had no idea who he was because she just didn't care.

It was refreshing.

He wanted to get to know her more because of it.

He turned the water off after he finished washing his body and quickly dried off before sliding under the covers.

He stared at his ceiling and remembered the smattering of stars that spread over him when he sat in the lawn chair next to Camden.

He was definitely going to get to know her better.

𝄞

Over the next few weeks, Jackson had a new favorite pastime: Camden watching.

It sounded much creepier than it was. They had the one class together on Tuesday and Thursday at nine in the morning. They usually met up once a week to work on their project and were ahead of schedule because of it.

He watched her in class and realized that she was genuine. He didn't have any doubt really, but he couldn't help but wonder if she treated everyone the same.

She did.

She was kind to everyone, even people who weren't kind to her.

He searched for her when he was on campus and even looked for her in the band section during one game. He didn't find her, but he planned to before the season ended. He wanted to see what she looked like in her uniform.

When he was at away games, he wanted to text her. He didn't let himself, though. He wasn't sure how she'd respond to it.

She was friendly, and she'd even joined him for coffee a few times after their study sessions if she wasn't busy. But that was the extent of it.

He was tempted to ask her to join him for lunch one day or even dinner. But he was certain she'd turn him down.

"Where's your head?" Ethan asked him one day during practice.

"What?"

"You're over here daydreaming, not even paying attention to how well Roscoe is playing."

Jackson turned his attention back to the field and realized that Ethan was right. He hadn't been paying attention. He wasn't that bothered by it, though.

"He can play well all he wants. He won't get my spot."

"Cocky."

"Is it cocky if it's true?" he asked, smirking at his friend.

Ethan lifted a shoulder and knocked his helmet against Jackson's. "Maybe not, but you need to keep your head in the game. All it'll take is one injury and you'll be toast."

Jackson nodded. Ethan was right. He needed to pull his head out of his ass and pay attention. They were undefeated so far this season and he planned to continue that streak with their upcoming home game. He couldn't let himself get distracted, no matter how much he wanted to think about Camden.

"Dove! Get your ass on the field!" the coach screamed, and he jogged out onto the grass, pulling his helmet on.

Roscoe passed him by and shoulder checked him, making Jackson pause and turn to look at the second-string quarterback. "You got a problem?"

Roscoe snorted. "With you? Please." He kept running and Jackson watched him for a few moments before shaking his head and turning back to the huddle behind him.

He jogged the last few feet and stood in the middle.

"You need to handle that, man," Ethan said, shaking his head.

"No kidding," Jim said. "He's getting mouthier and we don't like listening to his shit."

Jackson sighed and let his head hang for a few moments before looking at his offensive line. "I'll try to talk with him after practice and see what's up. I'm sure he just wants playing time."

"It's more than that, man," Dale said. "He's saying that he'll be the starting QB before the end of the season. I'd watch your back."

A chill worked its way up Jackson's spine at those words, but he hoped it didn't show to the guys standing around him.

He was their quarterback and captain. He needed to show that he wasn't rattled by what they'd just told him. He'd had second and third-string players try to threaten him and his position before. They hadn't gotten to him, so he wouldn't let some player that thought he was better than him take his position without a fight.

"Okay, let's get our heads in the game," Jackson said, pulling everyone's attention to him.

The rest of practice passed in a blur. When he got into the locker room, he looked for Roscoe and found him getting dressed at his locker. Jackson wanted a shower, but he knew he needed to have it out with Roscoe first.

"Hey, man. Can we talk?"

Roscoe snorted and rolled his eyes as he turned to face Jackson. "What?"

"Is there a problem?"

"Why the fuck would there be a problem?"

Jackson's eyes widened at the anger in Roscoe's voice. "I'm not sure," Jackson said slowly, "that's why I'm asking. It seems like there's a problem and we need to make sure we're a team."

"Oh, please," Roscoe said. "We're not a fucking team. You think you're so high and mighty, lording over everyone that you're an important football player. Please. You'll be washed up in two years, tops."

"Dude, I think you need to take a step back," Ethan said from behind Jackson.

"The day I listen to you is the day that I die, Ethan," Roscoe said.

No one said anything and Jackson looked around, realizing that the entire locker room was standing around looking at the showdown.

"What the fuck is your issue, man?" Ethan asked. "You got a problem with the team? With our captain?"

"I'd like to know that as well," Coach said from their right.

Roscoe paled, but he continued to glower at Jackson. He had to hand it to the guy. He wouldn't back down.

"Say what you got to say," Coach continued, stepping closer to them. "I'm sure we all want to hear it."

Roscoe dropped his gaze and clenched his jaw.

A few beats of silence passed before the Coach said, "Why don't you join me in my office and we can chat about this privately."

"I have class—" Roscoe started, but the coach quickly cut him off.

"Do I look like I'm asking?"

Roscoe huffed and stalked over to the coach's office.

Jackson met Coach's eyes, which were devoid of emotion, before turning back to his own locker and going through the motions of getting cleaned up after practice. He was more than ready for this day to be done.

Chapter Seven
Camden

Jackson was acting weird.

Camden didn't know him well—even though she wouldn't mind getting to know him better—but she could tell that something was up with him.

They still chatted, and he'd invited her and Corey to a few other events at the football house, so it wasn't like he'd suddenly changed how he was acting.

It was in the moments they weren't talking and she'd glimpse him. He looked worried and stressed, his mouth pulled tight.

She'd watched as the stressed look became more pronounced over a few weeks until it was the Thursday before fall break.

The football team had a bye week, so they didn't have to travel, but most were staying on campus for extra workouts. At least that was what Corey had told her. She'd become good friends with a few of the players since the two of them had been invited to the football house enough to be recognized.

The project she and Jackson had to do was due at the start of November and they'd be presenting it right before Thanksgiving, so they were trying to finish up the last of it before break. It was because of this that they were holed up in a study room in the library, putting the finishing touches on their paper and PowerPoint presentation.

"I think Dr. Head will like this," Jackson said as he clicked through the presentation. "We've hit all the points she wants in there plus a few extras. You were super thorough with your explanations too."

Camden shot him a smile before looking at her own screen and the bibliography she was trying to finish formatting. "Yeah, I think so too. I think she'll be impressed with how we made the cross-curricular connections too."

They lapsed into silence and a few minutes later, Camden finished formatting that last page. "I'm emailing you the paper for you to look over. If you think everything is ready, do you want to turn it in?"

Jackson shrugged. "Maybe? We still have two weeks after the break for the project. So I don't want her to think we rushed, you know?"

Camden nodded and turned to face him while he pulled the paper up. "Yeah, I get what you mean. I've heard she can be a hard-ass about stuff too. Maybe wait another week just in case?"

Jackson nodded, but he was reading over the paper, so he said nothing.

Camden used the opportunity to look at him. The stressed look that had been hounding him was still there, though he looked no more or less stressed than before. He was definitely tense though.

She sighed and dropped her gaze to her lap.

"What's wrong?" Jackson asked, making Camden jump in her seat.

"What?" She glanced at him in confusion.

"You sighed," he said, turning in his seat to face her more fully.

His turning made his knee graze her own, and she hoped that her face didn't reflect her reaction to that. A flutter started in her stomach and it continued as his knee continued to press into hers.

"Oh, you know..." she trailed off, not sure how to continue that. She wasn't sure what she should say. She didn't want to admit that she sighed because she was worried about him.

Yeah, they were friendly, but she wasn't sure their friendship extended to a conversation about what might be bothering Jackson.

"What's up?"

Camden looked away from him and cleared her throat. She needed to think of something to say that would distract him and get him away from why she sighed. But she wasn't very good at thinking on the fly. In fact, she was terrible at it.

"Nothing, just thinking about school work…" she said as she ran her fingers through her hair.

She froze when she realized what she was doing. That was one of her nervous tics and she did not need to do that in front of Jackson. He struck her as an observant person, so he might pick up on it.

"Nothing? You look like you've seen a ghost, and it's obvious something is bothering you. You're playing with your hair."

Camden grimaced and dropped her hands back down to her lap.

"So, what's up?"

She said nothing at first, hoping that he would drop it or someone would suddenly burst into the room to save her. But neither happened and Jackson continued to look at her expectantly.

She sighed and slumped. "I don't know how to tell you why I was sighing."

"Words usually work pretty well for that," he said drolly.

She shot him a look and saw the smirk on his face. "Ha ha. You know what I mean."

He nodded, and the smirk dropped. "I do. It's obvious that whatever this is is bothering you. You've looked worried for a few weeks now. I haven't brought it up yet because I didn't want you to feel pressured to tell me. But it's not getting better and as your friend, I think I have the right to ask you about it."

Camden sighed again. She was sighing all over the place today. "It's you."

Jackson's brows rose toward his hairline. "Me?"

Camden nodded. "Yeah. Just like you've noticed me, I've noticed you. Something is up and it's bothering you. You look stressed all the time. I wasn't sure if I should or could ask you about it…"

Jackson snorted. "Aren't we the pair? Too chicken shit to ask the important questions."

Camden chuckled. "We are apparently. I'm sorry if I've been worrying you. I've just been…worried about you."

Jackson dropped his gaze and all traces of humor left his face. He glanced at her. "Thanks for looking out. It means a lot that you've noticed, even if you said nothing. Never be scared to bring something up to me. We're friends and friends don't hide shit."

Camden's face heated at his words. "Okay."

She waited a few moments before asking, "So, what's up with you?"

It was his turn to sigh, and he ran a hand through his hair. "Just some football shit. It'll blow over."

Jackson looked at her head on before glancing at his phone and changing the subject. "It's a little early, but you want to get lunch off campus? My afternoon class was canceled because of break and I don't have practice either."

Camden's eyes widened in surprise. This was new territory. They'd never eaten together unless it was a quick snack in the study room. "Uh…" she said, trying to get her thoughts together. "What did you have in mind?"

Jackson shrugged and closed his laptop before packing his things away. "Doesn't matter to me. Whatever you want is fine. I'll eat just about anything."

Camden followed suit and started packing her things away as she turned the invitation over her in mind.

Did she want to go with him? Hell yes.

But she was nervous. They'd just established that they were friends and friends went to get food together all the time.

The only problem with that was she liked Jackson as more than a friend. Her feelings had been steadily growing the more time they spent together, and she was in the midst of a full-blown crush. It could fade over time. But she didn't see that happening anything time soon.

"How bout that Mexican place right off campus?" she asked.

Jackson nodded. "Sure, I love that place. Want to ride together?"

Camden blinked rapidly and stuttered. "Uhhh…sure?"

Jackson smiled. "Great. Let's go. You can keep your bag in my car and I'll take you home after."

As she followed Jackson out of the library and to his car, she wondered what she'd just agreed to.

Chapter Eight
Camden

The butterflies stayed with her as she followed Jackson to his car and rode the short distance to the restaurant.

She tried telling herself that it was Jackson and she was comfortable with him. There was nothing funny that was going to happen and it was a meal between friends.

That didn't help, though. Her body was in freak out mode. Butterflies were fluttering in her stomach. She was certain her face was red from her high emotion. Her hands felt clammy, and she really hoped she didn't have to touch Jackson because of it.

She was a mess.

Once he parked, she grabbed her wallet from her bag and followed behind him. He held the door open for them and told the hostess there were two of them.

As they followed the hostess, she was acutely aware of Jackson and how close he was to her. She was slightly in front of him and every so often, her arm would brush his front, sending a shock of electricity through her body. She needed to get herself together.

The hostess stopped by a table and placed the menus down. Camden felt a hand on her lower back and jerked. Her back stiffened until she realized it was Jackson and she relaxed.

He guided her into her side of the booth and her mouth dried.

As soon as she was seated, she opened her menu and tried to concentrate on what was in front of her and not how her body reacted to Jackson. He was a friend and nothing more. She needed to get control of herself before she made things awkward.

"Hello and welcome to El Cerro Grande. I'm Luke and I'll be your server today. What can I get you to drink?"

"A water, please," Jackson said.

Camden glanced up and met Jackson's gaze. She cleared her throat and looked at their server. "A Coke?"

"Pepsi fine?"

She nodded.

"Can we also get some queso to go with our chips and salsa?" Jackson asked.

Luke nodded and walked off.

Camden shifted in her seat, but forced herself to stop. She was uncomfortable, but she shouldn't be. If she discounted the fact that she was sitting across the table from the guy she was majorly crushing on, this was no different than when they were in the study room. It was fine. She was fine. Nothing was different.

Except it was.

They were at the restaurant together and while she knew it was as friends, she couldn't help but wonder what it would be like to go somewhere with Jackson as his date. As his girlfriend. As someone more than a friend and project partner.

"Camden."

Jackson said her name softly, and she glanced up when she heard it.

"Yeah?"

"You okay?"

She nodded as the waiter came back with their drinks, chips, salsa, and the cheese dip Jackson ordered.

"Y'all ready to order?"

She glanced at Jackson and he looked at her expectantly. "Are you ready? Or do you need a few?"

"Uh..." she glanced down and zeroed in on the a la carte taco menu. "Yep, I am. You go first though."

Jackson ordered, and she tried not to show her shock at how much he ordered. He was a football player, so he likely expended a lot of calories. But the amount of food he got was still insane.

Once he was done, she quickly ordered a variety of tacos.

They were alone again, and she tried to busy herself by taking the paper off her straw and sticking in her drink before taking a long pull.

Once she finished that, she concentrated on pouring salsa into her bowl and grabbing a chip to eat.

"Camden."

Jackson said her name again and Camden tensed as she looked at him. "Yeah?"

Talk about déjà vu.

"What's up with you? Are you uncomfortable? If so, we can leave and I'll take you home. I didn't intend to make you feel weird or anything by asking you to come to lunch with me."

"Oh, no. I'm just in my head, you know?"

Jackson nodded. "Yeah, I do. You want to talk about it?"

Her face burned at the thought of talking to Jackson about what she was thinking and feeling. That wouldn't happen in a million years.

"Nope, I'm good. Just being a girl, you know?"

He nodded and then started laughing. "I'm nodding, but I don't in fact know. If you're sure, then I believe you. Let's talk about something else. What are your plans for the break?"

Camden sagged with relief at the topic change. "Nothing much. I thought about going home, but it's a few hours away and my parents said I wasn't needed. They said I should stay here and relax. So I'm planning to be a couch potato."

Jackson nodded. "Should be fun."

"I hope so. What about you? You don't have a game, so do you have a lot of practice?"

Jackson shook his head. "Nah. We have to do some training, but we aren't doing full practices until next week. I'm glad because we're to the point of the season where we're all tired and need that break."

Camden nodded. "I'm sure. Y'all are playing well, so I imagine it takes a toll."

Jackson smirked at her. "How do you know we're playing well? Is Corey filling you in?"

Camden blushed. "Shut up…I pay attention and know a win when I see one."

Jackson laughed. "So, you've hit me with the extent of your knowledge?"

"You know I have," she muttered, embarrassed, though she knew she shouldn't be.

She'd tried to understand football, especially as she and Jackson got more and more friendly. But it still made little sense to her.

"No need to be embarrassed," Jackson said, reaching across the table and touching her hand.

She jerked at the contact. "I'm just teasing you," he continued.

She nodded. "Yeah."

Her voice sounded rough, and she cleared her throat, hoping he didn't notice.

"Since you'll be here also, we should totally hang out. You can come over to the football house."

Camden froze. This was uncharted territory. Yeah, she and Jackson were friendly, and he had invited her to the football parties. But they'd never done what they were doing today. Lunch. Talking about plans to hang out together over break.

They had five days of no classes including the weekend. That was five days they might hang out.

"Sure," she said. She was proud of herself for sounding so sure of her answer and not showing her inner-turmoil.

"You want to do anything special?" he asked.

She shook her head. "No, can't think of anything. Like I said, I planned to just hang out and watch some TV."

"We can't have you hole up the whole time."

She shrugged. "Why not? I've done it before."

"You've got me now."

Camden was saved from answering by the return of Luke with their food.

Once he was gone, she and Jackson both started eating and silence reigned between them.

She was thankful for it because it gave her the opportunity to get her thoughts together. She needed to make sure she didn't read too much into Jackson and what he was saying. She also needed to make sure there was some distance. They should hang out, but only once or twice over break. She'd make up some excuse to dodge him the other times.

As they ate, they started talking again and chatted about their other classes. Eventually he asked her about being in pep band and she talked about that a little, telling him how she got involved and how much she enjoyed it.

"So, will you become a music teacher?"

Camden shook her head. "No. I thought about it though. I enjoy music, but I don't think I'd enjoy trying to run a band or do chorus. So I'm going into my favorite subject: math."

Jackson's brows rose. "Math?"

She nodded. "Yeah. I know it seems weird, but it's the truth. I can see myself teaching math, so here we are. Your major is…physical education?"

Jackson smirked. "Are you stereotyping?"

Camden blushed. That was exactly what she was doing. "Maybe?"

He laughed. "I thought about it, but realized I wouldn't enjoy it. So I'm doing a double-major in history and English."

"Why a double?"

He shrugged and leaned back in his seat, pinning her with his gaze. "I enjoy both subjects. I haven't decided if I want to teach middle or high school, so I figured I'd double major in both just in case. If I want to teach middle, I have to have two certifications, anyway."

Camden leaned forward and propped her chin on her hand. "What got you into education?"

He shrugged and leaned forward, mimicking her stance. "I had a great teacher and coach when I was in high school. I realized that education was something I could see myself doing, especially when I did some observations my freshman year."

She tilted her head to the side. "Aren't you going pro?"

Jackson dropped his gaze and his cheeks turned red. She looked at him with a question in her eye, wondering what that was about.

"Yeah, I'm looking at going pro."

"Then why are you worried about getting your degree in education?"

He didn't answer at first and he kept his gaze trained on the table for a few moments. He eventually looked up at her, snagging her gaze. "They could have drafted me last year. I almost went ahead with it. But football won't be my entire life. I'll eventually have to retire or I'll be injured. If that happens sooner than I want, I want to have a career that I can fall back on. So many guys don't think about what happens after their pro career and they end up struggling. I don't want that to be me."

Camden stared at him, her mouth gaping a little. She was surprised and impressed by what he was saying.

"I think that's awesome. You see so many people that say they're going pro and they don't bother with a backup."

Jackson nodded. "Yeah. That's why I want to set myself apart."

Luke came back by the table and gathered their plates while dropping the check off. Camden grabbed her wallet to pull her card out. As she straightened, she saw that the check was missing, as was Luke.

"Where'd he go? I didn't give him my card?"

Jackson's cheeks turned red again. "Don't worry about it. I've got it."

She narrowed her eyes. "You don't have to do that. I want to pay my way."

"I invited you, so let me pay for you."

She shook her head. "No, I can't let you do that."

Jackson rubbed the back of his neck and looked away from her. "Please, let me."

She opened her mouth to say something else, but paused as she took in his body language. "Are you okay?" she asked as she noticed how tense he seemed.

"I'm fine."

She narrowed her eyes at him. He was still blushing, and he looked very uncomfortable. He was shifting in his seat and wouldn't look at her. Something was up.

"What's up? Something is bothering you, I can tell. Don't deny it."

Jackson snorted and shook his head. "Look at us. Finally speaking what's on our minds, huh?"

She didn't move or make a noise. She wouldn't let him distract her from whatever it was that was bothering him. She would figure it out.

Luke came back by and gave Jackson his card plus the slip to sign. As he put his card away and got ready to leave, she continued to look at him.

"Come on, let's go. I'll tell you when I drop you off."

She narrowed her eyes at him, not sure she believed him. But she went anyway.

As they walked to the car, she said, "Thank you for lunch. I really appreciate it."

"It's no problem."

She glanced at him and saw that he looked cool and collected. No hint of whatever was bothering him earlier. Either he'd gotten over it or he wasn't going to tell her what was up.

The ride to her apartment building was short and a few minutes later, he was parked in one spot outside it.

He turned his car off and his hands tightened, then relaxed on the steering wheel. Camden knew she needed to get out, but he'd told her he would tell her what was bothering him when they got to her place. She was going to hold him to that.

He sucked in a deep breath and slowly blew it out. She was worried that whatever he was going to say was going to be serious from the way he was acting. That worried her.

"Look, if you don't want to tell me, I won't push you," she said, trying to give him an out.

"I like you."

Chapter Nine
Jackson

Camden's mouth dropped open. Jackson watched her, waiting to see what her reaction would be.

He hoped for the best, but was preparing himself for the worst. When he asked her to lunch, he was hoping to feel her out, see if maybe she liked him too.

He should have come right out and told her he wanted it to be a date, especially with the standoff over the check at the end.

But he was too chicken-shit to do that. Instead, he had just blurted out that he liked Camden and she still hadn't said anything.

He cleared his throat and swallowed thickly before continuing. "When I say I like you, I mean as more than a friend."

Her mouth snapped shut, and she blinked rapidly at him. She had paled initially at his words, but now her face was slowly turning pink. Was it in embarrassment or was she about to break his heart?

He plowed on. "You're an awesome person. You're nice and patient and I enjoy spending time with you. I've wanted to ask you out for a while now, but because of our project, I've held off. I didn't want to make things awkward. I guess I've kinda fucked that up now, huh? I just had to say something—"

He was cut off by the feel of Camden's lips on his. He hadn't been paying attention to her, instead looking past her out the passenger window, concentrating on the pine trees that lined the parking lot.

He hadn't noticed her moving until she filled his vision and her lips touched his.

Neither of them moved at first. He was shocked at her move and he wondered if she was also since she seemed frozen.

He quickly snapped out of it, bringing a hand up to cup her cheek. He lightly ran his thumb across her skin as he pressed his lips more firmly against hers.

She sighed, and the tension seemed to leave her body. He moved his hand to the back of her neck, cradling her head as he tilted his head to the side to deepen the kiss.

Camden moaned low and opened her mouth, allowing him to caress her tongue with his own. They sat there in the front seat of his car for an untold amount of time kissing each other until he realized that anyone could walk by and see them. He didn't want someone to get a picture of them.

He slowed their kiss down until he finally pulled back.

He pressed his forehead against hers and panted lightly as he tried to catch his breath.

His gaze raked over her features, taking in her slightly swollen lights, flushed complexion, and now messy hair. He wanted to press his lips against hers again and lose himself.

But he wanted to make sure what that kiss meant first.

"Camden," he whispered.

Her eyes had been closed, and she slowly opened them at her name, blinking rapidly as her gaze focused on him.

"Hey," she breathed.

"Hey back," he said with a grin.

Silence stretched between them for a few beats before he forced himself to pull away from her, pulling his hand from her neck. He cleared his throat and said, "Sooo…"

"Sooo…" Camden mimicked.

"We kissed."

"We did."

They lapsed into silence again. This one was a little more awkward than the first.

He decided that he'd just rip the Band-Aid off and see what she said. "I wasn't lying. I like you. I asked you to lunch because I wanted to take you on a date. I just didn't say it earlier."

He'd glanced away from her with his confession, but at the end, he looked back at her face and she was staring at him intently.

"I like you, too."

He blinked at her, not sure he heard her right.

Apparently she wasn't done as she kept talking. "It seems a little crazy to think that the band nerd would get with the football star, which is why I said nothing. I didn't want to make it weird or anything. I want your friendship even if I can't have anything else."

"Hey," he said, stopping her. "It's not that crazy. You're kinda awesome, even for a band nerd."

He smirked at her so she'd know he was joking and she smiled in return. "I don't care that you're a band nerd or whatever else you might say about yourself. You're a great person and I'm attracted to you because of that."

"Really?"

"Really." He cleared his throat and asked, "Do you want to go on a real date with me?"

Camden arched a brow at him. "You mean lunch with you wasn't a real date?"

His heart was beating like crazy in his chest at her words. "I mean...uh...if you want..."

Camden laughed. "I'm just teasing you."

"I want lunch to be a date, but I don't want to pressure you."

She shook her head. "You aren't pressuring me if I want it too."

"Okay." His heartbeat slowed and he could breathe easier.

He'd dated before, but it had been a while since he'd had a steady girlfriend. The last one had been freshman year, and it was his high school sweetheart. They'd both come to the university together, and he was certain they'd stay together all four years.

That had quickly turned out to be false when he found her screwing his then roommate and best friend.

He hadn't cared about having a steady girlfriend after that. Camden was the first girl he'd wanted to try anything more than sex with since then.

"How about instead of another date, we hang out tonight? Your place or mine?" Camden asked, bringing him back to the present.

"Is your roommate still here?" he asked.

Camden nodded, and he considered his answer. He liked Corey; she was a lot of fun to hang out with. But he wanted to spend time with just Camden and he knew if they stayed at her place, that wouldn't happen.

"Mine okay?"

Camden nodded and smiled. "I was hoping you'd say that. I love Corey, but I'd like to spend time together just the two of us."

Jackson smiled. "Okay. Want me to wait for you and I'll drive you over now? Or you want to come over later?"

Camden bit her bottom lip and looked thoughtful. "I have a class at three. How about I come over after?"

He nodded. "Okay. That's fine."

Camden shot him a smile. "I'll see you then."

A few moments later, she was out of the car and he was alone, watching her walk toward the backdoor of the building.

He stayed there until he was sure she was inside before turning his car on and pointing it toward his house.

He was glad she'd said she'd come later. While his room and the house weren't a total mess, he definitely wanted a chance to tidy up some.

Once he was home, he quickly ran up the stairs to his room and changed the sheets on his bed. He didn't want to assume anything was happening there, but he didn't want to not change his sheets just in case.

He got them in the washer before he went into his ensuite bathroom and did a quick clean. He was never more thankful for his clean tendencies than right then. Some guys in the house were slobs. They had beard trimmings and pubes everywhere in their bathroom plus mold growing in the tub.

He kept an eye on the clock as he quickly vacuumed his room before making his way downstairs and into the kitchen and living room.

He started cleaning both and by the time he was finished loading the dishwasher, he had a small audience.

"What's up, man?" Ethan asked, sitting on a stool. "You're a neat freak, but you rarely touch the rest of the house."

Jackson nodded. "Nothing. Just felt like cleaning."

Jackson concentrated on wiping the counters down and hoped that Ethan would drop it. If the guys knew a girl was coming over, they'd tease him relentlessly.

"You never feel like cleaning down here unless you have a reason because you refuse to clean up after us."

Jackson sighed, but didn't respond to Ethan's statement. Ethan was right. He couldn't say anything in response, so he stayed silent instead.

Ethan said nothing for a few more minutes and he relaxed, thinking maybe Ethan would drop it.

"You got a chick, don't you?"

Jackson froze for a moment, but continued what he was doing.

Ethan continued. "That's why you're cleaning. You only get like this if your momma is coming or if you got a girl coming over. I know your momma ain't coming since I got an email from her the other day about your birthday saying she was going to see your sister this weekend. Who's the chick?"

Jackson continued to ignore him.

"You can't ignore me to get me to leave. I'll just keep my ass right here and you know it."

Jackson sighed and looked at his best friend. "Why do you want to know?"

"Why won't you tell me?" Ethan countered.

Jackson threw the rag into the sink and leaned against the counter, crossing his arms over his chest. "It's Camden."

"Your partner?" Ethan's brow furrowed.

Jackson nodded. "Yeah. I asked her out earlier."

Ethan's eyes widened. "You finally bit the bullet?"

Jackson glared at him. "What do you mean?"

Ethan laughed. "Dude, come on. It's obvious to me you like her. You find excuses to see her. You talk about her constantly. You invite her to the house for parties. She's a cool chick, but I've never seen you act like this about someone. She's coming over?"

Jackson nodded. Ethan grinned and Jackson braced himself for whatever Ethan was about to say. "Make sure you wrap it before you tap it."

"Get out of here, asshole!" Jackson said, lunging for his friend.

Ethan was already up and dancing away from him, laughing. "You'll make sweet, sweet love tonight. Enjoy it."

"Asshole," Jackson muttered as Ethan left the kitchen, leaving Jackson alone.

He sighed. The one good thing about Ethan coming in and talking to him was that it allowed him to calm down a little more. He'd cleaned everything he was going to clean, and he had some extra time, so he decided he'd take a quick shower before pulling some movies to watch with Camden.

He wanted it to be perfect.

Chapter Ten
Camden

"Wait, I need you to back up a second." Corey held up a hand as Camden flicked through her closet. "You're going to his house to *hang out?*"

Camden nodded. "Yeah. Why do you sound so shocked?"

Camden was trying very hard to play it cool, but she was sure she was failing. On the inside, she was freaking out. Jackson Dove, the star quarterback of King University and all around hot stud, had asked *her*, Camden North, to come hang with him at his house. The football house.

She was dying inside.

"Camden. It's Jackson Dove. Most popular guy at the university! I know you're friendly because of that class y'all have together, but...this is huge!"

Corey squealed and Camden shook her head as she found a shirt she didn't hate to change into. Corey started talking about different things related to Jackson and football, but Camden just tuned her out.

She was already psyched out enough as it was and hearing her best friend extol Jackson's virtues—including his tight ass—wasn't helping her not lose her shit.

She knew that Jackson inviting her over to hang out was just a friendly get together. They were hanging out as *friends*, nothing more. She just had to remind herself of that to make sure she didn't read too much into a situation. Yeah, they'd admitted they liked each other, but liking each other and doing other things was a huge leap.

She changed her shirt and fluffed her hair, finger-combing the tangles out. She turned to face Corey and held her hands out to the side. "Well, how do I look?"

Corey raked her gaze over Camden and shook her head. "Like you're not trying hard enough."

"Perfect. Exactly what I was going for."

Corey snorted. "I don't know why I bother."

"I don't know why you do, either."

Camden quickly gathered her things and tossed a wave over her shoulder to Corey before hopping in her car and driving the short distance to the football house.

It was the middle of the football season, so she was expecting a party to be going on at the house, even with break looming. But it surprised her to see only two cars parked outside as she pulled up to the curb and turned her car off.

She glanced at the clock and decided it was a little early for a party, so it was possible that one could happen later. She'd just try to be gone by then.

She gave herself a small pep talk in the car, reminding herself that Jackson was a friend and while he had a great ass and smile, she wouldn't rush anything.

A knock on the window next to her head made her scream. She whipped her head around and met Jackson's amused glare.

"You going to sit there all night?" he asked, his words slightly muffled through the glass.

She huffed and grabbed her purse before opening the door, wishing Jackson was still standing close enough she could have slammed it into him.

"What were you doing in there? You looked like you were talking to yourself?" he asked, a smirk on his lips.

She shrugged and locked her car before falling into step beside him. "I was giving myself a pep talk."

Jackson stopped walking toward the front door and turned to face her. "A pep talk?"

His brows were toward his hairline when she nodded. "What for?"

"You know, the usual. I agreed to come and we would have fun. I couldn't just bail on you without following through with my agreement."

Jackson said nothing at first. "You thought about not coming?"

She narrowed her eyes at him. His voice sounded a few octaves higher than normal when he asked that. "Yeah."

His mouth dropped open briefly before he snapped it closed. "Really? You didn't want to come?"

She shifted on her feet as she sorted through Jackson's tone. He sounded…hurt. "It's not that I didn't want to come…" she hedged, trying to figure out what to say so he would understand it wasn't that she didn't want to see him. "I'm just nervous around people I don't know that well. Yeah, I've met a few of the guys, but not many. I don't know what I'm walking into and I don't handle the unknown well either."

She peeked at Jackson and saw that he was nodding. "Okay, I can live with that. There's only me and Ethan here right now. Everyone else is out and shouldn't be back for a while. Some have already left to go home for the break."

Camden breathed a sigh of relief at his words. That made her feel much better to know that she wouldn't have to meet a ton of guys right then.

"Okay, lead the way then."

Jackson chuckled and turned back to the house. She fell into step behind him and followed him inside. There was a guy—she assumed Ethan—lying on the couch who waved as they walked through the living room.

Jackson waved, but didn't stop and led her upstairs to his bedroom.

She swallowed thickly as she walked inside, taking in his room. It was very neat. It was odd. Most of the guy's rooms she'd been in—which admittedly hadn't been many—were messy.

Jackson's room was neat as a pin. His bed was made with fluffed pillows on it, she couldn't see any clothing scattered, and even his desk was neat with his laptop sitting smack in the middle of it.

"So…" he said, trailing off. "We can check Netflix? Or we can look at Amazon or even run out to a Redbox to rent a DVD. I thought about ordering food, but didn't know what you wanted, so I waited."

"Netflix is cool," she said, nodding. "And I'm good with whatever food."

"I bought some snacks earlier. Make yourself comfortable and I'll go get them."

Camden narrowed her eyes at Jackson as he practically ran from his room. He'd seemed fine until they'd gotten upstairs, but as soon as they were in his room, it was a like a switch flipped. If she had to label it, she'd say that he seemed nervous. But that made little sense.

Jackson was the guy that threw long touchdown passes and stared at burly guys on the daily. There was no way he was nervous about her being at his house, let alone in his room.

She toed her shoes off and tucked them close to the wall, turning toward the door when she heard it open. Her eyes widened as she took in everything Jackson had in his arms.

"I wasn't sure what you'd like, so I tried to get a little bit of everything."

He dumped the bags on the bed. "I got some chips, cookies, popcorn…" He continued listing what he got before gesturing to the mini-fridge in his room. He'd put drinks in there.

She was impressed with how thorough he was with the food. With everything, really. He'd tried to do something to make sure she was comfortable, and it made her heart skip a beat.

She needed to get control of her errant heart and quickly. She was crushing hard, and she didn't want to set herself up for heartbreak.

She snapped back to reality when she heard a metallic snap and couldn't help but laugh as Jackson set up a small card table to put everything on.

"Really?" she asked, helping him lay their food out.

He shrugged, and she noticed that his ears turned red as he said, "I've found that it's smart to have an extra table around. I sometimes like to spread out when I study and this helps me not murder my back by sitting on my bed."

She said nothing else, but she secretly thought that was smart and she'd consider doing the same thing if she needed to in the future.

"Food is ready, so what do you want to watch?" he asked.

She shrugged and sat on the edge of his bed. "Why don't we see what there is?"

Jackson turned his TV on and navigated to Netflix. Once it loaded, she sucked in a breath, making Jackson jerk around to look at her. "What?"

"*The Witcher*. We should watch that."

"You want to watch it? Have you read the books?"

She shook her head. "Nope. No desire to either. But I want to watch that."

The picture beside the title was of Henry Cavill and she was certain her mouth was watering as she took him in. Yeah, he looked a little weird with the long white hair, but it didn't diminish his manliness.

"All right," Jackson said, chuckling as he queued up the first episode.

He walked over to the snack table and grabbed some things. She realized that she probably should too before she got sucked into watching the beautiful specimen that was Henry Cavill.

A few minutes later, they were both lying on his bed, propped against the headboard watching the sword fight on screen.

She couldn't help but let out a sigh at the beauty that was Henry Cavill. Even his grunts were something to behold.

She and Jackson didn't talk much through that first episode and he immediately started playing the second.

Before she knew it, three hours had passed. Jackson paused at the start of the fourth episode.

"Why do I get the feeling you were getting off on that?" he asked, looking at her.

She couldn't help it, she blushed. "I wasn't getting off on it…"

Jackson laughed. "Maybe not, but I definitely caught some drool coming out of your mouth."

Camden hunched down, embarrassed that Jackson had caught on to her crush.

"I'm not teasing you. That witch is hot as fuck. I'd totally do her too. I think it's cute."

Camden's breath froze in her throat, causing her to make a weird gargling noise. Cute? He thought it was cute?!

Defcon five in her brain as she tried to process that. Was being cute a good thing?

"You good?" he asked.

She nodded and cleared her throat. "Yeah, great. Want to take a break from watching and…"

Her words died in her throat as she tried to figure out what to continue with. She didn't know what else they could do.

Talk? She felt lame suggesting they talk.

Kiss? She'd die if she tried to suggest that one.

"Why don't we try to get to know each other better?" he asked, scooting down his bed until he was laying flat. He rolled to his side and looked at her expectantly.

She set the snacks she had left on the floor before mimicking his position, rolling so she was facing him.

"Don't you already know the important bit? I'm from the country. I play in the band. I don't get football. And I'm an education major."

He shrugged. "Yeah, but I feel like there's so much more to you."

"What do you want to know?"

He nibbled his lower lip before saying, "What's your favorite food?"

Chapter Eleven
Camden

The longer she talked to Jackson, the more relaxed Camden became until she was fighting off sleep when they started watching the next episode of *The Witcher*. Her head nodded a few times before she caught it, blinking rapidly and refocusing on the screen.

Eventually, she didn't catch it and fell asleep, waking later to a dark room. The television was off and the only light came from a small night light plugged in by the bathroom.

She swallowed, grimacing at how dry her mouth was. She smacked her lips a few times, trying to wet her mouth before taking stock of herself.

She was covered in a blanket. That hadn't been there earlier.

She wasn't wearing shoes still.

She was fully clothed, not that she thought he'd do anything to remove them. He didn't strike her as creepy like that.

Her eyes fully adjusted to the dark room, and she looked to her right and saw that Jackson was lying on his side facing her. She couldn't make out much of his face, just the general shape of his nose and the curve of his chin.

She grimaced as she swallowed again and knew she needed to get some water. And she'd head out too. She didn't want to overstay her welcome, especially since she fell asleep.

She slowly sat up and stretched as the blanket pooled in her lap. She squinted and tried to see where her phone had ended up. It wasn't on the bed or in her pocket, but when she looked toward the nightstand on her side, she caught what looked like a phone. She grabbed it and hit the home button, squinting and grimacing at the brightness of the screen.

It was her phone, so she thumbed to the flashlight option and turned it on so she could see better.

She kicked the blanket on her lap off and threw her legs over the side of the bed.

"What are you doing?" Jackson asked sleepily from behind her, making her freeze.

"Uh…" she said, not sure how to respond.

She was trying to leave, but she hadn't expected him waking. She shouldn't feel awkward about leaving in the middle of the night. It wasn't like they slept together or anything. Him waking up changed that though.

It made her feel weird knowing he was awake and aware she was leaving.

"Are you leaving?" He sounded more awake now and she could hear rustling.

A light clicked on behind her and she cringed before turning so she could see Jackson.

What little saliva still in her mouth dried up as she took him in. He wasn't wearing a shirt, which meant all his glorious muscles were on display. She knew he was ripped; he was a football player. They had to work out a lot to stay at the top of their game.

She'd also watched how his biceps bunched more than she would ever admit to anyone.

They were two perfectly round spheres that were just begging to be watched. She would be doing the women of the university a disservice if she didn't watch them.

But they had nothing on his chest. Good Lord, his chest.

When he sat up, the blankets had fallen to his lap, leaving every square inch of his torso on display for her to look at. His pecs were defined, as were his abs. It was a sight to behold.

And she was staring at him like he was the last piece of pizza at the buffet during exam week. She needed to get herself together.

She cleared her throat and looked at his face, catching the smirk there before his expression cleared.

"Are you leaving?" he repeated.

She nodded. "Yeah."

Her voice squeaked, and she hoped he hadn't noticed. She was already on edge because of the man flesh on display. She didn't need it to get worse because he picked up on her nerves.

"It's like three in the morning," he said, glancing at the clock. "Just stay."

He lay back down, but kept his gaze on her.

"I don't want to wear out my welcome…" she said, trying to think of an excuse to leave. She wasn't sure she'd survive staying in Jackson's bed with him.

"You won't. It's fine. You want some shorts or something? You've got jeans on."

Before she could respond, Jackson was already standing and striding toward his dresser, opening a drawer and pulling something out before throwing it at her.

She automatically held a hand up and caught it. It was a pair of mesh shorts.

"I've got to pee, so get changed."

He turned and walked into his bathroom and shut the door behind him.

She stared at the closed door for several moments before shaking her head and sighing. Guess she was staying then.

She quickly unbuttoned and unzipped her jeans before pushing them down and kicking them to the side. She pulled the shorts up and tightened the drawstrings so they didn't fall down her hips.

She heard the toilet flush, the water run, and then the door opened. She glanced at Jackson and tried not to ogle his chest again. Or notice how nice his butt looked in the shorts he was wearing.

She definitely wouldn't be thinking of *that* later. Insert sarcasm and an eye roll there. His butt would likely consume her thoughts once she was alone.

Jackson climbed back into the bed and slid under the covers while she gathered the blanket on her side and lay back down.

"You can get under the covers," he said.

She blushed.

"Just drop the blanket on the floor and I'll get it in the morning."

She balled the blanket up and tossed it to the left. She then wiggled until she got the comforter and sheet down and she could slide in.

Jackson clicked the light off while she tried to get more comfortable. But now she was acutely aware of the fact that she was laying next to a half-naked Jackson Dove while wearing a t-shirt and a pair of his shorts.

As she rolled to her side, the under wire of her bra dug into her breast, making her wince. She sat up and quickly undid the back before pulling it out of her sleeve. She dropped her bra to the floor.

When she lay back down, she was more comfortable physically, but that was it.

It was dark, and she was acutely aware of how close Jackson was to her. Then her mind flashed back to kissing him in the car. She was now nervous and horny.

She sighed.

"What's wrong?"

She squeaked. "Nothing."

Jackson sighed, and the bed shook before she felt a hand on her arm. "Roll to face me."

She did as he asked. Once she rolled, his hand slid up to her face and cupped her cheek. She held her breath as she felt him caress her cheek before his fingers traced her lips.

"Are you nervous?" he asked, his voice low.

"A little," she whispered back.

The kiss from earlier flashed into her mind again. She was regretting even kissing him if it was working her up this much, even if the situation seemed to beg for a kiss. He'd admitted that he liked her. And she'd kissed him.

Rustling.

One of Jackson's legs touched hers, making her jump. Slowly, he moved closer and pressed the rest of his body against hers.

He was close enough he could feel his breath fanning across her face and she wanted nothing more than to close the distance between them to press her lips against his. It was physically painful to be this close to him without touching, but her nerves were ruling the day right then.

"Don't be," he said, his nose brushing against her own. "I'd never do anything you don't want to. I'll be the perfect gentleman, even if the thought of you sitting in my bed without a bra on excites me more than you'll ever know."

Camden shivered at his words.

This time, she wasn't the one to make the first move; he was.

His lips lightly brushed her own, drawing a sigh from her before he slanted his lips over hers and kissed her more forcefully.

Though their mouths tried to devour each other, no other part of their body touched. Camden yearned to press against Jackson so she could feel every inch of him.

Instead, Jackson eased back and rubbed his nose against hers before saying, "Get some sleep. It's late."

She licked her lips, able to taste him there before she rolled over. One of Jackson's arms slid over her waist and pulled her so that her back was pressed to his front.

She gulped as she felt something long and hard pressed against her lower back. It was nice to know that she wasn't the only person affected by their situation.

But she wouldn't be acting on anything right then, and it was obvious Jackson wouldn't either. So instead, she closed her eyes and willed herself to fall asleep.

Chapter Twelve
Jackson

Waking up next to the girl of his dreams was unparalleled. The only issue with that was he was sporting major morning wood and his erection was nestled against Camden's ass crack.

He wanted to move back, but he had no way of knowing how lightly she slept. He didn't want to move and have her wake up suddenly, assuming he was trying something. She didn't seem like the type, but he didn't know what she was like in an intimate situation. She might freak.

She might also be all for some morning fun.

But he didn't want to push it.

He was just about to try moving his hips away when Camden sucked in a deep breath and arched her back, pushing her ass more firmly against his hips, making him stifle a groan.

Camden relaxed, but her butt stayed on his dick and he knew he needed to move.

"Morning," he said. He hoped he could distract her with some conversation and move his hips away without her noticing.

"Morning," she returned, her voice hoarse with sleep.

He couldn't resist leaning in and nuzzling against the back of her neck.

Camden sighed and leaned back against him, making him tighten his arm in response.

He wasn't a Casanova or Don Juan by any means, but he couldn't remember the last time he'd had a girl in his bed that just slept. Normally, the girls didn't stay the night if they were in his room, or he went to their place.

It was a nice change to wake up next to someone and just hold them. He wouldn't mind something a little more either, but he was content to hold as well.

They lay there together for several minutes, neither of them speaking and Jackson could feel himself starting to fall asleep again.

Camden laid a hand over one of his, lightly tracing his fingers with her own and he could feel himself relaxing further.

She laid her hand flat over his own and curled his fingers around the side of his hand, holding it.

Any sleep that was lingering suddenly fled as he waited to see what she would do. His hand was loosely hanging by her stomach, on top of her shirt.

Neither of them moved for several long moments until she started guiding their hands up her torso until his hand was cupping one of her breasts.

He froze. When he didn't move after several moments, she moved her hand directly on top of his and guided his fingers in a squeezing motion.

He sucked in a breath as she moved her hand away from his and he took over the caressing of her breast. He alternated between squeezing the globe of flesh and drawing a finger around one of her nipples, grinning when he felt it harden under his fingers.

He switched to her other breast, giving it the same treatment and taking delight in the little shivers working through her body and the light moans she let out every few seconds.

Each time she shivered, her butt brushed more forcefully against his erection and he had to stifle a few groans of his own.

They weren't even doing anything overly sexy, but he already felt toward the end of his leash, ready to blow.

Camden grabbed his hand and moved it away from her breast before turning over to face him. He swallowed thickly as he met her gaze.

She was still holding his hand and moved it back to her breast before curling the other one around his neck and pulling him to her for a kiss.

He normally worried about morning breath, but right then, he didn't give a shit. Camden was kissing him and he was going to take full advantage of that.

He abandoned her breast to drive his fingers into her hair and pull her more flush against him.

He jerked and pulled away from her when he felt her hand brush against his abs.

Camden didn't let him pull away any further, chasing his lips and claiming them for another kiss. He groaned low in his throat when she ran a finger along the top of his boxers, her finger just barely grazing the top of his dick.

While she toyed with him, he brought his hand down to the hem of her shirt and slipped his hand underneath, lightly tickling her as he moved back toward his breast, cupping it once he reached it.

As his hand cupped her breast, she finally, *finally* slipped her hand into his boxers and gripped him. They both groaned and their kisses became more consuming.

He pressed more fully against her and pushed her so that she was lying on her back and he could hover over her. She parted her legs, allowing him to settle between them and press his aching dick against her center.

He would give anything for those layers separating them to disappear so he could feel her. But he wouldn't rush this. If they just made out, he'd be fine with that. He'd probably end up with blue balls, but it would be worth it with the knowledge he'd made out with her and moved one step closer to what he wanted: her as his girlfriend.

Camden moaned and brought him back to the here and now. Her hand slipped between them and he moved his hips back so she could reach into his boxers and grip him again.

He couldn't help pressing his hips forward, thrusting through the circle her fingers made around him. He caressed her tongue with his own while he moved his hand from her breast and toward her center.

He went slow, wanting to give her a chance to say something and to stop him. But when she hadn't said anything by the time he reached the waist of her shorts, he pressed on, slipping his hand inside her panties.

He groaned when he felt how wet she was. She was so hot and slick, he could just imagine thrusting his dick against her before pressing in.

His dick twitched at his line of thoughts and he had to will himself to calm down. He didn't want to blow it right then and embarrass himself. She'd barely touched him.

He tried to focus on the task at hand and not on how amazing her hand felt on him.

He pressed lightly against her clit, making her hips jerk. She tore her lips from his and moaned as she threw her head back.

"Fuck," he muttered as he kissed her neck and sank two fingers into her. She was wet, warm, and tight.

He slowly thrust his fingers in and out of her while using his thumb to apply pressure to her clit.

"Oh my God," she moaned, and she grew wetter.

He lightly bit her neck before he started moving his fingers faster, taking pleasure in the sound of his fingers moving in and out of her.

Camden moaned again and started to ride his fingers, her hand in his pants forgotten as he helped her chase her orgasm.

A few moments later, she tensed and her back arched off the bed. Her walls fluttered around his fingers before clamping down. She was biting her lip to muffle a groan, but he could still hear it.

He continued to caress her as she came down from her high and pulled out only when she sagged back to the bed.

He pulled back and smirked at the dazed look on her face. He'd put that there, and he was damn proud of it.

He moved to his back beside her and tried not to pay attention to his dick. It was hard enough to pound nails. He'd have to handle it later though.

He wouldn't ask her to do anything about it.

He looked over at her and saw that she was staring at him.

Her mouth opened, but no sound came out. He fought back a grin as he watched her try to speak for several moments without success.

Finally, she said, "Holy shit."

He didn't stop the smirk that spread at her words. He was a smug shit at that.

Before he could register what she was doing, Camden was straddling his hips, her warm center pressed against him and her lips by his ear.

"I should return the favor, don't you think?"

Chapter Thirteen
Camden

Camden hoped the nerves she was feeling weren't showing on her face. She was trying to act cool and collected, but she was anything but inside.

Jackson had rocked her world with that orgasm and she wanted to return the favor for him. The only problem was she wasn't very experienced with pleasuring a guy. Her few run-ins with previous sexual partners were lackluster. Foreplay wasn't a word, and neither was orgasming.

She leaned down and acted like she was going to kiss him before moving to the side and pressing wet, open-mouthed kisses to the side of his neck.

Jackson groaned and shifted below her, pressing his dick closer to her.

She continued to kiss down his body, scraping her teeth along the ridges of his abs before hooking her fingers into the waistband of his shorts and boxers. She looked up at him and met his wide gaze. His pupils were so large there was almost no iris visible and he was staring at her intently.

She jerked on his shorts and he lifted his hips so she could pull them off.

His dick slapped his stomach and she couldn't help but stare at it. She knew he was nice and girthy from when she had her hand in his boxers, but seeing and feeling were two entirely different things.

She pulled his shorts and boxers all the way off before kneeling between his legs. She looked back up at Jackson and saw that he was still staring at her, his mouth opened and his fists clenched in the blankets.

She gave herself a quick mental pep talk before leaning forward and licking at the pre-cum beaded on the tip of his dick.

Jackson shuddered. "Fuck."

His voice was low and strained. It was heady to know that he was that way because of her and she hadn't even touched him yet.

She leaned forward again and licked him from root to tip this time, flattening her tongue over him before sliding back down.

Jackson's hips jerked, and he blew out a sharp breath as she repeated it once more.

She brought a hand up and lightly caressed his balls before sucking the tip of his erection into her mouth.

Jackson moaned and said something, but it was garbled.

She glanced up at him and saw that he had one arm thrown over his eyes while his other hand was still fisted into his sheets.

That wouldn't do. She wanted him to feel a fraction of what she felt when he touched her. She'd felt hot everywhere and thought she would go insane before she climaxed. When it hit, it felt like it had snuck up on her.

Her nipples had pebbled until they were hard points and it felt like a light touch anywhere on her body would send her off again as she came down.

She'd never felt like that.

She wanted to drive Jackson crazy too.

Even if she didn't know how to give a blowjob, she was going to be enthusiastic about it.

She wrapped a hand around the base of his dick and sucked as much of him into her mouth as possible.

He nudged the back of her throat and she backed off, stroking what hadn't fit into her mouth—which seemed to be most of him—with her hand.

She repeated the motion, smoothing her hand down his shaft and tried to find a rhythm easy for her to maintain while also driving him crazy.

Jackson shivered and his legs were growing restless.

She snuck another peek at him and took some satisfaction in the look of raw hunger on his face. He was looking at her again and the look on his face was feral.

He reached toward her and slid a hand into her hair. He lightly tugged on her hair, trying to pull her up, but she resisted.

"Camden, babe, please," he said, tugging again.

She released him with a pop and looked at him as she continued to stroke him. "What?"

"I—" He faltered slightly as his voice cracked.

He seemed lost for words. Camden wanted to lean down and pull him back into her mouth, but she also wanted to know what he felt like inside her.

Since this was a morning of firsts for her, she was going to do another first: make a move.

She slid down the bed and stood, keeping her eyes on Jackson. He watched her, his eyes dipping when her hands moved to the hem of her shirt. They widened when she pulled it up and off, tossing it into the corner of the room.

She then hooked her thumbs in the waistband of her shorts and underwear. Jackson's mouth fell open again as she pushed them down, letting them drop to the floor.

Jackson's eyes roamed her body before he met her gaze again.

"Come here," he said hoarsely.

She propped a knee on the bed, watching as he reached into his bedside table. He pulled a condom out and ripped it open, tossing the foil wrapper to the side before smoothing it down his erection.

His look was pure sex. His gaze raked over her body as she crawled up the bed toward him. He sat up and tugged her toward him when she was close enough, helping her settle over his hips.

He smoothed a hand down her side. "You sure?" he asked her.

She nodded. "So sure."

He huffed out a breath and leaned up to draw one of her nipples into his mouth. He laved it with his tongue before biting down on it lightly. She shuddered in his arms.

He released her with a pop, bringing a hand up to flick her nipple while one hand dipped between her legs. Tingles spread throughout her body at his light caresses.

Jackson was touching her softly, but she was now to the point of wanting more. She batted his hand away and reached between them to grasp him.

She sat up a little more and placed him at her entrance before slowly sinking down. She grimaced slightly at the burn of him stretching her in ways she hadn't been stretched before, but she rocked her hips and he finally slid all the way in.

"Fuck," he said, his hands grasping her ass and squeezing.

He encouraged her to rock against him and she gasped at the sensation of her clit rubbing against him.

Jackson lay back and bit his lip as he looked at her.

She grew bolder in her movements, circling her hips and bouncing up and down every so often.

Jackson's hands stayed on her hips and helped guide her as she faltered. It was hard work being on top.

"Roll," he said after a few minutes.

He rolled with her and was somehow able to stay inside her, pushing in further as her legs opened further as he settled between them.

They both groaned as he bottomed out.

He sat up and gripped her legs behind the knees as he slowly pulled up and snapped his hips back toward her.

She groaned as he repeated the motion, speeding up each time.

Soon the only sound was their slapping skin and their mingled moans as Jackson fucked her.

She was so close to another orgasm. She was teetering on the edge of it and all it took was a little pressure on her clit and she was shooting off into the stratosphere.

Her walls clamped down on Jackson, drawing a strangled moan from him as his thrusts sped up before he slammed in one final time before collapsing on top of her.

They both lay there, panting, for several minutes before Jackson rolled off her and walked into the bathroom.

She lay there for several moments, trying to get her brain to work again. It had short-circuited about the point he stuck his dick inside her.

"Hey," Jackson said as he padded toward the bed with a cloth in his hands.

She watched as he leaned over and pressed the warm cloth between her legs. She sighed, realizing just how sore she already was. That would teach her to go an extended period without having sex again.

He tossed the cloth into the corner of the room before lying next to her on the bed and gathering her into his arms.

She laid her head on his shoulder and tried not to think about how perfect it seemed to lay there with him. Neither of them spoke for several minutes and Camden used the silence to gather her thoughts.

She'd never slept with a guy she wasn't dating before. It was weird to think of having sex outside of a relationship because it wasn't something she thought she would ever do. Yet here she was, and she'd just done it with a guy she really liked.

He'd admitted to her he liked her as more than friends, but they hadn't talked about it since. A small part of her worried that now that she'd slept with him, that would be it. He would be done with her and the feelings he professed to have would disappear.

"Sooo…" he said a few moments later. "I'd planned to ask you this later, but considering what just happened, I want to do it now. Do you want to go out with me?"

She moved her head so she could look up at his face. He was already looking down at her.

"Go out with you?"

"Yeah. Not just on a date, but as my…girlfriend?"

His voice wavered at the end, revealing the nerves he was trying hard to hide. She knew it was weird, but knowing that he was nervous about asking her out made her feel just a little better. It was nice knowing she wasn't the only one that was nervous about being with the other person.

Though she couldn't imagine why he was nervous. He was a god on campus and any girl would jump at the chance to date him. So would she.

"Are you sure?" she couldn't help asking.

He arched a brow. "Am I sure?" he asked, chuckling. "I'm damn sure. I'd planned to ask you to go to breakfast with me and I'd talk to you about dating there. But considering we just had sex, I wanted to make sure I asked you now before you got it into your head that I was using you after admitting I liked you."

Camden's eyes widened at his words. She couldn't help but be surprised that he voiced what she'd been thinking. Was she obvious? She didn't think so, but she knew she had an expressive face.

He rolled onto his side and faced her.

"I'm all in. I know that you probably have some concerns considering the reputation of the football players here, but I want you to know that I'm not like that. I haven't had a serious girlfriend in a while and I want you to be it. I know things won't be easy…"

She grimaced at those words, Lisa popping into her head. "But I think we can make it work," he finished.

She licked her lips as she thought over his words. She wanted to date him so badly, but she couldn't help doubts creeping in.

She was just a band nerd. She'd never in a million years thought she'd meet up with the star quarterback of the football team, let alone have sex with him and have him ask her out.

They were two different people with two different groups of friends.

"How about this," he said, breaking into her thoughts. "Why don't we start with something easy: breakfast. Then we can plan another date after that. We don't have to label it or anything."

With those words, the panic bubbling inside her calmed, and she nodded.

"I can do that."

She felt bad that she freaked about being his girlfriend, but she couldn't get Lisa out of her mind. And she knew there were other girls just like her on campus that would be out to make her life a living hell.

She wanted to avoid that for as long as possible. But she wanted Jackson too. So she'd probably have to get used to it if she was going to be with him.

She was sure he'd be worth it based on what she already knew about him.

"So…breakfast?"

Chapter Fourteen
Camden

After agreeing to see how things went with Jackson, Camden expected things to change.

They didn't. They remained exactly the same.

She knew she should be happy with that, but she couldn't help waiting for the other shoe to drop. It finally came on one of their final practice days before their homecoming game. The marching band was practicing their half-time show with the dancers, color guard, baton twirlers, and a few other groups.

It was a grueling practice. The drum majors were on everyone's ass about being on their mark and marching correctly and Camden was noticing some glares coming her way from her *best friend* Lisa when the dancers weren't dancing.

She had a feeling that her time had run out.

Corey sidled up to her on their next water break. "Why are you getting glared at by that Lisa girl?"

Camden lifted one shoulder as she took a long sip from her bottle. "Who knows?"

"You think it's about…" Corey glanced around before leaning a little closer to Camden and dropping her voice, "you know who?"

Camden arched a brow. "Voldemort?"

Corey gasped. "You can't say his name! You'll invoke him!"

Camden rolled her eyes and screwed the top back on her bottle. "You realize he's not real, right?"

"You can't know that. Maybe he *is* real and we just don't know it because we're muggles."

Camden shook her head and set her bottle down. Some days she wondered why she was friends with Corey. Today was one of those days.

"If it isn't the nerd and loser, standing together."

Camden sighed at Lisa's voice. She'd been lucky to go this long without her coming to talk to her. Maybe if she let her get it over with, Lisa would leave her alone.

"Hey, Lisa," Camden said, turning to face the other girl.

Lisa was scowling at her, which made Camden falter. While Lisa wasn't pleasant to be around, she was more of an annoying gnat than anything. She wasn't nice, and she didn't seem to get that being mean wasn't the way to accomplish anything. But she hadn't been outright hostile like she was right then.

"I thought we talked about you and Jackson."

"I didn't realize you attacking me at practice was us talking."

If it was possible, Lisa glared at her even harder.

"Listen, bitch, just because you're working with him doesn't mean you get to encroach on *my territory*."

Camden's brows shot up. "Your territory?"

"Yeah, Jackson. He's mine. We've been friends for years and this is the year that he finally realizes what's been in front of him the entire time. Me."

Camden wasn't sure what to say, and she was sure shock was on her face, but she couldn't even bring herself to care.

She wasn't worried about what Lisa was saying. Jackson had already shown that he didn't care for her the night that he sat in the lawn chairs with Camden. He'd avoided Lisa.

What she was worried about was Lisa herself. Camden had seen mean girls in high school and how they bullied people they saw as lesser than. She hadn't seen it as much in college, but that didn't mean that it wasn't happening.

Lisa was just a mean girl. But it looked like she was a mean girl with an agenda and Camden was standing in the way of that. Lisa just didn't realize how much yet.

"I'm not sure why you're telling me this..." Camden said, trying to think of a way to get out of this confrontation. She had no desire to talk to Lisa, and she knew that if she wasn't careful, she'd end up getting demerits because of this.

Dr. Foster was very specific the last time Lisa accosted her. Camden could get in a lot of trouble when she hadn't even done anything.

"Because you're hanging around Jackson and it's pathetic. Do you think if you stare at him all wide-eyed that he'll have pity on you and fuck you?"

Camden's mind flashed back to the night that he had in fact fucked her. Her face flushed as she remembered what it felt like to have him touching her.

Lisa laughed, pulling her from her memory. "You're blushing. I should have known that's what you were hoping for. Get over it, loser. You're not his type and it's just...sad that you think you stand a chance."

Camden knew that she shouldn't let Lisa's words bother her, but she couldn't help it. She'd grown up so much since high school when she was shy and lacked self-confidence. But hearing Lisa tear her down reminded her of what it felt like to be known as the band nerd and teased because she was in the marching band. Don't even get her started on the jokes made about flute players.

"What's going on here?" Dr. Foster asked, coming to stand to the right of Camden.

Camden just looked at him, her voice gone. She didn't even have it in her to fight whatever punishment was going to be handed out right then, even if it wasn't deserved.

"I don't know," Lisa said, turning to face him and twirling her hair around her finger. "I was standing here talking to my friends, and she came up and starting yelling at me."

Dr. Foster shot Camden a look, and it looked like he didn't believe what Lisa was saying, but Camden remained silent.

"Is that true?" he asked Camden, giving her a chance to defend herself.

"Of course it's not!" Corey said, bumping Camden's shoulder. "Lisa has been glaring at her all practice and she came over here while we were getting water. Camden said nothing to her."

Dr. Foster looked between her and Lisa, his brow furrowing.

He rubbed a hand through his hair and shook his head. "Unless someone will corroborate what you're saying, you'll both be getting demerits. I'll talk to Coach Johnson about yours, Lisa."

Lisa gasped dramatically, and it surprised Camden she didn't faint and play the situation up further. "Dr. Foster! I didn't do anything!"

A round of snorts came from behind Camden and she glanced over her shoulder to see that there were several people from her section of the band standing there.

"Dr. Foster, Lisa came up while Camden was standing there talking to Corey. She barely said anything to the girl. Lisa was the one that was basically threatening her," Missy, another flute player, stated.

Dr. Foster looked at Camden again before looking at Missy. "Anyone else have anything to add to the situation?"

A few people murmured agreement with what Missy said and Dr. Foster sighed. "Lisa, I'll be talking to Johnson about this. Camden, stay after practice so you and I can discuss this further."

Camden jerkily nodded while Lisa stomped off to where the rest of her dance team was standing.

"Get ready to run through it again," Dr. Foster said, causing everyone to scatter. He walked back to his tower and Camden turned around to walk back to her starting mark.

"You need to speak up," Corey said, falling into step beside her. "Lisa is being a bitch and if you don't stand up for yourself, she won't stop."

Camden shrugged and stopped on her mark, getting ready to run through their routine.

She heard Corey sigh, but nothing else. She glanced over her shoulder and saw that Corey had moved into place a few rows over.

They started running through the start of their show and Camden found her mind wandering. It was a good thing she knew the halftime show like the back of her hand because she didn't remember much of the rest of practice. She was too caught up in her own mind.

She knew that Lisa was just one girl in a long string of girls that would likely be mad about Camden dating Jackson. She shouldn't let her words seep in. But she couldn't help it.

She *was* the band nerd that was trying to date the star quarterback. In what universe did this even make sense? People like her didn't date people like him. It just wasn't done.

By the time practice ended, she was exhausted and Lisa's words were ringing in her ears. She couldn't get them to stop playing on repeat in her head.

She packed her flute into its case and snagged her bag before walking over to Dr. Foster. He was busy talking to the drum majors, so she waited to the side until he was ready to talk to her.

A few minutes later, he turned to her and crossed his arms. Dr. Foster was one of her favorite people at the university. He was easygoing and nice. He was very knowledgeable and fair when the situation called for it.

Right then she didn't care about that though. All she cared about was being able to escape back to her apartment and wallowing a little in self-pity.

"Camden, want to talk to me about what happened earlier?"

He phrased it as a question, but she knew that he wasn't really asking. He expected her to speak up.

She sighed and dropped her gaze to the ground. "Not much to tell. Lisa came up to me and started talking to me."

"Is she harassing you?"

Camden raised one shoulder in a half-hearted shrug. To an extent, yeah, Lisa was harassing her. But it wasn't anything that hadn't happened before and that wouldn't happen again. She was used to it. It's why she kept her head down.

Dr. Foster sighed, drawing Camden's gaze back to him.

"I need you to be honest with me right now. I can't have one of my band members off her game because of someone, especially someone that's been causing issues with other people."

Camden's eyes widened at his words. Lisa was causing issues for other people?

Seeming to read the question in Camden's eyes, he said, "I can't tell you much about it, but know that you telling me what's going on with her will be helpful for the coach of the dance team. There are some issues there and she's trying to get all the information she can before deciding."

Camden bit her bottom lip at Dr. Foster's words. He implied that her information might help the coach decide about Lisa, which meant she would probably be kicked off the team.

That didn't sit well with her. She didn't want to be the reason that Lisa lost her place, but she also knew that she couldn't sit back and stay silent on the off chance that Lisa tried her act on someone else.

So she told him everything. About the first time Lisa came up to her at the start of the semester and the mean looks she'd gotten since culminating in today's confrontation.

When she finished, Dr. Foster smiled and said, "Thank you. Let me know if anything else happens."

Camden nodded and scurried away, ready to be back to her apartment.

As she unlocked her car, her phone buzzed, and she pulled it out of her pocket, an involuntary smile spreading across her face when she saw that it was Jackson.

Jackson: Your practice done yet? Want to hang out tonight?

She wanted to hang out tonight. She could use a good hug. But with Lisa's words still ringing in her ears, she wasn't sure she'd be able to face him and not spill what had happened.

Camden: Not tonight. I need to get some studying done for a test tomorrow. I'm planning to head right home to get started.

Jackson didn't immediately reply and Camden tossed her phone into the passenger seat with her bag. Her mind was already on getting home, showering, changing, and then trying to study and relax.

If only she could get Lisa's words out of her head.

Chapter Fifteen
Jackson

Camden might have said no to hanging out, but she didn't say no to eating together. So Jackson decided he'd surprise her with something to eat.

He'd texted her right after he'd walked into the locker room after practice. It had been brutal because of the upcoming homecoming game when they played their biggest rival, State.

King University had won for the last three years running and Jackson wanted to be sure they won this year too.

He wasn't the only one that wanted that. Most of the other guys were pushing harder to make sure they were ready.

He planned to shower and then run to get something to eat before surprising Camden at her place. He hoped she wouldn't be mad that he interrupted her study time, but outside of class, he hadn't had a chance to see her much recently. He wanted to spend a little bit of time together that wasn't dictated by their schedule.

"Dude, you talked to Camden?" Ethan asked as he walked up to his locker next to Jackson's.

"No, why?"

Ethan snorted and shook his head. "I just heard Roscoe talking about something going down at the marching band practice. Apparently Lisa tried to start something with her."

Jackson paused in pulling his pads off, gaping at Ethan. "What?"

Ethan nodded. "Yeah, man. I didn't hear much because once Roscoe realized I was standing there, he clammed up. But he said something about Lisa being pissed that Camden didn't get in trouble and that they would make sure Lisa got Camden back."

A sick feeling settled in his stomach. What Ethan was saying wasn't good. Lisa was relatively harmless, but Roscoe wasn't. Even though hazing was against the rules, that didn't stop Roscoe from trying to do it to the new players.

He'd been reprimanded the year before, so he'd been more careful about it this year. But Jackson had heard some guys talking about Roscoe. They didn't have proof, so they couldn't do anything about it except keep their eyes open.

Roscoe could easily do something to Camden, especially if he realized how important she was to Jackson.

"You going to do anything?" Ethan asked, tearing Jackson from his thoughts.

He shrugged. "Not sure what I can do. Unless he does something, I won't make the first move. That's a sure way to get my ass benched."

Ethan shot him an incredulous look. "Really? You're not going to do anything?"

Jackson shrugged. "I'll talk to Camden and find out about today. I'll make sure to warn her too, but I can't do anything if nothing is done."

Ethan shook his head. "I hope you know what you're doing, man. You know what Roscoe's like. You also know how vindictive Lisa is. I have a bad feeling about the two of them."

So did Jackson, but he didn't tell Ethan that. "I'll worry about it when it happens."

Ethan muttered under his breath, but Jackson said nothing else. He quickly stripped out of the rest of his gear and wrapped a towel around his waist before digging his shower stuff out of his locker.

He made his way into one shower and quickly rinsed off, his mind turning over what Ethan told him and his own worries and fears about Camden.

He knew he should try to head Roscoe off at the pass, but he wasn't sure how. Roscoe could be as slippery as an eel and Jackson knew he wouldn't get anything out of him if he were to ask. So that meant waiting.

And waiting sucked, especially when he was worried about what the guy would do to the girl he was with and cared about.

He finished his shower and quickly set about getting dressed. He waved to the guys as he stepped out of the locker room and hurried to his car, tossing his bag into the back.

He quickly went off campus to the Bojangles by the main entrance before driving the short distance to Camden's place.

Once he parked, he texted her.

Jackson: Can you come let me in?

His phone buzzed with a text a few moments later.

Camden: Let you in?

Jackson: Yeah. I brought food.

He stuffed his phone in the pocket of his shorts and grabbed the food before slamming his door shut and clicking the button for the locks.

He walked toward the back door and a few moments later, Camden opened it and looked around before spotting him.

She smiled as he walked closer. "Curbside service?"

He grinned. "Only for you."

She stepped to the side so he could slide past her and he paused just inside the door. He might have been to her building before, but he'd never been inside her apartment.

"You live with your best friend, right?" he asked as he followed her out of the stairwell and into a carpeted hallway.

Camden nodded and looked at him over her shoulder. "Yeah. We share a two-bedroom apartment. It's not the biggest or the nicest, but it is on campus and it's included in our tuition. We don't have to fight for parking, so I'll take it happily."

Jackson nodded. That would be kinda nice. They lived close enough to campus that they couldn't get parking passes, so they had to walk, ride a bike, or skateboard. But not having to worry about parking because you lived on campus would be nice.

"Here it is, home sweet home," she said as she unlocked a door and pushed it open.

He glanced around as he followed her in. At first glance, it reminded him a lot of hotel rooms. It had bland, generic furniture that he was certain matched every other apartment in the building. But he could see where Camden and Corey had tried to make the space their own. There were a few posters on the wall and he saw some blankets and pillows on the couch. It made it seem homier, but it also made him appreciate living in the football house off campus.

"I brought us Bojangles," he said, setting everything down on the small dining room table just inside the door.

Camden smiled. "Thanks."

He smirked. "Is that all I get for thanks?"

Her cheeks pinked as she stepped closer and tilted her head up so her lips were just a few scant inches from his own. He leaned down and kissed her softly, fighting the urge to sigh in contentment.

She pulled back and grabbed a chair while he did the same. "How was your day?" he asked, curious to see if she'd mention what he heard about Lisa.

She chatted about her classes and practice, mentioning how tired she was and how she just wanted to collapse. But nothing about Lisa.

He wasn't mad that she hadn't mentioned it, but there was a part of him that was upset about it. While they weren't defining their relationship with labels, he cared about Camden and wanted her to tell him if something had happened during the day. It was upsetting that she hadn't, and that he had to ask her about it.

"What happened with Lisa?" he asked when her chatter died down.

Camden paled, and she set her drink cup down. "How'd you hear about that?"

He kept his eyes on her, on the lookout for anything that would tell him what she was thinking when he answered. "Ethan overheard a guy talking about it. Apparently Lisa called him to bitch."

Camden's shoulders slumped, and she fiddled with the straw in her cup, making it screech in the plastic lid. Camden sighed after a few moments and looked at him. "It's nothing, really."

Jackson arched a brow. "Seems like something if Lisa called Roscoe about it. What happened?"

He listened as she told him about Lisa coming up to her and he worked hard to school his features so the scowl he wanted to wear didn't break through.

"That's ridiculous, I hope you know that," he told her when she finished. "Yeah, I've been friends with her, but I've never given her any sign I saw her as more than. I haven't even talked to her since that time you came into the study room and she was in there too."

Camden nodded, but remained silent. He narrowed his eyes as he took her in. Her shoulders were still slumped, and she looked like she was curling in on herself. She hadn't told him how she was feeling about it, but he had a feeling that Lisa's words were eating away at her.

He might not look it at this point in his life, but he struggled with self-esteem and confidence issues in middle school when he first tried out for the football team. He didn't make it his seventh grade year and was teased mercilessly about it because he cried when he saw he hadn't made the cut.

That had been the impetus to make him work harder so he would make it the next year.

He recognized that same defeated posture in Camden.

"Don't let Lisa get to you. It's what she wants," he said a little more harshly than he'd intended.

Camden's eyes snapped to him. "Excuse me?"

He softened his tone when he said, "Lisa just wants you to get upset and to back off of me. Don't let her do that. You know I like you and I know you like me. I'd shout it to the rooftops if you'd let me that you were my girlfriend. But I'm not going to push you to do something that makes you uncomfortable. And I'd love to say that you won't have to deal with people like Lisa ever, but that's just not the case. Lisa is just one of God knows how many women that will act the same because they're jealous bitches. And they should be jealous of you. You're amazing and I'm lucky to have met you."

He was babbling at first before he said that last sentence. Even though he hadn't set out to say all that, it didn't make it any less true. He was lucky to have met her. She was one of the kindest people he knew.

Camden sighed. "I know I shouldn't. But I can't help it. She hit on my insecurities."

"What can I do to help you see that she's just a jealous bitch?"

Camden smiled at him sadly. "Can you just keep being you and being there for me?"

He smiled and nodded. "I can definitely do that. I'm your man for all your needs."

He wiggled his eyebrows at the end of that sentence, making her laugh.

"I wasn't referring to that."

"You sure? I can be your star quarterback with that too."

Camden laughed. "Oh my, God. You're so inappropriate."

He leered at her. "And? I seem to remember you liking it."

Her face pinked, and she continued laughing. He joined her, glad that he'd gotten her to break her serious facade for a few minutes.

"Do I need to go?" he asked after their laughter died down. "I can. But I have my bag in the car and would love to stay here and study with you."

Camden nodded. "Okay, that's fine. You get your bag and I'll clean up?"

He stood quickly and almost ran out the door to his car. He propped the door to the building open so he could get back in without Camden since he forgot to ask her for her ID and then quickly made his way back inside.

By the time he stepped back in her apartment, she'd already spread her things over on half of the table and had her nose buried in a book. He reclaimed his seat and quickly did the same.

Even though they were just going to be studying, he couldn't help the feeling of happiness and contentment that came over him at spending the time with Camden.

Chapter Sixteen
Camden

"You're fucking the star quarterback. You kinda have to go," Corey said, dropping onto Camden's bed.

Camden shot her a look. "I'm not fucking him. We had sex once."

Corey rolled her eyes. "Please. You'd climb him like a tree if you both had more time and you know it. Still doesn't change the fact that y'all are dating—"

"We're just friends," Camden interrupted.

"Even if you haven't labeled it," Corey said, speaking over Camden, "you're still dating. You eat meals together, text, even study together. I'm surprised you haven't fucked him again though. He's primo meat."

"You're so disgusting sometimes," Camden muttered, turning back to her computer. "I'm not going."

Corey sighed. "Come on! You know you want to see him. If you don't go, Lisa or some other girl will be all up on him."

Camden's back stiffened before she turned to look at Corey. "Are you trying to say that he'll take advantage of me not being there to sleep with someone else?"

Corey's eyes widened, and she shook her head quickly. "No! That's not what I'm saying at all! I'm just saying…girls will see you not being there as an invitation to move in and shoot their shot."

Camden nibbled on her bottom lip at Corey's words. She knew she shouldn't let the thought of other girls hitting on and flirting with Jackson bother her, but she couldn't help it. Deep inside was that insecure girl that knew someone as popular as Jackson would never look her way.

"We'll go for a little while," Camden said, sighing. "I can't stay long though. I need to get to the library at some point tomorrow for some research for a paper."

Corey clasped her hands together in front of her chest and smiled at Camden. "I'll live with that. Get changed!"

Camden shook her head as Corey bounced out of her room and toward the other bedroom. She loved her friend, but Corey definitely knew how to push Camden's buttons a little too hard to get what she wanted.

Camden turned back to her computer and saved what she was working on before quickly changing into something that would be party appropriate, but still comfortable.

As she stepped out of her room, Corey was just stepping out of hers and grinned. "Ready?"

Camden nodded and followed Corey outside. "I'll drive since I don't plan on drinking."

Corey didn't put up a fight and a few minutes later they were trying to find parking near the football house. The street was already lined with cars and they ended up having to park two streets over and walk back to the house.

Camden didn't really mind. That meant she was less likely to get blocked in by someone and that it would be easier to leave at the end of the night.

The closer they drew to the house, the louder it got. It looked like every light in the place was blazing as they stopped on the sidewalk and gazed at the house.

Doors and windows were open and the sound of laughter and music spilled outside. She could just make out what looked like a beer pong table to the side of the house and she was certain the backyard was just as full as the house itself.

Corey grabbed her hand and pulled Camden behind her as she charged up the walk. A few moments later, they were inside the house and pushing through the crush of bodies in the living room.

A thin layer of sweat was already covering Camden by the time they reached the kitchen. Camden kept her eyes peeled for Jackson, but she hadn't seen him yet. She had seen some of Lisa's friends in the living room, but no Lisa either.

A funny feeling settled low in her gut. She knew she had nothing to worry about with Jackson and Lisa. He'd made his stance on her perfectly clear. But a little voice told her she shouldn't let her guard down. Just because Jackson wasn't into her didn't mean that Lisa wouldn't give up. It would probably make it worse.

They were beside the fridge and Camden quickly looked inside, snagging a bottle of water.

"Let's check the backyard!" Corey shouted into her ear before leading Camden to the back door.

Camden sighed in relief as soon as they stepped outside. It was still fairly hot and humid for November in North Carolina, but it was cooler than it was inside with all the bodies.

Camden scanned the people she saw on the porch and sighed when she realized that Jackson wasn't out there either. She pulled her phone out of her pocket and didn't see any texts or calls, so she wasn't sure where he was lurking.

She focused back on Corey and saw that she was standing next to Ethan, one of Jackson's friends, and flirting hard by the way she was twirling her hair around her fingers and batting her eyelashes at him.

That was fine. Camden would rather try to find the chair she'd sat in before and just be alone.

She walked down the steps and noticed that there were more lights in the backyard, though it was still dark.

It looked like they'd put some solar powered lights along the edge of the fence and some hanging lights periodically throughout the backyard. It ended up giving it a romantic glow and Camden worried she might stumble upon someone taking advantage of the low lighting.

It was college. Anything was possible.

She found the chair she'd sat in before—but no kiddie pool—and moved it closer to the fence so she was out of the way before settling down to people watch.

She was right. There were a lot of people in the yard now that she was looking. There were clusters throughout and a few that looked like they were up to no good along the fencing. But no one was near her and she was fine with that.

She cracked open the water bottle she'd grabbed from the kitchen earlier and took a small sip.

She sat there for an untold amount of time, not even really paying attention to what was going on around her until she was brought from her thoughts by someone standing over her.

"You mind if I sit?" a seriously jacked guy asked her, pointing to the chair that he was holding.

She shrugged. "Sure."

He set the chair down and settled into it. She winced as it creaked ominously and hoped that it didn't break under his weight. He was muscular enough that she imagined a lot of chairs creaked under his weight.

"I'm Roscoe. What's your name?" he asked, smiling at her while holding his right hand out for her to shake.

"Camden." She grasped his hand and gave it a quick shake before dropping his hand and surreptitiously wiping it on her jeans.

His hand was sweaty, which made no sense because it wasn't all that warm outside. Maybe he had bad social anxiety.

Neither of them spoke for several minutes and Camden almost forgot that he was sitting beside her until he asked, "Who do you know that lives here?"

She glanced at him from the corner of her eye. "Who says I know someone that lives here?"

Roscoe shrugged and drank from the beer bottle she didn't realize he had. "No one. Just assumed that you probably did. Coming to a football party usually means you know someone type of thing."

Camden shrugged. "My friend and I were invited. We came. Nothing to it."

"Hmmm." Roscoe said nothing else, but Camden cut her eyes to him again.

He hadn't said or done anything, but Camden couldn't say that she was comfortable sitting next to Roscoe. She couldn't put her finger on what it was, but she was definitely uneasy with him sitting next to her.

"You want a beer?" Roscoe asked, standing suddenly.

"Nope, I'm good." She held up her water bottle and shook it.

Roscoe nodded and disappeared. He returned a few minutes later with another beer and handed her a bottle of water.

She checked the seal and saw that it was open. While she thanked him for it, she knew she wouldn't be drinking from it. She didn't know Roscoe from Adam and she wouldn't take the chance that someone had put something in there.

"Tell me about yourself," Roscoe said after a few more minutes of silence. He scooted his chair closer to her.

Camden leaned away from him and wrinkled her nose. "Uh…what do you want to know?"

Roscoe shrugged and leaned back in his chair, trying to look relaxed, but he failed. There was an underlying tension in his shoulders and he'd started glancing around like he was looking for something.

It put her on edge and she couldn't help but glance around too.

That had to be why she saw Jackson as soon as he stepped out onto the back porch. Her heart beat faster as she looked him over, taking in the simple t-shirt and shorts he was wearing.

He paused beside Corey and Ethan, talking to them and looking her way when Corey pointed toward where she was sitting.

"Show time," she heard from her right and her brow furrowed.

She looked at Roscoe and saw that his attention was also taken by Jackson. The difference was Roscoe looked at Jackson with what Camden could only call hatred.

She looked back at Jackson and a smile spread across her face. That smile was quickly wiped away when Jackson was blocked and Roscoe was suddenly standing before her.

Before she could react, Roscoe pulled her up and into his arms. She tried to push away from him, but his arms were like steel bands and they were wrapped around her, keeping her pinned in place.

Before she could react, his lips were on her and she froze. What the fuck was going on right now?

She turned her head to the side and tried not to gag. "What are you doing?"

"Come on, baby, you know you want it."

Camden gagged again, and she renewed her efforts to get out of his arms. "What the fuck is your issue?" she spit at him.

He tried to capture her lips for another kiss, but Camden decided she'd had enough and brought her leg up to knee Roscoe in the balls.

Seeming to sense what she was doing, he jerked his hips back, so she missed her main target, but she still grazed something based on the groan he let out. His grip on her loosened and she could push him away.

She stumbled backward and wiped a hand across her lips, wishing she could get rid of the feel of his lips on hers.

"What the fuck?" Jackson said, coming to stand beside Camden. He glared between her and Roscoe. "What the fuck is going on here?"

"Camden got a little frisky is all," Roscoe said, straightening, only wincing slightly as he stood to his full height.

Camden's mouth dropped open. "What the fuck are you talking about? You pulled me into your arms and kissed me without making sure I was okay with it. That's assault."

Roscoe made a noise low in his throat. "Please. You were begging for it. Going on about how Jackson couldn't satisfy your needs."

For the second time, she was shocked. "I was not! I didn't even talk to you about him!"

Camden was fuming. What the fuck was his angle?

"Jackson!"

Camden looked past Roscoe and saw Lisa walking toward them, waving her hand in the air like they couldn't see her walking and she was at a polo match.

"Jackson, you left your phone upstairs."

Everything in Camden froze, and she held her breath. He'd been upstairs with *her*?

She cut her eyes to Jackson and saw the shock on his face. He patted his pockets; she assumed to check that his phone wasn't on him, before glowering at Lisa.

"How the fuck did you get my phone?" He snatched it from her hand and slipped it into his pocket.

Lisa giggled and flicked her hair over her shoulder. "You left it upstairs, silly. It must have fallen out of your pocket while we were in your bedroom."

Camden couldn't think as Lisa continued to talk, and she really didn't want to stick around to find out what else was going to be said. She just wanted to get away from the entire situation.

So she started walking, and she didn't turn around to look at whoever was calling her name. She was done.

Chapter Seventeen
Camden

She didn't make it far. Corey caught up to her first and took the keys from Camden. Thankfully, they hadn't been at the party long, otherwise Camden would have to drive and that wasn't a good idea. She was so angry that her hands were shaking.

They'd just reached the sidewalk when she heard Jackson behind her, calling her name. "Camden!"

Camden clenched her jaw and kept right on walking. She had nothing to say to him right then. She needed to calm down and think through what she wanted to say before she said something she regretted.

"Camden, wait!"

"You should hear what he has to say," Corey said.

Camden glared at her best friend. "Whose side are you on?"

Corey smiled sadly. "I'm on your side, always. But I think there's something fishy about what happened earlier."

Camden sighed and stopped walking.

"I'll bring the car around," Corey called over her shoulder.

Camden sucked in a deep breath and turned to face Jackson, crossing her arms over her chest as he came to a stop a few feet away. He put his hands into his front pocket and his shoulders curled forward. It was the first time she hadn't seen him looking like the confident quarterback that he was. It was odd to see him this way.

"I'm waiting," she said in a flat tone, wishing she hadn't stopped.

"I wasn't upstairs with Lisa."

Camden's brows rose to her hairline. "And I'm just supposed to believe you?"

He sighed and brought a hand up to rub the back of his neck. "I'll go get Josh and he can verify that I'd just gotten back from the store with him before I went out back looking for you."

Camden pursed her lips. "Get him out here."

Jackson fished his phone out of his pocket and fired off a quick text message before sliding his phone back into his pocket.

"Nothing happened."

"Okay."

A few beats passed and Jackson asked, "Are you okay?"

"Why wouldn't I be?"

He sighed. "Because Roscoe kissed you against your will."

Camden shrugged and feigned nonchalance. Honestly, she was really bothered by what happened with Roscoe. She hadn't liked that he'd kissed her like that and she felt violated. It was just a kiss, but it was against her will. No one should ever experience anything against his or her will.

"I'll be fine."

"'Sup?" a guy asked, Josh she assumed, as he came to stand next to Jackson.

"What were we doing right before I headed out back?"

The guy smiled and said, "We'd just got back from a beer run. Someone raided the good beer in the garage and we needed to stock up."

Jackson nodded and Josh walked back off. "That still doesn't explain how she got your phone."

Jackson sighed. "I know. I don't know how she did either. I realized I didn't have it with me when we left the house because I was going to text you that I would be back shortly, but thought nothing of it. Lisa came up to me when she first got here, so she probably got it then."

Camden studied his face, and she had a gut feeling that he was telling the truth. But she couldn't help the hurt that she was still feeling.

Not only had a douche-canoe violated her, she'd had the resident mean girl try to start some shit between her and her boyfriend. She knew she just needed to admit that they were boyfriend and girlfriend. She cared about him too much to continue to deny it.

"Come back to the party," he said, stepping closer to her.

Camden shook her head and took a step back, glancing over her shoulder when she heard a car slowing on the road. It was Corey in Camden's car and her friend was sitting behind the wheel staring at her and Jackson.

"I can't."

She didn't wait to see if he said or did anything else. She turned around and walked to the car, sliding into the passenger seat and saying, "Drive."

"I get that you're upset..." Corey said, making Camden look at her instead of the pancakes on her plate, "but don't you think you're overreacting?"

Camden said nothing and dropped her gaze back to her plate. There was a small part of her thought she was definitely overreacting. With a night to sleep on everything and turn it over in her mind, she could see that Roscoe and Lisa had planned what happened the night before with some precision.

She was sure if someone were to test that water bottle he'd given her, they would have found a roofie in it too. That made her wonder if something more sinister would have happened if the opportunity had arisen.

She shuddered at the thought.

So yes, she knew she was overreacting, but that didn't mean she had to let go of her anger.

"Camden." Corey set her silverware down with a clank. "Come on. Talk to me."

"What do you want me to say?" she asked, setting her own silverware down.

"I don't know. Rage at me about last night, get it off your chest. But you can't sit there and stew. It's not going to solve anything."

Camden opened her mouth to respond, but her words died as she caught sight of who walked into the restaurant they were eating breakfast in.

They were tucked into a booth in the middle of the restaurant at a breakfast place only a five-minute drive from campus. It was popular for lunch and dinner, but it usually didn't get a lot of college students until late morning. That's why she and Corey picked it. They wanted privacy.

But here were Roscoe and Lisa, walking behind a hostess and getting seated at the booth on the other side of the partition that separated their booths.

Camden slunk down in her chair and hoped they hadn't seen her.

"What's wrong?" Corey hissed, hunkering down as well.

"Roscoe and Lisa just walked in," she hissed.

Corey's eyes widened and Camden glanced toward the beveled glass between the booths.

Corey pointed toward it and Camden nodded and cupped a hand around her ear to mimic listening.

Corey nodded, and they both started eating again, but this time without talking.

Camden wouldn't pass up this opportunity. She knew that there was a good chance she wouldn't hear anything about what happened the night before, but she wanted to make sure she took full advantage of them sitting so close to her without knowing. Who knows what they might say.

She sat there while they ordered their food and when the waitress dropped their drinks off, but perked up when Lisa said, "I didn't get a chance to ask you last night. How'd it go with Camden?"

She heard the sound of a spoon hitting the side of a coffee cup before Roscoe replied, "We chatted and then I kissed her once Dove was in the backyard."

"What about the water you drugged? Did she take that?"

Camden stiffened at those words. She patted herself on the back for knowing not to drink that.

"Nah, she didn't drink it and I grabbed the bottle to take home with me. Didn't want someone finding it."

"Good. What are we going to do now? All last night accomplished was getting Camden to leave and Jackson to end the party early."

Camden's eyes widened as she looked at Corey. Jackson ended the party early? That seemed odd.

Roscoe sighed. "Maybe you should try something at your next practice that she's at. I can slip you some drugs to put in her water. It'll make her mess up and probably pass out mid-practice."

Camden hoped that Lisa would say no, but instead she heard Lisa agree before the sound of pills in a plastic bottle reached her ears. Surely he wasn't sitting in the middle of a restaurant handing off pills to Lisa. He couldn't be that stupid.

"Thanks. We have practice tomorrow and I'll slip it into her water first thing. She usually leaves it in her bag and won't even notice that I've messed with it."

Camden felt sick, and she honestly didn't want to listen to anything else. It was obvious that Lisa and Roscoe had some weird vendetta against her and Jackson. She understood Lisa's angle, to a point. She liked Jackson and didn't like that she didn't have him.

But she didn't know Roscoe and had no idea what his angle was.

She glanced at Corey and noticed that her phone was out and Corey was holding the speaker portion toward the partition. Camden looked at her with a questioning look in her eyes, but Corey ignored her and concentrated on what Lisa and Roscoe were saying.

Eventually the two stopped talking about the night before and moved on to a class they shared, which made Corey look at her as she stabbed at her screen.

They both leaned toward the middle of the table and Corey whispered, "I just recorded what they were saying. I think we need to go to Dr. Foster and the football coach with it. They admit to what they're doing. You can't not say something."

Camden nodded, but she really wasn't sure. Wasn't this hearsay or something?

"Camden, come on," Corey said. "Dr. Foster already wants you to make a statement about what Lisa's done before. If you go to him with this, maybe they can set it up to see if she does something. She could get in a lot of trouble. Besides, you already knew that last night was a setup. Don't think I don't remember you avoiding that earlier."

Camden nodded and sighed. She knew Corey was right. Just the thought of going to the band director with this made her stomach tie up in knots. She hated confrontation of any kind and she knew that if she pursued this, there would be a major confrontation in the works.

"Let's pay for breakfast and I'll drop you at Jackson's. I think you two need to have a real talk about everything going on."

Camden nodded and pulled her wallet out before sliding out of the booth.

She was sure they both looked ridiculous as they tried to slink down the line of booths until they reached the cashier, but neither of them wanted Lisa or Roscoe to see that they were there and might have overheard what was being said.

Camden could only imagine the showdown that would go down and she didn't have it in her to deal with more than one today. Talking to Jackson would be hard enough. She owed him an apology for the night before, there was no doubt about it.

After paying, they walked out to Corey's car, and they spent the short drive to the football house in silence.

Corey pulled up to the curb in front of the house and Camden stared at it before flicking her eyes to the cars parked outside. It was a Sunday, so most of the guys should be home, but a part of her worried that Jackson wasn't and that she'd have to track him down.

"Why are you still sitting out here? Go on!"

Camden glared at Corey, who just laughed, but she listened to her friend and pushed the door open.

"I hope I don't see you later and that you get the dicking of a lifetime!"

Camden rolled her eyes and slammed the door, ignoring Corey as she peeled away from the curb.

As she walked up to the door, her hands felt clammy, and she wiped them on her pants, hoping that she didn't get sick before she saw Jackson.

Once she reached the door, she paused once more and blew out a breath. It was now or never and she needed to pull her big girl panties on.

Heart Beats

    She knocked on the door and waited with bated breath to see who answered the door and if Jackson was home.

Chapter Eighteen
Jackson

"Jackson, there's someone at the door for you."

He sighed and rubbed his eyes at Ethan's words. "Okay, I'll be down in a min."

Everything was going to shit it seemed. The night before had been a fucking disaster of epic proportions and he was in the midst of studying for an exam coming up.

Camden wasn't talking to him and he honestly didn't care who was at the door for him. If he could get away with it, he'd probably stay in his room studying. But he didn't need it getting around that he was an asshole. He had goals and pissing people off wasn't a part of it.

He stood and stretched before sliding his phone into the pocket of his shorts and jogging down the stairs.

He nodded to the guys sitting in the living room and opened the door, stopping short when he saw Camden standing on the other side looking at her shoes.

"Camden?" he asked, thinking the studying had finally done him in and he was imaging her standing there.

"Hey," she said, looking at him with a shaky smile.

He raked his gaze over her and noticed that she had dark circles under her eyes and she was slouching. She looked very uncomfortable.

He glanced over his shoulder and saw that the guys sitting in the living room were watching him.

"Want to talk in my room?" he asked.

She nodded, and he stepped aside so she could enter. A few moments later, they were in his room with her sitting on the edge of his bed and him seated at his desk.

He wanted to join her on the bed, but he wasn't sure she'd appreciate that. So he had to be happy with sitting away from her.

"Sooo…" he said, rubbing his hand on the silky material of his shorts, trying to dry them off. They'd started sweating as soon as they entered his room.

"Sooo…" Camden mimicked, picking at the hem of her shirt while staring at the floor.

"About last night," Jackson finally said, leaning forward and propping his elbows on his knees. "I'm sorry that—"

Camden shook her head and his words died. She looked at him and he flinched at the sadness he could see reflected in her eyes.

"You don't need to apologize. You did absolutely nothing wrong." She paused and sucked in a shuddering breath. "Last night was a shit show and planned from the start."

She sighed and leaned to the side to pull her phone out of her back pocket. He watched as she unlocked it and tapped the screen a few times before Lisa and Roscoe's voice poured out of the speakers.

His eyes widened at first as he heard them talking, but then he started glowering. The guys had warned him that Roscoe was up to something, but he didn't think he'd take it that far.

Once the recording stopped, he took a few moments to get his thoughts together. "Are you reporting them?"

Camden nodded. "Yeah. I'm not sure much will happen since it's just a recording…"

"But it's better than saying nothing. Send me a copy and I'll talk to my coach."

Jackson sighed and rubbed a hand over his head. Things were much more complicated than he thought.

"I'm sorry for how I acted too."

He glanced at her and she was staring at him intently. "I shouldn't have run off last night—"

"I don't blame you for that. He forced himself on you. I'm not sure I could have been as calm about it as you were. He's lucky he was gone by the time I got back to the backyard. I fully planned on beating his ass."

A small smile flitted across Camden's face at his words. "I don't support violence, but in this instance, I would have been a-ok with it."

He smiled too. "Good to know."

An awkward silence stretched between them. Jackson felt like they were at the crossroads. Last night had been eye opening in a lot of ways, mainly in that he could see why Camden was worried about other people and what they might do.

He knew that they needed to talk about their relationship, whatever it was, and decide what was going to happen.

He sucked in a deep breath and bit the bullet. "I think we need to talk about us."

His words rushed out and he sounded harsher than he planned to, but there wasn't much he could do about it now. The words were out there.

Camden nodded. "Yeah, I agree."

She said nothing else, and he swallowed thickly. "I understand if you aren't interested in seeing me anymore—"

"Why would you think that?" Camden asked, interrupting him.

He shrugged. "With everything that happened last night…I didn't know if you decided it was too much dating me. There will be people like them no matter what. Maybe not that severe…but there will be people that are out to sabotage us and our relationship."

Camden was nodding and a lead ball settled into his stomach. Was she nodding because she agreed and wanted to break things off?

"I get what you're saying," Camden said, dropping her gaze to the floor before looking at him again with a fierce look on her face. "But I decided I don't give a shit."

His eyes widened at her words. "You don't give a shit?"

She shook her head. "Right. Yeah, there will be people that will try to bring us down and break us up, but after last night and hearing that shit this morning, I decided I don't care. I like you too much to let someone else dictate if I go out with you or not. If I walk out right now and say it's too hard…I'm letting them win. And I won't do that."

Before he could fully process what she was saying, she was moving across the small distance that separated them and straddling him in his chair. His eyes widened as her weight settled over him.

"Camden—" he started.

She cut him off with a hard kiss. She dominated the kiss, wrapping her arms around him and directing him on what to do. He brought his hands up to her waist and squeezed.

She undulated her hips, and he groaned at the feeling of her pressing down on him. His dick twitched, and he thrust up, trying to get more friction.

His fingers made their way to the hem of her shirt and he toyed with it for several moments before he quickly pushed it up, tearing his lips away from hers so he could pull it off. He quickly reached behind her and unclasped her bra before pulling that off too.

Before she could pull him to her for another kiss, he pulled one of her nipples into his mouth and bit down on it before swirling his tongue around it.

Camden moaned and gyrated against him.

As hot as it was to have her on his lap in the chair, he felt like he couldn't do much of anything while sitting there. Keeping his lips wrapped around her nipple, he moved his hands to her ass and stood, walking toward his bed carefully.

He lowered her to the bed slowly, his eyes raking over her as she leaned back on the bed, her hair fanning around her on his dark bedspread.

"Fuck." He'd seen nothing hotter.

She scooted back on the bed and he quickly pulled his shirt off before pushing his shorts and underwear off.

She arched a brow at him. "Cocky, aren't we?"

He smirked and wrapped a hand around the base of his dick and stroked. "I think I have reason to be."

Her gaze dropped to where he was stroking himself. He watched as her nostrils flared and her pupils dilated. Got 'em. She wasn't fooling anyone.

He leaned over her on the bed and hooked his fingers in the waistband of her pants and underwear, quickly pulling them off, pausing only to pull her shoes off before dropping them on the floor.

He met her eyes and slowly moved up the bed until he was kneeling between them, hovering over her.

He gazed down at her and sat back on his heels, watching her facial expressions as he slowly smoothed one of his hands over her upper thigh. She shivered and goosebumps rose.

A small smile curled one side of his mouth as he reacted it on the other leg.

She sucked in a shuddering breath as he gripped her behind the knees and pressed her legs toward her chest, opening her up to him further and allowing him to look more fully at her.

She was gorgeous with her hair mussed and her skin reddening, though he wasn't sure if that was from desire, embarrassment, or both.

Maintaining eye contact with her, he leaned down and licked her nether lips from back to front, making her hips buck off the bed.

He made a tsking noise in his throat. "Stay still."

He leaned down and licked her again, more firmly this time and settled down to feast on the nectar between her legs.

Camden panted above him as he slowly lapped at her clit and sucked her lips into his mouth before moving lower to her opening and spearing her with his tongue.

He could feel her walls contracting around it and he groaned as his mouth was flooded with more of her wetness. He brought one of his hands down and quickly pushed two fingers inside her while moving back to her clit and applying firm pressure there with his tongue before he started fluttering it.

"Oh my God," Camden moaned, her fingers curling into his hair and yanking.

He grunted at the pain, but he decided he liked it. It showed him he was doing his job right if she couldn't help herself.

Her walls clamped down around his fingers and her hips were rubbing against his face shamelessly. His mind flashed to what it might be like to have her sit on his face and he decided that it would happen at some point. He liked the thought of her taking pleasure from him.

As her spasms eased, he pulled away from her and reared up so he was sitting back on his heels again. Camden's eyes were closed, and she was panting.

He swiped at his mouth and watched as her eyes fluttered open.

"What the fuck did you do to me?" she asked.

He shrugged nonchalantly. "Nothing much."

She scoffed. "Right. Nothing much."

He grinned and reached into his bedside table for a condom, which he quickly opened and rolled on his length before settling between her thighs. "I can do nothing much again if you'd like."

"I'd like to see you try."

He just smiled and pushed in, taking enjoyment in how her breathing hitched. And he did nothing much again and again.

Epilogue
Camden
One year later…

It would be nice to say that everything went according to plan once Camden and Jackson met with the people they needed to about Lisa and Roscoe. But they didn't.

Because neither had done anything, they couldn't be punished. That didn't stop the university from investigating though.

At the next band practice, the one that Lisa said she'd drug Camden's water, they watched Lisa and when she went to put something into Camden's water, they stopped her. When they searched her bag, they found a pill bottle that was labeled Rohypnol. Camden was almost certain that was what she'd gotten from Roscoe, though she hadn't known that Lisa had her own stash.

They put Lisa on academic probation and eventually expelled her when members of the dance team came forward with proof of Lisa's bullying.

Roscoe's things were also searched, but they didn't find any drugs on him or in his things. It pissed Jackson off to no end to know that Roscoe escaped punishment for what he'd tried to do to Camden.

But karma was in action with him.

At the last football game of the year, he went to throw the ball, and another defender hit him by the hip, shattering his pelvis on impact. It ended his football career, and he ended up dropping out.

Camden was just waiting to hear that he'd been arrested or killed. Either way, he was out of their lives just like Lisa was and she would take it.

It was now the last home game of her and Jackson's senior year. They'd called all the seniors out and honored them on the field, along with her and the other senior marching band members, and they were gearing up for halftime.

It was bittersweet. The football team was likely going to the playoffs, which meant that the marching band season was over, but it was sad to think this would be her last official game playing with the band for halftime and throughout the game.

As they lined up along the sidelines as the clock ticked down to the start of halftime, Corey grinned at Camden almost maniacally. Camden was sure she could see the fillings in the back of her teeth.

Corey had been acting weird for the last few weeks, but wouldn't admit to anything being wrong or off. She just said that she was excited for the last game because that meant they'd finally be done with marching band.

Camden didn't believe her. Corey was majoring in music and loved marching band just as much, if not more, than Camden did.

The clock hit zero, and she turned her attention to the drum majors, waiting for their cue to go onto the field. A few minutes later, they were off and performing.

Almost seven minutes later, they were finishing their performance, and she had lowered her flute, ready to march off the field, when the surrounding people kept playing. She looked around with wide eyes, her heart beating fast. Had she forgotten part of the program?

As she listened, she realized she didn't recognize the song they were playing or the formation they were moving into.

She looked around, but couldn't figure out what was going on. She wanted to sprint off the field, but that would draw even more attention to herself than standing in the middle of a crowd of marching band people.

She was likely to be trampled if she tried to move. She valued her life, so she'd stay put.

She glanced toward the jumbotron, curious to see what they were making and everything about her froze.

Her breath froze in her lungs.

Her heart stopped beating.

Her body couldn't move.

On the screen she could see that they were spelling "Marry me."

Her eyes widened. What the fuck?

She heard cheers as she continued to study the formation on the screen.

She looked back in front of her and flinched when she saw that Jackson was standing in front of her in his sweaty glory, his hair hanging around his face, sweat dripping from his chin, and a wide grin directed right at her.

"Jackson?" she asked timidly.

"Camden." He spoke with quiet confidence as he reached into the helmet that she just realized was dangling from his fingers and pulled out a small velvet box.

Her mouth dried.

He dropped his helmet, and it bounced once before rolling to the side and he dropped to a knee and gazed up at her with the biggest smile she'd ever seen.

Her heart now felt like it was going to beat out of her chest.

"Jackson." No question this time. She knew what was coming and she couldn't believe he was doing it right then.

They'd talked marriage, but she thought it had been an after graduation type of thing. Apparently he didn't take it that way.

"I had this long speech where I was going to tell you all the reasons we shouldn't wait to get engaged. But it honestly doesn't matter. I love you. Marry me?"

He opened the box, and the sunlight winked across the diamond nestled inside.

Her mouth dropped open. Was this real life?

She nodded, unable to form any words and Jackson sagged in relief. He stood and pulled the ring from the box before grabbing her left hand and slipping it onto her finger.

He leaned down and kissed her, hard. When he pulled back, he said, "You're stuck with me now."

There were worse things that could happen.

Heart Beats

Strip Down

by

Ava Manello

Old friendships are rekindled when British male stripper troupe Naked Night's heads down under on tour.

Little did they know they'd be performing for the bikers from Severed MC.

With a mix of heat and humour this short read will have you worked up and laughing out loud.

Reconnect with some of your favourite characters from both England and Australia.

Prologue
Alex

The stage is in darkness with a smoke machine generating a subtle mist that is being revealed by tiny coloured spotlights that pass slowly from left to right. The heavy drum bass of the intro music breaks the silence.

It's 'Missile' by Dorothy. As the singing starts we enter the stage from both sides, matching our steps to the bass of the beat, one hand tapping over our heart with every other step, almost appearing as shadows through the smoke. We're dressed in beige combat trousers with sleeveless white baggy vests really showcasing the muscles we've been working on in the gym.

Sometimes less is more.

This venue suits the tease and the dance moves rather than stripping everything off. As the word light is sung the whole stage is bathed in bright white spotlights. They fade in and out rapidly creating the effect of the staccato flash of a camera, giving the jerky movements of the routine more emphasis. We pull at our vests stretching them in various directions as we swagger around the dance floor, posturing at each other with hips rolling in time to the music. The vests are cut with low sides ensuring the audience get the best possible view of our abs as we move. As the lead singer croons about being a missile we yank belts from the waistband of our combats, folding them in half and snapping them from side to side across our bodies. As the pace of the music changes from the steady beat we stand in place, hands either side of our heads, legs fixed in place and only move from the waist up as though we're shaking our heads in disbelief or confusion. When the beat returns the audience start a rhythmic clap to match it.

The atmosphere in here is intense.

As the song once again mentions a missile, we grab either side of our vests and rip them off in one swift move, balling them up and throwing them into the audience.

The flashing strobes highlight the oil on our chests, the tiny flecks of glitter glistening as we move. I know it was my idea and it looks great under the lights, but I'm going to regret this later as it's going to be showing up everywhere for days to come and it'll be a bitch to clean off. I'll be finding glitter in places I didn't know existed. Despite the song being about a missile we're not using weapons in the routine, it's more martial arts moves and boxing feints. We weave around each other easily, despite the stage being much smaller than we're used to. That's why this routine doesn't have lots of jumps and acrobatics. We're giving the impression that we're caged in this small area, never moving beyond the imaginary confines of the invisible prison we're contained within. As the last beat of the song plays the stage is bathed in a moment of light, long enough for us to rip off the combats and toss them aside, but not long enough to reveal the nude speedos we're wearing underneath.

As soon as the light has gone, we silently leave the stage to a chorus of cheering, applause and calls for more. This is a one routine gig so there won't be an encore. As we enter the small dressing room behind the stage to get dressed we can still hear the roar from the audience.

This is why I love my job. I'm a male stripper and I'm bloody good at it.

Chapter One
Alex

One week earlier

The heat hits me like a wall as I step outside of the air-conditioned comfort of the plane. Back home there was ice on the ground when I left and here, I am sweltering in temperatures that exceed anything I'm used to. I can't believe I've left winter behind and jumped ahead to summer; I feel like I've time travelled having missed out the whole season of spring. As much a contrast as the heat is, I welcome it. The sun is shining, the sky is blue and I'm going to make the most of it when we're not rehearsing or on stage.

The invitation to bring the Naked Night's to Australia was one we just couldn't turn down. Eric got on the phone as soon as the original call came through and made sure we had enough side bookings to cover the cost of the flights and hotels. Tiny interrupts my idling as he pushes up behind me, muttering about too small airline seats and no leg room. I must admit, I'm grateful to stretch my legs after being cooped up for so long, and I'm a fraction of the size that he is.

I deliberately slow my pace as I descend the plane's steps just so I can wind him up. Don't get me wrong, he's one of my best friends but I know if the roles were reversed, he'd be doing exactly the same thing to me. Probably not the best idea considering we'll be sharing a hotel room for the next few weeks. I'm sure he'll forgive me later.

Australia is one of the places on my bucket list, along with New York, New Orleans, New Zealand and Hawaii. I'm so fortunate that work has enabled me to cross this location off my list, and Eric managed to book everything to give us a few days off for sightseeing here and there. The main gig is in a large hotel complex, and they pretty much want the show that their General Manager saw when she was visiting the UK a few months ago.

However, the other venues are a lot smaller than we're used to so we're going to have to come up with some new routines or adapt others to suit. I'm really looking forward to the smaller venues as I'm sure it will be a very different vibe from the larger crowds we've become used to.

Once on the ground I pull my phone from my pocket to see if I've got a signal yet, I need to text Sally and let her know I arrived safely. As much as I wanted her to come with me, she couldn't get away from work for the four weeks we'll be over here. She's promised to try and get over for the last week of the tour, but knowing her she'll get caught up in work and not be able to join me. She's doing a lot more freelance work these days, and I think she'd like to quit her day job as a reporter altogether and write the book she's always talking about, but she's not quite there yet, or so she tells me. I'd love to be able to support the both of us, but stripping doesn't pay well enough for that and right now I can't see me changing career any time soon. If I'm honest I probably only have a few more years left of this and there aren't exactly a multitude of career options for an ex stripper.

The past year has been a whirlwind that I never saw coming, and I wouldn't change any part of it. Well, maybe just one, I'd have persuaded Chrissie to give Eric a chance and not go back home to the States. He's not been the same since she left, sure he puts on a good front, but I can see that the sparkle has gone from his eyes. I sometimes catch him watching Tiny and me when we're with Alison and Sally and he doesn't know I can see him, there's such a look of loss at those times.

Enough maudlin thoughts, we're in Australia! It's time to get down to work and have a shit load of fun.

Chapter Two
Alex

The hotel is pretty swish, but then again it is a complex in the middle of nowhere, it reminds me of a smaller version of a Vegas casino. Everything here is geared to letting your hair down and having fun. There are gaming tables, a huge spa, a theatre where we'll be performing, indoor and outdoor pools, boutique shops and even a cinema. The rooms are elegant without being overstated and the twin beds are a decent size, I could probably share my bed with Tiny and still have room to move. Now that's saying something. Tiny is a big guy, he's all muscle and solidly built. He's a total contrast to me, no matter how much I work out in the gym, beside him I'm always going to be lean. I think it's my dancing background.

We've been here almost a week now and this is the first day off we've had. I pull my phone from my pocket and unfold the piece of paper I've been carrying around since I last went to visit my parents. Our old neighbour Theresa and her Dad moved out to Australia several years ago and Mum asked me to check in on them and see how they're doing while I'm here. She's not heard from Elvis for a while and Mum being Mum, she's worried about him. They left the UK after his wife died. The phone rings and rings and I'm almost about to hang up when someone answers.

There's the sound of a baby crying in the background and a very harassed voice snaps out 'What do you want?" I almost laugh out loud, that's so like Theresa. She was never one for airs and graces and most definitely calls a spade a spade.

"Theresa, it's Alex, your old neighbour from England. I'm in Australia for a few weeks and Mum wanted me to check in and see how you and your Dad were setting in." There's an audible gasp from the other end of the phone then a moments silence. What did I say?

"Shit, I'm so sorry. I should have called your Mum but I was such a mess," she rushes the words out. "We lost my Dad last year…" there's a pause where I think she's going to continue, but then silence. There's some background noise and some mumbling, then a new voice comes on the line.

"Alex? How are you, I haven't seen you in forever?" I'm lost, I have no idea who I'm talking to right now. The woman on the other end must realise that. "Sorry, it's Eve, Theresa's best friend."

I'm even more confused now, Eve was Theresa's best friend back in England, what's she doing in Australia now? "Eve? What are you doing out here?" I ask.

"Long story," she laughs. "Sorry, Theresa was just a bit shocked at hearing from you, it's all still a bit raw from losing her Dad and now with baby brain she's all over the place."

"Baby brain?"

"Yep, she had a beautiful baby boy just before Christmas. He's a bit of a git when it comes to sleeping though so she's pretty much a zombie most of the time these days."

"Wow, I'm so behind. I'm over here for work for a few weeks and Mum wanted me to catch up with Theresa and her Dad while I'm here. I'm so sorry, I didn't know he'd passed away." Mum will be devastated; she had a real soft spot for Elvis and they'd been friends for a long time.

"Sounds good to me, I'm sure we can get someone to keep an eye on the baby and come meet you for a coffee. Where are you staying?"

When I tell her the name of the hotel she lets out a whistle. "Wow, you're moving in exalted circles. That place is pretty posh."

"I know what you mean," I reply. "I couldn't afford to stay here if I wasn't working here. I'm one of the entertainers."

"Oh yeah, what kind of entertainer? I don't remember you doing drama or singing back at school," she queries.

I take a breath before answering. I'm not ashamed of my job, but it's not the sort of thing you just blurt out. Sod it, this is Eve. I used to hang out with her and Theresa in the school playground and they were always pretty cool. "I'm a male stripper, I'm here with my group and we're performing at a few venues as well as here."

Eve lets out a long wolf whistle almost bursting my ear drum it's that loud. "Go you! Never saw that coming," she laughs again. "Maybe we'll have to come and see your show."

We arrange to meet tomorrow for coffee and a catch up and Eve says they'll come to me as she's always wanted to see the inside of this place, but that I'm buying. I happily agree. Who'd have thought I'd come half way around the world and be arranging to meet up with my old next-door neighbour. I guess it is a small world after all.

Chapter Three
Alex

The coffee lounge reminds me of a Costa back home with its own barista. I've arranged to meet the girls here in ten minutes, but I got bored of hanging around in my room listening to Tiny face time his girlfriend. I'm sure he'll be grateful for the privacy.

There's a stunning garden area outside that allows you to enjoy the sun with plenty of shady umbrellas to keep it comfortable. I hang around by the entrance so they don't have to go searching for me. A stunning blonde walks in through the front door and looks around, waving when she recognises me. Eve has certainly grown up since I last saw her. There's no sign of Theresa but there is an older woman I don't recognise with her. They walk over to me and Eve throws her arms around me.

"Hello stranger, long time no see!" I hug her back then step away to take her in.

She looks happy, really happy. I remember she had a hard time of it growing up, her Mum wasn't the most maternal and she seemed to spend most of her time round at Theresa's. We'd all hang out together, although granted not as much as we got older.

"This is Sue," Eve introduces me to her friend. "I'm sorry, Theresa couldn't make it today, she had a really rough night with the baby. She's going to try and get over before you leave if she can though." Eve rushes her words out, she seems really excited.

I nod a hello at Sue and gesture over to the counter. We all order black Americanos and the server offers to bring them out to us so we head outside and choose a table in the shade.

"So, what are you doing out here?" I ask Eve, "not that it's not great to see you, I just never expected to bump into you out here rather than in York." I quickly add.

"Long story," Eve sighs. "I came out last year for Theresa's wedding and almost got killed by a gang of bikers, then another gang of bikers saved my sorry ass and now I'm living with one of them."

I think my jaw must have dropped because Eve and Sue are laughing at my expression. "What?" I ask incredulously.

"Yeah, I saw something I shouldn't have done because I didn't listen to Theresa and wait for her to come get me," Eve shrugs her shoulders in a 'typical me' fashion. "Theresa's husband is the president of an MC and they took me in and kept me safe. There were a few more near misses, but it's all over now." Eve pauses for a moment and her face falls a little.

"Elvis didn't make it, he got killed when it all hit the fan." Sue reaches over and pats Eve's hand, a look passes between them. "Sue was Elvis's girlfriend, and she's Aaron's adopted grandma now."

At the mention of Aaron, a smile comes back to both their faces.

"Aaron?" I question.

"Sorry, Theresa's son is called Aaron Elvis," Eve offers. She pulls her phone out to show me some photos. He's cute as babies go, but I'm not really a baby guy. I can definitely take them or leave them. I make the appropriate complimentary noises.

"So, did you really say you're a stripper?" Eve looks at me with amusement.

"Erm, yeah." I agree. "Been doing it a while now, I actually really enjoy it, but it's not sleazy," I reassure her. "Eric wants the focus to be more on the dance than taking our clothes off which is cool by me."

"We'll have to see if we can't get along to one of your shows," Sue smiles at me.

"Hell, yes!" Eve exclaims.

"That would be so cool, we could really do with a girl's night out." Sue laughs at her enthusiasm. "You really think your menfolk are going to let you out on your own to go watch a male stripper?"

"But it's Alex!" Eve protests. "I've known him forever."

"Honey, you know what they're like when we just go to the pub in Severed on our own, they can't stay away." Sue reminds her.

"Well, they're welcome to come watch the show too as long as they stay out of our way." Eve grumbles, a slightly sulky expression on her face.

"Now this I have to see," Sue responds. "I bet that new man of yours is just as bad."

Eve sighs. "He's a bit of a silver fox and a biker too," she tells me.

Sue looks a little uncomfortable when the subject of her new man is raised. I got the impression that Elvis only died last year so perhaps she feels it's too soon to be in a new relationship, although I'm not judging her. Life's too short as far as I'm concerned, you should grab whatever happiness comes your way.

"So where are you living?" I ask Eve, trying to change the subject.

"We're about a half hour away in Severed, and Sue's about an hour the other way in Maldon. She pretty much splits her time between the two since Theresa had the baby."

I suppose it must be hard on Theresa, she's lost both her parents, she's a new mum and she's living in a different country to where she grew up. Theresa's a tough cookie though, I'm sure she'll be fine.

We spend the rest of the afternoon catching up, talking about old school friends and Eve's new family. It's obvious to anyone who looks at her that she's madly in love with her new man, and she deserves it after the rough ride she's had. I'm also glad to hear she's getting on better with her mother these days.

"So how long are you planning on staying out here for?" I ask her.

A frown falls over her face. "I'm not sure. I've managed to renew my visa for a few more months, but after that I don't know. I can try and apply for citizenship, but what do I have to offer? I can't ask Angel to move to England and give up everything here." Her voice is tinged with sadness.

"I'm sure you'll work something out," I try to reassure her.

Sue looks at her watch and starts to rise. "I hate to break this party up, but if I don't get you back soon that man of yours will be sending out a search party."

Eve smiles at the mention of him and starts to rise too. "It's been so good to see you again, now we've swapped numbers text me the dates and we'll see if we can't get a girls night out sorted and come see you guys." She embraces me in a hug before she leaves and I'm pleasantly surprised when Sue gives me one too.

I'm waving them goodbye when I feel a presence behind me, turning slightly I see its Tiny, he's finally finished his call home. He looks at me suspiciously.

"I thought you said you were catching up with an old schoolfriend?" There's a note of suspicion in his voice.

"That didn't look like an old schoolfriend to me, I thought you and Sally were solid?"

"What the hell?" I protest. "You've been spending too much time around Jacko, we don't all have loose morals. That *was* an old school friend, she's out here for a while and we caught up, that's all. Her and her friends are talking about coming to see one of the shows."

Tiny looks apologetic and so he should. "Sorry, guess I'm all wound up being so far away from my own girl."

There's only one thing for it when he's feeling like this, checking the time on my watch I suggest we hit the bar as it's open now. The best way to forget what we've left behind at home is a beer or two, or sod it three. We only have rehearsals tomorrow.

Chapter Four
Alex

I should have stopped at three drinks last night. My head is not happy and nor is my stomach. To be fair, neither is Eric.

"How old are you two!" He growls out to me and Tiny. "I expect you two to set an example to these other dickheads, not encourage them."

Jacko and the guys mutter at his words, but also have smug grins on their faces as for once they're not the ones in trouble.

"We need to get this routine sorted for tomorrow; the stage is smaller than we're used to so we're going to have to tweak some of the moves. Get your heads out of your arses and back in the game." He turns his back on us in disgust and heads over to the lighting and sound guys instead.

Eric's right. Tiny and I have always been professionals and this isn't how we behave normally. I guess we're both struggling a little more than we expected being so far away from our girls. Still, I have to admit, it was good to see Eve yesterday and have a small reminder of home.

We've already done a couple of shows and they've gone down well, but we have a new routine tomorrow night that we've got to prepare for. I snag a bottle of water from the cooler and take a long gulp. There's only one way to get over this hangover and that's to exercise it out of my system.

Eric begrudgingly gives us an hour to go workout in the gym then demands we're back and ready to get down to work. The gym is quiet at this time of day with just the odd guest running quietly on a treadmill or on a rowing machine. The rest of the guys have followed us and we all hit the weight machines. The girl behind the reception desk can't keep her eyes off Jacko, but the guys a sleaze and has a girl or two in every town, leaving a trail of broken hearts behind him. He's a good guy at heart, he just can't understand yet why he should settle down. He will one day, when he meets the right girl. Instead, right now, he's flirting outrageously with the poor girl. One of these days he's going to get shot down in flames, doesn't look like it's going to be today though as he escorts her out of the reception area and heads back to the lifts where our rooms are. I shake my head and turn back to concentrate on the machine I'm working out at. I don't want to incur Eric's wrath twice in one day.

There are a couple of teething issues with the routine due to the smaller stage, but eventually we work them out. It's coming together nicely. We're not used to only doing a couple of routines rather than a full evening, but I'm not complaining. Rehearsals take as much time as if we were doing a full show because of all the adjustments.

"Eric, any chance we can try something new?" I ask when we finally take a break. "I heard a cool song the other day, and I've got an idea."

Eric turns and looks at me with interest. "Talk to me," he offers.

"Well, you know we're doing a show near Maldon next week, I know some biker chicks are coming and I have an idea."

We talk it through as a team for the next half hour or so then put the track on the stereo and test out some moves.

"That is one sick routine," Jacko compliments me.

The rest of the guys nod in agreement, even Eric joins in. This is what I love about my job, we're a tight team and we gel perfectly together. I'm really looking forward to the new routine and seeing the girls reactions.

Chapter Five
Eve

I'm still not sure how we got the guys to agree to this night out watching male strippers, but I suspect it was only because we agreed to let them tag along. It's fine by me if Angel and the guys want to get their rocks off watching Alex and his group take their clothes off, just as long as they leave us girls in peace whilst we watch. Theresa made it, but only because we practically dragged her away from Aaron and Prez had insisted she come with us. He told her she deserved a night off, even if it was watching naked men, and besides she'd go home and appreciate him all the more when he got undressed in the future!

Men and their egos.

Sue brought a few of the women from her new man's MC. Rebel looks like a tough cookie with all her tattoos and sass, but I have to admit I admire her. She's grown up with bikers, she was actually abandoned at the club gates as a baby and they raised her, yet she's still found her own path in life. Maeve is a lot quieter and keeps casting glances at a huge biker at the back of the room when she thinks he's not looking. Sue said he's called Wrath and has only recently joined the club.

Chastity is Rebel's best friend and looks like the kind of girl who could end up going home with one of the strippers, she's a total flirt, yet I suspect that's masking something deep down. Sue raises her glass and announces a toast, "Here's to all the strong biker women I know, and the amazing biker men we love."

There's a round of 'hell yeahs!' from our table and we clink our glasses together. We've all had a few drinks with the exception of Theresa who's the only one on soda as she's still feeding Aaron herself.

While we're waiting for the show to start, I look around the room and see a lot of interest in our men at the back of the room. We tried to persuade them to wait out in the bar for us but no such luck. They're all far too territorial, yet they're good humoured enough to agree to us coming. In fairness their lurking is more about our safety than what we're going to see. Both Severed MC and Hellion MC have had a rough year or two and their women have been hurt in the process.

I glance back at Angel and see the smirk on his face when he catches me looking for him. He blows me a kiss and I feel my panties dampen just from his blazing look.

The lights fade into black and there's a hush of anticipation in the room. The music starts and I recognise the drum beat intro to Imagine Dragons 'Believer'. Spotlights shine on either side of the stage where the dancers are slowly appearing. I almost laugh out loud when I see their outfits. Alex, Tiny and Jacko are in biker gear in total contrast to the three guys opposite who look more like something from Fifty Shades in their grey suits and ties. The guys are punching the air towards each other as they move closer to the centre. It kind of reminds me of the rumble in West Side Story with the Jets and the Sharks.

I know which side I am on.

Alex moves centre stage and his moves are almost ballet like as he dances around Guido. They're feinting fighting moves but they're moving around the stage on the tip of their toes so gracefully. As Alex leans forward into Guido's space, Guido arches his back away from him, only their upper bodies moving to the beat of the music. Alex stands tall again and repeats the move on Guido's other side. The whole room is mesmerised by the dancers on the stage, they may be strippers but this is so tasteful and artistic. I'd normally expect catcalling and jeering, but everyone's too focused on the magic happening right in front of us.

Tiny moves towards Alex and Guido and grabbing Alex's wrist pulls him backwards, Alex pulls free, places one foot on Guido's thigh and before I can even gasp, he's claimed up Guido's body and done a backflip back to standing throwing his arm back in Guido's direction. Guido staggers backwards and the two remaining suits move in and catch him as he falls. Tiny and Alex move to the side of the stage and along with Jacko dance around the three suits in the middle. Guido is thrown up in the air and caught a couple of times by the suits before he's laid on the ground, arm flung wide and unmoving giving the impression that he's dead. At this point Alex moves in and sways back and forward over Guido's prone body while the suits and the bikers dance around each other, pushing and pulling in time to the music. At one point they stand back to back and hook arms, taking turns to lift and swing each other around. Their feet move left to right, front and back in a complicated step routine all the while this is happening.

As the music nears the end the two suits turn their backs to the audience and fall to their knees in front of the three bikers, heads bowed low. Alex moves forward and tips each head back to the audience before spinning on his heels and turning his back to them. He bows his head low and moves rhythmically from side to side. Tiny and Guido move forward in front of each suit and gesture with their hands. Just as the music is about to hit its crescendo the suits stand.

Tiny and Guido move forward and rip the suit jackets and shirts from them then toss off their own leather jackets. Everyone faces the front and in unison they perform what I can only describe as something resemble an Irish dance, their feet moving so perfectly in time with the music.

The lights shine off the oil on their abs, and sweat drips from their foreheads as they continue to move. At the last moment they rip their trousers off in unison and the stage goes black.

The crowd erupts in hoots and cheers and calls for more. What the hell did I just watch, that was nothing like I expected it to be. Chastity is fanning herself with the paper coaster from the table that her glass had been sitting on, "Holy hell! Did you see the hip action on those guys! I need me a piece of that," she's almost drooling as she speaks and Rebel starts laughing at her.

It's infectious, and before we know it we've all joined in.

That was one hell of a show.

Chapter Six
Eve

Now the routine is over a lot of the room has cleared out, meaning there's plenty of room for our guys to join us. They've not long sat down when Alex and the guys come over to us and ask if they can sit with us. I look warily at Angel but there's a huge grin as he welcomes them and organises extra chairs and scoots everybody around to fit in our new guests.

Angel has his arm around me, but not in a possessive way, it's just how he is. Looking round the table I see that most of our men are in similar positions. Chastity is sandwiched between Guido and Jacko and looks to be in her element. Maeve is in a Tiny and Alex sandwich and looks a little downcast if anything. I look for the guy she was eying up earlier but see he's still at the bar with a couple of the other single guys who came along. Angel is next to Alex and I can't help but wonder if he's acting as a buffer or he's genuinely interested in meeting my friend from back home. Watching the two of them enthusiastically talking to each other I settle for the latter.

Jackson, Sue's new man offers to make a run to the bar for more drinks. I ask for a soft drink and Angel looks at me quizzically. I shrug my shoulders back in response and comment that I'm doing it to support Theresa, who looks at me gratefully. It's no fun being the only teetotaller in a group I know. Besides, I'm not ready for that conversation with Angel yet. I distract him by asking Alex to share some stories of growing up next door to Theresa and he doesn't disappoint.

They're all silly little incidents but they do show that Theresa always had a temper on her, including the time when she almost knocked Alex out when he picked the cake she wanted from the plate at his birthday party. I think they were only about five at the time. Everyone is laughing and joking with each other, and I feel so at home here surrounded by my new family. Sometime soon I'm going to have to make a decision about my future with Angel, as much as I love him, I know my time here is finite.

Angel catches my expression and looks at me with concern. I paste a false smile on my face, tonight is about enjoying myself. I can worry about my future another day. Angel is grilling the guys about the amount of work that goes into their routine and when he finds out they have a couple of down days he invites them over to Severed so they can visit the MC and enjoy our hospitality.

"Show you what real bikers look like rather than those ballet dancers you were pretending to be." He laughs.

Eric has joined the group and Alex and the guys turn to him to look for their approval. "I'd love to say yes guys but you know how tight our time here is, you really need to hit the gym over the next couple of days."

The guys look crestfallen until Angel reminds them that we have a pretty good gym set up back at the clubhouse they can use.

"In that case we'd love to accept. I've always wanted to see if an MC is really like Sons of Anarchy."

There's a chorus of good natured disapproval around the table, our life is so different to SOA but outsiders always seem to think we live that way. They couldn't be more wrong.

"I'm looking forward to meeting the guy that tamed Theresa," Alex says and everyone tries talking over each other to assure Alex that there is no way anyone will ever tame Theresa. She huffs loudly, but there's a smile on her face that shows she doesn't really mean it.

Jackson returns to the table with the drinks and this time the big guy is with him, helping him out. Theresa watches Jackson when he goes back to sit next to Sue, and I wonder how she's really feeling about this new relationship. In some ways it's too soon, Elvis hasn't been gone that long, but I know that I don't begrudge Sue her chance at happiness. I'm not sure where Theresa's head is at over that.

Sue started pulling away from Severed shortly after Elvis passed, she still came over to make sure Theresa was okay, but you could tell that spending time around the club was painful for her.

Over the past year she and Jackson have become closer, and despite him being in another MC the club seems to have supported her. I guess it would have been a different story if he'd been a member of one of the violent MC's like Carnal, the club that almost cost me my life, but Hellion MC are good guys and seem to get on well enough with Severed MC.

If you'd have told me a year ago that I'd be sat here in a classy Australian hotel surrounded by male strippers and alpha male bikers I'd have laughed and called you insane. Look at me now, how my life has changed.

Who'd have thought these two different worlds would be sat around the same table for a start.

It's almost two am before the party breaks up and we've arranged for Alex and his guys to come stay over tomorrow night so we can show them some real MC hospitality. Looking around the table I already suspect there'll be a few sore heads in the morning and can guarantee that there'll be a hell of a lot more after spending the night with the MC.

Chapter Seven
Eve

I wake up and the bed is empty beside me, looking at the bedside clock I can see that Angel let me sleep. I was exhausted when we got back, after all it was almost three am. Still it wasn't too late for Angel to show me that I was most definitely his woman, and he was definitely all man. I smile smugly to myself at the memory. He doesn't know that I wasn't drinking at all last night, and I'm reminded why when a wave of nausea hits me. Groaning I rush for the bathroom and throw up, grateful that I haven't eaten yet so it's not as bad as it could have been. I open the cupboard under the sink and reach behind the tampons that I haven't needed for the last two months, feeling for the paper bag hidden at the back. I retrieve the pregnancy test with shaky hands. My life is up in the air enough at the moment without any extra complications. Sometime soon I'm going to have to make a decision, my visa won't last forever and Angel hasn't said anything about our future.

I pee on the stick, wash my hands and sit on the closed toilet seat to wait. My nerves are shot. Angel was as devastated as me when I had a miscarriage last year, but then he almost didn't touch me after as he felt I was too fragile. I think we've more than made up for that, especially in the last few months.

How will he react if I am pregnant?

He's amazing with my daughter Elizabeth, and I know he'd make a fantastic dad to his own child but I want him to ask me to stay because he wants me, not because I'm pregnant.

I need this test to hurry up, thinking about Elizabeth makes me yearn to see her. I'm getting used to her having sleepovers away from home now so that me and Angel can have grown up time together, but I still miss her.

The timer on my phone beeps and draws me out of my thoughts. Glancing at the test for the result, I know my future just got a hell of a lot more complicated. I put it back in the box and return it to its hiding place at the back of the cupboard again, just in time as I hear our bedroom door open.

"Eve, you in the bathroom? I brought you some coffee."

My stomach turns at the thought of coffee right now, but I cheerily shout back that I'll be out in a minute, I'm just going to grab a quick shower. No sooner has the water started than there's an extra body in the shower behind me. Angel needs no invitation. His strong arms pull me back into his chest and wrap around me protectively.

This right here is my happy place, safe in his embrace.

I love showering with Angel, although it more often than not involves us getting downright dirty before we get clean. This morning is no exception. As Angel reminds me how much he loves me, I put all thoughts of the future behind me, concentrating on the way he's making me feel right now.

I'm going to enjoy today.

Chapter Eight
Alex

There are a few sore heads around the breakfast table this morning, but everyone agrees it was a great night. We're all looking forward to visiting the MC later and putting some myths to rest.

Last night it was clear that this MC is all about family and looking out for each other. Yeah, the guys are alpha male as hell, but at the heart of it they're all about their women.

I respect that.

Saying that, if I spoke to Sally the way some of them speak to their women, I think I'd find myself slapped halfway into next week. Thinking of Sally makes me miss her, we're struggling to chat with the time differences, when I'm free she's either asleep or at work and vice versa. It's a couple of days since we spoke but we text each other often. We've still got just a little over two weeks to go before I'll see her again.

Tiny's an okay roommate but I'd much rather be sharing with my girl. By the time 11am comes around we're all in the lobby with our overnight bags and waiting for the lift that Angel arrived for us. We'd offered to hire a vehicle but he wouldn't hear of it.

Right on time two trucks pull up and a guy wearing a prospect cut comes to greet us, introducing himself as Scratch. Bearing in mind the conversation we had last night about biker names I really don't want to contemplate where his name comes from, and when he offers me his hand to shake, I take it reluctantly.

The ride over to Severed takes us through some beautiful countryside, it's a lot drier and dustier than back home, although there's still plenty of green around, certainly more than I'd expected.

The clubhouse isn't what I'd anticipated either, I guess we've all taken the scenes from SOA and expect that to be the reality. The inside of the clubhouse is bright and clean and not a stripper pole in sight, I'm almost disappointed as I have some great moves on a stripper pole. Eric wouldn't be too impressed though as they're prone to leave your legs covered in bruises where you grip the pole. It wouldn't go down well with our audience. At the left of the large room is a long bar and there are tables and chairs spread around the room. It reminds me of a working mens club back home in some respects, although fresher and more up to date.

Angel and Eve walk over to greet us and the big man almost growls when I greet Eve with a hug that goes on too long for his liking. I have to smile at his possessiveness, but I can't help liking the guy for the way he takes care of my friend.

I hear Theresa before I see her, she's with a guy I assume is her husband and she's chastising him for not holding the baby properly. He just looks at her with a goofy grin and ignores her.

"Hi, you must be Alex," he greets me. "Welcome to our clubhouse." He looks me up and down and smiles. "I guess I thought you'd look a bit like a pansy with being a stripper and all, but I'm impressed."

Theresa slaps his arm in protest. "You can't talk to him like that you bloody ape!"

I laugh, showing her I'm not offended. I take it as a compliment. We're not as ripped as some of these biker dudes, but we can hold our own, and I'm pretty certain we have more stamina than some of them. It's all the fitness training we do in the gym.

The girls turn to lead us out back where they've arranged a barbecue in our honour. I start to protest that they shouldn't have but am quickly cut short when they tell me they're always looking for a reason to get everyone together.

When we get out back it's a huge open compound area with garages along one side, a play park full of children running around at one corner and plenty of benches and tables full of families. It's definitely a far cry from SOA, but in a good way.

Chapter Nine
Eve

I've laughed so much this afternoon, I've really had a good time but it's nothing compared to this evening. Drink has been flowing since Alex and his guys got here, but no one has overdone it.

The MC has enjoyed meeting more crazy English folk as they call them, and the guys have relished a bit of home cooking, a refreshing change from hotel life. I get the impression they spend too much of the year in cheap hotels and not enough at home now some of them are settling down.

Theresa seems more relaxed today, I think having Alex here has brought back good memories and lifted a little of the sadness she feels every day at the loss of her Dad. I honestly think she has post-natal depression, after all the birth was pretty traumatic for her. Aaron arrived early after her waters broke at the clubhouse whilst her husband was in hospital having almost died after being caught in an explosion. All that on top of losing her Dad. I need to keep a close eye on her and make sure she gets help if she needs it, no matter how much she protests. I can see that Sue is keeping a protective eye on her as well.

The fun really starts when the younger kids have been put to bed, Cowboy calls the guys out on their dancing skills and Alex challenges him to a dance off.

Now this I have to see.

Cowboy's girlfriend Lucy is cheering him on loudly from the sidelines, she couldn't join us last night as she was working at Declan's bar in town.

Someone switches the music on the stereo and I almost fall off my chair when I hear 'I'm too sexy' by Right Said Fred.

Cowboy struts to the centre of the makeshift dance floor and starts to strut his stuff. It's mainly thrusting his hips suggestively, but there's the odd twist and turn in there that shows he's a little more nimble than I thought.

"That's right babe, you show him what a sex machine you are!" Lucy screeches from the sidelines.

What happened to that quiet girl we met last year, I guess that's what dating a biker does to you.

Alex strolls onto the dance floor and taps Cowboy on the shoulder, gesturing for him to move over. Alex is in a different league to Cowboy, the way he moves his hips has every woman swooning, it's not as overtly suggestive as Cowboy's moves, but the heat it generates in the females watching is off the scale. Cowboy watches Alex carefully and tries to emulate his moves. Alex realises and slows his movements down, almost coaching Cowboy which results in a visible improvement and raucous jeers and cat calls from the audience. Cowboy gestures for some of his friends to join him and I can't believe it when Angel and Prez join him along with a few others.

Sue brought Jackson, Rebel, Maeve and Chastity with her and she and Rebel are trying to coax Jackson onto the floor to join in. He's having none of it.

After a really tough year and losing some good people it's great to see everyone pulling together and enjoying themselves. We need more times like this, and every day we heal a little more.

Turning my focus back to the dance floor I almost wet myself with laughter as Alex twirls Cowboy away from him then back again, they're doing a bastardised version of something more fitted to Strictly Come Dancing. The track ends and they fall in a heap on the floor.

There's a murmur from Sue's table and they suddenly start calling out dance scores and the whole clubhouse erupts.

The track flicks over to something slow and I watch Angel as he stalks towards me, "Come dance with me baby," he pleads.

How can I resist my man when he looks so hot?

He pulls me close and holds me tight. We barely move our feet as we sway to the love song in the background. From the corner of my eye I'm aware of other couples joining us. Angel leans in and kisses me, there's so much intent behind it and I melt a little more into his arms. When he suggests we take this back to our room I don't object. My time is running out and I need to make as many memories as possible, just in case my future doesn't lie here.

Chapter Ten
Alex

Last night was pretty awesome, we were made to feel like part of the family and once again it was a very late finish. Eric didn't complain, but today he's going to make us work our arses off in the gym so we don't become slack. It's too easy to lose focus if we're not careful, and some parts of our routine are dangerous if that happens, especially when we're working in more confined spaces than we're used to.

Jacko lets out a whoop when we enter the gym at the clubhouse, its better equipped than half the gyms I've used back home. There's every piece of equipment I can think of, and rather than the focus being on a few treadmills and bikes like so many of the hotel gyms I'm familiar with, this place is a weightlifter's paradise. There's even a boxing ring and punchbag. Angel, Prez and Cowboy have joined us, they're interested to see what kind of routine Eric puts us through, especially as it's more about toning than bulk for us. We need to ensure we maintain our flexibility rather than just gain size.

I'm fascinated by the ink the guys have; I'd love to get a tattoo but I'm not sure Eric would approve. He's quite particular about our appearance. I make a mental note to chat with him about it later. Eric starts off with some floor work and it's a mix of yoga, Pilates and conditioning.

The bikers try their best to join in but struggle with some of the moves, Eric shows them ways they can adapt to suit their own level of fitness and it's all taken in good spirit. When we move to the weight machines the bikers suggest small tweaks to our routine that Eric approves of. They're speaking from years of experience that he respects. It's a two way street. Eric has decided that we're going to try the new routine back at the hotel tomorrow night, I'm flattered that he likes my choreography enough to use it at our main gig and we work it through again on the mats, trying a couple of extra moves we'll get away with on the slightly larger stage.

By the time we leave the gym we're hot, sweaty messes, all of us. That was a hell of a workout, but it's what we needed after a couple of nights of letting loose.

After showers and a late lunch, it's time for us to head back to the hotel. After our show tomorrow night, we're on the road for most of the rest of our stay in Australia but accept an invitation to a farewell party at the clubhouse before we fly home.

I hug Eve and Theresa before we leave and promise I'll be back to see them soon. The guys pull us all into man hugs much to the girl's amusement. We've not known them long but they've sure as hell made us feel welcome. As we leave, I find myself wishing the road dates were over and done with. I can't wait to get back and party with these guys.

Chapter Eleven
Alex

We're weary as hell as we walk back into the hotel after a gruelling few days on the road. Tomorrow night is our last show then we have a couple of days of R&R before we end the trip with the party back at the clubhouse. Right now I'm so ready for my bed, but I think everyone's decided to grab a beer or two along with something to eat. I'm following Tiny when I hear him whoop with joy and start running across the lobby, looking over I see Alison. A pang of hurt hits me that it's Tiny's girl and not mine, but I bite it back knowing that I'll be seeing Sally again in just a few days. I'm really pleased for him; I know he's missed her as much as I've missed Sally. I pull Alison into a hug and tell her how pleased I am to see her.

"I brought a couple of surprises with me," she smiles widely. Alison whistles, I never knew she could do that, and looks behind her.

I drop my bag suddenly and rush towards Sally as she appears around the corner, lifting her into a hug and swinging her around. "You're a sight for sore eyes," I tell her.

"I take it you're pleased to see me then," she laughs.

"You've no idea!" I respond, hugging her even tighter. "But how?" I question.

Sally nods over my shoulder towards Eric. "We had a bit of help setting up our surprise, and it's about to get a whole lot better," she smirks.

"How can it get any better than this?" I can't think how it could be better but then I see who else is here and I know it can.

Eric looks up in disbelief as the third girl makes her presence known. The rest of the guys are shocked into silence for a moment before they start whooping and hollering.

Chrissie walks towards Eric and stops in front of him. "Can you ever forgive me?" She looks so afraid right now. I get it, she broke the guys heart when she chose to leave him and go back home to the States.

"Nothing to forgive," Eric pulls her into a hug. He's got the biggest grin on his face. "How long do I have you for?" He asks hesitantly.

"That depends on you I guess," Chrissie bites at her lip nervously. "I had an offer to go back to the hospital in York and I thought I'd give it a shot if that's okay with you."

"You're back for work then?" Eric sounds disappointed.

"Well, I'm back for the man I love if he'll have me," she responds. "The job offer was just a bonus."

Eric's face lights up and he reaches in and kisses her deeply.

"Oh, and we booked extra rooms," Alison calls over.

"That settles it then," Eric announces. "Afternoon off guys, I'll see you all in the morning!" Eric practically drags Chrissie behind him to the lift, closely followed by me, Sally, Tiny and Alison.

We have some serious catching up to do!

Chapter Twelve
Eve

Angel almost caught me throwing up this morning, but I was lucky. I'm not sure how much longer I can keep it a secret. Sue's been giving me odd looks when she's been around, luckily Theresa's still too tied up with Aaron and exhaustion to have noticed.

I have to tell him what's going on, tonight at the party is as good a time as any I guess. It feels like I'm forcing him into a decision, and that's not how I wanted this to go. I'm resigned to the fact that I'm going to have to go home soon when my visa runs out, I've already had one extension and I'm doubtful I'd get another, especially as I'm not working. Angel doesn't want me to get a job and I'm pretty sure I can't anyway on the visa I'm on.

Looking around our home I'm going to miss it so much. This was the life I wanted for me and Elizabeth, but it doesn't look like it's the life I can have. Last time I didn't give Angel a chance, I just up and left and it almost got me killed. This time I know I have to talk to him first.

I head for the wardrobe and scan through the outfits on display, no idea what I'm going to wear this evening. It's more of a celebration than the last time we had Alex and the guys over for a barbecue so I decide on a little blue dress.

Angel walks in as I'm fastening the straps on my sandals and lets out a whistle of appreciation. There's a hungry look in his eyes and I'm grateful I haven't styled my hair yet as I know that look. We're going to be late to the party!

The party is in full swing by the time we get there and our guests have already arrived. I've been texting Alex so I know that his girlfriend Sally surprised him and will be attending tonight. I'm looking forward to meeting her.

He rushes over to greet me as we walk in and a look passes between him and Angel which I don't understand. Alex simply nods at some unspoken question. Men, I'll never understand them.

Sally, Alison and Chrissie are chatting with Sue and Rebel so I go over to join them, grabbing a soda on my way over, leaving the guys to talk. It's so refreshing to hear another English accent in the room, but I love Chrissy's American drawl. They're discussing the dance off at the barbecue and I join in the laughter.

The clubhouse is bouncing; they've brought a DJ in for the evening and cleared the tables back to create a makeshift dance floor. Elizabeth is running around shrieking with laughter while Lucy and Cowboy pretend to chase her. My little girl is growing up so fast. Without being aware that I'm doing it my hand moves protectively over my abdomen. Sue looks down at my hand and gives me a knowing look. I snatch my hand away quickly.

"Mummy, mummy, Daddy says he needs to talk to you!" Elizabeth comes racing over and pulls at my dress.

"In a minute darling," I smile down at her.

"Daddy said you'd say that and he said you have to come now." She insists.

I apologise to the girls and head over to where Angel is standing in the middle of the dance floor. His face looks serious. The music quietens down so it looks like he's getting ready to make an announcement. I look around the room to see where Alex and his friends are as I assume he's going to wish them good luck.

All the groups that were talking around the dance floor are now standing watching Angel with huge grins on their faces.

What the hell is going on?

Elizabeth pulls me closer to Angel and looks at him, "Now Daddy?" She questions.

'Now Darlin',' he acknowledges.

"Daddy loves you very much," she announces to the room whilst gripping tight to my dress. "He wants me to give you this." She holds up an envelope that I hadn't noticed she'd been clutching tightly in her hand.

Everyone is watching my reaction and I feel self-conscious as I open the envelope and pull out what looks to be a form. I've no idea what it is but it looks official.

What the hell is a subclass 300 form?

I look more closely and see that it's a prospective marriage visa. Does this mean what I think it does? I look from the form to Angel for clarification.

Angel grins at me and moves closer, dropping to one knee in front of me.

"Eve, you mean more to me than you could ever know. I love you with all my heart and I can't imagine my life without you in it. I know you've been stressing about your visa running out."

"How did you know?" I interrupt.

"Because I know you," he laughs. "Now stop interrupting." He reaches into his pocket and pulls out a little black box. Cracking it open he offers it to me. "Eve, please will you and Elizabeth do me the honour of becoming my wife and daughter, and make me the happiest man alive?"

I'm lost for words but the room around me is full of oohs and aahs.

"Answer him, Mummy!" Elizabeth pulls at my dress to get my attention. "Tell him we say yes," she pleads.

"Yes," I gasp out. "Yes, yes, yes and yes!"

The room erupts in cheers around us and we're surrounded by well-wishers and congratulations from every corner.

"Congratulations!" Alex pulls me into a hug.

I look at him and scrutinise his face. "You knew?" I question.

"I was the one tasked with looking after the ring," he smirks back at me.

"Thank you," I kiss him on the cheek.

"Hands off my woman you thieving Brit!" Angel shouts out, his laughter loud and clear.

Alex groans at Angel's pathetic attempt at an English accent but congratulates Angel warmly.

"Can I have a moment everyone," I raise my voice slightly. Angel looks at me, I can see the curiosity on his face.

The room stills and I look at Angel, my nerves almost getting the best of me.

"Do you think that proposal might have room for a plus one?" I ask, and reach for his hand placing it on my abdomen.

"Really?" His face is aglow with happiness. "We're pregnant?"

"We're pregnant," I confirm, a huge grin on my face.

"Can this night get any better?" He pulls me in and kisses me so deeply I feel it in my toes.
"Let's party everyone!" He shouts out. "This farewell party just turned into an engagement party."

The music volume goes back up and 'Congratulations' fills every corner of the room from the speakers.

Life can't get any better for me, and as I look around the room surrounded by so many friends and family I know that this is where I am meant to be.

The End... for now...

Park Life

by

Lucy Felthouse

Dee's tackling her usual Saturday afternoon housework tasks when some amazing singing floats in through her open window. She's reminded of the summer fayre in her local park. She hadn't been intending to go, but the magical female voice carrying on the air soon changes her mind. Before long, she's at the park, where she quickly discovers it's not only the woman's voice that is stunning—she's a gorgeous, curvy, pink-haired vision, and Dee is instantly smitten.

By the time the band finish their set, the pink-haired beauty has well and truly cast a spell over Dee—but will she pluck up the courage to ask her out?

Park Life

As Dee swept the duster over the sill of the open window, music floated in on the gentle summer breeze. Strains of a guitar—maybe two—drums, then, moments later, singing. A female voice. Too distant to make out the words, but Dee thought she recognised the song.

It was then she realised this was no tune being blasted out from someone's house or car stereo—this was a live band, playing in her local park. She'd forgotten all about the summer fayre, which was amazing really, since absolutely nothing ever happened in her neck of the woods, so the one event that *was* taking place should, by rights, have stuck in her mind.

The music and singing continued. Dee still couldn't quite work out what the song was, but it was bright and ballsy and stirring.

That's it. Bollocks to the cleaning. It can wait.

After abandoning the duster on the windowsill without a second thought, Dee raced into her bedroom. It might only be a little event in her neighbourhood park, but she didn't want to turn up looking like something the cat dragged in. She might see someone she knew.

Thanks to her short haircut and regular waxing habit, all she had to do was have a quick wash up, brush her teeth, and change her clothes. Maybe stick in a pair of earrings and whack on a bit of lip gloss.

Ten minutes later, Dee emerged onto the street in a pair of shorts, a vest top, her favourite Converse trainers, and her sunglasses. She'd stuck her purse, phone, keys and a bottle of water in a small handbag, which she slung over her shoulder as she headed for the park. Without the blocking effects of the windows and walls of her flat, the music was already louder, and slightly clearer. It danced on the air, taking on a life of its own. A wide grin spread over Dee's lips and she practically floated along, the combination of the music and the brilliant sunshine lifting her mood to an almost euphoric level.

God, if it's having this effect on me now, what's it going to be like when I'm actually at the fayre, with the band right in front of me? I hope I get there before their set finishes. They sound incredible.

She knew next to nothing about the Saturday afternoon event, having taken little notice of the posters she'd seen tacked up on lampposts and in shop windows, and the Facebook event that had repeatedly flashed up in her news feed. None of her local friends had seemed particularly interested, either, hence the whole thing almost passing her by until those notes had drifted in through her open window. She'd find out soon enough what was going on—the park was only a handful of streets away.

When she arrived in the sun-bathed green space, she was stunned to see how many people had turned out for the event. The whole thing was much bigger than she'd anticipated; with rows upon rows of market-style pop-up stalls; vans selling ice creams, hot dogs, burgers, and cold drinks; fairground-style games where you could win anything from a goldfish to an enormous teddy bear, and even a bloke making balloon animals for the kids. Everyone was clad in their summer gear, smiling and enjoying themselves, and the joyous atmosphere served to boost Dee's mood even further.

The music, of course, was much louder now, and she had no problem at all recognising what was being played. There'd been a brief pause and switch of song as she'd journeyed from home to the park, but the same band that had first caught her attention still played, with their amazing singer belting out a fairly recent chart hit. Dee grinned and began a fast walk to where a marquee had been set up at the far end of the area, eager to clap eyes on the owner of that haunting, melodic voice.

The scents of freshly cut grass and cooking food whirled around her and invaded her nostrils, a heady combination which made her smile and her stomach rumble in equal measure. But food would have to wait. First, the girl. No—the *woman*.

After what felt like an age, she reached the lawn area in front of the marquee. It was full of people watching and listening to the band. Some had come fully prepared and sat in deck chairs and camping chairs. Others sprawled on picnic blankets. The rest sat directly on the grass. Children ran around, playing and giggling, and dogs on leads sprawled out next to their owners or explored to the length of their restraints, sniffing around, hoping to find morsels of dropped food or someone to fuss them.

Despite the crowd, Dee was now plenty close enough to get a decent view of the band. There were four of them. A guy with a mop of blonde hair who looked more like he should be surfing played the drums. Two dark-haired blokes who had to be twins played the guitar and bass respectively.

And then, there was *her*. The lead singer. She was in a world of her own as she belted out lyrics, wiggling and strutting around as her wonderful voice filled the air. Long, screamingly-bright pink hair cascaded around her like a curtain, but did little to hide the tattoos, piercings, jewellery, and wacky clothes. She appeared to be the lovechild of a goth and a punk—a style all her own, and one she pulled off brilliantly. But the best part? Those *curves*. Boobs, belly, thighs, bum—Dee wanted to strip off that alternative outfit and explore the perfection beneath. Worship it, even. For hours. Days.

Dee sighed, half in love already. Who exactly *was* this gorgeous woman? And where the hell had she been *hiding?* It was only a small town—a stunning creature like her would stand out a mile.

Well, she'd get no closer to finding out by standing here, gawping like an idiot. She looked around for a spot to sit down, preferably close to the marquee so she could go and speak to Pink Hair once the band had finished their set. If she plucked up the courage, that was.

Having seen the perfect location in the shade of a tree—she hadn't realised the sun was so strong, and had stupidly forgotten to put sunscreen on in her haste to leave the flat—Dee scurried over and claimed it. It was off to one side of the performance area, and fairly close to one of the speakers, meaning she got quite the earful of music, and only an angled view of the band. But it also meant it was less likely anyone would notice quite how intently she was staring at Pink Hair. Even through her sunglasses it had to be apparent just who she was focusing on.

Dee parked her backside and relaxed against the tree trunk to continue enjoying the show. The band seemed to play quite the variety of covers—to provide something for everyone, she suspected. She swayed a little and bobbed her feet happily in time to the music, unable to wrench her gaze from the sexy vision before her.

Pink Hair's passion was palpable—Dee suspected she could start singing a song Dee hated, and she would still end up enjoying the performance, simply because of Pink Hair's pure joy and exuberance. Hopefully they wouldn't have to find out.

The tune ended to an enthusiastic round of applause from the audience, which Dee joined in with. Pink Hair thanked the crowd, then skipped off to the side of the marquee and retrieved a bottle of water from a small table. The hum of conversation, children screaming and laughing, dogs barking, and birdsong filled the temporary silence left by the band, who were all taking the opportunity to have a quick drink. No doubt singing and playing instruments was thirsty work, especially on such a hot day. Dee was grateful for her shaded spot. Her pale skin wouldn't have coped well, otherwise.

As she watched Pink Hair unscrew the lid of the bottle, then place it to her lips and tip her head back to down the contents, Dee's mouth went dry. She could make out the movement of Pink Hair's throat as she swallowed, and for some bizarre reason it sent a whole bunch of filthy thoughts rushing into her head. Unblinking, she groped for her bag and fumbled about until she'd managed to unzip it and pull out her own bottle of water. It was still nice and cold, since it had been in her fridge at home. She swept the chilly, condensated surface over her forehead, each of her cheeks, then down her neck and upper chest. Physically, it cooled her down, but mentally she was still on fire. Visions of exploring Pink Hair's dangerous curves assaulted her brain and resulted in a heat between her thighs that was nothing to do with the weather.

By now, the band had finished its mini-break, and they were all getting ready to begin playing again. They murmured amongst themselves for a moment, adjusted their kit, then the drummer counted them in. Another well-known song rang out, a feel-good, summery tune that resulted in a few delighted whoops from the crowd as they recognised it.

Dee smiled, cracked open the water, took a few long swallows, then settled back to enjoy the remainder of the gig. Her overwhelming lust for the lead singer aside, the band was very talented—all clearly having a great time and happily entertaining the visitors to the summer fayre. It was hardly Glastonbury, but it didn't seem to matter—not to anyone. It was a hot, sunny day and everyone was in a good mood.

All too soon, though, Pink Hair announced there were only a couple of tracks left in their set—but promised they would be crowd pleasers.

She wasn't kidding. The first got everyone singing along riotously, particularly during the chorus, almost drowning out the band, and the second—and last—resulted in arms and hands being thrust in the air and waved around, and lots of head bobbing. A few people even got to their feet and jumped up and down on the spot like they were in a mosh pit or something. Dee smirked, shook her head at their antics—perhaps alcohol had been taken—then turned her attention back to Pink Hair. She seemed to be in somewhat of a frenzy herself, thoroughly lost in the music, eyes closed, ring-clad fingers clutching the microphone as though it were at risk of running away if she didn't, head thrown back as the lyrics flowed from her like magic.

Dee supposed it *was* a kind of spell being woven over everyone. The crowd had been swept up in the words and melody, and euphoria reigned.

What a powerful—and wonderful—weapon to wield.

It had certainly brought Dee to her knees. Metaphorically, that was. In reality, she was still firmly sitting on her backside and leaning against the tree. Which she really ought to rectify if she wanted to go over and talk to Pink Hair before she disappeared. The last thing Dee wanted was to be thwarted by stiff limbs.

She took another long swallow of her water before putting the lid back on and slipping the bottle into her bag. Then she carefully clambered to her feet, wincing a little as her joints and muscles protested. The wisdom of those people who'd made the effort to bring chairs with them became apparent. She'd thought it seemed a lot of hassle to lug chairs into a summer fayre, but *they* weren't the ones grumbling and groaning as they got up from the ground. She brushed her hands across her bottom, legs, and back, dusting off any blades of grass, muck, or tree debris that might have stuck there. Then she tugged and tweaked at her clothes, straightened the strap of her bag over her shoulder, and ran her hands through her hair. In the absence of a mirror, she just had to trust that her walk to the park and the time she'd spent leaning against the tree hadn't rendered her completely unpresentable. She wanted to woo Pink Hair, not frighten the life out of her.

By the time the final song finished, Dee was ready—both physically and mentally. She continued psyching herself up as she applauded along with the rest of the crowd, even letting out a whoop or two of her own as she was swept up in the moment. Eventually, the clapping and cheering petered out, and a staid-looking man in a suit stepped up to the microphone and thanked the band, then launched into a rundown of what else was taking place at the fayre. Dee had no idea what he was saying—she'd already tuned him out in favour of carefully watching Pink Hair, who stood awkwardly off to one side of the bloke, presumably waiting for him to finish what he was saying and bugger off so she and her bandmates could start packing up.

Sure enough, the moment he took his leave—after turning to the four of them and shaking each of their hands in turn—they leapt into action.

So did Dee. Not giving herself the opportunity to chicken out, she pushed off from where she'd had one foot pressed against the tree trunk, and strode across the grass towards the marquee. Her ears buzzed a little from the volume of the music, having been so close to a speaker, but it was nothing she couldn't handle.

When she was a couple of steps away, she took a deep breath before launching herself into the structure and coming to an abrupt halt next to Pink Hair, who started and looked up at her, wide-eyed. "Oh, hello," she said, a tiny frown line appearing between her dark eyebrows, "can I help you?"

Dee grasped the strap of her handbag and twisted it between her suddenly-sweaty palms. Her heart pounded. "Er, I don't know, maybe?" She shook her head, realising she was coming across as the biggest kind of moron. The trouble was, up close, Pink Hair was more appealing than ever. The scent of her shampoo and perfume were adding another dimension to Dee's mental fantasies. She took another deep breath, straightened her spine, and said, "Your set was fantastic—well done. I really enjoyed it. Anyway, I was just wondering… would you like to come and get a drink with me? Maybe something to eat?"

Mentally, she chanted, *Please be into women, please be into women…*

Pink Hair's frown deepened, and colour stained her cheeks—but that could have been from the heat and exertion. She tucked her hair behind her ears, giving Dee a close-up glimpse of the silver rings adorning her fingers, then looked at her bandmates over her shoulder. They were busily packing away their instruments, but were clearly eavesdropping on the conversation. "I, er, I don't know. I need to help the guys—"

"No, you don't," piped up one of the twins, grinning between Pink Hair and Dee as he carefully rolled up a thick, black cable. "We can manage, it's fine."

"A-are you sure? But what about my…" She waved a hand at the microphone.

Her bandmate's smile widened. "We've got another gig tomorrow, remember? I'll just keep it in my van until then. It's not a problem. You go, have fun. We'll see you tomorrow, all right?"

Movement caught Dee's eye. She turned to see the other two men nodding emphatically, not even pretending to pack up now. "Yes," the blond said, "*go.* You must need a drink after all that singing."

"Er, well..." She turned a doubtful gaze to Dee, then her face softened. "All right—if you're sure you can manage. I'll see you guys tomorrow. Great set today!" She grabbed a backpack from the side of the marquee and hoiked it onto her shoulders, then grabbed a pair of sunglasses from a table and slotted them into place.

Three lots of murmured agreements rang out, and the men turned back to their respective tasks, but not before exchanging a glance and a knowing smirk.

A thrill shot through Dee's veins. *She said yes!* She clamped onto her bag strap again, trying to get a grip on her excitement. She pushed her nerves deep down inside, reminding herself that she'd done the hardest part—asking Pink Hair out. All she had to do now was spend some time with her and see where things went. "Okay," she said brightly, as they strode out of the marquee and across the grass towards the stalls, "what do you fancy, then? We can get some food, too, if you like. My treat."

Pink Hair gave a small smile and looked around as they reached the first row of stalls and food vans. "I *am* pretty hungry, actually. I haven't had any lunch, and doing a set in this heat has sapped my energy quite a bit. How about beer and a burger?"

Dee's eyebrows leapt up towards her hairline before she could stop them. God—could this woman *be* any more perfect? The word *woman* rang a bell in her mind, and she realised she'd skipped one of the most fundamental parts of meeting someone new—finding out their name. *Duh.* Supressing a sigh at her own stupidity—at least she could blame her nerves for the oversight—she replied, "That sounds great to me. I'm Dee, by the way."

They paused, shook hands. "Lovely to meet you, Dee. I'm Athena."

The physical contact having distracted her, Dee's filter didn't kick in, and she said with a smile, "Of *course* you are."

Athena frowned as she withdrew her hand. "Pardon?"

Heat scorched Dee's cheeks. *Shit. What did you say that for, you idiot?* "I-I..." She let out a weak laugh. "I just meant, well, Athena's a goddess, isn't she? And you're, well... *you*."

She realised the second Athena gasped and stepped back that her words had been taken completely the wrong way, but Athena spoke before Dee could explain.

"And what the hell is *that* supposed to mean?" she spat. "Is this some kind of prank? You asking me for a drink some kind of dare?"

Dee waved her hands, trying desperately to placate Athena, calm her down. People were starting to notice, and she didn't want to attract any more attention. "No! Christ, no! Just hear me out." She swallowed hard, willing her brain and mouth to communicate properly and not fuck things up even worse than she had already. "I asked you for a drink because I think you're gorgeous—stunning, actually—and I wanted to meet you, get to know you. You being named after a goddess seems very fitting to me."

Athena opened her mouth, then closed it again. She began fidgeting with the owl charm hanging from one of her necklaces, twisting it in her fingers. After a moment, her face relaxed into a smile. "Sorry. I didn't mean to bite your head off. I just… I guess I'm not used to compliments, so I automatically jumped to the wrong conclusion. People don't often find this," she wafted her free hand up and down to indicate her figure, "attractive enough to compare me to a goddess. Not even the one of wisdom and strategy." She winked.

Astounded that the woman who had commanded a crowd with such abandon not five minutes ago was insecure, Dee shook her head, and blinked. Then she shrugged. "People are stupid, then. Or blind. I think you're beautiful."

This time Athena *definitely* blushed. She dropped her gaze to the grass for a second or two, then lifted her head and smiled. "Thank you. You're gorgeous, too. I still can't quite believe you asked me for a drink."

Dee smiled back, then closed the gap between them and tucked her arm into Athena's. "Believe it. It's happening. Come on."

Athena allowed herself to be led towards the burger van and, five minutes later, they perched at the end of a picnic table, on opposite sides, with their burgers and beers. They were sharing their table with a young family so kept their chat light, child-friendly, just in case they were overheard. Unlikely, given the rowdy bunch were busy eating their own food and arguing with each other, but it was best to be careful.

Dee found she actually loved the fact they had to keep their conversation superficial. It meant they'd been forced to forego flirting and go back to basics. By the time the family packed up and left, Dee and Athena had told each other where they'd gone to school, what they did for a living, their hobbies, their birthdays, their favourite colours, books, films, and places to visit. Also, Athena had only moved to the area recently, which explained why Dee hadn't seen her around.

By now, they'd finished their burgers and were supping at their beers as they chatted. Dee was more enamoured with the smart, funny, self-deprecating Athena than ever, and was building up to asking her out on a date—something more formal than burgers and beers at a summer fayre.

"Hey," Athena said suddenly, interrupting Dee. She lifted her sunglasses and perched them on top of her head before squinting at Dee. "Did you put sunscreen on before you came out?"

Dee frowned and shook her head. "No, why?"

Her eyes widening, Athena replied, "Because your shoulders and upper arms have gone pretty red. Do you have a top you can put on—to cover up?"

"No." Dee removed her sunglasses and craned her neck to look at each of her shoulders in turn. They *were* starting to look quite colourful, and when she pressed a hand to one, the heat that reached her fingertips was intense. "Shit. It's scorching. Sorry, but I'd better find some shade. It might already be too late to avoid it peeling, but I don't want to make it any worse." She dropped her sunglasses back into place.

"Of course not." Athena replaced her own sunglasses, then scrambled off her seat, gathered up the trays their burgers had been in, and took them to the nearest litter bin. She dumped them, then returned to the table, where she scooped up her beer bottle. "Oh." She pouted as she jiggled it from side to side. "I'm almost out. Shall I get us another one before we find that shade?"

Dee did the same to her bottle, finding she only had dregs left, too. "Sure. Let's go." But as she swung her legs over the bench, sensation zinged through her upper body. "Ow!"

Athena rushed to her side. "What is it? What's up?"

With a wince, Dee replied, "When I moved—my arms, shoulders, back, chest. They all feel tight."

Her pink tresses waving as she shook her head, her expression stern, Athena said, "Right—never mind shade, we need to get you home and get you treated. Do you have any aloe vera moisturiser or after sun?"

"Yeah, but—" She didn't want their time together to end, not like this.

"But nothing. The sooner you get some cream on, the better. Finish your beer, and let's go."

Amused by the fact she'd been commanded to finish her beer, and touched by Athena's obvious concern, Dee did as she was told. As soon as she lowered the empty bottle, the other woman whisked it from her grasp and hurried over to throw it, along with hers, away.

She was back within seconds, and held out her hand. "You all right to walk? You don't feel faint or anything?"

"No, I'm fine. Honestly." But she took Athena's hand anyway, allowing her to help her up.

"Oh!" Athena paused, then quickly hitched her backpack from her shoulders, unzipped it, and began rummaging inside, muttering to herself. "I know it's in here somewhere." After a moment, she let out an exclamation, and pulled out a chiffon-type black scarf covered in lightning bolts. She held it out to Dee. "I know black isn't ideal, in this heat, but surely covering up with that is better than nothing at all? You said your flat is only a few minutes away, right?"

Taking the scarf with a grateful smile, Dee replied, "Yeah. Thanks." She unfolded the material and shook it out to its full size, then draped it over herself. It covered her shoulders, back, and upper arms—perfect. "I'll, er, give it to you next time I see you?" She had deliberately let her tone lift at the end, making the sentence into a question, hoping Athena would get the idea.

Athena wrinkled her nose. "Pfft. Never mind that—I'm coming with you. I want to see you get home safely, make sure you haven't got sunstroke, too. Now, stop waffling and start walking. Which way?" She zipped up her backpack and shouldered it.

Taken aback by Athena's sudden confidence and bossiness, Dee allowed herself to be steered away from the summer fayre. She pointed to the exit which led towards her place, and the pair of them made their way in silence across the grass, through the gate, and out onto the street.

"This way." Dee jerked her head, and they continued on, the journey from earlier in reverse, only this time she wasn't following the invisible trail of a beautiful voice. She was bringing the *owner* of the beautiful voice with her! How had that even happened?

Minutes later, they entered Dee's flat, and she cringed as she remembered she'd abandoned the cleaning to go to the park. "Er, sorry about the mess. I haven't finished my housework."

Athena closed the door behind them, removed her backpack, and placed it down in the hallway. She took off her sunglasses and tucked them into a side pocket of her bag. "Don't be silly. I'm not bothered what your flat looks like—I'm concerned about you. Right, first thing—water. We need to get you thoroughly hydrated. Tackle this from the inside as well as the outside."

"Oh. I've got some in my bag, actually. More bottles in the fridge."

"Good. Get that down you, and I'll grab you another. Kitchen?"

Dee pointed, then hurriedly retrieved the half-drunk bottle from her bag and followed Athena to the kitchen, sipping as she went. She found she didn't mind the fact the other woman was rooting around in her fridge, even though they'd just met. That had to be a good sign, right?

Athena seemed equally comfortable as she retrieved a bottle, cracked open the lid, then handed it to Dee. "Drink," she commanded.

"I haven't finished this one, yet."

"Then hurry," she urged. "Where's your cream, then?"

"Bathroom cabinet. It's an aloe vera after sun. Second door on your left."

"Perfect. You'd better be at least halfway down the second bottle by the time I get back, or you'll be in trouble." She shot Dee a wink to show she was joking, then was gone in a whirl of pink hair and jingling jewellery.

Dee blinked and shook her head, then realised she still had her sunglasses on. No wonder everything was dim. She hurriedly finished her first bottle of water, dumped it in the recycling, then took off her sunglasses, Athena's scarf, and her bag—careful not to touch any of her affected skin as she did so. That done, she retrieved the second bottle and began to guzzle the contents. She knew perfectly well where Athena was coming from—the sunburn would pull moisture to the surface of her skin and away from the rest of her body, but at the same time she was conscious she'd end up peeing like there was no tomorrow when the water made its way through her system. Still, she'd have to cross that bridge when she came to it. Better to be rushing to the loo than having a raging headache or feeling ill.

When Athena returned, green bottle aloft and a grin on her face, she glanced at Dee's hand and gave a firm nod. "All right—looks like you're not in trouble. Let's have a look at you, then."

Dee replaced the lid and put the bottle down on the table. She took a deep breath, then carefully hooked her thumbs into the straps of her vest top and bra, and lowered them. The trouble was, the scorching sensation went so far down her arms that she didn't want to rest the straps on her upper arms at all—it would hurt. *Thank God my legs were protected by the picnic table.*

Seeing her dilemma, Athena glanced towards the window, then, realising it wasn't overlooked, said, "Just slip your arms out of the straps altogether. Or do you want to just take the vest top off, then let your bra straps hang? It *would* make it easier for me to put the cream on your back—and I won't risk getting any on your clothes, then."

The increasing heat and tightness of her skin wiping out any hint of embarrassment she might have felt, Dee gingerly took off the vest top, then removed her arms from her bra straps and let them hang, as Athena had suggested. The bra was plenty firm enough to hold up by itself, anyway, so she was in no danger of flashing. She might have been fantasising about getting naked with Athena not so long ago, but their current circumstances weren't exactly erotic.

Athena winced as she regarded Dee's exposed skin. "Shit—that's gotta hurt. You got some ibuprofen?"

Dee nodded. "Is it that bad?"

"Pretty bad. Here, hold this." She passed Dee the aloe vera lotion, then began tugging off her chunky rings and bracelets and putting them on the table. "Last thing I want is these scraping your poor skin." That done, she took the lotion back, flipped open the lid, and squirted a big dollop into her palm. She gave Dee the bottle again, then rubbed her hands together. "Ready?" She raised an eyebrow in enquiry, then reached out when Dee nodded and gently placed her hands on Dee's shoulders.

Dee hissed at the initial contact, then sighed as Athena carefully swept her soft palms across her skin, smoothing the lotion over her. Unsurprisingly, her skin seemed to eat it up, so Athena patiently, painstakingly applied more and more of the cooling magic over her shoulders, arms, back, and chest until she was satisfied.

By the time she was done, Dee was almost in a trance. She'd long since closed her eyes and succumbed to the sensation of Athena's touch, and only the discomfort in her upper body counteracted the ache between her legs. She wobbled a little as she opened her eyes to see Athena stepping away.

"Right," she said, her expression and tone serious, "I think that's enough for now." She cleared her throat, then moved to the sink and washed her hands of the lotion. She grabbed a tea towel and turned back around, drying her hands. "I think you ought to take a couple of ibuprofen to help with the swelling, and keep drinking water. Take a cold shower or bath if you think you can stand it. If you do, though, make sure to slap a load more lotion on straight after—preferably while your skin is still damp. I'll come back in the morning to check on you, all right?"

Dee gaped. "Y-you're going?"

Athena looked away, then returned the tea towel to its hook. "I think that would be best. For today, at least." She met Dee's gaze, her blue eyes swirling with something she couldn't quite place. *Arousal? Regret? Both?* "I'll be back tomorrow morning—I promise."

"Er, okay then." She certainly wasn't going to beg her to stay. Plus, she *was* starting to feel pretty crappy. She'd hardly be the most scintillating company. No, better to spend the rest of the day feeling sorry for herself, hydrating, and whacking on as much sun lotion as her skin could stand.

And hoping like hell the morning would bring Athena.

Spoiler: it did. And their time apart might have given Dee a little time to heal, but it did nothing to dampen Dee and Athena's enthusiasm for each other. So much so, that Athena was almost late for her next gig.

It was worth it.

Acknowledgements

I never know what to say here. So, bear with me while I ramble on!

All the authors involved with this charity anthology have put in so much hard work and dedication to their stories that thank you never seems enough. But, THANK YOU, without you I wouldn't be able to put together this amazing anthology.

To all our readers, thank you for buying this book and supporting our chosen charity The Mercury Phoenix Trust, which helps provide care across the world for people with HIV and AIDS. I hope you enjoyed reading all these stories and found some new to you authors to stalk.

And finally thank you to my family and friends for putting up with my crazy ramblings about books!

You guys and girls are all amazing, thank you.

Until next year….happy reading.

Printed in Poland
by Amazon Fulfillment
Poland Sp. z o.o., Wrocław